Vittoria by George Meredith

George Meredith, OM, was born in Portsmouth, England on February 12th, 1828, a son and grandson of naval outfitters. His mother died when he was only five.

As a fourteen year old teenager he was sent to a Moravian School in Neuwied, Germany, staying there for two years.

After reading law he was articled as a solicitor, but quickly abandoned that career path for journalism and poetry. He collaborated with Edward Gryffydh Peacock, son of Thomas Love Peacock in publishing a privately circulated literary magazine, the Monthly Observer.

At age twenty-one he married Mary Ellen Nicolls, Edward Peacock's beautiful widowed sister, and mother of a child, on August 8th, 1849. Mary Ellen was twenty-eight. The marriage produced one child; Arthur (1853–1890).

Meredith collected his early writings, all previously published in periodicals, in an 1851 volume, Poems.

In 1856 he posed as the model for The Death of Chatterton, a well-known picture by the English Pre-Raphaelite painter Henry Wallis, which romantised the teenage Chatterton's demise.

Although Meredith received some publicity for this his wife received rather more attention from Wallis because of it. Mary Ellen ran off with Wallis in 1858, shortly before giving birth to a child that all assumed to be Wallis. Tragically she died three years later.

From that dreadful experience emerged a collection of sonnets entitled Modern Love in 1862 together with much of his first major novel; The Ordeal of Richard Feverel.

Meredith married Marie Vulliamy on September 20th, 1864 and they settled in Surrey. Together they had two children; William (born in 1865) and Mariette (born in 1874).

He continued writing novels and poetry, often inspired by nature. He had a keen understanding of comedy and his Essay on Comedy (1877) remains a reference work in the history of comic theory.

In The Egoist, published in 1879, he applies some of his theories of comedy in one of his most thoughtful and enduring novels.

During most of his career, he had difficulty crossing over from critical acclamation to popular success. It was only in 1885 that his first genuine commercial success appeared; Diana of the Crossways.

An artist's life throughout the ages, when not subsidised by a patron, is often difficult. Meredith found it no different. With an unreliable income stream he sought to bolster that with a job as a publisher's reader.

The company that gave him this lifeline was Chapman & Hall (an eminent publishing house who could include Charles Dickens, William Makepeace Thackeray, Elizabeth Barrett Browning and Anthony

Trollope on their roster). His advice to the company was very well received and made him influential in the world of letters.

To this influence he was able to add a circle of friends that included William and Dante Gabriel Rossetti, Algernon Charles Swinburne, Cotter Morison, Leslie Stephen, Robert Louis Stevenson, George Gissing and J. M. Barrie.

In 1868 Meredith was introduced to Thomas Hardy. Hardy had submitted his first novel, The Poor Man and the Lady. Meredith felt the book was too bitter a satire on the rich and told Hardy to put it aside as it was likely it would be savaged by reviewers and destroy his nascent career. Meredith had received the same reaction with The Ordeal of Richard Feverel. Although it had brought him success it was judged so shocking that Mudie's circulating library cancelled an order of 300 copies.

But these years, creatively, were very prolific and successful for Meredith. Novels and poems flowed from his pen including everything from The Adventures of Harry Richmond to Diana of the Crossways and many poetry volumes include The Lark Ascending (which later inspired the Vaughan Williams music)

In 1886, tragedy struck the Meredith household when his second wife, Marie Vulliamy, died of cancer.

Whilst his personal life was producing horrendous scars he was receiving many accolades. Oscar Wilde was a fan. In The Decay of Lying, (originally published in the January 1889 issue of The Nineteenth Century) he says of Meredith "Ah, Meredith! Who can define him? His style is chaos illumined by flashes of lightning".

In 1891 Meredith was even the subject of homage when Sir Arthur Conan Doyle in his Sherlock Holmes short story The Boscombe Valley Mystery, (published in the popular Strand magazine) when Sherlock Holmes turns to Watson during case discussions and says "And now let us talk about George Meredith, if you please, and we shall leave all minor matters until tomorrow."

Before his death, Meredith was honoured from many quarters: he succeeded Lord Tennyson as president of the Society of Authors; in 1905 he was appointed to the Order of Merit by King Edward VII.

George Meredith, aged 81, died at his home in Box Hill, Surrey on May 18th, 1909. He is buried in the cemetery at Dorking, Surrey.

Index of Contents
BOOK I
Chapter I - UP MONTE MOTTERONE
Chapter II - ON THE HEIGHTS
Chapter III - SIGNORINA VITTORIA
Chapter IV - AMMIANI'S INTERCESSION
Chapter V - THE SPY
Chapter VI - THE WARNING
Chapter VII - BARTO RIZZO
Chapter VIII - THE LETTER
BOOK II

Chapter IX - IN VERONA
Chapter X - THE POPE'S MOUTH
Chapter XI - LAURA PIAVENI
Chapter XII - THE BRONZE BUTTERFLY
Chapter XIII - THE PLOT OF THE SIGNOR ANTONIO
BOOK III
Chapter XIV - AT THE MAESTRO'S DOOR
Chapter XV - AMMIANI THROUGH THE MIDNIGHT
Chapter XVI - COUNTESS AMMIANI
Chapter XVII - IN THE PIAZZA D'ARMI
Chapter XVIII - THE NIGHT OF THE FIFTEENTH
Chapter XIX - THE PRIMA DONNA
BOOK IV
Chapter XX - THE OPERA OF CAMILLA
Chapter XXI - THE THIRD ACT
Chapter XXII - WILFRID COMES FORWARD
Chapter XXIII - FIRST HOURS OF THE FLIGHT
Chapter XXIV - ADVENTURES OF VITTORIA AND ANGELO
Chapter XXV - ACROSS THE MOUNTAINS
BOOK V
Chapter XXVI - THE DUEL IN THE PASS
Chapter XXVII - A NEW ORDEAL
Chapter XXVIII - THE ESCAPE OF ANGELO
BOOK VI
Chapter XXIX - EPISODES OF THE REVOLT AND THE WAR—THE TOBACCO RIOTS—RINALDO GUIDASCARPI
Chapter XXX - EPISODES OF THE REVOLT AND THE WAR—THE FIVE DAYS OF MILAN
Chapter XXXI - EPISODES OF THE REVOLT AND THE WAR—VITTORIA DISOBEYS HER LOVER
Chapter XXXII - EPISODES OF THE REVOLT AND THE WAR—THE TREACHERY OF PERICLES—THE WRITE UMBRELLA—THE DEATH OF RINALDO GUIDASCARPI
BOOK VII
Chapter XXXIII - EPISODES OF THE REVOLT AND THE WAR—COUNT KARL LENKENSTEIN—THE STORY OF THE GUIDASCARPI—THE VICTORY OF THE VOLUNTEERS
Chapter XXXIV - EPISODES OF THE REVOLT AND THE WAR—THE DEEDS OF BARTO RIZZO— THE MEETING AT ROVEREDO
Chapter XXXV - CLOSE OF THE LOMBARD CAMPAIGN—VITTORIA'S PERPLEXITY
Chapter XXXVI - A FRESH ENTANGLEMENT
Chapter XXXVII - ON LAGO MAGGIORE
Chapter XXXVIII -VIOLETTA D'ISORELLA
Chapter XXXIX - ANNA OF LENKENSTEIN
BOOK VIII
Chapter XL - THROUGH THE WINTER
Chapter XLI - THE INTERVIEW
Chapter XLII - THE SHADOW OF CONSPIRACY
Chapter XLIII - THE LAST MEETING IN MILAN
Chapter XLIV - THE WIFE AND THE HUSBAND
Chapter XLV - SHOWS MANY PATHS CONVERGING TO THE END
Chapter XLVI - THE LAST
EPILOGUE

GEORGE MEREDITH – A CONCISE BIBLIOGRAPHY

BOOK I

CHAPTER I

UP MONTE MOTTERONE

From Monte Motterone you survey the Lombard plain. It is a towering dome of green among a hundred pinnacles of grey and rust-red crags. At dawn the summit of the mountain has an eagle eye for the far Venetian boundary and the barrier of the Apennines; but with sunrise come the mists. The vast brown level is seen narrowing in; the Ticino and the Sesia waters, nearest, quiver on the air like sleepy lakes; the plain is engulphed up to the high ridges of the distant Southern mountain range, which lie stretched to a faint cloud-like line, in shape like a solitary monster of old seas crossing the Deluge. Long arms of vapour stretch across the urn-like valleys, and gradually thickening and swelling upward, enwrap the scored bodies of the ashen-faced peaks and the pastures of the green mountain, till the heights become islands over a forgotten earth. Bells of herds down the hidden run of the sweet grasses, and a continuous leaping of its rivulets, give the Motterone a voice of youth and homeliness amid that stern company of Titan-heads, for whom the hawk and the vulture cry. The storm has beaten at them until they have got the aspect of the storm. They take colour from sunlight, and are joyless in colour as in shade. When the lower world is under pushing steam, they wear the look of the revolted sons of Time, fast chained before scornful heaven in an iron peace. Day at last brings vigorous fire; arrows of light pierce the mist-wreaths, the dancing draperies, the floors of vapour; and the mountain of piled pasturages is seen with its foot on the shore of Lago Maggiore. Down an extreme gulf the full sunlight, as if darting on a jewel in the deeps, seizes the blue-green lake with its isles. The villages along the darkly-wooded borders of the lake show white as clustered swans; here and there a tented boat is visible, shooting from terraces of vines, or hanging on its shadow. Monte Boscero is unveiled; the semicircle of the Piedmontese and the Swiss peaks, covering Lake Orta, behind, on along the Ticinese and the Grisons, leftward toward and beyond the Lugano hills, stand bare in black and grey and rust-red and purple. You behold a burnished realm of mountain and plain beneath the royal sun of Italy. In the foreground it shines hard as the lines of an irradiated Cellini shield. Farther away, over middle ranges that are soft and clear, it melts, confusing the waters with hot rays, and the forests with darkness, to where, wavering in and out of view like flying wings, and shadowed like wings of archangels with rose and with orange and with violet, silverwhite Alps are seen. You might take them for mystical streaming torches on the border-ground between vision and fancy. They lean as in a great flight forward upon Lombardy.

The curtain of an early autumnal morning was everywhere lifted around the Motterone, save for one milky strip of cloud that lay lizard-like across the throat of Monte Boscero facing it, when a party of five footfarers, who had met from different points of ascent some way below, and were climbing the mountain together, stood upon the cropped herbage of the second plateau, and stopped to eye the landscape; possibly also to get their breath. They were Italians. Two were fair-haired muscular men, bronzed by the sun and roughly bearded, bearing the stamp of breed of one or other of the hill-cities under the Alps. A third looked a sturdy soldier, squareset and hard of feature, for whom beauties of scenery had few awakening charms. The remaining couple were an old man and a youth, upon whose shoulder the veteran leaned, and with a whimsical turn of head and eye, indicative of some playful cast of mind, poured out his remarks upon the objects in sight, and chuckled to himself, like one who has learnt the necessity to appreciate his own humour if he is disposed to indulge it. He was carelessly wrapped about in long loose woollen stuff, but the youth was dressed like a Milanese cavalier of the first quality, and was evidently one who would have been at home in the fashionable Corso. His face was of the sweetest virile Italian beauty. The head was long, like a hawk's, not too lean, and not sharply ridged from a rapacious beak, but enough to show characteristics of eagerness and promptitude. His eyes were darkest blue, the eyebrows and long disjoining eyelashes being very dark over them, which made their colour precious. The nose was straight and forward from the brows; a fluent black moustache ran with the curve of the upper lip, and lost its line upon a smooth olive cheek. The upper lip was firmly supported by the under, and the chin stood freely out from a fine neck and throat.

After a space an Austrian war-steamer was discerned puffing out of the harbour of Laveno.

"That will do," said the old man. "Carlo, thou son of Paolo, we will stump upward once more. Tell me, hulloa, sir! are the best peaches doomed to entertain vile, domiciliary, parasitical insects? I ask you, does nature exhibit motherly regard, or none, for the regions of the picturesque? None, I say. It is an arbitrary distinction of our day. To complain of the intrusion of that black-yellow flag and foul smoke-line on the lake underneath us is preposterous, since, as you behold, the heavens make no protestation. Let us up. There is comfort in exercise, even for an ancient creature such as I am. This mountain is my brother, and flatters me not—I am old."

"Take my arm, dear Agostino," said the youth.

"Never, my lad, until I need it. On, ahead of me, goat! chamois! and teach me how the thing used to be done in my time. Old legs must be the pupils of young ones mark that piece of humility, and listen with respectfulness to an old head by-and-by."

It was the autumn antecedent to that memorable Spring of the great Italian uprising, when, though for a tragic issue, the people of Italy first felt and acted as a nation, and Charles Albert, called the Sword of Italy, aspired, without comprehension of the passion of patriotism by which it was animated, to lead it quietly into the fold of his Piedmontese kingship.

There is not an easier or a pleasanter height to climb than the Motterone, if, in Italian heat, you can endure the disappointment of seeing the summit, as you ascend, constantly flit away to a farther station. It seems to throw its head back, like a laughing senior when children struggle up for kissings. The party of five had come through the vines from Stresa and from Baveno. The mountain was strange to them, and they had already reckoned twice on having the topmost eminence in view, when reaching it they found themselves on a fresh plateau, traversed by wild water-courses, and browsed by Alpine herds; and again the green dome was distant. They came to the highest chalet, where a hearty wiry young fellow, busily employed in making cheese, invited them to the enjoyment of shade and fresh milk. "For the sake of these adolescents, who lose much and require much, let it be so," said Agostino gravely, and not without some belief that he consented to rest on behalf of his companions. They allowed the young mountaineer to close the door, and sat about his fire like sagacious men. When cooled and refreshed, Agostino gave the signal for departure, and returned thanks for hospitality. Money was not offered and not expected. As they were going forth the mountaineer accompanied them to the step on the threshold, and with a mysterious eagerness in his eyes, addressed Agostino.

"Signore, is it true?—the king marches?"

"Who is the king, my friend?" returned Agostino. "If he marches out of his dominions, the king confers a blessing on his people perchance."

"Our king, signore!" The mountaineer waved his finger as from Novara toward Milan.

Agostino seemed to awaken swiftly from his disguise of an absolute gravity. A red light stood in his eyeballs, as if upon a fiery answer. The intemperate fit subsided. Smoothing dawn his mottled grey beard with quieting hands, he took refuge in his habitual sententious irony.

"My friend, I am not a hare in front of the king, nor am I a ram in the rear of him: I fly him not, neither do I propel him. So, therefore, I cannot predict the movements of the king. Will the wind blow from the north to-morrow, think you?"

The mountaineer sent a quick gaze up the air, as to descry signs.

"Who knows?" Agostino continued, though not playing into the smiles of his companions; "the wind will blow straight thither where there is a vacuum; and all that we can state of the king is, that there is a positive vacuum here. It would be difficult to predict the king's movements save by such weighty indications."

He laid two fingers hard against the rib which shields the heart. It had become apparently necessary for the speaker to relieve a mind surcharged with bile at the mention of the king; for, having done, he rebuked with an amazed frown the indiscretion of Carlo, who had shouted, "The Carbonaro king!"

"Carlo, my son, I will lean on your arm. On your mouth were better," Agostino added, under his voice, as they moved on.

"Oh, but," Carlo remonstrated, "let us trust somebody. Milan has made me sick of late. I like the look of that fellow."

"You allow yourself, my Carlo, an immense indulgence in permitting yourself to like the look of anything. Now, listen—Viva Carlo Alberto!"

The old man rang out the loyal salutation spiritedly, and awoke a prompt response from the mountaineer, who sounded his voice wide in the keen upper air.

"There's the heart of that fellow!" said Agostino. "He has but one idea—his king! If you confound it, he takes you for an enemy. These free mountain breezes intoxicate you. You would embrace the king himself if you met him here."

"I swear I would never be guilty of the bad joke of crying a 'Viva' to him anywhere upon earth," Carlo replied. "I offend you," he said quickly.

The old man was smiling.

"Agostino Balderini is too notoriously a bad joker to be offended by the comments of the perfectly sensible, boy of mine! My limbs were stiff, and the first three steps from a place of rest reminded me acutely of the king's five years of hospitality. He has saved me from all fatigue so long, that the necessity to exercise these old joints of mine touched me with a grateful sense of his royal bounty. I had from him a chair, a bed, and a table: shelter from sun and from all silly chatter. Now I want a chair or a bed. I should like to sit at a table; the sun burns me; my ears are afflicted. I cry 'Viva!' to him that I may be in harmony with the coming chorus of Italy, which I prophetically hear. That young fellow, in whom you confide so much, speaks for his country. We poor units must not be discordant. No! Individual opinion, my Carlo, is discord when there is a general delirium. The tide arriving, let us make the best of the tide. My voice is wisdom. We shall have to follow this king!"

"Shall we!" uttered one behind them gruffly. "When I see this king swallow one ounce of Austrian lead, I shall not be sorry to follow him!"

"Right, my dear Ugo," said Agostino, turning round to him; "and I will then compose his hymn of praise. He has swallowed enough of Austrian bread. He took an Austrian wife to his bed. Who knows? he may some day declare a preference for Austrian lead. But we shall have to follow him, or stay at home drivelling."

Agostino raised his eyes, that were glazed with the great heat of his frame.

"Oh, that, like our Dante, I had lived in the days when souls were damned! Then would I uplift another shout, believe me! As things go now, we must allow the traitor to hope for his own future, and we simply shrug. We cannot plant him neck-deep for everlasting in a burning marl, and hear him howling. We have no weapons in these times—none! Our curses come back to roost. This is one of the serious facts of the century, and controls violent language. What! are you all gathered about me? Oracles must be moving, too. There's no rest even for them, when they have got a mountain to scale."

A cry, "He is there!" and "Do you see him?" burst from the throats of men surrounding Agostino.

Looking up to the mountain's top, they had perceived the figure of one who stood with folded arms, sufficiently near for the person of an expected friend to be descried. They waved their hats, and Carlo shot ahead. The others trod after him more deliberately, but in glad excitement, speculating on the time which this sixth member of the party, who were engaged to assemble at a certain hour of the morning upon yonder height, had taken to reach the spot from Omegna, or Orta, or Pella, and rejoicing that his health should be so stout in despite of his wasting labours under city smoke.

"Yes, health!" said Agostino. "Is it health, do you think? It's the heart of the man! and a heart with a mill-stone about it—a heart to breed a country from! There stands the man who has faith in Italy, though she has been lying like a corpse for centuries. God bless him! He has no other comfort. Viva l'Italia!"

The exclamation went up, and was acknowledged by him on the eminence overhanging them; but at a repetition of it his hand smote the air sideways. They understood the motion, and were silent; while he, until Carlo breathed his name in his hearing, eyed the great scene stedfastly, with the absorbing simple passion of one who has endured long exile, and finds his clustered visions of it confronting the strange, beloved, visible life:—the lake in the arms of giant mountains: the far-spreading hazy plain; the hanging forests; the pointed crags; the gleam of the distant rose-shadowed snows that stretch for ever like an airy host, mystically clad, and baffling the eye as with the motions of a flight toward the underlying purple land.

CHAPTER II

He was a man of middle stature, thin, and even frail, as he stood defined against the sky; with the complexion of the student, and the student's aspect. The attentive droop of his shoulders and head, the straining of the buttoned coat across his chest, the air as of one who waited and listened, which distinguished his figure, detracted from the promise of other than contemplative energy, until his eyes were fairly seen and felt. That is, until the observer became aware that those soft and large dark meditative eyes had taken hold of him. In them lay no abstracted student's languor, no reflex burning of a solitary lamp; but a quiet grappling force engaged the penetrating look. Gazing upon them, you were drawn in suddenly among the thousand whirring wheels of a capacious and a vigorous mind, that was both reasoning and prompt, keen of intellect, acting throughout all its machinery, and having all under full command: an orbed mind, supplying its own philosophy, and arriving at the sword-stroke by logical steps,—a mind much less supple than a soldier's; anything but the mind of a Hamlet. The eyes were dark as the forest's border is dark; not as night is dark. Under favourable lights their colour was seen to be a deep rich brown, like the chestnut, or more like the hazel-edged sunset brown which lies upon our western rivers in the winter floods, when night begins to shadow them.

The side-view of his face was an expression of classic beauty rarely now to be beheld, either in classic lands or elsewhere. It was severe; the tender serenity of the full bow of the eyes relieved it. In profile they showed little of their intellectual quality, but what some might have thought a playful luminousness, and some a quick pulse of feeling. The chin was firm; on it, and on the upper lip, there was a clipped growth of black hair. The whole visage widened upward from the chin, though not very markedly before it reached the broad-lying brows. The temples were strongly indented by the swelling of the forehead above them: and on both sides of the head there ran a pregnant ridge, such as will sometimes lift men a deplorable half inch above the earth we tread. If this man was a problem to others, he was none to himself; and when others called him an idealist, he accepted the title, reading himself, notwithstanding, as one who was less flighty than many philosophers and professedly practical teachers of his generation. He saw far, and he grasped ends beyond obstacles: he was nourished by sovereign principles; he despised material present interests; and, as I have said, he was less supple than a soldier. If the title of idealist belonged to him, we will not immediately decide that it was opprobrious. The idealized conception of stern truths played about his head certainly for those who knew and who loved it. Such a man, perceiving a devout end to be reached, might prove less scrupulous in his course, possibly, and less remorseful, than revolutionary Generals. His smile was quite unclouded, and came softly as a curve in water. It seemed to flow with, and to pass in and out of, his thoughts, to be a part of his emotion and his meaning when it shone transiently full. For as he had an orbed mind, so had he an orbed nature. The passions were absolutely in harmony with the intelligence. He had the English manner; a remarkable simplicity contrasting with the demonstrative outcries and gesticulations of his friends when they joined him on the height. Calling them each by name, he received their caresses and took their hands; after which he touched the old man's shoulder.

"Agostino, this has breathed you?"

"It has; it has, my dear and best one!" Agostino replied. "But here is a good market-place for air. Down below we have to scramble for it in the mire. The spies are stifling down below. I don't know my own shadow. I begin to think that I am important. Footing up a mountain corrects the notion somewhat.

Yonder, I believe, I see the Grisons, where Freedom sits. And there's the Monte della Disgrazia. Carlo Alberto should be on the top of it, but he is invisible. I do not see that Unfortunate."

"No," said Carlo Ammiani, who chimed to his humour more readily than the rest, and affected to inspect the Grisons' peak through a diminutive opera-glass. "No, he is not there."

"Perhaps, my son, he is like a squirrel, and is careful to run up t'other side of the stem. For he is on that mountain; no doubt of it can exist even in the Boeotian mind of one of his subjects; myself, for example. It will be an effulgent fact when he gains the summit."

The others meantime had thrown themselves on the grass at the feet of their manifestly acknowledged leader, and looked up for Agostino to explode the last of his train of conceits. He became aware that the moment for serious talk had arrived, and bent his body, groaning loudly, and uttering imprecations against him whom he accused of being the promoter of its excruciating stiffness, until the ground relieved him of its weight. Carlo continued standing, while his eyes examined restlessly the slopes just surmounted by them, and occasionally the deep descent over the green-glowing Orta Lake. It was still early morning. The heat was tempered by a cool breeze that came with scents of thyme. They had no sight of human creature anywhere, but companionship of Alps and birds of upper air; and though not one of them seasoned the converse with an exclamation of joy and of blessings upon a place of free speech and safety, the thought was in their hunted bosoms, delicious as a woodland rivulet that sings only to the leaves overshadowing it.

They were men who had sworn to set a nation free,—free from the foreigner, to begin with.

(He who tells this tale is not a partisan; he would deal equally toward all. Of strong devotion, of stout nobility, of unswerving faith and self-sacrifice, he must approve; and when these qualities are displayed in a contest of forces, the wisdom of means employed, or of ultimate views entertained, may be questioned and condemned; but the men themselves may not be.)

These men had sworn their oath, knowing the meaning of it, and the nature of the Fury against whom men who stand voluntarily pledged to any great resolve must thenceforward match themselves. Many of the original brotherhood had fallen, on the battle-field, on the glacis, or in the dungeon. All present, save the youthfuller Carlo, had suffered. Imprisonment and exile marked the Chief. Ugo Corte, of Bergamo, had seen his family swept away by the executioner and pecuniary penalties. Thick scars of wounds covered the body and disfigured the face of Giulio Bandinelli. Agostino had crawled but half-a-year previously out of his Piedmontese cell, and Marco Sana, the Brescian, had in such a place tasted of veritable torture. But if the calamity of a great oath was upon them, they had now in their faithful prosecution of it the support which it gives. They were unwearied; they had one object; the mortal anguish they had gone through had left them no sense for regrets. Life had become the field of an endless engagement to them; and as in battle one sees beloved comrades struck down, and casts but a glance at their prostrate forms, they heard the mention of a name, perchance, and with a word or a sign told what was to be said of a passionate glorious heart at rest, thanks to Austrian or vassal-Sardinian mercy.

So they lay there and discussed their plans.

"From what quarter do you apprehend the surprise?" Ugo Corte glanced up from the maps and papers spread along the grass to question Carlo ironically, while the latter appeared to be keeping rigid watch over the safety of the position. Carlo puffed the smoke of a cigarette rapidly, and Agostino replied for him:—"From the quarter where the best donkeys are to be had."

It was supposed that Agostino had resumed the habit usually laid aside by him for the discussion of serious matters, and had condescended to father a coarse joke; but his eyes showed no spark of their well-known twinkling solicitation for laughter, and Carlo spoke in answer gravely:—"From Baveno it will be."

"From Baveno! They might as well think to surprise hawks from Baveno. Keep watch, dear Ammiani; a good start in a race is a kick from the Gods."

With that, Corte turned to the point of his finger on the map. He conceived it possible that Carlo Ammiani, a Milanese, had reason to anticipate the approach of people by whom he, or they, might not wish to be seen. Had he studied Carlo's face he would have been reassured. The brows of the youth were open, and his eyes eager with expectation, that showed the flying forward of the mind, and nothing of knotted distrust or wary watchfulness. Now and then he would move to the other side of the mountain, and look over upon Orta; or with the opera-glass clasped in one hand beneath an arm, he stopped in his sentinel-march, frowning reflectively at a word put to him, as if debating within upon all the bearings of it; but the only answer that came was a sharp assent, given after the manner of one who dealt conscientiously in definite affirmatives; and again the glass was in requisition. Marco Sana was a fighting soldier, who stated what he knew, listened, and took his orders. Giulio Bandinelli was also little better than the lieutenant in an enterprise. Corte, on the other hand, had the conspirator's head,—a head like a walnut, bulging above the ears,—and the man was of a sallying temper. He lay there putting bit by bit of his plot before the Chief for his approval, with a careful construction, that upon the expression of any doubt of its working smoothly in the streets of Milan, caused him to shout a defensive, "But Carlo says yes!"

This uniform character of Ammiani's replies, and the smile of Agostino on hearing them, had begun to strike the attention of the soldierly Marco Sana. He ran his hand across his shorn head, and puffed his burnt red mole-spotted cheeks, with a sidelong stare at the abstracted youth, "Said yes!" he remarked. "He might say no, for a diversion. He has yeses enough in his pay to earn a Cardinal's hat. 'Is Milan preparing to rise?' 'Yes.'—'Is she ready for the work?' 'Yes.'—'Is the garrison on its guard?' 'Yes.'—'Have you seen Barto Rizzo?' 'Yes.'—'Have the people got the last batch of arms?' 'Yes.'—And 'Yes,' the secret is well kept; 'Yes,' Barto Rizzo is steadily getting them together. We may rely on him: Carlo is his intimate friend: Yes, Yes:—There's a regiment of them at your service, and you may shuffle them as you will. This is the help we get from Milan: a specimen of what we may expect!"

Sana had puffed himself hot, and now blew for coolness.

"You are,"—Agostino addressed him,—"philosophically totally wrong, my Marco. Those affirmatives are fat worms for the catching of fish. They are the real pretty fruit of the Hesperides. Personally, you or I may be irritated by them: but I'm not sure they don't please us. Were Carlo a woman, of course he should learn to say no;—as he will now if I ask him, Is she in sight? I won't do it, you know; but as a man and a diplomatist, it strikes me that he can't say yes too often."

"Answer me, Count Ammiani, and do me the favour to attend to these trifles for the space of two minutes," said Corte. "Have you seen Barto Rizzo? Is he acting for Medole?"

"As mole, as reindeer, and as bloody northern Raven!" ejaculated Agostino: "perhaps to be jackal, by-and-by. But I do not care to abuse our Barto Rizzo, who is a prodigy of nature, and has, luckily for himself, embraced a good cause, for he is certain to be hanged if he is not shot. He has the prophetic owl's face. I have always a fancy of his hooting his own death-scrip. I wrong our Barto:—Medole would be the jackal, if it lay between the two."

Carlo Ammiani had corrected Corte's manner to him by a complacent readiness to give him distinct replies. He then turned and set off at full speed down the mountain.

"She is sighted at last," Agostino murmured, and added rapidly some spirited words under his breath to the Chief, whose chin was resting on his doubled hand.

Corte, Marco, and Giulio were full of denunciations against Milan and the Milanese, who had sent a boy to their councils. It was Brescia and Bergamo speaking in their jealousy, but Carlo's behaviour was odd, and called for reproof. He had come as the deputy of Milan to meet the Chief, and he had not spoken a serious word on the great business of the hour, though the plot had been unfolded, the numbers sworn to, and Brescia, and Bergamo, and Cremona, and Venice had spoken upon all points through their emissaries, the two latter cities being represented by Sana and Corte.

"We've had enough of this lad," said Corte. "His laundress is following him with a change of linen, I suppose, or it's a scent-bottle. He's an admirable representative of the Lombard metropolis!" Corte drawled out the words in prodigious mimicry. "If Milan has nothing better to send than such a fellow, we'll finish without her, and shame the beast that she is. She has been always a treacherous beast!"

"Poor Milan!" sighed the Chief; "she lies under the beak of the vulture, and has twice been devoured; but she has a soul: she proves it. Ammiani, too, will prove his value. I have no doubt of him. As to boys, or even girls, you know my faith is in the young. Through them Italy lives. What power can teach devotion to the old?"

"I thank you, signore," Agostino gesticulated.

"But, tell me, when did you learn it, my friend?"

In answer, Agostino lifted his hand a little boy's height from the earth.

The old man then said: "I am afraid, my dear Corte, you must accept the fellowship of a girl as well as of a boy upon this occasion. See! our Carlo! You recognize that dancing speck below there?—he has joined himself—the poor lad wishes he could, I dare swear!—to another bigger speck, which is verily a lady: who has joined herself to a donkey—a common habit of the sex, I am told; but I know them not. That lady, signor Ugo, is the signorina Vittoria. You stare? But, I tell you, the game cannot go on without her; and that is why I have permitted you to knock the ball about at your own pleasure for these forty minutes."

Corte drew his under-lip on his reddish stubble moustache. "Are we to have women in a conference?" he asked from eye to eye.

"Keep to the number, Ugo; and moreover, she is not a woman, but a noble virgin. I discern a distinction, though you may not. The Vestal's fire burns straight."

"Who is she?"

"It rejoices me that she should be so little known. All the greater the illumination when her light shines out! The signorina Vittoria is a cantatrice who is about to appear upon the boards."

"Ah! that completes it." Corte rose to his feet with an air of desperation. "We require to be refreshed with quavers and crescendos and trillets! Who ever knew a singer that cared an inch of flesh for her country? Money, flowers, flattery, vivas! but, money! money! and Austrian as good as Italian. I've seen the accursed wenches bow gratefully for Austrian bouquets:—bow? ay, and more; and when the Austrian came to them red with our blood. I spit upon their polluted cheeks! They get us an ill name wherever they go. These singers have no country. One—I knew her—betrayed Filippo Mastalone, and sang the night of the day he was shot. I heard the white demon myself. I could have taken her long neck till she twisted like a serpent and hissed. May heaven forgive me for not levelling a pistol at her head! If God, my friends, had put the thought into my brain that night!"

A flush had deadened Corte's face to the hue of nightshade.

"You thunder in a clear atmosphere, my Ugo," returned the old man, as he fell back calmly at full length.

"And who is this signorina Vittoria?" cried Corte.

"A cantatrice who is about to appear upon the boards, as I have already remarked: of La Scala, let me add, if you hold it necessary."

"And what does she do here?"

"Her object in coming, my friend? Her object in coming is, first, to make her reverence to one who happens to be among us this day; and secondly, but principally, to submit a proposition to him and to us."

"What's her age?" Corte sneered.

"According to what calendar would you have it reckoned? Wisdom would say sixty: Father Chronos might divide that by three, and would get scarce a month in addition, hungry as he is for her, and all of us! But Minerva's handmaiden has no age. And now, dear Ugo, you have your opportunity to denounce her as a convicted screecher by night. Do so."

Corte turned his face to the Chief, and they spoke together for some minutes: after which, having had names of noble devoted women, dead and living, cited to him, in answer to brutal bellowings against that sex, and hearing of the damsel under debate as one who was expected and was welcome, he flung himself upon the ground again, inviting calamity by premature resignation. Giulio Bandinelli stretched his hand for Carlo's glass, and spied the approach of the signorina.

"Dark," he said.

"A jewel of that complexion," added Agostino, by way of comment.

"She has scorching eyes."

"She may do mischief; she may do mischief; let it be only on the right Side!"

"She looks fat."

"She sits doubled up and forward, don't you see, to relieve the poor donkey. You, my Giulio, would call a swan fat if the neck were not always on the stretch."

"By Bacchus! what a throat she has!"

"And well interjected, Giulio! It runs down like wine, like wine, to the little ebbing and flowing wave! Away with the glass, my boy! You must trust to all that's best about you to spy what's within. She makes me young—young!"

Agostino waved his hand in the form of a salute to her on the last short ascent. She acknowledged it gracefully; and talking at intervals to Carlo Ammiani, who footed briskly by her side, she drew by degrees among the eyes fixed on her, some of which were not gentle; but hers were for the Chief, at whose feet, when dismounted by Ammiani's solicitous aid, she would have knelt, had he not seized her by her elbows, and put his lips to her cheek.

"The signorina Vittoria, gentlemen," said Agostino.

CHAPTER III

SIGNORINA VITTORIA

The old man had introduced her with much of the pride of a father displaying some noble child of his for the first time to admiring friends.

"She is one of us," he pursued; "a daughter of Italy! My daughter also; is it not so?"

He turned to her as for a confirmation. The signorina pressed his fingers. She was a little intimidated, and for the moment seemed shy and girlish. The shade of her broad straw hat partly concealed her vivid features.

"Now, gentlemen, if you please, the number is complete, and we may proceed to business," said Agostino, formally but as he conducted the signorina to place her at the feet of the Chief, she beckoned to her servant, who was holding the animal she had ridden. He came up to her, and presented himself in something of a military posture of attention to her commands. These were that he should take the poor brute to water, and then lead him back to Baveno, and do duty in waiting upon her mother. The first injunction was received in a decidedly acquiescent manner. On hearing the second, which directed his abandonment of his post of immediate watchfulness over her safety, the man flatly objected with a "Signorina, no."

He was a handsome bright-eyed fellow, with a soldier's frame and a smile as broad and beaming as laughter, indicating much of that mixture of acuteness, and simplicity which is a characteristic of the South, and means no more than that the extreme vivacity of the blood exceeds at times that of the brain.

A curious frown of half-amused astonishment hung on the signorina's face.

"When I tell you to go, Beppo!"

At once the man threw out his fingers, accompanied by an amazingly voluble delivery of his reasons for this revolt against her authority. Among other things, he spoke of an oath sworn by him to a foreign gentleman, his patron,—for whom, and for whomsoever he loved, he was ready to pour forth his heart's blood,—to the effect that he would never quit her side when she left the roof of her house.

"You see, Beppo," she remonstrated, "I am among friends."

Beppo gave a sweeping bow, but remained firm where he stood. Ammiani cast a sharp hard look at the man.

"Do you hear the signorina's orders?"

"I hear them, signore."

"Will you obey them?"

She interposed. "He must not hear quick words. Beppo is only showing his love for his master and for me. But you are wrong in this case, my Beppo. You shall give me your protection when I require it; and now, you are sensible, and must understand that it is not wanted. I tell you to go."

Beppo read the eyes of his young mistress.

"Signorina,"—he stooped forward mysteriously,—"signorina, that fellow is in Baveno. I saw him this morning."

"Good, good. And now go, my friend."

"The signor Agostino," he remarked loudly, to attract the old man; "the signor Agostino may think proper to advise you."

"The signor Agostino will laugh at nothing that you say to-day, Beppo. You will obey me. Go at once," she repeated, seeing him on tiptoe to gain Agostino's attention.

Beppo knew by her eyes that her ears were locked against him; and, though she spoke softly, there was an imperiousness in her voice not to be disregarded. He showed plainly by the lost rigidity of his attitude that he was beaten and perplexed. Further expostulations being disregarded, he turned his head to look at the poor panting beast under his charge, and went slowly up to him: they walked off together, a crest-fallen pair.

"You have gained the victory, signorina," said Ugo Corte.

She replied, smiling, "My poor Beppo! it's not difficult to get the best of those who love us."

"Ha!" cried Agostino; "here is one of their secrets, Carlo. Take heed of it, my boy. We shall have queens when kings are fossils, mark me!"

Ammiani muttered a courtly phrase, whereat Corte yawned in very grim fashion.

The signorina had dropped to the grass, at a short step from the Chief, to whom her face was now seriously given. In Ammiani's sight she looked a dark Madonna, with the sun shining bright gold through the edges of the summer hat, thrown back from her head. The full and steady contemplative eyes had taken their fixed expression, after a vanishing affectionate gaze of an instant cast upon Agostino. Attentive as they were, light played in them like water. The countenance was vivid in repose. She leaned slightly forward, clasping the wrist of one hand about her knee, and the sole of one little foot showed from under her dress.

Deliberately, but with no attempt at dramatic impressiveness, the Chief began to speak. He touched upon the condition of Italy, and the new lilt animating her young men and women. "I have heard many good men jeer," he said, "at our taking women to our counsel, accepting their help, and putting a great stake upon their devotion. You have read history, and you know what women can accomplish. They may be trained, equally as we are, to venerate the abstract idea of country, and be a sacrifice to it. Without their aid, and the fire of a fresh life being kindled in their bosoms, no country that has lain like ours in the death-trance can revive. In the death-trance, I say, for Italy does not die!"

"True," said other voices.

"We have this belief in the eternal life of our country, and the belief is the life itself. But let no strong man among us despise the help of women. I have seen our cause lie desperate, and those who despaired of it were not women. Women kept the flame alive. They worship in the temple of the cause."

Ammiani's eyes dwelt fervidly upon the signorina. Her look, which was fastened upon the Chief, expressed a mind that listened to strange matter concerning her very little. But when the plans for the rising of the Bergamascs and Brescians, the Venetians, the Bolognese, the Milanese, all the principal Northern cities, were recited, with a practical emphasis thrown upon numbers, upon the readiness of the organized bands, the dispositions of the leaders, and the amount of resistance to be expected at the various points indicated for the outbreak, her hands disjoined, and she stretched her fingers to the grass, supporting herself so, while her extended chin and animated features told how eagerly her spirit drank at positive springs, and thirsted for assurance of the coming storm.

"It is decided that Milan gives the signal," said the Chief; and a light, like the reflection of a beacon-fire upon the night, flashed over her.

He was pursuing, when Ugo Corte smote the air with his nervous fingers, crying out passionately, "Bunglers! are we again to wait for them, and hear that fifteen patriots have stabbed a Croat corporal, and wrestled hotly with a lieutenant of the guard? I say they are bunglers. They never mean the thing. Fifteen! There were just three Milanese among the last lot—the pick of the city; and the rest were made up of Trentini, and our lads from Bergamo and Brescia; and the order from the Council was, 'Go and do the business!' which means, 'Go and earn your ounce of Austrian lead.' They went, and we gave fifteen true men for one poor devil of a curst tight blue-leg. They can play the game on if we give them odds like that. Milan burns bad powder, and goes off like a drugged pistol. It's a nest of bunglers, and may it be razed! We could do without it, and well! If it were a family failing, should not I too be trusting them? My brother was one of the fifteen who marched out as targets to try the skill of those hell-plumed Tyrolese: and they did it thoroughly—shot him straight here." Corte struck his chest. "He gave a jump and a cry. Was it a viva for Milan? They swear that it was, and they can't translate from a living mouth, much more from a dead one; but I know my Niccolo better. I have kissed his lips a thousand times, and I know the poor boy meant, 'Scorn and eternal distrust of such peddling conspirators as these!' I can deal with traitors, but these flash-in-the-pan plotters—these shaking, jelly-bodied patriots!—trust to them again? Rather draw lots for another fifteen to bare their breasts and bandage their eyes, and march out in the grey morning, while the stupid Croat corporal goes on smoking his lumpy pipe! We shall hear that Milan is moving; we shall rise; we shall be hot at it; and the news will come that Milan has merely yawned and turned over to sleep on the other side. Twice she has done this trick, and the garrison there has sent five regiments to finish us—teach us to sleep soundly likewise! I say, let it be Bergamo; or be it Brescia, if you like; or Venice: she is ready. You trust to Milan, and you are fore-doomed. I would swear it with this hand in the flames. She give the signal? Shut your eyes, cross your hands flat on your breasts: you are dead men if you move. She lead the way? Spin on your heels, and you have followed her!"

Corte had spoken in a thick difficult voice, that seemed to require the aid of his vehement gestures to pour out as it did like a water-pipe in a hurricane of rain. He ceased, red almost to blackness, and knotted his arms, that were big as the cable of a vessel. Not a murmur followed his speech. The word was, given to the Chief, and he resumed:—"You have a personal feeling in this case, Ugo. You have not heard me. I came through Paris. A rocket will soon shoot up from Paris that will be a signal for Christendom. The keen French wit is sick of its compromise-king. All Europe is in convulsions in a few months: to-morrow it may be. The elements are in the hearts of the people, and nothing will contain them. We have sown them to reap them. The sowing asks for persistency; but the reaping demands skill and absolute truthfulness. We have now one of those occasions coming which are the flowers to be plucked by resolute and worthy hands: they are the tests of our sincerity. This time now rapidly approaching will try us all, and we must be ready for it. If we have believed in it, we stand prepared. If we have conceived our plan of action in purity of heart, we shall be guided to discern the means which may serve us. You will know speedily what it is that has prompted you to move. If passion blindfolds you, if you are foiled by a prejudice, I also shall know. My friend, the nursing of a single antipathy is a presumption that your motive force is personal—whether the thirst for vengeance or some internal union of a hundred indistinct little fits of egoism. I have seen brave and even noble men fail at the ordeal of such an hour: not fail in courage, not fail in the strength of their desire; that was the misery for them! They failed because midway they lost the vision to select the right instruments put in our way by heaven. That vision belongs solely to such as have clean and disciplined hearts. The hope in the bosom of a man whose fixed star is Humanity becomes a part of his blood, and is extinguished when his blood flows no more. To conquer him, the principle of life must be conquered. And he, my friend, will use all, because he serves all. I need not touch on Milan."

The signorina drew in her breath quickly, as if in this abrupt close she had a revelation of the Chief's whole meaning, and was startled by the sudden unveiling of his mastery. Her hands hung loose; her figure was tremulous. A murmur from Corte jarred within her like a furious discord, but he had not offended by refusing to disclaim his error, and had simply said in a gruff acquiescent way, "Proceed." Her sensations of surprise at the singular triumph of the Chief made her look curiously into the faces of the other men; but the pronouncing of her name engaged her attention.

"Your first night is the night of the fifteenth of next month?"

"It is, signore," she replied, abashed to find herself speaking with him who had so moved her.

"There is no likelihood of a postponement?"

"I am certain, signore, that I shall be ready."

"There are no squabbles of any serious kind among the singers?"

A soft dimple played for a moment on her lips. "I have heard something."

"Among the women?"

"Yes, and the men."

"But the men do not concern you?"

"No, signore. Except that the women twist them."

Agostino chuckled audibly. The Chief resumed:

"You believe, notwithstanding, that all will go well? The opera will be acted; and you will appear in it?"

"Yes, signore. I know one who has determined on it, and can do it."

"Good. The opera is Camilla?"

She was answering with an affirmative, when Agostino broke in,—"Camilla! And honour to whom honour is due! Let Caesar claim the writing of the libretto, if it be Caesar's! It has passed the censorship, signed Agostino Balderini—a disaffected person out of Piedmont, rendered tame and fangless by a rigorous imprisonment. The sources of the tale, O ye grave Signori Tedeschi? The sources are partly to be traced to a neat little French vaudeville, very sparkling—Camille, or the Husband Asserted; and again to a certain Chronicle that may be mediaeval, may be modern, and is just, as the great Shakespeare would say, 'as you like it.'"

Agostino recited some mock verses, burlesquing the ordinary libretti, and provoked loud laughter from Carlo Ammiani, who was familiar enough with the run of their nonsense.

"Camilla is the bride of Camillo. I give to her all the brains, which is a modern idea, quite! He does all the mischief, which is possibly mediaeval. They have both an enemy, which is mediaeval and modern. None of them know exactly what they are about; so there you have the modern, the mediaeval, and the antique, all in one. Finally, my friends, Camilla is something for you to digest at leisure. The censorship swallowed it at a gulp. Never was bait so handsomely taken! At present I have the joy of playing my fish. On the night of the fifteenth I land him. Camilla has a mother. Do you see? That mother is reported, is generally conceived, as dead. Do you see further? Camilla's first song treats of a dream she has had of that mother. Our signorina shall not be troubled to favour you with a taste of it, or, by Bacchus and his

Indian nymphs, I should speedily behold you jumping like peas in a pan, like trout on a bank! The earth would be hot under you, verily! As I was remarking, or meant to be, Camilla and her husband disagree, having agreed to. 'Tis a plot to deceive Count Orso—aha? You are acquainted with Count Orso! He is Camilla's antenuptial guardian. Now you warm to it! In that condition I leave you. Perhaps my child here will give you a taste of her voice. The poetry does much upon reflection, but it has to ripen within you— a matter of time. Wed this voice to the poetry, and it finds passage 'twixt your ribs, as on the point of a driven blade. Do I cry the sweetness and the coolness of my melons? Not I! Try them."

The signorina put her hand out for the scroll he was unfolding, and cast her eyes along bars of music, while Agostino called a "Silenzio tutti!" She sang one verse, and stopped for breath.

Between her dismayed breathings she said to the Chief:—"Believe me, signore, I can be trusted to sing when the time comes."

"Sing on, my blackbird—my viola!" said Agostino. "We all trust you. Look at Colonel Corte, and take him for Count Orso. Take me for pretty Camillo. Take Marco for Michiela; Giulio for Leonardo; Carlo for Cupid. Take the Chief for the audience. Take him for a frivolous public. Ah, my Pippo!" (Agostino laughed aside to him). "Let us lead off with a lighter piece; a trifle-tra-la-la! and then let the frisky piccolo be drowned in deep organ notes, as on some occasions in history the people overrun certain puling characters. But that, I confess, is an illustration altogether out of place, and I'll simply jot it down in my notebook."

Agostino had talked on to let her gain confidence. When he was silent she sang from memory. It was a song of flourishes: one of those be-flowered arias in which the notes flicker and leap like young flames. Others might have sung it; and though it spoke favourably of her aptitude and musical education, and was of a quality to enrapture easy, merely critical audiences, it won no applause from these men. The effect produced by it was exhibited in the placid tolerance shown by the uplifting of Ugo Corte's eyebrows, which said, "Well, here's a voice, certainly." His subsequent look added, "Is this what we have come hither to hear?"

Vittoria saw the look. "Am I on my trial before you?" she thought; and the thought nerved her throat. She sang in strong and grave contralto tones, at first with shut eyes. The sense of hostility left her, and left her soul free, and she raised them. The song was of Camilla dying. She pardons the treacherous hand, commending her memory and the strength of her faith to her husband:—

"Beloved, I am quickly out of sight:
I pray that you will love more than my dust.

Were death defeat, much weeping would be right;
'Tis victory when it leaves surviving trust.
You will not find me save when you forget
Earth's feebleness, and come to faith, my friend,
For all Humanity doth owe a debt
To all Humanity, until the end."

Agostino glanced at the Chief to see whether his ear had caught note of his own language.

The melancholy severity of that song of death changed to a song of prophetic triumph. The signorina stood up. Camilla has thrown off the mask, and has sung the name "Italia!" At the recurrence of it the men rose likewise.

"Italia, Italia, shall be free!"

Vittoria gave the inspiration of a dying voice: the conquest of death by an eternal truth seemed to radiate from her. Voice and features were as one expression of a rapture of belief built upon pathetic trustfulness.

"Italia, Italia shall be free!"

She seized the hearts of those hard and serious men as a wind takes the strong oak-trees, and rocks them on their knotted roots, and leaves them with the song of soaring among their branches. Italy shone about her; the lake, the plains, the peaks, and the shouldering flushed snowridges. Carlo Ammiani breathed as one who draws in fire. Grizzled Agostino glittered with suppressed emotion, like a frosted thorn-bush in the sunlight. Ugo Corte had his thick brows down, as a man who is reading iron matter. The Chief alone showed no sign beyond a half lifting of the hand, and a most luminous fixed observation of the fair young woman, from whom power was an emanation, free of effort. The gaze was sad In its thoughtfulness, such as our feelings translate of the light of evening.

She ceased, and he said, "You sing on the night of the fifteenth?"

"I do, signore."

"It is your first appearance?"

She bent her head.

"And you will be prepared on that night to sing this song?"

"Yes, signore."

"Save in the event of your being forbidden?"

"Unless you shall forbid me, I will sing it, signore."

"Should they imprison you?—"

"If they shoot me I shall be satisfied to know that I have sung a song that cannot be forgotten."

The Chief took her hand in a gentle grasp.

"Such as you will help to give our Italy freedom. You hold the sacred flame, and know you hold it in trust."

"Friends,"—he turned to his companions,—"you have heard what will be the signal for Milan."

CHAPTER IV

AMMIANI'S INTERCESSION

It was a surprise to all of them, save to Agostino Balderini, who passed his inspecting glance from face to face, marking the effect of the announcement. Corte gazed at her heavily, but not altogether disapprovingly. Giulio Bandinelli and Marco Sana, though evidently astonished, and to some extent incredulous, listened like the perfectly trusty lieutenants in an enterprise which they were. But Carlo Ammiani stood horror-stricken. The blood had left his handsome young olive-hued face, and his eyes were on the signorina, large with amazement, from which they deepened to piteousness of entreaty.

"Signorina!—you! Can it be true? Do you know?—do you mean it?"

"What, signor Carlo?"

"This; will you venture to do such a thing?"

"Oh, will I venture? What can you think of me? It is my own request."

"But, signorina, in mercy, listen and consider."

Carlo turned impetuously to the Chief. "The signorina can't know the danger she is running. She will be seized on the boards, and shut up between four walls before a man of us will be ready,—or more than one," he added softly. "The house is sure to be packed for a first night; and the Polizia have a suspicion of her. She has been off her guard in the Conservatorio; she has talked of a country called Italy; she has been indiscreet;—pardon, pardon, signorina! but it is true that she has spoken out from her noble heart. And this opera! Are they fools?—they must see through it. It will never,—it can't possibly be reckoned on to appear. I knew that the signorina was heart and soul with us; but who could guess that her object was to sacrifice herself in the front rank,—to lead a forlorn hope! I tell you it's like a Pagan rite. You are positively slaying a victim. I beg you all to look at the case calmly!"

A burst of laughter checked him; for his seniors by many years could not hear such veteran's counsel from a hurried boy without being shrewdly touched by the humour of it, while one or two threw a particular irony into their tones.

"When we do slay a victim, we will come to you as our augur, my Carlo," said Agostino.

Corte was less gentle. As a Milanese and a mere youth Ammiani was antipathetic to Corte, who closed his laughter with a windy rattle of his lips, and a "pish!" of some emphasis.

Carlo was quick to give him a challenging frown.

"What is it?" Corte bent his head back, as if inquiringly.

"It's I who claim that question by right," said Carlo.

"You are a boy."

"I have studied war."

"In books."

"With brains, Colonel Corte."

"War is a matter of blows, my little lad."

"Let me inform you, signor Colonel, that war is not a game between bulls, to be played with the horns of the head."

"You are prepared to instruct me?" The fiery Bergamasc lifted his eyebrows.

"Nay, nay!" said Agostino. "Between us two first;" and he grasped Carlo's arm, saying in an underbreath, "Your last retort was too long-winded. In these conflicts you must be quick, sharp as a rifle-crack that hits echo on the breast-bone and makes her cry out. I correct a student in the art of war." Then aloud: "My opera, young man!—well, it's my libretto, and you know we writers always say 'my opera' when we have put the pegs for the voice; you are certainly aware that we do. How dare you to make calumnious observations upon my opera? Is it not the ripe and admirable fruit of five years of confinement? Are not the lines sharp, the stanzas solid? and the stuff, is it not good? Is not the subject simple, pure from offence to sensitive authority, constitutionally harmless? Reply!"

"It's transparent to any but asses," said Carlo.

"But if it has passed the censorship? You are guilty, my boy, of bestowing upon those highly disciplined gentlemen who govern your famous city—what title? I trust a prophetic one, since that it comes from an animal whose custom is to turn its back before it delivers a blow, and is, they remark, fonder of encountering dead lions than live ones. Still, it is you who are indiscreet,—eminently so, I must add, if you will look lofty. If my opera has passed the censorship! eh, what have you to say?"

Carlo endured this banter till the end of it came.

"And you—you encourage her!" he cried wrathfully. "You know what the danger is for her, if they once lay hands on her. They will have her in Verona in four-and-twenty hours; through the gates of the Adige in a couple of days, and at Spielberg, or some other of their infernal dens of groans, within a week. Where is the chance of a rescue then? They torture, too, they torture! It's a woman; and insult will be one mode of torturing her. They can use rods—"

The excited Southern youth was about to cover his face, but caught back his hands, clenching them.

"All this," said Agostino, "is an evasion, manifestly, of the question concerning my opera, on which you have thought proper to cast a slur. The phrase, 'transparent to any but asses,' may not be absolutely objectionable, for transparency is, as the critics rightly insist, meritorious in a composition. And, according to the other view, if we desire our clever opponents to see nothing in something, it is notably skilful to let them see through it. You perceive, my Carlo. Transparency, then, deserves favourable comment. So, I do not complain of your phrase, but I had the unfortunate privilege of hearing it uttered. The method of delivery scarcely conveyed a compliment. Will you apologize?"

Carlo burst from him with a vehement question to the Chief: "Is it decided?"

"It is, my friend," was the reply.

"Decided! She is doomed! Signorina! what can you know of this frightful risk? You are going to the slaughter. You will be seized before the first verse is out of your lips, and once in their clutches, you will never breathe free air again. It's madness!—ah, forgive me!—yes, madness! For you shut your eyes; you rush into the trap blindfolded. And that is how you serve our Italy! She sees you an instant, and you are caught away;—and you who might serve her, if you would, do you think you can move dungeon walls?"

"Perhaps, if I have been once seen, I shall not be forgotten," said the signorina smoothly, and then cast her eyes down, as if she felt the burden of a little possible accusation of vanity in this remark. She raised them with fire.

"No; never!" exclaimed Carlo. "But, now you are ours. And—surely it is not quite decided?"

He had spoken imploringly to the Chief. "Not irrevocably?" he added.

"Irrevocably!"

"Then she is lost!"

"For shame, Carlo Ammiani;" said old Agostino, casting his sententious humours aside. "Do you not hear? It is decided! Do you wish to rob her of her courage, and see her tremble? It's her scheme and mine: a case where an old head approves a young one. The Chief says Yes! and you bellow still! Is it a Milanese trick? Be silent."

"Be silent!" echoed Carlo. "Do you remember the beast Marschatska's bet?" The allusion was to a black incident concerning a young Italian ballet girl who had been carried off by an Austrian officer, under the pretext of her complicity in one of the antecedent conspiracies.

"He rendered payment for it," said Agostino.

"He perished; yes! as we shake dust to the winds; but she!—it's terrible! You place women in the front ranks—girls! What can defenceless creatures do? Would you let the van-regiment in battle be the one without weapons? It's slaughter. She's like a lamb to them. You hold up your jewel to the enemy, and cry, 'Come and take it.' Think of the insults! think of the rough hands, and foul mouths! She will be seized on the boards—"

"Not if you keep your tongue from wagging," interposed Ugo Corte, fevered by this unseasonable exhibition of what was to him manifestly a lover's frenzied selfishness. He moved off, indifferent to Carlo's retort. Marco Sana and Giulio Bandinelli were already talking aside with the Chief.

"Signor Carlo, not a hand shall touch me," said the signorina. "And I am not a lamb, though it is good of you to think me one. I passed through the streets of Milan in the last rising. I was unharmed. You must have some confidence in me."

"Signorina, there's the danger," rejoined Carlo. "You trust to your good angels once, twice—the third time they fail you! What are you among a host of armed savages? You would be tossed like weed on the sea. In pity, do not look so scornfully! No, there is no unjust meaning in it; but you despise me for seeing danger. Can nothing persuade you? And, besides," he addressed the Chief, who alone betrayed no signs of weariness; "listen, I beg of you. Milan wants no more than a signal. She does not require to be excited. I came charged with several proposals for giving the alarm. Attend, you others! The night of the Fifteenth comes; it is passing like an ordinary night. At twelve a fire-balloon is seen in the sky. Listen, in the name of saints and devils!"

But even the Chief was observed to show signs of amusement, and the gravity of the rest forsook them altogether at the display of this profound and original conspiratorial notion.

"Excellent! excellent! my Carlo," said old Agostino, cheerfully. "You have thought. You must have thought, or whence such a conception? But, you really mistake. It is not the garrison whom we desire to put on their guard. By no means. We are not in the Imperial pay. Probably your balloon is to burst in due time, and, wind permitting, disperse printed papers all over the city?"

"What if it is?" cried Carlo fiercely.

"Exactly. I have divined your idea. You have thought, or, to correct the tense, are thinking, which is more hopeful, though it may chance not to seem so meritorious. But, if yours are the ideas of full-blown jackets, bear in mind that our enemies are coated and breeched. It may be creditable to you that your cunning is not the cunning of the serpent; to us it would be more valuable if it were. Continue."

"Oh! there are a thousand ways." Carlo controlled himself with a sharp screw of all his muscles. "I simply wish to save the signorina from an annoyance."

"Very mildly put," Agostino murmured assentingly.

"In our Journal," said Carlo, holding out the palm of one hand to dot the forefinger of the other across it, by way of personal illustration—"in our Journal we might arrange for certain letters to recur at distinct intervals in Roman capitals, which might spell out, 'This Night AT Twelve,' or 'At Once.'"

"Quite as ingenious, but on the present occasion erring on the side of intricacy. Aha! you want to increase the sale of your Journal, do you, my boy? The rogue!"

With which, and a light slap over Carlo's shoulder, Agostino left him.

The aspect of his own futile proposals stared the young man in the face too forcibly for him to nurse the spark of resentment which was struck out in the turmoil of his bosom. He veered, as if to follow Agostino, and remained midway, his chest heaving, and his eyelids shut.

"Signor Carlo, I have not thanked you." He heard Vittoria speak. "I know that a woman should never attempt to do men's work. The Chief will tell you that we must all serve now, and all do our best. If we fail, and they put me to great indignity, I promise you that I will not live. I would give this up to be done by anyone else who could do it better. It is in my hands, and my friends must encourage me."

"Ah, signorina!" the young man sighed bitterly. The knowledge that he had already betrayed himself in the presence of others too far, and the sob in his throat labouring to escape, kept him still.

A warning call from Ugo Corte drew their attention. Close by the chalet where the first climbers of the mountain had refreshed themselves, Beppo was seen struggling to secure the arms of a man in a high-crowned green Swiss hat, who was apparently disposed to give the signorina's faithful servant some trouble. After gazing a minute at this singular contention, she cried—"It's the same who follows me everywhere!"

"And you will not believe you are suspected," murmured Carlo in her ear.

"A spy?" Sana queried, showing keen joy at the prospect of scotching such a reptile on the lonely height. Corte went up to the Chief. They spoke briefly together, making use of notes and tracings on paper. The Chief then said "Adieu" to the signorina. It was explained to the rest by Corte that he had a meeting to attend near Pella about noon, and must be in Fobello before midnight. Thence his way would be to Genoa.

"So, you are resolved to give another trial to our crowned ex-Carbonaro," said Agostino.

"Without leaving him an initiative this time!" and the Chief embraced the old man. "You know me upon that point. I cannot trust him. I do not. But, if we make such a tide in Lombardy that his army must be drawn into it, is such an army to be refused? First, the tide, my friend! See to that."

"The king is our instrument!" cried Carlo Ammiani, brightening.

"Yes, if we were particularly well skilled in the use of that kind of instrument," Agostino muttered.

He stood apart while the Chief said a few words to Carlo, which made the blood play vividly across the visage of the youth. Carlo tried humbly to expostulate once or twice. In the end his head was bowed, and he signified a dumb acquiescence.

"Once more, good-bye." The Chief addressed the signorina in English.

She replied in the same tongue, "Good-bye," tremulously; and passion mounting on it, added—"Oh! when shall I see you again?"

"When Rome is purified to be a fit place for such as you."

In another minute he was hidden on the slope of the mountain lying toward Orta.

CHAPTER V

THE SPY

Beppo had effected a firm capture of his man some way down the slope. But it was a case of check that entirely precluded his own free movements. They hung together intertwisted in the characters of specious pacificator and appealing citizen, both breathless.

"There! you want to hand me up neatly; I know your vanity, my Beppo; and you don't even know my name," said the prisoner.

"I know your ferret of a face well enough," said Beppo. "You dog the signorina. Come up, and don't give trouble."

"Am I not a sheep? You worry me. Let me go."

"You're a wriggling eel."

"Catch me fast by the tail then, and don't hold me by the middle."

"You want frightening, my pretty fellow!"

"If that's true, my Beppo, somebody made a mistake in sending you to do it. Stop a moment. You're blown. I think you gulp down your minestra too hot; you drink beer."

"You dog the signorina! I swore to scotch you at last."

"I left Milan for the purpose—don't you see? Act fairly, my Beppo, and let us go up to the signorina together decently."

"Ay, ay, my little reptile! You'll find no Austrians here. Cry out to them to come to you from Baveno. If the Motterone grew just one tree! Saints! one would serve."

"Why don't you—fool that you are, my Beppo!—pray to the saints earlier? Trees don't grow from heaven."

"You'll be going there soon, and you'll know better about it."

"Thanks to the Virgin, then, we shall part at some time or other!"

The struggles between them continued sharply during this exchange of intellectual shots; but hearing Ugo Corte's voice, the prisoner's confident audacity forsook him, and he drew a long tight face like the mask of an admonitory exclamation addressed to himself from within.

"Stand up straight!" the soldier's command was uttered.

Even Beppo was amazed to see that the man had lost the power to obey or to speak.

Corte grasped him under the arm-pit. With the force of his huge fist he swung him round and stretched him out at arm's length, all collar and shanks. The man hung like a mole from the twig. Yet, while Beppo poured out the tale of his iniquities, his eyes gave the turn of a twinkle, showing that he could have answered one whom he did not fear. The charge brought against him was, that for the last six months he had been untiringly spying on the signorina.

Corte stamped his loose feet to earth, shook him and told him to walk aloft. The flexible voluble fellow had evidently become miserably disconcerted. He walked in trepidation, speechless, and when interrogated on the height his eyes flew across the angry visages with dismal uncertainty. Agostino perceived that he had undoubtedly not expected to come among them, and forthwith began to excite Giulio and Marco to the worst suspicions, in order to indulge his royal poetic soul with a study of a timorous wretch pushed to anticipations of extremity.

"The execution of a spy," he preluded, "is the signal for the ringing of joy-bells on this earth; not only because he is one of a pestiferous excess, in point of numbers, but that he is no true son of earth. He escaped out of hell's doors on a windy day, and all that we do is to puff out a bad light, and send him back. Look at this fellow in whom conscience is operating so that he appears like a corked volcano! You can see that he takes Austrian money; his skin has got to be the exact colour of Munz. He has the greenish-yellow eyes of those elective, thrice-abhorred vampyres who feed on patriot-blood. He is condemned without trial by his villainous countenance, like an ungrammatical preface to a book. His tongue refuses to confess, but nature is stronger:—observe his knees. Now this is guilt. It is execrable guilt. He is a nasty object. Nature has in her wisdom shortened his stature to indicate that it is left to us to shorten the growth of his offending years. Now, you dangling soul! answer me:—what name hailed you when on earth?"

The fan, with no clearly serviceable tongue, articulated, "Luigi."

"Luigi! the name Christian and distinctive. The name historic:-Luigi Porco?"

"Luigi Saracco, signore."

"Saracco: Saracco: very possibly a strip of the posterity of cut-throat Moors. To judge by your face, a Moor undoubtedly: glib, slippery! with a body that slides and a soul that jumps. Taken altogether, more serpent than eagle. I misdoubt that little quick cornering eye of yours. Do you ever remember to have blushed?"

"No, signore," said Luigi.

"You spy upon the signorina, do you?"

"You have Beppo's word for that," interposed Marco Sana, growling.

"And you are found spying on the mountain this particular day! Luigi Saracco, you are a fellow of a tremendous composition. A goose walking into a den of foxes is alone to be compared to you,—if ever such goose was! How many of us did you count, now, when you were, say, a quarter of a mile below?"

Marco interposed again: "He has already seen enough up here to make a rope of florins."

"The fellow's eye takes likenesses," said Giulio.

Agostino's question was repeated by Corte, and so sternly that Luigi, beholding kindness upon no other face save Vittoria's, watched her, and muttering "Six," blinked his keen black eyes piteously to get her sign of assent to his hesitated naming of that number. Her mouth and the turn of her head were expressive to him, and he cried "Seven."

"So; first six, and next seven," said Corte.

"Six, I meant, without the signorina," Luigi explained.

"You saw six of us without the signorina! You see we are six here, including the signorina. Where is the seventh?"

Luigi tried to penetrate Vittoria's eyes for a proper response; but she understood the grave necessity for getting the full extent of his observations out of him, and she looked as remorseless as the men. He feigned stupidity and sullenness, rage and cunning, in quick succession.

"Who was the seventh?" said Carlo.

"Was it the king?" Luigi asked.

This was by just a little too clever; and its cleverness, being seen, magnified the intended evasion so as to make it appear to them that Luigi knew well the name of the seventh.

Marco thumped a hand on his shoulder, shouting—"Here; speak out! You saw seven of us. Where has the seventh one gone?"

Luigi's wits made a dash at honesty. "Down Orta, signore."

"And down Orta, I think, you will go; deeper down than you may like."

Corte now requested Vittoria to stand aside. He motioned to her with his hand to stand farther, and still farther off; and finally told Carlo to escort her to Baveno. She now began to think that the man Luigi was in some perceptible danger, nor did Ammiani disperse the idea.

"If he is a spy, and if he has seen the Chief, we shall have to detain him for at least four-and-twenty hours," he said, "or do worse."

"But, Signor Carlo,"—Vittoria made appeal to his humanity,—"do they mean, if they decide that he is guilty, to hurt him?"

"Tell me, signorina, what punishment do you imagine a spy deserves?"

"To be called one!"

Carlo smiled at her lofty method of dealing with the animal.

"Then you presume him to have a conscience?"

"I am sure, Signor Carlo, that I could make him loathe to be called a spy."

They were slowly pacing from the group, and were on the edge of the descent, when the signorina's name was shrieked by Luigi. The man came running to her for protection, Beppo and the rest at his heels. She allowed him to grasp her hand.

"After all, he is my spy; he does belong to me," she said, still speaking on to Carlo. "I must beg your permission, Colonel Corte and Signor Marco, to try an experiment. The Signor Carlo will not believe that a spy can be ashamed of his name.—Luigi!"

"Signorina!"—he shook his body over her hand with a most plaintive utterance.

"You are my countryman, Luigi?"

"Yes, signorina."

"You are an Italian?"

"Certainly, signorina!"

"A spy!"

Vittoria had not always to lift her voice in music for it to sway the hearts of men. She spoke the word very simply in a mellow soft tone. Luigi's blood shot purple. He thrust his fists against his ears.

"See, Signor Carlo," she said; "I was right. Luigi, you will be a spy no more?"

Carlo Ammiani happened to be rolling a cigarette-paper. She put out her fingers for it, and then reached it to Luigi, who accepted it with singular contortions of his frame, declaring that he would confess everything to her. "Yes, signorina, it is true; I am a spy on you. I know the houses you visit. I know you eat too much chocolate for your voice. I know you are the friend of the Signora Laura, the widow of Giacomo Piaveni, shot—shot on Annunciation Day. The Virgin bless him! I know the turning of every street from your house near the Duomo to the signora's. You go nowhere else, except to the maestro's. And it's something to spy upon you. But think of your Beppo who spies upon me! And your little mother, the lady most excellent, is down in Baveno, and she is always near you when you make an expedition. Signorina, I know you would not pay your Beppo for spying upon me. Why does he do it? I do not sing 'Italia, Italia shall be free!' I have heard you when I was under the maestro's windows; and once you sang it to the Signor Agostino Balderini. Indeed, signorina, I am a sort of guardian of your voice. It is not gold of the Tedeschi I get from the Signor Antonio Pericles."

At the mention of this name, Agostino and Vittoria laughed out.

"You are in the pay of the Signor Antonio-Pericles," said Agostino. "Without being in our pay, you have done us the service to come up here among us! Bravo! In return for your disinterestedness, we kick you down, either upon Baveno or upon Stresa, or across the lake, if you prefer it.—The man is harmless. He is hired by a particular worshipper of the signorina's voice, who affects to have first discovered it when she was in England, and is a connoisseur, a millionaire, a Greek, a rich scoundrel, with one indubitable passion, for which I praise him. We will let his paid eavesdropper depart, I think. He is harmless."

Neither Ugo nor Marco was disposed to allow any description of spy to escape unscotched. Vittoria saw that Luigi's looks were against him, and whispered: "Why do you show such cunning eyes, Luigi?"

He replied: "Signorina, take me out of their hearing, and I will tell you everything."

She walked aside. He seemed immediately to be inspired with confidence, and stretched his fingers in the form of a grasshopper, at which sight they cried: "He knows Barto Rizzo—this rascal!" They plied him with signs and countersigns, and speedily let him go. There ensued a sharp snapping of altercation between Luigi and Beppo. Vittoria had to order Beppo to stand back.

"It is a poor dog, not of a good breed, signorina," Luigi said, casting a tolerant glance over his shoulder. "Faithful, but a poor nose. Ah! you gave me this cigarette. Not the Virgin could have touched my marrow as you did. That's to be remembered by-and-by. Now, you are going to sing on the night of the fifteenth of September. Change that night. The Signor Antonio-Pericles watches you, and he is a friend of the Government, and the Government is snoring for you to think it asleep. The Signor Antonio-Pericles pacifies the Tedeschi, but he will know all that you are doing, and how easy it will be, and how simple, for you to let me know what you think he ought to know, and just enough to keep him comfortable! So we work like a machine, signorina. Only, not through that Beppo, for he is vain of his legs, and his looks, and his service, and because he has carried a gun and heard it go off. Yes; I am a spy. But I am honest. I, too, have visited England. One can be honest and a spy. Signorina, I have two arms, but only one heart. If you will be gracious and consider! Say, here are two hands. One hand does this thing, one hand does that thing, and that thing wipes out this thing. It amounts to clear reasoning! Here are two eyes. Were they meant to see nothing but one side! Here is a tongue with a line down the middle almost to the tip of it—which is for service. That Beppo couldn't deal double, if he would; for he is imperfectly designed— a mere dog's pattern! But, only one heart, signorina—mind that. I will never forget the cigarette. I shall smoke it before I leave the mountain, and think—oh!"

Having illustrated the philosophy of his system, Luigi continued: "I am going to tell you everything. Pray, do not look on Beppo! This is important. The Signor Antonio-Pericles sent me to spy on you, because he expects some people to come up the mountain, and you know them; and one is an Austrian officer, and he is an Englishman by birth, and he is coming to meet some English friends who enter Italy from Switzerland over the Moro, and easily up here on mules or donkeys from Pella. The Signor Antonio-Pericles has gold ears for everything that concerns the signorina. 'A patriot is she!' he says; and he is jealous of your English friends. He thinks they will distract you from your studies; and perhaps"—Luigi nodded sagaciously before he permitted himself to say—"perhaps he is jealous in another way. I have heard him speak like a sonnet of the signorina's beauty. The Signor Antonio-Pericles thinks that you have come here to-day to meet them. When he heard that you were going to leave Milan for Baveno, he was mad, and with two fists up, against all English persons. The Englishman who is an Austrian officer is quartered at Verona, and the Signor Antonio Pericles said that the Englishman should not meet you yet, if he could help it."

Victoria stood brooding. "Who can it be,—who is an Englishman, and an Austrian officer, and knows me?"

"Signorina, I don't know names. Behold, that Beppo is approaching like the snow! What I entreat is, that the signorina will wait a little for the English party, if they come, so that I may have something to tell my patron. To invent upon nothing is most unpleasant, and the Signor Antonio can soon perceive whether one swims with corks. Signorina, I can dance on one rope—I am a man. I am not a midge—I cannot dance upon nothing."

The days of Vittoria's youth had been passed in England. It was not unknown to her that old English friends were on the way to Italy; the recollection of a quiet and a buried time put a veil across her features. She was perplexed by the mention of the Austrian officer by Luigi, as one may be who divines the truth too surely, but will not accept it for its loathsomeness. There were Englishmen in the army of Austria. Could one of them be this one whom she had cared for when she was a girl? It seemed hatefully cruel to him to believe it. She spoke to Agostino, begging him to remain with her on the height awhile to see whether the Signor Antonio-Pericles was right; to see whether Luigi was a truth-teller; to see whether these English persons were really coming. "Because," she said, "if they do come, it will at once dissolve any suspicions you may have of this Luigi. And I always long so much to know if the Signor Antonio is correct. I have never yet known him to be wrong."

"And you want to see these English," said Agostino. He frowned.

"Only to hear them. They shall not recognize me. I have now another name; and I am changed. My hat is enough to hide me. Let me hear them talk a little. You and the Signor Carlo will stay with me, and when they come, if they do come, I will remain no longer than just sufficient to make sure. I would refuse to know any of them before the night of the fifteenth; I want my strength too much. I shall have to hear a misery from them; I know it, I feel it; it turns my blood. But let me hear their voices! England is half my country, though I am so willing to forget her and give all my life to Italy. Stay with me, dear friend, my best father! humour me, for you know that I am always charming when I am humoured."

Agostino pressed his finger on a dimple in her cheeks. "You can afford to make such a confession as that to a greybeard. The day is your own. Bear in mind that you are so situated that it will be prudent for you to have no fresh relations, either with foreigners or others, until your work is done,—in which, my dear child, may God bless you!"

"I pray to him with all my might," Vittoria said in reply.

After a consultation with Agostino, Ugo Corte and Marco and Giulio bade their adieux to her. The task of keeping Luigi from their clutches was difficult; but Agostino helped her in that also. To assure them, after his fashion, of the harmlessness of Luigi, he seconded him in a contest of wit against Beppo, and the little fellow, now that he had shaken off his fears, displayed a quickness of retort and a liveliness "unknown to professional spies and impossible to the race," said Agostino; "so absolutely is the mind of man blunted by Austrian gold. We know that for a fact. Beppo is no match for him. Beppo is sententious; ponderously illustrative; he can't turn; he is long-winded; he, I am afraid, my Carlo, studies the journals. He has got your journalistic style, wherein words of six syllables form the relief to words of eight, and hardly one dares to stand by itself. They are like huge boulders across a brook. The meaning, do you, see, would run of itself, but you give us these impedimenting big stones to help us over it, while we profess to understand you by implication. For my part, I own, that to me, your parliamentary, illegitimate academic, modern crocodile phraseology, which is formidable in the jaws, impenetrable on the back, can't circumvent a corner, and is enabled to enter a common understanding solely by having a special highway prepared for it,—in short, the writing in your journals is too much for me. Beppo here is an example that the style is useless for controversy. This Luigi baffles him at every step."

"Some," rejoined Carlo, "say that Beppo has had the virtue to make you his study."

Agostino threw himself on his back and closed his eyes. "That, then, is more than you have done, signor Tuquoque. Look on the Bernina yonder, and fancy you behold a rout of phantom Goths; a sleepy rout, new risen, with the blood of old battles on their shroud-shirts, and a North-east wind blowing them upon our fat land. Or take a turn at the other side toward Orta, and look out for another invasion, by no means so picturesque, but preferable. Tourists! Do you hear them?"

Carlo Ammiani had descried the advanced troop of a procession of gravely-heated climbers ladies upon donkeys, and pedestrian guards stalking beside them, with courier, and lacqueys, and baskets of provisions, all bearing the stamp of pilgrims from the great Western Island.

CHAPTER VI

THE WARNING

A mountain ascended by these children of the forcible Isle, is a mountain to be captured, and colonized, and absolutely occupied for a term; so that Vittoria soon found herself and her small body of adherents observed, and even exclaimed against, as a sort of intruding aborigines, whose presence entirely dispelled the sense of romantic dominion which a mighty eminence should give, and which Britons expect when they have expended a portion of their energies. The exclamations were not complimentary; nevertheless, Vittoria listened with pleased ears, as one listens by a brookside near an old home, hearing a music of memory rather than common words. They talked of heat, of appetite, of chill, of thirst, of the splendour of the prospect, of the anticipations of good hotel accommodation below, of the sadness superinduced by the reflection that in these days people were found everywhere, and poetry was thwarted; again of heat, again of thirst, of beauty, and of chill. There was the enunciation of matronly advice; there was the outcry of girlish insubordination; there were sighings for English ale, and namings of the visible ranges of peaks, and indicatings of geographical fingers to show where Switzerland and Piedmont met, and Austria held her grasp on Lombardy; and "to this point we go to-night; yonder to-morrow; farther the next day," was uttered, soberly or with excitement, as befitted the age of the speaker.

Among these tourists there was one very fair English lady, with long auburn curls of the traditionally English pattern, and the science of Paris displayed in her bonnet and dress; which, if not as graceful as severe admirers of the antique in statuary or of the mediaeval in drapery demand, pleads prettily to be thought so, and commonly succeeds in its object, when assisted by an artistic feminine manner. Vittoria heard her answer to the name of Mrs. Sedley. She had once known her as a Miss Adela Pole. Amidst the cluster of assiduous gentlemen surrounding this lady it was difficult for Vittoria's stolen glances to discern her husband; and the moment she did discern him she became as indifferent to him as was his young wife, by every manifestation of her sentiments. Mrs. Sedley informed her lord that it was not expected of him to care, or to pretend to care, for such scenes as the Motterone exhibited; and having dismissed him to the shade of an umbrella near the provision baskets, she took her station within a few steps of Vittoria, and allowed her attendant gentlemen to talk while she remained plunged in a meditative rapture at the prospect. The talk indicated a settled scheme for certain members of the party to reach Milan from the Como road. Mrs. Sedley was asked if she expected her brother to join her here or in Milan.

"Here, if a man's promises mean anything," she replied languidly.

She was told that some one waved a handkerchief to them from below.

"Is he alone?" she said; and directing an operaglass upon the slope of the mountain, pursued, as in a dreamy disregard of circumstances: "That is Captain Gambier. My brother Wilfrid has not kept his appointment. Perhaps he could not get leave from the General; perhaps he is married; he is engaged to an Austrian Countess, I have heard. Captain Gambier did me the favour to go round to a place called Stresa to meet him. He has undertaken the journey for nothing. It is the way with all journeys though this" (the lady had softly reverted to her rapture) "this is too exquisite! Nature at least does not deceive."

Vittoria listened to a bubbling of meaningless chatter, until Captain Gambier had joined Mrs. Sedley; and at him, for she had known him likewise, she could not forbear looking up. He was speaking to Mrs. Sedley, but caught the look, and bent his head for a clearer view of the features under the broad straw hat. Mrs. Sedley commanded him imperiously to say on.

"Have you no letter from Wilfrid? Has the mountain tired you? Has Wilfrid failed to send his sister one word? Surely Mr. Pericles will have made known our exact route to him? And his uncle, General Pierson, could—I am certain he did—exert his influence to procure him leave for a single week to meet the dearest member of his family."

Captain Gambier gathered his wits to give serviceable response to the kindled lady, and letting his eyes fall from time to time on the broad straw hat, made answer—"Lieutenant Pierson, or, in other words, Wilfrid Pole—"

The lady stamped her foot and flushed.

"You know, Augustus, I detest that name."

"Pardon me a thousandfold. I had forgotten."

"What has happened to you?"

Captain Gambier accused the heat.

"I found a letter from Wilfrid at the hotel. He is apparently kept on constant service between Milan, and Verona, and Venice. His quarters are at Verona. He informs me that he is to be married in the Spring; that is, if all continues quiet; married in the Spring. He seems to fancy that there may be disturbances; not of a serious kind, of course. He will meet you in Milan. He has never been permitted to remain at Milan longer than a couple of days at a stretch. Pericles has told him that she is in Florence. Pericles has told me that Miss Belloni has removed to Florence."

"Say it a third time," the lady indulgently remarked.

"I do not believe that she has gone."

"I dare say not."

"She has changed her name, you know."

"Oh, dear, yes; she has done something fantastic, naturally! For my part, I should have thought her own good enough."

"Emilia Alessandra Belloni is good enough, certainly," said Captain Gambier.

The shading straw rim had shaken once during the colloquy. It was now a fixed defence.

"What is her new name?" Mrs. Sedley inquired.

"That I cannot tell. Wilfrid merely mentions that he has not seen her."

"I," said Mrs. Sedley, "when I reach Milan, shall not trust to Mr. Pericles, but shall write to the Conservatorio; for if she is going to be a great cantatrice, really, it will be agreeable to renew acquaintance with her. Nor will it do any mischief to Wilfrid, now that he is engaged. Are you very deeply attached to straw hats? They are sweet in a landscape."

Mrs. Sedley threw him a challenge from her blue eyes; but his reply to it was that of an unskilled youth, who reads a lady by the letters of her speech:—"One minute. I will be with you instantly. I want to have a look down on the lake. I suppose this is one of the most splendid views in Italy. Half a minute!"

Captain Gambier smiled brilliantly; and the lady, perceiving that polished shield, checked the shot of indignation on her astonished features, and laid it by. But the astonishment lingered there, like the lines of a slackened bow. She beheld her ideal of an English gentleman place himself before these recumbent foreign people, and turn to talk across them, with a pertinacious pursuit of the face under the bent straw hat. Nor was it singular to her that one of them at last should rise and protest against the continuation of the impertinence.

Carlo Ammiani, in fact, had opened matters with a scrupulously-courteous bow.

"Monsieur is perhaps unaware that he obscures the outlook?"

"Totally, monsieur," said Captain Gambier, and stood fast.

"Will monsieur do me the favour to take three steps either to the right or to the left?"

"Pardon, monsieur, but the request is put almost in the form of an order."

"Simply if it should prove inefficacious in the form of a request."

"What, may I ask, monsieur, is your immediate object?"

"To entreat you to behave with civility."

"I am at a loss, monsieur, to perceive any offence."

"Permit me to say, it is lamentable you do not know when you insult a lady."

"I have insulted a lady?" Captain Gambier looked profoundly incredulous. "Oh! then you will not take exception to my assuming the privilege to apologize to her in person?"

Ammiani arrested him as he was about to pass.

"Stay, monsieur; you determine to be impudent, I perceive; you shall not be obtrusive."

Vittoria had tremblingly taken old Agostino's hand, and had risen to her feet. Still keeping her face hidden, she walked down the slope, followed at an interval by her servant, and curiously watched by the English officer, who said to himself, "Well, I suppose I was mistaken," and consequently discovered that he was in a hobble.

A short duologue in their best stilted French ensued between him and Ammiani. It was pitched too high in a foreign tongue for Captain Gambier to descend from it, as he would fain have done, to ask the lady's name. They exchanged cards and formal salutes, and parted.

The dignified altercation had been witnessed by the main body of the tourists. Captain Gambier told them that he had merely interchanged amicable commonplaces with the Frenchman,—"or Italian," he added carelessly, reading the card in his hand. "I thought she might be somebody whom we knew," he said to Mrs. Sedley.

"Not the shadow of a likeness to her," the lady returned.

She had another opinion when later a scrap of paper bearing one pencilled line on it was handed round. A damsel of the party had picked it up near the spot where, as she remarked, "the foreigners had been sitting." It said:—

"Let none who look for safety go to Milan."

CHAPTER VII

BARTO RIZZO

A week following the day of meetings on the Motterone, Luigi the spy was in Milan, making his way across the Piazza de' Mercanti. He entered a narrow court, one of those which were anciently built upon the Oriental principle of giving shade at the small cost of excluding common air. It was dusky noon there through the hours of light, and thrice night when darkness fell. The atmosphere, during the sun's short passage overhead, hung with a glittering heaviness, like the twinkling iron-dust in a subterranean smithy. On the lower window of one of the houses there was a board, telling men that Barto Rizzo made and mended shoes, and requesting people who wished to see him to make much noise at the door, for he was hard of hearing. It speedily became known in the court that a visitor desired to see Barto Rizzo. The noise produced by Luigi was like that of a fanatical beater of the tomtom; he knocked and banged and danced against the door, crying out for his passing amusement an adaptation of a popular ballad:—
"Oh, Barto, Barto! my boot is sadly worn: The toe is seen that should be veiled from sight. The toe that

should be veiled like an Eastern maid: like a sultan's daughter: Shocking! shocking! One of a company of ten that were living a secluded life in chaste privacy! Oh, Barto, Barto! must I charge it to thy despicable leather or to my incessant pilgrimages? One fair toe! I fear presently the corruption of the remaining nine: Then, alas! what do I go on? How shall I come to a perfumed end, who walk on ten indecent toes? Well may the delicate gentlemen sneer at me and scorn me: As for the angelic Lady who deigns to look so low, I may say of her that her graciousness clothes what she looks at: To her the foot, the leg, the back: To her the very soul is bared: But she is a rarity upon earth. Oh, Barto, Barto, she is rarest in Milan! I might run a day's length and not find her. If, O Barto, as my boot hints to me, I am about to be stripped of my last covering, I must hurry to the inconvenient little chamber of my mother, who cannot refuse to acknowledge me as of this pattern: Barto, O shoemaker! thou son of artifice and right-hand-man of necessity, preserve me in the fashion of the time: Cobble me neatly: A dozen wax threads and I am remade:—Excellent! I thank you! Now I can plant my foot bravely: Oh, Barto, my shoemaker! between ourselves, it is unpleasant in these refined days to be likened at all to that preposterous Adam!"

The omission of the apostrophes to Barto left it one of the ironical, veiled Republican, semi-socialistic ballads of the time, which were sung about the streets for the sharpness and pith of the couplets, and not from a perception of the double edge down the length of them.

As Luigi was coming to the terminating line, the door opened. A very handsome sullen young woman, of the dark, thick-browed Lombard type, asked what was wanted; at the same time the deep voice of a man; conjecturally rising from a lower floor, called, and a lock was rattled. The woman told Luigi to enter. He sent a glance behind him; he had evidently been drained of his sprightliness in a second; he moved in with the slackness of limb of a gibbeted figure. The door shut; the woman led him downstairs. He could not have danced or sung a song now for great pay. The smell of mouldiness became so depressing to him that the smell of leather struck his nostrils refreshingly. He thought: "Oh, Virgin! it's dark enough to make one believe in every single thing they tell us about the saints." Up in the light of day Luigi had a turn for careless thinking on these holy subjects.

Barto Rizzo stood before him in a square of cellarage that was furnished with implements of his craft, too dark for a clear discernment of features.

"So, here you are!" was the greeting Luigi received.

It was a tremendous voice, that seemed to issue from a vast cavity. "Lead the gentleman to my sitting-room," said Barto. Luigi felt the wind of a handkerchief, and guessed that his eyes were about to be bandaged by the woman behind him. He petitioned to be spared it, on the plea, firstly, that it expressed want of confidence; secondly, that it took him in the stomach. The handkerchief was tight across his eyes while he was speaking. His hand was touched by the woman, and he commenced timidly an ascent of stairs. It continued so that he would have sworn he was a shorter time going up the Motterone; then down, and along a passage; lower down, deep into corpse-climate; up again, up another enormous mountain; and once more down, as among rats and beetles, and down, as among faceless horrors, and down, where all things seemed prostrate and with a taste of brass. It was the poor fellow's nervous imagination, preternaturally excited. When the handkerchief was caught away, his jaw was shuddering, his eyes were sickly; he looked as if impaled on the prongs of fright. It required just half a minute to reanimate this mercurial creature, when he found himself under the light of two lamps, and Barto Rizzo fronting him, in a place so like the square of cellarage which he had been led to with unbandaged eyes, that it relieved his dread by touching his humour. He cried, "Have I made the journey of the Signor Capofinale, who visited the other end of the world by standing on his head?"

Barto Rizzo rolled out a burly laugh.

"Sit," he said. "You're a poor sweating body, and must needs have a dry tongue. Will you drink?"

"Dry!" quoth Luigi. "Holy San Carlo is a mash in a wine-press compared with me."

Barto Rizzo handed him a liquor, which he drank, and after gave thanks to Providence. Barto raised his hand.

"We're too low down here for that kind of machinery," he said. "They say that Providence is on the side of the Austrians. Now then, what have you to communicate to me? This time I let you come to my house trust at all, trust entirely. I think that's the proverb. You are admitted: speak like a guest."

Luigi's preference happened to be for categorical interrogations. Never having an idea of spontaneously telling the whole truth, the sense that he was undertaking a narrative gave him such emotions as a bad swimmer upon deep seas may have; while, on the other hand, his being subjected to a series of questions seemed at least to leave him with one leg on shore, for then he could lie discreetly, and according to the finger-posts, and only when necessary, and he could recover himself if he made a false step. His ingenious mind reasoned these images out to his own satisfaction. He requested, therefore, that his host would let him hear what he desired to know.

Barto Rizzo's forefinger was pressed from an angle into one temple. His head inclined to meet it: so that it was like the support to a broad blunt pillar. The cropped head was flat as an owl's; the chest of immense breadth; the bulgy knees and big hands were those of a dwarf athlete. Strong colour, lying full on him from the neck to the forehead, made the big veins purple and the eyes fierier than the movements of his mind would have indicated. He was simply studying the character of his man. Luigi feared him; he was troubled chiefly because he was unaware of what Barto Rizzo wanted to know, and could not consequently tell what to bring to the market. The simplicity of the questions put to him was bewildering: he fell into the trap. Barto's eyes began to get terribly oblique. Jingling money in his pocket, he said:—"You saw Colonel Corte on the Motterone: you saw the Signor Agostino Balderini: good men, both! Also young Count Ammiani: I served his father, the General, and jogged the lad on my knee. You saw the Signorina Vittoria. The English people came, and you heard them talk, but did not understand. You came home and told all this to the Signor Antonio, your employer number one. You have told the same to me, your employer number two. There's your pay."

Barto summed up thus the information he had received, and handed Luigi six gold pieces. The latter, springing with boyish thankfulness and pride at the easy earning of them, threw in a few additional facts, as, that he had been taken for a spy by the conspirators, and had heard one of the Englishmen mention the Signorina Vittoria's English name. Barto Rizzo lifted his eyebrows queerly. "We'll go through another interrogatory in an hour," he said; "stop here till I return."

Luigi was always too full of his own cunning to suspect the same in another, until he was left alone to reflect on a scene; when it became overwhelmingly transparent. "But, what could I say more than I did say?" he asked himself, as he stared at the one lamp Barto had left. Finding the door unfastened, he took the lamp and lighted himself out, and along a cavernous passage ending in a blank wall, against which his heart knocked and fell, for his sensation was immediately the terror of imprisonment and helplessness. Mad with alarm, he tried every spot for an aperture. Then he sat down on his haunches;

he remembered hearing word of Barto Rizzo's rack:—certain methods peculiar to Barto Rizzo, by which he screwed matters out of his agents, and terrified them into fidelity. His personal dealings with Barto were of recent date; but Luigi knew him by repute: he knew that the shoemaking business was a mask. Barto had been a soldier, a schoolmaster: twice an exile; a conspirator since the day when the Austrians had the two fine Apples of Pomona, Lombardy and Venice, given them as fruits of peace. Luigi remembered how he had snapped his fingers at the name of Barto Rizzo. There was no despising him now. He could only arrive at a peaceful contemplation of Barto Rizzo's character by determining to tell all, and (since that seemed little) more than he knew. He got back to the leather-smelling chamber, which was either the same or purposely rendered exactly similar to the one he had first been led to.

At the end of a leaden hour Barto Rizzo returned.

"Now, to recommence," he said. "Drink before you speak, if your tongue is dry."

Luigi thrust aside the mention of liquor. It seemed to him that by doing so he propitiated that ill-conceived divinity called Virtue, who lived in the open air, and desired men to drink water. Barto Rizzo evidently understood the kind of man he was schooling to his service.

"Did that Austrian officer, who is an Englishman, acquainted with the Signor Antonio-Pericles, meet the lady, his sister, on the Motterone?"

Luigi answered promptly, "Yes."

"Did the Signorina Vittoria speak to the lady?"

"No."

"Not a word?"

"No."

"Not one communication to her?"

"No: she sat under her straw hat."

"She concealed her face?"

"She sat like a naughty angry girl."

"Did she speak to the officer?"

"Not she!"

"Did she see him?"

"Of course she did! As if a woman's eyes couldn't see through straw-plait!"

Barto paused, calculatingly, eye on victim.

"The Signorina Vittoria," he resumed, "has engaged to sing on the night of the Fifteenth; has she?"

A twitching of Luigi's muscles showed that he apprehended a necessary straining of his invention on another tack.

"On the night of the Fifteenth, Signor Barto Rizzo? That's the night of her first appearance. Oh, yes!"

"To sing a particular song?"

"Lots of them! ay-aie!"

Barto took him by the shoulder and pressed him into his seat till he howled, saying, "Now, there's a slate and a pencil. Expect me at the end of two hours, this time. Next time it will be four: then eight, then sixteen. Find out how many hours that will be at the sixteenth examination."

Luigi flew at the torturer and stuck at the length of his straightened arm, where he wriggled, refusing to listen to the explanation of Barto's system; which was that, in cases where every fresh examination taught him more, they were continued, after regularly-lengthening intervals, that might extend from the sowing of seed to the ripening of grain. "When all's delivered," said Barto, "then we begin to correct discrepancies. I expect," he added, "you and I will have done before a week's out."

"A week!" Luigi shouted. "Here's my stomach already leaping like a fish at the smell of this hole. You brute bear! it's a smell of bones. It turns my inside with a spoon. May the devil seize you when you're sleeping! You shan't go: I'll tell you everything—everything. I can't tell you anything more than I have told you. She gave me a cigarette—there! Now you know:—gave me a cigarette; a cigarette. I smoked it—there! Your faithful servant!"

"She gave you a cigarette, and you smoked it; ha!" said Barto Rizzo, who appeared to see something to weigh even in that small fact. "The English lady gave you the cigarette?"

Luigi nodded: "Yes;" pertinacious in deception. "Yes," he repeated; "the English lady. That was the person. What's the use of your skewering me with your eyes!"

"I perceive that you have never travelled, my Luigi," said Barto. "I am afraid we shall not part so early as I had supposed. I double the dose, and return to you in four hours' time."

Luigi threw himself flat on the ground, shrieking that he was ready to tell everything—anything. Not even the apparent desperation of his circumstances could teach him that a promise to tell the truth was a more direct way of speaking. Indeed, the hitting of the truth would have seemed to him a sort of artful archery, the burden of which should devolve upon the questioner, whom he supplied with the relation of "everything and anything."

All through a night Luigi's lesson continued. In the morning he was still breaking out in small and purposeless lies; but Barto Rizzo had accomplished his two objects: that of squeezing him, and that of subjecting his imagination. Luigi confessed (owing to a singular recovery of his memory) the gift of the cigarette as coming from the Signorina Vittoria. What did it matter if she did give him a cigarette?

"You adore her for it?" said Barto.

"May the Virgin sweep the floor of heaven into her lap!" interjected Luigi. "She is a good patriot."

"Are you one?" Barto asked.

"Certainly I am."

"Then I shall have to suspect you, for the good of your country."

Luigi could not see the deduction. He was incapable of guessing that it might apply forcibly to Vittoria, who had undertaken a grave, perilous, and imminent work. Nothing but the spontaneous desire to elude the pursuit of a questioner had at first instigated his baffling of Barto Rizzo, until, fearing the dark square man himself, he feared him dimly for Vittoria's sake; he could not have said why. She was a good patriot: wherefore the reason for wishing to know more of her? Barto Rizzo had compelled him at last to furnish a narrative of the events of that day on the Motterone, and, finding himself at sea, Luigi struck out boldly and swam as well as he could. Barto disentangled one succinct thread of incidents: Vittoria had been commissioned by the Chief to sing on the night of the Fifteenth; she had subsequently, without speaking to any of the English party, or revealing her features "keeping them beautifully hidden," Luigi said, with unaccountable enthusiasm—written a warning to them that they were to avoid Milan. The paper on which the warning had been written was found by the English when he was the only Italian on the height, lying thereto observe and note things in the service of Barto Rizzo. The writing was English, but when one of the English ladies—"who wore her hair like a planed shred of wood; like a torn vine; like a kite with two tails; like Luxury at the Banquet, ready to tumble over marble shoulders" (an illustration drawn probably from Luigi's study of some allegorical picture,—he was at a loss to describe the foreign female head-dress)—when this lady had read the writing, she exclaimed that it was the hand of "her Emilia!" and soon after she addressed Luigi in English, then in French, then in "barricade Italian" (by which phrase Luigi meant that the Italian words were there, but did not present their proper smooth footing for his understanding), and strove to obtain information from him concerning the signorina, and also concerning the chances that Milan would be an agitated city. Luigi assured her that Milan was the peacefullest of cities—a pure babe. He admitted his acquaintance with the Signorina Vittoria Campa, and denied her being "any longer" the Emilia Alessandra Belloni of the English lady. The latter had partly retained him in her service, having given him directions to call at her hotel in Milan, and help her to communicate with her old friend. "I present myself to her to-morrow, Friday," said Luigi.

"That's to-day," said Barto.

Luigi clapped his hand to his cheek, crying wofully, "You've drawn, beastly gaoler! a night out of my life like an old jaw-tooth."

"There's day two or three fathoms above us," said Barto; "and hot coffee is coming down."

"I believe I've been stewing in a pot while the moon looked so cool." Luigi groaned, and touched up along the sleeves of his arms: that which he fancied he instantaneously felt.

The coffee was brought by the heavy-browed young woman. Before she quitted the place Barto desired her to cast her eyes on Luigi, and say whether she thought she should know him again. She scarcely glanced, and gave answer with a shrug of the shoulders as she retired. Luigi at the time was drinking. He rose; he was about to speak, but yawned instead. The woman's carelessly-dropped upper eyelids seemed to him to be reading him through a dozen of his contortions and disguises, and checked the idea of liberty which he associated with getting to the daylight.

"But it is worth the money!" shouted Barto Rizzo, with a splendid divination of his thought. "You skulker! are you not paid and fattened to do business which you've only to remember, and it'll honey your legs in purgatory? You're the shooting-dog of that Greek, and you nose about the bushes for his birds, and who cares if any fellow, just for exercise, shoots a dagger a yard from his wrist and sticks you in the back? You serve me, and there's pay for you; brothers, doctors, nurses, friends,—a tight blanket if you fall from a housetop! and masses for your soul when your hour strikes. The treacherous cur lies rotting in a ditch! Do you conceive that when I employ you I am in your power? Your intelligence will open gradually. Do you know that here in this house I can conceal fifty men, and leave the door open to the Croats to find them? I tell you now—you are free; go forth. You go alone; no one touches you; ten years hence a skeleton is found with an English letter on its ribs—"

"Oh, stop! signor Barto, and be a blessed man," interposed Luigi, doubling and wriggling in a posture that appeared as if he were shaking negatives from the elbows of his crossed arms. "Stop. How did you know of a letter? I forgot—I have seen the English lady at her hotel. I was carrying the signorina's answer, when I thought 'Barto Rizzo calls me,' and I came like a lamb. And what does it matter? She is a good patriot; you are a good patriot; here it is. Consider my reputation, do; and be careful with the wax."

Barto drew a long breath. The mention of the English letter had been a shot in the dark. The result corroborated his devotional belief in the unerringness of his own powerful intuition. He had guessed the case, or hardly even guessed it—merely stated it, to horrify Luigi. The letter was placed in his hands, and he sat as strongly thrilled by emotion, under the mask of his hard face, as a lover hearing music. "I read English," he remarked.

After he had drawn the seal three or four times slowly over the lamp, the green wax bubbled and unsnapped. Vittoria had written the following lines in reply to her old English friend:—

"Forgive me, and do not ask to see me until we have passed the fifteenth of the month. You will see me that night at La Scala. I wish to embrace you, but I am miserable to think of your being in Milan. I cannot yet tell you where my residence is. I have not met your brother. If he writes to me it will make me happy, but I refuse to see him. I will explain to him why. Let him not try to see me. Let him send by this messenger. I hope he will contrive to be out of Milan all this month. Pray let me influence you to go for a time. I write coldly; I am tired, and forget my English. I do not forget my friends. I have you close against my heart. If it were prudent, and it involved me alone, I would come to you without a moment's loss of time. Do know that I am not changed, and am your affectionate

"Emilia."

When Barto Rizzo had finished reading, he went from the chamber and blew his voice into what Luigi supposed to be a hollow tube.

"This letter," he said, coming back, "is a repetition of the Signorina Vittoria's warning to her friends on the Motterone. The English lady's brother, who is in the Austrian service, was there, you say?"

Luigi considered that, having lately been believed in, he could not afford to look untruthful, and replied with a sprightly "Assuredly."

"He was there, and he read the writing on the paper?"

"Assuredly: right out loud, between puff-puff of his cigar."

"His name is Lieutenant Pierson. Did not Antonio-Pericles tell you his name? He will write to her: you will be the bearer of his letter to the signorina. I must see her reply. She is a good patriot; so am I; so are you. Good patriots must be prudent. I tell you, I must see her reply to this Lieutenant Pierson." Barto stuck his thumb and finger astride Luigi's shoulder and began rocking him gently, with a horrible meditative expression. "You will have to accomplish this, my Luigi. All fair excuses will be made, if you fail generally. This you must do. Keep upright while I am speaking to you! The excuses will be made; but I, not you, must make them: bear that in mind. Is there any person whom you, my Luigi, like best in the world?"

It was a winning question, and though Luigi was not the dupe of its insinuating gentleness, he answered, "The little girl who carries flowers every morning to the caffe La Scala."

"Ah! the little girl who carries flowers every morning to the caffe La Scala. Now, my Luigi, you may fail me, and I may pardon you. Listen attentively: if you are false; if you are guilty of one piece of treachery:—do you see? You can't help slipping, but you can help jumping. Restrain yourself from jumping, that's all. If you are guilty of treachery, hurry at once, straight off, to the little girl who carries flowers every morning to the caffe La Scala. Go to her, take her by the two cheeks, kiss her, say to her 'addio, addio,' for, by the thunder of heaven! you will never see her more."

Luigi was rocked forward and back, while Barto spoke in level tones, till the voice dropped into its vast hollow, when Barto held him fast a moment, and hurled him away by the simple lifting of his hand.

The woman appeared and bound Luigi's eyes. Barto did not utter another word. On his journey back to daylight, Luigi comforted himself by muttering oaths that he would never again enter into this trap. As soon as his eyes were unbandaged, he laughed, and sang, and tossed a compliment from his finger-tips to the savage-browed beauty; pretended that he had got an armful, and that his heart was touched by the ecstasy; and sang again: "Oh, Barto, Barto! my boot is sadly worn. The toe is seen," etc., half-way down the stanzas. Without his knowing it, and before he had quitted the court, he had sunk into songless gloom, brooding on the scenes of the night. However free he might be in body, his imagination was captive to Barto Rizzo. He was no luckier than a bird, for whom the cage is open that it may feel the more keenly with its little taste of liberty that it is tied by the leg.

CHAPTER VIII

THE LETTER

The importance of the matters extracted from Luigi does not lie on the surface; it will have to be seen through Barto Rizzo's mind. This man regarded himself as the mainspring of the conspiracy; specially its guardian, its wakeful Argus. He had conspired sleeplessly for thirty years; so long, that having no ideal reserve in his nature, conspiracy had become his professional occupation,—the wheel which it was his business to roll. He was above jealousy; he was above vanity. No one outstripping him cast a bad colour on him; nor did he object to bow to another as his superior. But he was prepared to suspect every one of insincerity and of faithlessness; and, being the master of the machinery of the plots, he was ready, upon a whispered justification, to despise the orders of his leader, and act by his own light in blunt disobedience. For it was his belief that while others speculated he knew all. He knew where the plots had failed; he knew the man who had bent and doubled. In the patriotic cause, perfect arrangements are crowned with perfect success, unless there is an imperfection of the instruments; for the cause is blessed by all superior agencies. Such was his governing idea. His arrangements had always been perfect; hence the deduction was a denunciation of some one particular person. He pointed out the traitor here, the traitor there; and in one or two cases he did so with a mildness that made those fret at their beards vaguely who understood his character. Barto Rizzo was, it was said, born in a village near Forli, in the dominions of the Pope; according to the rumour, he was the child of a veiled woman and a cowled paternity. If not an offender against Government, he was at least a wanderer early in life. None could accuse him of personal ambition. He boasted that he had served as a common soldier with the Italian contingent furnished by Eugene to the Moscow campaign; he showed scars of old wounds: brown spots, and blue spots, and twisted twine of white skin, dotting the wrist, the neck, the calf, the ankle, and looking up from them, he slapped them proudly. Nor had he personal animosities of any kind. One sharp scar, which he called his shoulder knot, he owed to the knife of a friend, by name Sarpo, who had things ready to betray him, and struck him, in anticipation of that tremendous moment of surprise and wrath when the awakened victim frequently is nerved with devil's strength; but, striking, like a novice, on the bone, the stilet stuck there; and Barto coolly got him to point the outlet of escape, and walked off, carrying the blade where the terrified assassin had planted it. This Sarpo had become a tradesman in Milan—a bookseller and small printer; and he was unmolested. Barto said of him, that he was as bad as a few odd persons thought himself to be, and had in him the making of a great traitor; but, that as Sarpo hated him and had sought to be rid of him for private reasons only, it was a pity to waste on such a fellow steel that should serve the Cause. "While I live," said Barto, "my enemies have a tolerably active conscience."

The absence of personal animosity in him was not due to magnanimity. He doubted the patriotism of all booksellers. He had been twice betrayed by women. He never attempted to be revenged on them; but he doubted the patriotism of all women. "Use them; keep eye on them," he said. In Venice he had conspired when he was living there as the clerk of a notary; in Bologna subsequently while earning his bread as a petty schoolmaster. His evasions, both of Papal sbirri and the Austrian polizia, furnished instances of astonishing audacity that made his name a byword for mastery in the hour of peril. His residence in Milan now, after seven years of exile in England and Switzerland, was an act of pointed defiance, incomprehensible to his own party, and only to be explained by the prevalent belief that the authorities feared to provoke a collision with the people by laying hands on him. They had only once made a visitation to his house, and appeared to be satisfied at not finding him. At that period Austria was simulating benevolence in her Lombardic provinces, with the half degree of persuasive earnestness which makes a Government lax in its vigilance, and leaves it simply open to the charge of effeteness. There were contradictory rumours as to whether his house had ever been visited by the polizia; but it was a legible fact that his name was on the window, and it was understood that he was not without elusive contrivances in the event of the authorities declaring war against him.

Of the nature of these contrivances Luigi had just learnt something. He had heard Barto Rizzo called 'The Miner' and 'The Great Cat,' and he now comprehended a little of the quality of his employer. He had entered a very different service from that of the Signor Antonio-Pericles, who paid him for nothing more than to keep eye on Vittoria, and recount her goings in and out; for what absolute object he was unaware, but that it was not for a political one he was certain. "Cursed be the day when the lust of gold made me open my hand to Barto Rizzo!" he thought; and could only reflect that life is short and gold is sweet, and that he was in the claws of the Great Cat. He had met Barto in a wine-shop. He cursed the habit which led him to call at that shop; the thirst which tempted him to drink: the ear which had been seduced to listen. Yet as all his expenses had been paid in advance, and his reward at the instant of his application for it; and as the signorina and Barto were both good patriots, and he, Luigi, was a good patriot, what harm could be done to her? Both she and Barto had stamped their different impressions on his waxen nature. He reconciled his service to them separately by the exclamation that they were both good patriots.

The plot for the rising in Milan city was two months old. It comprised some of the nobles of the city, and enjoyed the good wishes of the greater part of them, whose payment of fifty to sixty per cent to the Government on the revenue of their estates was sufficient reason for a desire to change masters, positively though they might detest Republicanism, and dread the shadow of anarchy. These looked hopefully to Charles Albert. Their motive was to rise, or to countenance a rising, and summon the ambitious Sardinian monarch with such assurances of devotion, that a Piedmontese army would be at the gates when the banner of Austria was in the dust. Among the most active members of the prospectively insurgent aristocracy of Milan was Count Medole, a young nobleman of vast wealth and possessed of a reliance on his powers of mind that induced him to take a prominent part in the opening deliberations, and speedily necessitated his hire of the friendly offices of one who could supply him with facts, with suggestions, with counsel, with fortitude, with everything to strengthen his pretensions to the leadership, excepting money. He discovered his man in Barto Rizzo, who quitted the ranks of the republican section to serve him, and wield a tool for his own party. By the help of Agostino Balderini, Carlo Ammiani, and others, the aristocratic and the republican sections of the conspiracy were brought near enough together to permit of a common action between them, though the maintaining of such harmony demanded an extreme and tireless delicacy of management. The presence of the Chief, whom we have seen on the Motterone, was claimed by other cities of Italy. Unto him solely did Barto Rizzo yield thorough adhesion. He being absent from Milan, Barto undertook to represent him and carry out his views. How far he was entitled to do so may be guessed when it is stated that, on the ground of his general contempt for women, he objected to the proposition that Vittoria should give the signal. The proposition was Agostino's. Count Medole, Barto, and Agostino discussed it secretly: Barto held resolutely against it, until Agostino thrust a sly-handed letter into his fingers and let him know that previous to any consultation on the subject he had gained the consent of his Chief. Barto then fell silent. He despatched his new spy, Luigi, to the Motterone, more for the purpose of giving him a schooling on the expedition, and on his return from it, and so getting hand and brain and soul service out of him. He expected no such a report of Vittoria's indiscretion as Luigi had spiced with his one foolish lie. That she should tell the relatives of an Austrian officer that Milan was soon to be a dangerous place for them;— and that she should write it on paper and leave it for the officer to read,—left her, according to Barto's reading of her, open to the alternative charges of imbecility or of treachery. Her letter to the English lady, the Austrian officer's sister, was an exaggeration of the offence, but lent it more the look of heedless folly. The point was to obtain sight of her letter to the Austrian officer himself. Barto was baffled during a course of anxious days that led closely up to the fifteenth. She had written no letter. Lieutenant Pierson, the officer in question, had ridden into the city once from Verona, and had called upon Antonio-Pericles to extract her address from him; the Greek had denied that she was in Milan. Luigi could tell no more. He described the officer's personal appearance, by saying that he was a recognizable Englishman in Austrian dragoon uniform;—white tunic, white helmet, brown moustache;—

ay! and eh! and oh! and ah! coming frequently from his mouth; that he stood square while speaking, and seemed to like his own smile; an extraordinary touch of portraiture, or else a scoff at insular self-satisfaction; at any rate, it commended itself to the memory. Barto dismissed him, telling him to be daily in attendance on the English lady.

Barto Rizzo's respect for the Chief was at war with his intense conviction that a blow should be struck at Vittoria even upon the narrow information which he possessed. Twice betrayed, his dreams and haunting thoughts cried "Shall a woman betray you thrice?" In his imagination he stood identified with Italy: the betrayal of one meant that of both. Falling into a deep reflection, Barto counted over his hours of conspiracy: he counted the Chief's; comparing the two sets of figures he discovered, that as he had suspected, he was the elder in the patriotic work therefore, if he bowed his head to the Chief, it was a voluntary act, a form of respect, and not the surrendering of his judgement. He was on the spot: the Chief was absent. Barto reasoned that the Chief could have had no experience of women, seeing that he was ready to trust in them. "Do I trust to my pigeon, my sling-stone?" he said jovially to the thickbrowed, splendidly ruddy young woman, who was his wife; "do I trust her? Not half a morsel of her!" This young woman, a peasant woman of remarkable personal attractions, served him with the fidelity of a fascinated animal, and the dumbness of a wooden vessel. She could have hanged him, had it pleased her. She had all his secrets: but it was not vain speaking on Barto Rizzo's part; he was master of her will; and on the occasions when he showed that he did not trust her, he was careful at the same time to shock and subdue her senses. Her report of Vittoria was, that she went to the house of the Signora, Laura Piaveni, widow of the latest heroic son of Milan, and to that of the maestro Rocco Ricci; to no other. It was also Luigi's report.

"She's true enough," the woman said, evidently permitting herself to entertain an opinion; a sign that she required fresh schooling.

"So are you," said Barto, and eyed her in a way that made her ask, "Now, what's for me to do?"

He thought awhile.

"You will see the colonel. Tell him to come in corporal's uniform. What's the little wretch twisting her body for? Shan't I embrace her presently if she's obedient? Send to the polizia. You believe your husband is in the city, and will visit you in disguise at the corporal's hour. They seize him. They also examine the house up to the point where we seal it. Your object is to learn whether the Austrians are moving men upon Milan. If they are-I learn something. When the house has been examined, our court here will have rest for a good month ahead; and it suits me not to be disturbed. Do this, and we will have a red-wine evening in the house, shut up alone, my snake! my pepper-flower!"

It happened that Luigi was entering the court to keep an appointment with Barto when he saw a handful of the polizia burst into the house and drag out a soldier, who was in the uniform, as he guessed it to be, of the Prohaska regiment. The soldier struggled and offered money to them. Luigi could not help shouting, "You fools! don't you see he's an officer?" Two of them took their captive aside. The rest made a search through the house. While they were doing so Luigi saw Barto Rizzo's face at the windows of the house opposite. He clamoured at the door, but Barto was denied to him there. When the polizia had gone from the court, he was admitted and allowed to look into every room. Not finding him, he said, "Barto Rizzo does not keep his appointments, then!" The same words were repeated in his ear when he had left the court, and was in the street running parallel with it. "Barto Rizzo does not keep his appointments, then!" It was Barto who smacked him on the back, and spoke out his own name with brown-faced laughter in the bustling street. Luigi was so impressed by his cunning and his recklessness that he at once told him more than he wished to tell:—The Austrian officer was with his sister, and had written to the signorina, and Luigi had delivered the letter; but the signorina was at the maestro's, Rocco Ricci's, and there was no answer: the officer was leaving for Verona in the morning. After telling so much, Luigi drew back, feeling that he had given Barto his full measure and owed to the signorina what remained.

Barto probably read nothing of the mind of his spy, but understood that it was a moment for distrust of him. Vittoria and her mother lodged at the house of one Zotti, a confectioner, dwelling between the Duomo and La Scala. Luigi, at Barto's bidding, left word with Zotti that he would call for the signorina's answer to a certain letter about sunrise. "I promised my Rosellina, my poppyheaded sipper, a red-wine evening, or I would hold this fellow under my eye till the light comes," thought Barto misgivingly, and let him go. Luigi slouched about the English lady's hotel. At nightfall her brother came forth. Luigi directed him to be in the square of the Duomo by sunrise, and slipped from his hold; the officer ran after him some distance. "She can't say I was false to her now," said Luigi, dancing with nervous ecstasy. At sunrise Barto Rizzo was standing under the shadow of the Duomo. Luigi passed him and went to Zotti's house, where the letter was placed in his hand, and the door shut in his face. Barto rushed to him, but Luigi, with a vixenish countenance, standing like a humped cat, hissed, "Would you destroy my reputation and have it seen that I deliver up letters, under the noses of the writers, to the wrong persons?—ha! pestilence!" He ran, Barto following him. They were crossed by the officer on horseback, who challenged Luigi to give up the letter, which was very plainly being thrust from his hand into his breast. The officer found it no difficult matter to catch him and pluck the letter from him; he opened it, reading it on the jog of the saddle as he cantered off. Luigi turned in a terror of expostulation to ward Barto's wrath. Barto looked at him hard, while he noted the matter down on the tablet of an ivory book. All he said was, "I have that letter!" stamping the assertion with an oath. Half-an-hour later Luigi saw Barto in the saddle, tight-legged about a rusty beast, evidently bound for the South-eastern gate, his brows set like a black wind. "Blessings on his going!" thought Luigi, and sang one of his street-songs:—
"O lemons, lemons, what a taste you leave in the mouth! I desire you, I love you, but when I suck you, I'm all caught up in a bundle and turn to water, like a wry-faced fountain. Why not be satisfied by a sniff at the blossoms? There's gratification. Why did you grow up from the precious little sweet chuck that you were, Marietta? Lemons, O lemons! such a thing as a decent appetite is not known after sucking at you."

His natural horror of a resolute man, more than fear (of which he had no recollection in the sunny Piazza), made him shiver and gave his tongue an acid taste at the prospect of ever meeting Barto Rizzo again. There was the prospect also that he might never meet him again.

BOOK II

CHAPTER IX

IN VERONA

The lieutenant read these lines, as he clattered through the quiet streets toward the Porta Tosa:

'DEAR FRIEND,—I am glad that you remind me of our old affection, for it assures me that yours is not dead. I cannot consent to see you yet. I would rather that we should not meet.

'I thought I would sign my name here, and say, "God bless you, Wilfrid; go!"

'Oh! why have you done this thing! I must write on. It seems like my past life laughing at me, that my old friend should have come here in Italy, to wear the detestable uniform. How can we be friends when we must act as enemies? We shall soon be in arms, one against the other. I pity you, for you have chosen a falling side; and when you are beaten back, you can have no pride in your country, as we Italians have; no delight, no love. They will call you a mercenary soldier. I remember that I used to have the fear of your joining our enemies, when we were in England, but it seemed too much for my reason.

'You are with a band of butchers. If I could see you and tell you the story of Giacomo Piaveni, and some other things, I believe you would break your sword instantly.

'There is time. Come to Milan on the fifteenth. You will see me then. I appear at La Scala. Promise me, if you hear me, that you will do exactly what I make you feel it right to do. Ah, you will not, though thousands will! But step aside to me, when the curtain falls, and remain—oh, dear friend! I write in honour to you; we have sworn to free the city and the country—remain among us: break your sword, tear off your uniform; we are so strong that we are irresistible. I know what a hero you can be on the field: then, why not in the true cause? I do not understand that you should waste your bravery under that ugly flag, bloody and past forgiveness.

'I shall be glad to have news of you all, and of England. The bearer of this is a trusty messenger, and will continue to call at the hotel. A. is offended that I do not allow my messenger to give my address; but I must not only be hidden, I must have peace, and forget you all until I have done my task. Addio. We have both changed names. I am the same. Can I think that you are? Addio, dear friend.

'VITTORIA.'

Lieutenant Pierson read again and again the letter of her whom he had loved in England, to get new lights from it, as lovers do when they have lost the power to take single impressions. He was the bearer of a verbal despatch from the commandant in Milan to the Marshal in Verona. At that period great favour was shown to Englishmen in the Austrian service, and the lieutenant's uncle being a General of distinction, he had a sort of semi-attachment to the Marshal's staff, and was hurried to and fro, for the purpose of keeping him out of duelling scrapes, as many of his friendlier comrades surmised. The right to the distinction of exercising staff-duties is, of course, only to be gained by stout competitorship in the Austrian service; but favour may do something for a young man even in that rigorous school of Arms. He had to turn to Brescia on his way, and calculated that if luck should put good horses under him, he would enter Verona gates about sunset. Meantime; there was Vittoria's letter to occupy him as he went.

We will leave him to his bronzing ride through the mulberries and the grapes, and the white and yellow and arid hues of the September plain, and make acquaintance with some of his comrades of that proud army which Vittoria thought would stand feebly against the pouring tide of Italian patriotism.

The fairest of the cities of the plain had long been a nest of foreign soldiery. The life of its beauty was not more visible then than now. Within the walls there are glimpses of it, that belong rather to the haunting spirit than to the life. Military science has made a mailed giant of Verona, and a silent one, save upon occasion. Its face grins of war, like a skeleton of death; the salient image of the skull and congregating worms was one that Italian lyrists applied naturally to Verona.

The old Field-Marshal and chief commander of the Austrian forces in Lombardy, prompted by the counsels of his sagacious adlatus, the chief of the staff, was engaged at that period in adding some of those ugly round walls and flanking bastions to Verona, upon which, when Austria was thrown back by the first outburst of the insurrection and the advance of the Piedmontese, she was enabled to plant a sturdy hind-foot, daring her foes as from a rock of defence.

A group of officers, of the cavalry, with a few infantry uniforms skirting them, were sitting in the pleasant cooling evening air, fanned by the fresh springing breeze, outside one of the Piazza Bra caffes, close upon the shadow of the great Verona amphitheatre. They were smoking their attenuated long straw cigars, sipping iced lemonade or coffee, and talking the common talk of the garrison officers, with perhaps that additional savour of a robust immorality which a Viennese social education may give. The rounded ball of the brilliant September moon hung still aloft, lighting a fathomless sky as well as the fair earth. It threw solid blackness from the old savage walls almost to a junction with their indolent outstretched feet. Itinerant street music twittered along the Piazza; officers walked arm-in-arm; now in moonlight bright as day, now in a shadow black as night: distant figures twinkled with the alternation. The light lay like a blade's sharp edge around the massive circle. Of Italians of a superior rank, Verona sent none to this resort. Even the melon-seller stopped beneath the arch ending the Stradone Porta Nuova, as if he had reached a marked limit of his popular customers.

This isolation of the rulers of Lombardy had commenced in Milan, but, owing to particular causes, was not positively defined there as it was in Verona. War was already rageing between the Veronese ladies and the officers of Austria. According to the Gallic Terpsichorean code, a lady who permits herself to make election of her partners and to reject applicants to the honour of her hand in the dance, when that hand is disengaged, has no just ground of complaint if a glove should smite her cheek. The Austrians had to endure this sort of rejection in Ballrooms. On the promenade their features were forgotten. They bowed to statues. Now, the officers of Austria who do not belong to a Croat regiment, or to one drawn from any point of the extreme East of the empire, are commonly gentlemanly men; and though they can be vindictive after much irritation, they may claim at least as good a reputation for forbearance in a conquered country as our officers in India. They are not ill-humoured, and they are not peevishly arrogant, except upon provocation. The conduct of the tender Italian dames was vexatious. It was exasperating to these knights of the slumbering sword to hear their native waltzes sounding of exquisite Vienna, while their legs stretched in melancholy inactivity on the Piazza pavement, and their arms encircled no ductile waists. They tried to despise it more than they disliked it, called their female foes Amazons, and their male by a less complimentary title, and so waited for the patriotic epidemic to pass.

A certain Captain Weisspriess, of the regiment named after a sagacious monarch whose crown was the sole flourishing blossom of diplomacy, particularly distinguished himself by insisting that a lady should remember him in public places. He was famous for skill with his weapons. He waltzed admirably; erect as under his Field-Marshal's eye. In the language of his brother officers, he was successful; that is, even as God Mars when Bellona does not rage. Captain Weisspriess (Johann Nepomuk, Freiherr von Scheppenhausen) resembled in appearance one in the Imperial Royal service, a gambling General of Division, for whom Fame had not yet blown her blast. Rumour declared that they might be relatives; a little-scrupulous society did not hesitate to mention how. The captain's moustache was straw-coloured; he wore it beyond the regulation length and caressed it infinitely. Surmounted by a pair of hot eyes, wavering in their direction, this grand moustache was a feature to be forgotten with difficulty, and

Weisspriess was doubtless correct in asserting that his face had endured a slight equal to a buffet. He stood high and square-shouldered; the flame of the moustache streamed on either side his face in a splendid curve; his vigilant head was loftily posted to detect what he chose to construe as insult, or gather the smiles of approbation, to which, owing to the unerring judgement of the sex, he was more accustomed. Handsome or not, he enjoyed the privileges of masculine beauty.

This captain of a renown to come pretended that a superb Venetian lady of the Branciani family was bound to make response in public to his private signals, and publicly to reply to his salutations. He refused to be as a particle in space floating airily before her invincible aspect. Meeting her one evening, ere sweet Italy had exiled herself from the Piazza, he bowed, and stepping to the front of her, bowed pointedly. She crossed her arms and gazed over him. He called up a thing to her recollection in resonant speech. Shameful lie, or shameful truth, it was uttered in the hearing of many of his brother officers, of three Italian ladies, and of an Italian gentleman, Count Broncini, attending them. The lady listened calmly. Count Broncini smote him on the face. That evening the lady's brother arrived from Venice, and claimed his right to defend her. Captain Weisspriess ran him through the body, and attached a sinister label to his corpse. This he did not so much from brutality; the man felt that henceforth while he held his life he was at war with every Italian gentleman of mettle. Count Broncini was his next victim. There, for a time, the slaughtering business of the captain stopped. His brother officers of the better kind would not have excused him at another season, but the avenger of their irritation and fine vindicator of the merits of Austrian steel, had a welcome truly warm, when at the termination of his second duel he strode into mess, or what serves for an Austrian regimental mess.

It ensued naturally that there was everywhere in Verona a sharp division between the Italians of all classes and their conquerors. The great green-rinded melons were never wheeled into the neighbourhood of the whitecoats. Damsels were no longer coquettish under the military glance, but hurried by in couples; and there was much scowling mixed with derisive servility, throughout the city, hard to be endured without that hostile state of the spirit which is the military mind's refuge in such cases. Itinerant musicians, and none but this fry, continued to be attentive to the dispensers of soldi.

The Austrian army prides itself upon being a brotherhood. Discipline is very strict, but all commissioned officers, when off duty, are as free in their intercourse as big boys. The General accepts a cigar from the lieutenant, and in return lifts his glass to him. The General takes an interest in his lieutenant's love-affairs: nor is the latter shy when he feels it his duty modestly to compliment his superior officer upon a recent conquest. There is really good fellowship both among the officers and in the ranks, and it is systematically encouraged.

The army of Austria was in those days the Austrian Empire. Outside the army the empire was a jealous congery of intriguing disaffected nationalities. The same policy which played the various States against one another in order to reduce all to subserviency to the central Head, erected a privileged force wherein the sentiment of union was fostered till it became a nationality of the sword. Nothing more fatal can be done for a country; but for an army it is a simple measure of wisdom. Where the password is MARCH, and not DEVELOP, a body of men, to be a serviceable instrument, must consent to act as one. Hannibal is the historic example of what a General can accomplish with tribes who are thus, enrolled in a new citizenship; and (as far as we know of him and his fortunes) he appears to be an example of the necessity of the fusing fire of action to congregated aliens in arms. When Austria was fighting year after year, and being worsted in campaign after campaign, she lost foot by foot, but she held together soundly; and more than the baptism, the atmosphere of strife has always been required to give her a healthy vitality as a centralized empire. She knew it; this (apart from the famous promptitude of the

Hapsburgs) was one secret of her dauntless readiness to fight. War did the work of a smithy for the iron and steel holding her together; and but that war costs money, she would have been an empire distinguished by aggressiveness. The next best medicinal thing to war is the military occupation of insurgent provinces. The soldiery soon feel where their home is, and feel the pride of atomies in unitive power, when they are sneered at, hooted, pelted, stabbed upon a gross misinterpretation of the slightest of moral offences, shamefully abused for doing their duty with a considerate sense of it, and too accurately divided from the inhabitants of the land they hold. In Italy, the German, the Czech, the Magyar, the Croft, even in general instances the Italian, clung to the standard for safety, for pay, for glory, and all became pre-eminently Austrian soldiers; little besides.

It was against a power thus bound in iron hoops, that Italy, dismembered, and jealous, and corrupt, with an organization promoted by passion chiefly, was preparing to rise. In the end, a country true to itself and determined to claim God's gift to brave men will overmatch a mere army, however solid its force. But an inspired energy of faith is demanded of it. The intervening chapters will show pitiable weakness, and such a schooling of disaster as makes men, looking on the surface of things, deem the struggle folly. As well, they might say, let yonder scuffling vagabonds up any of the Veronese side-streets fall upon the patrol marching like one man, and hope to overcome them! In Vienna there was often despair: but it never existed in the Austrian camp. Vienna was frequently double-dealing and time-serving her force in arms was like a trained man feeling his muscle. Thus, when the Government thought of temporizing, they issued orders to Generals whose one idea was to strike the blow of a mallet.

At this period there was no suspicion of any grand revolt being in process of development. The abounding dissatisfaction was treated as nothing more than the Italian disease showing symptoms here and there, and Vienna counselled measures mildly repressive,—'conciliating,' it was her pleasure to call them. Her recent commands with respect to turbulent Venice were the subject of criticism among the circle outside the Piazza Gaffe. An enforced inactivity of the military legs will quicken the military wits, it would appear, for some of the younger officers spoke hotly as to their notion of the method of ruling Venezia. One had bidden his Herr General to 'look here,' while he stretched forth his hand and declared that Italians were like women, and wanted—yes, wanted—(their instinct called for it) a beating, a real beating; as the emphatic would say in our vernacular, a thundering thrashing, once a month:-'Or so,' the General added acquiescingly. A thundering thrashing, once a month or so, to these unruly Italians, because they are like women! It was a youth who spoke, but none doubted his acquaintance with women, or cared to suggest that his education in that department of knowledge was an insufficient guarantee for his fitness to govern Venezia. Two young dragoon officers had approached during the fervid allocution, and after the salute to their superior, caught up chairs and stamped them down, thereupon calling for the loan of anybody's cigar-case. Where it is that an Austrian officer ordinarily keeps this instrument so necessary to his comfort, and obnoxious, one would suppose, to the rigid correctness of his shapely costume, we cannot easily guess. None can tell even where he stows away his pocket-handkerchief, or haply his purse. However, these things appear on demand. Several elongated cigar-cases were thrust forward, and then it was seen that the attire of the gallant youngsters was in disorder.

'Did you hunt her to earth?' they were asked.

The reply trenched on philosophy; and consisted in an inquiry as to who cared for the whole basketful— of the like description of damsels, being implied. Immoderate and uproarious laughter burst around them. Both seemed to have been clawed impartially. Their tightfitting coats bulged at the breast or opened at the waist, as though buttons were lacking, and the whiteness of that garment cried aloud for the purification of pipeclay. Questions flew. The damsel who had been pursued was known as a pretty girl, the daughter of a blacksmith, and no prolonged resistance was expected from one of her class. But, as it came out, she had said, a week past, 'I shall be stabbed if I am seen talking to you'; and therefore the odd matter was, not that she had, in tripping down the Piazza with her rogue-eyed cousin from Milan, looked away and declined all invitation to moderate her pace and to converse, but that, after doubling down and about lonely streets, the length of which she ran as swiftly as her feet would carry her, at a corner of the Via Colomba she allowed herself to be caught—wilfully, beyond a doubt, seeing that she was not a bit breathed—allowed one quick taste of her lips, and then shrieked as naturally as a netted bird, and brought a hustling crowd just at that particular point to her rescue: not less than fifty, and all men. 'Not a woman among them!' the excited young officer repeated.

A veteran in similar affairs could see that he had the wish to remain undisturbed in his bewilderment at the damsel's conduct. Profound belief in her partiality for him perplexed his recent experience rather agreeably. Indeed, it was at this epoch an article of faith with the Austrian military that nothing save terror of their males kept sweet Italian women from the expression of their preference for the broad-shouldered, thick-limbed, yellow-haired warriors—the contrast to themselves which is supposed greatly to inspirit genial Cupid in the selection from his quiver.

'What became of her? Did you let her go?' came pestering remarks, too absurd for replies if they had not been so persistent.

'Let her go? In the devil's name, how was I to keep my hold of her in a crowd of fifty of the fellows, all mowing, and hustling, and elbowing—every rascal stinking right under my nose like the pit?'

''Hem!' went the General present. 'As long as you did not draw! Unsheathe, a minute.'

He motioned for a sight of their naked swords.

The couple of young officers flushed.

'Herr General! Pardon!' they remonstrated.

'No, no. I know how boys talk; I've been one myself. Tutt! You tell the truth, of course; but the business is for me to know in what! how far! Your swords, gentlemen.'

'But, General!'

'Well? I merely wish to examine the blades.'

'Do you doubt our words?'

'Hark at them! Words? Are you lawyers? A soldier deals in acts. I don't want to know your words, but your deeds, my gallant lads. I want to look at the blades of your swords, my children. What was the last order? That on no account were we to provoke, or, if possibly to be avoided, accept a collision, etc., etc. The soldier in peace is a citizen, etc. No sword on any account, or for any excuse, to be drawn, etc. You all heard it? So, good! I receive your denial, my children. In addition, I merely desire to satisfy curiosity. Did the guard clear a way for you?'

The answer was affirmative.

'Your swords!'

One of them drew, and proffered the handle.

The other clasped the haft angrily, and with a resolute smack on it, settled it in the scabbard.

'Am I a prisoner, General?'

'Not at all!'

'Then I decline to surrender my sword.'

Another General officer happened to be sauntering by. Applauding with his hands, and choosing the Italian language as the best form of speech for the enunciation of ironical superlatives, he said:

'Eccellentemente! most admirable! of a distinguished loftiness of moral grandeur: "Then I decline," etc.: you are aware that you are quoting? "as the drummerboy said to Napoleon." I think you forgot to add that? It is the same young soldier who utters these immense things, which we can hardly get out of our mouths. So the little fellow towers! His moral greatness is as noisy as his drum. What's wrong?'

'General Pierson, nothing's wrong,' was replied by several voices; and some explained that Lieutenant Jenna had been called upon by General Schoneck to show his sword, and had refused.

The heroic defender of his sword shouted to the officer with whom General Pierson had been conversing: 'Here! Weisspriess!'

'What is it, my dear fellow? Speak, my good Jenna!'

The explanation was given, and full sympathy elicited from Captain Weisspriess, while the two Generals likewise whispered and nodded.

'Did you draw?' the captain inquired, yawning. 'You needn't say it in quite so many words, if you did. I shall be asked by the General presently; and owing to that duel pending 'twixt you and his nephew, of which he is aware, he may put a bad interpretation on your pepperiness.'

'The devil fetch his nephew!' returned the furious Lieutenant Jenna. 'He comes back to-night from Milan, and if he doesn't fight me to-morrow, I post him a coward. Well, about that business! My good Weisspriess, the fellows had got into a thick crowd all round, and had begun to knead me. Do you understand me? I felt their knuckles.'

'Ah, good, good!' said the captain. 'Then, you didn't draw, of course. What officer of the Imperial service would, under similar circumstances! That is my reply to the Emperor, if ever I am questioned. To draw would be to show that an Austrian officer relies on his good sword in the thick of his enemies; against which, as you know, my Jenna, the Government have issued an express injunction button. Did you sell it dear?'

'A fellow parted with his ear for it.'

Lieutenant Jenna illustrated a particular cut from a turn of his wrist.

'That oughtn't to make a noise?' he queried somewhat anxiously.

'It won't hear one any longer, at all events,' said Captain Weisspriess; and the two officers entered into the significance of the remark with enjoyment.

Meantime General Pierson had concluded an apparently humorous dialogue with his brother General, and the later, now addressing Lieutenant Jenna, said: 'Since you prefer surrendering your person rather than your sword—it is good! Report yourself at the door of my room to-night, at ten. I suspect that you have been blazing your steel, sir. They say, 'tis as ready to flash out as your temper.'

Several voices interposed: 'General! what if he did draw!'

'Silence. You have read the recent order. Orlando may have his Durindarda bare; but you may not. Grasp that fact. The Government wish to make Christians of you, my children. One cheek being smitten, what should you do?'

'Shall I show you, General?' cried a quick little subaltern.

'The order, my children, as received a fortnight since from our old Wien, commands you to offer the other cheek to the smiter.'

'So that a proper balance may be restored to both sides of the face,' General Pierson appended.

'And mark me,' he resumed. 'There may be doubts about the policy of anything, though I shouldn't counsel you to cherish them: but there's no mortal doubt about the punishment for this thing.' The General spoke sternly; and then relaxing the severity of his tone, he said, 'The desire of the Government is to make an army of Christians.'

'And a precious way of doing it!' interjected two or three of the younger officers. They perfectly understood how hateful the Viennese domination was to their chiefs, and that they would meet sympathy and tolerance for any extreme of irony, provided that they showed a disposition to be subordinate. For the bureaucratic order, whatever it was, had to be obeyed. The army might, and of course did, know best: nevertheless it was bound to be nothing better than a machine in the hands of the dull closeted men in Vienna, who judged of difficulties and plans of action from a calculation of numbers, or from foreign journals—from heaven knows what!

General Schoneck and General Pierson walked away laughing, and the younger officers were left to themselves. Half-a-dozen of them interlaced arms, striding up toward the Porta Nuova, near which, at the corner of the Via Trinita, they had the pleasant excitement of beholding a riderless horse suddenly in mid gallop sink on its knees and roll over. A crowd came pouring after it, and from the midst the voice of a comrade hailed them. 'It's Pierson,' cried Lieutenant Jenna. The officers drew their swords, and hailed the guard from the gates. Lieutenant Pierson dropped in among their shoulders, dead from want of breath. They held him up, and finding him sound, thumped his back. The blade of his sword was red. He coughed with their thumpings, and sang out to them to cease; the idle mob which had been at his heels drew back before the guard could come up with them. Lieutenant Pierson gave no explanation except that he had been attacked near Juliet's tomb on his way to General Schoneck's quarters. Fellows had stabbed his horse, and brought him to the ground, and torn the coat off his back. He complained in bitter mutterings of the loss of a letter therein, during the first candid moments of his anger: and, as he was known to be engaged to the Countess Lena von Lenkenstein, it was conjectured by his comrades that this lady might have had something to do with the ravishment of the letter. Great laughter surrounded him, and he looked from man to man. Allowance is naturally made for the irascibility of a brother officer coming tattered out of the hands of enemies, or Lieutenant Jenna would have construed his eye's challenge on the spot. As it was, he cried out, 'The letter! the letter! Charge, for the honour of the army, and rescue the letter!' Others echoed him: 'The letter! the letter! the English letter!' A foreigner in an army can have as much provocation as he pleases; if he is anything of a favourite with his superiors, his fellows will task his forbearance. Wilfrid Pierson glanced at the blade of his sword, and slowly sheathed it. 'Lieutenant Jenna is a good actor before a mob,' he said. 'Gentlemen, I rely upon you to make no noise about that letter; it is a private matter. In an hour or so, if any officer shall choose to question me concerning it, I will answer him.'

The last remnants of the mob had withdrawn. The officer in command at the gates threw a cloak over Wilfrid's shoulders; and taking the arm of a friend Wilfrid hurried to barracks, and was quickly in a position to report himself to his General, whose first remark, 'Has the dead horse been removed?' robbed him of his usual readiness to equivocate. 'When you are the bearer of a verbal despatch, come straight to quarters, if you have to come like a fig-tree on the north side of the wall in Winter,' said General Schoneck, who was joined presently by General Pierson.

'What 's this I hear of some letter you have been barking about all over the city?' the latter asked, after returning his nephew's on-duty salute.

Wilfrid replied that it was a letter of his sister's treating of family matters.

The two Generals, who were close friends, discussed the attack to which he had been subjected. Wilfrid had to recount it with circumstance: how, as he was nearing General Schoneck's quarters at a military trot, six men headed by a leader had dashed out on him from a narrow side-street, unhorsed him after a struggle, rifled the saddlebags, and torn the coat from his back, and had taken the mark of his sword, while a gathering crowd looked on, hooting. His horse had fled, and he confessed that he had followed his horse. General Schoneck spoke the name of Countess Lena suggestively. 'Not a bit,' returned General Pierson; 'the fellow courts her too hotly. The scoundrels here want a bombardment; that 's where it lies. A dose of iron pills will make Verona a healthy place. She must have it.'

General Schoneck said, 'I hope not,' and laughed at the heat of Irish blood. He led Wilfrid in to the Marshal, after which Wilfrid was free to seek Lieutenant Jenna, who had gained the right to a similar freedom by pledging his honour not to fight within a stipulated term of days. The next morning Wilfrid was roused by an orderly coming from his uncle, who placed in his hands a copy of Vittoria's letter: at the end of it his uncle had written, 'Rather astonishing. Done pretty well; but by a foreigner. "Affection" spelt with one "f." An Italian: you will see the letters are emphatic at "ugly flag"; also "bloody and past forgiveness" very large; the copyist had a dash of the feelings of a commentator, and did his (or her) best to add an oath to it. Who the deuce, sir, is this opera girl calling herself Vittoria? I have a lecture for you. German women don't forgive diversions during courtship; and if you let this Countess Lena slip, your chance has gone. I compliment you on your power of lying; but you must learn to show your right face to me, or the very handsome feature, your nose, and that useful box, your skull, will come to grief.

The whole business is a mystery. The letter (copy) was directed to you, brought to me, and opened in a fit of abstraction, necessary to commanding uncles who are trying to push the fortunes of young noodles pretending to be related to them. Go to Countess Lena. Count Paul is with her, from Bologna. Speak to her, and observe her and him. He knows English—has been attached to the embassy in London; but, pooh! the hand's Italian. I confess myself puzzled. We shall possibly have to act on the intimation of the fifteenth, and profess to be wiser than others. Something is brewing for business. See Countess Lena boldly, and then come and breakfast with me.'

Wilfrid read the miserable copy of Vittoria's letter, utterly unable to resolve anything in his mind, except that he would know among a thousand the leader of those men who had attacked him, and who bore the mark of his sword.

CHAPTER X

THE POPE'S MOUTH

Barto Rizzo had done what he had sworn to do. He had not found it difficult to outstrip the lieutenant (who had to visit Brescia on his way) and reach the gates of Verona in advance of him, where he obtained entrance among a body of grape-gatherers and others descending from the hills to meet a press of labour in the autumnal plains. With them he hoped to issue forth unchallenged on the following morning; but Wilfrid's sword had made lusty play; and, as in the case when the order has been given that a man shall be spared in life and limb, Barto and his fellow-assailants suffered by their effort to hold him simply half a minute powerless. He received a shrewd cut across the head, and lay for a couple of hours senseless in the wine-shop of one Battista—one of the many all over Lombardy who had pledged their allegiance to the Great Cat, thinking him scarcely vulnerable. He read the letter, dizzy with pain, and with the frankness proper to inflated spirits after loss of blood, he owned to himself that it was not worth much as a prize. It was worth the attempt to get possession of it, for anything is worth what it costs, if it be only as a schooling in resolution, energy, and devotedness:—regrets are the sole admission of a fruitless business; they show the bad tree;—so, according to his principle of action, he deliberated; but he was compelled to admit that Vittoria's letter was little else than a repetition of her want of discretion when she was on the Motterone. He admitted it, wrathfully: his efforts to convict this woman telling him she deserved some punishment; and his suspicions being unsatisfied, he resolved to keep them hungry upon her, and return to Milan at once. As to the letter itself, he purposed, since the harm in it was accomplished, to send it back honourably to the lieutenant, till finding it blood-stained, he declined to furnish the gratification of such a sight to any Austrian sword. For that reason, he copied it, while Battista's wife held double bandages tight round his head: believing that the letter stood transcribed in a precisely similar hand, he forwarded it to Lieutenant Pierson, and then sank and swooned. Two days he lay incapable and let his thoughts dance as they would. Information was brought to him that the gates were strictly watched, and that troops were starting for Milan. This was in the dull hour antecedent to the dawn. 'She is a traitress!' he exclaimed, and leaping from his bed, as with a brain striking fire, screamed, 'Traitress! traitress!' Battista and his wife had to fling themselves on him and gag him, guessing him as mad. He spoke pompously and theatrically; called himself the Eye of Italy, and said that he must be in Milan, or Milan would perish, because of the traitress: all with a great sullen air of composure and an odd distension of the eyelids. When they released him, he smiled and thanked them, though they knew, that had he chosen, he could have thrown off a dozen of them, such was his strength. The woman went down on her knees to him to get his consent that she should dress and bandage his head afresh. The sound of the regimental bugles drew him from the house, rather than any immediate settled scheme to watch at the gates.

Artillery and infantry were in motion before sunrise, from various points of the city, bearing toward the Palio and Zeno gates, and the people turned out to see them, for it was a march that looked like the beginning of things. The soldiers had green twigs in their hats, and kissed their hands good-humouredly to the gazing crowd, shouting bits of verses:

'I'm off! I'm off! Farewell, Mariandl! if I come back a sergeant-major or a Field-Marshal, don't turn up your nose at me: Swear you will be faithful all the while; because, when a woman swears, it's a comfort, somehow: Farewell! Squeeze the cow's udders: I shall be thirsty enough: You pretty wriggler! don't you know, the first cup of wine and the last, I shall float your name on it? Luck to the lads we leave behind! Farewell, Mariandl!'

The kindly fellows waved their hands and would take no rebuff. The soldiery of Austria are kindlier than most, until their blood is up. A Tyrolese regiment passed, singing splendidly in chorus. Songs of sentiment prevailed, but the traditions of a soldier's experience of the sex have informed his ballads with strange touches of irony, that help him to his (so to say) philosophy, which is recklessness. The Tyroler's 'Katchen' here, was a saturnine Giulia, who gave him no response, either of eye or lip.

'Little mother, little sister, little sweetheart, 'ade! ade!' My little sweetheart, your meadow is half-way up the mountain; it's such a green spot on the eyeballs of a roving boy! and the chapel just above it, I shall see it as I've seen it a thousand times; and the cloud hangs near it, and moves to the door and enters, for it is an angel, not a cloud; a white angel gone in to pray for Katerlein and me: Little mother, little sister, little sweetheart, 'ade! ade!' Keep single, Katerlein, as long as you can: as long as you can hold out, keep single: 'ade!''

Fifteen hundred men and six guns were counted as they marched on to one gate.

Barto Rizzo, with Battista and his wife on each side of him, were among the spectators. The black cock's feathers of the Tyrolese were still fluttering up the Corso, when the woman said, 'I 've known the tail of a regiment get through the gates without having to show paper.'

Battista thereupon asked Barto whether he would try that chance. The answer was a vacuous shake of the head, accompanied by an expression of unutterable mournfulness. 'There's no other way,' pursued Battista, 'unless you jump into the Adige, and swim down half-a-mile under water; and cats hate water—eh, my comico?'

He conceived that the sword-cut had rendered Barto imbecile, and pulled his hat down his forehead, and patted his shoulder, and bade him have cheer, patronizingly: but women do not so lightly lose their impression of a notable man. His wife checked him. Barto had shut his eyes, and hung swaying between them, as in drowsiness or drunkenness. Like his body, his faith was swaying within him. He felt it borne upon the reeling brain, and clung to it desperately, calling upon chance to aid him; for he was weak, incapable of a physical or mental contest, and this part of his settled creed that human beings alone failed the patriotic cause as instruments, while circumstances constantly befriended it—was shocked by present events. The image of Vittoria, the traitress, floated over the soldiery marching on Milan through her treachery. Never had an Austrian force seemed to him so terrible. He had to yield the internal fight, and let his faith sink and be blackened, in order that his mind might rest supine, according to his remembered system; for the inspiration which points to the right course does not come during mental strife, but after it, when faith summons its agencies undisturbed—if only men will have the faith, and will teach themselves to know that the inspiration must come, and will counsel them justly. This was a part of Barto Rizzo's sustaining creed; nor did he lose his grasp of it in the torment and the darkness of his condition.

He heard English voices. A carriage had stopped almost in front of him. A General officer was hat in hand, talking to a lady, who called him uncle, and said that she had been obliged to decide to quit Verona on account of her husband, to whom the excessive heat was unendurable. Her husband, in the same breath, protested that the heat killed him. He adorned the statement with all kinds of domestic and subterranean imagery, and laughed faintly, saying that after the fifteenth—on which night his wife insisted upon going to the Opera at Milan to hear a new singer and old friend—he should try a week at the Baths of Bormio, and only drop from the mountains when a proper temperature reigned, he being something of an invalid.

'And, uncle, will you be in Milan on the fifteenth?' said the lady; 'and Wilfrid, too?'

'Wilfrid will reach Milan as soon as you do, and I shall undoubtedly be there on the fifteenth,' said the General.

'I cannot possibly express to you how beautiful I think your army looks,' said the lady.

'Fine men, General Pierson, very fine men. I never saw such marching—equal to our Guards,' her husband remarked.

The lady named her Milanese hotel as the General waved his plumes, nodded, and rode off.

Before the carriage had started, Barto Rizzo dashed up to it; and 'Dear good English lady,' he addressed her, 'I am the brother of Luigi, who carries letters for you in Milan—little Luigi!—and I have a mother dying in Milan; and here I am in Verona, ill, and can't get to her, poor soul! Will you allow me that I may sit up behind as quiet as a mouse, and be near one of the lovely English ladies who are so kind to unfortunate persons, and never deaf to the name of charity? It's my mother who is dying, poor soul!'

The lady consulted her husband's face, which presented the total blank of one who refused to be responsible for an opinion hostile to the claims of charity, while it was impossible for him to fall in with foreign habits of familiarity, and accede to extraordinary petitions. Barto sprang up. 'I shall be your courier, dear lady,' he said, and commenced his professional career in her service by shouting to the vetturino to drive on. Wilfrid met them as he was trotting down from the Porta del Palio, and to him his sister confided her new trouble in having a strange man attached to her, who might be anything. 'We don't know the man,' said her husband; and Adela pleaded for him: 'Don't speak to him harshly, pray, Wilfrid; he says he has a mother dying in Milan.' Barto kept his head down on his arms and groaned; Adela gave a doleful little grimace. 'Oh, take the poor beggar,' said Wilfrid; and sang out to him in Italian: 'Who are you—what are you, my fine fellow?' Barto groaned louder, and replied in Swiss-French from a smothering depth: 'A poor man, and the gracious lady's servant till we reach Milan.'

'I can't wait,' said Wilfrid; 'I start in half-an-hour. It's all right; you must take him now you've got him, or else pitch him out—one of the two. If things go on quietly we shall have the Autumn manoeuvres in a week, and then you may see something of the army.' He rode away. Barto passed the gates as one of the licenced English family.

Milan was more strictly guarded than when he had quitted it. He had anticipated that it would be so, and tamed his spirit to submit to the slow stages of the carriage, spent a fiery night in Brescia, and entered the city of action on the noon of the fourteenth. Safe within the walls, he thanked the English lady, assuring her that her charitable deed would be remembered aloft. He then turned his steps in the direction of the Revolutionary post-office. This place was nothing other than a blank abutment of a corner house that had long been undergoing repair, and had a great bank of brick and mortar rubbish at its base. A stationary melonseller and some black fig and vegetable stalls occupied the triangular space fronting it. The removal of a square piece of cement showed a recess, where, chiefly during the night, letters and proclamation papers were deposited, for the accredited postman to disperse them. Hither, as one would go to a caffe for the news, Barto Rizzo came in the broad glare of noon, and flinging himself down like a tired man under the strip of shade, worked with a hand behind him, and drew out several folded scraps, of which one was addressed to him by his initials. He opened it and read:

'Your house is watched.

'A corporal of the P... ka regiment was seen leaving it this morning in time for the second bugle.

'Reply:—where to meet.

'Spies are doubled, troops coming.

'The numbers in Verona; who heads them.

'Look to your wife.

'Letters are called for every third hour.'

Barto sneered indolently at this fresh evidence of the small amount of intelligence which he could ever learn from others. He threw his eyes all round the vacant space while pencilling in reply:—'V. waits for M., but in a box' (that is, Verona for Milan). 'We take the key to her.

'I have no wife, but a little pupil.

'A Lieutenant Pierson, of the dragoons; Czech white coats, helmets without plumes; an Englishman, nephew of General Pierson: speaks crippled Italian; returns from V. to-day. Keep eye on him;—what house, what hour.'

Meditating awhile, Barto wrote out Vittoria's name and enclosed it in a thick black ring.

Beneath it he wrote

'The same on all the play-bills.

'The Fifteenth is cancelled.

'We meet the day after.

'At the house of Count M. to-night.'

He secreted this missive, and wrote Vittoria's name on numbers of slips to divers addresses, heading them, 'From the Pope's Mouth,' such being the title of the Revolutionary postoffice, to whatsoever spot it might in prudence shift. The title was entirely complimentary to his Holiness. Tangible freedom, as well as airy blessings, were at that time anticipated, and not without warrant, from the mouth of the successor of St. Peter. From the Pope's Mouth the clear voice of Italian liberty was to issue. This sentiment of the period was a natural and a joyful one, and endowed the popular ebullition with a sense of unity and a stamp of righteousness that the abstract idea of liberty could not assure to it before martyrdom. After suffering, after walking in the shades of death and despair, men of worth and of valour cease to take high personages as representative objects of worship, even when these (as the good Pope was then doing) benevolently bless the nation and bid it to have great hope, with a voice of authority. But, for an extended popular movement a great name is like a consecrated banner. Proclamations from the Pope's Mouth exacted reverence, and Barto Rizzo, who despised the Pope (because he was Pope, doubtless), did not hesitate to make use of him by virtue of his office.

Barto lay against the heap of rubbish, waiting for the approach of his trained lad, Checco, a lanky simpleton, cunning as a pure idiot, who was doing postman's duty, when a kick, delivered by that youth behind, sent him bounding round with rage, like a fish in air. The marketplace resounded with a clapping of hands; for it was here that Checco came daily to eat figs, and it was known that the 'povero,' the dear half-witted creature, would not tolerate an intruder in the place where he stretched his limbs to peel and suck in the gummy morsels twice or thrice a day. Barto seized and shook him. Checco knocked off his hat; the bandage about the wound broke and dropped, and Barto put his hand to his forehead, murmuring: 'What 's come to me that I lose my temper with a boy—an animal?'

The excitement all over the triangular space was hushed by an imperious guttural shout that scattered the groups. Two Austrian officers, followed by military servants, rode side by side. Dust had whitened their mustachios, and the heat had laid a brown-red varnish on their faces. Way was made for them, while Barto stood smoothing his forehead and staring at Checco.

'I see the very man!' cried one of the officers quickly. 'Weisspriess, there's the rascal who headed the attack on me in Verona the other day. It's the same!

'Himmel!' returned his companion, scrutinizing the sword-cut, 'if that's your work on his head, you did it right well, my Pierson! He is very neatly scored indeed. A clean stroke, manifestly!'

'But here when I left Milan! at Verona when I entered the North-west gate there; and the first man I see as I come back is this very brute. He dogs me everywhere! By the way, there may be two of them.'

Lieutenant Pierson leaned over his horse's neck, and looked narrowly at the man Barto Rizzo. He himself was eyed as in retort, and with yet greater intentness. At first Barto's hand was sweeping the air within a finger's length of his forehead, like one who fought a giddiness for steady sight. The mist upon his brain dispersing under the gaze of his enemy, his eyeballs fixed, and he became a curious picture of passive malice, his eyes seeming to say: 'It is enough for me to know your features, and I know them.' Such a look from a civilian is exasperating: it was scarcely to be endured from an Italian of the plebs.

'You appear to me to want more,' said the lieutenant audibly to himself; and he repeated words to the same effect to his companion, in bad German.

'Eh? You would promote him to another epaulette?' laughed Captain Weisspriess. 'Come off. Orders are direct against it. And we're in Milan—not like being in Verona! And my good fellow! remember your bet; the dozen of iced Rudesheimer. I want to drink my share, and dream I'm quartered in Mainz—the only place for an Austrian when he quits Vienna. Come.'

'No; but if this is the villain who attacked me, and tore my coat from my back,' cried Wilfrid, screwing in his saddle.

'And took your letter took your letter; a particular letter; we have heard of it,' said Weisspriess.

The lieutenant exclaimed that he should overhaul and examine the man, and see whether he thought fit to give him into custody. Weisspriess laid hand on his bridle.

'Take my advice, and don't provoke a disturbance in the streets. The truth is, you Englishmen and Irishmen get us a bad name among these natives. If this is the man who unhorsed you and maltreated you, and committed the rape of the letter, I'm afraid you won't get satisfaction out of him, to judge by his look. I'm really afraid not. Try it if you like. In any case, if you halt, I am compelled to quit your society, which is sometimes infinitely diverting. Let me remind you that you bear despatches. The other day they were verbal ones; you are now carrying paper.'

'Are you anxious to teach me my duty, Captain Weisspriess?'

'If you don't know it. I said I would "remind you." I can also teach you, if you need it.'

'And I can pay you for the instruction, whenever you are disposed to receive payment.'

'Settle your outstanding claims, my good Pierson!'

'When I have fought Jenna?'

'Oh! you're a Prussian—a Prussian!' Captain Weisspriess laughed. 'A Prussian, I mean, in your gross way of blurting out everything. I've marched and messed with Prussians—with oxen.'

'I am, as you are aware, an Englishman, Captain Weisspriess. I am due to Lieutenant Jenna for the present. After that you or any one may command me.'

'As you please,' said Weisspriess, drawing out one stream of his moustache. 'In the meantime, thank me for luring you away from the chances of a street row.'

Barto Rizzo was left behind, and they rode on to the Duomo. Glancing up at its pinnacles, Weisspriess said:

'How splendidly Flatschmann's jagers would pick them off from there, now, if the dogs were giving trouble in this part of the city!'

They entered upon a professional discussion of the ways and means of dealing with a revolutionary movement in the streets of a city like Milan, and passed on to the Piazza La Scala. Weisspriess stopped before the Play-bills. 'To-morrow's the fifteenth of the month,' he said. 'Shall I tell you a secret, Pierson? I am to have a private peep at the new prima donna this night. They say she's charming, and very pert. "I do not interchange letters with Germans." Benlomik sent her a neat little note to the conservatorio—he hadn't seen her only heard of her, and that was our patriotic reply. She wants taming. I believe I am called upon for that duty. At least, my friend Antonio-Pericles, who occasionally assists me with supplies, hints as much to me. You're an engaged man, or, upon my honour, I wouldn't trust you; but between ourselves, this Greek—and he's quite right—is trying to get her away from the set of snuffy vagabonds who are prompting her for mischief, and don't know how to treat her.'

While he was speaking Barto Rizzo pushed roughly between them, and with a black brush painted the circle about Vittoria's name.

'Do you see that?' said Weisspriess.

'I see,' Wilfrid retorted, 'that you are ready to meddle with the reputation of any woman who is likely to be talked about. Don't do it in my presence.'

It was natural for Captain Weisspriess to express astonishment at this outburst, and the accompanying quiver of Wilfrid's lip.

'Austrian military etiquette, Lieutenant Pierson,' he said, 'precludes the suspicion that the officers of the Imperial army are subject to dissension in public. We conduct these affairs upon a different principle. But I'll tell you what. That fellow's behaviour may be construed as a more than common stretch of incivility. I'll do you a service. I'll arrest him, and then you can hear tidings of your precious letter. We'll have his confession published.'

Weisspriess drew his sword, and commanded the troopers in attendance to lay hands on Barto; but the troopers called, and the officer found that they were surrounded. Weisspriess shrugged dismally. 'The brute must go, I suppose,' he said. The situation was one of those which were every now and then occurring in the Lombard towns and cities, when a chance provocation created a riot that became a revolt or not, according to the timidity of the ruling powers or the readiness of the disaffected. The extent and evident regulation of the crowd operated as a warning to the Imperial officers. Weisspriess sheathed his sword and shouted, 'Way, there!' Way was made for him; but Wilfrid lingered to scrutinize the man who, for an unaccountable reason, appeared to be his peculiar enemy. Barto carelessly threaded the crowd, and Wilfrid, finding it useless to get out after him, cried, 'Who is he? Tell me the name of that man?' The question drew a great burst of laughter around him, and exclamations of 'Englishman! Englishman!' He turned where there was a clear way left for him in the track of his brother officer.

Comments on the petty disturbance had been all the while passing at the Caffe La Scala, where sat Agostino Balderini, with, Count Medole and others, who, if the order for their arrest had been issued, were as safe in that place as in their own homes. Their policy, indeed, was to show themselves openly abroad. Agostino was enjoying the smoke of paper cigarettes, with all prudent regard for the well-being of an inflammable beard. Perceiving Wilfrid going by, he said, 'An Englishman! I continue to hope much from his countrymen. I have no right to do so, only they insist on it. They have promised, and more than once, to sail a fleet to our assistance across the plains of Lombardy, and I believe they will—probably in the watery epoch which is to follow Metternich. Behold my Carlo approaching. The heart of that lad doth so boil the brain of him, he can scarcely keep the lid on. What is it now? Speak, my son.'

Carlo Ammiani had to communicate that he had just seen a black circle to Vittoria's name on two public playbills. His endeavour to ape a deliberate gravity while he told the tale, roused Agostino's humouristic ire.

'Round her name?' said Agostino.

'Yes; in every bill.'

'Meaning that she is suspected!'

'Meaning any damnable thing you like.'

'It's a device of the enemy.'

Agostino, glad of the pretext to recur to his habitual luxurious irony, threw himself back, repeating 'It 's a device of the enemy. Calculate, my son, that the enemy invariably knows all you intend to do: determine simply to astonish him with what you do. Intentions have lungs, Carlo, and depend on the circumambient air, which, if not designedly treacherous, is communicative. Deeds, I need not remark, are a different body. It has for many generations been our Italian error to imagine a positive blood relationship—not to say maternity itself—existing between intentions and deeds. Nothing of the sort! There is only the intention of a link to unite them. You perceive? It's much to be famous for fine intentions, so we won't complain. Indeed, it's not our business to complain, but Posterity's; for fine intentions are really rich possessions, but they don't leave grand legacies; that is all. They mean to possess the future: they are only the voluptuous sons of the present. It's my belief, Carlino, from observation, apprehension, and other gifts of my senses, that our paternal government is not unacquainted with our intention to sing a song in a certain opera. And it may have learnt our clumsy method of enclosing names publicly, at the bidding of a non-appointed prosecutor, so to, isolate or extinguish them. Who can say? Oh, ay! Yes! the machinery that can so easily be made rickety is to blame; we admit that; but if you will have a conspiracy like a Geneva watch, you must expect any slight interference with the laws that govern it to upset the mechanism altogether. Ah-a! look yonder, but not hastily, my Carlo. Checco is nearing us, and he knows that he has fellows after him. And if I guess right, he has a burden to deliver to one of us.'

Checco came along at his usual pace, and it was quite evident that he fancied himself under espionage. On two sides of the square a suspicious figure threaded its way in the line of shade not far behind him. Checco passed the cafe looking at nothing but the huge hands he rubbed over and over. The manifest agents of the polizia were nearing when Checco ran back, and began mouthing as in retort at something that had been spoken from the cafe as he shot by. He made a gabbling appeal on either side, and addressed the pair of apparent mouchards, in what, if intelligible, should have been the language of earnest entreaty. At the first word which the caffe was guilty of uttering, a fit of exasperation seized him, and the exciteable creature plucked at his hat and sent it whirling across the open-air tables right through the doorway. Then, with a whine, he begged his followers to get his hat back for him. They complied.

'We only called "Illustrissimo!"' said Agostino, as one of the men returned from the interior of the caffe hat in hand.

'The Signori should have known better—it is an idiot,' the man replied. He was a novice: in daring to rebuke he betrayed his office.

Checco snatched his hat from his attentive friend grinning, and was away in a flash. Thereupon the caffe laughed, and laughed with an abashing vehemence that disconcerted the spies. They wavered in their choice of following Checco or not; one went a step forward, one pulled back; the loiterer hurried to rejoin his comrade, who was now for a retrograde movement, and standing together they swayed like two imperfectly jolly fellows, or ballet bandits, each plucking at the other, until at last the maddening laughter made them break, reciprocate cat-like hisses of abuse, and escape as they best could— lamentable figures.

'It says well for Milan that the Tedeschi can scrape up nothing better from the gutters than rascals the like of those for their service,' quoth Agostino. 'Eh, Signor Conte?'

'That enclosure about La Vittoria's name on the bills is correct,' said the person addressed, in a low tone. He turned and indicated one who followed from the interior of the caffe.

'If Barto is to be trusted she is not safe,' the latter remarked. He produced a paper that had been secreted in Checco's hat. Under the date and the superscription of the Pope's Mouth, 'LA VITTORIA' stood out in the ominous heavily-pencilled ring: the initials of Barto Rizzo were in a corner. Agostino began smoothing his beard.

'He has discovered that she is not trustworthy,' said Count Medole, a young man of a premature gravity and partial baldness, who spoke habitually with a forefinger pressed flat on his long pointed chin.

'Do you mean to tell me, Count Medole, that you attach importance to a communication of this sort?' said Carlo, forcing an amazement to conceal his anger.

'I do, Count Ammiani,' returned the patrician conspirator.

'You really listen to a man you despise?'

'I do not despise him, my friend.'

'You cannot surely tell us that you allow such a man, on his sole authority, to blacken the character of the signorina?'

'I believe that he has not.'

'Believe? trust him? Then we are all in his hands. What can you mean? Come to the signorina herself instantly. Agostino, you now conduct Count Medole to her, and save him from the shame of subscribing to the monstrous calumny. I beg you to go with our Agostino, Count Medole. It is time for you—I honour you for the part you have taken; but it is time to act according to your own better judgement.'

Count Medole bowed.

'The filthy rat!' cried Ammiani, panting to let out his wrath.

'A serviceable dog,' Agostino remarked correctingly. 'Keep true to the form of animal, Carlo. He has done good service in his time.'

'You listen to the man?' Carlo said, now thoroughly amazed.

'An indiscretion is possible to woman, my lad. She may have been indiscreet in some way I am compelled to admit the existence of possibilities.'

'Of all men, you, Agostino! You call her daughter, and profess to love her.'

'You forget,' said Agostino sharply. 'The question concerns the country, not the girl.' He added in an underbreath, 'I think you are professing that you love her a little too strongly, and scarce give her much help as an advocate. The matter must be looked into. If Barto shall be found to have acted without just grounds, I am certain that Count Medole'—he turned suavely to the nobleman—'will withdraw confidence from him; and that will be equivalent to a rope's-end for Barto. We shall see him to-night at your house?'

'He will be there,' Medole said.

'But the harm's done; the mischief's done! And what's to follow if you shall choose to consider this vile idiot justified?' asked Ammiani.

'She sings, and there is no rising,' said Medole.

'She is detached from the patriotic battery, for the moment: it will be better for her not to sing at all,' said Agostino. 'In fact, Barto has merely given us warning that—and things look like it—the Fifteenth is likely to be an Austrian feast-day. Your arm, my son. We will join you to-night, my dear Count. Now, Carlo, I was observing, it appears to me that the Austrians are not going to be surprised by us, and it affords me exquisite comfort. Fellows prepared are never more than prepared for one day and another day; and they are sure to be in a state of lax preparation after a first and second disappointment. On the contrary, fellows surprised'—Agostino had recovered his old smile again—'fellows surprised may be expected to make use of the inspirations pertaining to genius. Don't you see?'

'Oh, cruel! I am sick of you all!' Carlo exclaimed. 'Look at her; think of her, with her pure dream of Italy and her noble devotion. And you permit a doubt to be cast on her!'

'Now, is it not true that you have an idea of the country not being worthy of her?' said Agostino, slyly. 'The Chief, I fancy, did not take certain facts into his calculation when he pleaded that the conspiratrix was the sum and completion of the conspirator. You will come to Medole's to-night, Carlo. You need not be too sweet to him, but beware of explosiveness. I, a Republican, am nevertheless a practical exponent of the sacrifices necessary to unity. I accept the local leadership of Medole—on whom I can never look without thinking of an unfeathered pie; and I submit to be assisted by the man Barto Rizzo. Do thou likewise, my son. Let your enamoured sensations follow that duty, and with a breezy space between. A conspiracy is an epitome of humanity, with a boiling power beneath it. You're no more than a bit of mechanism—happy if it goes at all!'

Agostino said that he would pay a visit to Vittoria in the evening. Ammiani had determined to hunt out Barto Rizzo and the heads of the Clubs before he saw her. It was a relief to him to behold in the Piazza the Englishman who had exchanged cards with him on the Motterone. Captain Gambier advanced upon a ceremonious bow, saying frankly, in a more colloquial French than he had employed at their first interview, that he had to apologize for his conduct, and to request monsieur's excuse. 'If,' he pursued, 'that lady is the person whom I knew formerly in England as Mademoiselle Belloni, and is now known as Mademoiselle Vittoria Campa, may I beg you to inform her that, according to what I have heard, she is likely to be in some danger to-morrow?' What the exact nature of the danger was, Captain Gambier could not say.

Ammiani replied: 'She is in need of all her friends,' and took the pressure of the Englishman's hand, who would fair have asked more but for the stately courtesy of the Italian's withdrawing salute. Ammiani could no longer doubt that Vittoria's implication in the conspiracy was known.

CHAPTER XI

LAURA PIAVENI

After dark on the same day antecedent to the outbreak, Vittoria, with her faithful Beppo at her heels, left her mother to run and pass one comforting hour in the society of the Signora Laura Piaveni and her children.

There were two daughters of a parasitical Italian nobleman, of whom one had married the patriot Giacomo Piaveni, and one an Austrian diplomatist, the Commendatore Graf von Lenkenstein. Count Serabiglione was traditionally parasitical. His ancestors all had moved in Courts. The children of the House had illustrious sponsors. The House itself was a symbolical sunflower constantly turning toward Royalty. Great excuses are to be made for this, the last male descendant, whose father in his youth had been an Imperial page, and who had been nursed in the conception that Italy (or at least Lombardy) was a natural fief of Austria, allied by instinct and by interest to the holders of the Alps. Count Serabiglione mixed little with his countrymen,—the statement might be inversed,—but when, perchance, he was among them, he talked willingly of the Tedeschi, and voluntarily declared them to be gross, obstinate, offensive-bears, in short. At such times he would intimate in any cordial ear that the serpent was probably a match for the bear in a game of skill, and that the wisdom of the serpent was shown in his selection of the bear as his master, since, by the ordination of circumstances, master he must have. The count would speak pityingly of the poor depraved intellects which admitted the possibility of a coming Kingdom of Italy united: the lunatics who preached of it he considered a sort of self-elected targets for appointed files of Tyrolese jagers. But he was vindictive against him whom he called the professional doctrinaire, and he had vile names for the man. Acknowledging that Italy mourned her present woes, he charged this man with the crime of originating them:—and why? what was his object? He was, the count declared in answer, a born intriguer, a lover of blood, mad for the smell of it!—an Old Man of the Mountain; a sheaf of assassins; and more—the curse of Italy! There should be extradition treaties all over the world to bring this arch-conspirator to justice. The door of his conscience had been knocked at by a thousand bleeding ghosts, and nothing had opened to them. What was Italy in his eyes? A chess-board; and Italians were the chessmen to this cold player with live flesh. England nourished the wretch, that she might undermine the peace of the Continent.

Count Serabiglione would work himself up in the climax of denunciation, and then look abroad frankly as one whose spirit had been relieved. He hated bad men; and it was besides necessary for him to denounce somebody, and get relief of some kind. Italians edged away from him. He was beginning to feel that he had no country. The detested title 'Young Italy' hurried him into fits of wrath. 'I am,' he said, 'one of the Old Italians, if a distinction is to be made.' He assured his listeners that he was for his commune, his district, and aired his old-Italian prejudices delightedly; clapping his hands to the quarrels of Milan and Brescia; Florence and Siena—haply the feuds of villages—and the common North-Italian jealousy of the chief city. He had numerous capital tales to tell of village feuds, their date and origin, the stupid effort to heal them, and the wider consequent split; saying, 'We have, all Italians, the tenacity, the unforgiveness, the fervent blood of pure Hebrews; and a little more gaiety, perhaps; together with a love of fair things. We can outlive ten races of conquerors.'

In this fashion he philosophized, or forced a kind of philosophy. But he had married his daughter to an Austrian, which was what his countrymen could not overlook, and they made him feel it. Little by little, half acquiescing, half protesting, and gradually denationalized, the count was edged out of Italian society, save of the parasitical class, which he very much despised. He was not a happy man. Success at the Imperial Court might have comforted him; but a remorseless sensitiveness of his nature tripped his steps.

Bitter laughter rang throughout Lombardy when, in spite of his efforts to save his daughter's husband, Giacomo Piaveni suffered death. No harder blow had ever befallen the count: it was as good as a public proclamation that he possessed small influence. To have bent the knee was not afflicting to this nobleman's conscience: but it was an anguish to think of having bent the knee for nothing.

Giacomo Piaveni was a noble Italian of the young blood, son of a General loved by Eugene. In him the loss of Italy was deplorable. He perished by treachery at the age of twenty-three years. So splendid was this youth in appearance, of so sweet a manner with women, and altogether so-gentle and gallant, that it was a widowhood for women to have known him: and at his death the hearts of two women who had loved him in rivalry became bound by a sacred tie of friendship. He, though not of distinguished birth, had the choice of an almost royal alliance in the first blush of his manhood. He refused his chance, pleading in excuse to Count Serabiglione, that he was in love with that nobleman's daughter, Laura; which it flattered the count to hear, but he had ever after a contempt for the young man's discretion, and was observed to shrug, with the smooth sorrowfulness of one who has been a prophet, on the day when Giacomo was shot. The larger estates of the Piaveni family, then in Giacomo's hands, were in a famous cheese-making district, producing a delicious cheese:—'white as lambkins!' the count would ejaculate most dolefully; and in a rapture of admiration, 'You would say, a marble quarry when you cut into it.' The theme was afflicting, for all the estates of Giacomo were for the time forfeit, and the pleasant agitation produced among his senses by the mention of the cheese reminded him at the same instant that he had to support a widow with two children. The Signora Piaveni lived in Milan, and the count her father visited her twice during the summer months, and wrote to her from his fitful Winter residences in various capital cities, to report progress in the settled scheme for the recovery of Giacomo's property, as well for his widow as for the heirs of his body. 'It is a duty,' Count Serabiglione said emphatically. 'My daughter can entertain no proposal until her children are duly established; or would she, who is young and lovely and archly capricious, continue to decline the very best offers of the Milanese nobility, and live on one flat in an old quarter of the city, instead of in a bright and handsome street, musical with equipages, and full of the shows of life?'

In conjunction with certain friends of the signora, the count worked diligently for the immediate restitution of the estates. He was ably seconded by the young princess of Schyll-Weilingen,—by marriage countess of Fohrendorf, duchess of Graatli, in central Germany, by which title she passed,—an Austrian princess; she who had loved Giacomo, and would have given all for him, and who now loved his widow. The extreme and painful difficulty was that the Signora Piaveni made no concealment of her abhorrence of the House of Austria, and hatred of Austrian rule in Italy. The spirit of her dead husband had come to her from the grave, and warmed a frame previously indifferent to anything save his personal merits. It had been covertly communicated to her that if she performed due submission to the authorities, and lived for six months in good legal, that is to say, nonpatriotic odour, she might hope to have the estates. The duchess had obtained this mercy for her, and it was much; for Giacomo's scheme of revolt had been conceived with a subtlety of genius, and contrived on a scale sufficient to incense any despotic lord of such a glorious milch-cow as Lombardy. Unhappily the signora was more inspired by the remembrance of her husband than by consideration for her children. She received disaffected persons: she subscribed her money ostentatiously for notoriously patriotic purposes; and she who, in her father's Como villa, had been a shy speechless girl, nothing more than beautiful, had become celebrated for her public letters, and the ardour of declamation against the foreigner which characterized her style. In the face of such facts, the estates continued to be withheld from her governance. Austria could do that: she could wreak her spite against the woman, but she respected her own law even in a conquered land: the estates were not confiscated, and not absolutely sequestrated; and, indeed, money coming from them had been sent to her for the education of her children. It lay in unopened official envelopes, piled one upon another, quarterly remittances, horrible as blood of slaughter in her sight. Count Serabiglione made a point of counting the packets always within the first five minutes of a visit to his daughter. He said nothing, but was careful to see to the proper working of the lock of the cupboard where the precious deposits were kept, and sometimes in forgetfulness he carried off the key. When his daughter reclaimed it, she observed, 'Pray believe me quite as anxious as yourself to preserve these documents.' And the count answered, 'They represent the estates, and are of legal value, though the amount is small. They represent your protest, and the admission of your claim. They are priceless.'

In some degree, also, they compensated him for the expense he was put to in providing for his daughter's subsistence and that of her children. For there, at all events, visible before his eyes, was the value of the money, if not the money expended. He remonstrated with Laura for leaving it more than necessarily exposed. She replied,

'My people know what that money means!' implying, of course, that no one in her house would consequently touch it. Yet it was reserved for the count to find it gone.

The discovery was made by the astounded nobleman on the day preceding Vittoria's appearance at La Scala. His daughter being absent, he had visited the cupboard merely to satisfy an habitual curiosity. The cupboard was open, and had evidently been ransacked. He rang up the domestics, and would have charged them all with having done violence to the key, but that on reflection he considered this to be a way of binding faggots together, and he resolved to take them one by one, like the threading Jesuit that he was, and so get a Judas. Laura's return saved him from much exercise of his peculiar skill. She, with a cool 'Ebbene!' asked him how long he had expected the money to remain there. Upon which, enraged, he accused her of devoting the money to the accursed patriotic cause. And here they came to a curious open division.

'Be content, my father,' she said; 'the money is my husband's, and is expended on his behalf.'

'You waste it among the people who were the cause of his ruin!' her father retorted.

'You presume me to have returned it to the Government, possibly?'

'I charge you with tossing it to your so-called patriots.'

'Sir, if I have done that, I have done well.'

'Hear her!' cried the count to the attentive ceiling; and addressing her with an ironical 'madame,' he begged permission to inquire of her whether haply she might be the person in the pay of Revolutionists who was about to appear at La Scala, under the name of the Signorina Vittoria. 'For you are getting dramatic in your pose, my Laura,' he added, familiarizing the colder tone of his irony. 'You are beginning to stand easily in attitudes of defiance to your own father.'

'That I may practise how to provoke a paternal Government, you mean,' she rejoined, and was quite a match for him in dialectics.

The count chanced to allude further to the Signorina Vittoria.

'Do you know much of that lady?' she asked.

'As much as is known,' said he.

They looked at one another; the count thinking, 'I gave to this girl an excess of brains, in my folly!'

Compelled to drop his eyes, and vexed by the tacit defeat, he pursued, 'You expect great things from her?'

'Great,' said his daughter.

'Well, well,' he murmured acquiescingly, while sounding within himself for the part to play. 'Well-yes! she may do what you expect.'

'There is not the slightest doubt of her capacity,' said his daughter, in a tone of such perfect conviction that the count was immediately and irresistibly tempted to play the part of sagacious, kindly, tolerant but foreseeing father; and in this becoming character he exposed the risks her party ran in trusting anything of weight to a woman. Not that he decried women. Out of their sphere he did not trust them, and he simply objected to them when out of their sphere: the last four words being uttered staccato.

'But we trust her to do what she has undertaken to do,' said Laura.

The count brightened prodigiously from his suspicion to a certainty; and as he was still smiling at the egregious trap his clever but unskilled daughter had fallen into, he found himself listening incredulously to her plain additional sentence:—'She has easy command of three octaves.'

By which the allusion was transformed from politics to Art. Had Laura reserved this cunning turn a little further, yielding to the natural temptation to increase the shock of the antithetical battery, she would have betrayed herself: but it came at the right moment: the count gave up his arms. He told her that this

Signorina Vittoria was suspected. 'Whom will they not suspect!' interjected Laura. He assured her that if a conspiracy had ripened it must fail. She was to believe that he abhorred the part of a spy or informer, but he was bound, since she was reckless, to watch over his daughter; and also bound, that he might be of service to her, to earn by service to others as much power as he could reasonably hope to obtain. Laura signified that he argued excellently well. In a fit of unjustified doubt of her sincerity, he complained, with a querulous snap:

'You have your own ideas; you have your own ideas. You think me this and that. A man must be employed.'

'And this is to account for your occupation?' she remarked.

'Employed, I say!' the count reiterated fretfully. He was unmasking to no purpose, and felt himself as on a slope, having given his adversary vantage.

'So that there is no choice for you, do you mean?'

The count set up a staggering affirmative, but knocked it over with its natural enemy as soon as his daughter had said, 'Not being for Italy, you must necessarily be against her:—I admit that to be the position!'

'No!' he cried; 'no: there is no question of "for" or "against," as you are aware. "Italy, and not Revolution": that is my motto.'

'Or, in other words, "The impossible,"' said Laura. 'A perfect motto!'

Again the count looked at her, with the remorseful thought: 'I certainly gave you too much brains.'

He smiled: 'If you could only believe it not impossible!'

'Do you really imagine that "Italy without Revolution" does not mean "Austria"?' she inquired.

She had discovered how much he, and therefore his party, suspected, and now she had reasons for wishing him away. Not daring to show symptoms of restlessness, she offered him the chance of recovering himself on the crutches of an explanation. He accepted the assistance, praising his wits for their sprightly divination, and went through a long-winded statement of his views for the welfare of Italy, quoting his favourite Berni frequently, and forcing the occasion for that jolly poet. Laura gave quiet attention to all, and when he was exhausted at the close, said meditatively, 'Yes. Well; you are older. It may seem to you that I shall think as you do when I have had a similar, or the same, length of experience.'

This provoking reply caused her father to jump up from his chair and spin round for his hat. She rose to speed him forth.

'It may seem to me!' he kept muttering. 'It may seem to me that when a daughter gets married—addio! she is nothing but her husband.'

'Ay! ay! if it might be so!' the signora wailed out.

The count hated tears, considering them a clog to all useful machinery. He was departing, when through the open window a noise of scuffling in the street below arrested him.

'Has it commenced?' he said, starting.

'What?' asked the signora, coolly; and made him pause.

'But-but-but!' he answered, and had the grace to spare her ears. The thought in him was: 'But that I had some faith in my wife, and don't admire the devil sufficiently, I would accuse him point-blank, for, by Bacchus! you are as clever as he.'

It is a point in the education of parents that they should learn to apprehend humbly the compliment of being outwitted by their own offspring.

Count Serabiglione leaned out of the window and saw that his horses were safe and the coachman handy. There were two separate engagements going on between angry twisting couples.

'Is there a habitable town in Italy?' the count exclaimed frenziedly. First he called to his coachman to drive away, next to wait as if nailed to the spot. He cursed the revolutionary spirit as the mother of vices. While he was gazing at the fray, the door behind him opened, as he knew by the rush of cool air which struck his temples. He fancied that his daughter was hurrying off in obedience to a signal, and turned upon her just as Laura was motioning to a female figure in the doorway to retire.

'Who is this?' said the count.

A veil was over the strange lady's head. She was excited, and breathed quickly. The count brought forward a chair to her, and put on his best court manner. Laura caressed her, whispering, ere she replied: 'The Signorina Vittoria Romana!—Biancolla!—Benarriva!' and numerous other names of inventive endearment. But the count was too sharp to be thrown off the scent. 'Aha!' he said, 'do I see her one evening before the term appointed?' and bowed profoundly. 'The Signorina Vittoria!'

She threw up her veil.

'Success is certain,' he remarked and applauded, holding one hand as a snuff-box for the fingers of the other to tap on.

'Signor Conte, you—must not praise me before you have heard me.'

'To have seen you!'

'The voice has a wider dominion, Signor Conte.'

'The fame of the signorina's beauty will soon be far wider. Was Venus a cantatrice?'

She blushed, being unable to continue this sort of Mayfly-shooting dialogue, but her first charming readiness had affected the proficient social gentleman very pleasantly, and with fascinated eyes he hummed and buzzed about her like a moth at a lamp. Suddenly his head dived: 'Nothing, nothing, signorina,' he said, brushing delicately at her dress; 'I thought it might be paint.' He smiled to reassure her, and then he dived again, murmuring: 'It must be something sticking to the dress. Pardon me.' With that he went to the bell. 'I will ring up my daughter's maid. Or Laura—where is Laura?'

The Signora Piaveni had walked to the window. This antiquated fussiness of the dilettante little nobleman was sickening to her.

'Probably you expect to discover a revolutionary symbol in the lines of the signorina's dress,' she said.

'A revolutionary symbol!—my dear! my dear!' The count reproved his daughter. 'Is not our signorina a pure artist, accomplishing easily three octaves? aha! Three!' and he rubbed his hands. 'But, three good octaves!' he addressed Vittoria seriously and admonishingly. 'It is a fortune-millions! It is precisely the very grandest heritage! It is an army!'

'I trust that it may be!' said Vittoria, with so deep and earnest a ring of her voice that the count himself, malicious as his ejaculations had been, was astonished. At that instant Laura cried from the window: 'These horses will go mad.'

The exclamation had the desired effect.

'Eh?—pardon me, signorina,' said the count, moving half-way to the window, and then askant for his hat. The clatter of the horses' hoofs sent him dashing through the doorway, at which place his daughter stood with his hat extended. He thanked and blessed her for the kindly attention, and in terror lest the signorina should think evil of him as 'one of the generation of the hasty,' he said, 'Were it anything but horses! anything but horses! one's horses!—ha!' The audible hoofs called him off. He kissed the tips of his fingers, and tripped out.

The signora stepped rapidly to the window, and leaning there, cried a word to the coachman, who signalled perfect comprehension, and immediately the count's horses were on their hind-legs, chafing and pulling to right and left, and the street was tumultuous with them. She flung down the window, seized Vittoria's cheeks in her two hands, and pressed the head upon her bosom. 'He will not disturb us again,' she said, in quite a new tone, sliding her hands from the cheeks to the shoulders and along the arms to the fingers'-ends, which they clutched lovingly. 'He is of the old school, friend of my heart! and besides, he has but two pairs of horses, and one he keeps in Vienna. We live in the hope that our masters will pay us better! Tell me! you are in good health? All is well with you? Will they have to put paint on her soft cheeks to-morrow? Little, if they hold the colour as full as now? My Sandra! amica! should I have been jealous if Giacomo had known you? On my soul, I cannot guess! But, you love what he loved. He seems to live for me when they are talking of Italy, and you send your eyes forward as if you saw the country free. God help me! how I have been containing myself for the last hour and a half!'

The signora dropped in a seat and laughed a languid laugh.

'The little ones? I will ring for them. Assunta shall bring them down in their night-gowns if they are undressed; and we will muffle the windows, for my little man will be wanting his song; and did you not promise him the great one which is to raise Italy-his mother, from the dead? Do you remember our little fellow's eyes as he tried to see the picture? I fear I force him too much, and there's no need-not a bit.'

The time was exciting, and the signora spoke excitedly. Messing and Reggio were in arms. South Italy had given the open signal. It was near upon the hour of the unmasking of the great Lombard conspiracy, and Vittoria, standing there, was the beacon-light of it. Her presence filled Laura with transports of exultation; and shy of displaying it, and of the theme itself, she let her tongue run on, and satisfied herself by smoothing the hand of the brave girl on her chin, and plucking with little loving tugs at her skirts. In doing this she suddenly gave a cry, as if stung.

'You carry pins,' she said. And inspecting the skirts more closely, 'You have a careless maid in that creature Giacinta; she lets paper stick to your dress. What is this?'

Vittoria turned her head, and gathered up her dress to see.

'Pinned with the butterfly!' Laura spoke under her breath.

Vittoria asked what it meant.

'Nothing—nothing,' said her friend, and rose, pulling her eagerly toward the lamp.

A small bronze butterfly secured a square piece of paper with clipped corners to her dress. Two words were written on it:—

'SEI SOSPETTA.'

CHAPTER XII

THE BRONZE BUTTERFLY

The two women were facing one another in a painful silence when Carlo Ammiani was announced to them. He entered with a rapid stride, and struck his hands together gladly at sight of Vittoria.

Laura met his salutation by lifting the accusing butterfly attached to Vittoria's dress.

'Yes; I expected it,' he said, breathing quick from recent exertion. 'They are kind—they give her a personal warning. Sometimes the dagger heads the butterfly. I have seen the mark on the Play-bills affixed to the signorina's name.'

'What does it mean?' said Laura, speaking huskily, with her head bent over the bronze insect. 'What can it mean?' she asked again, and looked up to meet a covert answer.

'Unpin it.' Vittoria raised her arms as if she felt the thing to be enveloping her.

The signora loosened the pin from its hold; but dreading lest she thereby sacrificed some possible clue to the mystery, she hesitated in her action, and sent an intolerable shiver of spite through Vittoria's frame, at whom she gazed in a cold and cruel way, saying, 'Don't tremble.' And again, 'Is it the doing of that 'garritrice magrezza,' whom you call 'la Lazzeruola?' Speak. Can you trace it to her hand? Who put the plague-mark upon you?'

Vittoria looked steadily away from her.

'It means just this,' Carlo interposed; 'there! now it 's off; and, signorina, I entreat you to think nothing of it,—it means that any one who takes a chief part in the game we play, shall and must provoke all fools, knaves, and idiots to think and do their worst. They can't imagine a pure devotion. Yes, I see—"Sei sospetta." They would write their 'Sei sospetta' upon St. Catherine in the Wheel. Put it out of your mind. Pass it.'

'But they suspect her; and why do they suspect her?' Laura questioned vehemently. 'I ask, is it a Conservatorio rival, or the brand of one of the Clubs? She has no answer.'

'Observe.' Carlo laid the paper under her eyes.

Three angles were clipped, the fourth was doubled under. He turned it back and disclosed the initials B. R. 'This also is the work of our man-devil, as I thought. I begin to think that we shall be eternally thwarted, until we first clear our Italy of its vermin. Here is a weazel, a snake, a tiger, in one. They call him the Great Cat. He fancies himself a patriot,—he is only a conspirator. I denounce him, but he gets the faith of people, our Agostino among them, I believe. The energy of this wretch is terrific. He has the vigour of a fasting saint. Myself—I declare it to you, signora, with shame, I know what it is to fear this man. He has Satanic blood, and the worst is, that the Chief trusts him.'

'Then, so do I,' said Laura.

'And I,' Vittoria echoed her.

A sudden squeeze beset her fingers. 'And I trust you,' Laura said to her. 'But there has been some indiscretion. My child, wait: give no heed to me, and have no feelings. Carlo, my friend—my husband's boy—brother-in-arms! let her teach you to be generous. She must have been indiscreet. Has she friends among the Austrians? I have one, and it is known, and I am not suspected. But, has she? What have you said or done that might cause them to suspect you? Speak, Sandra mia.'

It was difficult for Vittoria to speak upon the theme, which made her appear as a criminal replying to a charge. At last she said, 'English: I have no foreign friends but English. I remember nothing that I have done.—Yes, I have said I thought I might tremble if I was led out to be shot.'

'Pish! tush!' Laura checked her. 'They flog women, they do not shoot them. They shoot men.'

'That is our better fortune,' said Ammiani.

'But, Sandra, my sister,' Laura persisted now, in melodious coaxing tones. 'Can you not help us to guess? I am troubled: I am stung. It is for your sake I feel it so. Can't you imagine who did it, for instance?'

'No, signora, I cannot,' Vittoria replied.

'You can't guess?'

I cannot help you.'

'You will not!' said the irritable woman. 'Have you noticed no one passing near you?'

'A woman brushed by me as I entered this street. I remember no one else. And my Beppo seized a man who was spying on me, as he said. That is all I can remember.'

Vittoria turned her face to Ammiani.

'Barto Rizzo has lived in England,' he remarked, half to himself. 'Did you come across a man called Barto Rizzo there, signorina? I suspect him to be the author of this.'

At the name of Barto Rizzo, Laura's eyes widened, awakening a memory in Ammiani; and her face had a spectral wanness.

'I must go to my chamber,' she said. 'Talk of it together. I will be with you soon.'

She left them.

Ammiani bent over to Vittoria's ear. 'It was this man who sent the warning to Giacomo, the signora's husband, which he despised, and which would have saved him.

It is the only good thing I know of Barto Rizzo. Pardon her.'

'I do,' said the girl, now weeping.

'She has evidently a rooted superstitious faith in these revolutionary sign-marks. They are contagious to her. She loves you, and believes in you, and will kneel to you for forgiveness by-and-by. Her misery is a disease. She thinks now, "If my husband had given heed to the warning!"

'Yes, I see how her heart works,' said Vittoria. 'You knew her husband, Signor Carlo?'

'I knew him. I served under him. He was the brother of my love. I shall have no other.'

Vittoria placed her hand for Ammiani to take it. He joined his own to the fevered touch. The heart of the young man swelled most ungovernably, but the perils of the morrow were imaged by him, circling her as with a tragic flame, and he had no word for his passion.

The door opened, when a noble little boy bounded into the room; followed by a little girl in pink and white, like a streamer in the steps of her brother. With shouts, and with arms thrown forward, they flung themselves upon Vittoria, the boy claiming all her lap, and the girl struggling for a share of the kingdom. Vittoria kissed them, crying, 'No, no, no, Messer Jack, this is a republic, and not an empire, and you are to have no rights of "first come"; and Amalia sits on one knee, and you on one knee, and you sit face to face, and take hands, and swear to be satisfied.'

'Then I desire not to be called an English Christian name, and you will call me Giacomo,' said the boy.

Vittoria sang, in mountain-notes, 'Giacomo!—Giacomo—Giac-giac-giac.. como!'

The children listened, glistening up at her, and in conjunction jumped and shouted for more.

'More?' said Vittoria; 'but is the Signor Carlo no friend of ours? and does he wear a magic ring that makes him invisible?'

'Let the German girl go to him,' said Giacomo, and strained his throat to reach at kisses.

'I am not a German girl,' little Amalia protested, refusing to go to Carlo Ammiani under that stigma, though a delightful haven of open arms and knees, and filliping fingers, invited her.

'She is not a German girl, O Signor Giacomo,' said Vittoria, in the theatrical manner.

'She has a German name.'

'It's not a German name!' the little girl shrieked.

Giacomo set Amalia to a miauling tune.

'So, you hate the Duchess of Graatli!' said Vittoria. 'Very well. I shall remember.'

The boy declared that he did not hate his mother's friend and sister's godmother: he rather liked her, he really liked her, he loved her; but he loathed the name 'Amalia,' and could not understand why the duchess would be a German. He concluded by miauling 'Amalia' in the triumph of contempt.

'Cat, begone!' said Vittoria, promptly setting him down on his feet, and little Amalia at the same time perceiving that practical sympathy only required a ring at the bell for it to come out, straightway pulled the wires within herself, and emitted a doleful wail that gave her sole possession of Vittoria's bosom, where she was allowed to bring her tears to an end very comfortingly. Giacomo meanwhile, his body bent in an arch, plucked at Carlo Ammiani's wrists with savagely playful tugs, and took a stout boy's lesson in the art of despising what he coveted. He had only to ask for pardon. Finding it necessary, he came shyly up to Vittoria, who put Amalia in his way, kissing whom, he was himself tenderly kissed.

'But girls should not cry!' Vittoria reproved the little woman.

'Why do you cry?' asked Amalia simply.

'See! she has been crying.' Giacomo appropriated the discovery, perforce of loudness, after the fashion of his sex.

'Why does our Vittoria cry?' both the children clamoured.

'Because your mother is such a cruel sister to her,' said Laura, passing up to them from the doorway. She drew Vittoria's head against her breast, looked into her eyes, and sat down among them. Vittoria sang one low-toned soft song, like the voice of evening, before they were dismissed to their beds. She could not obey Giacomo's demand for a martial air, and had to plead that she was tired.

When the children had gone, it was as if a truce had ended. The signora and Ammiani fell to a brisk counterchange of questions relating to the mysterious suspicion which had fallen upon Vittoria. Despite

Laura's love for her, she betrayed her invincible feeling that there must be some grounds for special or temporary distrust.

'The lives that hang on it knock at me here,' she said, touching under her throat with fingers set like falling arrows.

But Ammiani, who moved in the centre of conspiracies, met at their councils, and knew their heads, and frequently combated their schemes, was not possessed by the same profound idea of their potential command of hidden facts and sovereign wisdom. He said, 'We trust too much to one man. We are compelled to trust him, but we trust too much to him. I mean this man, this devil, Barto Rizzo. Signora, signora, he must be spoken of. He has dislocated the plot. He is the fanatic of the revolution, and we are trusting him as if he had full sway of reason. What is the consequence? The Chief is absent he is now, as I believe, in Genoa. All the plan for the rising is accurate; the instruments are ready, and we are paralyzed. I have been to three houses to-night, and where, two hours previously, there was union and concert, all are irresolute and divided. I have hurried off a messenger to the Chief. Until we hear from him, nothing can be done. I left Ugo Corte storming against us Milanese, threatening, as usual, to work without us, and have a Bergamasc and Brescian Republic of his own. Count Medole is for a week's postponement. Agostino smiles and chuckles, and talks his poetisms.'

'Until you hear from the Chief, nothing is to be done?' Laura said passionately. 'Are we to remain in suspense? Impossible! I cannot bear it. We have plenty of arms in the city. Oh, that we had cannon! I worship cannon! They are the Gods of battle! But if we surprise the citadel;—one true shock of alarm makes a mob of an army. I have heard my husband say so. Let there be no delay. That is my word.'

'But, signora, do you see that all concert about the signal is lost?'

'My friend, I see something'; Laura nodded a significant half-meaning at him. 'And perhaps it will be as well. Go at once. See that another signal is decided upon. Oh! because we are ready—ready. Inaction now is uttermost anguish—kills the heart. What number of the white butchers have we in the city to-night?'

'They are marching in at every gate. I saw a regiment of Hungarians coming up the Borgo della Stella. Two fresh squadrons of Uhlans in the Corso Francesco. In the Piazza d'Armi artillery is encamped.'

'The better for Brescia, for Bergamo, for Padua, for Venice!' exclaimed Laura. 'There is a limit to their power. We Milanese can match them. For days and days I have had a dream lying in my bosom that Milan was soon to breathe. Go, my brother; go to Barto Rizzo; gather him and Count Medole, Agostino, and Colonel Corte—to whom I kiss my fingers—gather them together, and squeeze their brains for the one spark of divine fire in this darkness which must exist where there are so many thorough men bent upon a sacred enterprise. And, Carlo,'—Laura checked her nervous voice, 'don't think I am declaiming to you from one of my "Midnight Lamps."' (She spoke of the title of her pamphlets to the Italian people.) 'You feel among us women very much as Agostino and Colonel Corte feel when the boy Carlo airs his impetuosities in their presence. Yes, my fervour makes a philosopher of you. That is human nature. Pity me, pardon me, and do my bidding.'

The comparison of Ammiani's present sentiments to those of the elders of the conspiracy, when his mouth was open in their midst, was severe and masterful, for the young man rose instantly without a thought in his head.

He remarked: 'I will tell them that the signorina does not give the signal.'

'Tell them that the name she has chosen shall be Vittoria still; but say, that she feels a shadow of suspicion to be an injunction upon her at such a crisis, and she will serve silently and humbly until she is rightly known, and her time comes. She is willing to appear before them, and submit to interrogation. She knows her innocence, and knowing that they work for the good of the country, she, if it is their will, is content to be blotted out of all participation:—all! She abjures all for the common welfare. Say that. And say, to-morrow night the rising must be. Oh! to-morrow night! It is my husband to me.'

Laura Piaveni crossed her arms upon her bosom.

Ammiani was moving from them with a downward face, when a bell-note of Vittoria's voice arrested him.

'Stay, Signor Carlo; I shall sing to-morrow night.'

The widow heard her through that thick emotion which had just closed her' speech with its symbolical sensuous rapture. Divining opposition fiercely, like a creature thwarted when athirst for the wells, she gave her a terrible look, and then said cajolingly, as far as absence of sweetness could make the tones pleasant, 'Yes, you will sing, but you will not sing that song.'

'It is that song which I intend to sing, signora.'

'When it is interdicted?'

'There is only one whose interdict I can acknowledge.'

'You will dare to sing in defiance of me?'

'I dare nothing when I simply do my duty.'

Ammiani went up to the window, and leaned there, eyeing the lights leading down to the crowding Piazza. He wished that he were among the crowd, and might not hear those sharp stinging utterances coming from Laura, and Vittoria's unwavering replies, less frequent, but firmer, and gravely solid. Laura spent her energy in taunts, but Vittoria spoke only of her resolve, and to the point. It was, as his military instincts framed the simile, like the venomous crackling of skirmishing rifles before a fortress, that answered slowly with its volume of sound and sweeping shot. He had the vision of himself pleading to secure her safety, and in her hearing, on the Motterone, where she had seemed so simple a damsel, albeit nobly enthusiastic: too fair, too gentle to be stationed in any corner of the conflict at hand. Partly abased by the remembrance of his brainless intercessions then, and of the laughter which had greeted them, and which the signora had recently recalled, it was nevertheless not all in self-abasement (as the momentary recognition of a splendid character is commonly with men) that he perceived the stature of Vittoria's soul. Remembering also what the Chief had spoken of women, Ammiani thought 'Perhaps he has known one such as she.' The passion of the young man's heart magnified her image. He did not wonder to see the signora acknowledge herself worsted in the conflict.

'She talks like the edge of a sword,' cried Laura, desperately, and dropped into a chair. 'Take her home, and convince her, if you can, on the way, Carlo. I go to the Duchess of Graatli to-night. She has a reception. Take this girl home. She says she will sing: she obeys the Chief, and none but the Chief. We will not suppose that it is her desire to shine. She is suspected; she is accused; she is branded; there is no general faith in her; yet she will hold the torch to-morrow night:—and what ensues? Some will move, some turn back, some run headlong over to treachery, some hang irresolute all are for the shambles! The blood is on her head.'

'I will excuse myself to you another time,' said Vittoria. 'I love you, Signora Laura.'

'You do, you do, or you would not think of excusing yourself to me,' said Laura. 'But now, go. You have cut me in two. Carlo Ammiani may succeed where I have failed, and I have used every weapon; enough to make a mean creature hate me for life and kiss me with transports. Do your best, Carlo, and let it be your utmost.'

It remained for Ammiani to assure her that their views were different.

'The signorina persists in her determination to carry out the programme indicated by the Chief, and refuses to be diverted from her path by the false suspicions of subordinates.' He employed a sententious phraseology instinctively, as men do when they are nervous, as well as when they justify the cynic's definition of the uses of speech. 'The signorina is, in my opinion, right. If she draws back, she publicly accepts the blot upon her name. I speak against my own feelings and my wishes.'

'Sandra, do you hear?' exclaimed Laura. 'This is a friend's interpretation of your inconsiderate wilfulness.'

Vittoria was content to reply, 'The Signor Carlo judges of me differently.'

'Go, then, and be fortified by him in this headstrong folly.' Laura motioned her hand, and laid it on her face.

Vittoria knelt and enclosed her with her arms, kissing her knees.

'Beppo waits for me at the house-door,' she said; but Carlo chose not to hear of this shadow-like Beppo.

'You have nothing to say for her save that she clears her name by giving the signal,' Laura burst out on his temperate 'Addio,' and started to her feet. 'Well, let it be so. Fruitless blood again! A 'rivederla' to you both. To-night I am in the enemy's camp. They play with open cards. Amalia tells me all she knows by what she disguises. I may learn something. Come to me to-morrow. My Sandra, I will kiss you. These shudderings of mine have no meaning.'

The signora embraced her, and took Ammiani's salute upon her fingers.

'Sour fingers!' he said. She leaned her cheek to him, whispering, 'I could easily be persuaded to betray you.'

He answered, 'I must have some merit in not betraying myself.'

'At each elbow!' she laughed. 'You show the thumps of an electric battery at each elbow, and expect your Goddess of lightnings not to see that she moves you. Go. You have not sided with me, and I am right, and I am a woman. By the way, Sandra mia, I would beg the loan of your Beppo for two hours or less.'

Vittoria placed Beppo at her disposal.

'And you run home to bed,' continued Laura. 'Reason comes to you obstinate people when you are left alone for a time in the dark.'

She hardly listened to Vittoria's statement that the chief singers in the new opera were engaged to attend a meeting at eleven at night at the house of the maestro Rocco Ricci.

CHAPTER XIII

THE PLOT OF THE SIGNOR ANTONIO

There was no concealment as to Laura's object in making request for the services of Beppo. She herself knew it to be obvious that she intended to probe and cross-examine the man, and in her wilfulness she chose to be obtuse to opinion. She did not even blush to lean a secret ear above the stairs that she might judge, by the tones of Vittoria's voice upon her giving Beppo the order to wait, whether she was at the same time conveying a hint for guardedness. But Vittoria said not a word: it was Ammiani who gave the order. 'I am despicable in distrusting her for a single second,' said Laura. That did not the less encourage her to question Beppo rigorously forthwith; and as she was not to be deceived by an Italian's affectation of simplicity, she let him answer two or three times like a plain fool, and then abruptly accused him of standing prepared with these answers. Beppo, within his own bosom, immediately ascribed to his sagacious instinct the mere spirit of opposition and dislike to serve any one save his own young mistress which had caused him to irritate the signora and be on his guard. He proffered a candid admission of the truth of the charge; adding, that he stood likewise prepared with an unlimited number of statements. 'Questions, illustrious signora, invariably put me on the defensive, and seem to cry for a return thrust; and this I account for by the fact that my mother—the blessed little woman now among the Saints!—was questioned, brows and heels, by a ferruginously—faced old judge at the momentous period when she carried me. So that, a question—and I show point; but ask me for a statement, and, ah, signora!' Beppo delivered a sweep of the arm, as to indicate the spontaneous flow of his tongue.

'I think,' said Laura, 'you have been a soldier, and a serving-man.'

'And a scene-shifter, most noble signora, at La Scala.'

'You accompanied the Signor Mertyrio to England when he was wounded?'

'I did.'

'And there you beheld the Signorina Vittoria, who was then bearing the name of Emilia Belloni?'

'Which name she changed on her arrival in Italy, illustrious signora, for that of Vittoria Campa—"sull' campo dells gloria"—ah! ah!—her own name being an attraction to the blow-flies in her own country. All this is true.'

'It should be a comfort to you! The Signor Mertyrio...'

Beppo writhed his person at the continuance of the questionings, and obtaining a pause, he rushed into his statement: 'The Signor Mertyrio was well, and on the point of visiting Italy, and quitting the wave-embraced island of fog, of beer, of moist winds, and much money, and much kindness, where great hearts grew. The signorina corresponded with him, and with him only.'

'You know that, and will swear to it?' Laura exclaimed.

Beppo thereby receiving the cue he had commenced beating for, swore to its truth profoundly, and straightway directed his statement to prove that his mistress had not been politically (or amorously, if the suspicion aimed at her in those softer regions) indiscreet or blameable in any of her actions. The signorina, he said, never went out from her abode without the companionship of her meritorious mother and his own most humble attendance. He, Beppo, had a master and a mistress, the Signor Mertyrio and the Signorina Vittoria. She saw no foreigners: though—a curious thing!—he had seen her when the English language was talked in her neighbourhood; and she had a love for that language: it made her face play in smiles like an infant's after it has had suck and is full;—the sort of look you perceive when one is dreaming and hears music. She did not speak to foreigners. She did not care to go to foreign cities, but loved Milan, and lived in it free and happy as an earwig in a ripe apricot. The circumvallation of Milan gave her elbow-room enough, owing to the absence of forts all round—'which knock one's funny-bone in Verona, signora.' Beppo presented a pure smile upon a simple bow for acceptance. 'The air of Milan,' he went on, with less confidence under Laura's steady gaze, and therefore more forcing of his candour—'the sweet air of Milan gave her a deep chestful, so that she could hold her note as long as five lengths of a fiddle-bow:—by the body of Sant' Ambrogio, it was true!' Beppo stretched out his arm, and chopped his hand edgeways five testificatory times on the shoulder-ridge. 'Ay, a hawk might fly from St. Luke's head (on the Duomo) to the stone on San Primo over Como, while the signorina held on her note! You listened, you gasped—you thought of a poet in his dungeon, and suddenly, behold, his chains are struck off!—you thought of a gold-shelled tortoise making his pilgrimage to a beatific shrine!—you thought—you knew not what you thought!'

Here Beppo sank into a short silence of ecstasy, and wakening from it, as with an ardent liveliness: 'The signora has heard her sing? How to describe it! Tomorrow night will be a feast for Milan.'

'You think that the dilettanti of Milan will have a delight to-morrow night?' said Laura; but seeing that the man's keen ear had caught note of the ironic reptile under the flower, and unwilling to lose further time, she interdicted his reply.

'Beppo, my good friend, you are a complete Italian—you waste your cleverness. You will gratify me by remembering that I am your countrywoman. I have already done you a similar favour by allowing you to air your utmost ingenuity. The reflection that it has been to no purpose will neither scare you nor instruct you. Of that I am quite assured. I speak solely to suit the present occasion. Now, don't seek to elude me. If you are a snake with friends as well as enemies, you are nothing but a snake. I ask you—you are not compelled to answer, but I forbid you to lie—has your mistress seen, or conversed and had correspondence with any one receiving the Tedeschi's gold, man or woman? Can any one, man or woman, call her a traitress?'

'Not twice!' thundered Beppo, with a furrowed red forehead.

There was a noble look about the fellow as he stood with stiff legs in a posture, frowning—theatrical, but noble also; partly the look of a Figaro defending his honour in extremity, yet much like a statue of a French Marshal of the Empire.

'That will do,' said Laura, rising. She was about to leave him, when the Duchess of Graatli's chasseur was ushered in, bearing a missive from Amalia, her friend. She opened it and read:—

'BEST BELOVED,—Am I soon to be reminded bitterly that there is a river of steel between my heart and me?

'Fail not in coming to-night. Your new Bulbul is in danger. The silly thing must have been reading Roman history. Say not no! It intoxicates you all. I watch over her for my Laura's sake: a thousand kisses I shower on you, dark delicious soul that you are! Are you not my pine-grove leading to the evening star? Come, that we may consult how to spirit her away during her season of peril. Gulfs do not close over little female madcaps, my Laura; so we must not let her take the leap. Enter the salle when you arrive: pass down it once and return upon your steps; then to my boudoir. My maid Aennchen will conduct you. Addio. Tell this messenger that you come. Laura mine, I am for ever thy

'AMALIA.'

Laura signalled to the chasseur that her answer was affirmative. As he was retiring, his black-plumed hat struck against Beppo, who thrust him aside and gave the hat a dexterous kick, all the while keeping a decorous front toward the signora. She stood meditating. The enraged chasseur mumbled a word or two for Beppo's ear, in execrable Italian, and went. Beppo then commenced bowing half toward the doorway, and tried to shoot through, out of sight and away, in a final droop of excessive servility, but the signora stopped him, telling him to consider himself her servant until the morning; at which he manifested a surprising readiness, indicative of nothing short of personal devotion, and remained for two minutes after she had quitted the room. So much time having elapsed, he ran bounding down the stairs and found the hall-door locked, and that he was a prisoner during the signora's pleasure. The discovery that he was mastered by superior cunning, instead of disconcerting, quieted him wonderfully; so he put by the resources of his ingenuity for the next opportunity, and returned stealthily to his starting-point, where the signora found him awaiting her with composure. The man was in mortal terror lest he might be held guilty of a trust betrayed, in leaving his mistress for an hour, even in obedience to her command, at this crisis: but it was not in his nature to state the case openly to the signora, whom he knew to be his mistress's friend, or to think of practising other than shrewd evasion to accomplish his duty and satisfy his conscience.

Laura said, without smiling, 'The street-door opens with a key,' and she placed the key in his hand, also her fan to carry. Once out of the house, she was sure that he would not forsake his immediate charge of the fan: she walked on, heavily veiled, confident of his following. The Duchess of Graatli's house neighboured the Corso Francesco; numerous carriages were disburdening their freights of fair guests, and now and then an Austrian officer in full uniform ran up the steps, glittering under the lamps. 'I go in among them,' thought Laura. It rejoiced her that she had come on foot. Forgetting Beppo, and her black fan, as no Italian woman would have done but she who paced in an acute quivering of the anguish of hopeless remembrances and hopeless thirst of vengeance, she suffered herself to be conducted in the midst of the guests, and shuddered like one who has taken a fever-chill as she fulfilled the duchess's directions; she passed down the length of the saloon, through a light of visages that were not human to her sensations.

Meantime Beppo, oppressed by his custody of the fan, and expecting that most serviceable lady's instrument to be sent for at any minute, stood among a strange body of semi-feudal retainers below, where he was soon singled out by the duchess's chasseur, a Styrian, who, masking his fury under jest, in the South-German manner, endeavoured to lead him up to an altercation. But Beppo was much too supple to be entrapped. He apologized for any possible offences that he might have committed, assuring the chasseur that he considered one hat as good as another, and some hats better than others: in proof of extreme cordiality, he accepted the task of repeating the chasseur's name, which was 'Jacob Baumwalder Feckelwitz,' a tolerable mouthful for an Italian; and it was with remarkable delicacy that Beppo contrived to take upon himself the whole ridicule of his vile pronunciation of the unwieldy name. Jacob Baumwalder Feckelwitz offered him beer to refresh him after the effort. While Beppo was drinking, he seized the fan. 'Good; good; a thousand thanks,' said Beppo, relinquishing it; 'convey it aloft, I beseech you.' He displayed such alacrity and lightness of limb at getting rid of it, that Jacob thrust it between the buttons of his shirtfront, returning it to his possession by that aperture. Beppo's head sank. A handful of black lace and cedarwood chained him to the spot! He entreated the men in livery to take the fan upstairs and deliver it to the Signora Laura Piaveni; but they, being advised by Jacob, refused. 'Go yourself,' said Jacob, laughing, and little prepared to see the victim, on whom he thought that for another hour at least he had got his great paw firmly, take him at his word. Beppo sprang into the hall and up the stairs. The duchess's maid, ivory-faced Aennchen, was flying past him. She saw a very taking dark countenance making eyes at her, leaned her ear shyly, and pretending to understand all that was said by the rapid foreign tongue, acted from the suggestion of the sole thing which she did understand. Beppo had mentioned the name of the Signora Piaveni. 'This way,' she indicated with her finger, supposing that of course he wanted to see the signora very urgently.

Beppo tried hard to get her to carry the fan; but she lifted her fingers in a perfect Susannah horror of it, though still bidding him to follow. Naturally she did not go fast through the dark passages, where the game of the fan was once more played out, and with accompaniments. The accompaniments she objected to no further than a fish is agitated in escaping from the hook; but 'Nein, nein!' in her own language, and 'No, no!' in his, burst from her lips whenever he attempted to transfer the fan to her keeping. 'These white women are most wonderful!' thought Beppo, ready to stagger between perplexity and impatience.

'There; in there!' said Aennchen, pointing to a light that came through the folds of a curtain. Beppo kissed her fingers as they tugged unreluctantly in his clutch, and knew by a little pause that the case was hopeful for higher privileges. What to do? He had not an instant to spare; yet he dared not offend a woman's vanity. He gave an ecstatic pressure of her hand upon his breastbone, to let her be sure she was adored, albeit not embraced. After this act of prudence he went toward the curtain, while the fair Austrian soubrette flew on her previous errand.

It was enough that Beppo found himself in a dark antechamber for him to be instantly scrupulous in his footing and breathing. As he touched the curtain, a door opened on the other side of the interior, and a tender gabble of fresh feminine voices broke the stillness and ran on like a brook coming from leaps to a level, and again leaping and making noise of joy. The Duchess of Graatli had clasped the Signora Laura's two hands and drawn her to an ottoman, and between kissings and warmer claspings, was questioning of the little ones, Giacomo and her goddaughter Amalia.

'When, when did I see you last?' she exclaimed. 'Oh! not since we met that morning to lay our immortelles upon his tomb. My soul's sister! kiss me, remembering it. I saw you in the gateway—it seemed to me, as in a vision, that we had both had one warning to come for him, and knock, and the door would be opened, and our beloved would come forth! That was many days back. It is to me like a day locked up forever in a casket of pearl. Was it not an unstained morning, my own! If I weep, it is with pleasure. But,' she added with precipitation, 'weeping of any kind will not do for these eyelids of mine.' And drawing forth a tiny gold-framed pocket-mirror she perceived convincingly that it would not do.

'They will think it is for the absence of my husband,' she said, as only a woman can say it who deplores nothing so little as that.

'When does he return from Vienna?' Laura inquired in the fallen voice of her thoughtfulness.

'I receive two couriers a week; I know not any more, my Laura. I believe he is pushing some connubial complaint against me at the Court. We have been married seventeen months. I submitted to the marriage because I could get no proper freedom without, and now I am expected to abstain from the very thing I sacrificed myself to get! Can he hear that in Vienna?' She snapped her fingers. 'If not, let him come and behold it in Milan. Besides, he is harmless. The Archduchess is all ears for the very man of whom he is jealous. This is my reply: You told me to marry: I obeyed. My heart 's in the earth, and I must have distractions. My present distraction is De Pyrmont, a good Catholic and a good Austrian soldier, though a Frenchman. I grieve to say—it's horrible—that it sometimes tickles me when I reflect that De Pyrmont is keen with the sword. But remember, Laura, it was not until after our marriage my husband told me he could have saved Giacomo by the lifting of a finger. Away with the man!—if it amuses me to punish him, I do so.'

The duchess kissed Laura's cheek, and continued:—'Now to the point where we stand enemies! I am for Austria, you are for Italy. Good. But I am always for Laura. So, there's a river between us and a bridge across it. My darling, do you know that we are much too strong for you, if you mean anything serious tomorrow night?'

'Are you?' Laura said calmly.

'I know, you see, that something is meant to happen to-morrow night.'

Laura said, 'Do you?'

'We have positive evidence of it. More than that: Your Vittoria—but do you care to have her warned? She will certainly find herself in a pitfall if she insists on carrying out her design. Tell me, do you care to have her warned and shielded? A year of fortress-life is not agreeable, is not beneficial for the voice. Speak, my Laura.'

Laura looked up in the face of her friend mildly with her large dark eyes, replying, 'Do you think of sending Major de Pyrmont to her to warn her?'

'Are you not wicked?' cried the duchess, feeling that she blushed, and that Laura had thrown her off the straight road of her interrogation. 'But, play cards with open hands, my darling, to-night. Look:—She is in danger. I know it; so do you. She will be imprisoned perhaps before she steps on the boards—who knows? Now, I—are not my very dreams all sworn in a regiment to serve my Laura?—I have a scheme. Truth, it is hardly mine. It belongs to the Greek, the Signor Antonio Pericles Agriolopoulos. It is simply'— the duchess dropped her voice out of Beppo's hearing—'a scheme to rescue her: speed her away to my chateau near Meran in Tyrol.' 'Tyrol' was heard by Beppo. In his frenzy at the loss of the context he indulged in a yawn, and a grimace, and a dance of disgust all in one; which lost him the next sentence likewise. 'There we purpose keeping her till all is quiet and her revolutionary fever has passed. Have you heard of this Signor Antonio? He could buy up the kingdom of Greece, all Tyrol, half Lombardy. The man has a passion for your Vittoria; for her voice solely, I believe. He is considered, no doubt truly, a great connoisseur. He could have a passion for nothing else, or alas!' (the duchess shook her head with doleful drollery) 'would he insist on written securities and mortgages of my private property when he lends me money? How different the world is from the romances, my Laura! But for De Pyrmont, I might fancy my smile was really incapable of ransoming an empire; I mean an emperor. Speak; the man is waiting to come; shall I summon him?'

Laura gave an acquiescent nod.

By this time Beppo had taken root to the floor. 'I am in the best place after all,' he said, thinking of the duties of his service. He was perfectly well acquainted with the features of the Signor Antonio. He knew that Luigi was the Signor Antonio's spy upon Vittoria, and that no personal harm was intended toward his mistress; but Beppo's heart was in the revolt of which Vittoria was to give the signal; so, without a touch of animosity, determined to thwart him, Beppo waited to hear the Signor Antonio's scheme.

The Greek was introduced by Aennchen. She glanced at the signora's lap, and seeing her still without her fan, her eye shot slyly up with her shining temple, inspecting the narrow opening in the curtain furtively. A short hush of preluding ceremonies passed.

Presently Beppo heard them speaking; he was aghast to find that he had no comprehension of what they were uttering. 'Oh, accursed French dialect!' he groaned; discovering the talk to be in that tongue. The Signor Antonio warmed rapidly from the frigid politeness of his introductory manner. A consummate acquaintance with French was required to understand him. He held out the fingers of one hand in regimental order, and with the others, which alternately screwed his moustache from its constitutional droop over the corners of his mouth, he touched the uplifted digits one by one, buzzing over them: flashing his white eyes, and shrugging in a way sufficient to madden a surreptitious listener who was aware that a wealth of meaning escaped him and mocked at him. At times the Signor Antonio pitched a note compounded half of cursing, half of crying, it seemed: both pathetic and objurgative, as if he whimpered anathemas and had inexpressible bitter things in his mind. But there was a remedy! He displayed the specific on a third finger. It was there. This being done (number three on the fingers), matters might still be well. So much his electric French and gesticulations plainly asserted. Beppo strained all his attention for names, in despair at the riddle of the signs. Names were pillars of light in the dark unintelligible waste. The signora put a question. It was replied to with the name of the Maestro Rocco Ricci. Following that, the Signor Antonio accompanied his voluble delivery with pantomimic action which seemed to indicate the shutting of a door and an instantaneous galloping of horses—a flight into air, any-whither. He whipped the visionary steeds with enthusiastic glee, and appeared to be off skyward like a mad poet, when the signora again put a question, and at once he struck his hand flat across his mouth, and sat postured to answer what she pleased with a glare of polite vexation. She spoke; he echoed her, and the duchess took up the same phrase. Beppo was assisted by the triangular recurrence of the words and their partial relationship to Italian to interpret them: 'This night.' Then the signora questioned further. The Greek replied: 'Mademoiselle Irma di Karski.'

'La Lazzeruola,' she said.

The Signor Antonio flashed a bit of sarcastic mimicry, as if acquiescing in the justice of the opprobrious term from the high point of view: but mademoiselle might pass, she was good enough for the public.

Beppo heard and saw no more. A tug from behind recalled him to his situation. He put out his arms and gathered Aennchen all dark in them: and first kissing her so heartily as to set her trembling on the verge of a betrayal, before she could collect her wits he struck the fan down the pretty hollow of her back, between her shoulder-blades, and bounded away. It was not his intention to rush into the embrace of Jacob Baumwalder Feckelwitz, but that perambulating chasseur received him in a semi-darkness where all were shadows, and exclaimed, 'Aennchen!' Beppo gave an endearing tenderness to the few words of German known to him: 'Gottschaf-donner-dummer!' and slipped from the hold of the astonished Jacob, sheer under his arm-pit. He was soon in the street, excited he knew not by what, or for what object. He shuffled the names he remembered to have just heard—'Rocco Ricci, and 'la Lazzeruola.' Why did the name of la Lazzeruola come in advance of la Vittoria? And what was the thing meant by 'this night,' which all three had uttered as in an agreement?—ay! and the Tyrol! The Tyrol—this night-Rocco Ricci la Lazzeruola!

Beppo's legs were carrying him toward the house of the Maestro Rocco Ricci ere he had arrived at any mental decision upon these imminent mysteries.

BOOK III

CHAPTER XIV

AT THE MAESTRO'S DOOR

The house of the Maestro Rocco Ricci turned off the Borgo della Stella. Carlo Ammiani conducted Vittoria to the maestro's door. They conversed very little on the way.

'You are a good swordsman?' she asked him abruptly.

'I have as much skill as belongs to a perfect intimacy with the weapon,' he answered.

'Your father was a soldier, Signor Carlo.'

'He was a General officer in what he believed to be the army of Italy. We used to fence together every day for two hours.'

'I love the fathers who do that,' said Vittoria.

After such speaking Ammiani was not capable of the attempt to preach peace and safety to her. He postponed it to the next minute and the next.

Vittoria's spirit was in one of those angry knots which are half of the intellect, half of the will, and are much under the domination of one or other of the passions in the ascendant. She was resolved to go forward; she felt justified in going forward; but the divine afflatus of enthusiasm buoyed her no longer, and she required the support of all that accuracy of insight and that senseless stubbornness which there might be in her nature. The feeling that it was she to whom it was given to lift the torch and plant the standard of Italy, had swept her as through the strings of a harp. Laura, and the horrible little bronze butterfly, and the 'Sei sospetta,' now made her duty seem dry and miserably fleshless, imaging itself to her as if a skeleton had been told to arise and walk:—say, the thing obeys, and fills a ghastly distension of men's eyelids for a space, and again lies down, and men get their breath: but who is the rosier for it? where is the glory of it? what is the good? This Milan, and Verona, Padua, Vicenza, Brescia, Venice, Florence, the whole Venetian, Tuscan, and Lombardic lands, down to far Sicily, and that Rome which always lay under the crown of a dead sunset in her idea—they too might rise; but she thought of them as skeletons likewise. Even the shadowy vision of Italy Free had no bloom on it, and stood fronting the blown trumpets of resurrection Lazarus-like.

At these moments young hearts, though full of sap and fire, cannot do common nursing labour for the little suckling sentiments and hopes, the dreams, the languors and the energies hanging about them for nourishment. Vittoria's horizon was within five feet of her. She saw neither splendid earth nor ancient heaven; nothing save a breach to be stepped over in defiance of foes and (what was harder to brave) of friends. Some wayward activity of old associations set her humming a quaint English tune, by which she was brought to her consciousness.

'Dear friend,' she said, becoming aware that there might be a more troubled depth in Ammiani's absence of speech than in her own.

'Yes?' said he, quickly, as for a sentence to follow. None came, and he continued, 'The Signora Laura is also your friend.'

She rejoined coldly, 'I am not thinking of her.'

Vittoria had tried to utter what might be a word of comfort for him, and she found she had not a thought or an emotion. Here she differed from Laura, who, if the mood to heal a favourite's little sore at any season came upon her, would shower out lively tendernesses and all cajoleries possible to the tongue of woman. Yet the irritation of action narrowed Laura more than it did Vittoria; fevered her and distracted her sympathies. Being herself a plaything at the time, she could easily play a part for others. Vittoria had not grown, probably never would grow, to be so plastic off the stage. She was stringing her hand to strike a blow as men strike, and women when they do that cannot be quite feminine.

'How dull the streets are,' she remarked.

'They are, just now,' said Ammiani, thinking of them on the night to come convulsed with strife, and of her, tossed perhaps like a weed along the torrent of bloody deluge waters. Her step was so firm, her face so assured, that he could not fancy she realized any prospect of the sort, and it filled him with pity and a wretched quailing.

If I speak now I shall be talking like a coward, he said to himself: and he was happily too prudent to talk to her in that strain. So he said nothing of peace and safety. She was almost at liberty to believe that he approved the wisdom of her resolution. At the maestro's door she thanked him for his escort, and begged for it further within an hour. 'And do bring me some chocolate.' She struck her teeth together champing in a pretty hunger for it. 'I have no chocolate in my pocket, and I hardly know myself.'

'What will your Signor Antonio say?'

Vittoria filliped her fingers. 'His rule is over, and he is my slave: I am not his. I will not eat much; but some some I must have.'

Ammiani laughed and promised to obtain it. 'That is, if there's any to be had.'

'Break open doors to get it for me,' she said, stamping with fun to inspirit him.

No sooner was she standing alone, than her elbow was gently plucked at on the other side: a voice was sibilating: 'S-s-signorina.' She allowed herself to be drawn out of the light of the open doorway, having no suspicion and no fear. 'Signorina, here is chocolate.' She beheld two hands in cup-shape, surcharged with packets of Turin chocolate.

'Lugi, it is you?'

The Motterone spy screwed his eyelids to an expression of the shrewdest secrecy.

'Hist! signorina. Take some. You shall have all, but wait:—by-and-by. Aha! you look at my eyes as you did on the Monterone, because one of them takes the shoulder-view; but, the truth is, my father was a contrabandist, and had his eye in his ear when the frontier guard sent a bullet through his back, cotton-bags and cutleries, and all! I inherit from him, and have been wry-eyed ever since. How does that touch a man's honesty, signorina? Not at all. Don't even suspect that you won't appreciate Luigi by-and-by. So, you won't ask me a word, signorina, but up you go to the maestro:—signorina, I swear I am your faithful servant—up to the maestro, and down first. Come down first not last:—first. Let the other one come down after you; and you come down first. Leave her behind, la Lazzeruola; and here,' 'Luigi displayed a black veil, the common head-dress of the Milanese women, and twisted his fingers round and round on his forehead to personate the horns of the veil; 'take it, signorina; you know how to wear it. Luigi and the saints watch over you.' Vittoria found herself left in possession of the veil and a packet of chocolate.

'If I am watched over by the saints and Luigi,' she thought, and bit at the chocolate.

When the door had closed upon her, Luigi resumed his station near it, warily casting his glances along the house-fronts, and moving his springy little legs like a heath-cock alert. They carried him sharp to an opposite corner of the street at a noise of some one running exposed to all eyes right down the middle of the road, straight to the house: in which foolish person he discerned Beppo, all of whose proceedings Luigi observed and commented on from the safe obscurity under eaves and starlight, while Beppo was in the light of the lamps. 'You thunder at the door, my Beppo. You are a fire-balloon: you are going to burn yourself up with what you carry. You think you can do something, because you read books and frequent the talking theatres—fourteen syllables to a word. Mother of heaven! will you never learn anything from natural intelligence? There you are, in at the door. And now you will disturb the signorina, and you will do nothing but make la Lazzeruola's ears lively. Bounce! you are up the stairs. Bounce! you are on the landing. Thrum! you drum at the door, and they are singing; they don't hear you. And now you're meek as a mouse. That's it—if you don't hit the mark when you go like a bullet, you 're stupid as lead. And they call you a clever fellow! Luigi's day is to come. When all have paid him all round, they will acknowledge Luigi's worth. You are honest enough, my Beppo; but you might as well be a countryman. You are the signorina's servant, but I know the turnings, said the rat to the cavaliere weazel.'

In a few minutes Beppo stepped from the house, and flung himself with his back against the lintel of the doorway.

'That looks like determination to stop on guard,' said Luigi.

He knew the exact feeling expressed by it, when one has come violently on an errand and has done no good.

'A flea, my feathery lad, will set you flying again.'

As it was imperative in Luigi's schemes that Beppo should be set flying again, he slipped away stealthily, and sped fast into the neighbouring Corso, where a light English closed carriage, drawn by a pair of the island horses, moved at a slow pace. Two men were on the driver's seat, one of whom Luigi hailed to come down then he laid a strip of paper on his knee, and after thumping on the side of his nose to get a notion of English-Italian, he wrote with a pencil, dancing upon one leg all the while for a balance:—

'Come, Beppo, daughter sake, now, at once, immediate,
Beppo, signor.'

'That's to the very extremity how the little signora Inglese would write,' said Luigi; yet cogitating profoundly in a dubitative twinkle of a second as to whether it might not be the English habit to wind up a hasty missive with an expediting oath. He had heard the oath of emphasis in that island: but he decided to let it go as it stood. The man he had summoned was directed to take it straightway and deliver it to one who would be found at the house-door of the Maestro Rocco Ricci.

'Thus, like a drunken sentinel,' said Luigi, folding his arms, crossing his legs, and leaning back. 'Forward, Matteo, my cherub.'

'All goes right?' the coachman addressed Luigi.

'As honey, as butter, as a mulberry leaf with a score of worms on it! The wine and the bread and the cream-cheeses are inside, my dainty one, are they? She must not starve, nor must I. Are our hampers fastened out side? Good. We shall be among the Germans in a day and a night. I 've got the route, and I pronounce the name of the chateau very perfectly—"Schloss Sonnenberg." Do that if you can.'

The unpractised Italian coachman declined to attempt it. He and Luigi compared time by their watches. In three-quarters of an hour he was to be within hail of the maestro's house. Thither Luigi quietly returned.

Beppo's place there was vacant.

'That's better than a draught of Asti,' said Luigi.

The lighted windows of the maestro's house, and the piano striking corrective notes, assured him that the special rehearsal was still going on; and as he might now calculate on two or three minutes to spare, he threw back his coat-collar, lifted his head, and distended his chest, apparently to chime in with the singing, but simply to listen to it. For him, it was imperative that he should act the thing, in order to apprehend and appreciate it.

A hurried footing told of the approach of one whom he expected.

'Luigi!'

'Here, padrone.'

'You have the chocolate?'

'Signor Antonio, I have deposited it in the carriage.'

'She is in up there?'

'I beheld her entering.'

'Good; that is fixed fact.' The Signor Antonio drove at his moustache right and left. 'I give you, see, Italian money and German money: German money in paper; and a paper written out by me to explain the value of the German paper-money. Silence, engine that you are, and not a man! I am preventive of stupidity, I am? Do I not know that, hein? Am I in need of the acclamation of you, my friend? On to the Chateau Sonnenberg:—drive on, drive on, and one who stops you, you drive over him: the gendarmes in white will peruse this paper, if there is any question, and will pass you and the cage, bowing; you hear? It is a pass; the military pass you when you show this paper. My good friend, Captain Weisspriess, on the staff of General Pierson, gives it, signed, and it is effectual. But you lose not the paper: put it away with the paper-money, quite safe. For yourself, this is half your pay—I give you napoleons; ten. Count. And now—once at the Chateau Sonnenberg, I repeat, you leave her in charge of two persons, one a woman, at the gate, and then back—frrrrr....'

Antonio-Pericles smacked on the flat of his hand, and sounded a rapid course of wheels.

'Back, and drop not a crumb upon the road. You have your map. It is, after Roveredo, straight up the Adige, by Bolzano... say "Botzen."'

'"Botz,"' said Luigi, submissively.

'"Botz"—"Botz"—ass! fool! double idiot! "Botzon!"' Antonio-Pericles corrected him furiously, exclaiming to the sovereign skies, 'Though I pay for brains, can I get them! No. But make a fiasco, Luigi, and not a second ten for you, my friend: and away, out of my sight, show yourself no more!'

Luigi humbly said that he was not the instrument of a fiasco.

Half spurning him, Antonio-Pericles snarled an end both to his advices and his prophetic disgust of the miserable tools furnished unto masterly minds upon this earth. He paced forward and back, murmuring in French, 'Mon Dieu! was there ever such a folly as in the head of this girl? It is her occasion:—Shall I be a Star? Shall I be a Cinder? It is tomorrow night her moment of Birth! No; she prefers to be extinguished. For what? For this thing she calls her country. It is infamous. Yes, vile little cheat! But, do you know Antonio-Pericles? Not yet. I will nourish you, I will imprison you: I will have you tortured by love, by the very devil of love, by the red-hot pincers of love, till you scream a music, and die to melt him with your voice, and kick your country to the gutter, and know your Italy for a birthplace and a cradle of Song, and no more, and enough! Bah!'

Having thus delivered himself of the effervescence of his internal agitation, he turned sharply round upon Luigi, with a military stamp of the foot and shout of the man's name.

'It is love she wants,' Antonio-Pericles resumed his savage soliloquy. 'She wants to be kindled on fire. Too much Government of brain; not sufficient Insurrection of heart! There it is. There it lies. But, little fool! you shall find people with arms and shots and cannon running all up and down your body, firing and crying out "Victory for Love!" till you are beaten, till you gasp "Love! love! love!" and then comes a beatific—oh! a heaven and a hell to your voice. I will pay,' the excited connoisseur pursued more deliberately: 'I will pay half my fortune to bring this about. I am fortified, for I know such a voice was sent to be sublime.' He exclaimed in an ecstasy: 'It opens the skies!' and immediately appended: 'It is destined to suffocate the theatres!'

Pausing as before a splendid vision: 'Money—let it go like dust! I have an object. Sandra Belloni—you stupid Vittoria Campa!—I have millions and the whole Austrian Government to back me, and you to be wilful, little rebel! I could laugh. It is only Love you want. Your voice is now in a marble chamber. I will put it in a palace of cedarwood. This Ammiani I let visit you in the hope that he would touch you.

Bah! he is a patriot—not a man! He cannot make you wince and pine, and be cold and be hot, and— Bah! I give a chance to some one else who is not a patriot. He has done mischief with the inflammable little Anna von Lenkenstein—I know it. Your proper lovers, you women, are the broad, the business lovers, and Weisspriess is your man.'

Antonio-Pericles glanced up at the maestro's windows. 'Hark! it is her voice,' he said, and drew up his clenched fists with rage, as if pumping. 'Cold as ice! Not a flaw. She is a lantern with no light in it— crystal, if you like. Hark now at Irma, the stork-neck. Aie! what a long way it is from your throat to your head, Mademoiselle Irma! You were reared upon lemons. The split hair of your mural crown is not thinner than that voice of yours. It is a mockery to hear you; but you are good enough for the people, my dear, and you do work, running up and down that ladder of wires between your throat and your head;—you work, it is true, you puss! sleek as a puss, bony as a puss, musical as a puss. But you are good enough for the people. Hola!'

This exclamation was addressed to a cavalier who was dismounting from his horse about fifty yards down the street, and who, giving the reins to a mounted servant, advanced to meet the Signor Antonio.

'It is you, Herr Captain von Weisspriess!'

'When he makes an appointment you see him, as a rule, my dear Pericles,' returned the captain.

'You are out of uniform—good. We will go up. Remember, you are a connoisseur, from Bonn—from Berlin—from Leipsic: not of the K.K. army! Abjure it, or you make no way with this mad thing. You shall see her and hear her, and judge if she is worth your visit to Schloss Sonnenberg and a short siege. Good: we go aloft. You bow to the maestro respectfully twice, as in duty; then a third time, as from a whisper of your soul. Vanitas, vanitatis! You speak of the 'UT de poitrine.' You remark: "Albrechtsberger has said—-," and you slap your head and stop. They think, "He is polite, and will not quote a German authority to us": and they think, "He will not continue his quotation; in truth, he scornfully considers it superfluous to talk of counterpoint to us poor Italians." Your Christian name is Johann?—you are Herr Johannes. Look at her well. I shall not expose you longer than ten minutes to their observation. Frown meditative; the elbow propped and two fingers in the left cheek; and walk into the room with a stoop: touch a note of the piano, leaning your ear to it as in detection of five-fifteenths of a shade of discord. Frown in trouble as of a tooth. So, when you smile, it is immense praise to them, and easy for you.'

The names of the Signor Antonio-Pericles and Herr Johannes were taken up to the maestro.

Tormented with curiosity, Luigi saw them enter the house. The face and the martial or sanguinary reputation of Captain Weisspriess were not unknown to him. 'What has he to do with this affair?' thought Luigi, and sauntered down to the captain's servant, who accepted a cigar from him, but was rendered incorruptible by ignorance of his language. He observed that the horses were fresh, and were furnished with saddle-bags as for an expedition. What expedition? To serve as escort to the carriage?—a nonsensical idea. But the discovery that an idea is nonsensical is not a satisfactory solution of a difficulty. Luigi squatted on his haunches beside the doorstep, a little under one of the lower windows of Rocco Ricci's house. Earlier than he expected, the captain and Signor Antonio came out; and as soon as the door had closed behind them, the captain exclaimed, 'I give you my hand on it, my brave Pericles. You have done me many services, but this is finest of all. She's superb. She's a nice little wild woman to tame. I shall go to the Sonnenberg immediately. I have only to tell General Pierson that his nephew is to be prevented from playing the fool, and I get leave at once, if there's no active work.'

'His nephew, Lieutenant Pierson, or Pole—hein?' interposed the Greek.

'That 's the man. He 's on the Marshal's staff. He 's engaged to the Countess Lena von Lenkenstein. She has fire enough, my Pericles.'

'The Countess Anna, you say?' The Greek stretched forward his ear, and was never so near getting it vigorously cuffed.

'Deafness is an unpardonable offence, my dear Pericles.'

Antonio-Pericles sniffed, and assented, 'It is the stupidity of the ear.'

'I said, the Countess Lena.'

'Von Lenkenstein; but I choose to be further deaf.'

'To the devil, sir. Do you pretend to be angry?' cried Weisspriess.

'The devil, sir, with your recommendation, is too black for me to visit him,' Antonio-Pericles rejoined.

'By heaven, Pericles, for less than what you allow yourself to say, I've sent men to him howling!'

They faced one another, pulling at their moustachios. Weisspriess laughed.

'You're not a fighting man, Pericles.'

The Greek nodded affably. 'One is in my way, I have him put out of my way. It is easiest.'

'Ah! easiest, is it?' Captain Weisspriess 'frowned meditative' over this remarkable statement of a system. 'Well, it certainly saves trouble. Besides, my good Pericles, none but an ass would quarrel with you. I was observing that General Pierson wants his nephew to marry the Countess Lena immediately; and if, as you tell me, this girl Belloni, who is called la Vittoria—the precious little woman!—has such power over him, it's quite as well, from the General's point of view, that she should be out of the way at Sonnenberg. I have my footing at the Duchess of Graath's. I believe she hopes that I shall some day challenge and kill her husband; and as I am supposed to have saved Major de Pyrmont's life, I am also an object of present gratitude. Do you imagine that your little brown-eyed Belloni scented one of her enemies in me?'

'I know nothing of imagination,' the Signor Antonio observed frigidly.

'Till we meet!' Captain Weisspriess kissed his fingers, half as up toward the windows, and half to the Greek. 'Save me from having to teach love to your Irma!'

He ran to join his servant.

Luigi had heard much of the conversation, as well as the last sentence.

'It shall be to la Irma if it is to anybody,' Luigi muttered.

'Let Weisspriess—he will not awake love in her—let him kindle hate, it will do,' said the Signor Antonio. 'She has seen him, and if he meets her on the route to Meran, she will think it her fascination.'

Looking at his watch and at the lighted windows, he repeated his special injunctions to Luigi. 'It is near the time. I go to sleep. I am getting old: I grow nervous. Ten-twenty in addition, you shall have, if all is done right. Your weekly pay runs on. Twenty—you shall have thirty! Thirty napoleons additional!'

Ten fingers were flashed thrice.

Luigi gave a jump. 'Padrone, they are mine.'

'Animal, that shake your belly-bag and brain-box, stand!' cried the Greek, who desired to see Luigi standing firm that he might inspire himself with confidence in his integrity. When Luigi's posture had satisfied him, he turned and went off at great strides.

'He does pay,' Luigi reflected, seeing that immense virtue in his patron. 'Yes, he pays; but what is he about? It is this question for me—"Do I serve my hand? or, Do I serve my heart?" My hand takes the money, and it is not German money. My heart gives the affection, and the signorina has my heart. She reached me that cigarette on the Motterone like the Madonna: it is never to be forgotten! I serve my heart! Now, Beppo, you may come; come quick for her. I see the carriage, and there are three stout fellows in it who could trip and muzzle you at a signal from me before you could count the letters of your father's baptismal name. Oh! but if the signorina disobeys me and comes out last!—the Signor Antonio will ask the maestro, who will say, "Yes, la Vittoria was here with me last of the two"; and I lose my ten, my twenty, my thirty napoleons.'

Luigi's chest expanded largely with a melancholy draught of air.

The carriage meantime had become visible at the head of the street, where it remained within hearing of a whistle. One of the Milanese hired vehicles drove up to the maestro's door shortly after, and Luigi cursed it. His worst fears for the future of the thirty napoleons were confirmed; the door opened and the Maestro Rocco Ricci, bareheaded and in his black silk dressing-gown, led out Irma di Karski, by some called rival to la Vittoria; a tall Slavic damsel, whose laughter was not soft and smooth, whose cheeks were bright, and whose eyes were deep in the head and dull. But she had vivacity both of lips and shoulders. The shoulders were bony; the lips were sharp and red, like winter-berries in the morning-time. Freshness was not absent from her aspect. The critical objection was that it seemed a plastered freshness and not true bloom; or rather it was a savage and a hard, not a sweet freshness. Hence perhaps the name which distinguished her la Lazzeruola (crab apple). It was a freshness that did not invite the bite; sour to Italian taste.

She was apparently in vast delight. 'There will be a perfect inundation to-morrow night from Prague and Vienna to see me even in so miserable a part as Michiella,' she said. 'Here I am supposed to be a beginner; I am no debutante there.'

'I can believe it, I can believe it,' responded Rocco, bowing for her speedy departure.

'You are not satisfied with my singing of Michiella's score! Now, tell me, kind, good, harsh old master! you think that Miss Vittoria would sing it better. So do I. And I can sing another part better. You do not know my capacities.'

'I am sure there is nothing you would not attempt,' said Rocco, bowing resignedly.

'There never was question of my courage.'

'Yes, but courage, courage! away with your courage!' Rocco was spurred by his personal grievances against her in a manner to make him forget his desire to be rid of her. 'Your courage sets you flying at once at every fioritura and bravura passage, to subdue, not to learn: not to accomplish, but to conquer it. And the ability, let me say, is not in proportion to the courage, which is probably too great to be easily equalled; but you have the opportunity to make your part celebrated to-morrow night, if, as you tell me, the house is to be packed with Viennese, and, signorina, you let your hair down.'

The hair of Irma di Karski was of singular beauty, and so dear to her that the allusion to the triumphant feature of her person passed off Rocco's irony in sugar.

'Addio! I shall astonish you before many hours have gone by,' she said; and this time they bowed together, and the maestro tripped back hurriedly, and shut his door.

Luigi's astonishment eclipsed his chagrin when he beheld the lady step from her place, bidding the driver move away as if he carried a freight, and indicating a position for him at the end of the street, with an imperative sway and deflection of her hand. Luigi heard the clear thin sound of a key dropped to her from one of the upper windows. She was quick to seize it; the door opened stealthily to her, and she passed out of sight without casting a look behind. 'That's a woman going to discover a secret, if she can,' remarked the observer; meaning that he considered the sex bad Generals, save when they have occasion to preserve themselves secret; then they look behind them carefully enough. The situation was one of stringent torment to a professional and natural spy. Luigi lost count of minutes in his irritation at the mystery, which he took as a personal offence. Some suspicion or wariness existed in the lighted room, for the maestro threw up a window, and inspected the street to right and left. Apparently satisfied he withdrew his head, and the window was closed.

In a little while Vittoria's voice rose audible out of the stillness, though she restrained its volume.

Its effect upon Luigi was to make him protest to her, whimpering with pathos as if she heard and must be melted: 'Signorina! signorina, most dear! for charity's sake! I am one of you; I am a patriot. Every man to his trade, but my heart is all with you.' And so on, louder by fits, in a running murmur, like one having his conscience ransacked, from which he was diverted by a side-thought of Irma di Karski, la Lazzeruola, listening, taking poison in at her ears; for Luigi had no hesitation in ascribing her behaviour to jealousy. 'Does not that note drive through your bosom, excellent lady? I can fancy the tremble going all down your legs. You are poisoned with honey. How you hate it! If you only had a dagger!'

Vittoria sang but for a short space. Simultaneously with the cessation of her song Ammiani reached the door, but had scarcely taken his stand there when, catching sight of Luigi, he crossed the street, and recognizing him, questioned him sternly as to his business opposite the maestro's house. Luigi pointed to a female figure emerging. 'See! take her home,' he said. Ammiani released him and crossed back hurriedly, when, smiting his forehead, Luigi cried in despair, 'Thirty napoleons and my professional reputation lost!' He blew a whistle; the carriage dashed down from the head of the street. While Ammiani was following the swiftly-stepping figure in wonderment (knowing it could not be Vittoria, yet supposing it must be, without any clear aim of his wits), the carriage drew up a little in advance of her; three men—men of bulk and sinew jumped from it; one threw himself upon Ammiani, the others grasped the affrighted lady, tightening a veil over her face, and the carriage-door shut sharp upon her. Ammiani's assailant then fell away: Luigi flung himself on the box and shouted, 'The signorina is behind you!' And Ammiani beheld Vittoria standing in alarm, too joyful to know that it was she. In the spasm of joy he kissed her hands. Before they could intercommunicate intelligibly the carriage was out of their sight, going at a gallop along the eastern strada of the circumvallation of the city.

CHAPTER XV

AMMIANI THROUGH THE MIDNIGHT

Ammiani hurried Vittoria out of the street to make safety sure. 'Home,' she said, ashamed of her excitement, and not daring to speak more words, lest the heart in her throat should betray itself. He saw what the fright had done for her. Perhaps also he guessed that she was trying to conceal her fancied cowardice from him. 'I have kissed her hands,' he thought, and the memory of it was a song of tenderness in his blood by the way.

Vittoria's dwelling-place was near the Duomo, in a narrow thoroughfare leading from the Duomo to the Piazza of La Scala, where a confectioner of local fame conferred upon the happier members of the population most piquant bocconi and tartlets, and offered by placard to give an emotion to the nobility, the literati, and the epicures of Milan, and to all foreigners, if the aforesaid would adventure upon a trial of his art. Meanwhile he let lodgings. It was in the house of this famous confectioner Zotti that Vittoria and her mother had lived after leaving England for Italy. As Vittoria came under the fretted shadow of the cathedral, she perceived her mother standing with Zotti at the house-door, though the night was far advanced. She laughed, and walked less hurriedly. Ammiani now asked her if she had been alarmed. 'Not alarmed,' she said, 'but a little more nervous than I thought I should be.'

He was spared from putting any further question by her telling him that Luigi, the Motterone spy, had in all probability done her a service in turning one or other f the machinations of the Signor Antonio. 'My madman,' she called this latter. 'He has got his Irma instead of me. We shall have to supply her place tomorrow; she is travelling rapidly, and on my behalf! I think, Signor Carlo, you would do well by going to the maestro when you leave me, and telling him that Irma has been caught into the skies. Say, "Jealous that earth should possess such overpowering loveliness," or "Attracted in spite of themselves by that combination of genius and beauty which is found united nowhere but in Irma, the spirits of heaven determined to rob earth of her Lazzeruola." Only tell it to him seriously, for my dear Rocco will have to work with one of the singers all day, and I ought to be at hand by them to help her, if I dared stir out. What do you think?'

Ammiani pronounced his opinion that it would be perilous for her to go abroad.

'I shall in truth, I fear, have a difficulty in getting to La Scala unseen,' she said; 'except that we are cunning people in our house. We not only practise singing and invent wonderful confectionery, but we do conjuring tricks. We profess to be able to deceive anybody whom we please.'

'Do the dupes enlist in a regiment?' said Ammiani, with an intonation that professed his readiness to serve as a recruit. His humour striking with hers, they smiled together in the bright fashion of young people who can lose themselves in a ray of fancy at any season.

Vittoria heard her mother's wailful voice. 'Twenty gnats in one,' she said.

Ammiani whispered quickly to know whether she had decided for the morrow. She nodded, and ran up to her mother, who cried:

'At this hour! And Beppo has been here after you, and he told me I wrote for him, in Italian, when not a word can I put to paper: I wouldn't!—and you are threatened by dreadful dangers, he declares. His behaviour was mad; they are all mad over in this country, I believe. I have put the last stitch to your dress. There is a letter or two upstairs for you. Always letters!'

'My dear good Zotti,' Vittoria turned to the artist in condiments, 'you must insist upon my mother going to bed at her proper time when I am out.'

'Signorina,' rejoined Zotti, a fat little round-headed man, with vivacious starting brown eyes, 'I have only to tell her to do a thing—I pull a dog by the collar; be it said with reverence.'

'However, I am very glad to see you both such good friends.'

'Yes, signorina, we are good friends till we quarrel again. I regret to observe to you that the respectable lady is incurably suspicious. Of me—Zotti! Mother of heaven!'

'It is you that are suspicious of me, sir,' retorted madame. 'Of me, of all persons! It's "tell me this, tell me that," all day with you; and because I can't answer, you are angry.'

'Behold! the signora speaks English; we have quarrelled again,' said Zotti.

'My mother thinks him a perfect web of plots,' Vittoria explained the case between them, laughing, to Ammiani; 'and Zotti is persuaded that she is an inveterate schemer. They are both entirely innocent, only they are both excessively timid. Out of that it grows.'

The pair dramatized her outline on the instant:

'"Did I not see him speak to an English lady, and he will not tell me a word about it, though she's my own countrywoman?"'

'"Is it not true that she received two letters this afternoon, and still does she pretend to be ignorant of what is going on?"'

'Happily,' said Vittoria, 'my mother is not a widow, or these quarrels might some day end in a fearful reconciliation.'

'My child,' her mother whimpered, 'you know what these autumn nights are in this country; as sure as you live, Emilia, you will catch cold, and then you're like a shop with shutters up for the dead.'

At the same time Zotti whispered: 'Signorina, I have kept the minestra hot for your supper; come in, come in. And, little things, little dainty bits!—do you live in Zotti's house for nothing? Sweetest delicacies that make the tongue run a stream!—just notions of a taste—the palate smacks and forgets; the soul seizes and remembers!'

'Oh, such seductions!' Vittoria exclaimed.

'It is,' Zotti pursued his idea, with fingers picturesquely twirling in a spider-like distension; 'it is like the damned, and they have but a crumb of a chance of Paradise, and down swoops St. Peter and has them in the gates fast! You are worthy of all that a man can do for you, signorina. Let him study, let him work, let him invent,—you are worthy of all.'

'I hope I am not too hungry to discriminate! Zotti I see Monte Rosa.'

'Signorina, you are pleased to say so when you are famishing. It is because—' the enthusiastic confectioner looked deep and oblique, as one who combined a remarkable subtlety of insight with profound reflection; 'it is because the lighter you get the higher you mount; up like an eagle of the peaks! But we'll give that hungry fellow a fall. A dish of hot minestra shoots him dead. Then, a tart of pistachios and chocolate and cream—and my head to him who shall reveal to me the flavouring!'

'When I wake in the morning, I shall have lived a month or two in Arabia, Zotti. Tell me no more; I will come in,' said Vittoria.

'Then, signorina, a little crisp filbert—biscuit—a composition! You crack it, and a surprise! And then, and then my dish; Zotti's dish, that is not yet christened. Signorina, let Italy rise first; the great inventor of the dish winked and nodded temperately. 'Let her rise. A battle or a treaty will do. I have two or three original conceptions, compositions, that only wait for some brilliant feat of arms, or a diplomatic triumph, and I send them forth baptized.'

Vittoria threw large eyes upon Ammiani, and set the underlids humorously quivering. She kissed her fingers: 'Addio; a rivederla.' He bowed formally: he was startled to find the golden thread of their companionship cut with such cruel abruptness. But it was cut; the door had closed on her. The moment it had closed she passed into his imagination. By what charm had she allayed the fever of his anxiety? Her naturalness had perforce given him assurance that peace must surround one in whom it shone so steadily, and smiling at the thought of Zotti's repast and her twinkle of subdued humour, he walked away comforted; which, for a lover in the season of peril means exalted, as in a sudden conflagration of the dry stock of his intelligence. 'She must have some great faith in her heart,' he thought, no longer attributing his exclusion from it to a lover's rivalry, which will show that more than imagination was on fire within him. For when the soul of a youth can be heated above common heat, the vices of passion shrivel up and aid the purer flame. It was well for Ammiani that he did perceive (dimly though it was perceived) the force of idealistic inspiration by which Vittoria was supported. He saw it at this one moment, and it struck a light to light him in many subsequent perplexities; it was something he had never seen before. He had read Tuscan poetry to her in old Agostino's rooms; he had spoken of secret preparations for the revolt; he had declaimed upon Italy,—the poetry was good though the declamation may have been bad,—but she had always been singularly irresponsive, with a practical turn for ciphers. A quick reckoning, a sharp display of figures in Italy's cause, kindled her cheeks and took her breath. Ammiani now understood that there lay an unspoken depth in her, distinct from her visible nature.

He had first an interview with Rocco Ricci, whom he prepared to replace Irma.

His way was then to the office of his Journal, where he expected to be greeted by two members of the Polizia, who would desire him to march before the central bureau, and exhibit proofs of articles and the items of news for inspection, for correction haply, and possibly for approval. There is a partial delight in the contemplated submission to an act of servitude for the last time. Ammiani stepped in with combative gaiety, but his stiff glance encountered no enemy. This astonished him. He turned back into the street and meditated. The Pope's Mouth might, he thought, hold the key to the riddle. It is not always most comfortable for a conspirator to find himself unsuspected: he reads the blank significantly. It looked ill that the authorities should allow anything whatsoever to be printed on such a morrow: especially ill, if they were on the alert. The neighbourhood by the Pope's Mouth was desolate under dark starlight. Ammiani got his fingers into the opening behind the rubbish of brick, and tore them on six teeth of a saw that had been fixed therein. Those teeth were as voluble to him as loud tongues. The Mouth was empty of any shred of paper. They meant that the enemy was ready to bite, and that the conspiracy had ceased to be active. He perceived that a stripped ivy-twig, with the leaves scattered around it, stretched at his feet. That was another and corroborative sign, clearer to him than printed capitals. The reading of it declared that the Revolt had collapsed. He wound and unwound his handkerchief about his fingers mechanically: great curses were in his throat. 'I would start for South America at dawn, but for her!' he said. The country of Bolivar still had its attractions for Italian youth. For a certain space Ammiani's soul was black with passion. He was the son of that fiery Paolo Ammiani who had cast his glove at Eugene's feet, and bade the viceroy deliver it to his French master. (The General was preparing to break his sword on his knee when Eugene rushed up to him and kissed him.)

Carlo was of this blood. Englishmen will hardly forgive him for having tears in his eyes, but Italians follow the Greek classical prescription for the emotions, while we take example by the Roman. There is no sneer due from us. He sobbed. It seemed that a country was lost.

Ammiani had moved away slowly: he was accidentally the witness of a curious scene. There came into the irregular triangle, and walking up to where the fruitstalls stood by day, a woman and a man. The man was an Austrian soldier. It was an Italian woman by his side. The sight of the couple was just then like an incestuous horror to Ammiani. She led the soldier straight up to the Mouth, directing his hand to it, and, what was far more wonderful, directing it so that he drew forth a packet of papers from where Ammiani had found none. Ammiani could see the light of them in his hand. The Austrian snatched an embrace and ran. Ammiani was moving over to her to seize and denounce the traitress, when he beheld another figure like an apparition by her side; but this one was not a whitecoat. Had it risen from the earth? It was earthy, for a cloud of dust was about it, and the woman gave a stifled scream. 'Barto! Barto!' she cried, pressing upon her eyelids. A strong husky laugh came from him. He tapped her shoulder heartily, and his 'Ha! ha!' rang in the night air.

'You never trust me,' she whimpered from shaken nerves.

He called her, 'Brave little woman! rare girl!'

'But you never trust me!'

'Do I not lay traps to praise you?'

'You make a woman try to deceive you.' If she could! If only she could!'

Ammiani was up with them.

'You are Barto Rizzo,' he spoke, half leaning over the man in his impetuosity.

Barto stole a defensive rearward step. The thin light of dawn had in a moment divided the extreme starry darkness, and Ammiani, who knew his face, had not to ask a second time. It was scored by a recent sword-cut. He glanced at the woman: saw that she was handsome. It was enough; he knew she must be Barto's wife, and, if not more cunning than Barto, his accomplice, his instrument, his slave.

'Five minutes ago I would have sworn you were a traitress he said to her.

She was expressionless, as if she had heard nothing; which fact, considering that she was very handsome, seemed remarkable to the young man. Youth will not believe that stupidity and beauty can go together.

'She is the favourite pupil of Bartolommeo Rizzo, Signor Carlo Ammiani,' quoth Barto, having quite regained his composure. 'She is my pretty puppet-patriot. I am not in the habit of exhibiting her; but since you see her, there she is.'

Barto had fallen into the Southern habit of assuming ease in quasi-rhetorical sentences, but with wary eyes over them. The peculiar, contracting, owl-like twinkle defied Ammiani's efforts to penetrate his look; so he took counsel of his anger, and spoke bluntly.

'She does your work?'

'Much of it, Signor Carlo: as the bullet does the work of the rifle.'

'Beast! was it your wife who pinned the butterfly to the Signorina Vittoria's dress?'

'Signor Carlo Ammiani, you are the son of Paolo, the General: you call me beast? I have dandled you in my arms, my little lad, while the bands played "There's yet a heart in Italy!" Do you remember it?' Barto sang out half-a-dozen bars. 'You call me beast? I'm the one man in Milan who can sing you that.'

'Beast or man, devil or whatever you are!' cried Ammiani, feeling nevertheless oddly unnerved, 'you have committed a shameful offence: you, or the woman, your wife, who serves you, as I see. You have thwarted the best of plots; you have dared to act in defiance of your Chief—'

'Eyes to him!' Barto interposed, touching over his eyeballs.

'And you have thrown your accursed stupid suspicions on the Signorina Vittoria. You are a mad fool. If I had the power, I would order you to be shot at five this morning; and that's the last rising of the light you should behold. Why did you do it? Don't turn your hellish eyes in upon one another, but answer at once! Why did you do it?'

'The Signorina Vittoria,' returned Barto—his articulation came forth serpent-like—'she is not a spy, you think. She has been in England: I have been in England. She writes; I can read. She is a thing of whims. Shall she hold the goblet of Italy in her hand till it overflows? She writes love-letters to an English whitecoat. I have read them. Who bids her write? Her whim! She warns her friends not to enter Milan. She—whose puppet is she? Not yours; not mine. She is the puppet of an English Austrian!'

Barto drew back, for Ammiani was advancing.

'What is it you mean?' he cried.

'I mean,' said Ammiani, still moving on him, 'I mean to drag you first before Count Medole, and next before the signorina; and you shall abjure your slander in her presence. After that I shall deal with you. Mark me! I have you: I am swifter on foot, and I am stronger. Come quietly.'

Barto smiled in grim contempt.

'Keep your foot fast on that stone, you're a prisoner,' he replied, and seeing Ammiani coming, 'Net him, my sling-stone! my serpent!' he signalled to his wife, who threw herself right round Ammiani in a tortuous twist hard as wire-rope. Stung with irritation, and a sense of disgrace and ridicule and pitifulness in one, Ammiani, after a struggle, ceased the attempt to disentwine her arms, and dragged her clinging to him. He was much struck by hearing her count deliberately, in her desperation, numbers from somewhere about twenty to one hundred. One hundred was evidently the number she had to complete, for when she had reached it she threw her arms apart. Barto was out of sight. Ammiani waved her on to follow in his steps: he was sick of her presence, and had the sensations of a shame-faced boy whom a girl has kissed. She went without uttering a word.

The dawn had now traversed the length of the streets, and thrown open the wide spaces of the city. Ammiani found himself singing, 'There's yet a heart in Italy!' but it was hardly the song of his own heart. He slept that night on a chair in the private room of his office, preferring not to go to his mother's house. 'There 's yet a heart in Italy!' was on his lips when he awoke with scattered sensations, all of which collected in revulsion against the song. 'There's a very poor heart in Italy!' he said, while getting his person into decent order; 'it's like the bell in the lunatic's tower between Venice and the Lido: it beats now and then for meals: hangs like a carrion-lump in the vulture's beak meanwhile!'

These and some other similar sentiments, and a heat about the brows whenever he set them frowning over what Barto had communicated concerning an English Austrian, assured Ammiani that he had no proper command of himself: or was, as the doctors would have told him, bilious. It seemed to him that he must have dreamed of meeting the dark and subtle Barto Rizzo overnight; on realizing that fact he could not realize how the man had escaped him, except that when he thought over it, he breathed deep and shook his shoulders. The mind will, as you may know, sometimes refuse to work when the sensations are shameful and astonished. He despatched a messenger with a 'good morrow' to his mother, and then went to a fencing-saloon that was fitted up in the house of Count Medole, where, among two or three, there was the ordinary shrugging talk of the collapse of the projected outbreak, bitter to hear. Luciano Romara came in, and Ammiani challenged him to small-sword and broadsword. Both being ireful to boiling point, and mad to strike at something, they attacked one another furiously, though they were dear friends, and the helmet-wires and the padding rattled and smoked to the thumps. For half an hour they held on to it, when, their blood being up, they flashed upon the men present, including the count, crying shame to them for letting a woman alone be faithful to her task that night. The blood forsook Count Medole's cheeks, leaving its dead hue, as when blotting-paper is laid on running-ink. He deliberately took a pair of foils, and offering the handle of one to Ammiani, broke the button off the end of his own, and stood to face an adversary. Ammiani followed the example: a streak of crimson was on his shirt-sleeve, and his eyes had got their hard black look, as of the flint-stone, before Romara in amazement discovered the couple to be at it in all purity of intention, on the sharp edge of the abyss. He knocked up their weapons and stood between them, puffing his cigarette leisurely.

'I fine you both,' he said.

He touched Ammiani's sword-arm, nodded with satisfaction to find that there was no hurt, and cried, 'You have an Austrian out on the ground by this time tomorrow morning. So, according to the decree!'

'Captain Weisspriess is in the city,' was remarked.

'There are a dozen on the list,' said little Pietro Cardi, drawing out a paper.

'If you are to be doing nothing else to-morrow morning,' added Leone Rufo, 'we may as well march out the whole dozen.'

These two were boys under twenty.

'Shall it be the first hit for Captain Weisspriess?' Count Medole said this while handing a fresh and fairly-buttoned foil to Ammiani.

Romara laughed: 'You will require to fence the round of Milan city, my dear count, to win a claim to Captain Weisspriess. In the first place, I yield him to no man who does not show himself a better man than I. It's the point upon which I don't pay compliments.'

Count Medole bowed.

'But, if you want occupation,' added Luciano, closing his speech with a merely interrogative tone.

'I scarcely want that, as those who know me will tell you,' said Medole, so humbly, that those who knew him felt that he had risen to his high seat of intellectual contempt. He could indulge himself, having shown his courage.

'Certainly not; if you are devising means of subsistence for the widows and orphans of the men who will straggle out to be slaughtered to-night,' said Luciano; 'you have occupation in that case.'

'I will do my best to provide for them,'—the count persisted in his air of humility, 'though it is a question with some whether idiots should live.' He paused effectively, and sucked in a soft smile of self-approbation at the stroke. Then he pursued: 'We meet the day after to-morrow. The Pope's Mouth is closed. We meet here at nine in the morning. The next day at eleven at Farugino's, the barber's, in Monza. The day following at Camerlata, at eleven likewise. Those who attend will be made aware of the dispositions for the week, and the day we shall name for the rising. It is known to you all, that without affixing a stigma on our new prima-donna, we exclude her from any share in this business. All the Heads have been warned that we yield this night to the Austrians. Gentlemen, I cannot be more explicit. I wish that I could please you better.'

'Oh, by all means,' said Pietro Cardi: 'but patience is the pestilence; I shall roam in quest of adventure. Another quiet week is a tremendous trial.'

He crossed foils with Leone Rufo, but finding no stop to the drawn 'swish' of the steel, he examined the end of his weapon with a lengthening visage, for it was buttonless. Ammiani burst into laughter at the spontaneous boyishness in the faces of the pair of ambitious lads. They both offered him one of the rapiers upon equal terms. Count Medole's example of intemperate vanity was spoiling them.

'You know my opinion,' Ammiani said to the count. 'I told you last night, and I tell you again to-day, that Barto Rizzo is guilty of gross misconduct, and that you must plead the same to a sort of excuseable treason. Count Medole, you cannot wind and unwind a conspiracy like a watch. Who is the head of this one? It is the man Barto Rizzo. He took proceedings before he got you to sanction them. You may be the vessel, but he commands, or at least, he steers it.'

The count waited undemonstratively until Ammiani had come to an end. 'You speak, my good Ammiani, with an energy that does you credit,' he said, 'considering that it is not in your own interest, but another person's. Remember, I can bear to have such a word as treason ascribed to my acts.'

Fresh visitors, more or less mixed, in the conspiracy, and generally willing to leave the management of it to Count Medole, now entered the saloon. These were Count Rasati, Angelo Dovili, a Piedmontese General, a Tuscan duke, and one or two aristocratic notabilities and historic nobodies. They were hostile to the Chief whom Luciano and Carlo revered and obeyed. The former lit a cigarette, and saying to his friend, 'Do you breakfast with your mother? I will come too,' slipped his hand on Ammiani's arm; they walked out indolently together, with the smallest shade of an appearance of tolerating scorn for those whom they left behind.

'Medole has money and rank and influence, and a kind of I-don't-know-what womanishness, that makes him push like a needle for the lead, and he will have the lead and when he has got the lead, there 's the last chapter of him,' said Luciano. 'His point of ambition is the perch of the weather-cock. Why did he set upon you, my Carlo? I saw the big V running up your forehead when you faced him. If you had finished him no great harm would have been done.'

'I saw him for a short time last night, and spoke to him in my father's style,' said Carlo. 'The reason was, that he defended Barto Rizzo for putting the ring about the Signorina Vittoria's name, and causing the black butterfly to be pinned to her dress.'

Luciano's brows stood up.

'If she sings to-night, depend upon it there will be a disturbance,' he said. 'There may be a rising in spite of Medole and such poor sparks, who're afraid to drop on powder, and twirl and dance till the wind blows them out. And mind, the chance rising is commonly the luckiest. If I get a command I march to the Alps. We must have the passes of the Tyrol. It seems to me that whoever holds the Alps must ride the Lombard mare. You spring booted and spurred into the saddle from the Alps.'

Carlo was hurt by his friend's indifference to the base injury done to Vittoria.

'I have told Medole that she will sing to-night in spite of him,' he was saying, with the intention of bringing round some reproach upon Luciano for his want of noble sympathy, when the crash of an Austrian regimental band was heard coming up the Corso. It stirred him to love his friend with all his warmth. 'At any rate, for my sake, Luciano, you will respect and uphold her.'

'Yes, while she's true,' said Luciano, unsatisfactorily. The regiment, in review uniform, followed by two pieces of artillery, passed by. Then came a squadron of hussars and one of Uhlans, and another foot regiment, more artillery, fresh cavalry.

'Carlo, if three generations of us pour out our blood to fertilize Italian ground, it's not too much to pay to chase those drilled curs.' Luciano spoke in vehement undertone.

'We 'll breakfast and have a look at them in the Piazza d'Armi, and show that we Milanese are impressed with a proper idea of their power,' said Carlo, brightening as he felt the correction of his morbid lover's anger in Luciano's reaching view of their duties as Italian citizens. The heat and whirl of the hour struck his head, for to-morrow they might be wrestling with that living engine which had marched past, and surely all the hate he could muster should be turned upon the outer enemy. He gained his mother's residence with clearer feelings.

CHAPTER XVI

COUNTESS AMMIANI

Countess Ammiani was a Venetian lady of a famous House, the name of which is as a trumpet sounding from the inner pages of the Republic. Her face was like a leaf torn from an antique volume; the hereditary features told the story of her days. The face was sallow and fireless; life had faded like a painted cloth upon the imperishable moulding. She had neither fire in her eyes nor colour on her skin. The thin close multitudinous wrinkles ran up accurately ruled from the chin to the forehead's centre, and touched faintly once or twice beyond, as you observe the ocean ripples run in threads confused to smoothness within a space of the grey horizon sky. But the chin was firm, the mouth and nose were firm, the forehead sat calmly above these shows of decay. It was a most noble face; a fortress face; strong and massive, and honourable in ruin, though stripped of every flower.

This lady in her girlhood had been the one lamb of the family dedicated to heaven. Paolo, the General, her lover, had wrenched her from that fate to share with him a life of turbulent sorrows till she should behold the blood upon his grave. She, like Laura Fiaveni, had bent her head above a slaughtered husband, but, unlike Laura, Marcellina Ammiani had not buried her heart with him. Her heart and all her energies had been his while he lived; from the visage of death it turned to her son. She had accepted the passion for Italy from Paolo; she shared it with Carlo. Italian girls of that period had as little passion of their own as flowers kept out of sunlight have hues. She had given her son to her country with that intensely apprehensive foresight of a mother's love which runs quick as Eastern light from the fervour of the devotion to the remote realization of the hour of the sacrifice, seeing both in one. Other forms of love, devotion in other bosoms, may be deluded, but hers will not be. She sees the sunset in the breast of the springing dawn. Often her son Carlo stood a ghost in her sight. With this haunting prophetic vision, it was only a mother, who was at the same time a supremely noble woman, that could feel all human to him notwithstanding. Her heart beat thick and fast when Carlo and Luciano entered the morning-room where she sat, and stopped to salute her in turn.

'Well?' she said without betraying anxiety or playing at carelessness.

Carlo answered, 'Let us eat and drink, for to-morrow we die. I think that's the language of peaceful men.'

'You are to be peaceful men to-morrow, my Carlo?'

'The thing is in Count Medole's hands,' said Luciano; 'and he is constitutionally of our Agostino's opinion that we are bound to wait till the Gods kick us into action; and, as Agostino says, Medole has raised himself upon our shoulders so as to be the more susceptible to their wishes when they blow a gale.'

He informed her of the momentary thwarting of the conspiracy, and won Carlo's gratitude by not speaking of the suspicion which had fallen on Vittoria.

'Medole,' he said, 'has the principal conduct of the business in Milan, as you know, countess. Our Chief cannot be everywhere at once; so Medole undertakes to decide for him here in old Milan. He decided yesterday afternoon to put off our holiday for what he calls a week. Checco, the idiot, in whom he confides, gave me the paper signifying the fact at four o'clock. There was no appeal; for we can get no place of general meeting under Medole's prudent management. He fears our being swallowed in a body if we all meet.'

The news sent her heart sinking in short throbs down to a delicious rest; but Countess Ammiani disdained to be servile to the pleasure, even as she had strengthened herself to endure the shocks of pain. It was a conquered heart that she and every Venetian and Lombard mother had to carry; one that played its tune according to its nature, shaping no action, sporting no mask. If you know what is meant by that phrase, a conquered heart, you will at least respect them whom you call weak women for having gone through the harshest schooling which this world can show example of. In such mothers Italy revived. The pangs and the martyrdom were theirs. Fathers could march to the field or to the grey glacis with their boys; there was no intoxication of hot blood to cheer those who sat at home watching the rise and fall of trembling scales which said life or death for their dearest. Their least shadowy hope could be but a shrouded contentment in prospect; a shrouded submission in feeling. What bloom of hope was there when Austria stood like an iron wall, and their own ones dashing against it were as little feeble waves that left a red mark and no more? But, duty to their country had become their religion; sacrifice they accepted as their portion; when the last stern evil befell them they clad themselves in a veil and walked upon an earth they had passed from for all purposes save service of hands. Italy revived in these mothers. Their torture was that of the re-animation of her frame from the death-trance.

Carlo and Luciano fell hungrily upon dishes of herb-flavoured cutlets, and Neapolitan maccaroni, green figs, green and red slices of melon, chocolate, and a dry red Florentine wine. The countess let them eat, and then gave her son a letter that been delivered at her door an hour back by the confectioner Zotti. It proved to be an enclosure of a letter addressed to Vittoria by the Chief. Genoa was its superscription. From that place it was forwarded by running relays of volunteer messengers. There were points of Italy which the Chief could reach four-and-twenty hours in advance of the Government with all its aids and machinery. Vittoria had simply put her initials at the foot of the letter. Carlo read it eagerly and cast it aside. It dealt in ideas and abstract phraseology; he could get nothing of it between his impatient teeth; he was reduced to a blank wonder at the reason for her sending it on to him. It said indeed—and so far it seemed to have a meaning for her:

'No backward step. We can bear to fall; we cannot afford to draw back.'

And again:

'Remember that these uprisings are the manifested pulsations of the heart of your country, so that none shall say she is a corpse, and knowing that she lives, none shall say that she deserves not freedom. It is the protest of her immortal being against her impious violator.'

Evidently the Chief had heard nothing of the counterstroke of Barto Rizzo, and of Count Medole's miserable weakness: but how, thought Carlo, how can a mind like Vittoria's find matter to suit her in such sentences? He asked himself the question, forgetting that a little time gone by, while he was aloof from the tumult and dreaming of it, this airy cloudy language and every symbolism, had been strong sustaining food, a vital atmosphere, to him. He did not for the moment (though by degrees he recovered his last night's conception of her) understand that among the noble order of women there is, when they plunge into strife, a craving for idealistic truths, which men are apt, under the heat and hurry of their energies, to put aside as stars that are meant merely for shining.

His mother perused the letter—holding it out at arm's length—and laid it by; Luciano likewise. Countess Ammiani was an aristocrat: the tone and style of the writing were distasteful to her. She allowed her son's judgement of the writer to stand for her own, feeling that she could surrender little prejudices in favour of one who appeared to hate the Austrians so mortally. On the other hand, she defended Count Medole. Her soul shrank at the thought of the revolution being yielded up to theorists and men calling themselves men of the people—a class of men to whom Paolo her soldier-husband's aversion had always been formidably pronounced. It was an old and a wearisome task for Carlo to explain to her that the times were changed and the necessities of the hour different since the day when his father conspired and fought for freedom. Yet he could not gainsay her when she urged that the nobles should be elected to lead, if they consented to lead; for if they did not lead, were they not excluded from the movement?

'I fancy you have defined their patriotism,' said Carlo.

'Nay, my son; but you are one of them.'

'Indeed, my dearest mother, that is not what they will tell you.'

'Because you have chosen to throw yourself into the opposite ranks.'

'You perceive that you divide our camp, madame my mother. For me there is no natural opposition of ranks. What are we? We are slaves: all are slaves. While I am a slave, shall I boast that I am of noble birth? "Proud of a coronet with gems of paste!" some one writes. Save me from that sort of pride! I am content to take my patent of nobility for good conduct in the revolution. Then I will be count, or marquis, or duke; I am not a Republican pure blood;—but not till then. And in the meantime—'

'Carlo is composing for his newspaper,' the countess said to Luciano.

'Those are the leaders who can lead,' the latter replied. 'Give the men who are born to it the first chance. Old Agostino is right—the people owe them their vantage ground. But when they have been tried and they have failed, decapitate them. Medole looks upon revolution as a description of conjuring trick. He shuffles cards and arranges them for a solemn performance, but he refuses to cut them if you look too serious or I look too eager; for that gives him a suspicion that you know what is going to turn up; and his object is above all things to produce a surprise.'

'You are both of you unjust to Count Medole,' said the countess. 'He imperils more than all of you.'

'Magnificent estates, it is true; but of head or of heart not quite so much as some of us,' said Luciano, stroking his thick black pendent moustache and chin-tuft. 'Ah, pardon me; yes! he does imperil a finer cock's comb.

'When he sinks, and his vanity is cut in two, Medole will bleed so as to flood his Lombard flats. It will be worse than death to him.'

Carlo said: 'Do you know what our Agostino says of Count Medole?'

'Oh, for ever Agostino with you young men!' the countess exclaimed. 'I believe he laughs at you.'

'To be sure he does: he laughs at all. But, what he says of Count Medole holds the truth of the thing, and may make you easier concerning the count's estates. He says that Medole is vaccine matter which the Austrians apply to this generation of Italians to spare us the terrible disease. They will or they won't deal gently with Medole, by-and-by; but for the present he will be handled tenderly. He is useful. I wish I could say that we thought so too. And now,' Carlo stooped to her and took her hand, 'shall we see you at La Scala to-night?'

The countess, with her hands lying in his, replied: 'I have received an intimation from the authorities that my box is wanted.'

'So you claim your right to occupy it!'

'That is my very humble protest for personal liberty.'

'Good: I shall be there, and shall much enjoy an introduction to the gentleman who disputes it with you. Besides, mother, if the Signorina Vittoria sings...'

Countess Ammiani's gaze fixed upon her son with a level steadiness. His voice threatened to be unequal. All the pleading force of his eyes was thrown into it, as he said: 'She will sing: and she gives the signal; that is certain. We may have to rescue her. If I can place her under your charge, I shall feel that she is safe, and is really protected.'

The countess looked at Luciano before she answered:

'Yes, Carlo, whatever I can do. But you know I have not a scrap of influence.'

'Let her lie on your bosom, my mother.'

'Is this to be another Violetta?'

'Her name is Vittoria,' said Carlo, colouring deeply. A certain Violetta had been his boy's passion.

Further distracting Austrian band-music was going by. This time it was a regiment of Italians in the white and blue uniform. Carlo and Luciano leaned over the balcony, smoking, and scanned the marching of their fellow-countrymen in the livery of servitude.

'They don't step badly,' said one; and the other, with a smile of melancholy derision, said, 'We are all brothers!'

Following the Italians came a regiment of Hungarian grenadiers, tall, swam-faced, and particularly light-limbed men, looking brilliant in the clean tight military array of Austria. Then a squadron of blue hussars, and Croat regiment; after which, in the midst of Czech dragoons and German Uhlans and blue Magyar light horsemen, with General officers and aides about him, the veteran Austrian Field-Marshal rode, his easy hand and erect figure and good-humoured smile belying both his age and his reputation among Italians. Artillery, and some bravely-clad horse of the Eastern frontier, possibly Serb, wound up the procession. It gleamed down the length of the Corso in a blinding sunlight; brass helmets and hussar feathers, white and violet surcoats, green plumes, maroon capes, bright steel scabbards, bayonet-points,—as gallant a show as some portentously-magnified summer field, flowing with the wind, might be; and over all the banner of Austria—the black double-headed eagle ramping on a yellow ground. This was the flower of iron meaning on such a field.

The two young men held their peace. Countess Ammiani had pushed her chair back into a dark corner of the room, and was sitting there when they looked back, like a sombre figure of black marble.

CHAPTER XVII

IN THE PIAZZA D'ARMI

Carlo and Luciano followed the regiments to the Piazza d'Armi, drawn after them by that irresistible attraction to youths who have as yet had no shroud of grief woven for them—desire to observe the aspect of a brilliant foe.

The Piazza d'Armi was the field of Mars of Milan, and an Austrian review of arms there used to be a tropical pageant. The place was too narrow for broad manoeuvres, or for much more than to furnish an inspection of all arms to the General, and a display (with its meaning) to the populace. An unusually large concourse of spectators lined the square, like a black border to a vast bed of flowers, nodding now this way, now that. Carlo and Luciano passed among the groups, presenting the perfectly smooth faces of young men of fashion, according to the universal aristocratic pattern handed down to querulous mortals from Olympus—the secret of which is to show a triumphant inaction of the heart and the brain, that are rendered positively subservient to elegance of limb. They knew the chances were in favour of their being arrested at any instant. None of the higher members of the Milanese aristocracy were visible; the people looked sullen. Carlo was attracted by the tall figure of the Signor Antonio-Pericles, whom he beheld in converse with the commandant of the citadel, out in the square, among chatting and laughing General officers. At Carlo's elbow there came a burst of English tongues; he heard Vittoria's English name spoken with animation. 'Admire those faces,' he said to Luciano, but the latter was interchanging quiet recognitions among various heads of the crowd; a language of the eyelids and the eyebrows. When he did look round he admired the fair island faces with an Italian's ardour: 'Their women are splendid!' and he no longer pushed upon Carlo's arm to make way ahead. In the English group were two sunny-haired girls and a blue-eyed lady with the famous English curls, full, and rounding richly. This lady talked of her brother, and pointed him out as he rode down the line in the Marshal's staff. The young officer indicated presently broke away and galloped up to her, bending over his horse's neck to join the conversation. Emilia Belloni's name was mentioned. He stared, and appeared to insist upon a contrary statement.

Carlo scrutinized his features. While doing so he was accosted, and beheld his former adversary of the Motter—one, with whom he had yesterday shaken hands in the Piazza of La Scala. The ceremony was cordially renewed. Luciano unlinked his arm from Carlo and left him.

'It appears that you are mistaken with reference to Mademoiselle Belloni,' said Captain Gambier. 'We hear on positive authority that she will not appear at La Scala to-night. It's a disappointment; though, from what you did me the honour to hint to me, I cannot allow myself to regret it.'

Carlo had a passionate inward prompting to trust this Englishman with the secret. It was a weakness that he checked. When one really takes to foreigners, there is a peculiar impulse (I speak of the people who are accessible to impulse) to make brothers of them. He bowed, and said, 'She does not appear?'

'She has in fact quitted Milan. Not willingly. I would have stopped the business if I had known anything of it; but she is better out of the way, and will be carefully looked after, where she is. By this time she is in the Tyrol.'

'And where?' asked Carlo, with friendly interest.

'At a schloss near Meran. Or she will be there in a very few hours. I feared—I may inform you that we were very good friends in England—I feared that when she once came to Italy she would get into political scrapes. I dare say you agree with me that women have nothing to do with politics. Observe: you see the lady who is speaking to the Austrian officer?—he is her brother. Like Mademoiselle Belloni he has adopted a fresh name; it's the name of his uncle, a General Pierson in the Austrian service. I knew him in England: he has been in our service. Mademoiselle Belloni lived with his sisters for some years two or three. As you may suppose, they are all anxious to see her. Shall I introduce you? They will be glad to know one of her Italian friends.'

Carlo hesitated; he longed to hear those ladies talk of Vittoria. 'Do they speak French?'

'Oh, dear, yes. That is, as we luckless English people speak it. Perhaps you will more easily pardon their seminary Italian. See there,' Captain Gambier pointed at some trotting squadrons; 'these Austrians have certainly a matchless cavalry. The artillery seems good. The infantry are fine men—very fine men. They have a "woodeny" movement; but that's in the nature of the case: tremendous discipline alone gives homogeneity to all those nationalities. Somehow they get beaten. I doubt whether anything will beat their cavalry.'

'They are useless in street-fighting,' said Carlo.

'Oh, street-fighting!' Captain Gambier vented a soldier's disgust at the notion. 'They're not in Paris. Will you step forward?'

Just then the tall Greek approached the party of English. The introduction was delayed.

He was addressed by the fair lady, in the island tongue, as 'Mr. Pericles.' She thanked him for his extreme condescension in deigning to notice them. But whatever his condescension had been, it did not extend to an admitted acquaintance with the poor speech of the land of fogs. An exhibition of aching deafness was presented to her so resolutely, that at last she faltered, 'What! have you forgotten English, Mr. Pericles? You spoke it the other day.'

'It is ze language of necessity—of commerce,' he replied.

'But, surely, Mr. Pericles, you dare not presume to tell me you choose to be ignorant of it whenever you please?'

'I do not take grits into ze teeth, madame; no more.' 'But you speak it perfectly.'

'Perfect it may be, for ze transactions of commerce. I wish to keep my teez.'

'Alas!' said the lady, compelled, 'I must endeavour to swim in French.'

'At your service, madame,' quoth the Greek, with an immediate doubling of the length of his body.

Carlo heard little more than he knew; but the confirmation of what we know will sometimes instigate us like fresh intelligence, and the lover's heart was quick to apprehend far more than he knew in one direction. He divined instantaneously that the English-Austrian spoken of by Barto Rizzo was the officer sitting on horseback within half-a-dozen yards of him. The certainty of the thought cramped his muscles. For the rest, it became clear to him that the attempt of the millionaire connoisseur to carry off Vittoria had received the tacit sanction of the Austrian authorities; for reasons quite explicable, Mr. Pericles, as the English lady called him, distinctly hinted it, while affirming with vehement self-laudation that his scheme had succeeded for the vindication of Art.

'The opera you will hear zis night,' he said, 'will be hissed. You will hear a chorus of screech-owls to each song of that poor Irma, whom the Italian people call "crabapple." Well; she pleases German ears, and if they can support her, it is well. But la Vittoria—your Belloni—you will not hear; and why? She has been false to her Art, false! She has become a little devil in politics. It is a Guy Fawkes femelle! She has been guilty of the immense crime of ingratitude. She is dismissed to study, to penitence, and to the society of her old friends, if they will visit her.'

'Of course we will,' said the English lady; 'either before or after our visit to Venice—delicious Venice!'

'Which you have not seen—hein?' Mr. Pericles snarled; 'and have not smelt. There is no music in Venice! But you have nothing but street tinkle-tinkle! A place to live in! mon Dieu!'

The lady smiled. 'My husband insists upon trying the baths of Bormio, and then we are to go over a pass for him to try the grape-cure at Meran. If I can get him to promise me one whole year in Italy, our visit to Venice may be deferred. Our doctor, monsieur, indicates our route. If my brother can get leave of absence, we shall go to Bormio and to Meran with him. He is naturally astonished that Emilia refused to see him; and she refused to see us too! She wrote a letter, dated from the Conservatorio to him, he had it in his saddlebag, and was robbed of it and other precious documents, when the wretched, odious people set upon him in Verona-poor boy! She said in the letter that she would see him in a few days after the fifteenth, which is to-day!

'Ah! a few days after the fifteenth, which is to-day,' Mr. Pericles repeated. 'I saw you but the day before yesterday, madame, or I could have brought you together.

She is now away-off—out of sight—the perfule! Ah false that she is; speak not of her. You remember her in England. There it was trouble, trouble; but here, we are a pot on a fire with her; speak not of her. She has used me ill, madame. I am sick.'

His violent gesticulation drooped. In a temporary abandonment to chagrin, he wiped the moisture from his forehead, unwilling or heedless of the mild ironical mouthing of the ladies, and looked about; for Carlo had made a movement to retire,—he had heard enough for discomfort.

'Ah! my dear Ammiani, the youngest editor in Europe! how goes it with you?' the Greek called out with revived affability.

Captain Gambier perceived that it was time to present his Italian acquaintance to the ladies by name, as a friend of Mademoiselle Belloni.

'My most dear Ammiani,' Antonio-Pericles resumed; he barely attempted to conceal his acrid delight in casting a mysterious shadow of coming vexation over the youth; 'I am afraid you will not like the opera Camilla, or perhaps it is the Camilla you will not like. But, shoulder arms, march!' (a foot regiment in motion suggested the form of the recommendation) 'what is not for to-day may be for to-morrow. Let us wait. I think, my Ammiani, you are to have a lemon and not an orange. Never mind. Let us wait.'

Carlo got his forehead into a show of smoothness, and said, 'Suppose, my dear Signor Antonio, the prophet of dark things were to say to himself, "Let us wait?"'

'Hein-it is deep.' Antonio-Pericles affected to sound the sentence, eye upon earth, as a sparrow spies worm or crumb. 'Permit me,' he added rapidly; an idea had struck him from his malicious reserve stores,—'Here is Lieutenant Pierson, of the staff of the Field-Marshal of Austria, unattached, an old friend of Mademoiselle Emilia Belloni,—permit me,—here is Count Ammiani, of the Lombardia Milanese journal, a new friend of the Signorina Vittoria Campa-Mademoiselle Belloni the Signorina Campa—it is the same person, messieurs; permit me to introduce you.'

Antonio-Pericles waved his arm between the two young men.

Their plain perplexity caused him to dash his fingers down each side of his moustachios in tugs of enjoyment.

For Lieutenant Pierson, who displayed a certain readiness to bow, had caught a sight of the repellent stare on Ammiani's face; a still and flat look, not aggressive, yet anything but inviting; like a shield.

Nevertheless, the lieutenant's head produced a stiff nod. Carlo's did not respond; but he lifted his hat and bowed humbly in retirement to the ladies.

Captain Gambier stepped aside with him.

'Inform Lieutenant Pierson, I beg you,' said Ammiani, 'that I am at his orders, if he should consider that I have insulted him.'

'By all means,' said Gambier; 'only, you know, it's impossible for me to guess what is the matter; and I don't think he knows.'

Luciano happened to be coming near. Carlo went up to him, and stood talking for half a minute. He then returned to Captain Gambier, and said, 'I put myself in the hands of a man of honour. You are aware that Italian gentlemen are not on terms with Austrian officers. If I am seen exchanging salutes with any one of them, I offend my countrymen; and they have enough to bear already.'

Perceiving that there was more in the background, Gambier simply bowed. He had heard of Italian gentlemen incurring the suspicion of their fellows by merely being seen in proximity to an Austrian officer.

As they were parting, Carlo said to him, with a very direct meaning in his eyes, 'Go to the opera tonight.'

'Yes, I suppose so,' the Englishman answered, and digested the look and the recommendation subsequently.

Lieutenant Pierson had ridden off. The war-machine was in motion from end to end: the field of flowers was a streaming flood; regiment by regiment, the crash of bands went by. Outwardly the Italians conducted themselves with the air of ordinary heedless citizens, in whose bosoms the music set no hell-broth boiling. Patrician and plebeian, they were chiefly boys; though here and there a middle-aged workman cast a look of intelligence upon Carlo and Luciano, when these two passed along the crowd. A gloom of hoarded hatred was visible in the mass of faces, ready to spring fierily.

Arms were in the city. With hatred to prompt the blow, with arms to strike, so much dishonour to avenge, we need not wonder that these youths beheld the bit of liberty in prospect magnified by their mighty obfuscating ardour, like a lantern in a fog. Reason did not act. They were in such a state when just to say 'Italia! Italia!' gave them nerve to match an athlete. So, the parading of Austria, the towering athlete, failed of its complete lesson of intimidation, and only ruffled the surface of insurgent hearts. It seemed, and it was, an insult to the trodden people, who read it as a lesson for cravens: their instinct commonly hits the bell. They felt that a secure supremacy would not have paraded itself: so they divined indistinctly that there was weakness somewhere in the councils of the enemy. When the show had vanished, their spirits hung pausing, like the hollow air emptied of big sound, and reacted. Austria had gained little more by her display than the conscientious satisfaction of the pedagogue who lifts the rod to advise intending juvenile culprits how richly it can be merited and how poor will be their future grounds of complaint.

But before Austria herself had been taught a lesson she conceived that she had but one man and his feeble instruments, and occasional frenzies, opposed to her, him whom we saw on the Motterone, which was ceasing to be true; though it was true that the whole popular movement flowed from that one man. She observed travelling sparks in the embers of Italy, and crushed them under her heel, without reflecting that a vital heat must be gathering where the spots of fire run with such a swiftness. It was her belief that if she could seize that one man, whom many of the younger nobles and all the people acknowledged as their Chief—for he stood then without a rival in his task—she would have the neck of conspiracy in her angry grasp. Had she caught him, the conspiracy for Italian freedom would not have crowed for many long seasons; the torch would have been ready, but not the magazine. He prepared it; it was he who preached to the Italians that opportunity is a mocking devil when we look for it to be revealed; or, in other words, wait for chance; as it is God's angel when it is created within us, the ripe fruit of virtue and devotion. He cried out to Italians to wait for no inspiration but their own; that they should never subdue their minds to follow any alien example; nor let a foreign city of fire be their beacon. Watching over his Italy; her wrist in his meditative clasp year by year; he stood like a mystic leech by the couch of a fair and hopeless frame, pledged to revive it by the inspired assurance, shared by none, that life had not forsaken it. A body given over to death and vultures-he stood by it in the desert. Is it a marvel to you that when the carrion-wings swooped low, and the claws fixed, and the beak plucked and savoured its morsel, he raised his arm, and urged the half-resuscitated frame to some vindicating show of existence? Arise! he said, even in what appeared most fatal hours of darkness. The slack limbs moved; the body rose and fell. The cost of the effort was the breaking out of innumerable wounds, old and new; the gain was the display of the miracle that Italy lived. She tasted her own blood, and herself knew that she lived.

Then she felt her chains. The time was coming for her to prove, by the virtues within her, that she was worthy to live, when others of her sons, subtle and adept, intricate as serpents, bold, unquestioning as well-bestridden steeds, should grapple and play deep for her in the game of worldly strife. Now—at this hour of which I speak—when Austrians marched like a merry flame down Milan streets, and Italians stood like the burnt-out cinders of the fire-grate, Italy's faint wrist was still in the clutch of her grave leech, who counted the beating of her pulse between long pauses, that would have made another think life to be heaving its last, not beginning.

The Piazza d'Armi was empty of its glittering show.

We quit the Piazza d'Armi. Rumour had its home in Milan. On their way to the caffe La Scala, Luciano and Carlo (who held together, determined to be taken together if the arrest should come) heard it said that the Chief was in Milan. A man passed by and uttered it, going. They stopped a second man, who was known to them, and he confirmed the rumour. Glad as sunlight once more, they hurried to Count Medole forgivingly. The count's servant assured them that his master had left the city for Monza. 'Is Medole a coward?' cried Luciano, almost in the servant's hearing. The fleeing of so important a man looked vile, now that they were sharpened by new eagerness. Forthwith they were off to Agostino, believing that he would know the truth. They found him in bed. 'Well, and what?' said Agostino, replying to their laughter. 'I am old; too old to stride across a day and night, like you giants of youth. I take my rest when I can, for I must have it.'

'But, you know, O conscript father,' said Carlo, willing to fall a little into his mood, 'you know that nothing will be done to-night.'

'Do I know so much?' Agostino murmured at full length.

'Do you know that the Chief is in the city?' said Luciano.

'A man who is lying in bed knows this,' returned Agostino, 'that he knows less than those who are up, though what he does know he perhaps digests better. 'Tis you who are the fountains, my boys, while I am the pool into which you play. Say on.'

They spoke of the rumour. He smiled at it. They saw at once that the rumour was false, for the Chief trusted Agostino.

'Proceed to Barto, the mole,' he said, 'Barto the miner; he is the father of daylight in the city: of the daylight of knowledge, you understand, for which men must dig deep. Proceed to him;—if you can find him.'

But Carlo brought flame into Agostino's eyes.

'The accursed beast! he has pinned the black butterfly to the signorina's dress.'

Agostino rose on his elbow. He gazed at them. 'We are followers of a blind mole,' he uttered with an inner voices while still gazing wrathfully, and then burst out in grief, '"Patria o mea creatrix, patria o mea genetrix!"'

'The signorina takes none of his warnings, nor do we. She escaped a plot last night, and to-night she sings.'

'She must not,' said Agostino imperiously.

'She does.'

'I must stop that.' Agostino jumped out of bed.

The young men beset him with entreaties to leave the option to her.

'Fools!' he cried, plunging a rageing leg into his garments. 'Here, Iris! Mercury! fly to Jupiter and say we are all old men and boys in Italy, and are ready to accept a few middleaged mortals as Gods, if they will come and help us. Young fools! Do you know that when you conspire you are in harness, and yoke-fellows, every one?'

'Yoked to that Barto Rizzo!'

'Yes; and the worse horse of the two. Listen, you pair of Nuremberg puppet-heads! If the Chief were here, I would lie still in my bed. Medole has stopped the outbreak. Right or wrong, he moves a mass; we are subordinates—particles. The Chief can't be everywhere. Milan is too hot for him. Two men are here, concealed—Rinaldo and Angelo Guidascarpi. The rumour springs from that. They have slain Count Paul Lenkenstein, and rushed to old Milan for work, with the blood on their swords. Oh, the tragedy!—when I have time to write it. Let me now go to my girl, to my daughter! The blood of the Lenkenstein must rust on the steel. Angelo slew him: Rinaldo gave him the cross to kiss. You shall have the whole story by-and-by; but this will be a lesson to Germans not to court our Italian damsels. Lift not that curtain, you Pannonian burglars! Much do we pardon; but bow and viol meet not, save that they be of one wood; especially not when signor bow is from yonderside the Rhoetian Alps, and donzella Viol is a growth of warm Lombardy. Witness to it, Angelo and Rinaldo Guidascarpi! bravo! You boys there—you stand like two Tyrolese salad-spoons! I say that my girl, my daughter, shall never help to fire blank shot. I sent my paternal commands to her yesterday evening. Does the wanton disobey her father and look up to a pair of rocket-headed rascals like you? Apes! if she sings that song to-night, the ear of Italy will be deaf to her for ever after. There's no engine to stir to-night; all the locks are on it; she will send half-a-dozen milkings like you to perdition, and there will be a circle of black blood about her name in the traditions of the insurrection—do you hear? Have I cherished her for that purpose? to have her dedicated to a brawl!'

Agostino fumed up and down the room in a confusion of apparel, savouring his epithets and imaginative peeps while he stormed, to get a relish out of something, as beseems the poetic temperament. The youths were silenced by him; Carlo gladly.

'Troop!' said the old man, affecting to contrast his attire with theirs; 'two graces and a satyr never yet went together, and we'll not frighten the classic Government of Milan. I go out alone. No, Signor Luciano, I am not sworn to Count Medole. I see your sneer contain it. Ah! what a thing is hurry to a mind like mine. It tears up the trees by the roots, floods the land, darkens utterly my poor quiet universe. I was composing a pastoral when you came in. Observe what you have done with my "Lovely Age of Gold!"'

Agostino's transfiguration from lymphatic poet to fiery man of action, lasted till his breath was short, when the necessity for taking a deep draught of air induced him to fall back upon his idle irony. 'Heads, you illustrious young gentlemen!—heads, not legs and arms, move a conspiracy. Now, you—think what you will of it—are only legs and arms in this business. And if you are insubordinate, you present the shocking fabular spirit of the members of the body in revolt; which is not the revolt we desire to see. I go to my daughter immediately, and we shall all have a fat sleep for a week, while the Tedeschi hunt and stew and exhaust their naughty suspicions. Do you know that the Pope's Mouth is closed? We made it tell a big lie before it shut tight on its teeth—a bad omen, I admit; but the idea was rapturously neat. Barto, the sinner—be sure I throttle him for putting that blot on my swan; only, not yet, not yet: he's a blind mole, a mad patriot; but, as I say, our beast Barto drew an Austrian to the Mouth last night, and led the dog to take a letter out of it, detailing the whole plot of tonight, and how men will be stationed at the vicolo here, ready to burst out on the Corso, and at the vicolo there, and elsewhere, all over the city, carrying fire and sword; a systematic map of the plot. It was addressed to Count Serabiglione—my boys! my boys! what do you think of it? Bravo! though Barto is a deadly beast if he—'Agostino paused. 'Yes, he went too far! too far!'

'Has he only gone too far, do you say?'

Carlo spoke sternly. His elder was provoked enough by his deadness of enthusiasm, and that the boy should dare to stalk on a bare egoistical lover's sentiment to be critical of him, Agostino, struck him as monstrous. With the treachery of controlled rage, Agostino drew near him, and whispered some sentences in his ear.

Agostino then called him his good Spartan boy for keeping brave countenance. 'Wait till you comprehend women philosophically. All's trouble with them till then. At La Scala tonight, my sons! We have rehearsed the fiasco; the Tedeschi perform it. Off with you, that I may go out alone!'

He seemed to think it an indubitable matter that he would find Vittoria and bend her will.

Agostino had betrayed his weakness to the young men, who read him with the keen eyes of a particular disapprobation. He delighted in the dark web of intrigue, and believed himself to be no ordinary weaver of that sunless work. It captured his imagination, filling his pride with a mounting gas. Thus he had become allied to Medole on the one hand, and to Barto Rizzo on the other. The young men read him shrewdly, but speaking was useless.

Before Carlo parted from Luciano, he told him the burden of the whisper, which had confirmed what he had heard on the Piazzi d'Armi. It was this: Barto Rizzo, aware that Lieutenant Pierson was the bearer of despatches from the Archduke in Milan to the marshal, then in Verona, had followed, and by extraordinary effort reached Verona in advance; had there tricked and waylaid him, and obtained, instead of despatches, a letter of recent date, addressed to him by Vittoria, which compromised the insurrectionary project.

'If that's the case, my Carlo!' said his friend, and shrugged, and spoke in a very worldly fashion of the fair sex.

Carlo shook him off. For the rest of the day he was alone, shut up with his journalistic pen. The pen traversed seas and continents like an old hack to whom his master has thrown the reins. Apart from the desperate perturbation of his soul, he thought of the Guidascarpi, whom he knew, and was allied to, and of the Lenkensteins, whom he knew likewise, or had known in the days when Giacomo Piaveni lived, and Bianca von Lenkenstein, Laura's sister, visited among the people of her country. Countess Anna and

Countess Lena von Lenkenstein were the German beauties of Milan, lively little women, and sweet. Between himself and Countess Lena there had been tender dealings about the age when sweetmeats have lost their attraction, and the charm has to be supplied. She was rich, passionate for Austria, romantic concerning Italy, a vixen in temper, but with a pearly light about her temples that kept her picture in his memory. And besides, during those days when women are bountiful to us as Goddesses, give they never so little, she had deigned to fondle hands with him; had set the universe rocking with a visible heave of her bosom; jingled all the keys of mystery; and had once (as to embalm herself in his recollection), once had surrendered her lips to him. Countess Lena would have espoused Ammiani, believing in her power to make an Austrian out of such Italian material. The Piaveni revolt had stopped that and all their intercourse by the division of the White Hand, as it was called; otherwise, the hand of the corpse. Ammiani had known also Count Paul von Lenkenstein. To his mind, death did not mean much, however pleasant life might be: his father and his friend had gone to it gaily; and he himself stood ready for the summons: but the contemplation of a domestic judicial execution, which the Guidascarpi seemed to have done upon Count Paul, affrighted him, and put an end to his temporary capacity for labour. He felt as if a spent shot were striking on his ribs; it was the unknown sensation of fear. Changeing, it became pity. 'Horrible deaths these Austrians die!' he said.

For a while he regarded their lot as the hardest. A shaft of sunlight like blazing brass warned him that the day dropped. He sent to his mother's stables, and rode at a gallop round Milan, dining alone in one of the common hotel gardens, where he was a stranger. A man may have good nerve to face the scene which he is certain will be enacted, who shrinks from an hour that is suspended in doubt. He was aware of the pallor and chill of his looks, and it was no marvel to him when two sbirri in mufti, foreign to Milan, set their eyes on him as they passed by to a vacant table on the farther side of the pattering gold-fish pool, where he sat. He divined that they might be in pursuit of the Guidascarpi, and alive to read a troubled visage. 'Yet neither Rinaldo nor Angelo would look as I do now,' he thought, perceiving that these men were judging by such signs, and had their ideas. Democrat as he imagined himself to be, he despised with a nobleman's contempt creatures who were so dead to the character of men of birth as to suppose that they were pale and remorseful after dealing a righteous blow, and that they trembled! Ammiani looked at his hand: no force of his will could arrest its palsy. The Guidascarpi were sons of Bologna. The stupidity of Italian sbirri is proverbial, or a Milanese cavalier would have been astonished to conceive himself mistaken for a Bolognese. He beckoned to the waiter, and said, 'Tell me what place has bred those two fellows on the other side of the fountain.' After a side-glance of scrutiny, the reply was, 'Neapolitans.' The waiter was ready to make an additional remark, but Ammiani nodded and communed with a toothpick. He was sure that those Neapolitans were recruits of the Bolognese Polizia; on the track of the Guidascarpi, possibly. As he was not unlike Angelo Guidascarpi in figure, he became uneasy lest they should blunder 'twixt him and La Scala; and the notion of any human power stopping him short of that destination, made Ammiani's hand perfectly firm. He drew on his gloves, and named the place whither he was going, aloud. 'Excellency,' said the waiter, while taking up and pretending to reckon the money for the bill: 'they have asked me whether there are two Counts Ammiani in Milan.' Carlo's eyebrows started. 'Can they be after me?' he thought, and said: 'Certainly; there is twice anything in this world, and Milan is the epitome of it.'

Acting a part gave him Agostino's catching manner of speech. The waiter, who knew him now, took this for an order to say 'Yes.' He had evidently a respect for Ammiani's name: Carlo supposed that he was one of Milan's fighting men. A sort of answer leading to 'Yes' by a circuit and the assistance of the hearer, was conveyed to the sbirri. They were true Neapolitans quick to suspect, irresolute upon their suspicions. He was soon aware that they were not to be feared more than are the general race of bunglers, whom the Gods sometimes strangely favour. They perplexed him: for why were they after him? and what had made them ask whether he had a brother? He was followed, but not molested, on his way to La Scala.

Ammiani's heart was in full play as he looked at the curtain of the stage. The Night of the Fifteenth had come. For the first few moments his strong excitement fronting the curtain, amid a great host of hearts thumping and quivering up in the smaller measures like his own, together with the predisposing belief that this was to be a night of events, stopped his consciousness that all had been thwarted; that there was nothing but plot, plot, counterplot and tangle, disunion, silly subtlety, jealousy, vanity, a direful congregation of antagonistic elements; threads all loose, tongues wagging, pressure here, pressure there, like an uncertain rage in the entrails of the undirected earth, and no master hand on the spot to fuse and point the intense distracted forces.

The curtain, therefore, hung like any common opera-screen; big only with the fate of the new prima donna. He was robbed even of the certainty that Vittoria would appear. From the blank aspect of the curtain he turned to the house, which was crowding fast, and was not like listless Milan about to criticize an untried voice. The commonly empty boxes of the aristocracy were full of occupants, and for a wonder the white uniforms were not in excess, though they were to be seen. The first person whom Ammiani met was Agostino, who spoke gruffly. Vittoria had been invisible to him. Neither the maestro, nor the impresario, nor the waiting-woman had heard of her. Uncertainty was behind the curtain, as well as in front; but in front it was the uncertainty which is tipped with expectation, hushing the usual noisy chatter, and setting a daylight of eyes forward. Ammiani spied about the house, and caught sight of Laura Piaveni with Colonel Corte by her side. The Lenkensteins were in the Archduke's box. Antonio-Pericles, and the English lady and Captain Gambier, were next to them. The appearance of a white uniform in his mother's box over the stage caused Ammiani to shut up his glass. He was making his way thither for the purpose of commencing the hostilities of the night, when Countess Ammiani entered the lobby, and took her son's arm with a grave face and a trembling touch.

CHAPTER XIX

THE PRIMA DONNA

'Whover is in my box is my guest,' said the countess, adding a convulsive imperative pressure on Carlo's arm, to aid the meaning of her deep underbreath. She was a woman who rarely exacted obedience, and she was spontaneously obeyed. No questions could be put, no explanations given in the crash, and they threaded on amid numerous greetings in a place where Milanese society had habitually ceased to gather, and found itself now in assembly with unconcealed sensations of strangeness. A card lay on the table of the countess's private retiring-room: it bore the name of General Pierson. She threw off her black lace scarf. 'Angelo Guidascarpi is in Milan,' she said. 'He has killed one of the Lenkensteins, sword to sword. He came to me an hour after you left; the sbirri were on his track; he passed for my son. He is now under the charge of Barto Rizzo, disguised; probably in this house. His brother is in the city. Keep the cowl on your head as long as possible; if these hounds see and identify you, there will be mischief.' She said no more, satisfied that she was understood, but opening the door of the box, passed in, and returned a stately acknowledgement of the salutations of two military officers. Carlo likewise bent his head to them; it was like bending his knee, for in the younger of the two intruders he recognized Lieutenant Pierson. The countess accepted a vacated seat; the cavity of her ear accepted the General's apologies. He informed her that he deeply regretted the intrusion; he was under orders to be present at the opera, and to be as near the stage as possible, the countess's box being designated. Her face had the unalterable composure of a painted head upon an old canvas. The General persisted in tendering excuses. She replied, 'It is best, when one is too weak to resist, to submit to an outrage quietly.' General Pierson at once took the position assigned to him; it was not an agreeable one. Between Carlo and the lieutenant no attempt at conversation was made.

The General addressed his nephew in English. 'Did you see the girl behind the scenes, Wilfrid?'

The answer was 'No.'

'Pericles has her fast shut up in the Tyrol: the best habitat for her if she objects to a whipping. Did you see Irma?'

'No; she has disappeared too.'

'Then I suppose we must make up our minds to an opera without head or tail. As Pat said of the sack of potatoes, "'twould be a mighty fine beast if it had them."'

The officers had taken refuge in their opera-glasses, and spoke while gazing round the house.

'If neither this girl nor Irma is going to appear, there is no positive necessity for my presence here,' said the General, reduced to excuse himself to himself. 'I'll sit through the first scene and then beat a retreat. I might be off at once; the affair looks harmless enough only, you know, when there's nothing to see, you must report that you have seen it, or your superiors are not satisfied.'

The lieutenant was less able to cover the irksomeness of his situation with easy talk. His glance rested on Countess Len a von Lenkenstein, a quick motion of whose hand made him say that he should go over to her.

'Very well,' said the General; 'be careful that you give no hint of this horrible business. They will hear of it when they get home: time enough!'

Lieutenant Pierson touched at his sister's box on the way. She was very excited, asked innumerable things,—whether there was danger? whether he had a whole regiment at hand to protect peaceable persons? 'Otherwise,' she said, 'I shall not be able to keep that man (her husband) in Italy another week. He refused to stir out to-night, though we know that nothing can happen. Your prima donna celestissima is out of harm's way.'

'Oh, she is safe,—ze minx'; cried Antonio-Pericles, laughing and saluting the Duchess of Graatli, who presented herself at the front of her box. Major de Pyrmont was behind her, and it delighted the Greek to point them out to the English lady, with a simple intimation of the character of their relationship, at which her curls shook sadly.

'Pardon, madame,' said Pericles. 'In Italy, a husband away, ze friend takes title: it is no more.'

'It is very disgraceful,' she said.

'Ze morales, madame, suit ze sun.'

Captain Gambier left the box with Wilfrid, expressing in one sentence his desire to fling Pericles over to the pit, and in another his belief that an English friend, named Merthyr Powys, was in the house.

'He won't be in the city four-and-twenty hours,' said Wilfrid.

'Well; you'll keep your tongue silent.'

'By heavens! Gambier, if you knew the insults we have to submit to! The temper of angels couldn't stand it. I'm sorry enough for these fellows, with their confounded country, but it's desperate work to be civil to them; upon my honour, it is! I wish they would stand up and let us have it over. We have to bear more from the women than the men.'

'I leave you to cool,' said Gambier.

The delayed absence of the maestro from his post at the head of the orchestra, where the musicians sat awaiting him, seemed to confirm a rumour that was now circling among the audience, warning all to prepare for a disappointment. His baton was brought in and laid on the book of the new overture. When at last he was seen bearing onward through the music-stands, a low murmur ran round. Rocco paid no heed to it. His demeanour produced such satisfaction in the breast of Antonio-Pericles that he rose, and was guilty of the barbarism of clapping his hands. Meeting Ammiani in the lobby, he said, 'Come, my good friend, you shall help me to pull Irma through to-night. She is vinegar—we will mix her with oil. It is only for to-night, to save that poor Rocco's opera.'

'Irma!' said Ammiani; 'she is by this time in Tyrol. Your Irma will have some difficulty in showing herself here within sixty hours.'

'How!' cried Pericles, amazed, and plucking after Carlo to stop him. 'I bet you—'

'How much?'

'I bet you a thousand florins you do not see la Vittoria to-night.'

'Good. I bet you a thousand florins you do not see Irma.'

'No Vittoria, I say!'

'And I say, no Lazzeruola!'

Agostino, who was pacing the lobby, sent Pericles distraught with the same tale of the rape of Irma. He rushed to Signora Piaveni's box and heard it repeated. There he beheld, sitting in the background, an old English acquaintance, with whom Captain Gambier was conversing.

'My dear Powys, you have come all the way from England to see your favourite's first night. You will be shocked, sir. She has neglected her Art. She is exiled, banished, sent away to study and to compose her mind.'

'I think you are mistaken,' said Laura. 'You will see her almost immediately.'

'Signora, pardon me; do I not know best?'

'You may have contrived badly.'

Pericles blinked and gnawed his moustache as if it were food for patience.

'I would wager a milliard of francs,' he muttered. With absolute pathos he related to Mr. Powys the aberrations of the divinely-gifted voice, the wreck which Vittoria strove to become, and from which he alone was striving to rescue her. He used abundant illustrations, coarse and quaint, and was half hysterical; flashing a white fist and thumping the long projection of his knee with a wolfish aspect. His grotesque sincerity was little short of the shedding of tears.

'And your sister, my dear Powys?' he asked, as one returning to the consideration of shadows.

'My sister accompanies me, but not to the opera.'

'For another campaign—hein?'

'To winter in Italy, at all events.'

Carlo Ammiani entered and embraced Merthyr Powys warmly. The Englishman was at home among Italians: Pericles, feeling that he was not so, and regarding them all as a community of fever-patients without hospital, retired. To his mind it was the vilest treason, the grossest selfishness, to conspire or to wink at the sacrifice of a voice like Vittoria's to such a temporal matter as this, which they called patriotism. He looked on it as one might look on the Hindoo drama of a Suttee. He saw in it just that stupid action of a whole body of fanatics combined to precipitate the devotion of a precious thing to extinction. And worse; for life was common, and women and Hindoo widows were common; but a Vittorian voice was but one in a generation—in a cycle of years. The religious belief of the connoisseur extended to the devout conception that her voice was a spiritual endowment, the casting of which priceless jewel into the bloody ditch of patriots was far more tragic and lamentable than any disastrous concourse of dedicated lives. He shook the lobby with his tread, thinking of the great night this might have been but for Vittoria's madness. The overture was coming to an end. By tightening his arms across his chest he gained some outward composure, and fixed his eyes upon the stage.

While sitting with Laura Piaveni and Merthyr Powys, Ammiani saw the apparition of Captain Weisspriess in his mother's box. He forgot her injunction, and hurried to her side, leaving the doors open. His passion of anger spurned her admonishing grasp of his arm, and with his glove he smote the Austrian officer on the face. Weisspriess plucked his sword out; the house rose; there was a moment like that of a wild beast's show of teeth. It passed: Captain Weisspriess withdrew in obedience to General Pierson's command. The latter wrote on a slip of paper that two pieces of artillery should be placed in position, and a squad of men about the doors: he handed it out to Weisspriess.

'I hope,' the General said to Carlo, 'we shall be able to arrange things for you without the interposition of the authorities.'

Carlo rejoined, 'General, he has the blood of our family on his hands. I am ready.'

The General bowed. He glanced at the countess for a sign of maternal weakness, saw none, and understood that a duel was down in the morrow's bill of entertainments, as well as a riot possibly before dawn. The house had revealed its temper in that short outburst, as a quivering of quick lightning-flame betrays the forehead of the storm.

Countess Ammiani bade her son make fast the outer door. Her sedate energies could barely control her agitation. In helping Angelo Guidascarpi to evade the law, she had imperilled her son and herself. Many of the Bolognese sbirri were in pursuit of Angelo. Some knew his person; some did not; but if those two before whom she had identified Angelo as being her son Carlo chanced now to be in the house, and to have seen him, and heard his name, the risks were great and various.

'Do you know that handsome young Count Ammiani?' Countess Lena said to Wilfrid. 'Perhaps you do not think him handsome? He was for a short time a play-fellow of mine. He is more passionate than I am, and that does not say a little; I warn you! Look how excited he is. No wonder. He is—everybody knows it—he is la Vittoria's lover.'

Countess Lena uttered that sentence in Italian. The soft tongue sent it like a coiling serpent through Wilfrid's veins. In English or in German it would not have possessed the deadly meaning.

She may have done it purposely, for she and her sister Countess Anna studied his face. The lifting of the curtain drew all eyes to the stage.

Rocco Ricci's baton struck for the opening of one of his spirited choruses; a chorus of villagers, who sing to the burden that Happiness, the aim of all humanity, has promised to visit the earth this day, that she may witness the union of the noble lovers, Camillo and Camilla. Then a shepherd sings a verse, with his hand stretched out to the impending castle. There lives Count Orso: will he permit their festivities to pass undisturbed? The puling voice is crushed by the chorus, which protests that the heavens are above Count Orso. But another villager tells of Orso's power, and hints at his misdeeds. The chorus rises in reply, warning all that Count Orso has ears wherever three are congregated; the villagers break apart and eye one another distrustfully, reuniting to the song of Happiness before they disperse. Camillo enters solus. Montini, as Camillo, enjoyed a warm reception; but as he advanced to deliver his canzone, it was seen that he and Rocco interchanged glances of desperate resignation. Camillo has had love passages with Michiella, Count Orso's daughter, and does not hesitate to declare that he dreads her. The orphan Camilla, who has been reared in yonder castle with her, as her sister, is in danger during all these last minutes which still retain her from his arms.

'If I should never see her—I who, like a poor ghost upon the shores of the dead river, have been flattered with the thought that she would fall upon my breast like a ray of the light of Elysium—if I should never see her more!' The famous tenore threw his whole force into that outcry of projected despair, and the house was moved by it: there were many in the house who shared his apprehension of a foul mischance.

Thenceforward the opera and the Italian audience were as one. All that was uttered had a meaning, and was sympathetically translated. Camilla they perceived to be a grave burlesque with a core to it. The quick-witted Italians caught up the interpretation in a flash. 'Count Orso' Austria; 'Michiella' is Austria's spirit of intrigue; 'Camillo' is indolent Italy, amorous Italy, Italy aimless; 'Camilla' is YOUNG ITALY!

Their eagerness for sight of Vittoria was now red-hot, and when Camillo exclaimed 'She comes!' many rose from their seats.

A scrap of paper was handed to Antonio-Pericles from Captain Weisspriess, saying briefly that he had found Irma in the carriage instead of the little 'v,' thanked him for the joke, and had brought her back. Pericles was therefore not surprised when Irma, as Michiella, came on, breathless, and looking in an excitement of anger; he knew that he had been tricked.

Between Camillo and Michiella a scene of some vivacity ensued—reproaches, threats of calamity, offers of returning endearment upon her part; a display of courtly scorn upon his. Irma made her voice claw at her quondam lover very finely; it was a voice with claws, that entered the hearing sharp-edged, and left it plucking at its repose. She was applauded relishingly when, after vainly wooing him, she turned aside and said—

'What change is this in one who like a reed
Bent to my twisting hands? Does he recoil?
Is this the hound whom I have used to feed
With sops of vinegar and sops of oil?'

Michiella's further communications to the audience make it known that she has allowed the progress toward the ceremonies of espousal between Camillo and Camilla, in order, at the last moment, to show her power over the youth and to plunge the detested Camilla into shame and wretchedness.

Camillo retires: Count Orso appears. There is a duet between father and daughter: she confesses her passion for Camillo, and entreats her father to stop the ceremony; and here the justice of the feelings of Italians, even in their heat of blood, was noteworthy. Count Orso says that he would willingly gratify his daughter, as it would gratify himself, but that he must respect the law. 'The law is of your own making,' says Michiella. 'Then, the more must I respect it,' Count Orso replies.

The audience gave Austria credit for that much in a short murmur.

Michiella's aside, 'Till anger seizes him I wait!' created laughter; it came in contrast with an extraordinary pomposity of self-satisfaction exhibited by Count Orso—the flower-faced, tun-bellied basso, Lebruno. It was irresistible. He stood swollen out like a morning cock. To make it further telling, he took off his yellow bonnet with a black-gloved hand, and thumped the significant colours prominently on his immense chest—an idea, not of Agostino's, but Lebruno's own; and Agostino cursed with fury. Both he and Rocco knew that their joint labour would probably have only one night's display of existence in the Austrian dominions, but they grudged to Lebruno the chief merit of despatching it to the Shades.

The villagers are heard approaching. 'My father!' cries Michiella, distractedly; 'the hour is near: it will be death to your daughter! Imprison Camillo: I can bring twenty witnesses to prove that he has sworn you are illegally the lord of this country. You will rue the marriage. Do as you once did. Be bold in time. The arrow-head is on the string-cut the string!'

'As I once did?' replies Orso with frown terrific, like a black crest. He turns broadly and receives the chorus of countrymen in paternal fashion—an admirably acted bit of grave burlesque.

By this time the German portion of the audience had, by one or other of the senses, dimly divined that the opera was a shadow of something concealed—thanks to the buffo-basso Lebruno. Doubtless they would have seen this before, but that the Austrian censorship had seemed so absolute a safeguard.

'My children! all are my children in this my gladsome realm!' Count Orso says, and marches forth, after receiving the compliment of a choric song in honour of his paternal government. Michiella follows him.

Then came the deep suspension of breath. For, as upon the midnight you count bell-note after bell-note of the toiling hour, and know not in the darkness whether there shall be one beyond it, so that you hang over an abysm until Twelve is sounded, audience and actors gazed with equal expectation at the path winding round from the castle, waiting for the voice of the new prima donna.

'Mia madre!' It issued tremblingly faint. None could say who was to appear.

Rocco Ricci struck twice with his baton, flung a radiant glance across his shoulders for all friends, and there was joy in the house. Vittoria stood before them.

BOOK IV

CHAPTER XX

THE OPERA OF CAMILLA

She was dressed like a noble damsel from the hands of Titian. An Italian audience cannot but be critical in their first glance at a prima donna, for they are asked to do homage to a queen who is to be taken on her merits: all that they have heard and have been taught to expect of her is compared swiftly with the observation of her appearance and her manner. She is crucially examined to discover defects. There is no boisterous loyalty at the outset. And as it was now evident that Vittoria had chosen to impersonate a significant character, her indications of method were jealously watched for a sign of inequality, either in her, motion, or the force of her eyes. So silent a reception might have seemed cruel in any other case; though in all cases the candidate for laurels must, in common with the criminal, go through the ordeal of justification. Men do not heartily bow their heads until they have subjected the aspirant to some personal contest, and find themselves overmatched. The senses, ready to become so slavish in adulation and delight, are at the beginning more exacting than the judgement, more imperious than the will. A figure in amber and pale blue silk was seen, such as the great Venetian might have sketched from his windows on a day when the Doge went forth to wed the Adriatic a superb Italian head, with dark banded hair-braid, and dark strong eyes under unabashed soft eyelids! She moved as, after long gazing at a painting of a fair woman, we may have the vision of her moving from the frame. It was an animated picture of ideal Italia. The sea of heads right up to the highest walls fronted her glistening, and she was mute as moonrise. A virgin who loosens a dove from her bosom does it with no greater effort than Vittoria gave out her voice. The white bird flutters rapidly; it circles and takes its flight. The voice seemed to be as little the singer's own.

The theme was as follows:—Camilla has dreamed overnight that her lost mother came to her bedside to bless her nuptials. Her mother was folded in a black shroud, looking formless as death, like very death, save that death sheds no tears. She wept, without change of voice, or mortal shuddering, like one whose nature weeps: 'And with the forth-flowing of her tears the knowledge of her features was revealed to me.' Behold the Adige, the Mincio, Tiber, and the Po!—such great rivers were the tears pouring from her eyes. She threw apart the shroud: her breasts and her limbs were smooth and firm as those of an immortal Goddess: but breasts and limbs showed the cruel handwriting of base men upon the body of a martyred saint. The blood from those deep gashes sprang out at intervals, mingling with her tears. She said:

'My child! were I a Goddess, my wounds would heal. Were I a Saint, I should be in Paradise. I am no Goddess, and no Saint: yet I cannot die. My wounds flow and my tears. My tears flow because of no fleshly anguish: I pardon my enemies. My blood flows from my body, my tears from my soul. They flow to wash out my shame. I have to expiate my soul's shame by my body's shame. Oh! how shall I tell you what it is to walk among my children unknown of them, though each day I bear the sun abroad like my beating heart; each night the moon, like a heart with no blood in it. Sun and moon they see, but not me! They know not their mother. I cry to God. The answer of our God is this:—"Give to thy children one by one to drink of thy mingled tears and blood:—then, if there is virtue in them, they shall revive, thou shaft revive. If virtue is not in them, they and thou shall continue prostrate, and the ox shall walk over you." From heaven's high altar, O Camilla, my child, this silver sacramental cup was reached to me. Gather my tears in it, fill it with my blood, and drink.'

The song had been massive in monotones, almost Gregorian in its severity up to this point.

'I took the cup. I looked my mother in the face. I filled the cup from the flowing of her tears, the flowing of her blood; and I drank!'

Vittoria sent this last phrase ringing out forcefully. From the inveterate contralto of the interview, she rose to pure soprano in describing her own action. 'And I drank,' was given on a descent of the voice: the last note was in the minor key—it held the ear as if more must follow: like a wail after a triumph of resolve. It was a masterpiece of audacious dramatic musical genius addressed with sagacious cunning and courage to the sympathizing audience present. The supposed incompleteness kept them listening; the intentness sent that last falling (as it were, broken) note travelling awakeningly through their minds. It is the effect of the minor key to stir the hearts of men with this particular suggestiveness. The house rose, Italians—and Germans together. Genius, music, and enthusiasm break the line of nationalities. A rain of nosegays fell about Vittoria; evvivas, bravas, shouts—all the outcries of delirious men surrounded her. Men and women, even among the hardened chorus, shook together and sobbed. 'Agostino!' and 'Rocco!' were called; 'Vittoria!' 'Vittoria!' above all, with increasing thunder, like a storm rushing down a valley, striking in broad volume from rock to rock, humming remote, and bursting up again in the face of the vale. Her name was sung over and over—'Vittoria! Vittoria!' as if the mouths were enamoured of it.

'Evviva la Vittoria a d' Italia!' was sung out from the body of the house.

An echo replied—'"Italia a il premio della VITTORIA!"' a well-known saying gloriously adapted, gloriously rescued from disgrace.

But the object and source of the tremendous frenzy stood like one frozen by the revelation of the magic the secret of which she has studiously mastered. A nosegay, the last of the tributary shower, discharged from a distance, fell at her feet. She gave it unconsciously preference over the rest, and picked it up. A little paper was fixed in the centre. She opened it with a mechanical hand, thinking there might be patriotic orders enclosed for her. It was a cheque for one thousand guineas, drawn upon an English banker by the hand of Antonio-Pericles Agriolopoulos; freshly drawn; the ink was only half dried, showing signs of the dictates of a furious impulse. This dash of solid prose, and its convincing proof that her Art had been successful, restored Vittoria's composure, though not her early statuesque simplicity. Rocco gave an inquiring look to see if she would repeat the song. She shook her head resolutely. Her opening of the paper in the bouquet had quieted the general ebullition, and the expression of her wish being seen, the chorus was permitted to usurp her place. Agostino paced up and down the lobby, fearful that he had been guilty of leading her to anticlimax.

He met Antonio-Pericles, and told him so; adding (for now the mask had been seen through, and was useless any further) that he had not had the heart to put back that vision of Camilla's mother to a later scene, lest an interruption should come which would altogether preclude its being heard. Pericles affected disdain of any success which Vittoria had yet achieved. 'Wait for Act the Third,' he said; but his irritable anxiousness to hold intercourse with every one, patriot or critic, German, English, or Italian, betrayed what agitation of exultation coursed in his veins. 'Aha!' was his commencement of a greeting; 'was Antonio-Pericles wrong when he told you that he had a prima donna for you to amaze all Christendom, and whose notes were safe and firm as the footing of the angels up and down Jacob's ladder, my friends? Aha!'

'Do you see that your uncle is signalling to you?' Countess Lena said to Wilfrid. He answered like a man in a mist, and looked neither at her nor at the General, who, in default of his obedience to gestures, came good-humouredly to the box, bringing Captain Weisspriess with him.

'We 're assisting at a pretty show,' he said.

'I am in love with her voice,' said Countess Anna.

'Ay; if it were only a matter of voices, countess.'

'I think that these good people require a trouncing,' said Captain Weisspriess.

'Lieutenant Pierson is not of your opinion,' Countess Anna remarked. Hearing his own name, Wilfrid turned to them with a weariness well acted, but insufficiently to a jealous observation, for his eyes were quick under the carelessly-dropped eyelids, and ranged keenly over the stage while they were affecting to assist his fluent tongue.

Countess Lena levelled her opera-glass at Carlo Ammiani, and then placed the glass in her sister's hand. Wilfrid drank deep of bitterness. 'That is Vittoria's lover,' he thought; 'the lover of the Emilia who once loved me!'

General Pierson may have noticed this by-play: he said to his nephew in the brief military tone: 'Go out; see that the whole regiment is handy about the house; station a dozen men, with a serjeant, at each of the backdoors, and remain below. I very much mistake, or we shall have to make a capture of this little woman to-night.'

'How on earth,' he resumed, while Wilfrid rose savagely and went out with his stiffest bow, 'this opera was permitted to appear, I can't guess! A child could see through it. The stupidity of our civil authorities passes my understanding—it's a miracle! We have stringent orders not to take any initiative, or I would stop the Fraulein Camilla from uttering another note.'

'If you did that, I should be angry with you, General,' said Countess Anna.

'And I also think the Government cannot do wrong,' Countess Lena joined in.

The General contented himself by saying: 'Well, we shall see.'

Countess Lena talked to Captain Weisspriess in an undertone, referring to what she called his dispute with Carlo Ammiani. The captain was extremely playful in rejoinders.

'You iron man!' she exclaimed.

'Man of steel would be the better phrase,' her sister whispered.

'It will be an assassination, if it happens.'

'No officer can bear with an open insult, Lena.'

'I shall not sit and see harm done to my old playmate, Anna.'

'Beware of betraying yourself for one who detests you.'

A grand duo between Montini and Vittoria silenced all converse. Camilla tells Camillo of her dream. He pledges his oath to discover her mother, if alive; if dead, to avenge her. Camilla says she believes her mother is in the dungeons of Count Orso's castle. The duo tasked Vittoria's execution of florid passages; it gave evidence of her sound artistic powers.

'I was a fool,' thought Antonio-Pericles; 'I flung my bouquet with the herd. I was a fool! I lost my head!'

He tapped angrily at the little ink-flask in his coat-pocket. The first act, after scenes between false Camillo and Michiella, ends with the marriage of Camillo and Camilla;—a quatuor composed of Montini, Vittoria, Irma, and Lebruno. Michiella is in despair; Count Orso is profoundly sonorous with paternity and devotion to the law. He has restored to Camilla a portion of her mother's sequestrated estates. A portion of the remainder will be handed over to her when he has had experience of her husband's good behaviour. The rest he considers legally his own by right of (Treaties), and by right of possession and documents his sword. Yonder castle he must keep. It is the key of all his other territories. Without it, his position will be insecure. (Allusion to the Austrian argument that the plains of Lombardy are the strategic defensive lines of the Alps.)

Agostino, pursued by his terror of anticlimax, ran from the sight of Vittoria when she was called, after the fall of the curtain. He made his way to Rocco Ricci (who had given his bow to the public from his perch), and found the maestro drinking Asti to counteract his natural excitement. Rocco told Agostino, that up to the last moment, neither he nor any soul behind the scenes knew Vittoria would be able to appear, except that she had sent a note to him with a pledge to be in readiness for the call. Irma had come flying in late, enraged, and in disorder, praying to take Camilla's part; but Montini refused to act with the seconda donna as prima donna. They had commenced the opera in uncertainty whether it could go on beyond the situation where Camilla presents herself. 'I was prepared to throw up my baton,' said Rocco, 'and publicly to charge the Government with the rape of our prima donna. Irma I was ready to replace. I could have filled that gap.' He spoke of Vittoria's triumph. Agostino's face darkened. 'Ha!' said he, 'provided we don't fall flat, like your Asti with the cork out. I should have preferred an enthusiasm a trifle more progressive. The notion of travelling backwards is upon me forcibly, after that tempest of acclamation.'

'Or do you think that you have put your best poetry in the first Act?' Rocco suggested with malice.

'Not a bit of it!' Agostino repudiated the idea very angrily, and puffed and puffed. Yet he said, 'I should not be lamenting if the opera were stopped at once.'

'No!' cried Rocco; 'let us have our one night. I bargain for that. Medole has played us false, but we go on. We are victims already, my Agostino.'

'But I do stipulate,' said Agostino, 'that my jewel is not to melt herself in the cup to-night. I must see her. As it is, she is inevitably down in the list for a week's or a month's incarceration.'

Antonio-Pericles had this, in his case, singular piece of delicacy, that he refrained from the attempt to see Vittoria immediately after he had flung his magnificent bouquet of treasure at her feet. In his intoxication with the success which he had foreseen and cradled to its apogee, he was now reckless of any consequences. He felt ready to take patriotic Italy in his arms, provided that it would succeed as Vittoria had done, and on the spot. Her singing of the severe phrases of the opening chant, or hymn, had turned the man, and for a time had put a new heart in him. The consolation was his also, that he had rewarded it the most splendidly—as it were, in golden italics of praise; so that her forgiveness of his disinterested endeavour to transplant her was certain, and perhaps her future implicit obedience or allegiance bought. Meeting General Pierson, the latter rallied him.

'Why, my fine Pericles, your scheme to get this girl out of the way was capitally concerted. My only fear is that on another occasion the Government will take another view of it and you.'

Pericles shrugged. 'The Gods, my dear General, decree. I did my best to lay a case before them; that is all.'

'Ah, well! I am of opinion you will not lay many other cases before the Gods who rule in Milan.'

'I have helped them to a good opera.'

'Are you aware that this opera consists entirely of political allusions?'

General Pierson spoke offensively, as the urbane Austrian military permitted themselves to do upon occasion when addressing the conquered or civilians.

'To me,' returned Pericles, 'an opera—it is music. I know no more.'

'You are responsible for it,' said the General, harshly. 'It was taken upon trust from you.'

'Brutal Austrians!' Pericles murmured. 'And you do not think much of her voice, General?'

'Pretty fair, sir.'

'What wonder she does not care to open her throat to these swine!' thought the changed Greek.

Vittoria's door was shut to Agostino. No voice within gave answer. He tried the lock of the door, and departed. She sat in a stupor. It was harder for her to make a second appearance than it was to make the first, when the shameful suspicion cruelly attached to her had helped to balance her steps with rebellious pride; and more, the great collected wave of her ambitious years of girlhood had cast her forward to the spot, as in a last effort for consummation. Now that she had won the public voice (love, her heart called it) her eyes looked inward; she meditated upon what she had to do, and coughed nervously. She frightened herself with her coughing, and shivered at the prospect of again going forward in the great nakedness of stagelights and thirsting eyes. And, moreover, she was not strengthened by the character of the music and the poetry of the second Act:—a knowledge of its somewhat inferior quality may possibly have been at the root of Agostino's dread of an anticlimax. The seconda donna had the chief part in it—notably an aria (Rocco had given it to her in compassion) that suited Irma's pure shrieks and the tragic skeleton she could be. Vittoria knew how low she was sinking when she found her soul in the shallows of a sort of jealousy of Irma. For a little space she lost all intimacy with herself; she looked at her face in the glass and swallowed water, thinking that she had strained a dream and confused her brain with it. The silence of her solitary room coming upon the blaze of light the colour and clamour of the house, and the strange remembrance of the recent impersonation of an ideal character, smote her with the sense of her having fallen from a mighty eminence, and that she lay in the dust. All those incense-breathing flowers heaped on her table seemed poisonous, and reproached her as a delusion. She sat crouching alone till her tirewomen called; horrible talkative things! her own familiar maid Giacinta being the worst to bear with.

Now, Michiella, by making love to Leonardo, Camillo's associate, discovers that Camillo is conspiring against her father. She utters to Leonardo very pleasant promises indeed, if he will betray his friend. Leonardo, a wavering baritono, complains that love should ask for any return save in the coin of the empire of love. He is seduced, and invokes a malediction upon his head should he accomplish what he has sworn to perform. Camilla reposes perfect confidence in this wretch, and brings her more doubtful husband to be of her mind.

Camillo and Camilla agree to wear the mask of a dissipated couple. They throw their mansion open; dicing, betting, intriguing, revellings, maskings, commence. Michiella is courted ardently by Camillo; Camilla trifles with Leonardo and with Count Orso alternately. Jealous again of Camilla, Michiella warns and threatens Leonardo; but she becomes Camillo's dupe, partly from returning love, partly from desire for vengeance on her rival. Camilla persuades Orso to discard Michiella. The infatuated count waxes as the personification of portentous burlesque; he is having everything his own way. The acting throughout—owing to the real gravity of the vast basso Lebruno's burlesque, and Vittoria's archness— was that of high comedy with a lurid background. Vittoria showed an enchanting spirit of humour. She sang one bewitching barcarole that set the house in rocking motion. There was such melancholy in her heart that she cast herself into all the flippancy with abandonment. The Act was weak in too distinctly revealing the finger of the poetic political squib at a point here and there. The temptation to do it of an Agostino, who had no other outlet, had been irresistible, and he sat moaning over his artistic depravity, now that it stared him in the face. Applause scarcely consoled him, and it was with humiliation of mind that he acknowledged his debt to the music and the singers, and how little they owed to him.

Now Camillo is pleased to receive the ardent passion of his wife, and the masking suits his taste, but it is the vice of his character that he cannot act to any degree subordinately in concert; he insists upon positive headship!—(allusion to an Italian weakness for sovereignties; it passed unobserved, and chuckled bitterly over his excess of subtlety). Camillo cannot leave the scheming to her. He pursues Michiella to subdue her with blandishments. Reproaches cease upon her part. There is a duo between them. They exchange the silver keys, which express absolute intimacy, and give mutual freedom of access. Camillo can now secrete his followers in the castle; Michiella can enter Camilla's blue-room, and ravage her caskets for treasonable correspondence. Artfully she bids him reflect on what she is forfeiting for him; and so helps him to put aside the thought of that which he also may be imperilling.

Irma's shrill crescendos and octave-leaps, assisted by her peculiar attitudes of strangulation, came out well in this scene. The murmurs concerning the sour privileges to be granted by a Lazzeruola were inaudible. But there has been a witness to the stipulation. The ever-shifting baritono, from behind a pillar, has joined in with an aside phrase here and there. Leonardo discovers that his fealty to Camilla is reviving. He determines to watch over her. Camillo now tosses a perfumed handkerchief under his nose, and inhales the coxcombical incense of the idea that he will do all without Camilla's aid, to surprise her; thereby teaching her to know him to be somewhat a hero. She has played her part so thoroughly that he can choose to fancy her a giddy person; he remarks upon the frequent instances of girls who in their girlhood were wild dreamers becoming after marriage wild wives. His followers assemble, that he may take advantage of the exchanged key of silver. He is moved to seek one embrace of Camilla before the conflict:—she is beautiful! There was never such beauty as hers! He goes to her in the fittest preparation for the pangs of jealousy. But he has not been foremost in practising the uses of silver keys. Michiella, having first arranged with her father to be before Camillo's doors at a certain hour with men-at-arms, is in Camilla's private chamber, with her hand upon a pregnant box of ebony wood, when she is startled by a noise, and slips into concealment. Leonardo bursts through the casement window. Camilla then appears. Leonardo stretches the tips of his fingers out to her; on his knees confesses his guilt and warns her. Camillo comes in. Thrusting herself before him, Michiella points to the stricken couple 'See! it is to show you this that I am here.' Behold occasion for a grand quatuor!

While confessing his guilt to Camilla, Leonardo has excused it by an emphatic delineation of Michiella's magic sway over him. (Leonardo, in fact, is your small modern Italian Machiavelli, overmatched in cunning, for the reason that he is always at a last moment the victim of his poor bit of heart or honesty: he is devoid of the inspiration of great patriotic aims.) If Michiella (Austrian intrigue) has any love, it is for such a tool. She cannot afford to lose him. She pleads for him; and, as Camilla is silent on his account, the cynical magnanimity of Camillo is predisposed to spare a fangless snake. Michiella withdraws him from the naked sword to the back of the stage. The terrible repudiation scene ensues, in which Camillo casts off his wife. If it was a puzzle to one Italian half of the audience, the other comprehended it perfectly, and with rapture. It was thus that YOUNG ITALY had too often been treated by the compromising, merely discontented, dallying aristocracy. Camilla cries to him, 'Have faith in me! have faith in me! have faith in me!' That is the sole answer to his accusations, his threats of eternal loathing, and generally blustering sublimities. She cannot defend herself; she only knows her innocence. He is inexorable, being the guilty one of the two. Turning from him with crossed arms, Camilla sings:

'Mother! it is my fate that I should know Thy miseries, and in thy footprints go. Grief treads the starry places of the earth: In thy long track I feel who gave me birth. I am alone; a wife without a lord; My home is with the stranger—home abhorr'd!—But that I trust to meet thy spirit there. Mother of Sorrows! joy thou canst not share: So let me wander in among the tombs, Among the cypresses and the withered blooms. Thy soul is with dead suns: there let me be; A silent thing that shares thy veil with thee.'

The wonderful viol-like trembling of the contralto tones thrilled through the house. It was the highest homage to Vittoria that no longer any shouts arose nothing but a prolonged murmur, as when one tells another a tale of deep emotion, and all exclamations, all ulterior thoughts, all gathered tenderness of sensibility, are reserved for the close, are seen heaping for the close, like waters above a dam. The flattery of beholding a great assembly of human creatures bound glittering in wizard subservience to the voice of one soul, belongs to the artist, and is the cantatrice's glory, pre-eminent over whatever poor glory this world gives. She felt it, but she felt it as something apart. Within her was the struggle of Italy calling to Italy: Italy's shame, her sadness, her tortures, her quenchless hope, and the view of Freedom. It sent her blood about her body in rebellious volumes. Once it completely strangled her notes. She dropped the ball of her chin in her throat; paused without ceremony; and recovered herself. Vittoria had too severe an artistic instinct to court reality; and as much as she could she from that moment corrected the underlinings of Agostino's libretto.

On the other hand, Irma fell into all his traps, and painted her Austrian heart with a prodigal waste of colour and frank energy:

'Now Leonardo is my tool:
Camilla is my slave:
And she I hate goes forth to cool
Her rage beyond the wave.
Joy! joy!
Paid am I in full coin for my caressing;
I take, but give nought, ere the priestly blessing.'

A subtle distinction. She insists upon her reverence for the priestly (papistical) blessing, while she confides her determination to have it dispensed with in Camilla's case. Irma's known sympathies with the Austrian uniform seasoned the ludicrousness of many of the double-edged verses which she sang or declaimed in recitative. The irony of applauding her vehemently was irresistible.

Camilla is charged with conspiracy, and proved guilty by her own admission.

The Act ends with the entry of Count Orso and his force; conspirators overawed; Camilla repudiated; Count Orso imperially just; Leonardo chagrined; Camillo pardoned; Michiella triumphant. Camillo sacrifices his wife for safety. He holds her estates; and therefore Count Orso, whose respect for law causes him to have a keen eye for matrimonial alliances, is now paternally willing, and even anxious to bestow Michiella upon him when the Pontifical divorce can be obtained; so that the long-coveted fruitful acres may be in the family. The chorus sings a song of praise to Hymen, the 'builder of great Houses.' Camilla goes forth into exile. The word was not spoken, but the mention of 'bread of strangers, strange faces, cold climes,' said sufficient.

'It is a question whether we ought to sit still and see a firebrand flashed in our faces,' General Pierson remarked as the curtain fell. He was talking to Major de Pyrmont outside the Duchess of Graatli's box. Two General officers joined them, and presently Count Serabiglione, with his courtly semi-ironical smile, on whom they straightway turned their backs. The insult was happily unseen, and the count caressed his shaven chin and smiled himself onward. The point for the officers to decide was, whether they dared offend an enthusiastic house—the fiery core of the population of Milan—by putting a stop to the opera before worse should come.

Their own views were entirely military; but they were paralyzed by the recent pseudo-liberalistic despatches from Vienna; and agreed, with some malice in their shrugs, that the odium might as well be left on the shoulders of the bureau which had examined the libretto. In fact, they saw that there would be rank peril in attempting to arrest the course of things within the walls of the house.

'The temper this people is changeing oddly,' said General Pierson. Major de Pyrmont listened awhile to what they had to say, and returned to the duchess. Amalia wrote these lines to Laura:—'If she sings that song she is to be seized on the wings of the stage. I order my carriage to be in readiness to take her whither she should have gone last night. Do you contrive only her escape from the house. Georges de P. will aid you. I adore the naughty rebel!'

Major de Pyrmont delivered the missive at Laura's box. He went down to the duchess's chasseur, and gave him certain commands and money for a journey. Looking about, he beheld Wilfrid, who implored him to take his place for two minutes. De Pyrmont laughed. 'She is superb, my friend. Come up with me. I am going behind the scenes. The unfortunate impresario is a ruined man; let us both condole with him. It is possible that he has children, and children like bread.'

Wilfrid was linking his arm to De Pyrmont's, when, with a vivid recollection of old times, he glanced at his uniform with Vittoria's eyes. 'She would spit at me!' he muttered, and dropped behind.

Up in her room Vittoria held council with Rocco, Agostino, and the impresario, Salvolo, who was partly their dupe. Salvolo had laid a freshly-written injunction from General Pierson before her, bidding him to exclude the chief solo parts from the Third Act, and to bring it speedily to a termination. His case was, that he had been ready to forfeit much if a rising followed; but that simply to beard the authorities was madness. He stated his case by no means as a pleader, although the impression made on him by the prima donna's success caused his urgency to be civil.

'Strike out what you please,' said Vittoria.

Agostino smote her with a forefinger. 'Rogue! you deserve an imperial crown. You have been educated for monarchy. You are ready enough to dispense with what you don't care for, and what is not your own.'

Much of the time was lost by Agostino's dispute with Salvolo. They haggled and wrangled laughingly over this and that printed aria, but it was a deplorable deception of the unhappy man; and with Vittoria's stronger resolve to sing the incendiary song, the more necessary it was for her to have her soul clear of deceit. She said, 'Signor Salvolo, you have been very kind to me, and I would do nothing to hurt your interests. I suppose you must suffer for being an Italian, like the rest of us. The song I mean to sing is not written or printed. What is in the book cannot harm you, for the censorship has passed it; and surely I alone am responsible for singing what is not in the book—I and the maestro. He supports me. We have both taken precautions' (she smiled) 'to secure our property. If you are despoiled, we will share with you. And believe, oh! in God's name, believe that you will not suffer to no purpose!'

Salvolo started from her in a horror of amazement. He declared that he had been miserably deceived and entrapped. He threatened to send the company to their homes forthwith. 'Dare to!' said Agostino; and to judge by the temper of the house, it was only too certain, that if he did so, La Scala would be a wrecked tenement in the eye of morning. But Agostino backed his entreaty to her to abjure that song; Rocco gave way, and half shyly requested her to think of prudence. She remembered Laura, and Carlo, and her poor little frightened foreign mother. Her intense ideal conception of her duty sank and danced within her brain as the pilot-star dances on the bows of a tossing vessel. All were against her, as the tempest is against the ship. Even light above (by which I would image that which she could appeal to pleading in behalf of the wisdom of her obstinate will) was dyed black in the sweeping obscuration; she failed to recollect a sentence that was to be said to vindicate her settled course. Her sole idea was her holding her country by an unseen thread, and of the everlasting welfare of Italy being jeopardized if she relaxed her hold. Simple obstinacy of will sustained her.

You mariners batten down the hatchways when the heavens are dark and seas are angry. Vittoria, with the same faith in her instinct, shut the avenues to her senses—would see nothing, hear nothing. The impresario's figure of despair touched her later. Giacinta drove him forth in the act of smiting his forehead with both hands. She did the same for Agostino and Rocco, who were not demonstrative.

They knew that by this time the agents of the Government were in all probability ransacking their rooms, and confiscating their goods.

'Is your piano hired?' quoth the former.

'No,' said the latter, 'are your slippers?'

They went their separate ways, laughing.

CHAPTER XXI

THE THIRD ACT

The libretto of the Third Act was steeped in the sentiment of Young Italy. I wish that I could pipe to your mind's hearing any notion of the fine music of Rocco Ricci, and touch you to feel the revelations which were in this new voice. Rocco and Vittoria gave the verses a life that cannot belong to them now; yet, as they contain much of the vital spirit of the revolt, they may assist you to some idea of the faith animating its heads, and may serve to justify this history.

Rocco's music in the opera of Camilla had been sprung from a fresh Italian well; neither the elegiac-melodious, nor the sensuous-lyrical, nor the joyous buffo; it was severe as an old masterpiece, with veins of buoyant liveliness threading it, and with sufficient distinctness of melody to enrapture those who like to suck the sugarplums of sound. He would indeed have favoured the public with more sweet things, but Vittoria, for whom the opera was composed, and who had been at his elbow, was young, and stern in her devotion to an ideal of classical music that should elevate and never stoop to seduce or to flatter thoughtless hearers. Her taste had directed as her voice had inspired the opera. Her voice belonged to the order of the simply great voices, and was a royal voice among them. Pure without attenuation, passionate without contortion, when once heard it exacted absolute confidence. On this night her theme and her impersonation were adventitious introductions, but there were passages when her artistic pre-eminence and the sovereign fulness and fire of her singing struck a note of grateful remembered delight. This is what the great voice does for us. It rarely astonishes our ears. It illumines our souls, as you see the lightning make the unintelligible craving darkness leap into long mountain ridges, and twisting vales, and spires of cities, and inner recesses of light within light, rose-like, toward a central core of violet heat.

At the rising of the curtain the knights of the plains, Rudolfo, Romualdo, Arnoldo, and others, who were conspiring to overthrow Count Orso at the time when Camillo's folly ruined all, assemble to deplore Camilla's banishment, and show, bereft of her, their helplessness and indecision. They utter contempt of Camillo, who is this day to be Pontifically divorced from his wife to espouse the detested Michiella. His taste is not admired.

They pass off. Camillo appears. He is, as he knows, little better than a pensioner in Count Orso's household. He holds his lands on sufferance. His faculties are paralyzed. He is on the first smooth shoulder-slope of the cataract. He knows that not only was his jealousy of his wife groundless, but it was forced by a spleenful pride. What is there to do? Nothing, save resignedly to prepare for his divorce from the conspiratrix Camilla and espousals with Michiella. The cup is bitter, and his song is mournful. He does the rarest thing a man will do in such a predicament—he acknowledges that he is going to get his deserts. The faithfulness and purity of Camilla have struck his inner consciousness. He knows not where she may be. He has secretly sent messengers in all directions to seek her, and recover her, and obtain her pardon: in vain. It is as well, perhaps, that he should never see her more. Accursed, he has cast off his sweetest friend. The craven heart could never beat in unison with hers.

'She is in the darkness: I am in the light. I am a blot upon the light; she is light in the darkness.'

Montini poured this out with so fine a sentiment that the impatience of the house for sight of its heroine was quieted. But Irma and Lebruno came forward barely under tolerance.

'We might as well be thumping a tambourine,' said Lebruno, during a caress. Irma bit her underlip with mortification. Their notes fell flat as bullets against a wall.

This circumstance aroused the ire of Antonio-Pericles against the libretto and revolutionists. 'I perceive,' he said, grinning savagely, 'it has come to be a concert, not an opera; it is a musical harangue in the marketplace. Illusion goes: it is politics here!'

Carlo Ammiani was sitting with his mother and Luciano breathlessly awaiting the entrance of Vittoria. The inner box-door was rudely shaken: beneath it a slip of paper had been thrust. He read a warning to him to quit the house instantly. Luciano and his mother both counselled his departure. The detestable initials 'B. R.,' and the one word 'Sbirri,' revealed who had warned, and what was the danger. His friend's advice and the commands of his mother failed to move him. 'When I have seen her safe; not before,' he said.

Countess Ammiani addressed Luciano: 'This is a young man's love for a woman.'

'The woman is worth it,' Luciano replied.

'No woman is worth the sacrifice of a mother and of a relative.'

'Dearest countess,' said Luciano, 'look at the pit; it's a cauldron. We shall get him out presently, have no fear: there will soon be hubbub enough to let Lucifer escape unseen. If nothing is done to-night, he and I will be off to the Lago di Garda to-morrow morning, and fish and shoot, and talk with Catullus.'

The countess gazed on her son with sorrowful sternness. His eyes had taken that bright glazed look which is an indication of frozen brain and turbulent heart—madness that sane men enamoured can be struck by. She knew there was no appeal to it.

A very dull continuous sound, like that of an angry swarm, or more like a rapid mufed thrumming of wires, was heard. The audience had caught view of a brown-coated soldier at one of the wings. The curious Croat had merely gratified a desire to have a glance at the semicircle of crowded heads; he withdrew his own, but not before he had awakened the wild beast in the throng. Yet a little while and the roar of the beasts would have burst out. It was thought that Vittoria had been seized or interdicted from appearing. Conspirators—the knights of the plains—meet: Rudolfos, Romualdos, Arnoldos, and others,—so that you know Camilla is not idle. She comes on in the great scene which closes the opera.

It is the banqueting hall of the castle. The Pontifical divorce is spread upon the table. Courtly friends, guards, and a choric bridal company, form a circle.

'I have obtained it,' says Count Orso: 'but at a cost.'

Leonardo, wavering eternally, lets us know that it is weighted with a proviso: IF Camilla shall not present herself within a certain term, this being the last day of it. Camillo comes forward. Too late, he has perceived his faults and weakness. He has cast his beloved from his arms to clasp them on despair. The choric bridal company gives intervening strophes. Cavaliers enter. 'Look at them well,' says Leonardo. They are the knights of the plains. 'They have come to mock me,' Camillo exclaims, and avoids them.

Leonardo, Michiella, and Camillo now sing a trio that is tricuspidato, or a three-pointed manner of declaring their divergent sentiments in harmony. The fast-gathering cavaliers lend masculine character to the choric refrains at every interval. Leonardo plucks Michiella entreatingly by the arm. She spurns him. He has served her; she needs him no more; but she will recommend him in other quarters, and bids him to seek them. 'I will give thee a collar for thy neck, marked "Faithful." It is the utmost I can do for thy species.' Leonardo thinks that he is insulted, but there is a vestige of doubt in him still. 'She is so fair! she dissembles so magnificently ever!' She has previously told him that she is acting a part, as Camilla did. Irma had shed all her hair from a golden circlet about her temples, barbarian-wise. Some Hunnish grandeur pertained to her appearance, and partly excused the infatuated wretch who shivered at her disdain and exulted over her beauty and artfulness.

In the midst of the chorus there is one veiled figure and one voice distinguishable. This voice outlives the rest at every strophe, and contrives to add a supplemental antiphonic phrase that recalls in turn the favourite melodies of the opera. Camillo hears it, but takes it as a delusion of impassioned memory and a mere theme for the recurring melodious utterance of his regrets. Michiella hears it. She chimes with the third notes of Camillo's solo to inform us of her suspicions that they have a serpent among them. Leonardo hears it. The trio is formed. Count Orso, without hearing it, makes a quatuor by inviting the bridal couple to go through the necessary formalities. The chorus changes its measure to one of hymeneals. The unknown voice closes it ominously with three bars in the minor key. Michiella stalks close around the rank singers like an enraged daughter of Attila. Stopping in front of the veiled figure, she says: 'Why is it thou wearest the black veil at my nuptials?'

'Because my time of mourning is not yet ended.'

'Thou standest the shadow in my happiness.'

'The bright sun will have its shadow.'

'I desire that all rejoice this day.'

'My hour of rejoicing approaches.'

'Wilt thou unveil?'

'Dost thou ask to look the storm in the face?'

'Wilt thou unveil?'

'Art thou hungry for the lightning?'

'I bid thee unveil, woman!'

Michiella's ringing shriek of command produces no response.

'It is she!' cries Michiella, from a contracted bosom; smiting it with clenched hands.

'Swift to the signatures. O rival! what bitterness hast thou come hither to taste.'

Camilla sings aside: 'If yet my husband loves me and is true.'

Count Orso exclaims: 'Let trumpets sound for the commencement of the festivities. The lord of his country may slumber while his people dance and drink!'

Trumpets flourish. Witnesses are called about the table. Camillo, pen in hand, prepares for the supreme act. Leonardo at one wing watches the eagerness of Michiella. The chorus chants to a muted measure of suspense, while Camillo dips pen in ink.

'She is away from me: she scorns me: she is lost to me. Life without honour is the life of swine. Union without love is the yoke of savage beasts. O me miserable! Can the heavens themselves plumb the depth of my degradation?'

Count Orso permits a half-tone of paternal severity to point his kindly hint that time is passing. When he was young, he says, in the broad and benevolently frisky manner, he would have signed ere the eye of the maiden twinkled her affirmative, or the goose had shed its quill.

Camillo still trifles. Then he dashes the pen to earth.

'Never! I have but one wife. Our marriage is irrevocable. The dishonoured man is the everlasting outcast. What are earthly possessions to me, if within myself shame faces me? Let all go. Though I have lost Camilla, I will be worthy of her. Not a pen no pen; it is the sword that I must write with. Strike, O count! I am here: I stand alone. By the edge of this sword, I swear that never deed of mine shall rob Camilla of her heritage; though I die the death, she shall not weep for a craven!'

The multitude break away from Camilla—veiled no more, but radiant; fresh as a star that issues through corrupting vapours, and with her voice at a starry pitch in its clear ascendency:

'Tear up the insufferable scroll!—
O thou, my lover and my soul!
It is the Sword that reunites;
The Pen that our perdition writes.'

She is folded in her husband's arms.

Michiella fronts them, horrid of aspect:—

'Accurst divorced one! dost thou dare
To lie in shameless fondness there?
Abandoned! on thy lying brow
Thy name shall be imprinted now.'

Camilla parts from her husband's embrace:

'My name is one I do not fear;
'Tis one that thou wouldst shrink to hear.
Go, cool thy penitential fires,
Thou creature, foul with base desires!'

CAMILLO (facing Count Orso).
'The choice is thine!'

COUNT ORSO (draws).
'The choice is made!'

CHORUS (narrowing its circle).
'Familiar is that naked blade.
Of others, of himself, the fate
How swift 'tis Provocation's mate!'

MICHIELLA (torn with jealous rage).
'Yea; I could smite her on the face.
Father, first read the thing's disgrace.
I grudge them, honourable death.
Put poison in their latest breath!'

ORSO (his left arm extended).
'You twain are sundered: hear with awe
The judgement of the Source of Law.'

CAMILLA (smiling confidently).
'Not such, when I was at the Source,

It said to me;—but take thy course.'

ORSO (astounded).
'Thither thy steps were bent?'

MICHIELLA (spurning verbal controversy).
'She feigns!
A thousand swords are in my veins.
Friends! soldiers I strike them down, the pair!'

CAMILLO (on guard, clasping his wife).
''Tis well! I cry, to all we share.
Yea, life or death, 'tis well! 'tis well!'

MICHIELLA (stamps her foot).
'My heart 's a vessel tossed on hell!'

LEONARDO (aside).
'Not in glad nuptials ends the day.'

ORSO (to Camilla).
'What is thy purpose with us?—say!'

CAMILLA (lowly).
'Unto my Father I have crossed
For tidings of my Mother lost.'

ORSO
'Thy mother dead!'

CAMILLA
'She lives!'

MICHIELLA
'Thou liest!
The tablets of the tomb defiest!
The Fates denounce, the Furies chase
The wretch who lies in Reason's face.'

CAMILLA.
'Fly, then; for we are match'd to try
Which is the idiot, thou or I'

MICHIELLA
Graceless Camilla!'

ORSO
'Senseless girl!

I cherished thee a precious pearl,
And almost owned thee child of mine.'

CAMILLA
'Thou kept'st me like a gem, to shine,
Careless that I of blood am made;
No longer be the end delay'd.
'Tis time to prove I have a heart—
Forth from these walls of mine depart!
The ghosts within them are disturb'd
Go forth, and let thy wrath be curb'd,
For I am strong: Camillo's truth
Has arm'd the visions of our youth.
Our union by the Head Supreme
Is blest: our severance was the dream.
We who have drunk of blood and tears,
Knew nothing of a mortal's fears.
Life is as Death until the strife
In our just cause makes Death as Life.'

ORSO
''Tis madness?'

LEONARDO
'Is it madness?'

CAMILLA.
'Men!
'Tis Reason, but beyond your ken.
There lives a light that none can view
Whose thoughts are brutish:—seen by few,
The few have therefore light divine
Their visions are God's legions!—sign,
I give you; for we stand alone,
And you are frozen to the bone.
Your palsied hands refuse their swords.
A sharper edge is in my words,
A deadlier wound is in my cry.
Yea, tho' you slay us, do we die?
In forcing us to bear the worst,
You made of us Immortals first.
Away! and trouble not my sight.'

Chorus of Cavaliers: RUDOLFO, ROMUALDO, ARNOLDO, and others.
'She moves us with an angel's might.
What if his host outnumber ours!
'Tis heaven that gives victorious powers.'

[They draw their steel. ORSO, simulating gratitude for their devotion to him, addresses them as to pacify their friendly ardour.]

MICHIELLA to LEONARDO (supplicating)
'Ever my friend I shall I appeal
In vain to see thy flashing steel?'

LEONARDO (finally resolved)
'Traitress! pray, rather, it may rest,
Or its first home will be thy breast.'

Chorus of Bridal Company
'The flowers from bright Aurora's head
 We pluck'd to strew a happy bed,
Shall they be dipp'd in blood ere night?
Woe to the nuptials! woe the sight!'

Rudolfo, Romualdo, Arnoldo, and the others, advance toward Camillo. Michiella calls to them encouragingly that it were well for the deed to be done by their hands. They bid Camillo to direct their lifted swords upon his enemies. Leonardo joins them. Count Orso, after a burst of upbraidings, accepts Camillo's offer of peace, and gives his bond to quit the castle. Michiella, gazing savagely at Camilla, entreats her for an utterance of her triumphant scorn. She assures Camilla that she knows her feelings accurately.

'Now you think that I am overwhelmed; that I shall have a restless night, and lie, after all my crying's over, with my hair spread out on my pillow, on either side my face, like green moss of a withered waterfall: you think you will bestow a little serpent of a gift from my stolen treasures to comfort me. You will comfort me with a lock of Camillo's hair, that I may have it on my breast to-night, and dream, and wail, and writhe, and curse the air I breathe, and clasp the abominable emptiness like a thousand Camillos. Speak!'

The dagger is seen gleaming up Michiella's wrist; she steps on in a bony triangle, faced for mischief: a savage Hunnish woman, with the hair of a Goddess—the figure of a cat taking to its forepaws. Close upon Camilla she towers in her whole height, and crying thrice, swift as the assassin trebles his blow, 'Speak,' to Camilla, who is fronting her mildly, she raises her arm, and the stilet flashes into Camilla's bosom.

'Die then, and outrage me no more.'

Camilla staggers to her husband. Camillo receives her falling. Michiella, seized by Leonardo, presents a stiffened shape of vengeance with fierce white eyes and dagger aloft. There are many shouts, and there is silence.

CAMILLA, supported by CAMILLO.
'If this is death, it is not hard to bear.
Your handkerchief drinks up my blood so fast
It seems to love it. Threads of my own hair
Are woven in it. 'Tis the one I cast

That midnight from my window, when you stood
Alone, and heaven seemed to love you so!
I did not think to wet it with my blood
When next I tossed it to my love below.'

CAMILLO (cherishing her)
'Camilla, pity! say you will not die.
 Your voice is like a soul lost in the sky.'

CAMILLA
'I know not if my soul has flown; I know
My body is a weight I cannot raise:
My voice between them issues, and
I go Upon a journey of uncounted days.
Forgetfulness is like a closing sea;
But you are very bright above me still.
My life I give as it was given to me
I enter on a darkness wide and chill.'

CAMILLO
'O noble heart! a million fires consume
The hateful hand that sends you to your doom.'

CAMILLA
'There is an end to joy: there is no end
To striving; therefore ever let us strive
In purity that shall the toil befriend,
And keep our poor mortality alive.
I hang upon the boundaries like light
Along the hills when downward goes the day
I feel the silent creeping up of night.
For you, my husband, lies a flaming way.'

CAMILLO
'I lose your eyes: I lose your voice: 'tis faint.
Ah, Christ! see the fallen eyelids of a saint.'

CAMILLA
'Our life is but a little holding, lent
To do a mighty labour: we are one
 With heaven and the stars when it is spent
To serve God's aim: else die we with the sun.'

She sinks. Camillo droops his head above her.

The house was hushed as at a veritable death-scene. It was more like a cathedral service than an operatic pageant. Agostino had done his best to put the heart of the creed of his Chief into these last verses. Rocco's music floated them in solemn measures, and Vittoria had been careful to articulate throughout the sacred monotony so that their full meaning should be taken.

In the printed book of the libretto a chorus of cavaliers, followed by one harmless verse of Camilla's adieux to them, and to her husband and life, concluded the opera.

'Let her stop at that—it's enough!—and she shall be untouched,' said General Pierson to Antonio-Pericles.

'I have information, as you know, that an extremely impudent song is coming.'

The General saw Wilfrid hanging about the lobby, in flagrant disobedience to orders. Rebuking his nephew with a frown, he commanded the lieutenant to make his way round to the stage and see that the curtain was dropped according to the printed book.

'Off, mon Dieu! off!' Pericles speeded him; adding in English, 'Shall she taste prison-damp, zat voice is killed.'

The chorus of cavaliers was a lamentation: the keynote being despair: ordinary libretto verses.

Camilla's eyes unclose. She struggles to be lifted, and, raised on Camillo's arm, she sings as if with the last pulsation of her voice, softly resonant in its rich contralto. She pardons Michiella. She tells Count Orso that when he has extinguished his appetite for dominion, he will enjoy an unknown pleasure in the friendship of his neighbours. Repeating that her mother lives, and will some day kneel by her daughter's grave—not mournfully, but in beatitude—she utters her adieu to all.

At the moment of her doing so, Montini whispered in Vittoria's ear. She looked up and beheld the downward curl of the curtain. There was confusion at the wings: Croats were visible to the audience. Carlo Ammiani and Luciano Romara jumped on the stage; a dozen of the noble youths of Milan streamed across the boards to either wing, and caught the curtain descending. The whole house had risen insurgent with cries of 'Vittoria.' The curtain-ropes were in the hands of the Croats, but Carlo, Luciano, and their fellows held the curtain aloft at arm's length at each side of her. She was seen, and she sang, and the house listened.

The Italians present, one and all, rose up reverently and murmured the refrain. Many of the aristocracy would, doubtless, have preferred that this public declaration of the plain enigma should not have rung forth to carry them on the popular current; and some might have sympathized with the insane grin which distorted the features of Antonio-Pericles, when he beheld illusion wantonly destroyed, and the opera reduced to be a mere vehicle for a fulmination of politics. But the general enthusiasm was too tremendous to permit of individual protestations. To sit, when the nation was standing, was to be a German. Nor, indeed, was there an Italian in the house who would willingly have consented to see Vittoria silenced, now that she had chosen to defy the Tedeschi from the boards of La Scala. The fascination of her voice extended even over the German division of the audience. They, with the Italians, said: 'Hear her! hear her!' The curtain was agitated at the wings, but in the centre it was kept above Vittoria's head by the uplifted arms of the twelve young men:—

'I cannot count the years,
That you will drink, like me,

The cup of blood and tears,
Ere she to you appears:—
Italia, Italia shall be free!'

So the great name was out, and its enemies had heard it.

'You dedicate your lives
To her, and you will be
The food on which she thrives,
Till her great day arrives
Italia, Italia shall be free!

'She asks you but for faith!
Your faith in her takes she
As draughts of heaven's breath,
Amid defeat and death:—
Italia, Italia shall be free!'

The prima donna was not acting exhaustion when sinking lower in Montini's arms. Her bosom rose and sank quickly, and she gave the terminating verse:—

'I enter the black boat
Upon the wide grey sea,
Where all her set suns float;
Thence hear my voice remote
Italia, Italia shall be free!'

The curtain dropped.

CHAPTER XXII

WILFRID COMES FORWARD

An order for the immediate arrest of Vittoria was brought round to the stage at the fall of the curtain by Captain Weisspriess, and delivered by him on the stage to the officer commanding, a pothered lieutenant of Croats, whose first proceeding was dictated by the military instinct to get his men in line, and who was utterly devoid of any subsequent idea. The thunder of the house on the other side of the curtain was enough to disconcert a youngster such as he was; nor have the subalterns of Croat regiments a very signal reputation for efficiency in the Austrian Service. Vittoria stood among her supporters apart; pale, and 'only very thirsty,' as she told the enthusiastic youths who pressed near her, and implored her to have no fear. Carlo was on her right hand; Luciano on her left. They kept her from going off to her room. Montini was despatched to fetch her maid Giacinta with cloak and hood for her mistress. The young lieutenant of Croats drew his sword, but hesitated. Weisspriess, Wilfrid, and Major de Pyrmont were at one wing, between the Italian gentlemen and the soldiery. The operatic company had fallen into the background, or stood crowding the side places of exit. Vittoria's name was being shouted with that angry, sea-like, horrid monotony of iteration which is more suggestive of menacing impatience and the positive will of the people, than varied, sharp, imperative calls. The people had got the lion in their throats. One shriek from her would bring them, like a torrent, on the boards, as the officers well knew; and every second's delay in executing the orders of the General added to the difficulty of their position. The lieutenant of Croats strode up to Weisspriess and Wilfrid, who were discussing a plan of action vehemently; while, amid hubbub and argument, De Pyrmont studied Vittoria's features through his opera-glass, with an admirable simple languor.

Wilfrid turned back to him, and De Pyrmont, without altering the level of his glass, said, 'She's as cool as a lemon-ice. That girl will be a mother of heroes. To have volcanic fire and the mastery of her nerves at the same time, is something prodigious. She is magnificent. Take a peep at her. I suspect that the rascal at her right is seizing his occasion to plant a trifle or so in her memory—the animal! It's just the moment, and he knows it.'

De Pyrmont looked at Wilfrid's face.

'Have I hit you anywhere accidentally?' he asked, for the face had grown dead-white.

'Be my friend, for heaven's sake!' was the choking answer. 'Save her! Get her away! She is an old acquaintance of mine—of mine, in England. Do; or I shall have to break my sword.'

'You know her? and you don't go over to her?' said De Pyrmont.

'I—yes, she knows me.'

'Then, why not present yourself?'

'Get her away. Talk Weisspriess down. He is for seizing her at all hazards. It 's madness to provoke a conflict. Just listen to the house! I may be broken, but save her I will. De Pyrmont, on my honour, I will stand by you for ever if you will help me to get her away.'

'To suggest my need in the hour of your own is not a bad notion,' said the cool Frenchman. 'What plan have you?'

Wilfrid struck his forehead miserably.

'Stop Lieutenant Zettlisch. Don't let him go up to her. Don't—'

De Pyrmont beheld in astonishment that a speechlessness such as affects condemned wretches in the supreme last minutes of existence had come upon the Englishman.

'I'm afraid yours is a bad case,' he said; 'and the worst of it is, it's just the case women have no compassion for. Here comes a parlementaire from the opposite camp. Let's hear him.'

It was Luciano Romara. He stood before them to request that the curtain should be raised. The officers debated together, and deemed it prudent to yield consent.

Luciano stipulated further that the soldiers were to be withdrawn.

'On one wing, or on both wings?' said Captain Weisspriess, twinkling eyes oblique.

'Out of the house,' said Luciano.

The officers laughed.

'You must confess,' said De Pyrmont, affably, 'that though the drum does issue command to the horse, it scarcely thinks of doing so after a rent in the skin has shown its emptiness. Can you suppose that we are likely to run when we see you empty-handed? These things are matters of calculation.'

'It is for you to calculate correctly,' said Luciano.

As he spoke, a first surge of the exasperated house broke upon the stage and smote the curtain, which burst into white zigzags, as it were a breast stricken with panic.

Giacinta came running in to her mistress, and cloaked and hooded her hurriedly.

Enamoured; impassioned, Ammiani murmured in Vittoria's ear: 'My own soul!'

She replied: 'My lover!'

So their first love-speech was interchanged with Italian simplicity, and made a divine circle about them in the storm.

Luciano returned to his party to inform them that they held the key of the emergency.

'Stick fast,' he said. 'None of you move. Whoever takes the first step takes the false step; I see that.'

'We have no arms, Luciano.'

'We have the people behind us.'

There was a fiercer tempest in the body of the house, and, on a sudden, silence. Men who had invaded the stage joined the Italian guard surrounding Vittoria, telling that the lights had been extinguished; and then came the muffled uproar of universal confusion. Some were for handing her down into the orchestra, and getting her out through the general vomitorium, but Carlo and Luciano held her firmly by them. The theatre was a rageing darkness; and there was barely a light on the stage. 'Santa Maria!' cried Giacinta, 'how dreadful that steel does look in the dark! I wish our sweet boys would cry louder.' Her mistress, almost laughing, bade her keep close, and be still. 'Oh! this must be like being at sea,' the poor creature whined, stopping her ears and shutting her eyes. Vittoria was in a thick gathering of her defenders; she could just hear that a parley was going on between Luciano and the Austrians. Luciano made his way back to her. 'Quick!' he said; 'nothing cows a mob like darkness. One of these officers tells me he knows you, and gives his word of honour—he's an Englishman—to conduct you out: come.'

Vittoria placed her hands in Carlo's one instant. Luciano cleared a space for them. She heard a low English voice.

'You do not recognize me? There is no time to lose. You had another name once, and I have had the honour to call you by it.'

'Are you an Austrian?' she exclaimed, and Carlo felt that she was shrinking back.

'I am the Wilfrid Pole whom you knew. You are entrusted to my charge; I have sworn to conduct you to the doors in safety, whatever it may cost me.'

Vittoria looked at him mournfully. Her eyes filled with tears. 'The night is spoiled for me!' she murmured.

'Emilia!'

'That is not my name.'

'I know you by no other. Have mercy on me. I would do anything in the world to serve you.'

Major de Pyrmont came up to him and touched his arm. He said briefly: 'We shall have a collision, to a certainty, unless the people hear from one of her set that she is out of the house.'

Wilfrid requested her to confide her hand to him.

'My hand is engaged,' she said.

Bowing ceremoniously, Wilfrid passed on, and Vittoria, with Carlo and Luciano and her maid Giacinta, followed between files of bayonets through the dusky passages, and downstairs into the night air.

Vittoria spoke in Carlo's ear: 'I have been unkind to him. I had a great affection for him in England.'

'Thank him; thank him,' said Carlo.

She quitted her lover's side and went up to Wilfrid with a shyly extended hand. A carriage was drawn up by the kerbstone; the doors of it were open. She had barely made a word intelligible; when Major de Pyrmont pointed to some officers approaching. 'Get her out of the way while there's time,' he said in French to Luciano. 'This is her carriage. Swiftly, gentlemen, or she's lost.'

Giacinta read his meaning by signs, and caught her mistress by the sleeve, using force. She and Major de Pyrmont placed Vittoria, bewildered, in the carriage; De Pyrmont shut the door, and signalled to the coachman. Vittoria thrust her head out for a last look at her lover, and beheld him with the arms of dark-clothed men upon him. La Scala was pouring forth its occupants in struggling roaring shoals from every door. Her outcry returned to her deadened in the rapid rolling of the carriage across the lighted Piazza. Giacinta had to hold her down with all her might. Great clamour was for one moment heard by them, and then a rushing voicelessness. Giacinta screamed to the coachman till she was exhausted. Vittoria sank shuddering on the lap of her maid, hiding her face that she might plunge out of recollection.

The lightnings shot across her brain, but wrote no legible thing; the scenes of the opera lost their outlines as in a white heat of fire. She tried to weep, and vainly asked her heart for tears, that this dry dreadful blind misery of mere sensation might be washed out of her, and leave her mind clear to grapple with evil; and then, as the lurid breaks come in a storm-driven night sky, she had the picture of her lover in the hands of enemies, and of Wilfrid in the white uniform; the torment of her living passion, the mockery of her passion by-gone. Recollection, when it came back, overwhelmed her; she swayed from recollection to oblivion, and was like a caged wild thing. Giacinta had to be as a mother with her. The poor trembling girl, who had begun to perceive that the carriage was bearing them to some unknown destination, tore open the bands of her corset and drew her mistress's head against the full warmth of her bosom, rocked her, and moaned over her, mixing comfort and lamentation in one offering, and so contrived to draw the tears out from her, a storm of tears; not fitfully hysterical, but tears that poured a black veil over the eyeballs, and fell steadily streaming. Once subdued by the weakness, Vittoria's nature melted; she shook piteously with weeping; she remembered Laura's words, and thought of what she had done, in terror and remorse, and tried to ask if the people would be fighting now, but could not. Laura seemed to stand before her like a Fury stretching her finger at the dear brave men whom she had hurled upon the bayonets and the guns. It was an unendurable anguish. Giacinta was compelled to let her cry, and had to reflect upon their present situation unaided. They had passed the city gates. Voices on the coachman's box had given German pass-words. She would have screamed then had not the carriage seemed to her a sanctuary from such creatures as foreign soldiers, whitecoats; so she cowered on. They were in the starry open country, on the high-road between the vine-hung mulberry trees. She held the precious head of her mistress, praying the Saints that strength would soon come to her to talk of their plight, or chatter a little comfortingly at least; and but for the singular sweetness which it shot thrilling to her woman's heart, she would have been fretted when Vittoria, after one long-drawn wavering sob, turned her lips to the bared warm breast, and put a little kiss upon it, and slept.

CHAPTER XXIII

FIRST HOURS OF THE FLIGHT

Vittoria slept on like an outworn child, while Giacinta nodded over her, and started, and wondered what embowelled mountain they might be passing through, so cold was the air and thick the darkness; and wondered more at the old face of dawn, which appeared to know nothing of her agitation. But morning was better than night, and she ceased counting over her sins forward and backward; adding comments on them, excusing some and admitting the turpitude of others, with 'Oh! I was naughty, padre mio! I was naughty—she huddled them all into one of memory's spare sacks, and tied the neck of it, that they should keep safe for her father-confessor. At such times, after a tumult of the blood, women have tender delight in one another's beauty. Giacinta doted on the marble cheek, upturned on her lap, with the black unbound locks slipping across it; the braid of the coronal of hair loosening; the chance flitting movement of the pearly little dimple that lay at the edge of the bow of the joined lips, like the cradling hollow of a dream. At whiles it would twitch; yet the dear eyelids continued sealed.

Looking at shut eyelids when you love the eyes beneath, is more or less a teazing mystery that draws down your mouth to kiss them. Their lashes seem to answer you in some way with infantine provocation; and fine eyelashes upon a face bent sideways, suggest a kind of internal smiling. Giacinta looked till she could bear it no longer; she kissed the cheek, and crooned over it, gladdened by a sense of jealous possession when she thought of the adored thing her mistress had been overnight. One of her hugs awoke Vittoria, who said, 'Shut my window, mother,' and slept again fast. Giacinta saw that they were nearer to the mountains. Mountain-shadows were thrown out, and long lank shadows of cypresses that climbed up reddish-yellow undulations, told of the sun coming. The sun threw a blaze of light into the carriage. He shone like a good friend, and helped Giacinta think, as she had already been disposed to imagine, that the machinery by which they had been caught out of Milan was amicable magic after all, and not to be screamed at. The sound medicine of sleep and sunlight was restoring livelier colour to her mistress. Giacinta hushed her now, but Vittoria's eyes opened, and settled on her, full of repose.

'What are you thinking about?' she asked.

'Signorina, my own, I was thinking whether those people I see on the hill-sides are as fond of coffee as I am.'

Vittoria sat up and tumbled questions out headlong, pressing her eyes and gathering her senses; she shook with a few convulsions, but shed no tears. It was rather the discomfort of their position than any vestige of alarm which prompted Giacinta to project her head and interrogate the coachman and chasseur. She drew back, saying, 'Holy Virgin! they are Germans. We are to stop in half-an-hour.' With that she put her hands to use in arranging and smoothing Vittoria's hair and dress—the dress of Camilla—of which triumphant heroine Vittoria felt herself an odd little ghost now. She changed her seat that she might look back on Milan. A letter was spied fastened with a pin to one of the cushions. She opened it, and read in pencil writing:

'Go quietly. You have done all that you could do for good or for ill. The carriage will take you to a safe place, where you will soon see your friends and hear the news. Wait till you reach Meran. You will see a friend from England. Avoid the lion's jaw a second time. Here you compromise everybody. Submit, or your friends will take you for a mad girl. Be satisfied. It is an Austrian who rescues you. Think yourself no longer appointed to put match to powder. Drown yourself if a second frenzy comes. I feel I could still love your body if the obstinate soul were out of it. You know who it is that writes. I might sign "Michiella" to this: I have a sympathy with her anger at the provoking Camilla. Addio! From La Scala.'

The lines read as if Laura were uttering them. Wrapping her cloak across the silken opera garb, Vittoria leaned back passively until the carriage stopped at a village inn, where Giacinta made speedy arrangements to satisfy as far as possible her mistress's queer predilection for bathing her whole person daily in cold water. The household service of the inn recovered from the effort to assist her sufficiently to produce hot coffee and sweet bread, and new green-streaked stracchino, the cheese of the district, which was the morning meal of the fugitives. Giacinta, who had never been so thirsty in her life, became intemperately refreshed, and was seized by the fatal desire to do something: to do what she could not tell; but chancing to see that her mistress had silken slippers on her feet, she protested loudly that stouter foot-gear should be obtained for her, and ran out to circulate inquiries concerning a shoemaker who might have a pair of country overshoes for sale. She returned to say that the coachman and his comrade, the German chasseur, were drinking and watering their horses, and were not going to start until after a rest of two hours, and that she proposed to walk to a small Bergamasc town within a couple of miles of the village, where the shoes could be obtained, and perhaps a stuff to replace the silken dress. Receiving consent, Giacinta whispered, 'A man outside wishes to speak to you, signorina. Don't be frightened. He pounced on me at the end of the village, and had as little breath to speak as a boy in love. He was behind us all last night on the carriage. He mentioned you by name. He is quite commonly dressed, but he's a gallant gentleman, and exactly like our Signor Carlo. My dearest lady, he'll be company for you while I am absent. May I beckon him to come into the room?'

Vittoria supposed at once that this was a smoothing of the way for the entrance of her lover and her joy. She stood up, letting all her strength go that he might the more justly take her and cherish her. But it was not Carlo who entered. So dead fell her broken hope that her face was repellent with the effort she made to support herself. He said, 'I address the Signorina Vittoria. I am a relative of Countess Ammiani. My name is Angelo Guidascarpi. Last night I was evading the sbirri in this disguise by the private door of La Scala, from which I expected Carlo to come forth. I saw him seized in mistake for me. I jumped up on the empty box-seat behind your carriage. Before we entered the village I let myself down. If I am seen and recognized, I am lost, and great evil will befall Countess Ammiani and her son; but if they are unable to confront Carlo and me, my escape ensures his safety!'

'What can I do?' said Vittoria.

He replied, 'Shall I answer you by telling you what I have done?'

'You need not, signore!'

'Enough that I want to keep a sword fresh for my country. I am at your mercy, signorina; and I am without anxiety. I heard the chasseur saying at the door of La Scala that he had the night-pass for the city gates and orders for the Tyrol. Once in Tyrol I leap into Switzerland. I should have remained in Milan, but nothing will be done there yet, and quiet cities are not homes for me.'

Vittoria began to admit the existence of his likeness to her lover, though it seemed to her a guilty weakness that she should see it.

'Will nothing be done in Milan?' was her first eager question.

'Nothing, signorina, or I should be there, and safe!'

'What, signore, do you require me to help you in?'

'Say that I am your servant.'

'And take you with me?'

'Such is my petition.'

'Is the case very urgent?'

'Hardly more, as regards myself, than a sword lost to Italy if I am discovered. But, signorina, from what Countess Ammiani has told me, I believe that you will some day be my relative likewise. Therefore I appeal not only to a charitable lady, but to one of my own family.'

Vittoria reddened. 'All that I can do I will do.'

Angelo had to assure her that Carlo's release was certain the moment his identity was established. She breathed gladly, saying, 'I wonder at it all very much. I do not know where they are carrying me, but I think I am in friendly hands. I owe you a duty. You will permit me to call you Beppo till our journey ends.'

They were attracted to the windows by a noise of a horseman drawing rein under it, whose imperious shout for the innkeeper betrayed the soldier's habit of exacting prompt obedience from civilians, though there was no military character in his attire. The innkeeper and his wife came out to the summons, and then both made way for the chasseur in attendance on Vittoria. With this man the cavalier conversed.

'Have you had food?' said Vittoria. 'I have some money that will serve for both of us three days. Go, and eat and drink. Pay for us both.'

She gave him her purse. He received it with a grave servitorial bow, and retired.

Soon after the chasseur brought up a message. Herr Johannes requested that he might have the honour of presenting his homage to her: it was imperative that he should see her. She nodded. Her first glance at Herr Johannes assured her of his being one of the officers whom she had seen on the stage last night, and she prepared to act her part. Herr Johannes desired her to recall to mind his introduction to her by the Signor Antonio-Pericles at the house of the maestro Rocco Ricci. 'It is true; pardon me,' said Vittoria.

He informed her that she had surpassed herself at the opera; so much so that he and many other Germans had been completely conquered by her. Hearing, he said, that she was to be pursued, he took horse and galloped all night on the road toward Schloss Sonnenberg, whither, as it had been whispered to him, she was flying, in order to counsel her to lie 'perdu' for a short space, and subsequently to conduct her to the schloss of the amiable duchess. Vittoria thanked him, but stated humbly that she preferred to travel alone. He declared that it was impossible: that she was precious to the world of Art, and must on no account be allowed to run into peril. Vittoria tried to assert her will; she found it unstrung. She thought besides that this disguised officer, with the ill-looking eyes running into one, might easily, since he had heard her, be a devotee of her voice; and it flattered her yet more to imagine him as a capture from the enemy—a vanquished subservient Austrian. She had seen him come on horseback; he had evidently followed her; and he knew what she now understood must be her destination.

Moreover, Laura had underlined 'it is an Austrian who rescues you.' This man perchance was the Austrian. His precise manner of speech demanded an extreme repugnance, if it was to be resisted; Vittoria's reliance upon her own natural fortitude was much too secure for her to encourage the physical revulsions which certain hard faces of men create in the hearts of young women.

'Was all quiet in Milan?' she asked.

'Quiet as a pillow,' he said.

'And will continue to be?'

'Not a doubt of it.'

'Why is there not a doubt of it, signore?'

'You beat us Germans on one field. On the other you have no chance. But you must lose no time. The Croats are on your track. I have ordered out the carriage.'

The mention of the Croats struck her fugitive senses with a panic.

'I must wait for my maid,' she said, attempting to deliberate.

'Ha! you have a maid: of course you have! Where is your maid?'

'She ought to have returned by this time. If not, she is on the road.'

'On the road? Good; we will pick up the maid on the road. We have not a minute to spare. Lady, I am your obsequious servant. Hasten out, I beg of you. I was taught at my school that minutes are not to be wasted. Those Croats have been drinking and what not on the way, or they would have been here before this. You can't rely on Italian innkeepers to conceal you.'

'Signore, are you a man of honour?'

'Illustrious lady, I am.'

She listened simply to the response without giving heed to the prodigality of gesture. The necessity for flight now that Milan was announced as lying quiet, had become her sole thought. Angelo was standing by the carriage.

'What man is this?' said Herr Johannes, frowning.

'He is my servant,' said Vittoria.

'My dear good lady, you told me your servant was a maid. This will never do. We can't have him.'

'Excuse me, signore, I never travel without him.'

'Travel! This is not a case of travelling, but running; and when you run, if you are in earnest about it, you must fling away your baggage and arms.'

Herr Johannes tossed out his moustache to right and left, and stamped his foot. He insisted that the man should be left behind.

'Off, sir! back to Milan, or elsewhere,' he cried.

'Beppo, mount on the box,' said Vittoria.

Her command was instantly obeyed. Herr Johannes looked her in the face. 'You are very decided, my dear lady.' He seemed to have lost his own decision, but handing Vittoria in, he drew a long cigar from his breastpocket, lit it, and mounted beside the coachman. The chasseur had disappeared.

Vittoria entreated that a general look-out should be kept for Giacinta. The road was straight up an ascent, and she had no fear that her maid would not be seen. Presently there was a view of the violet domes of a city. 'Is it Bergamo?—is it Brescia?' she longed to ask, thinking of her Bergamasc and Brescian friends, and of those two places famous for the bravery of their sons: one being especially dear to her, as the birthplace of a genius of melody, whose blood was in her veins. 'Did he look on these mulberry trees?—did he look on these green-grassed valleys?—did he hear these falling waters?' she asked herself, and closed her spirit with reverential thoughts of him and with his music. She saw sadly that they were turning from the city. A little ball of paper was shot into her lap. She opened it and read: 'An officer of the cavalry.—Beppo.' She put her hand out of the window to signify that she was awake to the situation. Her anxiety, however, began to fret. No sight of Giacinta was to be had in any direction. Her mistress commenced chiding the absent garrulous creature, and did so until she pitied her, when she accused herself of cowardice, for she was incapable of calling out to the coachman to stop. The rapid motion subdued such energy as remained to her, and she willingly allowed her hurried feelings to rest on the faces of rocks impending over long ravines, and of perched old castles and white villas and sub-Alpine herds. She burst from the fascination as from a dream, but only to fall into it again, reproaching her weakness, and saying, 'What a thing am I!' When she did make her voice heard by Herr Johannes and the coachman, she was nervous and ashamed, and met the equivocating pacification of the reply with an assent half-way, though she was far from comprehending the consolation she supposed that it was meant to convey. She put out her hand to communicate with Beppo. Another ball of pencilled writing answered to it. She read: 'Keep watch on this Austrian. Your maid is two hours in the rear. Refuse to be separated from me. My life is at your service.—Beppo.'

Vittoria made her final effort to get a resolve of some sort; ending it with a compassionate exclamation over poor Giacinta. The girl could soon find her way back to Milan. On the other hand, the farther from Milan, the less the danger to Carlo's relative, in whom she now perceived a stronger likeness to her lover. She sank back in the carriage and closed her eyes. Though she smiled at the vanity of forcing sleep in this way, sleep came. Her healthy frame seized its natural medicine to rebuild her after the fever of recent days.

She slept till the rocks were purple, and rose-purple mists were in the valleys. The stopping of the carriage aroused her. They were at the threshold of a large wayside hostelry, fronting a slope of forest and a plunging brook. Whitecoats in all attitudes leaned about the door; she beheld the inner court full of them. Herr Johannes was ready to hand her to the ground. He said: 'You have nothing to fear. These fellows are on the march to Cremona. Perhaps it will be better if you are served up in your chamber. You will be called early in the morning.'

She thanked him, and felt grateful. 'Beppo, look to yourself,' she said, and ran to her retirement.

'I fancy that 's about all that you are fit for,' Herr Johannes remarked, with his eyes on the impersonator of Beppo, who bore the scrutiny carelessly, and after seeing that Vittoria had left nothing on the carriage-seats, directed his steps to the kitchen, as became his functions. Herr Johannes beckoned to a Tyrolese maid-servant, of whom Beppo had asked his way. She gave her name as Katchen.

'Katchen, Katchen, my sweet chuck,' said Herr Johannes, 'here are ten florins for you, in silver, if you will get me the handkerchief of that man: you have just stretched your finger out for him.'

According to the common Austrian reckoning of them, Herr Johannes had adopted the right method for ensuring the devotion of the maidens of Tyrol. She responded with an amazed gulp of her mouth and a grimace of acquiescence. Ten florins in silver shortened the migratory term of the mountain girl by full three months. Herr Johannes asked her the hour when the officers in command had supper, and deferred his own meal till that time. Katchen set about earning her money. With any common Beppo it would have been easy enough—simple barter for a harmless kiss. But this Beppo appeared inaccessible; he was so courtly and so reserved; nor is a maiden of Tyrol a particularly skilled seductress. The supper of the officers was smoking on the table when Herr Johannes presented himself among them, and very soon the inn was shaken with an uproar of greeting. Katchen found Beppo listening at the door of the salle. She clapped her hands upon him to drag him away.

'What right have you to be leaning your head there?' she said, and threatened to make his proceedings known. Beppo had no jewel to give, little money to spare. He had just heard Herr Johannes welcomed among the officers by a name that half paralyzed him. 'You shall have anything you ask of me if you will find me out in a couple of hours,' he said. Katchen nodded truce for that period, and saw her home in the Oberinnthal still nearer—twelve mountain goats and a cow her undisputed property. She found him out, though he had strayed through the court of the inn, and down a hanging garden to the borders of a torrent that drenched the air and sounded awfully in the dark ravine below. He embraced her very mildly. 'One scream and you go,' he said; she felt the saving hold of her feet plucked from her, with all the sinking horror, and bit her under lip, as if keeping in the scream with bare stitches. When he released her she was perfectly mastered. 'You do play tricks,' she said, and quaked.

'I play no tricks. Tell me at what hour these soldiers march.'

'At two in the morning.'

'Don't be afraid, silly child: you're safe if you obey me. At what time has our carriage been ordered?'

'At four.'

'Now swear to do this:—rouse my mistress at a quarter past two: bring her down to me.'

'Yes, yes,' said Kitchen, eagerly: 'give me your handkerchief, and she will follow me. I do swear; that I do; by big St. Christopher! who's painted on the walls of our house at home.'

Beppo handed her sweet silver, which played a lively tune for her temporarily—vanished cow and goats. Peering at her features in the starlight, he let her take the handkerchief from his pocket.

'Oh! what have you got in there?' she said.

He laid his finger across her mouth, bidding her return to the house.

'Dear heaven!' Katchen went in murmuring; 'would I have gone out to that soft-looking young man if I had known he was a devil.'

Angelo Guidascarpi was aware that an officer without responsibility never sleeps faster than when his brothers-in-arms have to be obedient to the reveillee. At two in the morning the bugle rang out: many lighted cigars were flashing among the dark passages of the inn; the whitecoats were disposed in marching order; hot coffee was hastily swallowed; the last stragglers from the stables, the outhouses, the court, and the straw beds under roofs of rock, had gathered to the main body. The march set forward. A pair of officers sent a shout up to the drowsy windows, 'Good luck to you, Weisspriess!' Angelo descended from the concealment of the opposite trees, where he had stationed himself to watch the departure. The inn was like a sleeper who has turned over. He made Katchen bring him bread and slices of meat and a flask of wine, which things found a place in his pockets: and paying for his mistress and himself, he awaited Vittoria's foot on the stairs. When Vittoria came she asked no questions, but said to Katchen, 'You may kiss me'; and Kitchen began crying; she believed that they were lovers daring everything for love.

'You have a clear start of an hour and a half. Leave the high-road then, and turn left through the forest and ask for Bormio. If you reach Tyrol, and come to Silz, tell people that you know Katchen Giesslinger, and they will be kind to you.'

So saying, she let them out into the black-eyed starlight.

CHAPTER XXIV

ADVENTURES OF VITTORIA AND ANGELO

Nothing was distinguishable for the flying couple save the high-road winding under rock and forest, and here and there a coursing water in the depths of the ravines, that showed like a vein in black marble. They walked swiftly, keeping brisk ears for sound of hoof or foot behind them. Angelo promised her that she should rest after the morning light had come; but she assured him that she could bear fatigue, and her firm cheerfulness lent his heart vigour. At times they were hooded with the darkness, which came on them as if, as benighted children fancy, their faces were about to meet the shaggy breast of the forest. Rising up to lighter air, they had sight of distant twinklings: it might be city, or autumn weed, or fires of the woodmen, or beacon fires: they glimmered like eyelets to the mystery of the vast unseen land. Innumerable brooks went talking to the night: torrents in seasons of rain, childish voices now, with endless involutions of a song of three notes and a sort of unnoted clanging chorus, as if a little one sang and would sing on through the thumping of a tambourine and bells. Vittoria had these fancies: Angelo had none. He walked like a hunted man whose life is at stake.

'If we reach a village soon we may get some conveyance,' he said.

'I would rather walk than drive,' said Vittoria; 'it keeps me from thinking!'

'There is the dawn, signorina!'

Vittoria frightened him by taking a seat upon a bench of rock; while it was still dark about them, she drew off Camilla's silken shoes and stockings, and stood on bare feet.

'You fancied I was tired,' she said. 'No, I am thrifty; and I want to save as much of my finery as I can. I can go very well on naked feet. These shoes are no protection; they would be worn out in half-a-day, and spoilt for decent wearing in another hour.'

The sight of fair feet upon hard earth troubled Angelo; he excused himself for calling her out to endure hardship; but she said, 'I trust you entirely.' She looked up at the first thin wave of colour while walking.

'You do not know me,' said he.

'You are the Countess Ammiani's nephew.'

'I have, as I had the honour to tell you yesterday, the blood of your lover in my veins.'

'Do not speak of him now, I pray,' said Vittoria; 'I want my strength!

'Signorina, the man we have left behind us is his enemy;—mine. I would rather see you dead than alive in his hands. Do you fear death?'

'Sometimes; when I am half awake,' she confessed. 'I dislike thinking of it.'

He asked her curiously: 'Have you never seen it?'

'Death?' said she, and changed a shudder to a smile; 'I died last night.'

Angelo smiled with her. 'I saw you die!

'It seems a hundred years ago.'

'Or half-a-dozen minutes. The heart counts everything'

'Was I very much liked by the people, Signor Angelo?'

'They love you.'

'I have done them no good.'

'Every possible good. And now, mine is the duty to protect you.'

'And yesterday we were strangers! Signor Angelo, you spoke of sbirri. There is no rising in Bologna. Why are they after you? You look too gentle to give them cause.'

'Do I look gentle? But what I carry is no burden. Who that saw you last night would know you for Camilla? You will hear of my deeds, and judge. We shall soon have men upon the road; you must be hidden. See, there: there are our colours in the sky. Austria cannot wipe them out. Since I was a boy I have always slept in a bed facing East, to keep that truth before my eyes. Black and yellow drop to the earth: green, white, and red mount to heaven. If more of my countrymen saw these meanings!—but they are learning to. My tutor called them Germanisms. If so, I have stolen a jewel from my enemy.'

Vittoria mentioned the Chief.

'Yes,' said Angelo; 'he has taught us to read God's handwriting. I revere him. It's odd; I always fancy I hear his voice from a dungeon, and seeing him looking at one light. He has a fault: he does not comprehend the feelings of a nobleman. Do you think he has made a convert of our Carlo in that? Never! High blood is ineradicable.'

'I am not of high blood,' said Vittoria.

'Countess Ammiani overlooks it. And besides, low blood may be elevated without the intervention of a miracle. You have a noble heart, signorina. It may be the will of God that you should perpetuate our race. All of us save Carlo Ammiani seem to be falling.'

Vittoria bent her head, distressed by a broad beam of sunlight. The country undulating to the plain lay under them, the great Alps above, and much covert on all sides. They entered a forest pathway, following chance for safety. The dark leafage and low green roofing tasted sweeter to their senses than clear air and sky. Dark woods are home to fugitives, and here there was soft footing, a surrounding gentleness,—grass, and moss with dead leaves peacefully flat on it. The birds were not timorous, and when a lizard or a snake slipped away from her feet, it was amusing to Vittoria and did not hurt her tenderness to see that they were feared. Threading on beneath the trees, they wound by a valley's incline, where tumbled stones blocked the course of a green water, and filled the lonely place with one onward voice. When the sun stood over the valley they sat beneath a chestnut tree in a semicircle of orange rock to eat the food which Angelo had procured at the inn. He poured out wine for her in the hollow of a stone, deep as an egg-shell, whereat she sipped, smiling at simple contrivances; but no smile crossed the face of Angelo. He ate and drank to sustain his strength, as a weapon is sharpened; and having done, he gathered up what was left, and lay at her feet with his eyes fixed upon an old grey stone. She, too, sat brooding. The endless babble and noise of the water had hardened the sense of its being a life in that solitude. The floating of a hawk overhead scarce had the character of an animated thing. Angelo turned round to look at her, and looking upward as he lay, his sight was smitten by spots of blood upon one of her torn white feet, that was but half-nestled in the folds of her dress. Bending his head down, like a bird beaking at prey, he kissed the foot passionately. Vittoria's eyelids ran up; a chord seemed to snap within her ears: she stole the shamed foot into concealment, and throbbed, but not fearfully, for Angelo's forehead was on the earth. Clumps of grass, and sharp flint-dust stuck between his fists, which were thrust out stiff on either side of him. She heard him groan heavily. When he raised his face, it was white as madness. Her womanly nature did not shrink from caressing it with a touch of soothing hands.

She chanced to say, 'I am your sister.'

'No, by God! you are not my sister,' cried the young man. 'She died without a stain of blood; a lily from head to foot, and went into the vault so. Our mother will see that. She will kiss the girl in heaven and see that.' He rose, crying louder: 'Are there echoes here?' But his voice beat against the rocks undoubted.

She saw that a frenzy had seized him. He looked with eyes drained of human objects; standing square, with stiff half-dropped arms, and an intense melody of wretchedness in his voice.

'Rinaldo, Rinaldo!' he shouted: 'Clelia!—no answer from man or ghost. She is dead. We two said to her die! and she died. Therefore she is silent, for the dead have not a word. Oh! Milan, Milan! accursed betraying city! I should have found my work in you if you had kept faith. Now here am I, talking to the strangled throat of this place, and can get no answer. Where am I? The world is hollow: the miserable shell! They lied. Battle and slaughter they promised me, and enemies like ripe maize for the reaping-hook. I would have had them in thick to my hands. I would have washed my hands at night, and eaten and drunk and slept, and sung again to work in the morning. They promised me a sword and a sea to plunge it in, and our mother Italy to bless me. I would have toiled: I would have done good in my life. I would have bathed my soul in our colours. I would have had our flag about my body for a winding-sheet, and the fighting angels of God to unroll me. Now here am I, and my own pale mother trying at every turn to get in front of me. Have her away! It's a ghost, I know. She will be touching the strength out of me. She is not the mother I love and I serve. Go: cherish your daughter, you dead woman!'

Angelo reeled. 'A spot of blood has sent me mad,' he said, and caught for a darkness to cross his sight, and fell and lay flat.

Vittoria looked around her; her courage was needed in that long silence.

She adopted his language: 'Our mother Italy is waiting for us. We must travel on, and not be weary. Angelo, my friend, lend me your help over these stones.'

He rose quietly. She laid her elbow on his hand; thus supported she left a place that seemed to shudder. All the heavy day they walked almost silently; she not daring to probe his anguish with a question; and he calm and vacant as the hour following thunder. But, of her safety by his side she had no longer a doubt. She let him gather weeds and grasses, and bind them across her feet, and perform friendly services, sure that nothing earthly could cause such a mental tempest to recur. The considerate observation which at all seasons belongs to true courage told her that it was not madness afflicting Angelo.

Near nightfall they came upon a forester's hut, where they were welcomed by an old man and a little girl, who gave them milk and black bread, and straw to rest on. Angelo slept in the outer air. When Vittoria awoke she had the fancy that she had taken one long dive downward in a well; and on touching the bottom found her head above the surface. While her surprise was wearing off, she beheld the woodman's little girl at her feet holding up one end of her cloak, and peeping underneath, overcome by amazement at the flashing richness of the dress of the heroine Camilla. Entering into the state of her mind spontaneously, Vittoria sought to induce the child to kiss her; but quite vainly. The child's reverence for the dress allowed her only to be within reach of the hem of it, so as to delight her curiosity. Vittoria smiled when, as she sat up, the child fell back against the wall; and as she rose to her feet, the child scampered from the room. 'My poor Camilla! you can charm somebody, yet,' she said, limping; her visage like a broken water with the pain of her feet. 'If the bell rings for Camilla now, what sort of an entry will she make?' Vittoria treated her physical weakness and ailments with this spirit of humour. 'They may say that Michiella has bewitched you, my Camilla. I think your voice would sound as if it were dragging its feet after it just as a stork flies. O my Camilla! don't I wish I could do the same, and be ungraceful and at ease! A moan is married to every note of your treble, my Camilla, like December and May. Keep me from shrieking!'

The pangs shooting from her feet were scarce bearable, but the repression of them helped her to meet Angelo with a freer mind than, after the interval of separation, she would have had. The old woodman was cooking a queer composition of flour and milk sprinkled with salt for them. Angelo cut a stout cloth to encase each of her feet, and bound them in it. He was more cheerful than she had ever seen him, and now first spoke of their destination. His design was to conduct her near to Bormio, there to engage a couple of men in her service who would accompany her to Meran, by the Val di Sole, while he crossed the Stelvio alone, and turning leftward in the Tyrolese valley, tried the passage into Switzerland.

Bormio, if, when they quitted the forest, a conveyance could be obtained, was no more than a short day's distance, according to the old woodman's directions. Vittoria induced the little girl to sit upon her knee, and sang to her, but greatly unspirited the charm of her dress. The sun was rising as they bade adieu to the hut.

About mid-day they quitted the shelter of forest trees and stood on broken ground, without a path to guide them. Vittoria did her best to laugh at her mishaps in walking, and compared herself to a Capuchin pilgrim; but she was unused to going bareheaded and shoeless, and though she held on bravely, the strong beams of the sun and the stony ways warped her strength. She had to check fancies drawn from Arabian tales, concerning the help sometimes given by genii of the air and enchanted birds, that were so incessant and vivid that she found herself sulking at the loneliness and helplessness of the visible sky, and feared that her brain was losing its hold of things. Angelo led her to a half-shaded hollow, where they finished the remainder of yesterday's meat and wine. She set her eyes upon a gold-green lizard by a stone and slept.

'The quantity of sleep I require is unmeasured,' she said, a minute afterwards, according to her reckoning of time, and expected to see the lizard still by the stone. Angelo was near her; the sky was full of colours, and the earth of shadows.

'Another day gone!' she exclaimed in wonderment, thinking that the days of human creatures had grown to be as rapid and (save toward the one end) as meaningless as the gaspings of a fish on dry land. He told her that he had explored the country as far as he had dared to stray from her. He had seen no habitation along the heights. The vale was too distant for strangers to reach it before nightfall. 'We can make a little way on,' said Vittoria, and the trouble of walking began again. He entreated her more than once to have no fear. 'What can I fear?' she asked. His voice sank penitently: 'You can rely on me fully when there is anything to do for you.'

'I am sure of that,' she replied, knowing his allusion to be to his frenzy of yesterday. In truth, no woman could have had a gentler companion.

On the topmost ridge of the heights, looking over an interminable gulf of darkness they saw the lights of the vale. 'A bird might find his perch there, but I think there is no chance for us,' said Vittoria. 'The moment we move forward to them the lights will fly back. It is their way of behaving.'

Angelo glanced round desperately. Farther on along the ridge his eye caught sight of a low smouldering fire. When he reached it he had a great disappointment. A fire in the darkness gives hopes that men will be at hand. Here there was not any human society. The fire crouched on its ashes. It was on a little circular eminence of mossed rock; black sticks, and brushwood, and dry fern, and split logs, pitchy to the touch, lay about; in the centre of them the fire coiled sullenly among its ashes, with a long eye like a serpent's.

'Could you sleep here?' said Angelo.

'Anywhere!' Vittoria sighed with droll dolefulness.

'I can promise to keep you warm, signorina.'

'I will not ask for more till to-morrow, my friend.'

She laid herself down sideways, curling up her feet, with her cheek on the palm of her hand.

Angelo knelt and coaxed the fire, whose appetite, like that which is said to be ours, was fed by eating, for after the red jaws had taken half-a-dozen sticks, it sang out for more, and sent up flame leaping after flame and thick smoke. Vittoria watched the scene through a thin division of her eyelids; the fire, the black abyss of country, the stars, and the sentinel figure. She dozed on the edge of sleep, unable to yield herself to it wholly. She believed that she was dreaming when by-and-by many voices filled her ears. The fire was sounding like an angry sea, and the voices were like the shore, more intelligible, but confused in shriller clamour. She was awakened by Angelo, who knelt on one knee and took her outlying hand; then she saw that men surrounded them, some of whom were hurling the lighted logs about, some trampling down the outer rim of flames. They looked devilish to a first awakening glance. He told her that the men were friendly; they were good Italians. This had been the beacon arranged for the night of the Fifteenth, when no run of signals was seen from Milan; and yesterday afternoon it had been in mockery partially consumed. 'We have aroused the country, signorina, and brought these poor fellows out of their beds. They supposed that Milan must be up and at work. I have explained everything to them.'

Vittoria had rather to receive their excuses than to proffer her own. They were mostly youths dressed like the better class of peasantry. They laughed at the incident, stating how glad they would have been to behold the heights all across the lakes ablaze and promising action for the morrow. One square-shouldered fellow raised her lightly from the ground. She felt herself to be a creature for whom circumstance was busily plotting, so that it was useless to exert her mind in thought. The long procession sank down the darkness, leaving the low red fire to die out behind them.

Next morning she awoke in a warm bed, possessed by odd images of flames that stood up like crowing cocks, and cowered like hens above the brood. She was in the house of one of their new friends, and she could hear Angelo talking in the adjoining room. A conveyance was ready to take her on to Bormio. A woman came to her to tell her this, appearing to have a dull desire to get her gone. She was a draggled woman, with a face of slothful anguish, like one of the inner spectres of a guilty man. She said that her husband was willing to drive the lady to Bormio for a sum that was to be paid at once into his wife's hand; and little enough it was which poor persons could ever look for from your patriots and disturbers who seduced orderly men from their labour, and made widows and ruined households. This was a new Italian language to Vittoria, and when the woman went on giving instances of households ruined by a husband's vile infatuation about his country, she did not attempt to defend the reckless lord, but dressed quickly that she might leave the house as soon as she could. Her stock of money barely satisfied the woman's demand. The woman seized it, and secreted it in her girdle. When they had passed into the sitting-room, her husband, who was sitting conversing with Angelo, stretched out his hand and knocked the girdle.

'That's our trick,' he said. 'I guessed so. Fund up, our little Maria of the dirty fingers'-ends! We accept no money from true patriots. Grub in other ground, my dear!'

The woman stretched her throat awry, and set up a howl like a dog; but her claws came out when he seized her.

'Would you disgrace me, old fowl?'

'Lorenzo, may you rot like a pumpkin!'

The connubial reciprocities were sharp until the money lay on the table, when the woman began whining so miserably that Vittoria's sensitive nerves danced on her face, and at her authoritative interposition, Lorenzo very reluctantly permitted his wife to take what he chose to reckon a fair portion of the money, and also of his contempt. She seemed to be licking the money up, she bent over it so greedily.

'Poor wretch!' he observed; 'she was born on a hired bed.'

Vittoria felt that the recollection of this woman would haunt her. It was inconceivable to her that a handsome young man like Lorenzo should ever have wedded the unsweet creature, who was like a crawling image of decay; but he, as if to account for his taste, said that they had been of a common age once, when he married her; now she had grown old. He repeated that she 'was born on a hired bed.' They saw nothing further of her.

Vittoria's desire was to get to Meran speedily, that she might see her friends, and have tidings of her lover and the city. Those baffled beacon-flames on the heights had become an irritating indicative vision: she thirsted for the history. Lorenzo offered to conduct her over the Tonale Pass into the Val di Sole, or up the Val Furva, by the pass of the Corno dei Tre Signori, into the Val del Monte to Pejo, thence by Cles, or by Bolzano, to Meran. But she required shoeing and refitting; and for other reasons also, she determined to go on to Bormio. She supposed that Angelo had little money, and that in a place such as Bormio sounded to her ears she might possibly obtain the change for the great money-order which the triumph of her singing had won from Antonio-Pericles. In spite of Angelo's appeals to her to hurry on to the end of her journey without tempting chance by a single pause, she resolved to go to Bormio. Lorenzo privately assured her that there were bankers in Bormio. Many bankers, he said, came there from Milan, and that fact she thought sufficient for her purpose. The wanderers parted regretfully. A little chapel, on a hillock off the road, shaded by chestnuts, was pointed out to Lorenzo where to bring a letter for Angelo. Vittoria begged Angelo to wait till he heard from her; and then, with mutual wavings of hands, she was driven out of his sight.

CHAPTER XXV

ACROSS THE MOUNTAINS

After parting from Vittoria, Angelo made his way to an inn, where he ate and drank like a man of the fields, and slept with the power of one from noon till after morning. The innkeeper came up to his room, and, finding him awake, asked him if he was disposed to take a second holiday in bed. Angelo jumped up; as he did so, his stiletto slipped from under his pillow and flashed.

'That's a pretty bit of steel,' said the innkeeper, but could not get a word out of him. It was plain to Angelo that this fellow had suspicions. Angelo had been careful to tie up his clothes in a bundle; there was nothing for the innkeeper to see, save a young man in bed, who had a terrible weapon near his hand, and a look in his eyes of wary indolence that counselled prudent dealings. He went out, and returned a second and a third time, talking more and more confusedly and fretfully; but as he was again going to leave, 'No, no,' said Angelo, determined to give him a lesson, 'I have taken a liking to your company. Here, come here; I will show you a trick. I learnt it from the Servians when I was three feet high. Look; I lie quite still, you observe. Try to get on the other side of that door and the point of this blade shall scratch you through it.'

Angelo laid the blue stilet up his wrist, and slightly curled his arm. 'Try,' he repeated, but the innkeeper had stopped short in his movement to the door. 'Well, then, stay where you are,' said Angelo, 'and look; I'll be as good as my word. There's the point I shall strike.' With that he gave the peculiar Servian jerk of the muscles, from the wrist up to the arm, and the blade quivered on the mark. The innkeeper fell back in admiring horror. 'Now fetch it to me,' said Angelo, putting both hands carelessly under his head. The innkeeper tugged at the blade. 'Illustrious signore, I am afraid of breaking it,' he almost whimpered; 'it seems alive, does it not?'

'Like a hawk on a small bird,' said Angelo; 'that's the beauty of those blades. They kill, and put you to as little pain as a shot; and it 's better than a shot in your breast—there's something to show for it. Send up your wife or your daughter to take orders about my breakfast. It 's the breakfast of five mountaineers; and don't "Illustrious signore" me, sir, either in my hearing or out of it. Leave the knife sticking.'

The innkeeper sidled out with a dumb salute. 'I can count on his discretion for a couple of hours,' Angelo said to himself. He knew the effect of an exhibition of physical dexterity and strength upon a coward. The landlord's daughter came and received his orders for breakfast. Angelo inquired whether they had been visited by Germans of late. The girl told him that a German chasseur with a couple of soldiers had called them up last night.

'Wouldn't it have been a pity if they had dragged me out and shot me?' said Angelo.

'But they were after a lady,' she explained; 'they have gone on to Bormio, and expect to catch her there or in the mountains.'

'Better there than in the mountains, my dear; don't you think so?'

The girl said that she would not like to meet those fellows among the mountains.

'Suppose you were among the mountains, and those fellows came up with you; wouldn't you clap your hands to see me jumping down right in front of you all?' said Angelo.

'Yes, I should,' she admitted. 'What is one man, though!'

'Something, if he feeds like five. Quick! I must eat. Have you a lover?'

'Yes.'

'Fancy you are waiting on him.'

'He's only a middling lover, signore. He lives at Cles, over Val Pejo, in Val di Non, a long way, and courts me twice a year, when he comes over to do carpentering. He cuts very pretty Madonnas. He is a German.'

'Ha! you kneel to the Madonna, and give your lips to a German? Go.'

'But I don't like him much, signore; it's my father who wishes me to have him; he can make money.'

Angelo motioned to her to be gone, saying to himself, 'That father of hers would betray the Saints for a handful of florins.'

He dressed, and wrenched his knife from the door. Hearing the clatter of a horse at the porch, he stopped as he was descending the stairs. A German voice said, 'Sure enough, my jolly landlord, she's there, in Worms—your Bormio. Found her at the big hotel: spoke not a syllable; stole away, stole away. One chopin of wine! I'm off on four legs to the captain. Those lads who are after her by Roveredo and Trent have bad noses. "Poor nose—empty belly." Says the captain, "I stick at the point of the cross-roads." Says I, "Herr Captain, I'm back to you first of the lot." My business is to find the runaway lady-pretty Fraulein! pretty Fraulein! lai-ai! There's money on her servant, too; he's a disguised Excellency—a handsome boy; but he has cut himself loose, and he go hang. Two birds for the pride of the thing; one for satisfaction—I 'm satisfied. I've killed chamois in my time. Jacob, I am; Baumwalder, I am; Feckelwitz, likewise; and the very devil for following a track. Ach! the wine is good. You know the song?

"He who drinks wine, he may cry with a will,
Fortune is mine, may she stick to me still."

I give it you in German—the language of song! my own, my native 'lai-ai-lai-ai-la-la-lai-ai-i-ie!'

"While stars still sit
On mountain tops,
I take my gun,
Kiss little one
On mother's breast.
Ai-iu-e!

"My pipe is lit,
I climb the slopes,
I meet the dawn
A little one
On mother's breast.
Ai-aie: ta-ta-tai: iu-iu-iu-e!"

Another chopin, my jolly landlord. What's that you're mumbling? About the servant of my runaway young lady? He go hang! What——?'

Angelo struck his foot heavily on the stairs; the innkeeper coughed and ran back, bowing to his guest. The chasseur cried, 'I 'll drink farther on-wine between gaps!' A coin chinked on the steps in accompaniment to the chasseur's departing gallop. 'Beast of a Tedesco,' the landlord exclaimed as he picked up the money; 'they do the reckoning—not we. If I had served him with the worth of this, I should have had the bottle at my head. What a country ours is! We're ridden over, ridden over!' Angelo compelled the landlord to sit with him while he ate like five mountaineers. He left mere bones on the table. 'It's wonderful,' said the innkeeper; 'you can't know what fear is.'

'I think I don't,' Angelo replied; 'you do; cowards have to serve every party in turn. Up, and follow at my heels till I dismiss you. You know the pass into the Val Pejo and the Val di Sole.' The innkeeper stood entrenched behind a sturdy negative. Angelo eased him to submission by telling him that he only wanted the way to be pointed out. 'Bring tobacco; you're going to have an idle day,' said Angelo: 'I pay you when we separate.' He was deaf to entreaties and refusals, and began to look mad about the eyes; his poor coward plied him with expostulations, offered his wife, his daughter, half the village, for the service: he had to follow, but would take no cigars. Angelo made his daughter fetch bread and cigars, and put a handful in his pocket, upon which, after two hours of inactivity at the foot of the little chapel, where Angelo waited for the coming of Vittoria's messenger, the innkeeper was glad to close his fist. About noon Lorenzo came, and at once acted a play of eyes for Angelo to perceive his distrust of the man and a multitude of bad things about him he was reluctant, notwithstanding Angelo's ready nod, to bring out a letter; and frowned again, for emphasis to the expressive comedy. The letter said:

'I have fallen upon English friends. They lend me money. Fly to Lugano by the help of these notes: I inclose them, and will not ask pardon for it. The Valtellina is dangerous; the Stelvio we know to be watched. Retrace your way, and then try the Engadine. I should stop on a breaking bridge if I thought my companion, my Carlo's cousin, was near capture. I am well taken care of: one of my dearest friends, a captain in the English army, bears me company across. I have a maid from one of the villages, a willing girl. We ride up to the mountains; to-morrow we cross the pass; there is a glacier. Val di Non sounds Italian, but I am going into the enemy's land. You see I am well guarded. My immediate anxiety concerns you; for what will our Carlo ask of me? Lose not one moment. Away, and do not detain Lorenzo. He has orders to meet us up high in the mountain this evening. He is the best of servants but I always meet the best everywhere—that is, in Italy. Leaving it, I grieve. No news from Milan, except of great confusion there. I judge by the quiet of my sleep that we have come to no harm there.

'Your faithfullest

'VITTORIA.'

Lorenzo and the innkeeper had arrived at an altercation before Angelo finished reading. Angelo checked it, and told Lorenzo to make speed: he sent no message.

'My humanity,' Angelo then addressed his craven associate, 'counsels me that it's better to drag you some distance on than to kill you. You 're a man of intelligence, and you know why I have to consider the matter. I give you guide's pay up to the glacier, and ten florins buon'mano. Would you rather earn it with the blood of a countryman? I can't let that tongue of yours be on the high-road of running Tedeschi: you know it.

'Illustrious signore, obedience oils necessity,' quoth the innkeeper. 'If we had but a few more of my cigars!'

'Step on,' said Angelo sternly.

They walked till dark and they were in keen air. A hut full of recent grass-cuttings, on the border of a sloping wood, sheltered them. The innkeeper moaned for food at night and in the morning, and Angelo tossed him pieces of bread. Beyond the wood they came upon bare crag and commenced a sharper ascent, reached the height, and roused an eagle. The great bird went up with a sharp yelp, hanging over them with knotted claws. Its shadow stretched across sweeps of fresh snow. The innkeeper sent a mocking yelp after the eagle.

'Up here, one forgets one is a father—what's more, a husband,' he said, striking a finger on the side of his nose.

'And a cur, a traitor, carrion,' said Angelo.

'Ah, signore, one might know you were a noble. You can't understand our troubles, who carry a house on our heads, and have to fill mouths agape.'

'Speak when you have better to say,' Angelo replied.

'Padrone, one would really like to have your good opinion; and I'm lean as a wolf for a morsel of flesh. I could part with my buon'mano for a sight of red meat—oh! red meat dripping.'

'If,' cried Angelo, bringing his eyebrows down black on the man, 'if I knew that you had ever in your life betrayed one of us look below; there you should lie to be pecked and gnawed at.'

'Ah, Jacopo Cruchi, what an end for you when you are full of good meanings!' the innkeeper moaned. 'I see your ribs, my poor soul!'

Angelo quitted him. The tremendous excitement of the Alpine solitudes was like a stringent wine to his surcharged spirit. He was one to whom life and death had become as the yes and no of ordinary men: not more than a turning to the right or to the left. It surprised him that this fellow, knowing his own cowardice and his conscience, should consent to live, and care to eat to live.

When he returned to his companion, he found the fellow drinking from the flask of an Austrian soldier. Another whitecoat was lying near. They pressed Angelo to drink, and began to play lubberly pranks. One clapped hands, while another rammed the flask at the reluctant mouth, till Angelo tripped him and made him a subject for derision; whereupon they were all good friends. Musket on shoulder, the soldiers descended, blowing at their finger-nails and puffing at their tobacco—lauter kaiserlicher (rank Imperial), as with a sad enforcement of resignation they had, while lighting, characterized the universally detested Government issue of the leaf.

'They are after her,' said Jacopo, and he shot out his thumb and twisted an eyelid. His looks became insolent, and he added: 'I let them go on; but now, for my part, I must tell you, my worthy gentleman, I've had enough of it. You go your way, I go mine. Pay me, and we part. With the utmost reverence, I quit you. Climbing mountains at my time of life is out of all reason. If you want companions, I 'll signal to that pair of Tedeschi; they're within hail. Would you like it? Say the word, if you would—hey!'

Angelo smiled at the visible effect of the liquor.

'Barto Rizzo would be the man to take you in hand,' he remarked.

The innkeeper flung his head back to ejaculate, and murmured, 'Barto Rizzo! defend me from him! Why, he levies contribution upon us in the Valtellina for the good of Milan; and if we don't pay, we're all of us down in a black book. Disobey, and it's worse than swearing you won't pay taxes to the legitimate—perdition to it!—Government. Do you know Barto Rizzo, padrone? You don't know him, I hope? I'm sure you wouldn't know such a fellow.'

'I am his favourite pupil,' said Angelo.

'I'd have sworn it,' groaned the innkeeper, and cursed the day and hour when Angelo crossed his threshold. That done, he begged permission to be allowed to return, crying with tears of entreaty for mercy: 'Barto Rizzo's pupils are always out upon bloody business!' Angelo told him that he had now an opportunity of earning the approval of Barto Rizzo, and then said, 'On,' and they went in the track of the two whitecoats; the innkeeper murmuring all the while that he wanted the approval of Barto Rizzo as little as his enmity; he wanted neither frost nor fire. The glacier being traversed, they skirted a young stream, and arrived at an inn, where they found the soldiers regaling. Jacopo was informed by them that the lady whom they were pursuing had not passed. They pushed their wine for Angelo to drink: he declined, saying that he had sworn not to drink before he had shot the chamois with the white cross on his back.

'Come: we're two to one,' they said, 'and drink you shall this time!'

'Two to two,' returned Angelo: 'here is my Jacopo, and if he doesn't count for one, I won't call him father-in-law, and the fellow living at Cles may have his daughter without fighting for her.'

'Right so,' said one of the soldiers, 'and you don't speak bad German already.'

'Haven't I served in the ranks?' said Angelo, giving a bugle-call of the reveille of the cavalry.

He got on with them so well that they related the object of their expedition, which was, to catch a runaway young rebel lady and hold her fast down at Cles for the great captain—'unser tuchtiger Hauptmann.'

'Hadn't she a servant, a sort of rascal?' Angelo inquired.

'Right so; she had: but the doe's the buck in this chase.'

Angelo tossed them cigars. The valley was like a tumbled mountain, thick with crags and eminences, through which the river worked strenuously, sinuous in foam, hurrying at the turns. Angelo watched all the ways from a distant height till set of sun. He saw another couple of soldiers meet those two at the inn, and then one pair went up toward the vale-head. It seemed as if Vittoria had disconcerted them by having chosen another route.

'Padrone,' said Jacopo to him abruptly, when they descended to find a resting-place, 'you are, I speak humbly, so like the devil that I must enter into a stipulation with you, before I continue in your company, and take the worst at once. This is going to be the second night of my sleeping away from my wife: I merely mention it. I pinch her, and she beats me, and we are equal. But if you think of making me fight, I tell you I won't. If there was a furnace behind me, I should fall into it rather than run against a bayonet. I 've heard say that the nerves are in the front part of us, and that's where I feel the shock. Now we're on a plain footing. Say that I'm not to fight. I'll be your servant till you release me, but say I 'm not to fight; padrone, say that.'

'I can't say that: I'll say I won't make you fight,' Angelo pacified him by replying. From this moment Jacopo followed him less like a graceless dog pulled by his chain. In fact, with the sense of prospective security, he tasted a luxurious amazement in being moved about by a superior will, wafted from his inn, and paid for witnessing strange incidents. Angelo took care that he was fed well at the place where they slept, but himself ate nothing. Early after dawn they mounted the heights above the road. It was about noon that Angelo discerned a party coming from the pass on foot, consisting of two women and three men. They rested an hour at the village where he had slept overnight; the muskets were a quarter of a mile to the rear of them. When they started afresh, one of the muskets was discharged, and while the echoes were rolling away, a reply to it sounded in the front. Angelo, from his post of observation, could see that Vittoria and her party were marching between two guards, and that she herself must have perceived both the front and rearward couple. Yet she and her party held on their course at an even pace. For a time he kept them clearly in view; but it was tough work along the slopes of crag: presently Jacopo slipped and went down. 'Ah, padrone,' he said: 'I'm done for; leave me.'

'Not though I should have to haul you on my back,' replied Angelo. 'If I do leave you, I must cut out your tongue.'

'Rather than that, I'd go on a sprained ankle,' said Jacopo, and he strove manfully to conquer pain; limping and exclaiming, 'Oh, my little village! Oh, my little inn! When can a man say that he has finished running about the world! The moment he sits, in comes the devil.'

Angelo was obliged to lead him down to the open way, upon which they made slow progress.

'The noble gentleman might let me return—he might trust me now,' Jacopo whimpered.

'The devil trusts nobody,' said Angelo.

'Ah, padrone! there's a crucifix. Let me kneel by that.'

Angelo indulged him. Jacopo knelt by the wayside and prayed for an easy ankle and a snoring pillow and no wakeners. After this he was refreshed. The sun sank; the darkness spread around; the air grew icy. 'Does the Blessed Virgin ever consider what patriots have to endure?' Jacopo muttered to himself, and aroused a rare laugh from Angelo, who seized him under the arm, half-lifting him on. At the inn where they rested, he bathed and bandaged the foot.

'I can't help feeling a kindness to you for it,' said Jacopo.

'I can't afford to leave you behind,' Angelo accounted for his attention.

'Padrone, we've been understanding one another all along by our thumbs. It's that old inn of mine—the taxes! we have to sell our souls to pay the taxes. There's the tongue of the thing. I wouldn't betray you; I wouldn't.'

'I'll try you,' said Angelo, and put him to proof next day, when the soldiers stopped them as they were driving in a cart, and Jacopo swore to them that Angelo was his intended son-in-law.

There was evidently an unusual activity among the gendarmerie of the lower valley, the Val di Non; for Jacopo had to repeat his fable more than once, and Angelo thought it prudent not to make inquiries about travellers. In this valley they were again in summer heat. Summer splendours robed the broken ground. The Val di Non lies toward the sun, banked by the Val di Sole, like the southern lizard under a stone. Chestnut forest and shoulder over shoulder of vineyard, and meadows of marvellous emerald, with here and there central partly-wooded crags, peaked with castle-ruins, and ancestral castles that are still warm homes, and villages dropped among them, and a river bounding and rushing eagerly through the rich enclosure, form the scene, beneath that Italian sun which turns everything to gold. There is a fair breadth to the vale: it enjoys a great oval of sky: the falls of shade are dispersed, dot the hollow range, and are not at noontide a broad curtain passing over from right to left. The sun reigns and also governs in the Val di Non.

'The grape has his full benefit here, padrone,' said Jacopo.

But the place was too populous, and too much subjected to the general eye, to please Angelo. At Cles they were compelled to bear an inspection, and a little comedy occurred. Jacopo, after exhibiting Angelo as his son-in-law, seeing doubts on the soldiers' faces, mentioned the name of the German suitor for his daughter's hand—the carpenter, Johann Spellmann, to whose workshop he requested to be taken. Johann, being one of the odd Germans in the valley, was well known: he was carving wood astride a stool, and stopped his whistling to listen to the soldiers, who took the first word out of Jacopo's mouth, and were convinced, by Johann's droop of the chin, that the tale had some truth in it; and more when Johann yelled at the Valtelline innkeeper to know why, then, he had come to him, if he was prepared to play him false. One of the soldiers said bluntly, that as Angelo's appearance answered to the portrait of a man for whom they were on the lookout, they would, if their countryman liked, take him and give him a dose of marching and imprisonment.

'Ach! that won't make my little Rosetta love me better,' cried Johann, who commenced taking up a string of reproaches against women, and pitched his carving-blade and tools abroad in the wood-dust.

'Well, now, it 's queer you don't want to fight this lad,' said Jacopo; 'he's come to square it with you that way, if you think best.'

Johann spared a remark between his vehement imprecations against the sex to say that he was ready to fight; but his idea of vengeance was directed upon the abstract conception of a faithless womankind. Angelo, by reason of his detestation of Germans, temporarily threw himself into the part he was playing to the extent of despising him. Johann admitted to Jacopo that intervals of six months' duration in a courtship were wide jumps for Love to take.

'Yes; amor! amor!' he exclaimed with extreme dejection; 'I could wait. Well! since you've brought the young man, we'll have it out.'

He stepped before Angelo with bare fists. Jacopo had to interpose. The soldiers backed Johann, who now said to Angelo, 'Since you've come for it, we'll have it out.'

Jacopo had great difficulty in bringing him to see that it was a matter to talk over. Johann swore he would not talk about it, and was ready to fight a dozen Italians, man up man down.

'Bare-fisted?' screamed Jacopo.

'Hey! the old way! Give him knuckles, and break his back, my boy!' cried the soldiers; 'none of their steel this side of the mountain.'

Johann waited for Angelo to lift his hands; and to instigate his reluctant adversary, thumped his chest; but Angelo did not move. The soldiers roared.

'If she has you, she shall have a dolly,' said Johann, now heated with the prospect of presenting that sort of husband to his little Rosetta. At this juncture Jacopo threw himself between them.

'It shall be a real fight,' he said; 'my daughter can't make up her mind, and she shall have the best man. Leave me to arrange it all fairly; and you come here in a couple of hours, my children,' he addressed the soldiers, who unwillingly quitted the scene where there was a certainty of fun, on the assurance of there being a livelier scene to come.

When they had turned their heels on the shop, Jacopo made a face at Johann; Johann swung round upon Angelo, and met a smile. Then followed explanations.

'What's that you say? She's true—she's true?' exclaimed the astounded lover.

'True enough, but a girl at an inn wants hotter courting,' said Jacopo. 'His Excellency here is after his own sweetheart.'

Johann huzzaed, hugged at Angelo's hands, and gave a lusty filial tap to Jacopo on the shoulder. Bread and grapes and Tyrolese wine were placed for them, and Johann's mother soon produced a salad, eggs, and fowl; and then and there declared her willingness to receive Rosetta into the household, 'if she would swear at the outset never to have 'heimweh' (home-longing); as people—men and women, both—always did when they took a new home across a mountain.'

'She won't—will she?' Johann inquired with a dubious sparkle.

'Not she,' said Jacopo.

After the meal he drew Johann aside. They returned to Angelo, and Johann beckoned him to leave the house by a back way, leading up a slope of garden into high vine-poles. He said that he had seen a party pass out of Cles from the inn early, in a light car, on for Meran. The gendarmerie were busy on the road: a mounted officer had dashed up to the inn an hour later, and had followed them: it was the talk of the village.

'Padrone, you dismiss me now,' said Jacopo.

'I pay you, but don't dismiss you,' said Angelo, and handed him a bank-note.

'I stick to you, padrone, till you do dismiss me,' Jacopo sighed.

Johann offered to conduct them as far as the Monte Pallade pass, and they started, avoiding the high road, which was enviably broad and solid. Within view of a village under climbing woods, they discerned an open car, flanked by bayonets, returning to Cles. Angelo rushed ahead of them down the declivity, and stood full in the road to meet the procession. A girl sat in the car, who hung her head, weeping; Lorenzo was beside her; an Englishman on foot gave employment to a pair of soldiers to get him along. As they came near at marching pace, Lorenzo yawned and raised his hand to his cheek, keeping the thumb pointed behind him. Including the girl, there were four prisoners: Vittoria was absent. The Englishman, as he was being propelled forward, addressed Angelo in French, asking him whether he could bear to see an unoffending foreigner treated with wanton violation of law. The soldiers bellowed at their captive, and Angelo sent a stupid shrug after him. They rounded a bend of the road. Angelo tightened the buckle at his waist.

'Now I trust you,' he said to Jacopo. 'Follow the length of five miles over the pass: if you don't see me then, you have your liberty, tongue and all.'

With that he doubled his arms and set forth at a steady run, leaving his companions to speculate on his powers of endurance. They did so complacently enough, until Jacopo backed him for a distance and Johann betted against him, when behold them at intervals taking a sharp trot to keep him in view.

BOOK V

CHAPTER XXVI

THE DUEL IN THE PASS

Meanwhile Captain Weisspriess had not been idle. Standing at a blunt angle of the ways converging upon Vittoria's presumed destination, he had roused up the gendarmerie along the routes to Meran by Trent on one side, and Bormio on the other; and he soon came to the conclusion that she had rejected the valley of the Adige for the Valtelline, whence he supposed that she would be tempted either to cross the Stelvio or one of the passes into Southernmost Tyrol. He was led to think that she would certainly bear upon Switzerland, by a course of reasoning connected with Angelo Guidascarpi, who, fleeing under the cross of blood, might be calculated on to push for the mountains of the Republic; and he might judging by the hazards—conduct the lady thither, to enjoy the fruits of crime and love in security. The captain, when he had discovered Angelo's crest and name on the betraying handkerchief, had no doubts concerning the nature of their intimacy, and he was spurred by a new and thrice eager desire to capture the couple—the criminal for the purposes of justice, and the other because he had pledged his notable reputation in the chase of her. The conscience of this man's vanity was extremely active. He had engaged to conquer the stubborn girl, and he thought it possible that he might take a mistress from the patriot ranks, with a loud ha! ha! at revolutionists, and some triumph over his comrades. And besides, he was the favourite of Countess Anna of Lenkenstein, who yet refused to bring her estates to him; she dared to trifle; she also was a woman who required rude lessons. Weisspriess, a poor soldier bearing the heritage of lusty appetites, had an eye on his fortune, and served neither Mars alone nor Venus. Countess Anna was to be among that company assembled at the Castle of Sonnenberg in Meran; and if, while introducing Vittoria there with a discreet and exciting reserve, he at the same time handed over the assassin of Count Paul, a fine harvest of praise and various pleasant forms of female passion were to be looked for—a rich vista of a month's intrigue; at the end of it possibly his wealthy lady, thoroughly tamed, for a wife, and redoubled triumph over his comrades. Without these successes, what availed the fame of the keenest swordsman in the Austrian army?—The feast as well as the plumes of vanity offered rewards for the able exercise of his wits.

He remained at the sub-Alpine inn until his servant Wilhelm (for whom he had despatched the duchess's chasseur, then in attendance on Vittoria) arrived from Milan, bringing his uniform. The chasseur was directed on the Bormio line, with orders that he should cause the arrest of Vittoria only in the case of her being on the extreme limit of the Swiss frontier. Keeping his communications alert, Weisspriess bore that way to meet him. Fortune smiled on his strategy. Jacob Baumwalder Feckelwitz—full of wine, and discharging hurrahs along the road—met him on the bridge over the roaring Oglio, just out of Edolo, and gave him news of the fugitives. 'Both of them were at the big hotel in Bormio,' said Jacob; 'and I set up a report that the Stelvio was watched; and so it is.' He added that he thought they were going to separate; he had heard something to that effect; he believed that the young lady was bent upon crossing one of the passes to Meran. Last night it had devolved on him to kiss away the tears of the young lady's maid, a Valtelline peasant-girl, who deplored the idea of an expedition over the mountains, and had, with the usual cat-like tendencies of these Italian minxes, torn his cheek in return for his assiduities. Jacob displayed the pretty scratch obtained in the Herr Captain's service, and got his money for having sighted Vittoria and seen double. Weisspriess decided in his mind that Angelo had now separated from her (or rather, she from him) for safety. He thought it very probable that she would likewise fly to Switzerland. Yet, knowing that there was the attraction of many friends for her at Meran, he conceived that he should act more prudently by throwing himself on that line, and he sped Jacob Baumwalder along the Valtelline by Val Viola, up to Ponte in the Engadine, with orders to seize her if he could see her, and have her conveyed to Cles, in Tyrol. Vittoria being only by the gentlest interpretation of her conduct not under interdict, an unscrupulous Imperial officer might in those military times venture to employ the gendarmerie for his own purposes, if he could but give a plausible colour of devotion to the Imperial interests.

The chasseur sped lamentingly back, and Weisspriess, taking a guide from the skirting hamlet above Edolo, quitted the Val Camonica, climbed the Tonale, and reached Vermiglio in the branch valley of that name, scientifically observing the features of the country as he went. At Vermiglio he encountered a brother officer of one of his former regiments, a fat major on a tour of inspection, who happened to be a week behind news of the army, and detained him on the pretext of helping him on his car—a mockery that drove Weisspriess to the perpetual reply, 'You are my superior officer,' which reduced the major to ask him whether he had been degraded a step. As usual, Weisspriess was pushed to assert his haughtiness, backed by the shadow of his sword. 'I am a man with a family,' said the major, modestly. 'Then I shall call you my superior officer while they allow you to remain so,' returned Weisspriess, who scorned a married soldier.

'I aspired to the Staff once myself,' said the major. 'Unfortunately, I grew in girth—the wrong way for ambition. I digest, I assimilate with a fatal ease. Stout men are doomed to the obscurer paths. You may quote Napoleon as a contrary instance. I maintain positively that his day was over, his sun was eclipsed, when his valet had to loosen the buckles of his waistcoat and breech. Now, what do you say?'

'I say,' Weisspriess replied, 'that if there's a further depreciation of the paper currency, we shall none of us have much chance of digesting or assimilating either—if I know at all what those processes mean.'

'Our good Lombard cow is not half squeezed enough,' observed the major, confidentially in tone. 'When she makes a noise—quick! the pail at her udders and work away; that's my advice. What's the verse?— our Zwitterwitz's, I mean; the Viennese poet:—

"Her milk is good-the Lombard cow;
Let her be noisy when she pleases
But if she kicks the pail, I vow,
We'll make her used to sharper squeezes:
We'll write her mighty deeds in CHEESES:
(That is, if she yields milk enow)."

'Capital! capital!' the major applauded his quotation, and went on to speak of 'that Zwitterwitz' as having served in a border regiment, after creating certain Court scandal, and of his carrying off a Wallach lady from her lord and selling her to a Turk, and turning Turk himself and keeping a harem. Five years later he reappeared in Vienna with a volume of what he called 'Black Eagle Poems,' and regained possession of his barony. 'So far, so good,' said the major; 'but when he applied for his old commission in the army—that was rather too cool.'

Weisspriess muttered intelligibly, 'I've heard the remark, that you can't listen to a man five minutes without getting something out of him.'

'I don't know; it may be,' said the major, imagining that Weisspriess demanded some stronger flavours of gossip in his talk. 'There's no stir in these valleys. They arrested, somewhere close on Trent yesterday afternoon, a fellow calling himself Beppo, the servant of an Italian woman—a dancer, I fancy. They're on the lookout for her too, I'm told; though what sort of capers she can be cutting in Tyrol, I can't even guess.'

The major's car was journeying leisurely toward Cles. 'Whip that brute!' Weisspriess sang out to the driver, and begging the major's pardon, requested to know whither he was bound. The major informed him that he hoped to sup in Trent. 'Good heaven! not at this pace,' Weisspriess shouted. But the pace was barely accelerated, and he concealed his reasons for invoking speed. They were late in arriving at Trent, where Weisspriess cast eye on the imprisoned wretch, who declared piteously that he was the trusted and innocent servant of the Signorina Vittoria, and had been visiting all the castles of Meran in search of her. The captain's man Wilhelm had been the one to pounce on poor Beppo while the latter was wandering disconsolately. Leaving him to howl, Weisspriess procured the loan of a horse from a colonel of cavalry at the Buon Consiglio barracks, and mounted an hour before dawn, followed by Wilhelm. He reached Cles in time to learn that Vittoria and her party had passed through it a little in advance of him. Breakfasting there, he enjoyed the first truly calm cigar of many days. Gendarmes whom he had met near the place came in at his heels. They said that the party would positively be arrested, or not allowed to cross the Monte Pallade. The passes to Meran and Botzen, and the road to Trent, were strictly guarded. Weisspriess hurried them forward with particular orders that they should take into custody the whole of the party, excepting the lady; her, if arrested with the others, they were to release: her maid and the three men were to be marched back to Cles, and there kept fast.

The game was now his own: he surveyed its pretty intricate moves as on a map. The character of Herr Johannes he entirely discarded: an Imperial officer in his uniform, sword in belt, could scarcely continue that meek performance. 'But I may admire music, and entreat her to give me a particular note, if she has it,' said the captain, hanging in contemplation over a coming scene, like a quivering hawk about to close its wings. His heart beat thick; which astonished him: hitherto it had never made that sort of movement.

From Cles he despatched a letter to the fair chatelaine at Meran, telling her that by dainty and skilful management of the paces, he was bringing on the intractable heroine of the Fifteenth, and was to be expected in about two or three days. The letter was entrusted to Wilhelm, who took the borrowed horse back to Trent.

Weisspriess was on the mule-track a mile above the last village ascending to the pass, when he observed the party of prisoners, and climbed up into covert. As they went by he discerned but one person in female garments; the necessity to crouch for obscurity prevented him from examining them separately. He counted three men and beheld one of them between gendarmes. 'That must be my villain,' he said.

It was clear that Vittoria had chosen to go forward alone. The captain praised her spirit, and now pushed ahead with hunter's strides. He passed an inn, closed and tenantless: behind him lay the Val di Non; in front the darker valley of the Adige: where was the prey? A storm of rage set in upon him with the fear that he had been befooled. He lit a cigar, to assume ease of aspect, whatever the circumstances might be, and gain some inward serenity by the outer reflection of it—not altogether without success. 'My lady must be a doughty walker,' he thought; 'at this rate she will be in the Ultenthal before sunset.' A wooded height ranged on his left as he descended rapidly. Coming to a roll of grass dotted with grey rock, he climbed it, and mounting one of the boulders, beheld at a distance of half-a-dozen stone-throws downward, the figure of a woman holding her hand cup-shape to a wayside fall of water. The path by which she was going rounded the height he stood on. He sprang over the rocks, catching up his clattering steel scabbard; and plunging through tinted leafage and green underwood, steadied his heels on a sloping bank, and came down on the path with stones and earth and brambles, in time to appear as a seated pedestrian when Vittoria turned the bend of the mountain way.

Gracefully withdrawing the cigar from his mouth, and touching his breast with turned-in fingers, he accosted her with a comical operatic effort at her high notes

'Italia!'

She gathered her arms on her bosom and looked swiftly round: then at the apparition of her enemy.

It is but an ironical form of respect that you offer to the prey you have been hotly chasing and have caught. Weisspriess conceived that he had good reasons for addressing her in the tone best suited to his character: he spoke with a ridiculous mincing suavity:

'My pretty sweet! are you not tired? We have not seen one another for days! Can you have forgotten the enthusiastic Herr Johannes? You have been in pleasant company, no doubt; but I have been all—all alone. Think of that! What an exceedingly fortunate chance this is! I was smoking dolefully, and imagining anything but such a rapture.—No, no, mademoiselle, be mannerly.' The captain blocked her passage. 'You must not leave me while I am speaking. A good governess would have taught you that in the nursery. I am afraid you had an inattentive governess, who did not impress upon you the duty of recognizing friends when you meet them! Ha! you were educated in England, I have heard. Shake hands. It is our custom—I think a better one—to kiss on the right cheek and the left, but we will shake hands.'

'In God's name, sir, let me go on,' Vittoria could just gather voice to utter.

'But,' cried the delighted captain, 'you address me in the tones of a basso profundo! It is absurd. Do you suppose that I am to be deceived by your artifice?—rogue that you are! Don't I know you are a woman? a sweet, an ecstatic, a darling little woman!'

He laughed. She shivered to hear the solitary echoes. There was sunlight on the farthest Adige walls, but damp shade already filled the East-facing hollows.

'I beg you very earnestly, to let me go on,' said Vittoria.

'With equal earnestness, I beg you to let me accompany you,' he replied. 'I mean no offence, mademoiselle; but I have sworn that I and no one but I shall conduct you to the Castle of Sonnenberg, where you will meet the Lenkenstein ladies, with whom I have the honour to be acquainted. You see, you have nothing to fear if you play no foolish pranks, like a kicking filly in the pasture.'

'If it is your pleasure,' she said gravely; but he obtruded the bow of an arm. She drew back. Her first blank despair at sight of the trap she had fallen into, was clearing before her natural high courage.

'My little lady! my precious prima donna! do you refuse the most trifling aid from me? It's because I'm a German.'

'There are many noble gentlemen who are Germans,' said Vittoria.

'It 's because I'm a German; I know it is. But, don't you see, Germany invades Italy, and keeps hold of her? Providence decrees it so—ask the priests! You are a delicious Italian damsel, and you will take the arm of a German.'

Vittoria raised her face. 'Do you mean that I am your prisoner?'

'You did not look braver at La Scala'; the captain bowed to her.

'Ah, I forgot,' said she; 'you saw me there. If, signore, you will do me the favour to conduct me to the nearest inn, I will sing to you.'

'It is precisely my desire, signorina.

You are not married to that man Guidascarpi, I presume? No, no: you are merely his... friend. May I have the felicity of hearing you call me your friend? Why, you tremble! are you afraid of me?'

'To tell the truth, you talk too much to please me,' said Vittoria.

The captain praised her frankness, and he liked it. The trembling of her frame still fascinated his eyes, but her courage and the absence of all womanly play and cowering about her manner impressed him seriously. He stood looking at her, biting his moustache, and trying to provoke her to smile.

'Conduct you to the nearest inn; yes,' he said, as if musing. 'To the nearest inn, where you will sing to me; sing to me. It is not an objectionable scheme. The inns will not be choice: but the society will be exquisite. Say first, I am your sworn cavalier?'

'It does not become me to say that,' she replied, feigning a demure sincerity, on the verge of her patience.

'You allow me to say it?'

She gave him a look of fire and passed him; whereat, following her, he clapped hands, and affected to regard the movement as part of an operatic scene. 'It is now time to draw your dagger,' he said. 'You have one, I'm certain.'

'Anything but touch me!' cried Vittoria, turning on him. 'I know that I am safe. You shall teaze me, if it amuses you.'

'Am I not, now, the object of your detestation?'

'You are near being so.'

'You see! You put on no disguise; why should I?'

This remark struck her with force.

'My temper is foolish,' she said softly. 'I have always been used to kindness.'

He vowed that she had no comprehension of kindness; otherwise would she continue defiant of him? She denied that she was defiant: upon which he accused the hand in her bosom of clutching a dagger. She cast the dagger at his feet. It was nobly done, and he was not insensible to the courage and inspiration of the act; for it checked a little example of a trial of strength that he had thought of exhibiting to an armed damsel.

'Shall I pick it up for you?' he said.

'You will oblige me,' was her answer; but she could not control a convulsion of her underlip that her defensive instinct told her was best hidden.

'Of course, you know you are safe,' he repeated her previous words, while examining the silver handle of the dagger. 'Safe? certainly! Here is C. A. to V.... A. neatly engraved: a gift; so that the young gentleman may be sure the young lady will defend herself from lions and tigers and wild boars, if ever she goes through forests and over mountain passes. I will not obtrude my curiosity, but who is V.... A.?'

The dagger was Carlo's gift to her; the engraver, by singular misadventure, had put a capital letter for the concluding letter of her name instead of little a; she remembered the blush on Carlo's face when she had drawn his attention to the error, and her own blush when she had guessed its meaning.

'It spells my name,' she said.

'Your assumed name of Vittoria. And who is C. A.?'

'Those are the initials of Count Carlo Ammiani.'

'Another lover?'

'He is my sole lover. He is my betrothed. Oh, good God!' she threw her eyes up to heaven; 'how long am I to endure the torture of this man in my pathway? Go, sir, or let me go on. You are intolerable. It 's the spirit of a tiger. I have no fear of you.'

'Nay, nay,' said Weisspriess, 'I asked the question because I am under an obligation to run Count Carlo Ammiani through the body, and felt at once that I should regret the necessity. As to your not fearing me, really, far from wishing to hurt you—'

Vittoria had caught sight of a white face framed in the autumnal forest above her head. So keen was the glad expression of her face, that Weisspriess looked up.

'Come, Angelo, come to me;' she said confidently.

Weisspriess plucked his sword out, and called to him imperiously to descend.

Beckoned downward by white hand and flashing blade, Angelo steadied his feet and hands among drooping chestnut boughs, and bounded to Vittoria's side.

'Now march on,' Weisspriess waved his sword; 'you are my prisoners.'

'You,' retorted Angelo; 'I know you; you are a man marked out for one of us. I bid you turn back, if you care for your body's safety.'

'Angelo Guidascarpi, I also know you. Assassin! you double murderer! Defy me, and I slay you in the sight of your paramour.'

'Captain Weisspriess, what you have spoken merits death. I implore of my Maker that I may not have to kill you.'

'Fool! you are unarmed.'

Angelo took his stilet in his fist.

'I have warned you, Captain Weisspriess. Here I stand. I dare you to advance.'

'You pronounce my name abominably,' said the captain, dropping his sword's point. 'If you think of resisting me, let us have no women looking on.' He waved his left hand at Vittoria.

Angelo urged her to go. 'Step on for our Carlo's sake.' But it was asking too much of her.

'Can you fight this man?' she asked.

'I can fight him and kill him.'

'I will not step on,' she said. 'Must you fight him?'

'There is no choice.' Vittoria walked to a distance at once.

Angelo directed the captain's eyes to where, lower in the pass, there was a level plot of meadow.

Weisspriess nodded. 'The odds are in my favour, so you shall choose the ground.'

All three went silently to the meadow.

It was a circle of green on a projecting shoulder of the mountain, bounded by woods that sank toward the now shadowy South-flowing Adige vale, whose Western heights were gathering red colour above a strongly-marked brown line. Vittoria stood at the border of the wood, leaving the two men to their work. She knew when speech was useless.

Captain Weisspriess paced behind Angelo until the latter stopped short, saying, 'Here!'

'Wherever you please,' Weisspriess responded. 'The ground is of more importance to you than to me.'

They faced mutually; one felt the point of his stilet, the other the temper of his sword.

'Killing you, Angelo Guidascarpi, is the killing of a dog. But there are such things as mad dogs. This is not a duel. It is a righteous execution, since you force me to it: I shall deserve your thanks for saving you from the hangman. I think you have heard that I can use my weapon. There's death on this point for you. Make your peace with your Maker.'

Weisspriess spoke sternly. He delayed the lifting of his sword that the bloody soul might pray.

Angelo said, 'You are a good soldier: you are a bad priest. Come on.'

A nod of magnanimous resignation to the duties of his office was the captain's signal of readiness. He knew exactly the method of fighting which Angelo must adopt, and he saw that his adversary was supple, and sinewy, and very keen of eye. But, what can well compensate for even one additional inch of steel? A superior weapon wielded by a trained wrist in perfect coolness means victory, by every reasonable reckoning. In the present instance, it meant nothing other than an execution, as he had said. His contemplation of his own actual share in the performance was nevertheless unpleasant; and it was but half willingly that he straightened out his sword and then doubled his arm. He lessened the odds in his favour considerably by his too accurate estimation of them. He was also a little unmanned by the thought that a woman was to see him using his advantage; but she stood firm in her distant corner, refusing to be waved out of sight. Weisspriess had again to assure himself that it was not a duel, but the enforced execution of a criminal who would not surrender, and who was in his way. Fronting a creature that would vainly assail him, and temporarily escape impalement by bounding and springing, dodging and backing, now here now there, like a dangling bob-cherry, his military gorge rose with a sickness of disgust. He had to remember as vividly as he could realize it, that this man's life was forfeited, and that the slaughter of him was a worthy service to Countess Anna; also, that there were present reasons for desiring to be quit of him. He gave Angelo two thrusts, and bled him. The skill which warded off the more vicious one aroused his admiration.

'Pardon my blundering,' he said; 'I have never engaged a saltimbanque before.'

They recommenced. Weisspriess began to weigh the sagacity of his opponent's choice of open ground, where he could lengthen the discourse of steel by retreating and retreating, and swinging easily to right or to left. In the narrow track the sword would have transfixed him after a single feint. He was amused. Much of the cat was in his combative nature. An idea of disabling or dismembering Angelo, and forwarding him to Meran, caused him to trifle further with the edge of the blade. Angelo took a cut, and turned it on his arm; free of the deadly point, he rushed in and delivered a stab; but Weisspriess saved his breast. Quick, they resumed their former positions.

'I am really so unused to this game!' said Weisspriess, apologetically.

He was pale: his unsteady breathing, and a deflection of his dripping sword-wrist, belied his coolness. Angelo plunged full on him, dropped, and again reached his right arm; they hung, getting blood for blood, with blazing interpenetrating eyes; a ghastly work of dark hands at half lock thrusting, and savage eyes reading the fiery pages of the book of hell. At last the Austrian got loose from the lock and hurled him off.

'That bout was hotter,' he remarked; and kept his sword-point out on the whole length of the arm: he would have scorned another for so miserable a form either of attack or defence.

Vittoria beheld Angelo circling round the point, which met him everywhere; like the minute hand of a clock about to sound his hour, she thought.

He let fall both his arms, as if beaten, which brought on the attack: by sheer evasion he got away from the sword's lunge, and essayed a second trial of the bite of steel at close quarters; but the Austrian backed and kept him to the point, darting short alluring thrusts, thinking to tempt him on, or to wind him, and then to have him. Weisspriess was chilled by a more curious revulsion from this sort of engagement than he at first experienced. He had become nervously incapable of those proper niceties of sword-play which, without any indecent hacking or maiming, should have stretched Angelo, neatly slain, on the mat of green, before he had a chance. Even now the sight of the man was distressing to an honourable duellist. Angelo was scored with blood-marks. Feeling that he dared not offer another chance to a fellow so desperately close-dealing, Weisspriess thrust fiercely, but delayed his fatal stroke. Angelo stooped and pulled up a handful of grass and soft earth in his left hand.

'We have been longer about it than I expected,' said Weisspriess.

Angelo tightened his fingers about the stringy grasstuft; he stood like a dreamer, leaning over to the sword; suddenly he sprang on it, received the point right in his side, sprang on it again, and seized it in his hand, and tossed it up, and threw it square out in time to burst within guard and strike his stilet below the Austrian's collar-bone. The blade took a glut of blood, as when the wolf tears quick at dripping flesh. It was at a moment when Weisspriess was courteously bantering him with the question whether he was ready, meaning that the affirmative should open the gates of death to him.

The stilet struck thrice. Weisspriess tottered, and hung his jaw like a man at a spectre: amazement was on his features.

'Remember Broncini and young Branciani!'

Angelo spoke no other words throughout the combat.

Weisspriess threw himself forward on a feeble lunge of his sword, and let the point sink in the ground, as a palsied cripple supports his frame, swayed, and called to Angelo to come on, and try another stroke, another—one more! He fell in a lump: his look of amazement was surmounted by a strong frown.

His enemy was hanging above him panting out of wide nostrils, like a hunter's horse above the long-tongued quarry, when Vittoria came to them.

She reached her strength to the wounded man to turn his face to heaven.

He moaned, 'Finish me'; and, as he lay with his back to earth, 'Good-evening to the old army!'

A vision of leaping tumbrils, and long marching columns about to deploy, passed before his eyelids: he thought he had fallen on the battle-field, and heard a drum beat furiously in the back of his head; and on streamed the cavalry, wonderfully caught away to such a distance that the figures were all diminutive, and the regimental colours swam in smoke, and the enemy danced a plume here and there out of the sea, while his mother and a forgotten Viennese girl gazed at him with exactly the same unfamiliar countenance, and refused to hear that they were unintelligible in the roaring of guns and floods and hurrahs, and the thumping of the tremendous big drum behind his head—'somewhere in the middle of the earth': he tried to explain the locality of that terrible drumming noise to them, and Vittoria conceived him to be delirious; but he knew that he was sensible; he knew her and Angelo and the mountain-pass, and that he had a cigar-case in his pocket worked in embroidery of crimson, blue, and gold, by the hands of Countess Anna. He said distinctly that he desired the cigar-case to be delivered to Countess Anna at the Castle of Sonnenberg, and rejoiced on being assured that his wish was comprehended and should be fulfilled; but the marvel was, that his mother should still refuse to give him wine, and suppose him to be a boy: and when he was so thirsty and dry-lipped that though Mina was bending over him, just fresh from Mariazell, he had not the heart to kiss her or lift an arm to her!—His horse was off with him-whither?—He was going down with a company of infantry in the Gulf of Venice: cards were in his hands, visible, though he could not feel them, and as the vessel settled for the black plunge, the cards flushed all honours, and his mother shook her head at him: he sank, and heard Mina sighing all the length of the water to the bottom, which grated and gave him two horrid shocks of pain: and he cried for a doctor, and admitted that his horse had managed to throw him; but wine was the cure, brandy was the cure, or water, water! Water was sprinkled on his forehead and put to his lips.

He thanked Vittoria by name, and imagined himself that General, serving under old Wurmser, of whom the tale is told that being shot and lying grievously wounded on the harsh Rivoli ground, he obtained the help of a French officer in as bad case as himself, to moisten his black tongue and write a short testamentary document with his blood, and for a way of returning thanks to the Frenchman, he put down among others, the name of his friendly enemy's widow; whereupon both resigned their hearts to death; but the Austrian survived to find the sad widow and espouse her.

His mutterings were full of gratitude, showing a vividly transient impression to what was about him, that vanished in a narrow-headed flight through clouds into lands of memory. It pained him, he said, that he could not offer her marriage; but he requested that when his chin was shaved his moustache should be brushed up out of the way of the clippers, for he and all his family were conspicuous for the immense amount of life which they had in them, and his father had lain six-and-thirty hours bleeding on the field of Wagram, and had yet survived to beget a race as hearty as himself:—'Old Austria! thou grand old Austria!'

The smile was proud, though faint, which accompanied the apostrophe, addressed either to his country or to his father's personification of it; it was inexpressibly pathetic to Vittoria, who understood his 'Oesterreich,' and saw the weak and helpless bleeding man, with his eyeballs working under the lids, and the palms of his hands stretched out open-weak as a corpse, but conquering death.

The arrival of Jacopo and Johann furnished help to carry him onward to the nearest place of shelter. Angelo would not quit her side until he had given money and directions to both the trembling fellows, together with his name, that they might declare the author of the deed at once if questioned. He then bowed to Vittoria slightly and fled. They did not speak.

The last sunbeams burned full crimson on the heights of the Adige mountains as Vittoria followed the two pale men who bore the wounded officer between them at a slow pace for the nearest village in the descent of the pass.

Angelo watched them out of sight. The far-off red rocks spun round his eyeballs; the meadow was a whirling thread of green; the brown earth heaved up to him. He felt that he was diving, and had the thought that there was but water enough to moisten his red hands when his senses left him.

CHAPTER XXVII

A NEW ORDEAL

The old city of Meran faces Southward to the yellow hills of Italy, across a broad vale, between two mountain-walls and torrent-waters. With one hand it takes the bounding green Passeyr, and with the other the brown-rolling Adige, and plunges them together in roaring foam under the shadow of the Western wall. It stands on the spur of a lower central eminence crowned by a grey castle, and the sun has it from every aspect. The shape of a swan in water may describe its position, for the Vintschgau and the stony Passeyrthal make a strong curve on two sides as they descend upon it with their rivers, and the bosom of the city projects, while the head appears bending gracefully backward. Many castles are in view of it; the loud and tameless Passeyr girdles it with an emerald cincture; there is a sea of arched vineyard foliage at his feet.

Vittoria reached the Castle of Sonnenberg about noon, and found empty courts and open doors. She sat in the hall like a supplicant, disregarded by the German domestics, who beheld a travel-stained humble-faced young Italian woman, and supposed that their duty was done in permitting her to rest; but the duchess's maid Aennchen happening to come by, questioned her in moderately intelligible Italian, and hearing her name gave a cry, and said that all the company were out hunting, shooting, and riding, in the vale below or the mountain above. "Ah, dearest lady, what a fright we have all been in about you! Signora Piaveni has not slept a wink, and the English gentleman has made great excursions every day to find you. This morning the soldier Wilhelm arrived with news that his master was bringing you on."

Vittoria heard that Laura and her sister and the duchess had gone down to Meran. Countess Lena von Lenkenstein was riding to see her betrothed shoot on a neighbouring estate. Countess Anna had disappeared early, none knew where. Both these ladies, and their sister-in-law, were in mourning for the terrible death of their brother, Count Paul Aennchen repeated what she knew of the tale concerning him.

The desire to see Laura first, and be embraced and counselled by her, and lie awhile in her arms to get a breath of home, made Vittoria refuse to go up to her chamber, and notwithstanding Aennchen's persuasions, she left the castle, and went out and sat in the shaded cart-track. On the winding ascent she saw a lady in a black riding habit, leading her horse and talking to a soldier, who seemed to be receiving orders from her, and presently saluted and turned his steps downward. The lady came on, and passed her without a glance. After entering the courtyard, where she left her horse, she reappeared, and stood hesitating, but came up to Vittoria and said bluntly, in Italian:

"Are you the signorina Campa, or Belloni, who is expected here?"

The Austrian character and colouring of her features told Vittoria that this must be the Countess Anna or her sister.

"I think I have been expected," she replied.

"You come alone?"

"I am alone."

"I am Countess Anna von Lenkenstein; one of the guests of the castle."

"My message is to the Countess Anna."

"You have a message?"

Vittoria lifted the embroidered cigar-case. Countess Anna snatched it from her hand.

"What does this mean? Is it insolence? Have the kindness, if you please, not to address me in enigmas. Do you"—Anna was deadly pale as she turned the cigarcase from side to side—"do you imagine that I smoke, 'par hasard?'" She tried to laugh off her intemperate manner of speech; the laugh broke at sight of a blood-mark on one corner of the case; she started and said earnestly, "I beg you to let me hear what the meaning of this may be?"

"He lies in the Ultenthal, wounded; and his wish was that I should deliver it to you." Vittoria spoke as gently as the harsh tidings would allow.

"Wounded? My God! my God!" Anna cried in her own language. "Wounded?-in the breast, then! He carried it in his breast. Wounded by what? by what?"

"I can tell you no more."

"Wounded by whom?"

"It was an honourable duel."

"Are you afraid to tell me he has been assassinated?"

"It was an honourable duel."

"None could match him with the sword."

"His enemy had nothing but a dagger."

"Who was his enemy?"

"It is no secret, but I must leave him to say."

"You were a witness of the fight?"

"I saw it all."

"The man was one of your party!

"Ah!" exclaimed Vittoria, "lose no time with me, Countess Anna, go to him at once, for though he lived when I left him, he was bleeding; I cannot say that he was not dying, and he has not a friend near."

Anna murmured like one overborne by calamity. "My brother struck down one day—he the next!" She covered her face a moment, and unclosed it to explain that she wept for her brother, who had been murdered, stabbed in Bologna.

"Was it Count Ammiani who did this?" she asked passionately.

Vittoria shook her head; she was divining a dreadful thing in relation to the death of Count Paul.

"It was not?" said Anna. "They had a misunderstanding, I know. But you tell me the man fought with a dagger. It could not be Count Ammiani. The dagger is an assassin's weapon, and there are men of honour in Italy still."

She called to a servant in the castle-yard, and sent him down with orders to stop the soldier Wilhelm.

"We heard this morning that you were coming, and we thought it curious," she observed; and called again for her horse to be saddled. "How far is this place where he is lying? I have no knowledge of the Ultenthal. Has he a doctor attending him? When was he wounded? It is but common humanity to see that he is attended by an efficient doctor. My nerves are unstrung by the recent blow to our family; that is why—Oh, my father! my holy father!" she turned to a grey priest's head that was rising up the ascent, "I thank God for you! Lena is away riding; she weeps constantly when she is within four walls. Come in and give me tears, if you can; I am half mad for the want of them. Tears first; teach me patience after."

The old priest fanned his face with his curled hat, and raised one hand as he uttered a gentle chiding in reproof of curbless human sorrow. Anna said to Vittoria, coldly, "I thank you for your message:" she walked into the castle by his side, and said to him there: "The woman you saw outside has a guilty conscience. You will spend your time more profitably with her than with me. I am past all religious duties at this moment. You know, father, that I can open my heart. Probe this Italian woman; search her through and through. I believe her to be blood-stained and abominable. She hates us. She has sworn an oath against us. She is malignant."

It was not long before Anna issued forth and rode down to the vale. The priest beckoned to Vittoria from the gates. He really supposed her to have come to him with a burdened spirit.

"My daughter," he addressed her. The chapter on human error was opened: "We are all of one family—all of us erring children—all of us bound to abnegate hatred: by love alone are we saved. Behold the Image of Love—the Virgin and Child. Alas! and has it been visible to man these more than eighteen hundred years, and humankind are still blind to it? Are their ways the ways of comfort and blessedness? Their ways are the ways of blood; paths to eternal misery among howling fiends. Why have they not chosen the sweet ways of peace, which are strewn with flowers, which flow with milk?"—The priest spread his hand open for Vittoria's, which she gave to his keeping, and he enclosed it softly, smoothing it with his palms, and retaining it as a worldly oyster between spiritual shells. "Why, my daughter, why, but because we do not bow to that Image daily, nightly, hourly, momently! We do not worship it that its seed may be sown in us. We do not cling to it, that in return it may cling to us."

He spoke with that sensuous resource of rich feeling which the contemplation of the Image does inspire. And Vittoria was not led reluctantly into the oratory of the castle to pray with him; but she refused to confess. Thereupon followed a soft discussion that was as near being acerb as nails are near velvet paws.

Vittoria perceived his drift, and also the dear good heart of the old man, who meant no harm to her, and believed that he was making use of his professional weapons for her ultimate good. The inquisitions and the kindness went musically together; she responded to the kindness, but rebutted the inquisitions; at which he permitted a shade of discontent to traverse his features, and asked her with immense tenderness whether she had not much on her mind; she expressing melodious gratitude for his endeavours to give her comfort. He could not forbear directing an admonishment to her stubborn spirit, and was obliged, for the sake of impressiveness, to speak it harshly; until he saw, that without sweetness of manner and unction of speech, he left her untouched; so he was driven back to the form of address better suited to his nature and habits; the end of which was that both were cooing.

Vittoria was ashamed to tell herself how much she liked him and his ghostly brethren, whose preaching was always of peace, while the world was full of lurid hatred, strife, and division. She begged the baffled old man to keep her hand in his. He talked in Latinized Italian, and only appeared to miss the exact meaning of her replies when his examination of the state of her soul was resumed. They sat in the soft colour of the consecrated place like two who were shut away from earth. Often he thought that her tears were about to start and bring her low; for she sighed heavily; at the mere indication of the displacement of her hand, she looked at him eagerly, as if entreating him not to let it drop.

"You are a German, father?" she said.

"I am of German birth, my daughter."

"That makes it better. Remain beside me. The silence is sweet music."

The silence was broken at intervals by his murmur of a call for patience! patience!

This strange scene concluded with the entry of the duchess, who retired partly as soon as she saw them. Vittoria smiled to the old man, and left him: the duchess gave her a hushed welcome, and took her place. Vittoria was soon in Laura's arms, where, after a storm of grief, she related the events of the journey following her flight from Milan. Laura interrupted her but once to exclaim, "Angelo Guidascarpi!" Vittoria then heard from her briefly that Milan was quiet, Carlo Ammiani in prison. It had been for tidings of her lover that she had hastened over the mountains to Meran. She craved for all that could be told of him, but Laura repeated, as in a stupefaction, "Angelo Guidascarpi!" She answered Vittoria's question by saying, "You could not have had so fatal a companion."

"I could not have had so devoted a protector."

"There is such a thing as an evil star. We are all under it at present, to some degree; but he has been under it from his birth. My Sandra, my beloved, I think I have pardoned you, if I ever pardon anyone! I doubt it; but it is certain that I love you. You have seen Countess Anna, or I would have told you to rest and get over your fatigue. The Lenkensteins are here—my poor sister among them. You must show yourself. I was provident enough to call at your mother's for a box of your clothes before I ran out of wretched Milan."

Further, the signora stated that Carlo might have to remain in prison. She made no attempt to give dark or fair colour to the misery of the situation; telling Vittoria to lie on her bed and sleep, if sleep could be persuaded to visit her, she went out to consult with the duchess. Vittoria lay like a dead body on the bed, counting the throbs of her heart. It helped her to fall into a state of insensibility. When she awoke, the room was dark; she felt that some one had put a silken cushion across her limbs. The noise of a storm traversing the vale rang through the castle, and in the desolation of her soul, that stealthy act of kindness wrought in her till she almost fashioned a vow upon her lips that she would leave the world to toss its wrecks, and dedicate her life to God.

For, O heaven! of what avail is human effort? She thought of the Chief, whose life was stainless, but who stood proscribed because his aim was too high to be attained within compass of a mortal's years. His error seemed that he had ever aimed at all. He seemed less wise than the old priest of the oratory. She could not disentangle him from her own profound humiliation and sense of fallen power. Her lover's imprisonment accused her of some monstrous culpability, which she felt unrepentingly, not as we feel a truth, but as we submit to a terrible force of pressure.

The morning light made her realize Carlo's fate, to whom it would penetrate through a hideous barred loophole—a defaced and dreadful beam. She asked herself why she had fled from Milan. It must have been some cowardly instinct that had prompted her to fly. "Coward, coward! thing of vanity! you, a mere woman!" she cried out, and succeeded in despising herself sufficiently to think it possible that she had deserved to forfeit her lover's esteem.

It was still early when the duchess's maid came to her, bringing word that her mistress would be glad to visit her. From the duchess Vittoria heard of the charge against Angelo. Respecting Captain Weisspriess, Amalia said that she had perceived his object in wishing to bring the great cantatrice to the castle; and that it was a well-devised audacious scheme to subdue Countess Anna:—"We Austrians also can be jealous. The difference between us is, that it makes us tender, and you Italians savage." She asked pointedly for an affirmative, that Vittoria was glad to reply with, when she said: "Captain Weisspriess was perfectly respectful to you?" She spoke comforting words of Carlo Ammiani, whom she hoped to see released as soon as the excitement had subsided. The chief comfort she gave was by saying that he had been originally arrested in mistake for his cousin Angelo.

"I will confide what is now my difficulty here frankly to you," said the duchess. "The Lenkensteins are my guests; I thought it better to bring them here. Angelo Guidascarpi has slain their brother—a base deed! It does not affect you in my eyes; you can understand that in theirs it does. Your being present—Laura has told me everything—at the duel, or fight, between that young man and Captain Weisspriess, will make you appear as his accomplice—at least, to Anna it will; she is the most unreasoning, the most implacable of women. She returned from the Ultenthal last night, and goes there this morning, which is a sign that Captain Weisspriess lives. I should be sorry if we lost so good an officer. As she is going to take Father Bernardus with her, it is possible that the wound is serious. Do you know you have mystified the worthy man exceedingly? What tempted you to inform him that your conscience was heavily burdened, at the same time that you refused to confess?"

"Surely he has been deluded about me," said Vittoria.

"I do but tell you his state of mind in regard to you," the duchess pursued. "Under all the circumstances, this is what I have to ask: you are my Laura's guest, therefore the guest of my heart. There is another one here, an Englishman, a Mr. Powys; and also Lieutenant Pierson, whom, naughty rebel that you are, you have been the means of bringing into disgrace; naturally you would wish to see them: but my request is, that you should keep to these rooms for two or three days: the Lenkensteins will then be gone. They can hardly reproach me for retaining an invalid. If you go down among them, it will be a cruel meeting."

Vittoria thankfully consented to the arrangement. They agreed to act in accordance with it.

The signora was a late riser. The duchess had come on a second visit to Vittoria when Laura joined them, and hearing of the arrangement, spurned the notion of playing craven before the Lenkensteins, who, she said, might think as it pleased them to think, but were never to suppose that there was any fear of confronting them. "And now, at this very moment, when they have their triumph, and are laughing over Viennese squibs at her, she has an idea of hiding her head—she hangs out the white flag! It can't be. We go or we stay; but if we stay, the truth is that we are too poor to allow our enemies to think poorly of us. You, Amalia, are victorious, and you may snap your fingers at opinion. It is a luxury we cannot afford. Besides, I wish her to see my sister and make acquaintance with the Austrianized-Italian—such a wonder as is nowhere to be seen out of the Serabiglione and in the Lenkenstein family. Marriage is, indeed, a tremendous transformation. Bianca was once declared to be very like me."

The brow-beaten duchess replied to the outburst that she had considered it right to propose the scheme for Vittoria's seclusion on account of the Guidascarpi.

"Even if that were a good reason, there are better on the other side," said Laura; adding, with many little backward tosses of the head, "That story has to be related in full before I denounce Angelo and Rinaldo."

"It cannot be denied that they are assassins," returned the duchess.

"It cannot be denied that they have killed one man or more. For you, Justice drops from the bough: we have to climb and risk our necks for it. Angelo stood to defend my darling here. Shall she be ashamed of him?"

"You will never persuade me to tolerate assassination," said the duchess colouring.

"Never, never; I shall never persuade you; never persuade—never attempt to persuade any foreigner that we can be driven to extremes where their laws do not apply to us—are not good for us—goad a subjected people till their madness is pardonable. Nor shall I dream of persuading you that Angelo did right in defending her from that man."

"I maintain that there are laws applicable to all human creatures," said the duchess. "You astonish me when you speak compassionately of such a criminal."

"No; not of such a criminal, of such an unfortunate youth, and my countryman, when every hand is turned against him, and all tongues are reviling him. But let Angelo pass; I pray to heaven he may escape. All who are worth anything in our country are strained in every fibre, and it's my trick to be half in love with anyone of them when he is persecuted. I fancy he is worth more than the others, and is simply luckless. You must make allowances for us, Amalia—pity captive Judah!"

"I think, my Laura, you will never be satisfied till I have ceased to be Babylonian," said the duchess, smiling and fondling Vittoria, to whom she said, "Am I not a complaisant German?"

Vittoria replied gently, "If they were like you!"

"Yes, if they were like the duchess," said Laura, "nothing would be left for us then but to hate ourselves. Fortunately, we deal with brutes."

She was quite pitiless in prompting Vittoria to hasten down, and marvelled at the evident reluctance in doing this slight duty, of one whose courage she had recently seen rise so high. Vittoria was equally amazed by her want of sympathy, which was positive coldness, and her disregard for the sentiments of her hostess. She dressed hesitatingly, responding with forlorn eyes to Laura's imperious "Come." When at last she was ready to descend, Laura took her dawn, full of battle. The duchess had gone in advance to keep the peace.

The ladies of the Lenkenstein family were standing at one window of the morning room conversing. Apart from them, Merthyr Powys and Wilfrid were examining one of the cumbrous antique arms ranged along the wall. The former of these old English friends stepped up to Vittoria quickly and kissed her forehead. Wilfrid hung behind him; he made a poor show of indifference, stammered English and reddened; remembering that he was under observation he recovered wonderfully, and asked, like a patron, "How is the voice?" which would have been foolish enough to Vittoria's more attentive hearing. She thanked him for the service he had rendered her at La Scala. Countess Lena, who looked hard at both, saw nothing to waken one jealous throb.

"Bianca, you expressed a wish to give a salute to my eldest daughter," said Laura.

The Countess of Lenkenstein turned her head. "Have I done so?"

"It is my duty to introduce her," interposed the duchess, and conducted the ceremony with a show of its embracing these ladies, neither one of whom changed her cold gaze.

Careful that no pause should follow, she commenced chatting to the ladies and gentlemen alternately, keeping Vittoria under her peculiar charge. Merthyr alone seconded her efforts to weave the web of converse, which is an armistice if not a treaty on these occasions.

"Have you any fresh caricatures from Vienna?" Laura continued to address her sister.

"None have reached me," said the neutral countess.

"Have they finished laughing?"

"I cannot tell."

"At any rate, we sing still," Laura smiled to Vittoria. "You shall hear us after breakfast. I regret excessively that you were not in Milan on the Fifteenth. We will make amends to you as much as possible. You shall hear us after breakfast. You will sing to please my sister, Sandra mia, will you not?"

Vittoria shook her head. Like those who have become passive, she read faces—the duchess's imploring looks thrown from time to time to the Lenkenstein ladies, Wilfrid's oppressed forehead, the resolute neutrality of the countess—and she was not only incapable of seconding Laura's aggressive war, but shrank from the involvement and sickened at the indelicacy. Anna's eyes were fixed on her and filled her with dread lest she should be resolving to demand a private interview.

"You refuse to sing?" said Laura; and under her breath, "When I bid you not, you insist!"

"Can she possibly sing before she grows accustomed to the air of the place?" said the duchess.

Merthyr gravely prescribed a week's diet on grapes antecedent to the issuing of a note. "Have you never heard what a sustained grape-diet will do for the bullfinches?"

"Never," exclaimed the duchess. "Is that the secret of their German education?"

"Apparently, for we cannot raise them to the same pitch of perfection in England."

"I will try it upon mine. Every morning they shall have two big bunches."

"Fresh plucked, and with the first sunlight on them. Be careful of the rules."

Wilfrid remarked, "To make them exhibit the results, you withdraw the benefit suddenly, of course?"

"We imitate the general run of Fortune's gifts as much as we can," said Merthyr.

"That is the training for little shrill parrots: we have none in Italy," Laura sighed, mock dolefully; "I fear the system would fail among us."

"It certainly would not build Como villas," said Lena.

Laura cast sharp eyes on her pretty face.

"It is adapted for caged voices that are required to chirrup to tickle the ears of boors."

Anna said to the duchess: "I hope your little birds are all well this morning."

"Come to them presently with me and let our ears be tickled," the duchess laughed in answer; and the spiked dialogue broke, not to revive.

The duchess had observed the constant direction of Anna's eyes upon Vittoria during the repast, and looked an interrogation at Anna, who replied to it firmly. "I must be present," the duchess whispered.

She drew Vittoria away by the hand, telling Merthyr Powys that it was unkind to him, but that he should be permitted to claim his fair friend from noon to the dinner-bell.

Laura and Bianca were discussing the same subject as the one for which Anna desired an interview with Vittoria. It was to know the conditions and cause of the duel between Angelo Guidascarpi and Captain Weisspriess, and whither Angelo had fled. "In other words, you cry for vengeance under the name of justice," Laura phrased it, and put up a prayer for Angelo's escape.

The countess rebuked her. "It is men like Angelo who are a scandal to Italy."

"Proclaimed so; but by what title are they judged?" Laura retorted. "I have heard that his duel with Count Paul was fair, and that the grounds for it were just. Deplore it; but to condemn an Italian gentleman without hearing his personal vindication, is infamous; nay, it is Austrian. I know next to nothing of the story. Countess Ammiani has assured me that the brothers have a clear defence—not from your Vienna point of view: Italy and Vienna are different sides of the shield."

Vittoria spoke most humbly before Anna; her sole irritating remark was, that even if she were aware of the direction of Angelo's flight, she would not betray him.

The duchess did her utmost to induce her to see that he was a criminal, outlawed from common charity. "These Italians are really like the Jews," she said to Anna; "they appear to me to hold together by a bond of race: you cannot get them to understand that any act can be infamous when one of their blood is guilty of it."

Anna thought gloomily: "Then, why do you ally yourself to them?"

The duchess, with Anna, Lena, and Wilfrid, drove to the Ultenthal. Vittoria and Merthyr had a long afternoon of companionship. She had been shyer in meeting him than in meeting Wilfrid, whom she had once loved. The tie between herself and Wilfrid was broken; but Merthyr had remained true to his passionless affection, which ennobled him to her so that her heart fluttered, though she was heavily depressed. He relieved her by letting her perceive that Carlo Ammiani's merits were not unknown to him. Merthyr smiled at Carlo for abjuring his patrician birth. He said: "Count Ammiani will be cured in time of those little roughnesses of his adopted Republicanism. You must help to cure him. Women are never so foolish as men in these things."

When Merthyr had spoken thus, she felt that she might dare to press his hand. Sharing friendship with this steadfast nature and brotherly gentleman; who was in the ripe manhood of his years; who loved Italy and never despaired; who gave great affection, and took uncomplainingly the possible return for it;—seemed like entering on a great plain open to boundless heaven. She thought that friendship was sweeter than love. Merthyr soon left the castle to meet his sister at Coire. Laura and Vittoria drove some distance up the Vintschgau, on the way to the Engadine, with him. He affected not to be downcast by the failure of the last attempt at a rising in Milan. "Keep true to your Art; and don't let it be subservient to anything," he said, and his final injunction to her was that she should get a German master and practise rigidly.

Vittoria could only look at Laura in reply.

"He is for us, but not of us," said Laura, as she kissed her fingers to him.

"If he had told me to weep and pray," Vittoria murmured, "I think I should by-and-by lift up my head."

"By-and-by! By-and-by I think I see a convent for me," said Laura.

Their faces drooped.

Vittoria cried: "Ah! did he mean that my singing at La Scala was below the mark?"

At this, Laura's laughter came out in a volume. "And that excellent Father Bernardus thinks he is gaining a convert!" she said.

Vittoria's depression was real, though her strong vitality appeared to mock it. Letters from Milan, enclosed to the duchess, spoke of Carlo Ammiani's imprisonment as a matter that might be indefinitely prolonged. His mother had been subjected to an examination; she had not hesitated to confess that she had received her nephew in her house, but it could not be established against her that it was not Carlo whom she had passed off to the sbirri as her son. Countess Ammiani wrote to Laura, telling her she scarcely hoped that Carlo would obtain his liberty save upon the arrest of Angelo:—"Therefore, what I most desire, I dare not pray for!" That line of intense tragic grief haunted Vittoria like a veiled head thrusting itself across the sunlight. Countess Ammiani added that she must give her son what news she could gather;—"Concerning you," said Laura, interpreting the sentence: "Bitter days do this good, they make a proud woman abjure the traditions of her caste." A guarded answer was addressed, according to the countess's directions, to Sarpo the bookseller, in Milan. For purposes of such a nature, Barto Rizzo turned the uneasy craven to account.

It happened that one of the maids at Sonnenberg was about to marry a peasant, of Meran, part proprietor of a vineyard, and the nuptials were to be celebrated at the castle. Among those who thronged the courtyard on the afternoon of the ceremony, Vittoria beheld her faithful Beppo, who related the story of his pursuit of her, and the perfidy of Luigi;—a story so lengthy, that his voluble tongue running at full speed could barely give the outlines of it. He informed her, likewise, that he had been sent for, while lying in Trent, by Captain Weisspriess, whom he had seen at an inn of the Ultenthal, weak but improving. Beppo was the captain's propitiatory offering to Vittoria. Meanwhile the ladies sat on a terrace, overlooking the court, where a stout fellow in broad green braces and blue breeches lay half across a wooden table, thrumming a zither, which set the groups in motion. The zither is a melancholy little instrument; in range of expression it is to the harp what the winchat is to the thrush; or to the violin, what that bird is to the nightingale; yet few instruments are so exciting: here and there along these mountain valleys you may hear a Tyrolese maid set her voice to its plaintive thin tones; but when the strings are swept madly there is mad dancing; it catches at the nerves. "Andreas! Andreas!" the dancers shouted to encourage the player. Some danced with vine-poles; partners broke and wandered at will, taking fresh partners, and occasionally huddling in confusion, when the poles were levelled and tilted at them, and they dispersed. Beppo, dancing mightily to recover the use of his legs, met his acquaintance Jacob Baumwalder Feckelwitz, and the pair devoted themselves to a rivalry of capers; jump, stamp, shuffle, leg aloft, arms in air, yell and shriek: all took hands around them and streamed, tramping the measure, and the vine-poles guarded the ring. Then Andreas raised the song: "Our Lady is gracious," and immediately the whole assemblage were singing praise to the Lady of the castle. Following which, wine being brought to Andreas, he drank to his lady, to his lady's guests, to the bride, to the bridegroom, to everybody. He was now ready to improvize, and dashed thumb and finger on the zither, tossing up his face, swarthy-flushed: "There was a steinbock with a beard." Half-a-dozen voices repeated it, as to proclaim the theme.

"Alas! a beard indeed, for there is no end to this animal. I know him;" said the duchess dolefully.

"There was a steinbock with a beard;
Of no gun was he afeard
Piff-paff left of him: piff-paff right of him
Piff-paff everywhere, where you get a sight of him."

The steinbock led through the whole course of a mountaineer's emotions and experiences, with piff-paff continually left of him and right of him and nothing hitting him. The mountaineer is perplexed; an able man, a dead shot, who must undo the puzzle or lose faith in his skill, is a tremendous pursuer, and the mountaineer follows the steinbock ever. A 'sennderin' at a 'sennhutchen' tells him that she admitted the steinbock last night, and her curled hair frizzled under the steinbock's eyes. The case is only too clear: my goodness! the steinbock is the—"Der Teu!..." said Andreas, with a comic stop of horror, the rhyme falling cleverly to "ai." Henceforth the mountaineer becomes transformed into a champion of humanity, hunting the wicked bearded steinbock in all corners; especially through the cabinet of those dark men who decree the taxes detested in Tyrol.

The song had as yet but fairly commenced, when a break in the 'piff-paff' chorus warned Andreas that he was losing influence, women and men were handing on a paper and bending their heads over it; their responses hushed altogether, or were ludicrously inefficient.

"I really believe the poor brute has come to a Christian finish—this Ahasuerus of steinbocks!" said the duchess.

The transition to silence was so extraordinary and abrupt, that she called to her chasseur to know the meaning of it. Feckelwitz fetched the paper and handed it up. It exhibited a cross done in blood under the word 'Meran,' and bearing that day's date. One glance at it told Laura what it meant. The bride in the court below was shedding tears: the bridegroom was lighting his pipe and consoling her; women were chattering, men shrugging. Some said they had seen an old grey-haired hag (hexe) stand at the gates and fling down a piece of paper. A little boy whose imagination was alive with the tale of the steinbock, declared that her face was awful, and that she had only the use of one foot. A man patted him on the shoulder, and gave him a gulp of wine, saying with his shrewdest air: "One may laugh at the devil once too often, though!" and that sentiment was echoed; the women suggested in addition the possibility of the bride Lisa having something on her conscience, seeing that she had lived in a castle two years and more. The potential persuasions of Father Bernardus were required to get the bride to go away to her husband's roof that evening: when she did make her departure, the superstitious peasantry were not a merry party that followed at her heels.

At the break-up of the festivities Wilfrid received an intimation that his sister had arrived in Meran from Bormio. He went down to see her, and returned at a late hour. The ladies had gone to rest. He wrote a few underlined words, entreating Vittoria to grant an immediate interview in the library of the castle. The missive was entrusted to Aennchen. Vittoria came in alarm.

"My sister is perfectly well," said Wilfrid. "She has heard that Captain Gambier has been arrested in the mountains; she had some fears concerning you, which I quieted. What I have to tell you, does not relate to her. The man Angelo Guidascarpi is in Meran. I wish you to let the signora know that if he is not carried out of the city before sunset to-morrow, I must positively inform the superior officer of the district of his presence there."

This was their first private interview. Vittoria (for she knew him) had acceded to it, much fearing that it would lead to her having to put on her sex's armour. To collect her wits, she asked tremblingly how Wilfrid had chanced to see Angelo. An old Italian woman, he said, had accosted him at the foot of the mountain, and hearing that he was truly an Englishman—"I am out of my uniform," Wilfrid remarked with intentional bitterness—had conducted him to the house of an Italian in the city, where Angelo Guidascarpi was lying.

"Ill?" said Vittoria.

"Just recovering. After that duel, or whatever it may be called with Weisspriess, he lay all night out on the mountains. He managed to get the help of a couple of fellows, who led him at dusk into Meran, saw an Italian name over a shop, and—I will say for them that the rascals hold together. There he is, at all events."

"Would you denounce a sick man, Wilfrid?"

"I certainly cannot forget my duty upon every point"

"You are changed!"

"Changed! Am I the only one who is changed?"

"He must have supposed that it would be Merthyr. I remember speaking of Merthyr to him as our unchangeable friend. I told him Merthyr would be here."

"Instead of Merthyr, he had the misfortune to see your changeable friend, if you will have it so."

"But how can it be your duty to denounce him, Wilfrid. You have quitted that army."

"Have I? I have forfeited my rank, perhaps."

"And Angelo is not guilty of a military offence."

"He has slain one of a family that I am bound to respect."

"Certainly, certainly," said Vittoria hurriedly.

Her forehead showed distress of mind; she wanted Laura's counsel.

"Wilfrid, do you know the whole story?"

"I know that he inveigled Count Paul to his house and slew him; either he or his brother, or both."

"I have been with him for days, Wilfrid. I believe that he would do no dishonourable thing. He is related——".

"He is the cousin of Count Ammiani."

"Ah! would you plunge us in misery?"

"How?"

"Count Ammiani is my lover."

She uttered it unblushingly, and with tender eyes fixed on him.

"Your lover!" he exclaimed, with vile emphasis.

"He will be my husband," she murmured, while the mounting hot colour burned at her temples.

"Changed—who is changed?" he said, in a vehement underneath. "For that reason I am to be false to her who does me the honour to care for me!"

"I would not have you false to her in thought or deed."

"You ask me to spare this man on account of his relationship to your lover, and though he has murdered the brother of the lady whom I esteem. What on earth is the meaning of the petition? Really, you amaze me."

"I appeal to your generosity, Wilfrid, I am Emilia."

"Are you?"

She gave him her hand. He took it, and felt at once the limit of all that he might claim. Dropping the hand, he said:

"Will nothing less than my ruin satisfy you? Since that night at La Scala, I am in disgrace with my uncle; I expect at any moment to hear that I am cashiered from the army, if not a prisoner. What is it that you ask of me now? To conspire with you in shielding the man who has done a mortal injury to the family of which I am almost one. Your reason must perceive that you ask too much. I would willingly assist you in sparing the feelings of Count Ammiani; and, believe me, gratitude is the last thing I require to stimulate my services. You ask too much; you must see that you ask too much."

"I do," said Vittoria. "Good-night, Wilfrid."

He was startled to find her going, and lost his equable voice in trying to detain her. She sought relief in Laura's bosom, to whom she recapitulated the interview.

"Is it possible," Laura said, looking at her intently, "that you do not recognize the folly of telling this Lieutenant Pierson that you were pleading to him on behalf of your lover? Could anything be so monstrous, when one can see that he is malleable to the twist of your little finger? Are you only half a woman, that you have no consciousness of your power? Probably you can allow yourself—enviable privilege!—to suppose that he called you down at this late hour simply to inform you that he is compelled to do something which will cause you unhappiness! I repeat, it is an enviable privilege. Now, when the real occasion has come for you to serve us, you have not a single weapon—except these tears, which you are wasting on my lap. Be sure that if he denounces Angelo, Angelo's life cries out against you. You have but to quicken your brain to save him. Did he expose his life for you or not? I knew that he was in Meran," the signora continued sadly. "The paper which frightened the silly peasants, revealed to me that he was there, needing help. I told you Angelo was under an evil star. I thought my day to-morrow would be a day of scheming. The task has become easy, if you will."

"Be merciful; the task is dreadful," said Vittoria.

"The task is simple. You have an instrument ready to your hands. You can do just what you like with him—make an Italian of him; make him renounce his engagement to this pert little Lena of Lenkenstein, break his sword, play Arlecchino, do what you please. He is not required for any outrageous performance. A week, and Angelo will have recovered his strength; you likewise may resume the statuesque demeanour which you have been exhibiting here. For the space of one week you are asked for some natural exercise of your wits and compliancy. Hitherto what have you accomplished, pray?" Laura struck spitefully at Vittoria's degraded estimation of her worth as measured by events. "You have done nothing—worse than nothing. It gives me horrors to find it necessary to entreat you to look your duty in the face and do it, that even three or four Italian hearts—Carlo among them—may thank you. Not Carlo, you say?" (Vittoria had sobbed, "No, not Carlo.") "How little you know men! How little do you think how the obligations of the hour should affect a creature deserving life! Do you fancy that Carlo wishes you to be for ever reading the line of a copy-book and shaping your conduct by it? Our Italian girls do this; he despises them. Listen to me; do not I know what is meant by the truth of love? I pass through fire, and keep constant to it; but you have some vile Romance of Chivalry in your head; a modern sculptor's figure, 'MEDITATION;' that is the sort of bride you would give him in the stirring days of Italy. Do you think it is only a statue that can be true? Perceive—will you not—that this Lieutenant Pierson is your enemy. He tells you as much; surely the challenge is fair? Defeat him as you best can. Angelo shall not be abandoned."

"O me! it is unendurable; you are merciless," said Vittoria, shuddering.

She saw the vile figure of herself aping smirks and tender meanings to her old lover. It was a picture that she dared not let her mind rest on: how then could she personate it? All through her life she had been frank; as a young woman, she was clear of soul; she felt that her, simplicity was already soiled by the bare comprehension of the abominable course indicated by Laura. Degradation seemed to have been a thing up to this moment only dreamed of; but now that it was demanded of her to play coquette and trick her womanhood with false allurements, she knew the sentiment of utter ruin; she was ashamed. No word is more lightly spoken than shame. Vittoria's early devotion to her Art, and subsequently to her Italy, had carried her through the term when she would otherwise have showed the natural mild attack of the disease. It came on her now in a rush, penetrating every chamber of her heart, overwhelming her; she could see no distinction between being ever so little false and altogether despicable. She had loathings of her body and her life. With grovelling difficulty of speech she endeavoured to convey the sense of her repugnance to Laura, who leaned her ear, wondering at such bluntness of wit in a woman, and said, "Are you quite deficient in the craft of your sex, child? You can, and you will, guard yourself ten times better when your aim is simply to subject him." But this was not reason to a spirit writhing in the serpent-coil of fiery blushes.

Vittoria said, "I shall pity him so."

She meant she would pity Wilfrid in deluding him. It was a taint of the hypocrisy which comes with shame.

The signora retorted: "I can't follow the action of your mind a bit."

Pity being a form of tenderness, Laura supposed that she would intuitively hate the man who compelled her to do what she abhorred.

They spent the greater portion of the night in this debate.

CHAPTER XXVIII

THE ESCAPE OF ANGELO

Vittoria knew better than Laura that the task was easy; she had but to override her aversion to the show of trifling with a dead passion; and when she thought of Angelo lying helpless in the swarm of enemies, and that Wilfrid could consent to use his tragic advantage to force her to silly love-play, his selfishness wrought its reflection, so that she became sufficiently unjust to forget her marvellous personal influence over him. Even her tenacious sentiment concerning his white uniform was clouded. She very soon ceased to be shamefaced in her own fancy. At dawn she stood at her window looking across the valley of Meran, and felt the whole scene in a song of her heart, with the faintest recollection of her having passed through a tempest overnight. The warm Southern glow of the enfoliaged valley recalled her living Italy, and Italy her voice. She grew wakefully glad: it was her nature, not her mind, that had twisted in the convulsions of last night's horror of shame. The chirp of healthy blood in full-flowing veins dispersed it; and as a tropical atmosphere is cleared by the hurricane, she lost her depression and went down among her enemies possessed by an inner delight, that was again of her nature, not of her mind. She took her gladness for a happy sign that she had power to rise buoyant above circumstances; and though aware that she was getting to see things in harsh outlines, she was unconscious of her haggard imagination.

The Lenkensteins had projected to escape the blandishments of Vienna by residing during the winter in Venice, where Wilfrid and his sister were to be the guests of the countess:—a pleasant prospect that was dashed out by an official visit from Colonel Zofel of the Meran garrison, through whom it was known that Lieutenant Pierson, while enjoying his full liberty to investigate the charms of the neighbourhood, might not extend his excursions beyond a pedestrian day's limit;—he was, in fact, under surveillance. The colonel formally exacted his word of honour that he would not attempt to pass the bounds, and explained to the duchess that the injunction was favourable to the lieutenant, as implying that he must be ready at any moment to receive the order to join his regiment. Wilfrid bowed with a proper soldierly submission. Respecting the criminal whom his men were pursuing, Colonel Zofel said that he was sparing no efforts to come on his traces; he supposed, from what he had heard in the Ultenthal, that Guidascarpi was on his back somewhere within a short range of Meran. Vittoria strained her ears to the colonel's German; she fancied his communication to be that he suspected Angelo's presence in Meran.

The official part of his visit being terminated, the colonel addressed some questions to the duchess concerning the night of the famous Fifteenth at La Scala. He was an amateur, and spoke with enthusiasm of the reports of the new prima donna. The duchess perceived that he was asking for an introduction to the heroine of the night, and graciously said that perhaps that very prima donna would make amends, to him for his absence on the occasion. Vittoria checked a movement of revolt in her frame. She cast an involuntary look at Wilfrid. "Now it begins," she thought, and went to the piano: she had previously refused to sing. Wilfrid had to bend his head over his betrothed and listen to her whisperings. He did so, carelessly swaying his hand to the measure of the aria, with an increasing bitter comparison of the two voices. Lena persisted in talking; she was indignant at his abandonment of the journey to Venice; she reproached him as feeble, inconsiderate, indifferent. Then for an instant she would pause to hear the voice, and renew her assault. "We ought to be thankful that she is not singing a song of death and destruction to us! The archduchess is coming to Venice. If you are presented to her and please her, and get the writs of naturalization prepared, you will be one of us completely, and your fortune is made. If you stay here—why should you stay? It is nothing but your uncle's caprice. I am too angry to care for music. If you stay, you will earn my contempt. I will not be buried another week in such a place. I am tired of weeping. We all go to Venice: Captain Weisspriess follows us. We are to have endless Balls, an opera, a Court there—with whom am I to dance, pray, when I am out of mourning? Am I to sit and govern my feet under a chair, and gaze like an imbecile nun? It is too preposterous. I am betrothed to you; I wish, I wish to behave like a betrothed. The archduchess herself will laugh to see me chained to a chair. I shall have to reply a thousand times to 'Where is he?' What can I answer? 'Wouldn't come,' will be the only true reply."

During this tirade, Vittoria was singing one of her old songs, well known to Wilfrid, which brought the vision of a foaming weir, and moonlight between the branches of a great cedar-tree, and the lost love of his heart sitting by his side in the noising stillness. He was sure that she could be singing it for no one but for him. The leap taken by his spirit from this time to that, was shorter than from the past back to the present.

"You do not applaud," said Lena, when the song had ceased.

He murmured: "I never do, in drawing-rooms."

"A cantatrice expects it everywhere; these creatures live on it."

"I'll tell her, if you like, what we thought of it, when I take her down to my sister, presently."

"Are you not to take me down?"

"The etiquette is to hand her up to you."

"No, no!" Lena insisted, in abhorrence of etiquette; but Wilfrid said pointedly that his sister's feelings must be spared. "Her husband is an animal: he is a millionaire city-of-London merchant; conceive him! He has drunk himself gouty on Port wine, and here he is for the grape-cure."

"Ah! in that England of yours, women marry for wealth," said Lena.

"Yes, in your Austria they have a better motive" he interpreted her sentiment.

"Say, in our Austria."

"In our Austria, certainly."

"And with our holy religion?"

"It is not yet mine."

"It will be?" She put the question eagerly.

Wilfrid hesitated, and by his adept hesitation succeeded in throwing her off the jealous scent.

"Say that it will be, my Wilfrid!"

"You must give me time"

"This subject always makes you cold."

"My own Lena!"

"Can I be, if we are doomed to be parted when we die?"

There is small space for compunction in a man's heart when he is in Wilfrid's state, burning with the revival of what seemed to him a superhuman attachment. He had no design to break his acknowledged bondage to Countess Lena, and answered her tender speech almost as tenderly.

It never occurred to him, as he was walking down to Meran with Vittoria, that she could suppose him to be bartering to help rescue the life of a wretched man in return for soft confidential looks of entreaty; nor did he reflect, that when cast on him, they might mean no more than the wish to move him for a charitable purpose. The completeness of her fascination was shown by his reading her entirely by his own emotions, so that a lowly-uttered word, or a wavering unwilling glance, made him think that she was subdued by the charm of the old days.

"Is it here?" she said, stopping under the first Italian name she saw in the arcade of shops.

"How on earth have you guessed it?" he asked, astonished.

She told him to wait at the end of the arcade, and passed in. When she joined him again, she was downcast. They went straight to Adela's hotel, where the one thing which gave her animation was the hearing that Mr. Sedley had met an English doctor there, and had placed himself in his hands. Adela dressed splendidly for her presentation to the duchess. Having done so, she noticed Vittoria's depressed countenance and difficult breathing. She commanded her to see the doctor. Vittoria consented, and made use of him. She could tell Laura confidently at night that Wilfrid would not betray Angelo, though she had not spoken one direct word to him on the subject.

Wilfrid was peculiarly adept in the idle game he played. One who is intent upon an evil end is open to expose his plan. But he had none in view; he lived for the luxurious sensation of being near the woman who fascinated him, and who was now positively abashed when by his side. Adela suggested to him faintly—she believed it was her spontaneous idea—that he might be making his countess jealous. He assured her that the fancy sprang from scenes which she remembered, and that she could have no idea of the pride of a highborn Austrian girl, who was incapable of conceiving jealousy of a person below her class. Adela replied that it was not his manner so much as Emilia's which might arouse the suspicion; but she immediately affected to appreciate the sentiments of a highborn Austrian girl toward a cantatrice, whose gifts we regard simply as an aristocratic entertainment. Wilfrid induced his sister to relate Vittoria's early history to Countess Lena; and himself almost wondered, when he heard it in bare words, at that haunting vision of the glory of Vittoria at La Scala—where, as he remembered, he would have run against destruction to cling to her lips. Adela was at first alarmed by the concentrated wrathfulness which she discovered in the bosom of Countess Anna, who, as their intimacy waxed, spoke of the intruding opera siren in terms hardly proper even to married women; but it seemed right, as being possibly aristocratic. Lena was much more tolerant. "I have just the same enthusiasm for soldiers that my Wilfrid has for singers," she said; and it afforded Adela exquisite pleasure to hear her tell how that she had originally heard of the 'eccentric young Englishman,' General Pierson's nephew, as a Lustspiel— a comedy; and of his feats on horseback, and his duels, and his—"he was very wicked over here, you know;" Lena laughed. She assumed the privileges of her four-and-twenty years and her rank. Her marriage was to take place in the Spring. She announced it with the simplicity of an independent woman of the world, adding, "That is, if my Wilfrid will oblige me by not plunging into further disgrace with the General."

"No; you will not marry a man who is under a cloud," Anna subjoined.

"Certainly not a soldier," said Lena. "What it was exactly that he did at La Scala, I don't know, and don't care to know, but he was then ignorant that she had touched the hand of that Guidascarpi. I decide by this—he was valiant; he defied everybody: therefore I forgive him. He is not in disgrace with me. I will reinstate him."

"You have your own way of being romantic," said Anna. "A soldier who forgets his duty is in my opinion only a brave fool."

"It seems to me that a great many gallant officers are fond of fine voices," Lena retorted.

"No doubt it is a fashion among them," said Anna.

Adela recoiled with astonishment when she began to see the light in which the sisters regarded Vittoria; and she was loyal enough to hint and protest on her friend's behalf. The sisters called her a very good soul. "It may not be in England as over here," said Anna. "We have to submit to these little social scourges."

Lena whispered to Adela, "An angry woman will think the worst. I have no doubt of my Wilfrid. If I had!—"

Her eyes flashed. Fire was not wanting in her.

The difficulties which tasked the amiable duchess to preserve an outward show of peace among the antagonistic elements she gathered together were increased by the arrival at the castle of Count Lenkenstein, Bianca's husband, and head of the family, from Bologna. He was a tall and courtly man, who had one face for his friends and another for the reverse party; which is to say, that his manners could be bad. Count Lenkenstein was accompanied by Count Serabiglione, who brought Laura's children with their Roman nurse, Assunta. Laura kissed her little ones, and sent them out of her sight. Vittoria found her home in their play and prattle. She needed a refuge, for Count Lenkenstein was singularly brutal in his bearing toward her. He let her know that he had come to Meran to superintend the hunt for the assassin, Angelo Guidascarpi. He attempted to exact her promise in precise speech that she would be on the spot to testify against Angelo when that foul villain should be caught. He objected openly to Laura's children going about with her. Bitter talk on every starting subject was exchanged across the duchess's table. She herself was in disgrace on Laura's account, and had to practise an overflowing sweetness, with no one to second her efforts. The two noblemen spoke in accord on the bubble revolution. The strong hand—ay, the strong hand! The strong hand disposes of vermin. Laura listened to them, pallid with silent torture. "Since the rascals have taken to assassination, we know that we have them at the dregs," said Count Lenkenstein. "A cord round the throats of a few scores of them, and the country will learn the virtue of docility."

Laura whispered to her sister: "Have you espoused a hangman?"

Such dropping of deadly shells in a quiet society went near to scattering it violently; but the union was necessitous. Count Lenkenstein desired to confront Vittoria with Angelo; Laura would not quit her side, and Amalia would not expel her friend. Count Lenkenstein complained roughly of Laura's conduct; nor did Laura escape her father's reproof. "Sir, you are privileged to say what you will to me," she responded, with the humility which exasperated him.

"Yes, you bend, you bend, that you may be stiff-necked when it suits you," he snapped her short.

"Surely that is the text of the sermon you preach to our Italy!"

"A little more, as you are running on now, madame, and our Italy will be froth on the lips. You see, she is ruined."

"Chi lo fa, lo sa," hummed Laura; "but I would avoid quoting you as that authority."

"After your last miserable fiasco, my dear!"

"It was another of our school exercises. We had not been good boys and girls. We had learnt our lesson imperfectly. We have received our punishment, and we mean to do better next time."

"Behave seasonably, fittingly; be less of a wasp; school your tongue."

"Bianca is a pattern to me, I am aware," said Laura.

"She is a good wife."

"I am a poor widow."

"She is a good daughter."

"I am a wicked rebel."

"And you are scheming at something now," said the little nobleman, sagacious so far; but he was too eager to read the verification of the tentative remark in her face, and she perceived that it was a guess founded on her show of spirit.

"Scheming to contain my temper, which is much tried," she said. "But I suppose it supports me. I can always keep up against hostility."

"You provoke it; you provoke it."

"My instinct, then, divines my medicine."

"Exactly, my dear; your personal instinct. That instigates you all. And none are so easily conciliated as these Austrians. Conciliate them, and you have them." Count Serabiglione diverged into a repetition of his theory of the policy and mission of superior intelligences, as regarded his system for dealing with the Austrians.

Nurse Assunta's jealousy was worked upon to separate the children from Vittoria. They ran down with her no more to meet the vast bowls of grapes in the morning and feather their hats with vine leaves. Deprived of her darlings, the loneliness of her days made her look to Wilfrid for commiseration. Father Bernardus was too continually exhortative, and fenced too much to "hit the eyeball of her conscience," as he phrased it, to afford her repose. Wilfrid could tell himself that he had already done much for her; for if what he had done were known, his career, social and military, was ended. This idea being accompanied by a sense of security delighted him; he was accustomed to inquire of Angelo's condition, and praise the British doctor who was attending him gratuitously. "I wish I could get him out of the way," he said, and frowned as in a mental struggle. Vittoria heard him repeat his "I wish!" It heightened greatly her conception of the sacrifice he would be making on her behalf and charity's. She spoke with a reverential tenderness, such as it was hard to suppose a woman capable of addressing to other than the man who moved her soul. The words she uttered were pure thanks; it was the tone which sent them winged and shaking seed. She had spoken partly to prompt his activity, but her self-respect had been sustained by his avoidance of the dreaded old themes, and that grateful feeling made her voice musically rich.

"I dare not go to him, but the doctor tells me the fever has left him, Wilfrid; his wounds are healing; but he is bandaged from head to foot. The sword pierced his side twice, and his arms and hands are cut horribly. He cannot yet walk. If he is discovered he is lost. Count Lenkenstein has declared that he will stay at the castle till he has him his prisoner. The soldiers are all round us. They know that Angelo is in the ring. They have traced him all over from the Valtellina to this Ultenthal, and only cannot guess where he is in the lion's jaw. I rise in the morning, thinking, 'Is this to be the black day?' He is sure to be caught."

"If I could hit on a plan," said Wilfrid, figuring as though he had a diorama of impossible schemes revolving before his eyes.

"I could believe in the actual whispering of an angel if you did. It was to guard me that Angelo put himself in peril."

"Then," said Wilfrid, "I am his debtor. I owe him as much as my life is worth."

"Think, think," she urged; and promised affection, devotion, veneration, vague things, that were too like his own sentiments to prompt him pointedly. Yet he so pledged himself to her by word, and prepared his own mind to conceive the act of service, that (as he did not reflect) circumstance might at any moment plunge him into a gulf. Conduct of this sort is a challenge sure to be answered.

One morning Vittoria was gladdened by a letter from Rocco Ricci, who had fled to Turin. He told her that the king had promised to give her a warm welcome in his capital, where her name was famous. She consulted with Laura, and they resolved to go as soon as Angelo could stand on his feet. Turin was cold—Italy, but it was Italy; and from Turin the Italian army was to flow, like the Mincio from the Garda lake. "And there, too, is a stage," Vittoria thought, in a suddenly revived thirst for the stage and a field for work. She determined to run down to Meran and see Angelo. Laura walked a little way with her, till Wilfrid, alert for these occasions, joined them. On the commencement of the zig-zag below, there were soldiers, the sight of whom was not confusing. Military messengers frequently came up to the castle where Count Lenkenstein, assisted by Count Serabiglione, examined their depositions, the Italian in the manner of a winding lawyer, the German of a gruff judge. Half-way down the zig-zag Vittoria cast a preconcerted signal back to Laura. The soldiers had a pair of prisoners between their ranks; Vittoria recognized the men who had carried Captain Weisspriess from the ground where the duel was fought. A quick divination told her that they held Angelo's life on their tongues. They must have found him in the mountain-pass while hurrying to their homes, and it was they who had led him to Meran. On the Passeyr bridge, she turned and said to Wilfrid, "Help me now. Send instantly the doctor in a carriage to the place where he is lying."

Wilfrid was intent on her flushed beauty and the half-compressed quiver of her lip.

She quitted him and hurried to Angelo. Her joy broke out in a cry of thankfulness at sight of Angelo; he had risen from his bed; he could stand, and he smiled.

"That Jacopo is just now the nearest link to me," he said, when she related her having seen the two men guarded by soldiers; he felt helpless, and spoke in resignation. She followed his eye about the room till it rested on the stilet. This she handed to him. "If they think of having me alive!" he said softly. The Italian and his wife who had given him shelter and nursed him came in, and approved his going, though they did not complain of what they might chance to have incurred. He offered them his purse, and they took it. Minutes of grievous expectation went by; Vittoria could endure them no longer; she ran out to the hotel, near which, in the shade of a poplar, Wilfrid was smoking quietly. He informed her that his sister and the doctor had driven out to meet Captain Gambier; his brother-in-law was alone upstairs. Her look of amazement touched him more shrewdly than scorn, and he said, "What on earth can I do?"

"Order out a carriage. Send your brother-in-law in it. If you tell him 'for your health,' he will go."

"On my honour, I don't know where those three words would not send him," said Wilfrid; but he did not move, and was for protesting that he really could not guess what was the matter, and the ground for all this urgency.

Vittoria compelled her angry lips to speak out her suspicions explicitly, whereupon he glanced at the sun-glare in a meditation, occasionally blinking his eyes. She thought, "Oh, heaven! can he be waiting for me to coax him?" It was the truth, though it would have been strange to him to have heard it. She grew sure that it was the truth; never had she despised living creature so utterly as when she murmured, "My best friend! my brother! my noble Wilfrid! my old beloved! help me now, without loss of a minute."

It caused his breath to come and go unevenly.

"Repeat that—once, only once," he said.

She looked at him with the sorrowful earnestness which, as its meaning was shut from him, was so sweet.

"You will repeat it by-and-by?—another time? Trust me to do my utmost. Old beloved! What is the meaning of 'old beloved'? One word in explanation. If it means anything, I would die for you! Emilia, do you hear?—die for you! To me you are nothing old or by-gone, whatever I may be to you. To me—yes, I will order the carriage you are the Emilia—listen! listen! Ah! you have shut your ears against me. I am bound in all seeming, but I—you drive me mad; you know your power. Speak one word, that I may feel—that I may be convinced,... or not a single word; I will obey you without. I have said that you command my life."

In a block of carriages on the bridge, Vittoria perceived a lifted hand. It was Laura's; Beppo was in attendance on her. Laura drove up and said: "You guessed right; where is he?" The communications between them were more indicated than spoken. Beppo had heard Jacopo confess to his having conducted a wounded Italian gentleman into Meran. "That means that the houses will be searched within an hour," said Laura; "my brother-in-law Bear is radiant." She mimicked the Lenkenstein physiognomy spontaneously in the run of her speech. "If Angelo can help himself ever so little, he has a fair start." A look was cast on Wilfrid; Vittoria nodded—Wilfrid was entrapped.

"Englishmen we can trust," said Laura, and requested him to step into her carriage. He glanced round the open space. Beppo did the same, and beheld the chasseur Jacob Baumwalder Feckelwitz crossing the bridge on foot, but he said nothing. Wilfrid was on the step of the carriage, for what positive object neither he nor the others knew, when his sister and the doctor joined them. Captain Gambier was still missing.

"He would have done anything for us," Vittoria said in Wilfrid's hearing.

"Tell us what plan you have," the latter replied fretfully.

She whispered: "Persuade Adela to make her husband drive out. The doctor will go too, and Beppo. They shall take Angelo. Our carriage will follow empty, and bring Mr. Sedley back."

Wilfrid cast his eyes up in the air, at the monstrous impudence of the project. "A storm is coming on," he suggested, to divert her reading of his grimace; but she was speaking to the doctor, who readily answered her aloud: "If you are certain of what you say." The remark incited Wilfrid to be no subordinate in devotion; handing Adela from the carriage, while the doctor ran up to Mr. Sedley, he drew her away. Laura and Vittoria watched the motion of their eyes and lips.

"Will he tell her the purpose?" said Laura.

Vittoria smiled nervously: "He is fibbing."

Marking the energy expended by Wilfrid in this art, the wiser woman said: "Be on your guard the next two minutes he gets you alone."

"You see his devotion."

"Does he see his compensation? But he must help us at any hazard."

Adela broke away from her brother twice, and each time he fixed her to the spot more imperiously. At last she ran into the hotel; she was crying. "A bad economy of tears," said Laura, commenting on the dumb scene, to soothe her savage impatience. "In another twenty minutes we shall have the city gates locked."

They heard a window thrown up; Mr. Sedley's head came out, and peered at the sky. Wilfrid said to Vittoria: "I can do nothing beyond what I have done, I fear."

She thought it was a petition for thanks, but Laura knew better; she said: "I see Count Lenkenstein on his way to the barracks."

Wilfrid bowed: "I may be able to serve you in that quarter."

He retired: whereupon Laura inquired how her friend could reasonably suppose that a man would ever endure being thanked in public.

"I shall never understand and never care to understand them," said Vittoria.

"It is a knowledge that is forced on us, my dear. May heaven make the minds of our enemies stupid for the next five hours!—Apropos of what I was saying, women and men are in two hostile camps. We have a sort of general armistice and everlasting strife of individuals—Ah!" she clapped hands on her knees, "here comes your doctor; I could fancy I see a pointed light on his head. Men of science, my Sandra, are always the humanest."

The chill air of wind preceding thunder was driving round the head of the vale, and Mr. Sedley, wrapped in furs, and feebly remonstrating with his medical adviser, stepped into his carriage. The doctor followed him, giving a grave recognition of Vittoria's gaze. Both gentlemen raised their hats to the ladies, who alighted as soon as they had gone in the direction of the Vintschgau road.

"One has only to furnish you with money, my Beppo," said Vittoria, complimenting his quick apprehensiveness. "Buy bread and cakes at one of the shops, and buy wine. You will find me where you can, when you have seen him safe. I have no idea of where my home will be. Perhaps England."

"Italy, Italy! faint heart," said Laura.

Furnished with money, Beppo rolled away gaily.

The doubt was in Laura whether an Englishman's wits were to be relied on in such an emergency; but she admitted that the doctor had looked full enough of serious meaning, and that the Englishman named Merthyr Powys was keen and ready. They sat a long half-hour, that thumped itself out like an alarm-bell, under the poplars, by the clamouring Passeyr, watching the roll and spring of the waters, and the radiant foam, while band-music played to a great company of visitors, and sounds of thunder drew near. Over the mountains above the Adige, the leaden fingers of an advance of the thunder-cloud pushed slowly, and on a sudden a mighty gale sat heaped blank on the mountain-top and blew. Down went the heads of the poplars, the river staggered in its leap, the vale was shuddering grey. It was like the transformation in a fairy tale; Beauty had taken her old cloak about her, and bent to calamity. The poplars streamed their length sideways, and in the pauses of the strenuous wind nodded and dashed wildly and white over the dead black water, that waxed in foam and hissed, showing its teeth like a beast enraged. Laura and Vittoria joined hands and struggled for shelter. The tent of a travelling circus from the South, newly-pitched on a grassplot near the river, was caught up and whirled in the air and flung in the face of a marching guard of soldiery, whom it swathed and bore sheer to earth, while on them and around them a line of poplars fell flat, the wind whistling over them. Laura directed Vittoria's eyes to the sight. "See," she said, and her face was set hard with cold and excitement, so that she looked a witch in the uproar; "would you not say the devil is loose now Angelo is abroad?" Thunder and lightning possessed the vale, and then a vertical rain. At the first gleam of sunlight, Laura and Vittoria walked up to the Laubengasse—the street of the arcades, where they made purchases of numerous needless articles, not daring to enter the Italian's shop. A woman at a fruitstall opposite to it told them that no carriage could have driven up there. During their great perplexity, mud and rain-stained soldiers, the same whom they had seen borne to earth by the flying curtain, marched before the shop; the shop and the house were searched; the Italian and his old liming wife were carried away.

"Tell me now, that storm was not Angelo's friend!" Laura muttered.

"Can he have escaped?" said Vittoria.

"He is 'on horseback.'" Laura quoted the Italian proverb to signify that he had flown; how, she could not say, and none could inform her. The joy of their hearts rose in one fountain.

"I shall feel better blood in my body from this moment," Laura said; and Vittoria, "Oh! we can be strong, if we only resolve."

"You want to sing?"

"I do."

"I shall find pleasure in your voice now."

"The wicked voice!"

"Yes, the very wicked voice! But I shall be glad to hear it. You can sing to-night, and drown those Lenkensteins."

"If my Carlo could hear me!"

"Ah!" sighed the signora, musing. "He is in prison now. I remember him, the dearest little lad, fencing with my husband for exercise after they had been writing all day. When Giacomo was imprisoned, Carlo sat outside the prison walls till it was time for him to enter; his chin and upper lip were smooth as a girl's. Giacomo said to him, 'May you always have the power of going out, or not have a wife waiting for you.' Here they come." (She spoke of tears.) "It's because I am joyful. The channel for them has grown so dry that they prick and sting. Oh, Sandra! it would be pleasant to me if we might both be buried for seven days, and have one long howl of weakness together. A little bite of satisfaction makes me so tired. I believe there's something very bad for us in our always being at war, and never, never gaining ground. Just one spark of triumph intoxicates us. Look at all those people pouring out again. They are the children of fair weather. I hope the state of their health does not trouble them too much. Vienna sends consumptive patients here. If you regard them attentively, you will observe that they have an anxious air. Their constitutions are not sound; they fear they may die."

Laura's irony was unforced; it was no more than a subtle discord naturally struck from the scene by a soul in contrast with it.

They beheld the riding forth of troopers and a knot of officers hotly conversing together. At another point the duchess and the Lenkenstein ladies, Count Lenkenstein, Count Serabiglione, and Wilfrid paced up and down, waiting for music. Laura left the public places and crossed an upper bridge over the Passeyr, near the castle, by which route she skirted vines and dropped over sloping meadows to some shaded boulders where the Passeyr found a sandy bay, and leaped in transparent green, and whitened and swung twisting in a long smooth body down a narrow chasm, and noised below. The thundering torrent stilled their sensations: and the water, making battle against great blocks of porphyry and granite, caught their thoughts. So strong was the impression of it on Vittoria's mind, that for hours after, every image she conceived seemed proper to the inrush and outpour; the elbowing, the tossing, the foaming, the burst on stones, and silvery bubbles under and silvery canopy above, the chattering and huzzaing; all working on to the one-toned fall beneath the rainbow on the castle-rock.

Next day, the chasseur Jacob Baumwalder Feckelwitz deposed in full company at Sonnenberg, that, obeying Count Serabiglione's instructions, he had gone down to the city, and had there seen Lieutenant Pierson with the ladies in front of the hotel; he had followed the English carriage, which took up a man who was standing ready on crutches at the corner of the Laubengasse, and drove rapidly out of the North-western gate, leading to Schlanders and Mals and the Engadine. He had witnessed the transfer of the crippled man from one carriage to another, and had raised shouts and given hue and cry, but the intervention of the storm had stopped his pursuit.

He was proceeding to say what his suppositions were. Count Lenkenstein lifted his finger for Wilfrid to follow him out of the room. Count Serabiglione went at their heels. Then Count Lenkenstein sent for his wife, whom Anna and Lena accompanied.

"How many persons are you going to ruin in the course of your crusade, my dear?" the duchess said to Laura.

"Dearest, I am penitent when I succeed," said Laura.

"If that young man has been assisting you, he is irretrievably ruined."

"I am truly sorry for him."

"As for me, the lectures I shall get in Vienna are terrible to think of. This is the consequence of being the friend of both parties, and a peace-maker."

Count Serabiglione returned alone from the scene at the examination, rubbing his hands and nodding affably to his daughter. He maliciously declined to gratify the monster of feminine curiosity in the lump, and doled out the scene piecemeal. He might state, he observed, that it was he who had lured Beppo to listen at the door during the examination of the prisoners; and who had then planted a spy on him—following the dictation of precepts exceedingly old. "We are generally beaten, duchess; I admit it; and yet we generally contrive to show the brain. As I say, wed brains to brute force!—but my Laura prefers to bring about a contest instead of an union, so that somebody is certain to be struck, and"—the count spread out his arms and bowed his head—"deserves the blow." He informed them that Count Lenkenstein had ordered Lieutenant Pierson down to Meran, and that the lieutenant might expect to be cashiered within five days. "What does it matter?" he addressed Vittoria. "It is but a shuffling of victims; Lieutenant Pierson in the place of Guidascarpi! I do not object."

Count Lenkenstein withdrew his wife and sisters from Sonnenberg instantly. He sent an angry message of adieu to the duchess, informing her that he alone was responsible for the behaviour of the ladies of his family. The poor duchess wept. "This means that I shall be summoned to Vienna for a scolding, and have to meet my husband," she said to Laura, who permitted herself to be fondled, and barely veiled her exultation in her apology for the mischief she had done. An hour after the departure of the Lenkensteins, the castle was again officially visited by Colonel Zofel. Vittoria and Laura received an order to quit the district of Meran before sunset. The two firebrands dropped no tears. "I really am sorry for others when I succeed," said Laura, trying to look sad upon her friend.

"No; the heart is eaten out of you both by excitement," said the duchess.

Her tender parting, "Love me," in the ear of Vittoria, melted one heart of the two.

Count Serabiglione continued to be buoyed up by his own and his daughter's recent display of a superior intellectual dexterity until the carriage was at the door and Laura presented her cheek to him. He said, "You will know me a wise man when I am off the table." His gesticulations expressed "Ruin, headlong ruin!" He asked her how she could expect him to be for ever repairing her follies. He was going to Vienna; how could he dare to mention her name there? Not even in a trifle would she consent to be subordinate to authority. Laura checked her replies—the surrendering, of a noble Italian life to the Austrians was such a trifle! She begged only that a poor wanderer might depart with a father's blessing. The count refused to give it; he waved her off in a fury of reproof; and so got smoothly over the fatal moment when money, or the promise of money, is commonly extracted from parental sources, as Laura explained his odd behaviour to her companion. The carriage-door being closed, he regained his courtly composure; his fury was displaced by a chiding finger, which he presently kissed. Father. Bernardus was on the steps beside the duchess, and his blessing had not been withheld from Vittoria, though he half confessed to her that she was a mystery in his mind, and would always be one.

"He can understand robust hostility," Laura said, when Vittoria recalled the look of his benevolent forehead and drooping eyelids; "but robust ductility does astonish him. He has not meddled with me; yet I am the one of the two who would be fair prey for an enterprising spiritual father, as the destined roan of heaven will find out some day."

She bent and smote her lap. "How little they know us, my darling! They take fever for strength, and calmness for submission. Here is the world before us, and I feel that such a man, were he to pounce on me now, might snap me up and lock me in a praying-box with small difficulty. And I am the inveterate rebel! What is it nourishes you and keeps you always aiming straight when you are alone? Once in Turin,

I shall feel that I am myself. Out of Italy I have a terrible craving for peace. It seems here as if I must lean down to him, my beloved, who has left me."

Vittoria was in alarm lest Wilfrid should accost her while she drove from gate to gate of the city. They passed under the archway of the gate leading up to Schloss Tyrol, and along the road bordered by vines. An old peasant woman stopped them with the signal of a letter in her hand. "Here it is," said Laura, and Vittoria could not help smiling at her shrewd anticipation of it.

"May I follow?"

Nothing more than that was written.

But the bearer of the missive had been provided with a lead pencil to obtain the immediate reply.

"An admirable piece of foresight!" Laura's honest exclamation burst forth.

Vittoria had to look in Laura's face before she could gather her will to do the cruel thing which was least cruel. She wrote firmly:—"Never follow me."

BOOK VI

CHAPTER XXIX

EPISODES OF THE REVOLT AND THE WAR—THE TOBACCO-RIOTS—RINALDO GUIDASCARPI

Anna von Lenkenstein was one who could wait for vengeance. Lena punished on the spot, and punished herself most. She broke off her engagement with Wilfrid, while at the same time she caused a secret message to be conveyed to him, telling him that the prolongation of his residence in Meran would restore him to his position in the army.

Wilfrid remained at Meran till the last days of December.

It was winter in Milan, turning to the new year—the year of flames for continental Europe. A young man with a military stride, but out of uniform, had stepped from a travelling carriage and entered a cigar-shop. Upon calling for cigars, he was surprised to observe the woman who was serving there keep her arms under her apron. She cast a look into the street, where a crowd of boys and one or two lean men had gathered about the door. After some delay, she entreated her customer to let her pluck his cloak halfway over the counter; at the same time she thrust a cigar-box under that concealment, together with a printed song in the Milanese dialect. He lifted the paper to read it, and found it tough as Russ. She translated some of the more salient couplets. Tobacco had become a dead business, she said, now that the popular edict had gone forth against 'smoking gold into the pockets of the Tedeschi.' None smoked except officers and Englishmen.

"I am an Englishman," he said.

"And not an officer?" she asked; but he gave no answer. "Englishmen are rare in winter, and don't like being mobbed," said the woman.

Nodding to her urgent petition, he deferred the lighting of his cigar. The vetturino requested him to jump up quickly, and a howl of "No smoking in Milan—fuori!—down with tobacco-smokers!" beset the carriage. He tossed half-a-dozen cigars on the pavement derisively. They were scrambled for, as when a pack of wolves are diverted by a garment dropped from the flying sledge, but the unluckier hands came after his heels in fuller howl. He noticed the singular appearance of the streets. Bands of the scum of the population hung at various points: from time to time a shout was raised at a distance, "Abasso il zigarro!" and "Away with the cigar!" went an organized file-firing of cries along the open place. Several gentlemen were mobbed, and compelled to fling the cigars from their teeth. He saw the polizta in twos and threes taking counsel and shrugging, evidently too anxious to avoid a collision. Austrian soldiers and subalterns alone smoked freely; they puffed the harder when the yells and hootings and whistlings thickened at their heels. Sometimes they walked on at their own pace; or, when the noise swelled to a crisis, turned and stood fast, making an exhibition of curling smoke, as a mute form of contempt. Then commenced hustlings and a tremendous uproar; sabres were drawn, the whitecoats planted themselves back to back. Milan was clearly in a condition of raging disease. The soldiery not only accepted the challenge of the mob, but assumed the offensive. Here and there they were seen crossing the street to puff obnoxiously in the faces of people. Numerous subalterns were abroad, lively for strife, and bright with the signal of their readiness. An icy wind blew down from the Alps, whitening the housetops and the ways, but every street, torso, and piazza was dense with loungers, as on a summer evening; the clamour of a skirmish anywhere attracted streams of disciplined rioters on all sides; it was the holiday of rascals.

Our traveller had ordered his vetturino to drive slowly to his hotel, that he might take the features of this novel scene. He soon showed his view of the case by putting an unlighted cigar in his mouth. The vetturino noted that his conveyance acted as a kindling-match to awaken cries in quiet quarters, looked round, and grinned savagely at the sight of the cigar.

"Drop it, or I drop you," he said; and hearing the command to drive on, pulled up short.

They were in a narrow way leading to the Piazza de' Mercanti. While the altercation was going on between them, a great push of men emerged from one of the close courts some dozen paces ahead of the horse, bearing forth a single young officer in their midst.

"Signore, would you like to be the froth of a boiling of that sort?" The vetturino seized the image at once to strike home his instance of the danger of outraging the will of the people.

Our traveller immediately unlocked a case that lay on the seat in front of him, and drew out a steel scabbard, from which he plucked the sword, and straightway leaped to the ground. The officer's cigar had been dashed from his mouth: he stood at bay, sword in hand, meeting a rush with a desperate stroke. The assistance of a second sword got him clear of the fray. Both hastened forward as the crush melted with the hiss of a withdrawing wave. They interchanged exclamations: "Is it you, Jenna!"

"In the devil's name, Pierson, have you come to keep your appointment in mid-winter?"

"Come on: I'll stick beside you."

"On, then!"

They glanced behind them, heeding little the tail of ruffians whom they had silenced.

"We shall have plenty of fighting soon, so we'll smoke a cordial cigar together," said Lieutenant Jenna, and at once struck a light and blazed defiance to Milan afresh—an example that was necessarily followed by his comrade. "What has happened to you, Pierson? Of course, I knew you were ready for our bit of play—though you'll hear what I said of you. How the deuce could you think of running off with that opera girl, and getting a fellow in the mountains to stab our merry old Weisspriess, just because you fancied he was going to slip a word or so over the back of his hand in Countess Lena's ear? No wonder she's shy of you now."

"So, that's the tale afloat," said Wilfrid. "Come to my hotel and dine with me. I suppose that cur has driven my luggage there."

Jenna informed him that officers had to muster in barracks every evening.

"Come and see your old comrades; they'll like you better in bad luck—there's the comfort of it: hang the human nature! She's a good old brute, if you don't drive her hard. Our regiment left Verona in November. There we had tolerable cookery; come and take the best we can give you."

But this invitation Wilfrid had to decline.

"Why?" said Jenna.

He replied: "I've stuck at Meran three months. I did it, in obedience to what I understood from Colonel Zofel to be the General's orders. When I was as perfectly dry as a baked Egyptian, I determined to believe that I was not only in disgrace, but dismissed the service. I posted to Botzen and Riva, on to Milan; and here I am. The least I can do is to show myself here."

"Very well, then, come and show yourself at our table," said Jenna. "Listen: we'll make a furious row after supper, and get hauled in by the collar before the General. You can swear you have never been absent from duty: swear the General never gave you forcible furlough. I'll swear it; all our fellows will swear it. The General will say, 'Oh! a very big lie's equal to a truth; big brother to a fact, or something; as he always does, you know. Face it out. We can't spare a good stout sword in these times. On with me, my Pierson."

"I would," said Wilfrid, doubtfully.

A douse of water from a window extinguished their cigars.

Lieutenant Jenna wiped his face deliberately, and lighting another cigar, remarked—"This is the fifth poor devil who has come to an untimely end within an hour. It is brisk work. Now, I'll swear I'll smoke this one out."

The cigar was scattered in sparks from his lips by a hat skilfully flung. He picked it up miry and cleaned it, observing that his honour was pledged to this fellow. The hat he trampled into a muddy lump. Wilfrid found it impossible to ape his coolness. He swung about for an adversary. Jenna pulled him on.

"A salute from a window," he said. "We can't storm the houses. The time'll come for it—and then, you cats!"

Wilfrid inquired how long this state of things had been going on. Jenna replied that they appeared to be in the middle of it;—nearly a week. Another week, and their day would arrive; and then!

"Have you heard anything of a Count Ammiani here?" said Wilfrid.

"Oh! he's one of the lot, I believe. We have him fast, as we'll have the bundle of them. Keep eye on those dogs behind us, and manoeuvre your cigar. The plan is, to give half-a-dozen bright puffs, and then keep it in your fist; and when you see an Italian head, volcano him like fury. Yes, I've heard of that Ammiani. The scoundrels, made an attempt to get him out of prison—I fancy he's in the city prison—last Friday night. I don't know exactly where he is; but it's pretty fair reckoning to say that he'll enjoy a large slice of the next year in the charming solitude of Spielberg, if Milan is restless. Is he a friend of yours?"

"Not by any means," said Wilfrid.

"Mio prigione!" Jenna mouthed with ineffable contemptuousness; "he'll have time to write his memoirs, as, one of the dogs did. I remember my mother crying over, the book. I read it? Not I! I never read books. My father said—the stout old colonel—'Prison seems to make these Italians take an interest in themselves.' 'Oh!' says my mother, 'why can't they be at peace with us?' 'That's exactly the question,' says my father, 'we're always putting to them.' And so I say. Why can't they let us smoke our cigars in peace?"

Jenna finished by assaulting a herd of faces with smoke.

"Pig of a German!" was shouted; and "Porco, porco," was sung in a scale of voices. Jenna received a blinding slap across the eyes. He staggered back; Wilfrid slashed his sword in defence of him. He struck a man down. "Blood! blood!" cried the gathering mob, and gave space, but hedged the couple thickly. Windows were thrown up; forth came a rain of household projectiles. The cry of "Blood! blood!" was repeated by numbers pouring on them from the issues to right and left. It is a terrible cry in a city. In a city of the South it rouses the wild beast in men to madness. Jenna smoked triumphantly and blew great clouds, with an eye aloft for the stools, basins, chairs, and water descending. They were in the middle of one of the close streets of old Milan. The man felled by Wilfrid was raised on strong arms, that his bleeding head might be seen of all, and a dreadful hum went round. A fire of missiles, stones, balls of wax, lumps of dirt, sticks of broken chairs, began to play. Wilfrid had a sudden gleam of the face of his Verona assailant. He and Jenna called "Follow me," in one breath, and drove forward with sword-points, which they dashed at the foremost; by dint of swift semicirclings of the edges they got through, but a mighty voice of command thundered; the rearward portion of the mob swung rapidly to the front, presenting a scattered second barrier; Jenna tripped on a fallen body, lost his cigar, and swore that he must find it. A dagger struck his sword-arm. He staggered and flourished his blade in the air, calling "On!" without stirring. "This infernal cigar!" he said; and to the mob, "What mongrel of you took my cigar?" Stones thumped on his breast; the barrier-line ahead grew denser. "I'll go at them first; you're bleeding," said Wilfrid. They were refreshed by the sound of German cheering, as in approach. Jenna uplifted a crow of the regimental hurrah of the charge; it was answered; on they went and got through the second fence, saw their comrades, and were running to meet them, when a weighted ball hit Wilfrid on the back of the head. He fell, as he believed, on a cushion of down, and saw thousands of saints dancing with lamps along cathedral aisles.

The next time he opened his eyes he fancied he had dropped into the vaults of the cathedral. His sensation of sinking was so vivid that he feared lest he should be going still further below. There was a lamp in the chamber, and a young man sat reading by the light of the lamp. Vision danced fantastically on Wilfrid's brain. He saw that he rocked as in a ship, yet there was no noise of the sea; nothing save the remote thunder haunting empty ears at strain for sound. He looked again; the young man was gone, the lamp was flickering. Then he became conscious of a strong ray on his eyelids; he beheld his enemy gazing down on him and swooned. It was with joy, that when his wits returned, he found himself looking on the young man by the lamp. "That other face was a dream," he thought, and studied the aspect of the young man with the unwearied attentiveness of partial stupor, that can note accurately, but cannot deduce from its noting, and is inveterate in patience because it is unideaed. Memory wakened first.

"Guidascarpi!" he said to himself.

The name was uttered half aloud. The young man started and closed his book.

"You know me?" he asked.

"You are Guidascarpi?"

"I am."

"Guidascarpi, I think I helped to save your life in Meran."

The young man stooped over him. "You speak of my brother Angelo. I am Rinaldo. My debt to you is the same, if you have served him."

"Is he safe?"

"He is in Lugano."

"The signorina Vittoria?"

"In Turin."

"Where am I?"

The reply came from another mouth than Rinaldo's.

"You are in the poor lodging of the shoemaker, whose shoes, if you had thought fit to wear them, would have conducted you anywhere but to this place."

"Who are you?" Wilfrid moaned.

"You ask who I am. I am the Eye of Italy. I am the Cat who sees in the dark." Barto Rizzo raised the lamp and stood at his feet. "Look straight. You know me, I think."

Wilfrid sighed, "Yes, I know you; do your worst."

His head throbbed with the hearing of a heavy laugh, as if a hammer had knocked it. What ensued he knew not; he was left to his rest. He lay there many days and nights, that were marked by no change of light; the lamp burned unwearyingly. Rinaldo and a woman tended him. The sign of his reviving strength was shown by a complaint he launched at the earthy smell of the place.

"It is like death," said Rinaldo, coming to his side. "I am used to it, and familiar with death too," he added in a musical undertone.

"Are you also a prisoner here?" Wilfrid questioned him.

"I am."

"The brute does not kill, then?"

"No; he saves. I owe my life to him. He has rescued yours."

"Mine?" said Wilfrid.

"You would have been torn to pieces in the streets but for Barto Rizzo."

The streets were the world above to Wilfrid; he was eager to hear of the doings in them. Rinaldo told him that the tobacco-war raged still; the soldiery had recently received orders to smoke abroad, and street battles were hourly occurring. "They call this government!" he interjected.

He was a soft-voiced youth; slim and tall and dark, like Angelo, but with a more studious forehead. The book he was constantly reading was a book of chemistry. He entertained Wilfrid with very strange talk. He spoke of the stars and of a destiny. He cited certain minor events of his life to show the ground of his present belief in there being a written destiny for each individual man. "Angelo and I know it well. It was revealed to us when we were boys. It has been certified to us up to this moment. Mark what I tell you," he pursued in a devout sincerity of manner that baffled remonstrance, "my days end with this new year. His end with the year following. Our house is dead."

Wilfrid pressed his hand. "Have you not been too long underground?"

"That is the conviction I am coming to. But when I go out to breathe the air of heaven, I go to my fate. Should I hesitate? We Italians of this period are children of thunder and live the life of a flash. The worms may creep on: the men must die. Out of us springs a better world. Romara, Ammiani, Mercadesco, Montesini, Rufo, Cardi, whether they see it or not, will sweep forward to it. To some of them, one additional day of breath is precious. Not so for Angelo and me. We are unbeloved. We have neither mother nor sister, nor betrothed. What is an existence that can fly to no human arms? I have been too long underground, because, while I continue to hide, I am as a drawn sword between two lovers."

The previous mention of Ammiani's name, together with the knowledge he had of Ammiani's relationship to the Guidascarpi, pointed an instant identification of these lovers to Wilfrid.

He asked feverishly who they were, and looked his best simplicity, as one who was always interested by stories of lovers.

The voice of Barto Rizzo, singing "Vittoria!" stopped Rinaldo's reply: but Wilfrid read it in his smile at that word. He was too weak to restrain his anguish, and flung on the couch and sobbed. Rinaldo supposed that he was in fear of Barto, and encouraged him to meet the man confidently. A lusty "Viva l'Italia! Vittoria!" heralded Barto's entrance. "My boy! my noblest! we have beaten them the cravens! Tell me now—have I served an apprenticeship to the devil for nothing? We have struck the cigars out of their mouths and the monopoly-money out of their pockets. They have surrendered. The Imperial order prohibits soldiers from smoking in the streets of Milan, and so throughout Lombardy! Soon we will have the prisons empty, by our own order. Trouble yourself no more about Ammiani. He shall come out to the sound of trumpets. I hear them! Hither, my Rosellina, my plump melon; up with your red lips, and buss me a Napoleon salute—ha! ha!"

Barto's wife went into his huge arm, and submissively lifted her face. He kissed her like a barbaric king, laughing as from wine.

Wilfrid smothered his head from his incarnate thunder. He was unnoticed by Barto. Presently a silence told him that he was left to himself. An idea possessed him that the triumph of the Italians meant the release of Ammiani, and his release the loss of Vittoria for ever. Since her graceless return of his devotion to her in Meran, something like a passion—arising from the sole spring by which he could be excited to conceive a passion—had filled his heart. He was one of those who delight to dally with gentleness and faith, as with things that are their heritage; but the mere suspicion of coquettry and indifference plunged him into a fury of jealous wrathfulness, and tossed so desireable an image of beauty before him that his mad thirst to embrace it seemed love. By our manner of loving we are known. He thought it no meanness to escape and cause a warning to be conveyed to the Government that there was another attempt brewing for the rescue of Count Ammiani. Acting forthwith on the hot impulse, he seized the lamp. The door was unlocked. Luckier than Luigi had been, he found a ladder outside, and a square opening through which he crawled; continuing to ascend along close passages and up narrow flights of stairs, that appeared to him to be fashioned to avoid the rooms of the house. At last he pushed a door, and found himself in an armoury, among stands of muskets, swords, bayonets, cartouche-boxes, and, most singular of all, though he observed them last, small brass pieces of cannon, shining with polish. Shot was piled in pyramids beneath their mouths. He examined the guns admiringly. There were rows of daggers along shelves; some in sheath, others bare; one that had been hastily wiped showed a smear of ropy blood. He stood debating whether he should seize a sword for his protection. In the act of trying its temper on the floor, the sword-hilt was knocked from his hand, and he felt a coil of arms around him. He was in the imprisoning embrace of Barto Rizzo's wife. His first, and perhaps natural, impression accused her of a violent display of an eccentric passion for his manly charms; and the tighter she locked him, the more reasonably was he held to suppose it; but as, while stamping on the floor, she offered nothing to his eyes save the yellow poll of her neck, and hung neither panting nor speaking, he became undeceived. His struggles were preposterous; his lively sense of ridicule speedily stopped them. He remained passive, from time to time desperately adjuring his living prison to let him loose, or to conduct him whither he had come; but the inexorable coil kept fast—how long there was no guessing—till he could have roared out tears of rage, and that is extremity for an Englishman. Rinaldo arrived in his aid; but the woman still clung to him. He was freed only by the voice of Barto Rizzo, who marched him back. Rinaldo subsequently told him that his discovery of the armoury necessitated his confinement.

"Necessitates it!" cried Wilfrid. "Is this your Italian gratitude?"

The other answered: "My friend, you risked your fortune for my brother; but this is a case that concerns our country."

He deemed these words to be an unquestionable justification, for he said no more. After this they ceased to converse.

Each lay down on his strip of couch-matting; rose and ate, and passed the dreadful untamed hours; nor would Wilfrid ask whether it was day or night. We belong to time so utterly, that when we get no note of time, it wears the shrouded head of death for us already. Rinaldo could quit the place as he pleased; he knew the hours; and Wilfrid supposed that it must be hatred that kept him from voluntarily divulging that blessed piece of knowledge. He had to encourage a retorting spirit of hatred in order to mask his intense craving. By an assiduous calculation of seconds and minutes, he was enabled to judge that the lamp burned a space of six hours before it required replenishing. Barto Rizzo's wife trimmed it regularly, but the accursed woman came at all seasons. She brought their meals irregularly, and she would never open her lips: she was like a guardian of the tombs. Wilfrid abandoned his dream of the variation of night and day, and with that the sense of life deadened, as the lamp did toward the sixth hour. Thenceforward his existence fed on the movements of his companion, the workings of whose mind he began to read with a marvellous insight. He knew once, long in advance of the act or an indication of it, that Rinaldo was bent on prayer. Rinaldo had slightly closed his eyelids during the perusal of his book; he had taken a pencil and traced lines on it from memory, and dotted points here and there; he had left the room, and returned to resume his study. Then, after closing the book softly, he had taken up the mark he was accustomed to place in the last page of his reading, and tossed it away. Wilfrid was prepared to clap hands when he should see the hated fellow drop on his knees; but when that sight verified his calculation, he huddled himself exultingly in his couch-cloth:—it was like a confirming clamour to him that he was yet wholly alive. He watched the anguish of the prayer, and was rewarded for the strain of his faculties by sleep. Barto Rizzo's rough voice awakened him. Barto had evidently just communicated dismal tidings to Rinaldo, who left the vault with him, and was absent long enough to make Wilfrid forget his hatred in an irresistible desire to catch him by the arm and look in his face.

"Ah! you have not forsaken me," the greeting leaped out.

"Not now," said Rinaldo.

"Do you think of going?"

"I will speak to you presently, my friend."

"Hound!" cried Wilfrid, and turned his face to the wall.

Until he slept, he heard the rapid travelling of a pen; on his awakening, the pen vexed him like a chirping cricket that tells us that cock-crow is long distant when we are moaning for the dawn. Great drops of sweat were on Rinaldo's forehead. He wrote as one who poured forth a history without pause. Barto's wife came to the lamp and beckoned him out, bearing the lamp away. There was now for the first time darkness in this vault. Wilfrid called Rinaldo by name, and heard nothing but the fear of the place, which seemed to rise bristling at his voice and shrink from it. He called till dread of his voice held him dumb. "I am, then, a coward," he thought. Nor could he by-and-by repress a start of terror on hearing Rinaldo speak out of the darkness. With screams for the lamp, and cries that he was suffering slow murder, he underwent a paroxysm in the effort to conceal his abject horror. Rinaldo sat by his side patiently. At last, he said: "We are both of us prisoners on equal terms now." That was quieting intelligence to Wilfrid, who asked eagerly: "What hour is it?"

It was eleven of the forenoon. Wilfrid strove to dissociate his recollection of clear daylight from the pressure of the hideous featureless time surrounding him. He asked: "What week?" It was the first week in March. Wilfrid could not keep from sobbing aloud. In the early period of such a captivity, imagination, deprived of all other food, conjures phantasms for the employment of the brain; but there is still some consciousness within the torpid intellect wakeful to laugh at them as they fly, though they have held us at their mercy. The face of time had been imaged like the withering mask of a corpse to him. He had felt, nevertheless, that things had gone on as we trust them to do at the closing of our eyelids: he had preserved a mystical remote faith in the steady running of the world above, and hugged it as his most precious treasure. A thunder was rolled in his ears when he heard of the flight of two months at one bound. Two big months! He would have guessed, at farthest, two weeks. "I have been two months in one shirt? Impossible!" he exclaimed. His serious idea (he cherished it for the support of his reason) was, that the world above had played a mad prank since he had been shuffled off its stage.

"It can't be March," he said. "Is there sunlight overhead?"

"It is a true Milanese March," Rinaldo replied.

"Why am I kept a prisoner?"

"I cannot say. There must be some idea of making use of you."

"Have you arms?"

"I have none."

"You know where they're to be had."

"I know, but I would not take them if I could. They, my friend, are for a better cause."

"A thousand curses on your country!" cried Wilfrid. "Give me air; give me freedom, I am stifled; I am eaten up with dirt; I am half dead. Are we never to have the lamp again?"

"Hear me speak," Rinaldo stopped his ravings. "I will tell you what my position is. A second attempt has been made to help Count Ammiani's escape; it has failed. He is detained a prisoner by the Government under the pretence that he is implicated in the slaying of an Austrian noble by the hands of two brothers, one of whom slew him justly—not as a dog is slain, but according to every honourable stipulation of the code. I was the witness of the deed. It is for me that my cousin, Count Ammiani, droops in prison when he should be with his bride. Let me speak on, I pray you. I have said that I stand between two lovers. I can release him, I know well, by giving myself up to the Government. Unless I do so instantly, he will be removed from Milan to one of their fortresses in the interior, and there he may cry to the walls and iron-bars for his trial. They are aware that he is dear to Milan, and these two miserable attempts have furnished them with their excuse. Barto Rizzo bids me wait. I have waited: I can wait no longer. The lamp is withheld from me to stop my writing to my brother, that I may warn him of my design, but the letter is written; the messenger is on his way to Lugano. I do not state my intentions before I have taken measures to accomplish them. I am as much Barto Rizzo's prisoner now as you are."

The plague of darkness and thirst for daylight prevented Wilfrid from having any other sentiment than gladness that a companion equally unfortunate with himself was here, and equally desirous to go forth. When Barto's wife brought their meal, and the lamp to light them eating it, Rinaldo handed her pen, ink, pencil, paper, all the material of correspondence; upon which, as one who had received a stipulated exchange, she let the lamp remain. While the new and thrice-dear rays were illumining her dark-coloured solid beauty, I know not what touch of man-like envy or hurt vanity led Wilfrid to observe that the woman's eyes dwelt with a singular fulness and softness on Rinaldo. It was fulness and softness void of fire, a true ox-eyed gaze, but human in the fall of the eyelids; almost such as an early poet of the brush gave to the Virgin carrying her Child, to become an everlasting reduplicated image of a mother's strong beneficence of love. He called Rinaldo's attention to it when the woman had gone. Rinaldo understood his meaning at once.

"It will have to be so, I fear," he said; "I have thought of it. But if I lead her to disobey Barto, there is little hope for the poor soul." He rose up straight, like one who would utter grace for meat. "Must we, O my God, give a sacrifice at every step?"

With that he resumed his seat stiffly, and bent and murmured to himself. Wilfrid had at one time of his life imagined that he was marked by a peculiar distinction from the common herd; but contact with this young man taught him to feel his fellowship to the world at large, and to rejoice at it, though it partially humbled him.

They had no further visit from Barto Rizzo. The woman tended them in the same unswerving silence, and at whiles that adorable maternity of aspect. Wilfrid was touched by commiseration for her. He was too bitterly fretful on account of clean linen and the liberty which fluttered the prospect of it, to think much upon what her fate might be: perhaps a beating, perhaps the knife. But the vileness of wearing one shirt two months and more had hardened his heart; and though he was considerate enough not to prompt his companion very impatiently, he submitted desperate futile schemes to him, and suggested— "To-night?—tomorrow?—the next day?" Rinaldo did not heed him. He lay on his couch like one who bleeds inwardly, thinking of the complacent faithfulness of that poor creature's face. Barto Rizzo had sworn to him that there should be a rising in Milan before the month was out; but he had lost all confidence in Milanese risings. Ammiani would be removed, if he delayed; and he knew that the moment his letter reached Lugano, Angelo would start for Milan and claim to surrender in his stead. The woman came, and went forth, and Rinaldo did not look at her until his resolve was firm.

He said to Wilfrid in her presence, "Swear that you will reveal nothing of this house."

Wilfrid spiritedly pronounced his gladdest oath.

"It is dark in the streets," Rinaldo addressed the woman. "Lead us out, for the hour has come when I must go."

She clutched her hands below her bosom to stop its great heaving, and stood as one smitten by the sudden hearing of her sentence. The sight was pitiful, for her face scarcely changed; the anguish was expressionless. Rinaldo pointed sternly to the door.

"Stay," Wilfrid interposed. "That wretch may be in the house, and will kill her."

"She is not thinking of herself," said Rinaldo.

"But, stay," Wilfrid repeated. The woman's way of taking breath shocked and enfeebled him.

Rinaldo threw the door open.

"Must you? must you?" her voice broke.

"Waste no words."

"You have not seen a priest?"

"I go to him."

"You die."

"What is death to me? Be dumb, that I may think well of you till my last moment."

"What is death to me? Be dumb!"

She had spoken with her eyes fixed on his couch. It was the figure of one upon the scaffold, knitting her frame to hold up a strangled heart.

"What is death to me? Be dumb!" she echoed him many times on the rise and fall of her breathing, and turned to get him in her eyes. "Be dumb! be dumb!" She threw her arms wide out, and pressed his temples and kissed him.

The scene was like hot iron to Wilfrid's senses. When he heard her coolly asking him for his handkerchief to blind him, he had forgotten the purpose, and gave it mechanically. Nothing was uttered throughout the long mountings and descent of stairs. They passed across one corridor where the walls told of a humming assemblage of men within. A current of keen air was the first salute Wilfrid received from the world above; his handkerchief was loosened; he stood foolish as a blind man, weak as a hospital patient, on the steps leading into a small square of visible darkness, and heard the door shut behind him. Rinaldo led him from the court to the street.

"Farewell," he said. "Get some housing instantly; avoid exposure to the air. I leave you."

Wilfrid spent his tongue in a fruitless and meaningless remonstrance. "And you?" he had the grace to ask.

"I go straight to find a priest. Farewell."

So they parted.

The same hand which brought Rinaldo's letter to his brother delivered a message from Barto Rizzo, bidding Angelo to start at once and head a stout dozen or so of gallant Swiss. The letter and the message appeared to be grievous contradictions: one was evidently a note of despair, while the other sang like a trumpet. But both were of a character to draw him swiftly on to Milan. He sent word to his Lugano friends, naming a village among the mountains between Como and Varese, that they might join him there if they pleased.

Toward nightfall, on the nineteenth of the month, he stood with a small band of Ticinese and Italian fighting lads two miles distant from the city. There was a momentary break in long hours of rain; the air was full of inexplicable sounds, that floated over them like a toning of multitudes wailing and singing fitfully behind a swaying screen. They bent their heads. At intervals a sovereign stamp on the pulsation of the uproar said, distinct as a voice in the ear—Cannon. "Milan's alive!" Angelo cried, and they streamed forward under the hurry of stars and scud, till thumping guns and pattering musket-shots, the long big boom of surgent hosts, and the muffled voluming and crash of storm-bells, proclaimed that the insurrection was hot. A rout of peasants bearing immense ladders met them, and they joined with cheers, and rushed to the walls. As yet no gate was in the possession of the people. The walls showed bayonet-points: a thin edge of steel encircled a pit of fire. Angelo resolved to break through at once. The peasants hesitated, but his own men were of one mind to follow, and, planting his ladder in the ditch, he rushed up foremost. The ladder was full short; he called out in German to a soldier to reach his hand down, and the butt-end of a musket was dropped, which he grasped, and by this aid sprang to the parapet, and was seized. "Stop," he said, "there's a fellow below with my brandy-flask and portmanteau." The soldiers were Italians; they laughed, and hauled away at man after man of the mounting troop, calling alternately "brandy-flask!—portmanteau!" as each one raised a head above the parapet. "The signor has a good supply of spirits and baggage," they remarked. He gave them money for porterage, saying, "You see, the gates are held by that infernal people, and a quiet traveller must come over the walls. Viva l'Italia! who follows me?" He carried away three of those present. The remainder swore that they and their comrades would be on his side on the morrow. Guided by the new accession to his force, Angelo gained the streets. All shots had ceased; the streets were lighted with torches and hand-lamps; barricades were up everywhere, like a convulsion of the earth. Tired of receiving challenges and mounting the endless piles of stones, he sat down at the head of the Corso di Porta Nuova, and took refreshments from the hands of ladies. The house-doors were all open. The ladies came forth bearing wine and minestra, meat and bread, on trays; and quiet eating and drinking, and fortifying of the barricades, went on. Men were rubbing their arms and trying rusty gun-locks. Few of them had not seen Barto Rizzo that day; but Angelo could get no tidings of his brother. He slept on a door-step, dreaming that he was blown about among the angels of heaven and hell by a glorious tempest. Near morning an officer of volunteers came to inspect the barricade defences. Angelo knew him by sight; it was Luciano Romara. He explained the position of the opposing forces. The Marshal, he said, was clearly no street-fighter. Estimating the army under his orders in Milan at from ten to eleven thousand men of all arms, it was impossible for him to guard the gates and then walls, and at the same time fight the city. Nor could he provision his troops. Yesterday the troops had made one: charge and done mischief, but they had immediately retired. "And if they take to cannonading us to-day, we shall know what that means," Romara concluded. Angelo wanted to join him. "No, stay here," said Romara. "I think you are a man who won't give ground." He had not seen either Rinaldo or Ammiani, but spoke of both as certain to be rescued.

Rain and cannon filled the weary space of that day. Some of the barricades fronting the city gates had been battered down by nightfall; they were restored within an hour. Their defenders entered the houses right and left during the cannonade, waiting to meet the charge; but the Austrians held off. "They have no plan," Romara said on his second visit of inspection; "they are waiting on Fortune, and starve meanwhile. We can beat them at that business."

Romara took Angelo and his Swiss away with him. The interior of the city was abandoned by the Imperialists, who held two or three of the principal buildings and the square of the Duomo. Clouds were driving thick across the cold-gleaming sky when the storm-bells burst out with the wild Jubilee-music of insurrection—a carol, a jangle of all discord, savage as flame. Every church of the city lent its iron tongue to the peal; and now they joined and now rolled apart, now joined again and clanged like souls shrieking across the black gulfs of an earthquake; they swam aloft with mournful delirium, tumbled together, were scattered in spray, dissolved, renewed, died, as a last worn wave casts itself on an unfooted shore, and rang again as through rent doorways, became a clamorous host, an iron body, a pressure as of a down-drawn firmament, and once more a hollow vast, as if the abysses of the Circles were sounded through and through. To the Milanese it was an intoxication; it was the howling of madness to the Austrians—a torment and a terror: they could neither sing, nor laugh, nor talk under it. Where they stood in the city, the troops could barely hear their officers' call of command. No sooner had the bells broken out than the length of every street and Corso flashed with the tri-coloured flag; musket-muzzles peeped from the windows; men with great squares of pavement lined the roofs. Romara mounted a stiff barricade and beheld a scattered regiment running the gauntlet of storms of shot and missiles, in full retreat upon the citadel. On they came, officers in front for the charge, as usual with the Austrians; fire on both flanks, a furious mob at their heels, and the barricade before them. They rushed at Romara, and were hurled back, and stood in a riddled lump. Suddenly Romara knocked up the rifles of the couching Swiss; he yelled to the houses to stop firing. "Surrender your prisoners,—you shall pass," he called. He had seen one dear head in the knot of the soldiery. No answer was given. Romara, with Angelo and his Swiss and the ranks of the barricade, poured over and pierced the streaming mass, steel for steel.

"Ammiani! Ammiani!" Romara cried; a roar from the other side, "Barto! Barto! the Great Cat!" met the cry. The Austrians struck up a cheer under the iron derision of the bells; it was ludicrous, it was as if a door had slammed on their mouths, ringing tremendous echoes in a vaulted roof. They stood sweeping fire in two oblong lines; a show of military array was preserved like a tattered robe, till Romara drove at their centre and left the retreat clear across the barricade. Then the whitecoats were seen flowing over, the motley surging hosts from the city in pursuit—foam of a storm-torrent hurled forward by the black tumult of precipitous waters. Angelo fell on his brother's neck; Romara clasped Carlo Ammiani. These two were being marched from the prison to the citadel when Barto Rizzo, who had prepared to storm the building, assailed the troops. To him mainly they were indebted for their rescue.

Even in that ecstasy of meeting, the young men smiled at the preternatural transport on his features as he bounded by them, mad for slaughter, and mounting a small brass gun on the barricade, sent the charges of shot into the rear of the enemy. He kissed the black lip of his little thunderer in, a rapture of passion; called it his wife, his naked wife; the best of mistresses, who spoke only when he charged her to speak; raved that she was fair, and liked hugging; that she was true, and the handsomest daughter of Italy; that she would be the mother of big ones—none better than herself, though they were mountains of sulphur big enough to make one gulp of an army.

His wife in the flesh stood at his feet with a hand-grenade and a rifle, daggers and pistols in her belt. Her face was black with powder-smoke as the muzzle of the gun. She looked at Rinaldo once, and Rinaldo at her; both dropped their eyes, for their joy at seeing one another alive was mighty.

Dead Austrians were gathered in a heap. Dead and wounded Milanese were taken into the houses. Wine was brought forth by ladies and household women. An old crutched beggar, who had performed a deed of singular intrepidity in himself kindling a fire at the door of one of the principal buildings besieged by the people, and who showed perforated rags with a comical ejaculation of thanks to the Austrians for knowing how to hit a scarecrow and make a beggar holy, was the object of particular attention. Barto seated him on his gun, saying that his mistress and beauty was honoured; ladies were proud in waiting on the fine frowzy old man. It chanced during that morning that Wilfrid Pierson had attached himself to Lieutenant Jenna's regiment as a volunteer. He had no arms, nothing but a huge white umbrella, under which he walked dry in the heavy rain, and passed through the fire like an impassive spectator of queer events. Angelo's Swiss had captured them, and the mob were maltreating them because they declined to shout for this valorous ancient beggarman. "No doubt he's a capital fellow," said Jenna; "but 'Viva Scottocorni' is not my language;" and the spirited little subaltern repeated his "Excuse me," with very good temper, while one knocked off his shako, another tugged at his coat-skirts. Wilfrid sang out to the Guidascarpi, and the brothers sprang to him and set them free; but the mob, like any other wild beast gorged with blood, wanted play, and urged Barto to insist that these victims should shout the viva in exaltation of their hero.

"Is there a finer voice than mine?" said Barto, and he roared the 'viva' like a melodious bull. Yet Wilfrid saw that he had been recognized. In the hour of triumph Barto Rizzo had no lust for petty vengeance. The magnanimous devil plumped his gorge contentedly on victory. His ardour blazed from his swarthy crimson features like a blown fire, when scouts came running down with word that all about the Porta Camosina, Madonna del Carmine, and the Gardens, the Austrians were reaping the white flag of the inhabitants of that district. Thitherward his cry of "Down with the Tedeschi!" led the boiling tide. Rinaldo drew Wilfrid and Jenna to an open doorway, counselling the latter to strip the gold from his coat and speak his Italian in monosyllables. A woman of the house gave her promise to shelter and to pass them forward. Romara, Ammiani, and the Guidascarpi, went straight to the Casa Gonfalonieri, where they hoped to see stray members of the Council of War, and hear a correction of certain unpleasant rumours concerning the dealings of the Provisional Government with Charles Albert.

The first crack of a division between the patriot force and the aristocracy commenced this day; the day following it was a breach.

A little before dusk the bells of the city ceased their hammering, and when they ceased, all noises of men and musketry seemed childish. The woman who had promised to lead Wilfrid and Jenna to the citadel, feared no longer either for herself or them, and passed them on up the Corso Francesco past the Contrada del Monte. Jenna pointed out the Duchess of Graatli's house, saying, "By the way, the Lenkensteins are here; they left Venice last week. Of course you know, or don't you?—and there they must stop, I suppose." Wilfrid nodded an immediate good-bye to him, and crossed to the house-door. His eccentric fashion of acting had given him fame in the army, but Jenna stormed at it now, and begged him to come on and present himself to General Schoneck, if not to General Pierson. Wilfrid refused even to look behind him. In fact, it was a part of the gallant fellow's coxcombry (or nationality) to play the Englishman. He remained fixed by the housedoor till midnight, when a body of men in the garb of citizens, volubly and violently Italian in their talk, struck thrice at the door. Wilfrid perceived Count

Lenkenstein among them. The ladies Bianca, Anna, and Lena issued mantled and hooded between the lights of two barricade watchfires. Wilfrid stepped after them. They had the password, for the barricades were crossed. The captain of the head-barricade in the Corso demurred, requiring a counter-sign. Straightway he was cut down. He blew an alarm-call, when up sprang a hundred torches. The band of Germans dashed at the barricade as at the tusks of a boar. They were picked men, most of them officers, but a scanty number in the thick of an armed populace. Wilfrid saw the lighted passage into the great house, and thither, throwing out his arms, he bore the affrighted group of ladies, as a careful shepherd might do. Returning to Count Lenkenstein's side, "Where are they?" the count said, in mortal dread. "Safe," Wilfrid replied. The count frowned at him inquisitively. "Cut your way through, and on!" he cried to three or four who hung near him; and these went to the slaughter.

"Why do you stand by me, sir?" said the count. Interior barricades were pouring their combatants to the spot; Count Lenkenstein was plunged upon the door-steps. Wilfrid gained half-a-minute's parley by shouting in his foreign accent, "Would you hurt an Englishman?" Some one took him by the arm, and helping to raise the count, hurried them both into the house.

"You must make excuses for popular fury in times like these," the stranger observed.

The Austrian nobleman asked him stiffly for his name. The name of Count Ammiani was given. "I think you know it," Carlo added.

"You escaped from your lawful imprisonment this day, did you not?—you and your cousin, the assassin. I talk of law! I might as justly talk of honour. Who lives here?" Carlo contained himself to answer, "The present occupant is, I believe, if I have hit the house I was seeking, the Countess d'Isorella."

"My family were placed here, sir?" Count Lenkenstein inquired of Wilfrid. But Wilfrid's attention was frozen by the sight of Vittoria's lover. A wifely call of "Adalbert" from above quieted the count's anxiety.

"Countess d'Isorella," he said. "I know that woman. She belongs to the secret cabinet of Carlo Alberto—a woman with three edges. Did she not visit you in prison two weeks ago? I speak to you, Count Ammiani. She applied to the Archduke and the Marshal for permission to visit you. It was accorded. To the devil with our days of benignity! She was from Turin. The shuffle has made her my hostess for the nonce. I will go to her. You, sir," the count turned to Wilfrid—"you will stay below. Are you in the pay of the insurgents?"

Wilfrid, the weakest of human beings where women were involved with him, did one of the hardest things which can task a young man's fortitude: he looked his superior in the face, and neither blenched, nor frowned, nor spoke.

Ammiani spoke for him. "There is no pay given in our ranks."

"The licence to rob is supposed to be an equivalent," said the count.

Countess d'Isorella herself came downstairs, with profuse apologies for the absence of all her male domestics, and many delicate dimples about her mouth in uttering them. Her look at Ammiani struck Wilfrid as having a peculiar burden either of meaning or of passion in it. The count grimaced angrily when he heard that his sister Lena was not yet able to bear the fatigue of a walk to the citadel. "I fear you must all be my guests, for an hour at least," said the countess.

Wilfrid was left pacing the hall. He thought he had never beheld so splendid a person, or one so subjugatingly gracious. Her speech and manner poured oil on the uncivil Austrian nobleman. What perchance had stricken Lena?

He guessed; and guessed it rightly. A folded scrap of paper signed by the Countess of Lenkenstein was brought to him.

It said:—"Are you making common cause with the rebels? Reply. One asks who should be told."

He wrote:—"I am an outcast of the army. I fight as a volunteer with the K. K. troops. Could I abandon them in their peril?"

The touch of sentiment he appended for Lena's comfort. He was too strongly impressed by the new vision of beauty in the house for his imagination to be flushed by the romantic posture of his devotion to a trailing flag.

No other message was delivered. Ammiani presently descended and obtained a guard from the barricade; word was sent on to the barricades in advance toward the citadel. Wilfrid stood aside as Count Lenkenstein led the ladies to the door, bearing Lena on his arm. She passed her lover veiled. The count said, "You follow." He used the menial second person plural of German, and repeated it peremptorily.

"I follow no civilian," said Wilfrid.

"Remember, sir, that if you are seen with arms in your hands, and are not in the ranks, you run the chances of being hanged."

Lena broke loose from her brother; in spite of Anna's sharp remonstrance and the count's vexed stamp of the foot, she implored her lover:—"Come with us; pardon us; protect me—me! You shall not be treated harshly. They shall not Oh! be near me. I have been ill; I shrink from danger. Be near me!"

Such humble pleading permitted Wilfrid's sore spirit to succumb with the requisite show of chivalrous dignity. He bowed, and gravely opened his enormous umbrella, which he held up over the heads of the ladies, while Ammiani led the way. All was quiet near the citadel. A fog of plashing rain hung in red gloom about the many watchfires of the insurgents, but the Austrian head-quarters lay sombre and still. Close at the gates, Ammiani saluted the ladies. Wilfrid did the same, and heard Lena's call to him unmoved.

"May I dare to hint to you that it would be better for you to join your party?" said Ammiani.

Wilfrid walked on. After appearing to weigh the matter, he answered, "The umbrella will be of no further service to them to-night."

Ammiani laughed, and begged to be forgiven; but he could have done nothing more flattering.

Sore at all points, tricked and ruined, irascible under the sense of his injuries, hating everybody and not honouring himself, Wilfrid was fast growing to be an eccentric by profession. To appear cool and careless was the great effort of his mind.

"We were introduced one day in the Piazza d'Armi," said Ammiani. "I would have found means to convey my apologies to you for my behaviour on that occasion, but I have been at the mercy of my enemies. Lieutenant Pierson, will you pardon me? I have learnt how dear you and your family should be to me. Pray, accept my excuses and my counsel. The Countess Lena was my friend when I was a boy. She is in deep distress."

"I thank you, Count Ammiani, for your extremely disinterested advice," said Wilfrid; but the Italian was not cut to the quick by his irony; and he added: "I have hoisted, you perceive, the white umbrella instead of wearing the white coat. It is almost as good as an hotel in these times; it gives as much shelter and nearly as much provision, and, I may say, better attendance. Good-night. You will be at it again about daylight, I suppose?"

"Possibly a little before," said Ammiani, cooled by the false ring of this kind of speech.

"It's useless to expect that your infernal bells will not burst out like all the lunatics on earth?"

"Quite useless, I fear. Good-night."

Ammiani charged one of the men at an outer barricade to follow the white umbrella and pass it on.

He returned to the Countess d'Isorella, who was awaiting him, and alone.

This glorious head had aroused his first boyish passion. Scandal was busy concerning the two, when Violetta d'Asola, the youthfullest widow in Lombardy and the loveliest woman, gave her hand to Count d'Isorella, who took it without question of the boy Ammiani. Carlo's mother assisted in that arrangement; a maternal plot, for which he could thank her only after he had seen Vittoria, and then had heard the buzz of whispers at Violetta's name. Countess d'Isorella proved her friendship to have survived the old passion, by travelling expressly from Turin to obtain leave to visit him in prison. It was a marvellous face to look upon between prison walls. Rescued while the soldiers were marching him to the citadel that day, he was called by pure duty to pay his respects to the countess as soon as he had heard from his mother that she was in the city. Nor was his mother sorry that he should go. She had patiently submitted to the fact of his betrothal to Vittoria, which was his safeguard in similar perils; and she rather hoped for Violetta to wean him from his extreme republicanism. By arguments? By influence, perhaps. Carlo's republicanism was preternatural in her sight, and she presumed that Violetta would talk to him discreetly and persuasively of the noble designs of the king.

Violetta d'Isorella received him with a gracious lifting of her fingers to his lips; congratulating him on his escape, and on the good fortune of the day. She laughed at the Lenkensteins and the singular Englishman; sat down to a little supper-tray, and pouted humorously as she asked him to feed on confects and wine; the huge appetites of the insurgents had devoured all her meat and bread.

"Why are you here?" he said.

She did well in replying boldly, "For the king."

"Would you tell another that it is for the king?"

"Would I speak to another as I speak to you?"

Ammiani inclined his head.

They spoke of the prospects of the insurrection, of the expected outbreak in Venice, the eruption of Paris and Vienna, and the new life of Italy; touching on Carlo Alberto to explode the truce in a laughing dissension. At last she said seriously, "I am a born Venetian, you know; I am not Piedmontese. Let me be sure that the king betrays the country, and I will prefer many heads to one. Excuse me if I am more womanly just at present. The king has sent his accredited messenger Tartini to the Provisional Government, requesting it to accept his authority. Why not? why not? on both sides. Count Medole gives his adhesion to the king, but you have a Council of War that rejects the king's overtures—a revolt within a revolt.

"It is deplorable. You must have an army. The Piedmontese once over the Ticino, how can you act in opposition to it? You must learn to take a master. The king is only, or he appears, tricksy because you compel him to wind and counterplot. I swear to you, Italy is his foremost thought. The Star of Italy sits on the Cross of Savoy."

Ammiani kept his eyelids modestly down. "Ten thousand to plead for him, such as you!" he said. "But there is only one!"

"If you had been headstrong once upon a time, and I had been weak, you see, my Carlo, you would have been a domestic tyrant, I a rebel. You will not admit the existence of a virtue in an opposite opinion. Wise was your mother when she said 'No' to a wilful boy!"

Violetta lit her cigarette and puffed the smoke lightly.

"I told you in that horrid dungeon, my Carlo Amaranto—I call you by the old name—the old name is sweet!—I told you that your Vittoria is enamoured of the king. She blushes like a battle-flag for the king. I have heard her 'Viva il Re!' It was musical."

"So I should have thought."

"Ay, but my amaranto-innamorato, does it not foretell strife? Would you ever—ever take a heart with a king's head stamped on it into your arms?"

"Give me the chance!"

He was guilty of this ardent piece of innocence though Violetta had pitched her voice in the key significant of a secret thing belonging to two memories that had not always flowed dividedly.

"Like a common coin?" she resumed.

"A heart with a king's head stamped on it like a common coin."

He recollected the sentence. He had once, during the heat of his grief for Giacomo Piaveni, cast it in her teeth.

Violetta repeated it, as to herself, tonelessly; a method of making an old unkindness strike back on its author with effect.

"Did we part good friends? I forget," she broke the silence.

"We meet, and we will be the best of friends," said Ammiani.

"Tell your mother I am not three years older than her son,—I am thirty. Who will make me young again? Tell her, my Carlo, that the genius for intrigue, of which she accuses me, develops at a surprising rate. As regards my beauty," the countess put a tooth of pearl on her soft under lip.

Ammiani assured her that he would find words of his own for her beauty.

"I hear the eulogy, I know the sonnet," said Violetta, smiling, and described the points of a brunette: the thick black banded hair, the full brown eyes, the plastic brows couching over them;—it was Vittoria's face: Violetta was a flower of colour, fair, with but one shade of dark tinting on her brown eye-brows and eye-lashes, as you may see a strip of night-cloud cross the forehead of morning. She was yellow-haired, almost purple-eyed, so rich was the blue of the pupils. Vittoria could be sallow in despondency; but this Violetta never failed in plumpness and freshness. The pencil which had given her aspect the one touch of discord, endowed it with a subtle harmony, like mystery; and Ammiani remembered his having stood once on the Lido of Venice, and eyed the dawn across the Adriatic, and dreamed that Violetta was born of the loveliness and held in her bosom the hopes of morning. He dreamed of it now, feeling the smooth roll of a torrent.

A cry of "Arms!" rang down the length of the Corso.

He started to his feet thankfully.

"Take me to your mother," she said. "I loathe to hear firing and be alone."

Ammiani threw up the window. There was a stir of lamps and torches below, and the low sky hung red. Violetta stood quickly thick-shod and hooded.

"Your mother will admit my companionship, Carlo?"

"She desires to thank you."

"She has no longer any fear of me?"

"You will find her of one mind with you."

"Concerning the king!"

"I would say, on most subjects."

"But that you do not know my mind! You are modest. Confess that you are thinking the hour you have passed with me has been wasted."

"I am, now I hear the call to arms."

"If I had all the while entertained you with talk of your Vittoria! It would not have been wasted then, my amaranto. It is not wasted for me. If a shot should strike you—"

"Tell her I died loving her with all my soul!" cried Ammiani.

Violetta's frame quivered as if he had smitten her.

They left the house. Countess Ammiani's door was the length of a barricade distant: it swung open to them, like all the other house-doors which were, or wished to be esteemed, true to the cause, and hospitable toward patriots.

"Remember, when you need a refuge, my villa is on Lago Maggiore," Violetta said, and kissed her finger-tips to him.

An hour after, by the light of this unlucky little speech, he thought of her as a shameless coquette. "When I need a refuge? Is not Milan in arms?—Italy alive? She considers it all a passing epidemic; or, perhaps, she is to plead for me to the king!"

That set him thinking moodily over the things she had uttered of Vittoria's strange and sudden devotion to the king.

Rainy dawn and the tongues of the churches ushered in the last day of street fighting. Ammiani found Romara and Colonel Corte at the head of strong bodies of volunteers, well-armed, ready to march for the Porta 'rosa. All three went straight to the house where the Provisional Government sat, and sword in hand denounced Count Medole as a traitor who sold his country to the king. Corte dragged him to the window to hear the shouts for the Republic. Medole wrote their names down one by one, and said, "Shall I leave the date vacant?" They put themselves at the head of their men, and marched in the ringing of the bells. The bells were their sacro-military music. Barto Rizzo was off to make a spring at the Porta Ticinese. Students, peasants, noble youths of the best blood, old men and young women, stood ranged in the drenching rain, eager to face death for freedom. At mid-day the bells were answered by cannon and the blunt snap of musketry volleys; dull, savage responses, as of a wounded great beast giving short howls and snarls by the interminable over-roaring of a cataract. Messengers from the gates came running to the quiet centre of the city, where cool men discoursed and plotted. Great news, big lies, were shouted:—Carlo Alberto thundered in the plains; the Austrians were everywhere retiring; the Marshal was a prisoner; the flag of surrender was on the citadel! These things were for the ears of thirsty women, diplomatists, and cripples.

Countess Ammiani and Countess d'Isorella sat together throughout the agitation of the day.

The life prayed for by one seemed a wisp of straw flung on this humming furnace.

Countess Ammiani was too well used to defeat to believe readily in victory, and had shrouded her head in resignation too long to hope for what she craved. Her hands were joined softly in her lap. Her visage had the same unmoved expression when she conversed with Violetta as when she listened to the ravings of the Corso.

Darkness came, and the bells ceased not rolling by her open windows: the clouds were like mists of conflagration.

She would not have the windows closed. The noise of the city had become familiar and akin to the image of her boy. She sat there cloaked.

Her heart went like a time-piece to the two interrogations to heaven: "Alive?—or dead?"

The voice of Luciano Romara was that of an angel's answering. He entered the room neat and trim as a cavalier dressed for social evening duty, saying with his fine tact, "We are all well;" and after talking like a gazette of the Porta Tosa taken by the volunteers, Barto Rizzo's occupation of the gate opening on the Ticino, and the bursting of the Porta Camosina by the freebands of the plains, he handed a letter to Countess Ammiani.

"Carlo is on the march to Bergamo and Brescia, with Corte, Sana, and about fifty of our men," he said.

"And is wounded—where?" asked Violetta.

"Slightly in the hand—you see, he can march," Romara said, laughing at her promptness to suspect a subterfuge, until he thought, "Now, what does this mean, madam?"

A lamp was brought to Countess Ammiani. She read:

"MY MOTHER!

"Cotton-wool on the left fore-finger. They deigned to give me no other memorial of my first fight. I am not worthy of papa's two bullets. I march with Corte and Sana to Brescia. We keep the passes of the Tyrol. Luciano heads five hundred up to the hills to-morrow or next day. He must have all our money. Then go from door to door and beg subscriptions. Yes, my Chief! it is to be like God, and deserving of his gifts to lay down all pride, all wealth. This night send to my betrothed in Turin. She must be with no one but my mother. It is my command. Tell her so. I hold imperatively to it.

"I breathe the best air of life. Luciano is a fine leader in action, calm as in a ball-room. What did I feel? I will talk of it with you by-and-by;—my father whispered in my ears; I felt him at my right hand. He said, 'I died for this day.' I feel now that I must have seen him. This is imagination. We may say that anything is imagination. I certainly heard his voice. Be of good heart, my mother, for I can swear that the General wakes up when I strike Austrian steel. He loved Brescia; so I go there. God preserve my mother! The eyes of heaven are wide enough to see us both. Vittoria by your side, remember! It is my will.

"CARLO."

Countess Ammiani closed her eyes over the letter, as in a dead sleep. "He is more his father than himself, and so suddenly!" she said. She was tearless. Violetta helped her to her bed-room under the pretext of a desire to hear the contents of the letter.

That night, which ended the five days of battle in Milan, while fires were raging at many gates, bells were rolling over the roof-tops, the army of Austria coiled along the North-eastern walls of the city, through rain and thick obscurity, and wove its way like a vast worm into the outer land.

Countess d'Isorella's peculiar mission to Milan was over with the victory of the city. She undertook personally to deliver Carlo's injunction to Vittoria on her way to the king. Countess Ammiani deemed it sufficient that her son's wishes should be repeated verbally; and as there appeared to be no better messenger than one who was bound for Turin and knew Vittoria's place of residence, she entrusted the duty to Violetta.

The much which hangs on little was then set in motion:

Violetta was crossing the Ticino when she met a Milanese nobleman who had received cold greeting from the king, and was returning to Milan with word that the Piedmontese declaration of war against Austria had been signed. She went back to Milan, saw and heard, and gathered a burden for the royal ears. This was a woman, tender only to the recollection of past days, who used her beauty and her arts as weapons for influence. She liked kings because she saw neither master nor dupe in a republic; she liked her early lover because she could see nothing but a victim in any new one. She was fond of Carlo, as greatly occupied minds may be attached to an old garden where they have aforetime sown fair seed. Jealousy of a rival in love that was disconnected with political business and her large expenditure, had never yet disturbed the lady's nerves.

At Turin she found Vittoria singing at the opera, and winning marked applause from the royal box. She thought sincerely that to tear a prima donna from her glory would be very much like dismissing a successful General to his home and gabbling family. A most eminent personage agreed with her. Vittoria was carelessly informed that Count Ammiani had gone to Brescia, and having regard for her safety, desired her to go to Milan to be under the protection of his mother, and that Countess Ammiani was willing to receive her.

Now, with her mother, and her maid Giacinta, and Beppo gathered about her, for three weeks Vittoria had been in full operatic career, working, winning fame, believing that she was winning influence, and establishing a treasury. The presence of her lover in Milan would have called her to the noble city; but he being at Brescia, she asked herself why she should abstain from labours which contributed materially to the strength of the revolution and made her helpful. It was doubtful whether Countess Ammiani would permit her to sing at La Scala; or whether the city could support an opera in the throes of war. And Vittoria was sending money to Milan. The stipend paid to her by the impresario, the jewels, the big bouquets—all flowed into the treasury of the insurrection. Antonio-Pericles advanced her a large sum on the day when the news of the Milanese uprising reached Turin: the conditions of the loan had simply been that she should continue her engagement to sing in Turin. He was perfectly slavish to her, and might be trusted to advance more. Since the great night at La Scala, she had been often depressed by a secret feeling that there was divorce between her love of her country and devotion to her Art. Now that both passions were in union, both active, each aiding the fire of the other, she lived a consummate life.

She could not have abandoned her path instantly though Carlo had spoken his command to her in person. Such were her first spontaneous seasonings, and Laura Piaveni seconded them; saying, "Money, money! we must be Jews for money. We women are not allowed to fight, but we can manage to contribute our lire and soldi; we can forge the sinews of war."

Vittoria wrote respectfully to Countess Ammiani stating why she declined to leave Turin. The letter was poorly worded. While writing it she had been taken by a sentiment of guilt and of isolation in presuming to disobey her lover. "I am glad he will not see it," she remarked to Laura, who looked rapidly across the lines, and said nothing. Praise of the king was in the last sentence. Laura's eyes lingered on it half-a-minute.

"Has he not drawn his sword? He is going to march," said Vittoria.

"Oh, yes," Laura replied coolly; "but you put that to please Countess Ammiani."

Vittoria confessed she had not written it purposely to defend the king. "What harm?" she asked.

"None. Only this playing with shades allows men to call us hypocrites."

The observation angered Vittoria. She had seen the king of late; she had breathed Turin incense and its atmosphere; much that could be pleaded on the king's behalf she had listened to with the sympathetic pity which can be woman's best judgement, and is the sentiment of reason. She had also brooded over the king's character, and had thought that if the Chief could have her opportunities for studying this little impressible, yet strangely impulsive royal nature, his severe condemnation of him would be tempered. In fact, she was doing what makes a woman excessively tender and opinionated; she was petting her idea of the misunderstood one: she was thinking that she divined the king's character by mystical intuition; I will dare to say, maternally apprehended it. And it was a character strangely open to feminine perceptions, while to masculine comprehension it remained a dead blank, done either in black or in white.

Vittoria insisted on praising the king to Laura.

"With all my heart," Laura said, "so long as he is true to Italy."

"How, then, am I hypocritical?"

"My Sandra, you are certainly perverse. You admitted that you did something for the sake of pleasing Countess Ammiani."

"I did. But to be hypocritical one must be false."

"Oh!" went Laura.

"And I write to Carlo. He does not care for the king; therefore it is needless for me to name the king to him; and I shall not."

Laura said, "Very well." She saw a little deeper than the perversity, though she did not see the springs. In Vittoria's letter to her lover, she made no allusion to the Sword of Italy.

Countess Ammiani forwarded both letters on to Brescia.

When Carlo had finished reading them, he heard all Brescia clamouring indignantly at the king for having disarmed volunteers on Lago Maggiore and elsewhere in his dominions. Milan was sending word by every post of the overbearing arrogance of the Piedmontese officers and officials, who claimed a prostrate submission from a city fresh with the ardour of the glory it had won for itself, and that would fain have welcomed them as brothers. Romara and others wrote of downright visible betrayal. It was a time of passions;—great readiness for generosity, equal promptitude for undiscriminating hatred. Carlo read Vittoria's praise of the king with insufferable anguish. "You—you part of me, can write like this!" he struck the paper vehemently. The fury of action transformed the gentle youth. Countess Ammiani would not have forwarded the letter addressed to herself had she dreamed the mischief it might do. Carlo saw double-dealing in the absence of any mention of the king in his own letter.

"Quit Turin at once," he dashed hasty lines to Vittoria; "and no 'Viva il Re' till we know what he may merit. Old delusions are pardonable; but you must now look abroad with your eyes. Your words should be the echoes of my soul. Your acts are mine. For the sake of the country, do nothing to fill me with shame. The king is a traitor. I remember things said of him by Agostino; I subscribe to them every one. Were you like any other Italian girl, you might cry for him—who would care! But you are Vittoria. Fly to my mother's arms, and there rest. The king betrays us. Is a stronger word necessary? I am writing too harshly to you;—and here are the lines of your beloved letter throbbing round me while I write; but till the last shot is fired I try to be iron, and would hold your hand and not kiss it—not be mad to fall between your arms—not wish for you—not think of you as a woman, as my beloved, as my Vittoria; I hope and pray not, if I thought there was an ace of work left to do for the country. Or if one could say that you cherished a shred of loyalty for him who betrays it. Great heaven! am I to imagine that royal flatteries—My hand is not my own! You shall see all that it writes. I will seem to you no better than I am. I do not tell you to be a Republican, but an Italian. If I had room for myself in my prayers—oh! one half-instant to look on you, though with chains on my limbs. The sky and the solid ground break up when I think of you. I fancy I am still in prison. Angelo was music to me for two whole days (without a morning to the first and a night to the second). He will be here to-morrow and talk of you again. I long for him more than for battle—almost long for you more than for victory for our Italy.

"This is Brescia, which my father said he loved better than his wife.

"General Paolo Ammiani is buried here. I was at his tombstone this morning. I wish you had known him.

"You remember, we talked of his fencing with me daily. 'I love the fathers who do that.' You said it. He will love you. Death is the shadow—not life. I went to his tomb. It was more to think of Brescia than of him. Ashes are only ashes; tombs are poor places. My soul is the power.

"If I saw the Monte Viso this morning, I saw right over your head when you were sleeping.

"Farewell to journalism—I hope, for ever. I jump at shaking off the journalistic phraseology Agostino laughs at. Yet I was right in printing my 'young nonsense.' I did, hold the truth, and that was felt, though my vehicle for delivering it was rubbish.

"In two days Corte promises to sing his song, 'Avanti.' I am at his left hand. Venice, the passes of the Adige, the Adda, the Oglio are ours. The room is locked; we have only to exterminate the reptiles inside it. Romara, D'Arci, Carnischi march to hold the doors. Corte will push lower; and if I can get him to enter the plains and join the main army I shall rejoice."

The letter concluded with a postscript that half an Italian regiment, with white coats swinging on their bayonet-points, had just come in.

It reached Vittoria at a critical moment.

Two days previously, she and Laura Piaveni had talked with the king. It was an unexpected honour. Countess, d'Isorella conducted them to the palace. The lean-headed sovereign sat booted and spurred, his sword across his knees; he spoke with a peculiar sad hopefulness of the prospects of the campaign, making it clear that he was risking more than anyone risked, for his stake was a crown. The few words he uttered of Italy had a golden ring in them; Vittoria knew not why they had it. He condemned the Republican spirit of Milan more regretfully than severely. The Republicans were, he said, impracticable. Beyond the desire for change, they knew not what they wanted. He did not state that he should avoid Milan in his march. On the contrary, he seemed to indicate that he was about to present himself to the people of Milan. "To act against the enemy successfully, we must act as one, under one head, with one aim." He said this, adding that no heart in Italy had yearned more than his own for the signal to march for the Mincio and the Adige.

Vittoria determined to put him to one test. She summoned her boldness to crave grace for Agostino Balderini to return to Piedmont. The petition was immediately granted. Alluding to the libretto of Camilla, the king complimented Vittoria for her high courage on the night of the Fifteenth of the foregoing year. "We in Turin were prepared, though we had only then the pleasure of hearing of you," he said.

"I strove to do my best to help. I wish to serve our cause now," she replied, feeling an inexplicable new sweetness running in her blood.

He asked her if she did not know that she had the power to move multitudes.

"Sire, singing appears so poor a thing in time of war."

He remarked that wine was good for soldiers, singing better, such a voice as hers best of all.

For hours after the interview, Vittoria struggled with her deep blushes. She heard the drums of the regiments, the clatter of horses, the bugle-call of assembly, as so many confirmatory notes that it was a royal hero who was going forth.

"He stakes a crown," she said to Laura.

"Tusk! it tumbles off his head if he refuses to venture something," was Laura's response.

Vittoria reproached her for injustice.

"No," Laura said; "he is like a young man for whom his mother has made a match. And he would be very much in love with his bride if he were quite certain of winning her, or rather, if she would come a little more than halfway to meet him. Some young men are so composed. Genoa and Turin say, 'Go and try.'

Milan and Venice say, 'Come and have faith in us.' My opinion is that he is quite as much propelled as attracted."

"This is shameful," said Vittoria.

"No; for I am quite willing to suspend my judgement. I pray that fortune may bless his arms. I do think that the stir of a campaign, and a certain amount of success will make him in earnest."

"Can you look on his face and not see pure enthusiasm?"

"I see every feminine quality in it, my dear."

"What can it be that he is wanting in?"

"Masculine ambition."

"I am not defending him," said Vittoria hastily.

"Not at all; and I am not attacking him. I can excuse his dread of Republicanism. I can fancy that there is reason for him just now to fear Republicanism worse than Austria. Paris and Milan are two grisly phantoms before him. These red spectres are born of earthquake, and are more given to shaking thrones than are hostile cannonshot. Earthquakes are dreadfuller than common maladies to all of us. Fortune may help him, but he has not the look of one who commands her. The face is not aquiline. There's a light over him like the ray of a sickly star."

"For that reason!" Vittoria burst out.

"Oh, for that reason we pity men, assuredly, my Sandra, but not kings. Luckless kings are not generous men, and ungenerous men are mischievous kings."

"But if you find him chivalrous and devoted; if he proves his noble intentions, why not support him?"

"Dandle a puppet, by all means," said Laura.

Her intellect, not her heart, was harsh to the king; and her heart was not mistress of her intellect in this respect, because she beheld riding forth at the head of Italy one whose spirit was too much after the pattern of her supple, springing, cowering, impressionable sex, alternately ardent and abject, chivalrous and treacherous, and not to be confided in firmly when standing at the head of a great cause.

Aware that she was reading him very strictly by the letters of his past deeds, which were not plain history to Vittoria, she declared that she did not countenance suspicion in dealing with the king, and that it would be a delight to her to hear of his gallant bearing on the battle-field. "Or to witness it, my Sandra, if that were possible;—we two! For, should he prove to be no General, he has the courage of his family."

Vittoria took fire at this. "What hinders our following the army?"

"The less baggage the better, my dear."

"But the king said that my singing—I have no right to think it myself." Vittoria concluded her sentence with a comical intention of humility.

"It was a pretty compliment," said Laura. "You replied that singing is a poor thing in time of war, and I agree with you. We might serve as hospital nurses."

"Why do we not determine?"

"We are only considering possibilities."

"Consider the impossibility of our remaining quiet."

"Fire that goes to flame is a waste of heat, my Sandra."

The signora, however, was not so discreet as her speech. On all sides there was uproar and movement. High-born Italian ladies were offering their hands for any serviceable work. Laura and Vittoria were not alone in the desire which was growing to be resolution to share the hardships of the soldiers, to cherish and encourage them, and by seeing, to have the supreme joy of feeling the blows struck at the common enemy.

The opera closed when the king marched. Carlo Ammiani's letter was handed to Vittoria at the fall of the curtain on the last night.

Three paths were open to her: either that she should obey her lover, or earn an immense sum of money from Antonio-Pericles by accepting an immediate engagement in London, or go to the war. To sit in submissive obedience seemed unreasonable; to fly from Italy impossible. Yet the latter alternative appealed strongly to her sense of duty, and as it thereby threw her lover's commands into the background, she left it to her heart to struggle with Carlo, and thought over the two final propositions. The idea of being apart from Italy while the living country streamed forth to battle struck her inflamed spirit like the shock of a pause in martial music. Laura pretended to take no part in Vittoria's decision, but when it was reached, she showed her a travelling-carriage stocked with lint and linen, wine in jars, chocolate, cases of brandy, tea, coffee, needles, thread, twine, scissors, knives; saying, as she displayed them, "there, my dear, all my money has gone in that equipment, so you must pay on the road."

"This doesn't leave me a choice, then," said Victoria, joining her humour.

"Ah, but think over it," Laura suggested.

"No! not think at all," cried Vittoria.

"You do not fear Carlo's anger?"

"If I think, I am weak as water. Let us go."

Countess d'Isorella wrote to Carlo: "Your Vittoria is away after the king to Pavia. They tell me she stood up in her carriage on the Ponte del Po-'Viva il Re d'Italia!' waving the cross of Savoy. As I have previously assured you, no woman is Republican. The demonstration was a mistake. Public characters should not let their personal preferences betrumpeted: a diplomatic truism:—but I must add, least of all a cantatrice for a king. The famous Greek amateur—the prop of failing finances—is after her to arrest her for breach of engagement. You wished to discover an independent mind in a woman, my Carlo; did you not? One would suppose her your wife—or widow. She looked a superb thing the last night she sang. She is not, in my opinion, wanting in height. If, behind all that innocence and candour, she has any trained artfulness, she will beat us all. Heaven bless your arms!"

The demonstration mentioned by the countess had not occurred.

Vittoria's letter to her lover missed him. She wrote from Pavia, after she had taken her decisive step.

Carlo Ammiani went into the business of the war with the belief that his betrothed had despised his prayer to her.

He was under Colonel Corte, operating on the sub-Alpine range of hills along the line of the Chiese South-eastward. Here the volunteers, formed of the best blood of Milan, the gay and brave young men, after marching in the pride of their strength to hold the Alpine passes and bar Austria from Italy while the fight went on below, were struck by a sudden paralysis. They hung aloft there like an arm cleft from the body. Weapons, clothes, provisions, money, the implements of war, were withheld from them. The Piedmontese officers despatched to watch their proceedings laughed at them like exasperating senior scholars examining the accomplishments of a lower form. It was manifest that Count Medole and the Government of Milan worked everywhere to conquer the people for the king before the king had done a stroke to conquer the Austrians for the people; while, in order to reduce them to the condition of Piedmontese soldiery, the flame of their patriotic enthusiasm was systematically damped, and instead of apprentices in war, who possessed at any rate the elementary stuff of soldiers, miserable dummies were drafted into the royal service. The Tuscans and the Romans had good reason to complain on behalf of their princes, as had the Venetians and the Lombards for the cause of their Republic. Neither Tuscans, Romans, Venetians, nor Lombards were offering up their lives simply to obtain a change of rulers; though all Italy was ready to bow in allegiance to a king of proved kingly quality. Early in the campaign the cry of treason was muttered, and on all sides such became the temper of the Alpine volunteers, that Angelo and Rinaldo Guidascarpi were forced to join their cousin under Corte, by the dispersion of their band, amounting to something more than eighteen hundred fighting lads, whom a Piedmontese superior officer summoned peremptorily to shout for the king. They thundered as one voice for the Italian Republic, and instantly broke up and disbanded. This was the folly of the young: Carlo Ammiani confessed that it was no better; but he knew that a breath of generous confidence from the self-appointed champion of the national cause would have subdued his impatience at royalty and given heart and cheer to his sickening comrades. He began to frown angrily when he thought of Vittoria. "Where is she now?—where now?" he asked himself in the season of his most violent wrath at the king. Her conduct grew inseparable in his mind from the king's deeds. The sufferings, the fierce irony, the very deaths of the men surrounding him in aims, rose up in accusation against the woman he loved.

CHAPTER XXXI

EPISODES OF THE REVOLT AND THE WAR—THE TREACHERY OF PERICLES—THE WHITE UMBRELLA—THE DEATH OF RINALDO GUIDASCARPI

The king crossed the Mincio. The Marshal, threatened on his left flank, drew in his line from the farther Veronese heights upon a narrowed battle front before Verona. Here they manoeuvred, and the opening successes fell to the king. Holding Peschiera begirt, with one sharp passage of arms he cleared the right bank of the Adige and stood on the semicircle of hills, master of the main artery into Tyrol.

The village of Pastrengo has given its name to the day. It was a day of intense heat coming after heavy rains. The arid soil steamed; the white powder-smoke curled in long horizontal columns across the hazy ring of the fight. Seen from a distance it was like a huge downy ball, kicked this way and that between the cypresses by invisible giants. A pair of eager-eyed women gazing on a battle-field for the first time could but ask themselves in bewilderment whether the fate of countries were verily settled in such a fashion. Far in the rear, Vittoria and Laura heard the cannon-shots; a sullen dull sound, as of a mallet striking upon rotten timber. They drove at speed. The great thumps became varied by musketry volleys, that were like blocks of rockboulder tumbled in the roll of a mountain torrent. These, then, were the voices of Italy and Austria speaking the devilish tongue of the final alternative. Cannon, rockets, musketry, and now the run of drums, now the ring of bugles, now the tramp of horses, and the field was like a landslip. A joyful bright black death-wine seemed to pour from the bugles all about. The women strained their senses to hear and see; they could realize nothing of a reality so absolute; their feelings were shattered, and crowded over them in patches;—horror, glory, panic, hope, shifted lights within their bosoms. The fascination and repulsion of the image of Force divided them. They feared; they were prostrate; they sprang in praise. The image of Force was god and devil to their souls. They strove to understand why the field was marked with blocks of men who made a plume of vapour here, and hurried thither. The action of their intellects resolved to a blank marvel at seeing an imminent thing—an interrogation to almighty heaven treated with method, not with fury streaming forward. Cleave the opposing ranks! Cry to God for fire? Cut them through! They had come to see the Song of Deborah performed before their eyes, and they witnessed only a battle. Blocks of infantry gathered densely, thinned to a line, wheeled in column, marched: blocks of cavalry changed posts: artillery bellowed from one spot and quickly selected another. Infantry advanced in the wake of tiny smokepuffs, halted, advanced again, rattled files of shots, became struck into knots, faced half about as from a blow of the back of a hand, retired orderly. Cavalry curved like a flickering scimetar in their rear; artillery plodded to its further station. Innumerable tiny smoke-puffs then preceded a fresh advance of infantry. The enemy were on the hills and looked mightier, for they were revealed among red flashes of their guns, and stood partly visible above clouds of hostile smoke and through clouds of their own, which grasped viscously by the skirts of the hills. Yet it seemed a strife of insects, until, one by one, soldiers who had gone into yonder white pit for the bloody kiss of death, and had got it on their faces, were borne by Vittoria and Laura knelt in this horrid stream of mortal anguish to give succour from their stores in the carriage. Their natural emotions were distraught. They welcomed the sight of suffering thankfully, for the poor blotted faces were so glad at sight of them. Torture was their key to the reading of the battle. They gazed on the field no longer, but let the roaring wave of combat wash up to them what it would.

The hill behind Pastrengo was twice stormed. When the bluecoats first fell back, a fine charge of Piedmontese horse cleared the slopes for a second effort, and they went up and on, driving the enemy from hill to hill. The Adige was crossed by the Austrians under cover of Tyrolese rifleshots.

Then, with Beppo at their heels, bearing water, wine, and brandy, the women walked in the paths of carnage, and saw the many faces of death. Laura whispered strangely, "How light-hearted they look!" The wounded called their comforters sweet names. Some smoked and some sang, some groaned; all were quick to drink. Their jokes at the dead were universal. They twisted their bodies painfully to stick a cigar between dead lips, and besprinkle them with the last drops of liquor in their cups, laughing a benediction. These scenes put grievous chains on Vittoria's spirit, but Laura evidently was not the heavier for them. Glorious Verona shone under the sunset as their own to come; Peschiera, on the blue lake, was in the hollow of their hands. "Prizes worth any quantity of blood," said Laura. Vittoria confessed that she had seen enough of blood, and her aspect provoked Laura to utter, "For God's sake, think of something miserable;—cry, if you can!"

Vittoria's underlip dropped sickly with the question, "Why?"

Laura stated the physical necessity with Italian naivete.

"If I can," said Vittoria, and blinked to get a tear; but laughter helped as well to relieve her, and it came on their return to the carriage. They found the spy Luigi sitting beside the driver. He informed them that Antonio-Pericles had been in the track of the army ever since their flight from Turin; daily hurrying off with whip of horses at the sound of cannon-shot, and gradually stealing back to the extreme rear. This day he had flown from Oliosi to Cavriani, and was, perhaps, retracing his way already as before, on fearful toe-tips. Luigi acted the caution of one who stepped blindfolded across hot iron plates. Vittoria, without a spark of interest, asked why the Signor Antonio should be following the army.

"Why, it's to find you, signorina."

Luigi's comical emphasis conjured up in a jumbled picture the devotion, the fury, the zeal, the terror of Antonio-Pericles—a mixture of demoniacal energy and ludicrous trepidation. She imagined his long figure, fantastical as a shadow, off at huge strides, and back, with eyes sliding swiftly to the temples, and his odd serpent's head raised to peer across the plains and occasionally to exclaim to the reasonable heavens in anger at men and loathing of her. She laughed ungovernably. Luigi exclaimed that, albeit in disgrace with the signor Antonio, he had been sent for to serve him afresh, and had now been sent forward to entreat the gracious signorina to grant her sincerest friend and adorer an interview. She laughed at Pericles, but in truth she almost loved the man for his worship of her Art, and representation of her dear peaceful practice of it.

The interview between them took place at Oliosi. There, also, she met Georgiana Ford, the half-sister of Merthyr Powys, who told her that Merthyr and Augustus Gambier were in the ranks of a volunteer contingent in the king's army, and might have been present at Pastrengo. Georgiana held aloof from battle-fields, her business being simply to serve as Merthyr's nurse in case of wounds, or to see the last of him in case of death. She appeared to have no enthusiasm. She seconded strongly the vehement persuasions addressed by Pericles to Vittoria. Her disapproval of the presence of her sex on fields of battle was precise. Pericles had followed the army to give Vittoria one last chance, he said, and drag her away from this sick country, as he called it, pointing at the dusty land from the windows of the inn. On first seeing her he gasped like one who has recovered a lost thing. To Laura he was a fool; but Vittoria enjoyed his wildest outbursts, and her half-sincere humility encouraged him to think that he had captured her at last. He enlarged on the perils surrounding her voice in dusty bellowing Lombardy, and on the ardour of his friendship in exposing himself to perils as tremendous, that he might rescue her. While speaking he pricked a lively ear for the noise of guns, hearing a gun in everything, and jumping to the window with horrid imprecations. His carriage was horsed at the doors below. Let the horses die, he said, let the coachman have sun-stroke. Let hundreds perish, if Vittoria would only start in an hour-in two—to-night—to-morrow.

"Because, do you see,"—he turned to Laura and Georgiana, submitting to the vexatious necessity of seeming reasonable to these creatures,—"she is a casket for one pearl. It is only one, but it is ONE, mon Dieu! and inscrutable heaven, mesdames, has made the holder of it mad. Her voice has but a sole skin; it is not like a body; it bleeds to death at a scratch. A spot on the pearl, and it is perished—pfoof! Ah, cruel thing! impious, I say. I have watched, I have reared her. Speak to me of mothers! I have cherished her for her splendid destiny—to see it go down, heels up, among quarrels of boobies! Yes; we have war in Italy. Fight! Fight in this beautiful climate that you may be dominated by a blue coat, not by a white coat. We are an intelligent race; we are a civilized people; we will fight for that. What has a voice of the very heavens to do with your fighting? I heard it first in England, in a firwood, in a month of Spring, at night-time, fifteen miles and a quarter from the city of London—oh, city of peace! Sandra you will come there. I give you thousands additional to the sum stipulated. You have no rival. Sandra Belloni! no rival, I say"—he invoked her in English, "and you hear—you, to be a draggle-tail vivandiere wiz a brandy-bottle at your hips and a reputation going like ze brandy. Ah! pardon, mesdames; but did mankind ever see a frenzy like this girl's? Speak, Sandra. I could cry it like Michiella to Camilla—Speak!"

Vittoria compelled him to despatch his horses to stables. He had relays of horses at war-prices between Castiglione and Pavia, and a retinue of servants; nor did he hesitate to inform the ladies that, before entrusting his person to the hazards of war, he had taken care to be provided with safe-conduct passes for both armies, as befitted a prudent man of peace—"or sense; it is one, mesdames."

Notwithstanding his terror at the guns, and disgust at the soldiery and the bad fare at the inn, Vittoria's presence kept him lingering in this wretched place, though he cried continually, "I shall have heart-disease." He believed at first that he should subdue her; then it became his intention to carry her off.

It was to see Merthyr that she remained. Merthyr came there the day after the engagement at Santa Lucia. They had not met since the days at Meran. He was bronzed, and keen with strife, and looked young, but spoke not over-hopefully. He scolded her for wishing to taste battle, and compared her to a bad swimmer on deep shores. Pericles bounded with delight to hear him, and said he had not supposed there was so much sense in Powys. Merthyr confessed that the Austrians had as good as beaten them at Santa Lucia. The tactical combinations of the Piedmontese were wretched. He was enamoured of the gallantly of the Duke of Savoy, who had saved the right wing of the army from rout while covering the backward movement. Why there had been any fight at all at Santa Lucia, where nothing was to be gained, much to be lost, he was incapable of telling; but attributed it to an antique chivalry on the part of the king, that had prompted the hero to a trial of strength, a bout of blood-letting.

"You do think he is a hero?" said Vittoria.

"He is; and he will march to Venice."

"And open the opera at Venice," Pericles sneered. "Powys, mon cher, cure her of this beastly dream. It is a scandal to you to want a woman's help. You were defeated at Santa Lucia. I say bravo to anything that brings you to reason. Bravo! You hear me."

The engagement at Santa Lucia was designed by the king to serve as an instigating signal for the Veronese to rise in revolt; and this was the secret of Charles Albert's stultifying manoeuvres between Peschiera and Mantua. Instead of matching his military skill against the wary old Marshal's, he was offering incentives to conspiracy. Distrusting the revolution, which was a force behind him, he placed such reliance on its efforts in his front as to make it the pivot of his actions.

"The volunteers North-east of Vicenza are doing the real work for us, I believe," said Merthyr; and it seemed so then, as it might have been indeed, had they not been left almost entirely to themselves to do it.

These tidings of a fight lost set Laura and Vittoria quivering with nervous irritation. They had been on the field of Pastrengo, and it was won. They had been absent from Santa Lucia. What was the deduction? Not such as reason would have made for them; but they were at the mercy of the currents of the blood. "Let us go on," said Laura. Merthyr refused to convoy them. Pericles drove with him an hour on the road, and returned in glee, to find Vittoria and Laura seated in their carriage, and Luigi scuffling with Beppo.

"Padrone, see how I assist you," cried Luigi.

Upon this Beppo instantly made a swan's neck of his body and trumpeted: "A sally from the fortress for forage."

"Whip! whip!" Pericles shouted to his coachman, and the two carriages parted company at the top of their speed.

Pericles fell a victim to a regiment of bersaglieri that wanted horses, and unceremoniously stopped his pair and took possession of them on the route for Peschiera. He was left in a stranded carriage between a dusty ditch and a mulberry bough. Vittoria and Laura were not much luckier. They were met by a band of deserters, who made no claim upon the horses, but stood for drink, and having therewith fortified their fine opinion of themselves, petitioned for money. A kiss was their next demand. Money and good humour saved the women from indignity. The band of rascals went off with a 'Viva l'Italia.' Such scum is upon every popular rising, as Vittoria had to learn. Days of rain and an incomprehensible inactivity of the royal army kept her at a miserable inn, where the walls were bare, the cock had crowed his last. The guns of Peschiera seemed to roam over the plain like an echo unwillingly aroused that seeks a hollow for its further sleep. Laura sat pondering for hours, harsh in manner, as if she hated her. "I think," she said once, "that women are those persons who have done evil in another world:" The "why?" from Vittoria was uttered simply to awaken friendly talk, but Laura relapsed into her gloom. A village priest, a sleek gentle creature, who shook his head to earth when he hoped, and filled his nostrils with snuff when he desponded, gave them occasional companionship under the title of consolation. He wished the Austrians to be beaten, remarking, however, that they were good Catholics, most fervent Catholics. As the Lord decided, so it would end! "Oh, delicious creed!" Laura broke out: "Oh, dear and sweet doctrine! that results and developments in a world where there is more evil than good are approved by heaven." She twisted the mild man in supple steel of her irony so tenderly that Vittoria marvelled to hear her speak of him in abhorrence when they quitted the village. "Not to be born a woman, and voluntarily to be a woman!" ejaculated Laura. "How many, how many are we to deduct from the male population of Italy? Cross in hand, he should be at the head of our arms, not whimpering in a corner for white bread. Wretch! he makes the marrow in my bones rage at him. He chronicled pig that squeaked."

"Why had she been so gentle with him?"

"Because, my dear, when I loathe a thing I never care to exhaust my detestation before I can strike it," said the true Italian.

They were on the field of Goito; it was won. It was won against odds. At Pastrengo they witnessed an encounter; this was a battle. Vittoria perceived that there was the difference between a symphony and a lyric song. The blessedness of the sensation that death can be light and easy dispossessed her of the meaner compassion, half made up of cowardice, which she had been nearly borne down by on the field of Pastrengo. At an angle on a height off the left wing of the royal army the face of the battle was plain to her: the movements of the troops were clear as strokes on a slate. Laura flung her life into her eyes, and knelt and watched, without summing one sole thing from what her senses received.

Vittoria said, "We are too far away to understand it."

"No," said Laura, "we are too far away to feel it."

The savage soul of the woman was robbed of its share of tragic emotion by having to hold so far aloof. Flashes of guns were but flashes of guns up there where she knelt. She thirsted to read the things written by them; thirsted for their mystic terrors, somewhat as souls of great prophets have craved for the full revelation of those fitful underlights which inspired their mouths.

Charles Albert's star was at its highest when the Piedmontese drums beat for an advance of the whole line at Goito.

Laura stood up, white as furnace-fire. "Women can do some good by praying," she said. She believed that she had been praying. That was her part in the victory.

Rain fell as from the forehead of thunder. From black eve to black dawn the women were among dead and dying men, where the lanterns trailed a slow flame across faces that took the light and let it go. They returned to their carriage exhausted. The ways were almost impassable for carriage-wheels. While they were toiling on and exchanging their drenched clothes, Vittoria heard Merthyr's voice speaking to Beppo on the box. He was saying that Captain Gambier lay badly wounded; brandy was wanted for him. She flung a cloak over Laura, and handed out the flask with a naked arm. It was not till she saw him again that she remembered or even felt that he had kissed the arm. A spot of sweet fire burned on it just where the soft fulness of a woman's arm slopes to the bend. He chid her for being on the field and rejoiced in a breath, for the carriage and its contents helped to rescue his wounded brother in arms from probable death. Gambier, wounded in thigh and ankle by rifle-shot, was placed in the carriage. His clothes were saturated with the soil of Goito; but wounded and wet, he smiled gaily, and talked sweet boyish English. Merthyr gave the driver directions to wind along up the Mincio. "Georgiana will be at the nearest village—she has an instinct for battle-fields, or keeps spies in her pay," he said.

"Tell her I am safe. We march to cut them (the enemy) off from Verona, and I can't leave. The game is in our hands. We shall give you Venice."

Georgiana was found at the nearest village. Gambier's wounds had been dressed by an army-surgeon. She looked at the dressing, and said that it would do for six hours. This singular person had fully qualified herself to attend on a soldier-brother. She had studied medicine for that purpose, and she had served as nurse in a London hospital. Her nerves were completely under control. She could sit in attendance by a sick-bed for hours, hearing distant cannon, and the brawl of soldiery and vagabonds in the street, without a change of countenance. Her dress was plain black from throat to heel, with a skull cap of white, like a Moravian sister. Vittoria reverenced her; but Georgiana's manner in return was cold aversion, so much more scornful than disdain that it offended Laura, who promptly put her finger on the blot in the fair character with the word 'Jealousy;' but a single word is too broad a mark to be exactly true. "She is a perfect example of your English," Laura said. "Brave, good, devoted, admirable—ice at the heart. The judge of others, of course. I always respected her; I never liked her; and I should be afraid of a comparison with her. Her management of the household of this inn is extraordinary."

Georgiana condescended to advise Vittoria once more not to dangle after armies.

"I wish to wait here to assist you in nursing our friend," said Vittoria.

Georgiana replied that her strength was unlikely to fail.

After two days of incessant rain, sunshine blazed over 'the watery Mantuan flats. Laura drove with Beppo to see whether the army was in motion, for they were distracted by rumours. Vittoria clung to her wounded friend, whose pleasure was the hearing her speak. She expected Laura's return by set of sun. After dark a messenger came to her, saying that the signora had sent a carriage to fetch her to Valeggio. Her immediate supposition was that Merthyr might have fallen. She found Luigi at the carriage-door, and listened to his mysterious directions and remarks that not a minute must be lost, without suspicion. He said that the signora was in great trouble, very anxious to see the signorina instantly; there was but a distance of five miles to traverse.

She thought it strange that the carriage should be so luxuriously fitted with lights and silken pillows, but her ideas were all of Merthyr, until she by chance discovered a packet marked I chocolate, which told her at once that she was entrapped by Antonio-Pericles. Luigi would not answer her cry to him. After some fruitless tremblings of wrath, she lay back relieved by the feeling that Merthyr was safe, come what might to herself. Things could lend to nothing but an altercation with Pericles, and for this scene she prepared her mind. The carriage stopped while she was dozing. Too proud to supplicate in the darkness, she left it to the horses to bear her on, reserving her energies for the morning's interview, and saying, "The farther he takes me the angrier I shall be." She dreamed of her anger while asleep, but awakened so frequently during the night that morning was at her eyelids before they divided. To her amazement, she saw the carriage surrounded by Austrian troopers. Pericles was spreading cigars among them, and addressing them affably. The carriage was on a good road, between irrigated flats, that flashed a lively green and bright steel blue for miles away. She drew down the blinds to cry at leisure; her wings were clipped, and she lost heart. Pericles came round to her when the carriage had drawn up at an inn. He was egregiously polite, but modestly kept back any expressions of triumph. A body of Austrians, cavalry and infantry, were breaking camp. Pericles accorded her an hour of rest. She perceived that he was anticipating an outbreak of the anger she had nursed overnight, and baffled him so far by keeping dumb. Luigi was sent up to her to announce the expiration of her hour of grace.

"Ah, Luigi!" she said. "Signorina, only wait, and see how Luigi can serve two," he whispered, writhing under the reproachfulness of her eyes. At the carriage-door she asked Pericles whither he was taking her. "Not to Turin, not to London, Sandra Belloni!" he replied; "not to a place where you are wet all night long, to wheeze for ever after it. Go in." She entered the carriage quickly, to escape from staring officers, whose laughter rang in her ears and humbled her bitterly; she felt herself bringing dishonour on her lover. The carriage continued in the track of the Austrians. Pericles was audibly careful to avoid the border regiments. He showered cigars as he passed; now and then he exhibited a paper; and on one occasion he brought a General officer to the carriage-door, opened it and pointed in. A white-helmeted dragoon rode on each side of the carriage for the remainder of the day. The delight of the supposition that these Austrians were retreating before the invincible arms of King Carlo Alberto kept her cheerful;

but she heard no guns in the rear. A blocking of artillery and waggons compelled a halt, and then Pericles came and faced her. He looked profoundly ashamed of himself, ready as he was for an animated defence of his proceedings.

"Where are you taking me, sir?" she said in English.

"Sandra, will you be a good child? It is anywhere you please, if you will promise—"

"I will promise nothing."

"Zen, I lock you up in Verona."

"In Verona!"

"Sandra, will you promise to me?"

"I will promise nothing."

"Zen I lock you up in Verona. It is settled. No more of it. I come to say, we shall not reach a village. I am sorry. We have soldiers for a guard. You draw out a board and lodge in your carriage as in a bed. Biscuits, potted meats, prunes, bon-bona, chocolate, wine—you shall find all at your right hand and your left. I am desolate in offending you. Sandra, if you will promise—"

"I will promise—this is what I will promise," said Vittoria.

Pericles thrust his ear forward, and withdrew it as if it had been slapped.

She promised to run from him at the first opportunity, to despise him ever after, and never to sing again in his hearing. With the darkness Luigi appeared to light her lamp; he mouthed perpetually, "To-morrow, to-morrow." The watch-fires of Austrians encamped in the fields encircled her; and moving up and down, the cigar of Antonio-Pericles was visible. He had not eaten or drunk, and he was out there sleepless; he walked conquering his fears in the thick of war troubles: all for her sake. She watched critically to see whether the cigar-light was puffed in fretfulness. It burned steadily; and the thought of Pericles supporting patience quite overcame her. In a fit of humour that was almost tears, she called to him and begged him to take a place in the carriage and have food. "If it is your pleasure," he said; and threw off his cloak. The wine comforted him. Thereupon he commenced a series of strange gesticulations, and ended by blinking at the window, saying, "No, no; it is impossible to explain. I have no voice; I am not, gifted. It is," he tapped at his chest, "it is here. It is, imprisoned in me."

"What?" said Vittoria, to encourage him.

"It can never be explained, my child. Am I not respectful to you? Am I not worshipful to you? But, no! it can never be explained. Some do call me mad. I know it; I am laughed at. Oh! do I not know zat? Perfectly well. My ancestors adored Goddesses. I discover ze voice of a Goddess: I adore it. So you call me mad; it is to me what you call me—juste ze same. I am possessed wiz passion for her voice. So it will be till I go to ashes. It is to me ze one zsing divine in a pig, a porpoise world. It is to me—I talk! It is unutterable—impossible to tell."

"But I understand it; I know you must feel it," said Vittoria.

"But you hate me, Sandra. You hate your Pericles."

"No, I do not; you are my good friend, my good Pericles."

"I am your good Pericles? So you obey me?"

"In what?"

"You come to London?"

"I shall not."

"You come to Turin?"

"I cannot promise."

"To Milan?"

"No; not yet."

"Ungrateful little beast! minx! temptress! You seduce me into your carriage to feed me, to fill me, for to coax me," cried Pericles.

"Am I the person to have abuse poured on me?" Vittoria rejoined, and she frowned. "Might I not have called you a wretched whimsical money-machine, without the comprehension of a human feeling? You are doing me a great wrong—to win my submission, as I see, and it half amuses me; but the pretence of an attempt to carry me off from my friends is an offence that I should take certain care to punish in another. I do not give you any promise, because the first promise of all—the promise to keep one—is not in my power. Shut your eyes and sleep where you are, and in the morning think better of your conduct!"

"Of my conduct, mademoiselle!" Pericles retained this sentence in his head till the conclusion of her animated speech,—"of my conduct I judge better zan to accept of such a privilege as you graciously offer to me;" and he retired with a sour grin, very much subdued by her unexpected capacity for expression. The bugles of the Austrians were soon ringing. There was a trifle of a romantic flavour in the notes which Vittoria tried not to feel; the smart iteration of them all about her rubbed it off, but she was reduced to repeat them, and take them in various keys. This was her theme for the day.

They were in the midst of mulberries, out of sight of the army; green mulberries, and the green and the bronze young vine-leaf. It was a delicious day, but she began to fear that she was approaching Verona, and that Pericles was acting seriously. The bronze young vine-leaf seemed to her like some warrior's face, as it would look when beaten by weather, burned by the sun. They came now to inns which had been visited by both armies. Luigi established communication with the innkeepers before the latter had stated the names of villages to Pericles, who stood map in hand, believing himself at last to be no more conscious of his position than an atom in a whirl of dust. Vittoria still refused to give him any promise, and finally, on a solitary stretch of the road, he appealed to her mercy. She was the mistress of the carriage, he said; he had never meant to imprison her in Verona; his behaviour was simply dictated by his adoration—alas! This was true or not true, but it was certain that the ways were confounded to them. Luigi, despatched to reconnoitre from a neighbouring eminence, reported a Piedmontese encampment far ahead, and a walking tent that was coming on their route. The walking tent was an enormous white umbrella. Pericles advanced to meet it; after an interchange of opening formalities, he turned about and clapped hands. The umbrella was folded. Vittoria recognized the last man she would then have thought of meeting; he seemed to have jumped out of an ambush from Meran in Tyrol:—it was Wilfrid. Their greeting was disturbed by the rushing up of half-a-dozen troopers. The men claimed him as an Austrian spy. With difficulty Vittoria obtained leave to drive him on to their commanding officer. It appeared that the white umbrella was notorious for having been seen on previous occasions threading the Piedmontese lines into and out of Peschiera. These very troopers swore to it; but they could not swear to Wilfrid, and white umbrellas were not absolutely uncommon. Vittoria declared that Wilfrid was an old English friend; Pericles vowed that Wilfrid was one of their party. The prisoner was clearly an Englishman. As it chanced, the officer before whom Wilfrid was taken had heard Vittoria sing on the great night at La Scala. "Signorina, your word should pass the Austrian Field-Marshal himself," he said, and merely requested Wilfrid to state on his word of honour that he was not in the Austrian service, to which Wilfrid unhesitatingly replied, "I am not."

Permission was then accorded to him to proceed in the carriage.

Vittoria held her hand to Wilfrid. He took the fingers and bowed over them.

He was perfectly self-possessed, and cool even under her eyes. Like a pedlar he carried a pack on his back, which was his life; for his business was a combination of scout and spy.

"You have saved me from a ditch to-day," he said; "every fellow has some sort of love for his life, and I must thank you for the odd luck of your coming by. I knew you were on this ground somewhere. If the rascals had searched me, I should not have come off so well. I did not speak falsely to that officer; I am not in the Austrian service. I am a volunteer spy. I am an unpaid soldier. I am the dog of the army— fetching and carrying for a smile and a pat on the head. I am ruined, and I am working my way up as best I can. My uncle disowns me. It is to General Schoneck that I owe this chance of re-establishing myself. I followed the army out of Milan. I was at Melegnano, at Pastrengo, at Santa Lucia. If I get nothing for it, the Lenkensteins at least shall not say that I abandoned the flag in adversity. I am bound for Rivoli. The fortress (Peschiera) has just surrendered. The Marshal is stealing round to make a dash on Vicenza." So far he spoke like one apart from her, but a flush crossed his forehead. "I have not followed you. I have obeyed your brief directions. I saw this carriage yesterday in the ranks of our troops. I saw Pericles. I guessed who might be inside it. I let it pass me. Could I do more?"

"Not if you wanted to punish me," said Vittoria.

She was afflicted by his refraining from reproaches in his sunken state.

Their talk bordered the old life which they had known, like a rivulet, coming to falls where it threatens to be e, torrent and a flood; like flame bubbling the wax of a seal. She was surprised to find herself expecting tenderness from him: and, startled by the languor in her veins, she conceived a contempt for her sex and her own weak nature. To mask that, an excessive outward coldness was assumed. "You can serve as a spy, Wilfrid!"

The answer was ready: "Having twice served as a traitor, I need not be particular. It is what my uncle and the Lenkensteins call me. I do my best to work my way up again. Despise me for it, if you please."

On the contrary, she had never respected him so much. She got herself into opposition to him by provoking him to speak with pride of his army; but the opposition was artificial, and she called to Carlo Ammiani in heart. "I will leave these places, cover up my head, and crouch till the struggle is decided."

The difficulty was now to be happily rid of Wilfrid by leaving him in safety. Piedmontese horse scoured the neighbourhood, and any mischance that might befall him she traced to her hand. She dreaded at every instant to hear him speak of his love for her; yet how sweet it would have been to hear it,—to hear him speak of passionate love; to shape it in deep music; to hear one crave for what she gave to another! "I am sinking: I am growing degraded," she thought. But there was no other way for her to quicken her imagination of her distant and offended lover. The sights on the plains were strange contrasts to these conflicting inner emotions: she seemed to be living in two divided worlds.

Pericles declared anew that she was mistress of the carriage. She issued orders: "The nearest point to Rivoli, and then to Brescia."

Pericles broke into shouts. "She has arrived at her reason! Hurrah for Brescia! I beheld you," he confessed to Wilfrid,—"it was on ze right of Mincio, my friend. I did not know you were so true for Art, or what a hand I would have reached to you! Excuse me now. Let us whip on. I am your banker. I shall desire you not to be shot or sabred. You are deserving of an effigy on a theatral grand stair-case!" His gratitude could no further express itself. In joy he whipped the horses on. Fools might be fighting—he was the conqueror. From Brescia, one leap took him in fancy to London. He composed mentally a letter to be forwarded immediately to a London manager, directing him to cause the appearance of articles in the journals on the grand new prima donna, whose singing had awakened the people of Italy.

Another day brought them in view of the Lago di Garda. The flag of Sardinia hung from the walls of Peschiera. And now Vittoria saw the Pastrengo hills—dear hills, that drove her wretched languor out of her, and made her soul and body one again. The horses were going at a gallop. Shots were heard. To the left of them, somewhat in the rear, on higher ground, there was an encounter of a body of Austrians and Italians: Tyrolese riflemen and the volunteers. Pericles was raving. He refused to draw the reins till they had reached the village, where one of the horses dropped. From the windows of the inn, fronting a clear space, Vittoria beheld a guard of Austrians surrounding two or more prisoners. A woman sat near them with her head buried in her lap. Presently an officer left the door of the inn and spoke to the soldiers. "That is Count Karl von Lenkenstein," Wilfrid said in a whisper. Pericles had been speaking with Count Karl and came up to the room, saying, "We are to observe something; but we are safe; it is only fortune of war." Wilfrid immediately went out to report himself. He was seen giving his papers, after which Count Karl waved his finger back to the inn, and he returned. Vittoria sprang to her feet at the words he uttered. Rinaldo Guidascarpi was one of the prisoners. The others Wilfrid professed not to know. The woman was the wife of Barto Rizzo.

In the great red of sunset the Tyrolese riflemen and a body of Italians in Austrian fatigue uniform marched into the village. These formed in the space before the inn. It seemed as if Count Karl were declaiming an indictment. A voice answered, "I am the man." It was clear and straight as a voice that goes up in the night. Then a procession walked some paces on. The woman followed. She fell prostrate at the feet of Count Karl. He listened to her and nodded. Rinaldo Guidascarpi stood alone with bandaged eyes. The woman advanced to him; she put her mouth on his ear; there she hung.

Vittoria heard a single shot. Rinaldo Guidascarpi lay stretched upon the ground and the woman stood over him.

BOOK VII

CHAPTER XXXIII

EPISODES OF THE REVOLT AND THE WAR—COUNT KARL LENKENSTEIN—THE STORY OF THE GUIDASCARPI—THE VICTORY OF THE VOLUNTEERS

The smoke of a pistol-shot thinned away while there was yet silence.

"It is a saving of six charges of Austrian ammunition," said Pericles.

Vittoria stared at the scene, losing faith in her eyesight. She could in fact see no distinct thing beyond what appeared as an illuminated copper medallion, held at a great distance from her, with a dead man and a towering female figure stamped on it.

The events following were like a rush of water on her senses. There was fighting up the street of the village, and a struggle in the space where Rinaldo had fallen; successive yellowish shots under the rising moonlight, cries from Italian lips, quick words of command from German in Italian, and one sturdy bull's roar of a voice that called across the tumult to the Austro-Italian soldiery, "Venite fratelli!—come, brothers, come under our banner!" She heard "Rinaldo!" called.

This was a second attack of the volunteers for the rescue of their captured comrades. They fought more desperately than on the hill outside the village: they fought with steel. Shot enfiladed them; yet they bore forward in a scattered body up to that spot where Rinaldo lay, shouting for him. There they turned,—they fled.

Then there was a perfect stillness, succeeding the strife as quickly, Vittoria thought, as a breath yielded succeeds a breath taken.

She accused the heavens of injustice.

Pericles, prostrate on the floor, moaned that he was wounded. She said, "Bleed to death!"

"It is my soul, it is my soul is wounded for you, Sandra."

"Dreadful craven man!" she muttered.

"When my soul is shaking for your safety, Sandra Belloni!" Pericles turned his ear up. "For myself—not; it is for you, for you."

Assured of the cessation of arms by delicious silence he jumped to his feet.

"Ah! brutes to fight. It is 'immonde;' it is unnatural!"

He tapped his finger on the walls for marks of shot, and discovered a shot-hole in the wood-work, that had passed an arm's length above her head, into which he thrust his finger in an intense speculative meditation, shifting eyes from it to her, and throwing them aloft.

He was summoned to the presence of Count Karl, with whom he found Captain Weisspriess, Wilfrid, and officers of jagers and the Italian battalion. Barto Rizzo's wife was in a corner of the room. Weisspriess met him with a very civil greeting, and introduced him to Count Karl, who begged him to thank Vittoria for the aid she had afforded to General Schoneck's emissary in crossing the Piedmontese lines. He spoke in Italian. He agreed to conduct Pericles to a point on the route of his march, where Pericles and his precious prima donna—"our very good friend," he said, jovially—could escape the risk of unpleasant mishaps, and arrive at Trent and cities of peace by easy stages. He was marching for the neighbourhood of Vicenza.

A little before dawn Vittoria came down to the carriage. Count Karl stood at the door to hand her in. He was young and handsome, with a soft flowing blonde moustache and pleasant eyes, a contrast to his brother Count Lenkenstein. He repeated his thanks to her, which Pericles had not delivered; he informed her that she was by no means a prisoner, and was simply under the guardianship of friends— "though perhaps, signorina, you will not esteem this gentleman to be one of your friends." He pointed to Weisspriess. The officer bowed, but kept aloof. Vittoria perceived a singular change in him: he had become pale and sedate. "Poor fellow! he has had his dose," Count Karl said. "He is, I beg to assure you, one of your most vehement admirers."

A piece of her property that flushed her with recollections, yet made her grateful, was presently handed to her, though not in her old enemy's presence, by a soldier. It was the silver-hilted dagger, Carlo's precious gift, of which Weisspriess had taken possession in the mountain-pass over the vale of Meran, when he fought the duel with Angelo. Whether intended as a peace-offering, or as a simple restitution, it helped Vittoria to believe that Weisspriess was no longer the man he had been.

The march was ready, but Barto Rizzo's wife refused to move a foot. The officers consulted. She, was brought before them. The soldiers swore with jesting oaths that she had been carefully searched for weapons, and only wanted a whipping. "She must have it," said Weisspriess. Vittoria entreated that she might have a place beside her in the carriage. "It is more than I would have asked of you; but if you are not afraid of her," said Count Karl, with an apologetic shrug.

Her heart beat fast when she found herself alone with the terrible woman.

Till then she had never seen a tragic face. Compared with this tawny colourlessness, this evil brow, this shut mouth, Laura, even on the battle-field, looked harmless. It was like the face of a dead savage. The eyeballs were full on Vittoria, as if they dashed at an obstacle, not embraced an image. In proportion as they seemed to widen about her, Vittoria shrank. The whole woman was blood to her gaze.

When she was capable of speaking, she said entreatingly:

"I knew his brother."

Not a sign of life was given in reply.

Companionship with this ghost of broad daylight made the flattering Tyrolese feathers at both windows a welcome sight.

Precautions had been taken to bind the woman's arms. Vittoria offered to loosen the cords, but she dared not touch her without a mark of assent.

"I know Angelo Guidascarpi, Rinaldo's brother," she spoke again.

The woman's nostrils bent inward, as when the breath we draw is keen as a sword to the heart. Vittoria was compelled to look away from her.

At the mid-day halt Count Karl deigned to justify to her his intended execution of Rinaldo—the accomplice in the slaying of his brother Count Paula. He was evidently eager to obtain her good opinion of the Austrian military. "But for this miserable spirit of hatred against us," he said, "I should have espoused an Italian lady;" and he asked, "Why not? For that matter, in all but blood we Lenkensteins are half Italian, except when Italy menaces the empire. Can you blame us for then drawing the sword in earnest?"

He proffered his version of the death of Count Paul. She kept her own silent in her bosom.

Clelia Guidascarpi, according to his statement, had first been slain by her brothers. Vittoria believed that Clelia had voluntarily submitted to death and died by her own hand. She was betrothed to an Italian nobleman of Bologna, the friend of the brothers. They had arranged the marriage; she accepted the betrothal. "She loved my brother, poor thing!" said Count Karl. "She concealed it, and naturally. How could she take a couple of wolves into her confidence? If she had told the pair of ruffians that she was plighted to an Austrian, they would have quieted her at an earlier period. A woman! a girl—signorina! The intolerable cowardice amazes me. It amazes me that you or anyone can uphold the character of such brutes. And when she was dead they lured my brother to the house and slew him; fell upon him with daggers, stretched him at the foot of her coffin, and then—what then?—ran! ran for their lives. One has gone to his account. We shall come across the other. He is among that volunteer party which attacked us yesterday. The body was carried off by them; it is sufficient testimony that Angelo Guidascarpi is in the neighbourhood. I should be hunting him now but that I am under orders to march South-east."

The story, as Vittoria knew it, had a different, though yet a dreadful, colour.

"I could have hanged Rinaldo," Count Karl said further. "I suppose the rascals feared I should use my right, and that is why they sent their mad baggage of a woman to spare any damage to the family pride. If I had been a man to enjoy vengeance, the rope would have swung for him. In spite of provocation, I shall simply shoot the other; I pledge my word to it. They shall be paid in coin. I demand no interest."

Weisspriess prudently avoided her. Wilfrid held aloof. She sat in garden shade till the bugle sounded. Tyrolese and Italian soldiers were gibing at her haggard companion when she entered the carriage. Fronting this dumb creature once more, Vittoria thought of the story of the brothers. She felt herself reading it from the very page. The woman looked that evil star incarnate which Laura said they were born under.

This is in brief the story of the Guidascarpi.

They were the offspring of a Bolognese noble house, neither wealthy nor poor. In her early womanhood, Clelia was left to the care of her brothers. She declined the guardianship of Countess Ammiani because of her love for them; and the three, with their passion of hatred to the Austrians inherited from father and mother, schemed in concert to throw off the Austrian yoke. Clelia had soft features of no great mark; by her colouring she was beautiful, being dark along the eyebrows, with dark eyes, and a surpassing richness of Venetian hair. Bologna and Venice were married in her aspect. Her brothers conceived her to possess such force of mind that they held no secrets from her. They did not know that the heart of their sister was struggling with an image of Power when she uttered hatred of it. She was in truth a woman of a soft heart, with a most impressionable imagination.

There were many suitors for the hand of Clelia Guidascarpi, though her dowry was not the portion of a fat estate. Her old nurse counselled the brothers that they should consent to her taking a husband. They fulfilled this duty as one that must be done, and she became sorrowfully the betrothed of a nobleman of Bologna; from which hour she had no cheerfulness. The brothers quitted Bologna for Venice, where there was the bed of a conspiracy. On their return they were shaken by rumours of their sister's misconduct. An Austrian name was allied to hers in busy mouths. A lady, their distant relative, whose fame was light, had withdrawn her from the silent house, and made display of her. Since she had seen more than an Italian girl should see, the brothers proposed to the nobleman her betrothed to break the treaty; but he was of a mind to hurry on the marriage, and recollecting now that she was but a woman, the brothers fixed a day for her espousals, tenderly, without reproach. She had the choice of taking the vows or surrendering her hand. Her old nurse prayed for the day of her espousals to come with a quicker step.

One night she surprised Count Paul Lenkenstein at Clelia's window. Rinaldo was in the garden below. He moved to the shadow of a cypress, and was seen moving by the old nurse. The lover took the single kiss he had come for, was led through the chamber, and passed unchallenged into the street. Clelia sat between locked doors and darkened windows, feeling colder to the brothers she had been reared with than to all other men upon the earth. They sent for her after a lapse of hours. Her old nurse was kneeling at their feet. Rinaldo asked for the name of her lover. She answered with it. Angelo said, "It will be better for you to die: but if you cannot do so easy a thing as that, prepare widow's garments." They forced her to write three words to Count Paul, calling him to her window at midnight. Rinaldo fetched a priest: Angelo laid out two swords. An hour before the midnight, Clelia's old nurse raised the house with her cries. Clelia was stretched dead in her chamber. The brothers kissed her in turn, and sat, one at her head, one at her feet. At midnight her lover stood among them. He was gravely saluted, and bidden to look upon the dead body. Angelo said to him, "Had she lived you should have wedded her hand. She is gone of her own free choice, and one of us follows her." With the sweat of anguish on his forehead, Count Paul drew sword. The window was barred; six male domestics of the household held high lights in the chamber; the priest knelt beside one corpse, awaiting the other.

Vittoria's imagination could not go beyond that scene, but she looked out on the brother of the slain youth with great pity, and with a strange curiosity. The example given by Clelia of the possible love of an Italian girl for the white uniform, set her thinking whether so monstrous a fact could ever be doubled in this world. "Could it happen to me?" she asked herself, and smiled, as she half-fashioned the words on her lips, "It is a pretty uniform."

Her reverie was broken by a hiss of "Traitress!" from the woman opposite.

She coloured guiltily, tried to speak, and sat trembling. A divination of intense hatred had perhaps read the thought within her breast: or it was a mere outburst of hate. The woman's face was like the wearing away of smoke from a spot whence shot has issued. Vittoria walked for the remainder of the day. That fearful companion oppressed her. She felt that one who followed armies should be cast in such a frame, and now desired with all her heart to render full obedience to Carlo, and abide in Brescia, or even in Milan—a city she thought of shyly.

The march was hurried to the slopes of the Vicentino, for enemies were thick in this district. Pericles refused to quit the soldiers, though Count Karl used persuasion. The young nobleman said to Vittoria, "Be on your guard when you meet my sister Anna. I tell you, we can be as revengeful as any of you: but you will exonerate me. I do my duty; I seek to do no more."

At an inn that they reached toward evening she saw the innkeeper shoot a little ball of paper at an Italian corporal, who put his foot on it and picked it up. The soldier subsequently passed through the ranks of his comrades, gathering winks and grins. They were to have rested at the inn, but Count Karl was warned by scouts, which was sufficient to make Pericles cling to him in avoidance of the volunteers, of whom mainly he was in terror. He looked ague-stricken. He would not listen to her, or to reason in any shape. "I am on the sea—shall I trust a boat? I stick to a ship," he said. The soldiers marched till midnight. It was arranged that the carriage should strike off for Schio at dawn. The soldiers bivouacked on the slope of one of the low undulations falling to the Vicentino plain. Vittoria spread her cloak, and lay under bare sky, not suffering the woman to be ejected from the carriage. Hitherto Luigi had avoided her. Under pretence of doubling Count Karl's cloak as a pillow for her head, he whispered, "If the signorina hears shots let her lie on the ground flat as a sheet." The peacefulness surrounding her precluded alarm. There was brilliant moonlight, and the host of stars, all dim; and first they beckoned her up to come away from trouble, and then, through long gazing, she had the fancy that they bent and swam about her, making her feel that she lay in the hollows of a warm hushed sea. She wished for her lover.

Men and officers were lying at a stone's-throw distant. The Tyrolese had lit a fire for cooking purposes, by which four of them stood, and, lifting hands, sang one of their mountain songs, that seemed to her to spring like clear water into air, and fall wavering as a feather falls, or the light about a stone in water. It lulled her to a half-sleep, during which she fancied hearing a broad imitation of a cat's-call from the mountains, that was answered out of the camp, and a talk of officers arose in connection with the response, and subsided. The carriage was in the shadows of the fire. In a little while Luigi and the driver began putting the horses to, and she saw Count Karl and Weissspriess go up to Luigi, who declared loudly that it was time. The woman inside was aroused. Weissspriess helped to drag her out. Luigi kept making much noise, and apologized for it by saying that he desired to awaken his master, who was stretched in a secure circle among the Tyrolese. Presently Vittoria beheld the woman's arms thrown out free; the next minute they were around the body of Weissspriess, and a shrewd cry issued from Count Karl. Shots rang from the outposts; the Tyrolese sprang to arms; "Sandra!" was shouted by Pericles; and once more she heard the 'Venite fratelli!' of the bull's voice, and a stream of volunteers dashed at the Tyrolese with sword and dagger and bayonet. The Austro-Italians stood in a crescent line—the ominous form of incipient military insubordination. Their officers stormed at them, and called for Count Karl and for Weissspriess. The latter replied like a man stifling, but Count Karl's voice was silent.

"Weissspriess! here, to me!" the captain sang out in Italian.

"Ammiani! here, to me!" was replied.

Vittoria struck her hands together in electrical gladness at her lover's voice and name. It rang most cheerfully. Her home was in the conflict where her lover fought, and she muttered with ecstasy, "We have met! we have met!" The sound of the keen steel, so exciting to dream of, paralyzed her nerves in a way that powder, more terrible for a woman's imagination, would not have done, and she could only feebly advance. It was a spacious moonlight, but the moonlight appeared to have got of a brassy hue to her eyes, though the sparkle of the steel was white; and she felt too, and wondered at it, that the cries and the noise went to her throat, as if threatening to choke her. Very soon she found herself standing there, watching for the issue of the strife, almost as dead as a weight in scales, incapable of clear vision.

Matched against the Tyrolese alone, the volunteers had an equal fight in point of numbers, and the advantage of possessing a leader; for Count Karl was down, and Weisspriess was still entangled in the woman's arms. When at last Wilfrid got him free, the unsupported Tyrolese were giving ground before Carlo Ammiani and his followers. These fought with stern fury, keeping close up to their enemy, rarely shouting. They presented something like the line of a classic bow, with its arrow-head; while the Tyrolese were huddled in groups, and clubbed at them, and fell back for space, and ultimately crashed upon their betraying brothers in arms, swinging rifles and flying. The Austro-Italians rang out a Viva for Italy, and let them fly: they were swept from the scene.

Vittoria heard her lover addressing his followers. Then he and Angelo stood over Count Karl, whom she had forgotten. Angelo ran up to her, but gave place the moment Carlo came; and Carlo drew her by the hand swiftly to an obscure bend of the rolling ground, and stuck his sword in the earth, and there put his arms round her and held her fast.

"Obey me now," were his first words.

"Yes," she answered.

He was harsh of eye and tongue, not like the gentle youth she had been torn from at the door of La Scala.

"Return; make your way to Brescia. My mother is in Brescia. Milan is hateful. I throw myself into Vicenza. Can I trust you to obey?"

"Carlo, what evil have you heard of me?"

"I listen to no tales."

"Let me follow you to Vicenza and be your handmaid, my beloved."

"Say that you obey."

"I have said it."

He seemed to shut her in his heart, so closely was she enfolded.

"Since La Scala," she murmured; and he bent his lips to her ear, whispering, "Not one thought of another woman! and never till I die."

"And I only of you, Carlo, and for you, my lover, my lover!"

"You love me absolutely?"

"I belong to you."

"I could be a coward and pray for life to live to hear you say it."

"I feel I breathe another life when you are away from me."

"You belong to me; you are my own?"

"You take my voice, beloved."

"And when I claim you, I am to have you?"

"Am I not in your hands?"

"The very instant I make my claim you will say yes?"

"I shall not have strength for more than to nod."

Carlo shuddered at the delicious image of her weakness.

"My Sandra! Vittoria, my soul! my bride!"

"O my Carlo! Do you go to Vicenza? And did you know I was among these people?"

"You will hear everything from little Leone Rufo, who is wounded and accompanies you to Brescia. Speak of nothing. Speak my name, and look at me. I deserve two minutes of blessedness."

"Ah! my dearest, if I am sweet to you, you might have many!"

"No; they begin to hum a reproach at me already, for I must be marching. Vicenza will soon bubble on a fire, I suspect. Comfort my mother; she wants a young heart at her elbow. If she is alone, she feeds on every rumour; other women scatter in emotions what poisons her. And when my bride is with her, I am between them."

"Yes, Carlo, I will go," said Vittoria, seeing her duty at last through tenderness.

Carlo sprang from her side to meet Angelo, with whom he exchanged some quick words. The bugle was sounding, and Barto Rizzo audible. Luigi came to, her, ruefully announcing that the volunteers had sacked the carriage behaved worse than the Austrians; and that his padrone, the signor Antonio-Pericles, was off like a gossamer. Angelo induced her to remain on the spot where she stood till the carriage was seen on the Schio road, when he led her to it, saying that Carlo had serious work to do.

Count Karl Lenkenstein was lying in the carriage, supported by Wilfrid and by young Leone Rufo, who sat laughing, with one eye under a cross-bandage and an arm slung in a handkerchief. Vittoria desired to wait that she might see her lover once more; but Angelo entreated her that she should depart, too earnestly to leave her in doubt of there being good reason for it and for her lover's absence. He pointed to Wilfrid: "Barto Rizzo captured this man; Carlo has released him. Take him with you to attend on his superior officer." She drew Angelo's observation to the first morning colours over the peaks. He looked up, and she knew that he remembered that morning of their flight from the inn. Perhaps he then had the image of his brother in his mind, for the colours seemed to be plucking at his heart, and he said, "I have lost him."

"God help you, my friend!" said Vittoria, her throat choking.

Angelo pointed at the insensible nobleman: "These live. I do not grudge him his breath or his chances; but why should these men take so much killing? Weisspriess has risen, as though I struck the blow of a babe. But we one shot does for us! Nevertheless, signorina," Angelo smiled firmly, "I complain of nothing while we march forward."

He kissed his hand to her, and turned back to his troop. The carriage was soon under the shadows of the mountains.

CHAPTER XXXIV

EPISODES OF THE REVOLT AND THE WAR THE DEEDS OF BARTO RIZZO—THE MEETING AT ROVEREDO

At Schio there was no medical attendance to be obtained for Count Karl, and he begged so piteously to be taken on to Roveredo, that, on his promising to give Leone Rufo a pass, Vittoria decided to work her way round to Brescia by the Alpine route. She supposed Pericles to have gone off among the Tyrolese, and wished in her heart that Wilfrid had gone likewise, for he continued to wear that look of sad stupefaction which was the harshest reproach to her. Leone was unconquerably gay in spite of his wounds. He narrated the doings of the volunteers, with proud eulogies of Carlo Ammiani's gallant leadership; but the devices of Barto Rizzo appeared to have struck his imagination most. "He is positively a cat—a great cat," Leone said. "He can run a day; he can fast a week; he can climb a house; he can drop from a crag; and he never lets go his hold. If he says a thing to his wife, she goes true as a bullet to the mark. The two make a complete piece of artillery. We are all for Barto, though our captain Carlo is often enraged with him. But there's no getting on without him. We have found that."

Rinaldo and Angelo Guidascarpi and Barto Rizzo had done many daring feats. They had first, heading about a couple of dozen out of a force of sixty, endeavoured to surprise the fortress Rocca d'Anfo in Lake Idro—an insane enterprise that touched on success, and would have been an achievement had all the men who followed them been made of the same desperate stuff. Beaten off, they escaped up the Val di Ledro, and secretly entered Trent, where they hoped to spread revolt, but the Austrian commandant knew what a quantity of dry wood was in the city, and stamped his heel on sparks. A revolt was prepared notwithstanding the proclamation of imprisonment and death. Barto undertook to lead a troop against the Buon Consiglio barracks, while Angelo and Rinaldo cleared the ramparts. It chanced, whether from treachery or extra-vigilance was unknown, that the troops paid domiciliary visits an hour before the intended outbreak, and the three were left to accomplish their task alone. They remained in the city several days, hunted from house to house, and finally they were brought to bay at night on the roof of a palace where the Lenkenstein ladies were residing. Barto took his dagger between his teeth and dropped to the balcony of Lena's chamber. The brothers soon after found the rooftrap opened to them, and Lena and Anna conducted them to the postern-door. There Angelo asked whom they had to thank. The terrified ladies gave their name; upon hearing which, Rinaldo turned and said that he would pay for a charitable deed to the extent of his power, and would not meanly allow them to befriend persons who were to continue strangers to them. He gave the name of Guidascarpi, and relieved his brother, as well as himself, of a load of obligation, for the ladies raised wild screams on the instant. In falling from the walls to the road, Rinaldo hurt his foot. Barto lifted him on his back, and journeyed with him so till at the appointed place he met his wife, who dressed the foot, and led them out of the line of pursuit, herself bending under the beloved load. Her adoration of Rinaldo was deep as a mother's, pure as a virgin's, fiery as a saint's. Leone Rufo dwelt on it the more fervidly from seeing Vittoria's expression of astonishment. The woman led them to a cave in the rocks, where she had stored provision and sat two days expecting the signal from Trent. They saw numerous bands of soldiers set out along the valleys—merry men whom it was Barto's pleasure to beguile by shouts, as a relief for his parched weariness upon the baking rock. Accident made it an indiscretion. A glass was levelled at them by a mounted officer, and they had quickly to be moving. Angelo knew the voice of Weisspriess in the word of command to the soldiers, and the call to him to surrender. Weisspriess followed them across the mountain track, keeping at their heels, though they doubled and adopted all possible contrivances to shake him off. He was joined by Count Karl Lenkenstein on the day when Carlo Ammiani encountered them, with the rear of Colonel Corte's band marching for Vicenza. In the collision between the Austrians and the volunteers, Rinaldo was taken fighting upon his knee-cap. Leone cursed the disabled foot which had carried the hero in action, to cast him at the mercy of his enemies; but recollection of that sight of Rinaldo fighting far ahead and alone, half-down-like a scuttled ship, stood like a flower in the lad's memory. The volunteers devoted themselves to liberate or avenge him. It was then that Barto Rizzo sent his wife upon her mission. Leone assured Vittoria that Angelo was aware of its nature, and approved it—hoped that the same might be done for himself. He shook his head when she asked if Count Ammiani approved it likewise.

"Signorina, Count Ammiani has a grudge against Barto, though he can't help making use of him. Our captain Carlo is too much of a mere soldier. He would have allowed Rinaldo to be strung up, and Barto does not owe him obedience in those things."

"But why did this Barto Rizzo employ a woman's hand?"

"The woman was capable. No man could have got permission to move freely among the rascal Austrians, even in the character of a deserter. She did, and she saved him from the shame of execution. And besides, it was her punishment. You are astonished? Barto Rizzo punishes royally. He never forgives, and he never persecutes; he waits for his opportunity. That woman disobeyed him once—once only; but once was enough. It occurred in Milan, I believe. She released an Austrian, or did something—I don't know the story exactly—and Barto said to her, 'Now you can wash out your crime and send your boy to heaven unspotted, with one blow.' I saw her set out to do it. She was all teeth and eyes, like a frightened horse; she walked like a Muse in a garden."

Vittoria discovered that her presence among the Austrians had been known to Carlo. Leone alluded slightly to Barto Rizzo's confirmed suspicion of her, saying that it was his weakness to be suspicious of women. The volunteers, however, were all in her favour, and had jeered at Barto on his declaring that she might, in proof of her willingness to serve the cause, have used her voice for the purpose of subjugating the wavering Austro-Italians, who wanted as much coaxing as women. Count Karl had been struck to earth by Barto Rizzo. "Not with his boasted neatness, I imagine," Leone said. In fact, the dagger had grazed an ivory portrait of a fair Italian head wreathed with violets in Count Karl's breast.

Vittoria recognized the features of Violetta d'Isorella as the original of the portrait.

They arrived at Roveredo late in the evening. The wounded man again entreated Vittoria to remain by him till a messenger should bring one of his sisters from Trent. "See," she said to Leone, "how I give grounds for suspicion of me; I nurse an enemy."

"Here is a case where Barto is distinctly to blame," the lad replied. "The poor fellow must want nursing, for he can't smoke."

Anna von Lenkenstein came from Trent to her brother's summons. Vittoria was by his bedside, and the sufferer had fallen asleep with his head upon her arm. Anna looked upon this scene with more hateful amazement than her dull eyelids could express. She beckoned imperiously for her to come away, but Vittoria would not allow him to be disturbed, and Anna sat and faced her. The sleep was long. The eyes of the two women met from time to time, and Vittoria thought that Barto Rizzo's wife, though more terrible, was pleasanter to behold, and less brutal, than Anna. The moment her brother stirred, Anna repeated her imperious gesture, murmuring, "Away! out of my sight!" With great delicacy of touch she drew the arm from the pillow and thrust it back, and then motioning in an undisguised horror, said, "Go." Vittoria rose to go.

"Is it my Lena?" came from Karl's faint lips.

"It is your Anna."

"I should have known," he moaned.

Vittoria left them.

Some hours later, Countess Lena appeared, bringing a Trentino doctor. She said when she beheld Vittoria, "Are you our evil genius, then?" Vittoria felt that she must necessarily wear that aspect to them.

Still greater was Lena's amazement when she looked on Wilfrid. She passed him without a sign.

Vittoria had to submit to an interview with both sisters before her departure. Apart from her distress on their behalf, they had always seemed as very weak, flippant young women to her, and she could have smiled in her heart when Anna pointed to a day of retribution in the future.

"I shall not seek to have you assassinated," Anna said; "do not suppose that I mean the knife or the pistol. But your day will come, and I can wait for it. You murdered my brother Paul: you have tried to murder my brother Karl. I wish you to leave this place convinced of one thing:—you shall be repaid for it."

There was no direct allusion either to Weisspriess or to Wilfrid.

Lena spoke of the army. "You think our cause is ruined because we have insurrection on all sides of us: you do not know our army. We can fight the Hungarians with one hand, and you Italians with the other—with a little finger. On what spot have we given way? We have to weep, it is true; but tears do not testify to defeat; and already I am inclined to pity those fools who have taken part against us. Some have experienced the fruits of their folly."

This was the nearest approach to a hint at Wilfrid's misconduct.

Lena handed Leone's pass to Vittoria, and drawing out a little pocket almanac, said, "You proceed to Milan, I presume. I do not love your society; mademoiselle Belloni or Campa: yet I do not mind making an appointment—the doctor says a month will set my brother on his feet again,—I will make an appointment to meet you in Milan or Como, or anywhere in your present territories, during the month of August. That affords time for a short siege and two pitched battles."

She appeared to be expecting a retort.

Vittoria replied, "I could beg one thing on my knees of you, Countess Lena."

"And that is—?" Lena threw her head up superbly.

"Pardon my old friend the service he did me through friendship."

The sisters interchanged looks. Lena flushed angrily.

Anna said, "The person to whom you allude is here."

"He is attending on your brother."

"Did he help this last assassin to escape, perchance?"

Vittoria sickened at the cruel irony, and felt that she had perhaps done ill in beginning to plead for Wilfrid.

"He is here; let him speak for himself: but listen to him, Countess Lena."

"A dishonourable man had better be dumb," interposed Anna.

"Ah! it is I who have offended you."

"Is that his excuse?"

Vittoria kept her eyes on the fiercer sister, who now declined to speak.

"I will not excuse my own deeds; perhaps I cannot. We Italians are in a hurricane; I cannot reflect. It may be that I do not act more thinkingly than a wild beast."

"You have spoken it," Anna exclaimed.

"Countess Lena, he fights in your ranks as a common soldier. He encounters more than a common soldier's risks."

"The man is brave,—we knew that," said Anna.

"He is more than brave, he is devoted. He fights against us, without hope of reward from you. Have I utterly ruined him?"

"I imagine that you may regard it as a fact that you have utterly ruined him," said Anna, moving to break up the parting interview. Lena turned to follow her.

"Ladies, if it is I who have hardened your hearts, I am more guilty than I thought." Vittoria said no more. She knew that she had been speaking badly, or ineffectually, by a haunting flatness of sound, as of an unstrung instrument, in her ears: she was herself unstrung and dispirited, while the recollection of Anna's voice was like a sombre conquering monotony on a low chord, with which she felt insufficient to compete.

Leone was waiting in the carriage to drive to the ferry across the Adige. There was news in Roveredo of the king's advance upon Rivoli; and Leone sat trying to lift and straighten out his wounded arm, with grimaces of laughter at the pain of the effort, which resolutely refused to acknowledge him to be an able combatant. At the carriage-door Wilfrid bowed once over Vittoria's hand.

"You see that," Anna remarked to her sister.

"I should have despised him if he had acted indifference," replied Lena.

She would have suspected him—that was what her heart meant; the artful show of indifference had deceived her once. The anger within her drew its springs much more fully from his refusal to respond to her affection, when she had in a fit of feminine weakness abased herself before him on the night of the Milanese revolt, than from the recollection of their days together in Meran. She had nothing of her sister's unforgivingness. And she was besides keenly curious to discover the nature of the charm Vittoria threw on him, and not on him solely. Vittoria left Wilfrid to better chances than she supposed. "Continue fighting with your army," she said, when they parted. The deeper shade which traversed his features told her that, if she pleased, her sway might still be active; but she had no emotion to spare for sentimental regrets. She asked herself whether a woman who has cast her lot in scenes of strife does not lose much of her womanhood and something of her truth; and while her imagination remained depressed, her answer was sad. In that mood she pitied Wilfrid with a reckless sense of her inability to repay him for the harm she had done him. The tragedies written in fresh blood all about her, together with that ever-present image of the fate of Italy hanging in the balance, drew her away from personal reflections. She felt as one in a war-chariot, who has not time to cast more than a glance on the fallen. At the place where the ferry is, she was rejoiced by hearing positive news of the proximity of the Royal army. There were none to tell her that Charles Albert had here made his worst move by leaving Vicenza to the operations of the enemy, that he might become master of a point worthless when Vicenza fell into the enemy's hands. The old Austrian Field-Marshal had eluded him at Mantua on that very night when Vittoria had seen his troops in motion. The daring Austrian flank-march on Vicenza, behind the fortresses of the Quadrilateral, was the capital stroke of the campaign. But the presence of a Piedmontese vanguard at Rivoli flushed the Adige with confidence, and Vittoria went on her way sharing the people's delight. She reached Brescia to hear that Vicenza had fallen. The city was like a landscape smitten black by the thunder-cloud. Vittoria found Countess Ammiani at her husband's tomb, stiff, colourless, lifeless as a monument attached to the tomb.

CHAPTER XXXV

CLOSE OF THE LOMBARD CAMPAIGN—VITTORIA'S PERPLEXITY

The fall of Vicenza turned a tide that had overflowed its barriers with force enough to roll it to the Adriatic. From that day it was as if a violent wind blew East over Lombardy; flood and wind breaking here and there a tree, bowing everything before them. City, fortress, and battle-field resisted as the eddy whirls. Venice kept her brave colours streaming aloft in a mighty grasp despite the storm, but between Venice and Milan there was this unutterable devastation,—so sudden a change, so complete a reversal of the shield, that the Lombards were at first incredulous even in their agony, and set their faces against it as at a monstrous eclipse, as though the heavens were taking false oath of its being night when it was day. From Vicenza and Rivoli, to Sommacampagna, and across Monte Godio to Custozza, to Volta on the right of the Mincio, up to the gates of Milan, the line of fire travelled, with a fantastic overbearing swiftness that, upon the map, looks like the zig-zag elbowing of a field-rocket. Vicenza fell on the 11th of June; the Austrians entered Milan on the 6th of August. Within that short time the Lombards were struck to the dust.

Countess Ammiani quitted Brescia for Bergamo before the worst had happened; when nothing but the king's retreat upon the Lombard capital, after the good fight at Volta, was known. According to the king's proclamation the Piedmontese army was to defend Milan, and hope was not dead. Vittoria succeeded in repressing all useless signs of grief in the presence of the venerable lady, who herself showed none, but simply recommended her accepted daughter to pray daily. "I can neither confess nor pray," Vittoria said to the priest, a comfortable, irritable ecclesiastic, long attached to the family, and little able to deal with this rebel before Providence, that would not let her swollen spirit be bled. Yet she admitted to him that the countess possessed resources which she could find nowhere; and she saw the full beauty of such inimitable grave endurance. Vittoria's foolish trick of thinking for herself made her believe, nevertheless, that the countess suffered more than she betrayed, was less consoled than her spiritual comforter imagined. She continued obstinate and unrepentant, saying, "If my punishment is to come, it will at least bring experience with it, and I shall know why I am punished. The misery now is that I do not know, and do not see, the justice of the sentence."

Countess Ammiani thought better of her case than the priest did; or she was more indulgent, or half indifferent. This girl was Carlo's choice;—a strange choice, but the times were strange, and the girl was robust. The channels of her own and her husband's house were drying on all sides; the house wanted resuscitating. There was promise that the girl would bear children of strong blood. Countess Ammiani would not for one moment have allowed the spiritual welfare of the children to hang in dubitation, awaiting their experience of life; but a certain satisfaction was shown in her faint smile when her confessor lamented over Vittoria's proud stony state of moral revolt. She said to her accepted daughter, "I shall expect you to be prepared to espouse my son as soon as I have him by my side;" nor did Vittoria's silent bowing of her face assure her that strict obedience was implied. Precise words—"I will," and "I will not fail"—were exacted. The countess showed some emotion after Vittoria had spoken. "Now, may God end this war quickly, if it is to go against us," she exclaimed, trembling in her chair visibly a half-minute, with dropped eyelids and lips moving.

Carlo had sent word that he would join his mother as early as he was disengaged from active service, and meantime requested her to proceed to a villa on Lago Maggiore. Vittoria obtained permission from the countess to order the route of the carriage through Milan, where she wished to take up her mother and her maid Giacinta. For other reasons she would have avoided the city. The thought of entering it was painful with the shrewdest pain. Dante's profoundly human line seemed branded on the forehead of Milan.

The morning was dark when they drove through the streets of Bergamo. Passing one of the open places, Vittoria beheld a great concourse of volunteer youth and citizens, all of them listening to the voice of one who stood a few steps above them holding a banner. She gave an outcry of bitter joy. It was the Chief. On one side of him was Agostino, in the midst of memorable heads that were unknown to her. The countess refused to stay, though Vittoria strained her hands together in extreme entreaty that she might for a few moments hear what the others were hearing. "I speak for my son, and I forbid it," Countess Ammiani said. Vittoria fell back and closed her eyes to cherish the vision. All those faces raised to the one speaker under the dark sky were beautiful. He had breathed some new glory of hope in them, making them shine beneath the overcast heavens, as when the sun breaks from an evening cloud and flushes the stems of a company of pine-trees.

Along the road to Milan she kept imagining his utterance until her heart rose with music. A delicious stream of music, thin as poor tears, passed through her frame, like a life reviving. She reached Milan in a mood to bear the idea of temporary defeat. Music had forsaken her so long that celestial reassurance seemed to return with it.

Her mother was at Zotti's, very querulous, but determined not to leave the house and the few people she knew. She had, as she told her daughter, fretted so much on her account that she hardly knew whether she was glad to see her. Tea, of course, she had given up all thoughts of; but now coffee was rising, and the boasted sweet bread of Lombardy was something to look at! She trusted that Emilia would soon think of singing no more, and letting people rest: she might sing when she wanted money. A letter recently received from Mr. Pericles said that Italy was her child's ruin, and she hoped Emilia was ready to do as he advised, and hurry to England, where singing did not upset people, and people lived like real Christians, not——Vittoria flapped her hand, and would not hear of the unchristian crimes of the South. As regarded the expected defence of Milan, the little woman said, that if it brought on a bombardment, she would call it unpardonable wickedness, and only hoped that her daughter would repent.

Zotti stood by, interpreting the English to himself by tones. "The amiable donnina is not of our persuasion," he observed. "She remains dissatisfied with patriotic Milan. I have exhibited to her my dabs of bread through all the processes of making and baking. It is in vain. She rejects analogy. She is wilful as a principessina: 'Tis so! 'tis not so! 'tis my will! be silent, thou! Signora, I have been treated in that way by your excellent mother."

"Zotti has not been paid for three weeks, and he certainly has not mentioned it or looked it, I will say, Emilia."

"Zotti has had something to think of during the last three weeks," said Vittoria, touching him kindly on the arm.

The confectioner lifted his fingers and his big brown eyes after them, expressive of the unutterable thoughts. He informed her that he had laid in a stock of flour, in the expectation that Carlo Alberto would defend the city: The Milanese were ready to aid him, though some, as Zotti confessed, had ceased to effervesce; and a great number who were perfectly ready to fight regarded his tardy appeal to Italian patriotism very coldly. Zotti set out in person to discover Giacinta. The girl could hardly fetch her breath when she saw her mistress. She was in Laura's service, and said that Laura had brought a wounded Englishman from the field of Custozza. Vittoria hurried to Laura, with whom she found Merthyr, blue-white as a corpse, having been shot through the body. His sister was in one of the Lombard hamlets, unaware of his fall; Beppo had been sent to her.

They noticed one another's embrowned complexions, but embraced silently. "Twice widowed!" Laura said when they sat together. Laura hushed all speaking of the war or allusion to a single incident of the miserable campaign, beyond the bare recital of Vittoria's adventures; yet when Vicenza by chance was mentioned, she burst out: "They are not cities, they are living shrieks. They have been made impious for ever. Burn them to ashes, that they may not breathe foul upon heaven!" She had clung to the skirts of the army as far as the field of Custozza. "He," she said, pointing to the room where Merthyr lay,—"he groans less than the others I have nursed. Generally, when they looked at me, they appeared obliged to recollect that it was not I who had hurt them. Poor souls! some ended in great torment. 'I think of them as the happiest; for pain is a cloak that wraps you about, and I remember one middle-aged man who died softly at Custozza, and said, 'Beaten!' To take that thought as your travelling companion into the gulf, must be worse than dying of agony; at least, I think so."

Vittoria was too well used to Laura's way of meeting disaster to expect from her other than this ironical fortitude, in which the fortitude leaned so much upon the irony. What really astonished her was the conception Laura had taken of the might of Austria. Laura did not directly speak of it, but shadowed it in allusive hints, much as if she had in her mind the image of an iron roller going over a field of flowers— hateful, imminent, irresistible. She felt as a leaf that has been flying before the gale.

Merthyr's wound was severe: Vittoria could not leave him. Her resolution to stay in Milan brought her into collision with Countess Ammiani, when the countess reminded her of her promise, sedately informing her that she was no longer her own mistress, and had a primary duty to fulfil. She offered to wait three days, or until the safety of the wounded man was medically certified to. It was incomprehensible to her that Vittoria should reject her terms; and though it was true that she would not have listened to a reason, she was indignant at not hearing one given in mitigation of the offence. She set out alone on her journey, deeply hurt. The reason was a feminine sentiment, and Vittoria was naturally unable to speak it. She shrank with pathetic horror from the thought of Merthyr's rising from his couch to find her a married woman, and desired most earnestly that her marriage should be witnessed by him. Young women will know how to reconcile the opposition of the sentiment. Had Merthyr been only slightly wounded, and sound enough to seem to be able to bear a bitter shock, she would not have allowed her personal feelings to cause chagrin to the noble lady. The sight of her dear steadfast friend prostrate in the cause of Italy, and who, if he lived to rise again, might not have his natural strength to bear the thought of her loss with his old brave firmness, made it impossible for her to act decisively in one direct line of conduct.

Countess Ammiani wrote brief letters from Luino and Pallanza on Lago Maggiore. She said that Carlo was in the Como mountains; he would expect to find his bride, and would accuse his mother; "but his mother will be spared those reproaches," she added, "if the last shot fired kills, as it generally does, the bravest and the dearest."

"If it should!"—the thought rose on a quick breath in Vittoria's bosom, and the sentiment which held her away dispersed like a feeble smoke, and showed her another view of her features. She wept with longing for love and dependence. She was sick of personal freedom, tired of the exercise of her will, only too eager to give herself to her beloved. The blessedness of marriage, of peace and dependence, came on her imagination like a soft breeze from a hidden garden, like sleep. But this very longing created the resistance to it in the depths of her soul. There was a light as of reviving life, or of pain comforted, when it was she who was sitting by Merthyr's side, and when at times she saw the hopeless effort of his hand to reach to hers, or during the long still hours she laid her head on his pillow, and knew that he breathed gratefully. The sweetness of helping him, and of making his breathing pleasant to him, closed much of the world which lay beyond her windows to her thoughts, and surprised her with an unknown emotion, so strange to her that when it first swept up her veins she had the fancy of her having been touched by a supernatural hand, and heard a flying accord of instruments. She was praying before she knew what prayer was. A crucifix hung over Merthyr's head. She had looked on it many times, and looked on it still, without seeing more than the old sorrow. In the night it was dim. She found herself trying to read the features of the thorn-crowned Head in the solitary night. She and it were alone with a life that was faint above the engulphing darkness. She prayed for the life, and trembled, and shed tears, and would have checked them; they seemed to be bearing away her little remaining strength. The tears streamed. No answer was given to her question, "Why do I weep?" She wept when Merthyr had passed the danger, as she had wept when the hours went by, with shrouded visages; and though she felt the difference m the springs of her tears, she thought them but a simple form of weakness showing shade and light.

These tears were a vanward wave of the sea to follow; the rising of her voice to heaven was no more than a twitter of the earliest dawn before the coming of her soul's outcry.

"I have had a weeping fit," she thought, and resolved to remember it tenderly, as being associated with her friend's recovery, and a singular masterful power absolutely to look on the Austrians marching up the streets of Milan, and not to feel the surging hatred, or the nerveless despair, which she had supposed must be her alternatives.

It is a mean image to say that the entry of the Austrians into the reconquered city was like a river of oil permeating a lake of vinegar, but it presents the fact in every sense. They demanded nothing more than submission, and placed a gentle foot upon the fallen enemy; and wherever they appeared they were isolated. The deepest wrath of the city was, nevertheless, not directed against them, but against Carlo Alberto, who had pledged his honour to defend it, and had forsaken it. Vittoria committed a public indiscretion on the day when the king left Milan to its fate: word whereof was conveyed to Carlo Ammiani, and he wrote to her.

"It is right that I should tell you what I have heard," the letter said. "I have heard that my bride drove up to the crowned traitor, after he had unmasked himself, and when he was quitting the Greppi palace, and that she kissed his hand before the people—poor bleeding people of Milan! This is what I hear in the Val d'Intelvi:—that she despised the misery and just anger of the people, and, by virtue of her name and mine, obtained a way for him. How can she have acted so as to give a colour to this infamous scandal? True or false, it does not affect my love for her. Still, my dearest, what shall I say? You keep me divided in two halves. My heart is out of me; and if I had a will, I think I should be harsh with you. You are absent from my mother at a time when we are about to strike another blow. Go to her. It is kindness; it is charity: I do not say duty. I remember that I did write harshly to you from Brescia. Then our march was so clear in view that a little thing ruffled me. Was it a little thing? But to applaud the Traitor now! To uphold him who has spilt our blood only to hand the country over to the old gaolers! He lent us his army like a Jew, for huge interest. Can you not read him? If not, cease, I implore you, to think at all for yourself.

"Is this a lover's letter? I know that my beloved will see the love in it. To me your acts are fair and good as the chronicle of a saint. I find you creating suspicion—almost justifying it in others, and putting your name in the mouth of a madman who denounces you. I shall not speak more of him. Remember that my faith in you is unchangeable, and I pray you to have the same in me.

"I sent you a greeting from the Chief. He marched in the ranks from Bergamo. I saw him on the line of march strip off his coat to shelter a young lad from the heavy rain. He is not discouraged; none are who have been near him.

"Angelo is here, and so is our Agostino; and I assure you he loads and fires a carbine much more deliberately than he composes a sonnet. I am afraid that your adored Antonio-Pericles fared badly among our fellows, but I could gather no particulars.

"Oh! the bright two minutes when I held you right in my heart. That spot on the Vicentino is alone unclouded. If I live I will have that bit of ground. I will make a temple of it. I could reach it blindfolded."

A townsman of Milan brought this letter to Vittoria. She despatched Luigi with her reply, which met the charge in a straightforward affirmative.

"I was driving to Zotti's by the Greppi palace, when I saw the king come forth, and the people hooted him. I stood up, and petitioned to kiss his hand. The people knew me. They did not hoot any more for some time.

"So that you have heard the truth, and you must judge me by it. I cannot even add that I am sorry, though I strive to wish that I had not been present. I might wish it really, if I did not feel it to be a cowardly wish.

"Oh, my Carlo! my lover! my husband! you would not have me go against my nature? I have seen the king upon the battle-field. He has deigned to speak to me of Italy and our freedom. I have seen him facing our enemy; and to see him hooted by the people, and in misfortune and with sad eyes!—he looked sad and nothing else—and besides, I am sure I know the king. I mean that I understand him. I am half ashamed to write so boldly, even to you. I say to myself you should know me, at least; and if I am guilty of a piece of vanity, you should know that also. Carlo Alberto is quite unlike other men. He worships success as, much; but they are not, as he is, so much bettered by adversity. Indeed I do not believe that he has exact intentions of any sort, or ever had the intention to betray us, or has done so in reality, that is, meaningly, of his own will. Count Medole and his party did, as you know, offer Lombardy to him; and Venice gave herself—brave, noble Venice! Oh! if we two were there—Venice has England's sea-spirit. But, did we not flatter the king? And ask yourself, my Carlo, could a king move in such an enterprise as a common person? Ought we not to be in union with Sardinia? How can we be if we reject her king? Is it not the only positive army that, we can look to—I mean regular army? Should we not; make some excuses for one who is not in our position?

"I feel that I push my questions like waves that fall and cannot get beyond—they crave so for answers agreeing to them. This should make me doubt myself, perhaps; but they crowd again, and seem so conclusive until I have written them down. I am unworthy to struggle with your intellect; but I say to myself, how unworthy of you I should be if I did not use my own, such as it is! The poor king; had to conclude an armistice to save his little kingdom. Perhaps we ought to think of that sternly. My heart is; filled with pity.

"It cannot but be right that you should know the worst; of me. I call you my husband, and tremble to be permitted to lean my head on your bosom for hours, my sweet lover! And yet my cowardice, if I had let the king go by without a reverential greeting from me, in his adversity, would have rendered me insufferable to myself. You are hearing me, and I am compelled to say, that rather than behave so basely I would forfeit your love, and be widowed till death should offer us for God to join us. Does your face change to me?

"Dearest, and I say it when the thought of you sets me almost swooning. I find my hands clasped, and I am muttering I know not what, and I am blushing. The ground seems to rock; I can barely breathe; my heart is like a bird caught in the hands of a cruel boy: it will not rest. I fear everything. I hear a whisper, 'Delay not an instant!' and it is like a furnace; 'Hasten to him! Speed!' and I seem to totter forward and drop—I think I have lost you—I am like one dead.

"I remain here to nurse our dear friend Merthyr. For that reason I am absent from your mother. It is her desire that we should be married.

"Soon, soon, my own soul!

"I seem to be hanging on a tree for you, swayed by such a teazing wind.

"Oh, soon! or I feel that I shall hate any vestige of will that I have in this head of mine. Not in the heart— it is not there!

"And sometimes I am burning to sing. The voice leaps to my lips; it is quite like a thing that lives apart— my prisoner.

"It is true, Laura is here with Merthyr.

"Could you come at once?—not here, but to Pallanza? We shall both make our mother happy. This she wishes, this she lives for, this consoles her—and oh, this gives me peace! Yes, Merthyr is recovering! I can leave him without the dread I had; and Laura confesses to the feminine sentiment, if her funny jealousy of a rival nurse is really simply feminine. She will be glad of our resolve, I am sure. And then you will order all my actions; and I shall be certain that they are such as I would proudly call mine; and I shall be shut away from the world. Yes; let it be so! Addio. I reserve all sweet names for you. Addio. In Pallanza:—no not Pallanza—Paradise!

"Hush! and do not smile at me:—it was not my will, I discover, but my want of will, that distracted me.

"See my last signature of—not Vittoria; for I may sign that again and still be Emilia Alessandra Ammiani.

"SANDRA BELLONI"

The letter was sealed; Luigi bore it away, and a brief letter to Countess Ammiani, in Pallanza, as well.

Vittoria was relieved of her anxiety concerning Merthyr by the arrival of Georgiana, who had been compelled to make her way round by Piacenza and Turin, where she had left Gambier, with Beppo in attendance on him. Georgiana at once assumed all the duties of head-nurse, and the more resolutely because of her brother's evident moral weakness in sighing for the hand of a fickle girl to smooth his pillow. "When he is stronger you can sit beside him a little," she said to Vittoria, who surrendered her post without a struggle, and rarely saw him, though Laura told her that his frequent exclamation was her name, accompanied by a soft look at his sister—"which would have stirred my heart like poor old Milan last March," Laura added, with a lift of her shoulders.

Georgiana's icy manner appeared infinitely strange to Vittoria when she heard from Merthyr that his sister had become engaged to Captain Gambier.

"Nothing softens these women," said Laura, putting Georgiana in a class.

"I wish you could try the effect of your winning Merthyr," Vittoria suggested.

"I remember that when I went to my husband, I likewise wanted every woman of my acquaintance to be married." Laura sighed deeply. "What is this poor withered body of mine now? It feels like an old volcano, cindery, with fire somewhere:—a charming bride! My dear, if I live till my children make me a grandmother, I shall look on the love of men and women as a toy that I have played with. A new husband? I must be dragged through the Circles of Dante before I can conceive it, and then I should loathe the stranger."

News came that the volunteers were crushed. It was time for Vittoria to start for Pallanza, and she thought of her leave-taking; a final leave-taking, in one sense, to the friends who had cared too much for her. Laura delicately drew Georgiana aside in the sick-room, which she would not quit, and alluded to the necessity for Vittoria's departure without stating exactly wherefore: but Georgiana was a Welshwoman. Partly to show her accurate power of guessing, and chiefly that she might reprove Laura's insulting whisper, which outraged and irritated her as much as if "Oh! your poor brother!" had been exclaimed, she made display of Merthyr's manly coldness by saying aloud, "You mean, that she is going to her marriage." Laura turned her face to Merthyr. He had striven to rise on his elbow, and had dropped flat in his helplessness. Big tears were rolling down his cheeks. His articulation failed him, beyond a reiterated "No, no," pitiful to hear, and he broke into childish sobs. Georgiana hurried Laura from the room. By-and-by the doctor was promptly summoned, and it was Georgiana herself, miserably humbled, who obtained Vittoria's sworn consent to keep the life in Merthyr by lingering yet awhile.

Meantime Luigi brought a letter from Pallanza in Carlo's handwriting. This was the burden of it:

"I am here, and you are absent. Hasten!"

CHAPTER XXXVI

A FRESH ENTANGLEMENT

The Lenkenstein ladies returned to Milan proudly in the path of the army which they had followed along the city walls on the black March midnight. The ladies of the Austrian aristocracy generally had to be exiles from Vienna, and were glad to flock together even in an alien city. Anna and Lena were aware of Vittoria's residence in Milan, through the interchange of visits between the Countess of Lenkenstein and her sister Signora Piaveni. They heard also of Vittoria's prospective and approaching marriage to Count Ammiani. The Duchess of Graatli, who had forborne a visit to her unhappy friends, lest her Austrian face should wound their sensitiveness, was in company with the Lenkensteins one day, when Irma di Karski called on them. Irma had come from Lago Maggiore, where she had left her patron, as she was pleased to term Antonio-Pericles. She was full of chatter of that most worthy man's deplorable experiences of Vittoria's behaviour to him during the war, and of many things besides. According to her account, Vittoria had enticed him from place to place with promises that the next day, and the next day, and the day after, she would be ready to keep her engagement to go to London, and at last she had given him the slip and left him to be plucked like a pullet by a horde of volunteer banditti, out of whose hands Antonio-Pericles-"one of our richest millionaires in Europe, certainly our richest amateur," said Irma—escaped in fit outward condition for the garden of Eden.

Count Karl was lying on the sofa, and went into endless invalid's laughter at the picture presented by Irma of the 'wild man' wanderings of poor infatuated Pericles, which was exaggerated, though not intentionally, for Irma repeated the words and gestures of Pericles in the recital of his tribulations. Being of a somewhat similar physical organization, she did it very laughably. Irma declared that Pericles was cured of his infatuation. He had got to Turin, intending to quit Italy for ever, when—"he met me," said Irma modestly.

"And heard that the war was at an end," Count Karl added.

"And he has taken the superb Villa Ricciardi, on Lago Maggiore, where he will have a troupe of singers, and perform operas, in which I believe I may possibly act as prima donna. The truth is, I would do anything to prevent him from leaving the country."

But Irma had more to say; with "I bear no malice," she commenced it. The story she had heard was that Count Ammiani, after plighting himself to a certain signorina, known as Vittoria Campa, had received tidings that she was one of those persons who bring discredit on Irma's profession. "Gifted by nature, I can acknowledge," said Irma; "but devoured by vanity—a perfect slave to the appetite for praise; ready to forfeit anything for flattery! Poor signor Antonio-Pericles!—he knows her." And now Count Ammiani, persuaded to reason by his mother, had given her up. There was nothing more positive, for Irma had seen him in the society of Countess Violetta d'Isorella.

Anna and Lena glanced at their brother Karl.

"I should not allude to what is not notorious," Irma pursued. "They are always together. My dear Antonio-Pericles is most amusing in his expressions of delight at it. For my part, though she served me an evil turn once,—you will hardly believe, ladies, that in her jealousy of me she was guilty of the most shameful machinations to get me out of the way on the night of the first performance of Camilla,—but, for my part, I bear no malice. The creature is an inveterate rebel, and I dislike her for that, I do confess."

"The signorina Vittoria Campa is my particular and very dear friend," said the duchess.

"She is not the less an inveterate rebel," said Anna.

Count Karl gave a long-drawn sigh. "Alas, that she should have brought discredit on Fraulein di Karski's profession!"

The duchess hurried straightway to Laura, with whom was Count Serabiglione, reviewing the present posture of affairs from the condescending altitudes of one that has foretold it. Laura and Amalia embraced and went apart. During their absence Vittoria came down to the count and listened to a familiar illustration of his theory of the relations which should exist between Italy and Austria, derived from the friendship of those two women.

"What I wish you to see, signorina, is that such an alliance is possible; and, if we supply the brains, as we do, is by no means likely to be degrading. These bears are absolutely on their knees to us for good fellowship. You have influence, you have amazing wit, you have unparalleled beauty, and, let me say it with the utmost sadness, you have now had experience. Why will you not recognize facts? Italian unity! I have exposed the fatuity—who listens? Italian freedom! I do not attempt to reason with my daughter. She is pricked by an envenomed fly of Satan. Yet, behold her and the duchess! It is the very union I preach; and I am, I declare to you, signorina, in great danger. I feel it, but I persist. I am in danger" (Count Serabiglione bowed his head low) "of the transcendent sin of scorn of my species."

The little nobleman swayed deploringly in his chair. "Nothing is so perilous for a soul's salvation as that. The one sane among madmen! The one whose reason is left to him among thousands who have forsaken it! I beg you to realize the idea. The Emperor, as I am given to understand, is about to make public admission of my services. I shall be all the more hated. Yet it is a considerable gain. I do not deny that I esteem it as a promotion for my services. I shall not be the first martyr in this world, signorina."

Count Serabiglione produced a martyr's smile.

"The profits of my expected posts will be," he was saying, with a reckoning eye cast upward into his cranium for accuracy, when Laura returned, and Vittoria ran out to the duchess. Amalia repeated Irma's tattle. A curious little twitching of the brows at Violetta d'Isorella's name marked the reception of it.

"She is most lovely," Vittoria said.

"And absolutely reckless."

"She is an old friend of Count Ammiani's."

"And you have an old friend here. But the old friend of a young woman—I need not say further than that it is different."

The duchess used the privilege of her affection, and urged Vittoria not to trifle with her lover's impatience.

Admitted to the chamber where Merthyr lay, she was enabled to make allowance for her irresolution. The face of the wounded man was like a lake-water taking light from Vittoria's presence.

"This may go on for weeks," she said to Laura.

Three days later, Vittoria received an order from the Government to quit the city within a prescribed number of hours, and her brain was racked to discover why Laura appeared so little indignant at the barbarous act of despotism. Laura undertook to break the bad news to Merthyr. The parting was as quiet and cheerful as, in the opposite degree, Vittoria had thought it would be melancholy and regretful. "What a Government!" Merthyr said, and told her to let him hear of any changes. "All changes that please my friends please me."

Vittoria kissed his forehead with one grateful murmur of farewell to the bravest heart she had ever known. The going to her happiness seemed more like going to something fatal until she reached the Lago Maggiore. There she saw September beauty, and felt as if the splendour encircling her were her bridal decoration. But no bridegroom stood to greet her on the terrace-steps between the potted orange and citron-trees. Countess Ammiani extended kind hands to her at arms' length.

"You have come," she said. "I hope that it is not too late."

Vittoria was a week without sight of her lover: nor did Countess Ammiani attempt to explain her words, or speak of other than common daily things. In body and soul Vittoria had taken a chill. The silent blame resting on her in this house called up her pride, so that she would not ask any questions; and when Carlo came, she wanted warmth to melt her. Their meeting was that of two passionless creatures. Carlo kissed her loyally, and courteously inquired after her health and the health of friends in Milan, and then he rallied his mother. Agostino had arrived with him, and the old man, being in one of his soft moods, unvexed by his conceits, Vittoria had some comfort from him of a dull kind. She heard Carlo telling his mother that he must go in the morning. Agostino replied to her quick look at him, "I stay;" and it seemed like a little saved from the wreck, for she knew that she could speak to Agostino as she could not to the countess. When his mother prepared to retire, Carlo walked over to his bride, and repeated rapidly and brightly his inquiries after friends in Milan. She, with a pure response to his natural-unnatural manner, spoke of Merthyr Powys chiefly: to which he said several times, "Dear fellow!" and added, "I shall always love Englishmen for his sake."

This gave her one throb. "I could not leave him, Carlo."

"Certainly not, certainly not," said Carlo. "I should have been happy to wait on him myself. I was busy; I am still. I dare say you have guessed that I have a new journal in my head: the Pallanza Iris is to be the name of it;—to be printed in three colours, to advocate three principles, in three styles. The Legitimists, the Moderates, and the Republicans are to proclaim themselves in its columns in prose, poetry, and hotch-potch. Once an editor, always an editor. The authorities suspect that something of the sort is about to be planted, so I can only make occasional visits here:—therefore, as you will believe,"—Carlo let his voice fall—"I have good reason to hate them still. They may cease to persecute me soon."

He insisted upon lighting his mother to her room. Vittoria and Agostino sat talking of the Chief and the minor events of the war—of Luciano, Marco, Giulio, and Ugo Corte—till the conviction fastened on them that Carlo would not return, when Agostino stood up and said, yawning wearily, "I'll talk further to you, my child, tomorrow."

She begged that it might be now.

"No; to-morrow," said he.

"Now, now!" she reiterated, and brought down a reproof from his fore-finger.

"The poetic definition of 'now' is that it is a small boat, my daughter, in which the female heart is constantly pushing out to sea and sinking. 'To-morrow' is an island in the deeps, where grain grows. When I land you there, I will talk to you."

She knew that he went to join Carlo after he had quitted her.

Agostino was true to his promise next day. He brought her nearer to what she had to face, though he did not help her vision much. Carlo had gone before sunrise.

They sat on the terrace above the lake, screened from the sunlight by thick myrtle bushes. Agostino smoked his loosely-rolled cigarettes, and Vittoria sipped chocolate and looked upward to the summit of Motterone, with many thoughts and images in her mind.

He commenced by giving her a love-message from Carlo. "Hold fast to it that he means it: conduct is never a straight index where the heart's involved," said the chuckling old man; "or it is not in times like ours. You have been in the wrong, and your having a good excuse will not help you before the deciding fates. Woman that you are! did you not think that because we were beaten we were going to rest for a very long while, and that your Carlo of yesterday was going to be your Carlo of to-day?"

Vittoria tacitly confessed to it.

"Ay," he pursued, "when you wrote to him in the Val d'Intelvi, you supposed you had only to say, 'I am ready,' which was then the case. You made your summer and left the fruits to hang, and now you are astounded that seasons pass and fruits drop. You should have come to this place, if but for a pair of days, and so have fixed one matter in the chapter. This is how the chapter has run on. I see I talk to a stunned head; you are thinking that Carlo's love for you can't have changed: and it has not, but occasion has gone and times have changed. Now listen. The countess desired the marriage. Carlo could not go to you in Milan with the sword in his hand. Therefore you had to come to him. He waited for you, perhaps for his own preposterous lover's sake as much as to make his mother's heart easy. If she loses him she loses everything, unless he leaves a wife to her care and the hope that her House will not be extinct, which is possibly not much more the weakness of old aristocracy than of human nature.

"Meantime, his brothers in arms had broken up and entered Piedmont, and he remained waiting for you still. You are thinking that he had not waited a month. But if four months finished Lombardy, less than one month is quite sufficient to do the same for us little beings. He met the Countess d'Isorella here. You have to thank her for seeing him at all, so don't wrinkle your forehead yet. Luciano Romara is drilling his men in Piedmont; Angelo Guidascarpi has gone there. Carlo was considering it his duty to join Luciano, when he met this lady, and she has apparently succeeded in altering his plans. Luciano and his band will go to Rome. Carlo fancies that another blow will be struck for Lombardy. This lady should know; the point is, whether she can be trusted. She persists in declaring that Carlo's duty is to remain, and—I cannot tell how, for I am as a child among women—she has persuaded him of her sincerity. Favour me now with your clearest understanding, and deliver it from feminine sensations of any description for just two minutes."

Agostino threw away the end of a cigarette and looked for firmness in Vittoria's eyes.

"This Countess d'Isorella is opposed to Carlo's marriage at present. She says that she is betraying the king's secrets, and has no reliance on a woman. As a woman you will pardon her, for it is the language of your sex. You are also denounced by Barto Rizzo, a madman—he went mad as fire, and had to be chained at Varese. In some way or other Countess d'Isorella got possession of him; she has managed to subdue him. A sword-cut he received once in Verona has undoubtedly affected his brain, or caused it to be affected under strong excitement. He is at her villa, and she says—perhaps with some truth—that Carlo would in several ways lose his influence by his immediate marriage with you. The reason must have weight; otherwise he would fulfil his mother's principal request, and be at the bidding of his own desire. There; I hope I have spoken plainly."

Agostino puffed a sigh of relief at the conclusion of his task.

Vittoria had been too strenuously engaged in defending the steadiness of her own eyes to notice the shadow of an assumption of frankness in his.

She said that she understood.

She got away to her room like an insect carrying a load thrice its own size. All that she could really gather from Agostino's words was, that she felt herself rocking in a tower, and that Violetta d'Isorella was beautiful. She had striven hard to listen to him with her wits alone, and her sensations subsequently revenged themselves in this fashion. The tower rocked and struck a bell that she discovered to be her betraying voice uttering cries of pain. She was for hours incapable of meeting Agostino again. His delicate intuition took the harshness off the meeting. He led her even to examine her state of mind, and to discern the fancies from the feelings by which she was agitated. He said shrewdly and bluntly, "You can master pain, but not doubt. If you show a sign of unhappiness, remember that I shall know you doubt both what I have told you, and Carlo as well."

Vittoria fenced: "But is there such a thing as happiness?"

"I should imagine so," said Agostino, touching her cheek, "and slipperiness likewise. There's patience at any rate; only you must dig for it. You arrive at nothing, but the eternal digging constitutes the object gained. I recollect when I was a raw lad, full of ambition, in love, and without a franc in my pockets, one night in Paris, I found myself looking up at a street lamp; there was a moth in it. He couldn't get out, so he had very little to trouble his conscience. I think he was near happiness: he ought to have been happy. My luck was not so good, or you wouldn't see me still alive, my dear."

Vittoria sighed for a plainer speaker.

CHAPTER XXXVII

ON LAGO MAGGIORE

Carlo's hours were passed chiefly across the lake, in the Piedmontese valleys. When at Pallanza he was restless, and he shunned the two or three minutes of privacy with his betrothed which the rigorous Italian laws besetting courtship might have allowed him to take. He had perpetually the look of a man starting from wine. It was evident that he and Countess d'Isorella continued to hold close communication, for she came regularly to the villa to meet him. On these occasions Countess Ammiani accorded her one ceremonious interview, and straightway locked herself in her room. Violetta's grace of ease and vivacity soared too high to be subject to any hostile judgement of her character. She seemed to rely entirely on the force of her beauty, and to care little for those who did not acknowledge it. She accepted public compliments quite royally, nor was Agostino backward in offering them. "And you have a voice, you know," he sometimes said aside to Vittoria; but she had forgotten how easily she could swallow great praise of her voice; she had almost forgotten her voice. Her delight was to hang her head above inverted mountains in the lake, and dream that she was just something better than the poorest of human creatures. She could not avoid putting her mind in competition with this brilliant woman's, and feeling eclipsed; and her weakness became pitiable. But Countess d'Isorella mentioned once that Pericles was at the Villa Ricciardi, projecting magnificent operatic entertainments. The reviving of a passion to sing possessed Vittoria like a thirst for freedom, and instantly confused all the reflected images within her, as the fury of a sudden wind from the high Alps scourges the glassy surface of the lake. She begged Countess Ammiani's permission that she might propose to Pericles to sing in his private operatic company, in any part, at the shortest notice.

"You wish to leave me?" said the countess, and resolutely conceived it.

Speaking to her son on this subject, she thought it necessary to make some excuse for a singer's instinct, who really did not live save on the stage. It amused Carlo; he knew when his mother was really angry with persons she tried to shield from the anger of others; and her not seeing the wrong on his side in his behaviour to his betrothed was laughable. Nevertheless she had divined the case more correctly than he: the lover was hurt. After what he had endured, he supposed, with all his forgiveness, that he had an illimitable claim upon his bride's patience. He told his another to speak to her openly.

"Why not you, my Carlo?" said the countess.

"Because, mother, if I speak to her, I shall end by throwing out my arms and calling for the priest."

"I would clap hands to that."

"We will see; it may be soon or late, but it can't be now."

"How much am I to tell her, Carlo?"

"Enough to keep her from fretting."

The countess then asked herself how much she knew. Her habit of receiving her son's word and will as supreme kept her ignorant of anything beyond the outline of his plans; and being told to speak openly of them to another, she discovered that her acquiescing imagination supplied the chief part of her knowledge. She was ashamed also to have it thought, even by Carlo, that she had not gathered every detail of his occupation, so that she could not argue against him, and had to submit to see her dearest wishes lightly swept aside.

"I beg you to tell me what you think of Countess d'Isorella; not the afterthought," she said to Vittoria.

"She is beautiful, dear Countess Ammiani."

"Call me mother now and then. Yes; she is beautiful. She has a bad name."

"Envy must have given it, I think."

"Of course she provokes envy. But I say that her name is bad, as envy could not make it. She is a woman who goes on missions, and carries a husband into society like a passport. You have only thought of her beauty?"

"I can see nothing else," said Vittoria, whose torture at the sight of the beauty was appeased by her disingenuous pleading on its behalf.

"In my time Beauty was a sinner," the countess resumed. "My confessor has filled my ears with warnings that it is a net to the soul, a weapon for devils. May the saints of Paradise make bare the beauty of this woman. She has persuaded Carlo that she is serving the country. You have let him lie here alone in a fruitless bed, silly girl. He stayed for you while his comrades called him to Vercelli, where they are assembled. The man whom he salutes as his Chief gave him word to go there. They are bound for Rome. Ah me! Rome is a great name, but Lombardy is Carlo's natal home, and Lombardy bleeds. You were absent—how long you were absent! If you could know the heaviness of those days of his waiting for you. And it was I who kept him here! I must have omitted a prayer, for he would have been at Vercelli now with Luciano and Emilio, and you might have gone to him; but he met this woman, who has convinced him that Piedmont will make a Winter march, and that his marriage must be delayed." The countess raised her face and drooped her hands from the wrists, exclaiming, "If I have lately omitted one prayer, enlighten me, blessed heaven! I am blind; I cannot see for my son; I am quite blind. I do not love the woman; therefore I doubt myself. You, my daughter, tell me your thought of her, tell me what you think. Young eyes observe; young heads are sometimes shrewd in guessing."

Vittoria said, after a pause, "I will believe her to be true, if she supports the king." It was hardly truthful speaking on her part.

"How can Carlo have been persuaded!" the countess sighed.

"By me?" Victoria asked herself, and for a moment she was exulting.

She spoke from that emotion when it had ceased to animate her.

"Carlo was angry with the king. He echoed Agostino, but Agostino does not sting as he did, and Carlo cannot avoid seeing what the king has sacrificed. Perhaps the Countess d'Isorella has shown him promises of fresh aid in the king's handwriting. Suffering has made Carlo Alberto one with the Republicans, if he had other ambitions once. And Carlo dedicates his blood to Lombardy: he does rightly. Dear countess—my mother! I have made him wait for me; I will be patient in waiting for him. I know that Countess d'Isorella is intimate with the king. There is a man named Barto Rizzo, who thinks me a guilty traitress, and she is making use of this man. That must be her reason for prohibiting the marriage. She cannot be false if she is capable of uniting extreme revolutionary agents and the king in one plot, I think; I do not know." Vittoria concluded her perfect expression of confidence with this atoning doubtfulness.

Countess Ammiani obtained her consent that she would not quit her side.

After Violetta had gone, Carlo, though he shunned secret interviews, addressed his betrothed as one who was not strange to his occupation and the trial his heart was undergoing. She could not doubt that she was beloved, in spite of the colourlessness and tonelessness of a love that appealed to her intellect. He showed her a letter he had received from Laura, laughing at its abuse of Countess d'Isorella, and the sarcasms levelled at himself.

In this letter Laura said that she was engaged in something besides nursing.

Carlo pointed his finger to the sentence, and remarked, "I must have your promise—a word from you is enough—that you will not meddle with any intrigue."

Vittoria gave the promise, half trusting it to bring the lost bloom of their love to him; but he received it as a plain matter of necessity. Certain of his love, she wondered painfully that it should continue so barren of music.

"Why am I to pledge myself that I will be useless?" she asked. "You mean, my Carlo, that I am to sit still, and watch, and wait."

He answered, "I will tell you this much: I can be struck vitally through you. In the game I am playing, I am able to defend myself. If you enter it, distraction begins. Stay with my mother."

"Am I to know nothing?"

"Everything—in good time."

"I might—might I not help you, my Carlo?"

"Yes; and nobly too. And I show you the way."

Agostino and Carlo made an expedition to Turin. Before he went, Carlo took her in his arms.

"Is it coming?" she said, shutting her eyelids like a child expecting the report of firearms.

He pressed his lips to the closed eyes. "Not yet; but are you growing timid?"

His voice seemed to reprove her.

She could have told him that keeping her in the dark among unknown terrors ruined her courage; but the minutes were too precious, his touch too sweet. In eyes and hands he had become her lover again. The blissful minutes rolled away like waves that keep the sunshine out at sea.

Her solitude in the villa was beguiled by the arrival of the score of an operatic scena, entitled "HAGAR," by Rocco Ricci, which she fancied that either Carlo or her dear old master had sent, and she devoured it. She thought it written expressly for her. With HAGAR she communed during the long hours, and sang herself on to the verge of an imagined desert beyond the mountain-shadowed lake and the last view of her beloved Motterone. Hagar's face of tears in the Brerawas known to her; and Hagar in her 'Addio' gave the living voice to that dumb one. Vittoria revelled in the delicious vocal misery. She expanded with the sorrow of poor Hagar, whose tears refreshed her, and parted her from her recent narrowing self-consciousness. The great green mountain fronted her like a living presence. Motterone supplied the place of the robust and venerable patriarch, whom she reproached, and worshipped, but with a fathomless burdensome sense of cruel injustice, deeper than the tears or the voice which spoke of it: a feeling of subjected love that was like a mother's giving suck to a detested child. Countess Ammiani saw the abrupt alteration of her step and look with a dim surprise. "What do you conceal from me?" she asked, and supplied the answer by charitably attributing it to news that the signora Piaveni was coming.

When Laura came, the countess thanked her, saying, "I am a wretched companion for this boiling head."

Laura soon proved to her that she had been the best, for after very few hours Vittoria was looking like the Hagar on the canvas.

A woman such as Violetta d'Isorella was of the sort from which Laura shrank with all her feminine power of loathing; but she spoke of her with some effort at personal tolerance until she heard of Violetta's stipulation for the deferring of Carlo's marriage, and contrived to guess that Carlo was reserved and unfamiliar with his betrothed. Then she cried out, "Fool that he is! Is it ever possible to come to the end of the folly of men? She has inflamed his vanity. She met him when you were holding him waiting, and no doubt she commenced with lamentations over the country, followed by a sigh, a fixed look, a cheerful air, and the assurance to him that she knew it—uttered as if through the keyhole of the royal cabinet—she knew that Sardinia would break the Salasco armistice in a mouth:—if only, if the king could be sure of support from the youth of Lombardy."

"Do you suspect the unhappy king?" Vittoria interposed.

"Grasp your colours tight," said Laura, nodding sarcastic approbation of such fidelity, and smiling slightly. "There has been no mention of the king. Countess d'Isorella is a spy and a tool of the Jesuits, taking pay from all parties—Austria as well, I would swear. Their object is to paralyze the march on Rome, and she has won Carlo for them. I am told that Barto Rizzo is another of her conquests. Thus she has a madman and a fool, and what may not be done with a madman and a fool? However, I have set a watch on her. She must have inflamed Carlo's vanity. He has it, just as they all have. There's trickery: I would rather behold the boy charging at the head of a column than putting faith in this base creature. She must have simulated well," Laura went on talking to herself.

"What trickery?" said Vittoria.

"He was in love with the woman when he was a lad," Laura replied, and pertinently to Vittoria's feelings. This threw the moist shade across her features.

Beppo in Turin and Luigi on the lake were the watch set on Countess d'Isorella; they were useless except to fortify Laura's suspicions. The Duchess of Graatli wrote mere gossip from Milan. She mentioned that Anna of Lenkenstein had visited with her the tomb of her brother Count Paul at Bologna, and had returned in double mourning; and that Madame Sedley—"the sister of our poor ruined Pierson"—had obtained grace, for herself at least, from Anna, by casting herself at Anna's feet,—and that they were now friends.

Vittoria felt ashamed of Adela.

When Carlo returned, the signora attacked him boldly with all her weapons; reproached him; said, "Would my husband have treated me in such a manner?" Carlo twisted his moustache and stroked his young beard for patience. They passed from room to balcony and terrace, and Laura brought him back into company without cessation of her fire of questions and sarcasms, saying, "No, no; we will speak of these things publicly." She appealed alternately to Agostino, Vittoria, and Countess Ammiani for support, and as she certainly spoke sense, Carlo was reduced to gloom and silence. Laura then paused. "Surely you have punished your bride enough?" she said; and more softly, "Brother of my Giacomo! you are under an evil spell."

Carlo started up in anger. Bending to Vittoria, he offered her his hand to lead her out, They went together.

"A good sign," said the countess.

"A bad sign!" Laura sighed. "If he had taken me out for explanation! But tell me, my Agostino, are you the woman's dupe?"

"I have been," Agostino admitted frankly.

"You did really put faith in her?"

"She condescends to be so excessively charming."

"You could not advance a better reason."

"It is one of our best; perhaps our very best, where your sex is concerned, signora."

"You are her dupe no more?"

"No more. Oh, dear no!"

"You understand her now, do you?"

"For the very reason, signora, that I have been her dupe. That is, I am beginning to understand her. I am not yet in possession of the key."

"Not yet in possession!" said Laura contemptuously; "but, never mind. Now for Carlo."

"Now for Carlo. He declares that he never has been deceived by her."

"He is perilously vain," sighed the signora.

"Seriously"—Agostino drew out the length of his beard—"I do not suppose that he has been—boys, you know, are so acute. He fancies he can make her of service, and he shows some skill."

"The skill of a fish to get into the net!"

"My dearest signora, you do not allow for the times. I remember"—Agostino peered upward through his eyelashes in a way that he had—"I remember seeing in a meadow a gossamer running away with a spider-thread. It was against all calculation. But, observe: there were exterior agencies at work: a stout wind blew. The ordinary reckoning is based on calms. Without the operation of disturbing elements, the spider-thread would have gently detained the gossamer."

"Is that meant for my son?" Countess Ammiani asked slowly, with incredulous emphasis.

Agostino and Laura, laughing in their hearts at the mother's mysterious veneration for Carlo, had to explain that 'gossamer' was a poetic, generic term, to embrace the lighter qualities of masculine youth.

A woman's figure passed swiftly by the window, which led Laura to suppose that the couple outside had parted. She ran forth, calling to one of them, but they came hand in hand, declaring that they had seen neither woman nor man. "And I am happy," Vittoria whispered. She looked happy, pale though she was.

"It is only my dreadful longing for rest which makes me pale," she said to Laura, when they were alone. "Carlo has proved to me that he is wiser than I am."

"A proof that you love Carlo, perhaps," Laura rejoined.

"Dearest, he speaks more gently of the king."

"It may be cunning, or it may be carelessness."

"Will nothing satisfy you, wilful sceptic? He is quite alive to the Countess d'Isorella's character. He told me how she dazzled him once."

"Not how she has entangled him now?"

"It is not true. He told me what I should like to dream over without talking any more to anybody. Ah, what a delight! to have known him, as you did, when he was a boy. Can one who knew him then mean harm to him? I am not capable of imagining it. No; he will not abandon poor broken Lombardy, and he is right; and it is my duty to sit and wait. No shadow shall come between us. He has said it, and I have said it. We have but one thing to fear, which is contemptible to fear; so I am at peace."

"Love-sick," was Laura's mental comment. Yet when Carlo explained his position to her next day, she was milder in her condemnation of him, and even admitted that a man must be guided by such brains as he possesses. He had conceived that his mother had a right to claim one month from him at the close of the war; he said this reddening. Laura nodded. He confessed that he was irritated when he met the Countess d'Isorella, with whom, to his astonishment, he found Barto Rizzo. She had picked him up, weak from a paroxysm, on the high-road to Milan. "And she tamed the brute," said Carlo, in admiration of her ability; "she saw that he was plot-mad, and she set him at work on a stupendous plot; agents running nowhere, and scribblings concentring in her work-basket. You smile at me, as if I were a similar patient, signora. But I am my own agent. I have personally seen all my men in Turin and elsewhere. Violetta has not one grain of love for her country; but she can be made to serve it. As for me, I have gone too far to think of turning aside and drilling with Luciano. He may yet be diverted from Rome, to strike another blow for Lombardy. The Chief, I know, has some religious sentiment about Rome. So might I have; it is the Head of Italy. Let us raise the body first. And we have been beaten here. Great Gods! we will have another fight for it on the same spot, and quickly. Besides, I cannot face Luciano and tell him why I was away from him in the dark hour. How can I tell him that I was lingering to bear a bride to the altar? while he and the rest—poor fellows! Hard enough to have to mention it to you, signora!"

She understood his boyish sense of shame. Making smooth allowances for a feeling natural to his youth and the circumstances, she said, "I am your sister, for you were my husband's brother in arms, Carlo. We two speak heart to heart: I sometimes fancy you have that voice: you hurt me with it more than you know; gladden me too! My Carlo, I wish to hear why Countess d'Isorella objects to your marriage."

"She does not object."

"An answer that begins by quibbling is not propitious. She opposes it."

"For this reason: you have not forgotten the bronze butterfly?"

"I see more clearly," said Laura, with a start.

"There appears to be no cure for the brute's mad suspicion of her," Carlo pursued: "and he is powerful among the Milanese. If my darling takes my name, he can damage much of my influence, and—you know what there is to be dreaded from a fanatic."

Laura nodded, as if in full agreement with him, and said, after meditating a minute, "What sort of a lover is this!"

She added a little laugh to the singular interjection.

"Yes, I have also thought of a secret marriage," said Carlo, stung by her penetrating instinct so that he was enabled to read the meaning in her mind.

"The best way, when you are afflicted by a dilemma of such a character, my Carlo," the signora looked at him, "is to take a chess-table and make your moves on it. 'King—my duty;' 'Queen—my passion;' 'Bishop—my social obligation;' 'Knight—my what-you-will and my round-the-corner wishes.' Then, if you find that queen may be gratified without endangering king, and so forth, why, you may follow your inclinations; and if not, not. My Carlo, you are either enviably cool, or you are an enviable hypocrite."

"The matter is not quite so easily settled as that," said Carlo.

On the whole, though against her preconception, Laura thought him an honest lover, and not the player of a double game. She saw that Vittoria should have been with him in the critical hour of defeat, when his passions were down, and heaven knows what weakness of our common manhood, that was partly pride, partly love-craving, made his nature waxen to every impression; a season, as Laura knew, when the mistress of a loyal lover should not withhold herself from him. A nature tender like Carlo's, and he bearing an enamoured heart, could not, as Luciano Romara had done, pass instantly from defeat to drill. And vain as Carlo was (the vanity being most intricate and subtle, like a nervous fluid), he was very open to the belief that he could diplomatize as well as fight, and lead a movement yet better than follow it. Even so the signora tried to read his case.

They were all, excepting Countess Ammiani ("who will never, I fear, do me this honour," Violetta wrote, and the countess said, "Never," and quoted a proverb), about to pass three or four days at the villa of Countess d'Isorella. Before they set out, Vittoria received a portentous envelope containing a long scroll, that was headed "YOUR CRIMES," and detailing a lest of her offences against the country, from the revelation of the plot in her first letter to Wilfrid, to services rendered to the enemy during the war, up to the departure of Charles Albert out of forsaken Milan.

"B. R." was the undisguised signature at the end of the scroll.

Things of this description restored her old war-spirit to Vittoria. She handed the scroll to Laura; Laura, in great alarm, passed it on to Carlo. He sent for Angelo Guidascarpi in haste, for Carlo read it as an ante-dated justificatory document to some mischievous design, and he desired that hands as sure as his own, and yet more vigilant eyes, should keep watch over his betrothed.

CHAPTER XXXVIII

VIOLETTA D'ISORELLA

The villa inhabited by Countess d'Isorella was on the water's edge, within clear view of the projecting Villa Ricciardi, in that darkly-wooded region of the lake which leads up to the Italian-Swiss canton.

Violetta received here an envoy from Anna of Lenkenstein, direct out of Milan: an English lady, calling herself Mrs. Sedley, and a particular friend of Countess Anna. At the first glance Violetta saw that her visitor had the pretension to match her arts against her own; so, to sound her thoroughly, she offered her the hospitalities of the villa for a day or more. The invitation was accepted. Much to Violetta's astonishment, the lady betrayed no anxiety to state the exact terms of her mission: she appeared, on the contrary, to have an unbounded satisfaction in the society of her hostess, and prattled of herself and Antonio-Pericles, and her old affection for Vittoria, with the wiliest simplicity, only requiring to be assured at times that she spoke intelligible Italian and exquisite French. Violetta supposed her to feel that she commanded the situation. Patient study of this woman revealed to Violetta the amazing fact that she was dealing with a born bourgeoise, who, not devoid of petty acuteness, was unaffectedly enjoying her noble small-talk, and the prospect of a footing in Italian high society. Violetta smiled at the comedy she had been playing in, scarcely reproaching herself for not having imagined it. She proceeded to the point of business without further delay.

Adela Sedley had nothing but a verbal message to deliver. The Countess Anna of Lenkenstein offered, on her word of honour as a noblewoman, to make over the quarter of her estate and patrimony to the Countess d'Isorella, if the latter should succeed in thwarting—something.

Forced to speak plainly, Adela confessed she thought she knew the nature of that something.

To preclude its being named, Violetta then diverged from the subject.

"We will go round to your friend the signor Antonio-Pericles at Villa Ricciardi," she said. "You will see that he treats me familiarly, but he is not a lover of mine. I suspect your 'something' has something to do with the Jesuits."

Adela Sedley replied to the penultimate sentence: "It would not surprise me, indeed, to hear of any number of adorers."

"I have the usual retinue, possibly," said Violetta.

"Dear countess, I could be one of them myself!" Adela burst out with tentative boldness.

"Then, kiss me."

And behold, they interchanged that unsweet feminine performance.

Adela's lips were unlocked by it.

"How many would envy me, dear Countess d'Isorella!"

She really conceived that she was driving into Violetta's heart by the great high-road of feminine vanity. Violetta permitted her to think as she liked.

"Your countrywomen, madame, do not make large allowances for beauty, I hear."

"None at all. But they are so stiff! so frigid! I know one, a Miss Ford, now in Italy, who would not let me have a male friend, and a character, in conjunction."

"You are acquainted with Count Karl Lenkenstein?"

Adela blushingly acknowledged it.

"The whisper goes that I was once admired by him," said Violetta.

"And by Count Ammiani."

"By count? by milord? by prince? by king?"

"By all who have good taste."

"Was it jealousy, then, that made Countess Anna hate me?"

"She could not—or she cannot now."

"Because I have not taken possession of her brother."

"I could not—may I say it?—I could not understand his infatuation until Countess Anna showed me the portrait of Italy's most beautiful living woman. She told me to look at the last of the Borgia family."

Violetta laughed out clear music. "And now you see her?"

"She said that it had saved her brother's life. It has a star and a scratch on the left cheek from a dagger. He wore it on his heart, and an assassin struck him there: a true romance. Countess Anna said to me that it had saved one brother, and that it should help to avenge the other. She has not spoken to me of Jesuits."

"Nothing at all of the Jesuits?" said Violetta carelessly. "Perhaps she wishes to use my endeavours to get the Salaseo armistice prolonged, and tempts me, knowing I am a prodigal. Austria is victorious, you know, but she wants peace. Is that the case? I do not press you to answer."

Adela replied hesitatingly: "Are you aware, countess, whether there is any truth in the report that Countess Lena has a passion for Count Ammiani?"

"Ah, then," said Violetta, "Countess Lena's sister would naturally wish to prevent his contemplated marriage! We may have read the riddle at last. Are you discreet? If you are, you will let it be known that I had the honour of becoming intimate with you in Turin—say, at the Court. We shall meet frequently there during winter, I trust, if you care to make a comparison of the Italian with the Austrian and the English nobility."

An eloquent "Oh!" escaped from Adela's bosom. She had certainly not expected to win her way with this estimable Italian titled lady thus rapidly. Violetta had managed her so well that she was no longer sure whether she did know the exact nature of her mission, the words of which she had faithfully transmitted as having been alone confided to her. It was with chagrin that she saw Pericles put his fore-finger on a salient dimple of the countess's cheek when he welcomed them. He puffed and blew like one working simultaneously at bugle and big drum on hearing an allusion to Victoria. The mention of the name of that abominable traitress was interdicted at Villa Ricciardi, he said; she had dragged him at two armies' tails to find his right senses at last: Pericles was cured of his passion for her at last. He had been mad, but he was cured—and so forth, in the old strain. His preparations for a private operatic performance diverted him from these fierce incriminations, and he tripped busily from spot to spot, conducting the ladies over the tumbled lower floors of the spacious villa, and calling their admiration on the desolation of the scene. Then they went up to the maestro's room. Pericles became deeply considerate for the master's privacy. "He is my slave; the man has ruined himself for la Vittoria; but I respect the impersonation of art," he said under his breath to the ladies as they stood at the door; "hark!" The piano was touched, and the voice of Irma di Karski broke out in a shrill crescendo. Rocco Ricci within gave tongue to the vehement damnatory dance of Pericles outside. Rocco struck his piano again encouragingly for a second attempt, but Irma was sobbing. She was heard to say: "This is the fifteenth time you have pulled me down in one morning. You hate me; you do; you hate me." Rocco ran his fingers across the keys, and again struck the octave for Irma. Pericles wiped his forehead, when, impenitent and unteachable, she took the notes in the manner of a cock. He thumped at the door violently and entered.

"Excellent! horrid! brava! abominable! beautiful! My Irma, you have reached the skies. You ascend like a firework, and crown yourself at the top. No more to-day; but descend at your leisure, my dear, and we will try to mount again by-and-by, and not so fast, if you please. Ha! your voice is a racehorse. You will learn to ride him with temper and judgement, and you will go. Not so, my Rocco? Irma, you want repose, my dear. One thing I guarantee to you—you will please the public. It is a minor thing that you should please me."

Countess d'Isorella led Irma away, and had to bear with many fits of weeping, and to assent to the force of all the charges of vindictive conspiracy and inveterate malice with which the jealous creature assailed Vittoria's name. The countess then claimed her ear for half-a-minute.

"Have you had any news of Countess Anna lately?"

Irma had not; she admitted it despondently. "There is such a vile conspiracy against me in Italy—and Italy is a poor singer's fame—that I should be tempted to do anything. And I detest la Vittoria. She has such a hold on this Antonio-Pericles, I don't see how I can hurt her, unless I meet her and fly at her throat."

"You naturally detest her," said the countess. "Repeat Countess Anna's proposal to you."

"It was insulting—she offered me money."

"That you should persuade me to assist you in preventing la Vittoria's marriage to Count Ammiani?"

"Dear lady, you know I did not try to persuade you."

"You knew that you would not succeed, my Irma. But Count Ammiani will not marry her; so you will have a right to claim some reward. I do not think that la Vittoria is quite idle. Look out for yourself, my child. If you take to plotting, remember it is a game of two."

"If she thwarts me in one single step, I will let loose that madman on her," said Irma, trembling.

"You mean the signor Antonio-Pericles?"

"No; I mean that furious man I saw at your villa, dear countess."

"Ah! Barto Rizzo. A very furious man. He bellowed when he heard her name, I remember. You must not do it. But, for Count Ammiani's sake, I desire to see his marriage postponed, at least."

"Where is she?" Irma inquired.

The countess shrugged. "Even though I knew, I could not prudently tell you in your present excited state."

She went to Pericles for a loan of money. Pericles remarked that there was not much of it in Turin. "But, countess, you whirl the gold-pieces like dust from your wheels; and a spy, my good soul, a lovely secret emissary, she will be getting underpaid if she allows herself to want money. There is your beauty; it is ripe, but it is fresh, and it is extraordinary. Yes; there is your beauty." Before she could obtain a promise of the money, Violetta had to submit to be stripped to her character, which was hard; but on the other hand, Pericles exacted no interest on his money, and it was not often that he exacted a return of it in coin. Under these circumstances, ladies in need of money can find it in their hearts to pardon mere brutality of phrase. Pericles promised to send it to the countess on one condition; which condition he cancelled, saying dejectedly, "I do not care to know where she is. I will not know."

"She has the score of Hagar, wherever she is," said Violetta, "and when she hears that you have done the scene without her aid, you will have stuck a dagger in her bosom."

"Not," Pericles cried in despair, "not if she should hear Irma's Hagar! To the desert with Irma. It is the place for a crab-apple. Bravo, Abraham! you were wise."

Pericles added that Montini was hourly expected, and that there was to be a rehearsal in the evening.

When she had driven home, Violetta found Barto Rizzo's accusatory paper laid on her writing-desk. She gathered the contents in a careless glance, and walked into the garden alone, to look for Carlo.

He was leaning on the balustrade of the terrace, near the water-gate, looking into the deep clear lake-water. Violetta placed herself beside him without a greeting.

"You are watching fish for coolness, my Carlo?"

"Yes," he said, and did not turn to her face.

"You were very angry when you arrived?"

She waited for his reply.

"Why do you not speak, Carlino?"

"I am watching fish for coolness," he said.

"Meantime," said Violetta, "I am scorched."

He looked up, and led her to an arch of shade, where he sat quite silent.

"Can anything be more vexing than this?" she was reduced to exclaim.

"Ah!" said he, "you would like the catalogue to be written out for you in a big bold hand, possibly, with a terrific initials at the end of the page."

"Carlo, you have done worse than that. When I saw you first here, what crimes did you not accuse me of? what names did you not scatter on my head? and what things did I not, confess to? I bore the unkindness, for you were beaten, and you wanted a victim. And, my dear friend, considering that I am after all a woman, my forbearance has subsequently been still greater."

"How?" he asked. Her half-pathetic candour melted him.

"You must, have a lively memory for the uses of forgetfulness, Carlo, When you had scourged me well, you thought it proper to raise me up and give me comfort. I was wicked for serving the king, and therefore the country, as a spy; but I was to persevere, and cancel my iniquities by betraying those whom I served to you. That was your instructive precept. Have I done it or not? Answer, too have I done it for any payment beyond your approbation? I persuaded you to hope for Lombardy, and without any vaunting of my own patriotism. You have seen and spoken to the men I directed you to visit. If their heads master yours, I shall be reprobated for it, I know surely; but I am confident as yet that you can match them. In another month I expect to see the king over the Ticino once more, and Carlo in Brescia with his comrades. You try to penetrate my eyes. That's foolish; I can make them glass. Read me by what I say and what I do. I do not entreat you to trust me; I merely beg that you will trust your own judgement of me by what I have helped you to do hitherto. You and I, my dear boy, have had some trifling together. Admit that another woman would have refused to surrender you as I did when your unruly Vittoria was at last induced to come to you from Milan. Or, another woman would have had her revenge on discovering that she had been a puppet of soft eyes and a lover's quarrel with his mistress. Instead of which, I let you go. I am opposed to the marriage, it's true; and you know why."

Carlo had listened to Violetta, measuring the false and the true in this recapitulation of her conduct with cool accuracy until she alluded to their personal relations. Thereat his brows darkened.

"We had I some trifling together," he said, musingly.

"Is it going to be denied in these sweeter days?" Violetta reddened.

"The phrase is elastic. Suppose my bride were to hear it?"

"It was addressed to your ears, Carlo."

"It cuts two ways. Will you tell me when it was that I last had the happiness of saluting you, lip to lip?"

"In Brescia—before I had espoused an imbecile—two nights before my marriage—near the fountain of the Greek girl with a pitcher."

Pride and anger nerved the reply. It was uttered in a rapid low breath. Coming altogether unexpectedly, it created an intense momentary revulsion of his feelings by conjuring up his boyish love in a scene more living than the sunlight.

He lifted her hand to his mouth. He was Italian enough, though a lover, to feel that she deserved more. She had reddened deliciously, and therewith hung a dewy rosy moisture on her underlids. Raising her eyes, she looked like a cut orange to a thirsty lip. He kissed her, saying, "Pardon."

"Keep it secret, you mean?" she retorted. "Yes, I pardon that wish of yours. I can pardon much to my beauty."

She stood up as majestically as she had spoken.

"You know, my Violetta, that I am madly in love."

"I have learnt it."

"You know it:—what else would?... If I were not lost in love, could I see you as I do and let Brescia be the final chapter?"

Violetta sighed. "I should have preferred its being so rather than this superfluous additional line to announce an end, like a foolish staff on the edge of a cliff. You thought that you were saluting a leper, or a saint?"

"Neither. If ever we can talk together again, as we have done," Carlo said gloomily, "I will tell you what I think of myself."

"No, but Richelieu might have behaved.... Ah! perhaps not quite in the same way," she corrected her flowing apology for him. "But then, he was a Frenchman. He could be flighty without losing his head. Dear Italian Carlo! Yes, in the teeth of Barto Rizzo, and for the sake of the country, marry her at once. It will be the best thing for you; really the best. You want to know from me the whereabout of Barto Rizzo. He may be in the mountain over Stresa, or in Milan. He also has thrown off my yoke, such as it was! I do assure you, Carlo, I have no command over him: but, mind, I half doat on the wretch. No man made me desperately in love with myself before he saw me, when I stopped his raving in the middle of the road with one look of my face. There was foam on his beard and round his eyes; the poor wretch took out his handkerchief, and he sobbed. I don't know how many luckless creatures he had killed on his way; but when I took him into my carriage—king, emperor, orator on stilts, minister of police not one has flattered me as he did, by just gazing at me. Beauty can do as much as music, my Carlo."

Carlo thanked heaven that Violetta had no passion in her nature. She had none: merely a leaning toward evil, a light sense of shame, a desire for money, and in her heart a contempt for the principles she did not possess, but which, apart from the intervention of other influences, could occasionally sway her actions. Friendship, or rather the shadowy recovery of a past attachment that had been more than friendship, inclined her now and then to serve a master who failed distinctly to represent her interests; and when she met Carlo after the close of the war, she had really set to work in hearty kindliness to rescue him from what she termed "shipwreck with that disastrous Republican crew." He had obtained greater ascendency over her than she liked; yet she would have forgiven it, as well as her consequent slight deviation from direct allegiance to her masters in various cities, but for Carlo's commanding personal coolness. She who had tamed a madman by her beauty, was outraged, and not unnaturally, by the indifference of a former lover.

Later in the day, Laura and Vittoria, with Agostino, reached the villa; and Adela put her lips to Vittoria's ear, whispering: "Naughty! when are you to lose your liberty to turn men's heads?" and then she heaved a sigh with Wilfrid's name. She had formed the acquaintance of Countess d'Isorella in Turin, she said, and satisfactorily repeated her lesson, but with a blush. She was little more than a shade to Vittoria, who wondered what she had to live for. After the early evening dinner, when sunlight and the colours of the sun were beyond the western mountains, they pushed out on the lake. A moon was overhead, seeming to drop lower on them as she filled with light.

Agostino and Vittoria fell upon their theme of discord, as usual—the King of Sardinia.

"We near the vesper hour, my daughter," said Agostino; "you would provoke me to argumentation in heaven itself. I am for peace. I remember looking down on two cats with arched backs in the solitary arena of the Verona amphitheatre. We men, my Carlo, will not, in the decay of time, so conduct ourselves."

Vittoria looked on Laura and thought of the cannon-sounding hours, whose echoes rolled over their slaughtered hope. The sun fell, the moon shone, and the sun would rise again, but Italy lay face to earth.

They had seen her together before the enemy. That recollection was a joy that stood, though the winds beat at it, and the torrents. She loved her friend's worn eyelids and softly-shut mouth; the after-glow of battle seemed on them; the silence of the field of carnage under heaven;—and the patient turning of Laura's eyes this way and that to speakers upon common things, covered the despair of her heart as with a soldier's cloak.

Laura met the tender study of Vittoria's look, and smiled.

They neared the Villa Ricciardi, and heard singing. The villa was lighted profusely, so that it made a little mock-sunset on the lake.

"Irma!" said Vittoria, astonished at the ring of a well-known voice that shot up in firework fashion, as Pericles had said of it. Incredulous, she listened till she was sure; and then glanced hurried questions at all eyes. Violetta laughed, saying, "You have the score of Rocco Ricci's Hagar."

The boat drew under the blazing windows, and half guessing, half hearing, Vittoria understood that Pericles was giving an entertainment here, and had abjured her. She was not insensible to the slight. This feeling, joined to her long unsatisfied craving to sing, led her to be intolerant of Irma's style, and visibly vexed her.

Violetta whispered: "He declares that your voice is cracked: show him! Burst out with the 'Addio' of Hagar. May she not, Carlo? Don't you permit the poor soul to sing? She cannot contain herself."

Carlo, Adela, Agostino, and Violetta prompted her, and, catching a pause in the villa, she sang the opening notes of Hagar's 'Addio' with her old glorious fulness of tone and perfect utterance.

The first who called her name was Rocco Ricci, but Pericles was the first to rush out and hang over the boat. "Witch! traitress! infernal ghost! heart of ice!" and in English "humbug!" and in French "coquin!":—these were a few of the titles he poured on her. Rocco Ricci and Montini kissed hands to her, begging her to come to them. She was very willing outwardly, and in her heart most eager; but Carlo bade the rowers push off. Then it was pitiful to hear the shout of abject supplication from Pericles. He implored Count Ammiani's pardon, Vittoria's pardon, for telling her what she was; and as the boat drew farther away, he offered her sums of money to enter the villa and sing the score of Hagar. He offered to bear the blame of her bad behaviour to him, said he would forget it and stamp it out; that he would pay for the provisioning of a regiment of volunteers for a whole month; that he would present her marriage trousseau to her—yes, and let her marry. "Sandra! my dear! my dear!" he cried, and stretched over the parapet speechless, like a puppet slain.

So strongly did she comprehend the sincerity of his passion for her voice that she could or would see nothing extravagant in this demonstration, which excited unrestrained laughter in every key from her companions in the boat. When the boat was about a hundred yards from the shore, and in full moonlight, she sang the great "Addio" of Hagar. At the close of it, she had to feel for her lover's hand blindly. No one spoke, either at the Villa Ricciardi, or about her. Her voice possessed the mountain-shadowed lake.

The rowers pulled lustily home through chill air.

Luigi and Beppo were at the villa, both charged with news from Milan. Beppo claiming the right to speak first, which Luigi granted with a magnificent sweep of his hand, related that Captain Weisspriess, of the garrison, had wounded Count Medole in a duel severely. He brought a letter to Vittoria from Merthyr, in which Merthyr urged her to prevent Count Ammiani's visiting Milan for any purpose whatever, and said that he was coming to be present at, her marriage. She was reading this while Luigi delivered his burden; which was, that in a subsequent duel, the slaughtering captain had killed little Leone Rufo, the gay and gallant boy, Carlo's comrade, and her friend.

Luigi laughed scornfully at his rival, and had edged away—out of sight before he could be asked who had sent him. Beppo ignominiously confessed that he had not heard of this second duel. At midnight he was on horseback, bound for Milan, with a challenge to the captain from Carlo, who had a jealous fear that Luciano at Vercelli might have outstripped him. Carlo requested the captain to guarantee him an hour's immunity in the city on a stated day, or to name any spot on the borders of Piedmont for the meeting. The challenge was sent with Countess Ammiani's approbation and Laura's. Vittoria submitted.

That done, Carlo gave up his heart to his bride. A fight in prospect was the hope of wholesome work after his late indecision and double play. They laughed at themselves, accused hotly, and humbly excused themselves, praying for mutual pardon.

She had behaved badly in disobeying his mandate from Brescia.

Yes, but had he not been over-imperious?

True; still she should have remembered her promise in the Vicentino.

She did indeed; but how could she quit her wounded friend Merthyr?

Perhaps not: then, why had she sent word to him from Milan that she would be at Pallanza?

This question knocked at a sealed chamber. She was silent, and Carlo had to brood over something as well. He gave her hints of his foolish pique, his wrath and bitter baffled desire for her when, coming to Pallanza, he came to an empty house. But he could not help her to see, for he did not himself feel, that he had been spurred by silly passions, pique, and wrath, to plunge instantly into new political intrigue; and that some of his worst faults had become mixed up with his devotion to his country. Had he taken Violetta for an ally in all purity of heart? The kiss he had laid on the woman's sweet lips had shaken his absolute belief in that. He tried to set his brain travelling backward, in order to contemplate accurately the point of his original weakness. It being almost too severe a task for any young head, Carlo deemed it sufficient that he should say—and this he felt—that he was unworthy of his beloved.

Could Vittoria listen to such stuff? She might have kissed him to stop the flow of it, but kissings were rare between them; so rare, that when they had put mouth to mouth, a little quivering spire of flame, dim at the base, stood to mark the spot in their memories. She moved her hand, as to throw aside such talk. Unfretful in blood, chaste and keen, she at least knew the foolishness of the common form of lovers' trifling when there is a burning love to keep under, and Carlo saw that she did, and adored her for this highest proof of the passion of her love.

"In three days you will be mine, if I do not hear from Milan? within five, if I do?" he said.

Vittoria gave him the whole beauty of her face a divine minute, and bowed it assenting. Carlo then led her to his mother, before whom he embraced her for the comfort of his mother's heart. They decided that there should be no whisper of the marriage until the couple were one. Vittoria obtained the countess's permission to write for Merthyr to attend her at the altar. She had seen Weisspriess fall in combat, and she had perfect faith in her lover's right hand.

CHAPTER XXXIX

ANNA OF LENKENSTEIN

Captain Weisspriess replied to Carlo Ammiani promptly, naming Camerlata by Como, as the place where he would meet him.

He stated at the end of some temperate formal lines, that he had given Count Ammiani the preference over half-a-dozen competitors for the honour of measuring swords with him; but that his adversary must not expect him to be always ready to instruct the young gentlemen of the Lombardo-Venetian province in the arts of fence; and therefore he begged to observe, that his encounter with Count Ammiani would be the last occasion upon which he should hold himself bound to accept a challenge from Count Ammiani's countrymen.

It was quite possible, the captain said, drawing a familiar illustration from the gaming-table, to break the stoutest Bank in the world by a perpetual multiplication of your bets, and he was modest enough to remember that he was but one man against some thousands, to contend with all of whom would be exhausting.

Consequently the captain desired Count Ammiani to proclaim to his countrymen that the series of challenges must terminate; and he requested him to advertize the same in a Milanese, a Turin, and a Neapolitan journal.

"I am not a butcher," he concluded. "The task you inflict upon me is scarcely bearable. Call it by what name you will, it is having ten shots to one, which was generally considered an equivalent to murder. My sword is due to you, Count Ammiani; and, as I know you to be an honourable nobleman, I would rather you were fighting in Venice, though your cause is hopeless, than standing up to match yourself against me. Let me add, that I deeply respect the lady who is engaged to be united to you, and would not willingly cross steel either with her lover or her husband. I shall be at Camerlata at the time appointed. If I do not find you there, I shall understand that you have done me the honour to take my humble advice, and have gone where your courage may at least appear to have done better service. I shall sheathe my sword and say no more about it."

All of this, save the concluding paragraph, was written under the eyes of Countess Anna of Lenkenstein.

He carried it to his quarters, where he appended the as he deemed it—conciliatory passage: after which he handed it to Beppo, in a square of the barracks, with a buon'mano that Beppo received bowing, and tossed to an old decorated regimental dog of many wounds and a veteran's gravity. For this offence a Styrian grenadier seized him by the shoulders, lifting him off his feet and swinging him easily, while the dog arose from his contemplation of the coin and swayed an expectant tail. The Styrian had dashed

Beppo to earth before Weisspriess could interpose, and the dog had got him by the throat. In the struggle Beppo tore off the dog's medal for distinguished conduct on the field of battle. He restored it as soon as he was free, and won unanimous plaudits from officers and soldiers for his kindly thoughtfulness and the pretty manner with which he dropped on one knee, and assuaged the growls, and attached the medal to the old dog's neck. Weisspriess walked away. Beppo then challenged his Styrian to fight. The case was laid before a couple of sergeants, who shook their heads on hearing his condition to be that of a serving-man, the Styrian was ready to waive considerations of superiority; but the "judge" pronounced their veto. A soldier in the Imperial Royal service, though he was merely a private in the ranks, could not accept a challenge from civilians below the rank of notary, secretary, hotel- or inn-keeper, and suchlike: servants and tradesmen he must seek to punish in some other way; and they also had their appeal to his commanding officer. So went the decision of the military tribunal, until the Styrian, having contrived to make Beppo understand, by the agency of a single Italian verb, that he wanted a blow, Beppo spun about and delivered a stinging smack on the Styrian's cheek; which altered the view of the case, for, under peculiar circumstances—supposing that he did not choose to cut him down—a soldier might condescend to challenge his civilian inferiors: "in our regiment," said the sergeants, meaning that they had relaxed the stringency of their laws.

Beppo met his Styrian outside the city walls, and laid him flat. He declined to fight a second; but it was represented to him, by the aid of an interpreter, that the officers of the garrison were subjected to successive challenges, and that the first trial of his skill might have been nothing finer than luck; and besides, his adversary had a right to call a champion. "We all do it," the soldiers assured him. "Now your blood's up you're ready for a dozen of us;" which was less true of a constitution that was quicker in expending its heat. He stood out against a young fellow almost as limber as himself, much taller, and longer in the reach, by whom he was quickly disabled with cuts on thigh and head. Seeing this easy victory over him, the soldiers, previously quite civil, cursed him for having got the better of their fallen comrade, and went off discussing how he had done the trick, leaving him to lie there. A peasant carried him to a small suburban inn, where he remained several days oppressed horribly by a sense that he had forgotten something. When he recollected what it was, he entrusted the captain's letter to his landlady;—a good woman, but she chanced to have a scamp of a husband, who snatched it from her and took it to his market. Beppo supposed the letter to be on its way to Pallauza, when it was in General Schoneck's official desk; and soon after the breath of a scandalous rumour began to circulate.

Captain Weisspriess had gone down to Camerlata, accompanied by a Colonel Volpo, of an Austro-Italian regiment, and by Lieutenant Jenna. At Camerlata a spectacled officer, Major Nagen, joined them. Weisspriess was the less pleased with his company on hearing that he had come to witness the meeting, in obedience to an express command of a person who was interested in it. Jenna was the captain's friend: Volpo was seconding him for the purpose of getting Count Ammiani to listen to reason from the mouth of a countryman. There could be no doubt in the captain's mind that this Major Nagen was Countess Anna's spy as well as his rival, and he tried to be rid of him; but in addition to the shortness of sight which was Nagen's plea for pushing his thin transparent nose into every corner, he enjoyed at will an intermittent deafness, and could hear anything without knowing of it. Brother officers said of Major Nagen that he was occasionally equally senseless in the nose, which had been tweaked without disturbing the repose of his features. He waited half-an-hour on the ground after the appointed time, and then hurried to Milan. Weisspriess waited an hour. Satisfied that Count Ammiani was not coming, he exacted from Volpo and from Jenna their word of honour as Austrian officers that they would forbear-to cast any slur on the courage of his adversary, and would be so discreet on the subject as to imply that the duel was a drawn affair. They pledged themselves accordingly. "There's Nagen, it's true," said Weisspriess, as a man will say and feel that he has done his best to prevent a thing inevitable.

Milan, and some of the journals of Milan, soon had Carlo Ammiani's name up for challenging Weisspriess and failing to keep his appointment. It grew to be discussed as a tremendous event. The captain received fifteen challenges within two days; among these a second one from Luciano Romara, whom he was beginning to have a strong desire to encounter. He repressed it, as quondam drunkards fight off the whisper of their lips for liquor. "No more blood," was his constant inward cry. He wanted peace; but as he also wanted Countess Anna of Lenkenstein and her estates, it may possibly be remarked of him that what he wanted he did not want to pay for.

At this period Wilfrid had resumed the Austrian uniform as a common soldier in the ranks of the Kinsky regiment. General Schoneck had obtained the privilege for him from the Marshal, General Pierson refusing to lift a finger on his behalf. Nevertheless the uncle was not sorry to hear the tale of his nephew's exploits during the campaign, or of the eccentric intrepidity of the white umbrella; and both to please him, and to intercede for Wilfrid, the tatter's old comrades recited his deeds as a part of the treasured familiar history of the army in its late arduous struggle.

General Pierson was chiefly anxious to know whether Countess Lena would be willing to give her hand to Wilfrid in the event of his restoration to his antecedent position in the army. He found her extremely excited about Carlo Ammiani, her old playmate, and once her dear friend. She would not speak of Wilfrid at all. To appease the chivalrous little woman, General Pierson hinted that his nephew, being under the protection of General Schoneck, might get some intelligence from that officer. Lena pretended to reject the notion of her coming into communication with Wilfrid for any earthly purpose. She said to herself, however, that her object was pre-eminently unselfish; and as the General pointedly refused to serve her in a matter that concerned an Italian nobleman, she sent directions to Wilfrid to go before General Schoeneck the moment he was off duty, and ask his assistance, in her name, to elucidate the mystery of Count Ammiani's behaviour. The answer was a transmission of Captain Weisspriess's letter to Carlo. Lena caused the fact of this letter having missed its way to be circulated in the journals, and then she carried it triumphantly to her sister, saying:

"There! I knew these reports were abase calumny."

"Reports, to what effect?" said Anna.

"That Carlo Ammiani had slunk from a combat with your duellist."

"Oh! I knew that myself," Anna remarked.

"You were the loudest in proclaiming it."

"Because I intend to ruin him."

"Carlo Ammiani? What has he done to you?"

Anna's eyes had fallen on the additional lines of the letter which she had not dictated. She frowned and exclaimed:

"What is this? Does the man play me false? Read those lines, Lena, and tell me, does the man mean to fight in earnest who can dare to write them? He advises Ammiani to go to Venice. It's treason, if it is not cowardice. And see here—he has the audacity to say that he deeply respects the lady Ammiani is going to marry. Is Ammiani going to marry her? I think not."

Anna dashed the letter to the floor.

"But I will make use of what's within my reach," she said, picking it up.

"Carlo Ammiani will marry her, I presume," said Lena.

"Not before he has met Captain Weisspriess, who, by the way, has obtained his majority. And, Lena, my dear, write to inform him that we wish to offer him our congratulations. He will be a General officer in good time."

"Perhaps you forget that Count Ammiani is a perfect swordsman, Anna."

"Weisspriess remembers it for me, perhaps;—is that your idea, Lena?"

"He might do so profitably. You have thrown him on two swords."

"Merely to provoke the third. He is invincible. If he were not, where would his use be?"

"Oh, how I loathe revenge!" cried Lena.

"You cannot love!" her sister retorted. "That woman calling herself Vittoria Campa shall suffer. She has injured and defied me. How was it that she behaved to us at Meran? She is mixed up with assassins; she is insolent—a dark-minded slut; and she catches stupid men. My brother, my country, and this weak Weisspriess, as I saw him lying in the Ultenthal, cry out against her. I have no sleep. I am not revengeful. Say it, say it, all of you! but I am not. I am not unforgiving. I worship justice, and a black deed haunts me. Let the wicked be contrite and washed in tears, and I think I can pardon them. But I will have them on their knees. I hate that woman Vittoria more than I hate Angelo Guidascarpi. Look, Lena. If both were begging for life to me, I would send him to the gallows and her to her bedchamber; and all because I worship justice, and believe it to be the weapon of the good and pious. You have a baby's heart; so has Karl. He declines to second Weisspriess; he will have nothing to do with duelling; he would behold his sisters mocked in the streets and pass on. He talks of Paul's death like a priest. Priests are worthy men; a great resource! Give me a priests lap when I need it. Shall I be condemned to go to the priest and leave that woman singing? If I did, I might well say the world's a snare, a sham, a pitfall, a horror! It's what I don't think in any degree. It's what you think, though. Yes, whenever you are vexed you think it. So do the priests, and so do all who will not exert themselves to chastise. I, on the contrary, know that the world is not made up of nonsense. Write to Weisspriess immediately; I must have him here in an hour."

Weisspriess, on visiting the ladies to receive their congratulations, was unprepared for the sight of his letter to Carlo Ammiani, which Anna thrust before him after he had saluted her, bidding him read it aloud. He perused it in silence. He was beginning to be afraid of his mistress.

"I called you Austria once, for you were always ready," Anna said, and withdrew from him, that the sung of her words might take effect.

"God knows, I have endeavoured to earn the title in my humble way," Weisspriess appealed to Lena.

"Yes, Major Weisspriess, you have," she said. "Be Austria still, and forbear toward these people as much as you can. To beat them is enough, in my mind. I am rejoiced that you have not met Count Ammiani, for if you had, two friends of mine, equally dear and equally skilful, would have held their lives at one another's mercy."

"Equally!" said Weisspriess, and pulled out the length of his moustache.

"Equally courageous," Lena corrected herself. "I never distrusted Count Ammiani's courage, nor could distrust yours."

"Equally dear!" Weisspriess tried to direct a concentrated gaze on her.

Lena evaded an answer by speaking of the rumour of Count Ammiani's marriage.

Weisspriess was thinking with all the sagacious penetration of the military mind, that perhaps this sister was trying to tell him that she would be willing to usurp the piece of the other in his affections; and if so, why should she not?

"I may cherish the idea that I am dear to you, Countess Lena?"

"When you are formally betrothed to my sister, you will know you are very dear to me, Major Weisspriess."

"But," said he, perceiving his error, "how many persons am I to call out before she will consent to a formal betrothal?"

Lena was half smiling at the little tentative bit of sentiment she had so easily turned aside. Her advice to him was to refuse to fight, seeing that he had done sufficient for glory and his good name.

He mentioned Major Nagen as a rival.

Upon this she said: "Hear me one minute. I was in my sister's bed-room on the first night when she knew of your lying wounded in the Ultenthal. She told you just now that she called you Austria. She adores our Austria in you. The thought that you had been vanquished seemed like our Austria vanquished, and she is so strong for Austria that it is really out of her power to fancy you as defeated without suspecting foul play. So when she makes you fight, she thinks you safe. Many are to go down because you have gone down. Do you not see? And now, Major Weisspriess, I need not expose my sister to you any more, I hope, or depreciate Major Nagen for your satisfaction."

Weisspriess had no other interview with Anna for several days. She shunned him openly. Her carriage moved off when he advanced to meet her at the parade, or review of arms; and she did not scruple to speak in public with Major Nagen, in the manner of those who have begun to speak together in private. The offender received his punishment gracefully, as men will who have been taught that it flatters them. He refused every challenge. From Carlo Ammiani there came not a word.

It would have been a deadly lull to any fiery temperament engaged in plotting to destroy a victim, but Anna had the patience of hatred—that absolute malignity which can measure its exultation rather by the gathering of its power to harm than by striking. She could lay it aside, or sink it to the bottom of her emotions, at will, when circumstances appeared against it. And she could do this without fretful regrets, without looking to the future. The spirit of her hatred extracted its own nourishment from things, like an organized creature. When foiled she became passive, and she enjoyed—forced herself compliantly to enjoy—her redoubled energy of hatred voluptuously, if ever a turn in events made wreck of her scheming. She hated Vittoria for many reasons, all of them vague within her bosom because the source of them was indefinite and lay in the fact of her having come into collision with an opposing nature, whose rivalry was no visible rivalry, whose triumph was an ignorance of scorn—a woman who attracted all men, who scattered injuries with insolent artlessness, who never appealed to forgiveness, and was a low-born woman daring to be proud. By repute Anna was implacable, but she had, and knew she had, the capacity for magnanimity of a certain kind; and her knowledge of the existence of this unsuspected fund within her justified in some degree her reckless efforts to pull her enemy down on her knees. It seemed doubly right that she should force Vittoria to penitence, as being good for the woman, and an end that exonerated her own private sins committed to effect it.

Yet she did not look clearly forward to the day of Vittoria's imploring for mercy. She had too many vexations to endure: she was an insufficient schemer, and was too frequently thwarted to enjoy that ulterior prospect. Her only servile instruments were Major Nagen, and Irma, who came to her from the Villa Ricciardi, hot to do her rival any deadly injury; but though willing to attempt much, these were apparently able to perform little more than the menial work of vengeance. Major Nagen wrote in the name of Weisspriess to Count Ammiani, appointing a second meeting at Como, and stating that he would be at the villa of the Duchess of Graatli there. Weisspriess was unsuspectingly taken down to the place by Anna and Lena. There was a gathering of such guests as the duchess alone among her countrywomen could assemble, under the patronage of the conciliatory Government, and the duchess projected to give a series of brilliant entertainments in the saloons of the Union, as she named her house-roof. Count Serabiglione arrived, as did numerous Moderates and priest-party men, Milanese garrison officers and others. Laura Piaveni travelled with Countess d'Isorella and the happy Adela Sedley, from Lago Maggiore.

Laura came, as she cruelly told her friend, for the purpose of making Victoria's excuses to the duchess. "Why can she not come herself?" Amalia persisted in asking, and began to be afflicted with womanly curiosity. Laura would do nothing but shrug and smile, and repeat her message. A little after sunset, when the saloons were lighted, Weisspriess, sitting by his Countess Anna's side, had a slip of paper placed in his hands by one of the domestics. He quitted his post frowning with astonishment, and muttered once, "My appointment!" Laura noticed that Anna's heavy eyelids lifted to shoot an expressive glance at Violetta d'Isorella. She said: "Can that have been anything hostile, do you suppose?" and glanced slyly at her friend.

"No, no," said Amalia; "the misunderstanding is explained, and Major Weisspriess is just as ready as Count Ammiani to listen to reason. Besides, Count Ammiani is not so unfriendly but that if he came so near he would come up to me, surely."

Laura brought Amalia's observation to bear upon Anna and Violetta by turning pointedly from one to the other as she said: "As for reason, perhaps you have chosen the word. If Count Ammiani attended an appointment this time, he would be unreasonable."

A startled "Why?"—leaped from Anna's lips. She reddened at her impulsive clumsiness.

Laura raised her shoulders slightly: "Do you not know?" The expression of her face reproved Violetta, as for remissness in transmitting secret intelligence. "You can answer why, countess," she addressed the latter, eager to exercise her native love of conflict with this doubtfully-faithful countrywoman;—the Austrian could feel that she had beaten her on the essential point, and afford to give her any number of dialectical victories.

"I really cannot answer why," Violetta said; "unless Count Ammiani is, as I venture to hope, better employed."

"But the answer is charming and perfect," said Laura.

"Enigmatical answers are declared to be so when they come from us women," the duchess remarked; "but then, I fancy, women must not be the hearers, or they will confess that they are just as much bewildered and irritated as I am. Do speak out, my dearest. How is he better employed?"

Laura passed her eyes around the group of ladies. "If any hero of yours had won the woman he loves, he would be right in thinking it folly to be bound by the invitation to fight, or feast, or what you will, within a space of three months or so; do you not agree with me?"

The different emotions on many visages made the scene curious.

"Count Ammiani has married her!" exclaimed the duchess.

"My old friend Carlo is really married!" said Lena.

Anna stared at Violetta.

The duchess, recovering from her wonder, confirmed the news by saying that she now knew why M. Powys had left Milan in haste, three or four days previously, as she was aware that the bride had always wished him to be present at the ceremony of her marriage.

"Signora, may I ask you, were you present?" Violetta addressed Laura.

"I will answer most honestly that I was not," said Laura.

"The marriage was a secret one; perhaps?"

"Even for friends, you see."

"Necessarily, no doubt," Lena said, with an idea of easing her sister's stupefaction by a sarcasm foreign to her sentiments.

Adela Sedley, later in exactly comprehending what had been spoken, glanced about for some one who would not be unsympathetic to her exclamation, and suddenly beheld her brother entering the room with Weisspriess. "Wilfrid! Wilfrid! do you know she is married?"

"So they tell me," Wilfrid replied, while making his bow to the duchess. He was much broken in appearance, but wore his usual collected manner. Who had told him of the marriage? A person downstairs, he said; not Count Ammiani; not signor Balderini; no one whom he saw present, no one whom he knew.

"A very mysterious person," said the duchess.

"Then it's true after all," cried Laura. "I did but guess it." She assured Violetta that she had only guessed it.

"Does Major Weisspriess know it to be true?" The question came from Anna.

Weisspriess coolly verified it, on the faith of a common servant's communication.

The ladies could see that some fresh piece of mystery lay between him and Wilfrid.

"With whom have you had an interview, and what have you heard?" asked Lena, vexed by Wilfrid's pallid cheeks.

Both men stammered and protested, out of conceit, and were as foolish as men are when pushed to play at mutual concealment.

The duchess's chasseur, Jacob Baumwalder Feckelwitz, stepped up to his mistress and whispered discreetly. She gazed straight at Laura. After hesitation she shook her head, and the chasseur retired. Amalia then came to the rescue of the unhappy military wits that were standing a cross-fire of sturdy interrogation.

"Do you not perceive what it is?" she said to Anna. "Major Weisspriess meets Private Pierson at the door of my house, and forgets that he is well-born and my guest. I may be revolutionary, but I declare that in plain clothes Private Pierson is the equal of Major Weisspriess. If bravery made men equals, who would be Herr Pierson's superior? Ire has done me the honour, at a sacrifice of his pride, I am sure, to come here and meet his sister, and rejoice me with his society. Major Weisspriess, if I understand the case correctly, you are greatly to blame."

"I beg to assert," Weisspriess was saying as the duchess turned her shoulder on him.

"There is really no foundation," Wilfrid began, with similar simplicity.

"What will sharpen the wits of these soldiers!" the duchess murmured dolefully to Laura.

"But Major Weisspriess was called out of his room by a message—was that from Private Pierson?" said Anna.

"Assuredly; I should presume so," the duchess answered for them.

"Ay; undoubtedly," Weisspriess supported her.

"Then," Laura smiled encouragement to Wilfrid, "you know nothing of Count Ammiani's marriage after all?"

Wilfrid launched his reply on a sharp repression of his breath, "Nothing whatever."

"And the common servant's communication was not made to you?" Anna interrogated Weisspriess.

"I simply followed in the track of Pierson," said that officer, masking his retreat from the position with a duck of his head and a smile, tooth on lip.

"How could you ever suppose, child, that a common servant would be sent to deliver such tidings? and to Major Weisspriess!" the duchess interposed.

This broke up the Court of inquiry.

Weisspriess shortly after took his leave, on the plea that he wished to prove his friendliness by accompanying Private Pierson, who had to be on duty early next day in Milan. Amalia had seen him breaking from Anna in extreme irritation, and he had only to pledge his word that he was really bound for Milan to satisfy her. "I believe you to be at heart humane," she said meaningly.

"Duchess, you may be sure that I would not kill an enemy save on the point of my sword," he answered her.

"You are a gallant man," said Amalia, and pride was in her face as she looked on him.

She willingly consented to Wilfrid's sudden departure, as it was evident that some shot had hit him hard.

On turning to Laura, the duchess beheld an aspect of such shrewd disgust that she was provoked to exclaim: "What on earth is the matter now?"

Laura would favour her with no explanation until they were alone in the duchess's boudoir, when she said that to call Weisspriess a gallant man was an instance of unblushing adulation of brutal strength: "Gallant for slaying a boy? Gallant because he has force of wrist?"

"Yes; gallant;—an honour to his countrymen: and an example to some of yours," Amalia rejoined.

"See," cried Laura, "to what a degeneracy your excess of national sentiment reduces you!"

While she was flowing on, the duchess leaned a hand across her shoulder, and smiling kindly, said she would not allow her to utter words that she would have to eat. "You saw my chasseur step up to me this evening, my Laura? Well, not to torment you, he wished to sound an alarm cry after Angelo Guidascarpi. I believe my conjecture is correct, that Angelo Guidascarpi was seen by Major Weisspriess below, and allowed to pass free. Have you no remark to make?"

"None," said Laura.

"You cannot admit that he behaved like a gallant man?" Laura sighed deeply. "Perhaps it was well for you to encourage him!"

The mystery of Angelo's interview with Weisspriess was cleared the next night, when in the midst of a ball-room's din, Aennchen, Amalia's favourite maid, brought a letter to Laura from Countess Ammiani. These were the contents:

"DEAREST SIGNORA,

"You now learn a new and blessed thing. God make the marriage fruitful! I have daughter as well as son. Our Carlo still hesitated, for hearing of the disgraceful rumours in Milan, he fancied a duty lay there for him to do. Another menace came to my daughter from the madman Barto Rizzo. God can use madmen to bring about the heavenly designs. We decided that Carlo's name should cover her. My son was like a man who has awakened up. M. Powys was our good genius. He told her that he had promised you to bring it about. He, and Angelo, and myself, were the witnesses. So much before heaven! I crossed the lake with them to Stress. I was her tirewoman, with Giacinta, to whom I will give a husband for the tears of joy she dropped upon the bed. Blessed be it! I placed my daughter in my Carlo's arms. Both kissed their mother at parting.

"This is something fixed. I had great fears during the war. You do not yet know what it is to have a sonless son in peril. Terror and remorse haunted me for having sent the last Ammiani out to those fields, unattached to posterity.

"An envelope from Milan arrived on the morning of his nuptials. It was intercepted by me. The German made a second appointment at Como. Angelo undertook to assist me in saving my son's honour. So my Carlo had nothing to disturb his day. Pray with me, Laura Piaveni, that the day and the night of it may prove fresh springs of a river that shall pass our name through the happier mornings of Italy! I commend you to God, my dear, and am your friend,

"MARCCELLINA, COUNTESS AMMIANI.

"P.S. Countess Alessandra will be my daughter's name."

The letter was read and re-read before the sweeter burden it contained would allow Laura to understand that Countess Ammiani had violated a seal and kept a second hostile appointment hidden from her son.

"Amalia, you detest me," she said, when they had left the guests for a short space, and the duchess had perused the letter, "but acknowledge Angelo Guidascarpi's devotion. He came here in the midst of you Germans, at the risk of his life, to offer battle for his cousin."

The duchess, however, had much more to say for the magnanimity of Major Weisspriess, who, if he saw him, had spared him; she compelled Laura to confess that Weisspriess must have behaved with some nobleness, which Laura did, humming and I 'brumming,' and hinting at the experience he had gained of Angelo's skill. Her naughtiness provoked first, and then affected Amalia; in this mood the duchess had the habit of putting on a grand air of pitying sadness. Laura knew it well, and never could make head against it. She wavered, as a stray floating thing detached from an eddy whirls and passes on the flood. Close on Amalia's bosom she sobbed out: "Yes; you Austrians have good qualities some: many! but you choose to think us mean because we can't readily admit them when we are under your heels. Just see me; what a crumb feeds me! I am crying with delight at a marriage!"

The duchess clasped her fondly.

"It's not often one gets you so humble, my Laura."

"I am crying with delight at a marriage! Amalia, look at me: you would suppose it a mighty triumph. A marriage! two little lovers lying cheek to cheek! and me blessing heaven for its goodness! and there may be dead men unburied still on the accursed Custozza hill-top!"

Amalia let her weep. The soft affection which the duchess bore to her was informed with a slight touch of envy of a complexion that could be torn with tears one minute, and the next be fit to show in public. No other thing made her regard her friend as a southern—that is, a foreign-woman.

"Be patient," Laura said.

"Cry; you need not be restrained," said Amalia.

"You sighed."

"No!"

"A sort of sigh. My fit's over. Carlo's marriage is too surprising and delicious. I shall be laughing presently. I hinted at his marriage—I thought it among the list of possible things, no more—to see if that crystal pool, called Violetta d'Isorella, could be discoloured by stirring. Did you watch her face? I don't know what she wanted with Carlo, for she's cold as poison—a female trifler; one of those women whom I, and I have a chaste body, despise as worse than wantons; but she certainly did not want him to be married. It seems like a victory—though we're beaten. You have beaten us, my dear!"

"My darling! it is your husband kisses you," said Amalia, kissing Laura's forehead from a full heart.

BOOK VIII

CHAPTER XL

THROUGH THE WINTER

Weisspriess and Wilfrid made their way toward Milan together, silently smoking, after one attempt at conversation, which touched on Vittoria's marriage; but when they reached Monza the officer slapped his degraded brother in arms upon the shoulder, and asked him whether he had any inclination to crave permission to serve in Hungary. For his own part, Weisspriess said that he should quit Italy at once; he had here to skewer the poor devils, one or two weekly, or to play the mightily generous; in short, to do things unsoldierly; and he was desirous of getting away from the country. General Schoneck was at Monza, and might arrange the matter for them both. Promotion was to be looked for in Hungary; the application would please the General; one battle would restore the lieutenant's star to Wilfrid's collar. Wilfrid, who had been offended by his companion's previous brooding silence, nodded briefly, and they stopped at Monza, where they saw General Schoneck in the morning, and Wilfrid being by extraordinary favour in civilian's dress during his leave of absence, they were jointly invited to the General's table at noon, though not to meet any other officer. General Schoneck agreed with Weisspriess that Hungary would be a better field for Wilfrid; said he would do his utmost to serve them in the manner they wished, and dismissed them after the second cigar. They strolled about the city, glad for reasons of their own to be out of Milan as long as the leave permitted. At night, when they were passing a palace in one of the dark streets, a feather, accompanied by a sharp sibilation from above, dropped on Wilfrid's face. Weisspriess held the feather up, and judged by its length that it was an eagle's, and therefore belonging to the Hungarian Hussar regiment stationed in Milan. "The bird's aloft," he remarked. His voice aroused a noise of feet that was instantly still. He sent a glance at the doorways, where he thought he discerned men. Fetching a whistle in with his breath, he unsheathed his sword, and seeing that Wilfrid had no weapon, he pushed him to a gate of the palace-court that had just cautiously turned a hinge. Wilfrid found his hand taken by a woman's hand inside. The gate closed behind him. He was led up to an apartment where, by the light of a darkly-veiled lamp, he beheld a young Hungarian officer and a lady clinging to his neck, praying him not to go forth. Her Italian speech revealed how matters stood in this house. The officer accosted Wilfrid: "But you are not one of us!" He repeated it to the lady: "You see, the man is not one of us!"

She assured him that she had seen the uniform when she dropped the feather, and wept protesting it.

"Louis, Louis! why did you come to-night! why did I make you come! You will be slain. I had my warning, but I was mad."

The officer hushed her with a quick squeeze of her inter-twisted fingers.

"Are you the man to take a sword and be at my back, sir?" he said; and resumed in a manner less contemptuous toward the civil costume: "I request it for the sole purpose of quieting this lady's fears."

Wilfrid explained who and what he was. On hearing that he was General Pierson's nephew the officer laughed cheerfully, and lifted the veil from the lamp, by which Wilfrid knew him to be Colonel Prince Radocky, a most gallant and the handsomest cavalier in the Imperial service. Radocky laughed again when he was told of Weisspriess keeping guard below.

"Aha! we are three, and can fight like a pyramid."

He flourished his hand above the lady's head, and called for a sword. The lady affected to search for one while he stalked up and down in the jaunty fashion of a Magyar horseman; but the sword was not to be discovered without his assistance, and he was led away in search of it. The moment he was alone Wilfrid burst into tears. He could bear anything better than the sight of fondling lovers. When they rejoined him, Radocky had evidently yielded some point; he stammered and worked his underlip on his moustache. The lady undertook to speak for him. Happily for her, she said, Wilfrid would not compromise her; and taking her lover's hand, she added with Italian mixture of wit and grace: "Happily for me, too, he does. The house is surrounded by enemies; it is a reign of terror for women. I am dead, if they slay him; but if they recognize him, I am lost."

Wilfrid readily leaped to her conclusion. He offered his opera-hat and civil mantle to Radocky, who departed in them, leaving his military cloak in exchange. During breathless seconds the lady hung kneeling at the window. When the gate opened there was a noise as of feet preparing to rush; Weisspriess uttered an astonished cry, but addressed Radocky as "my Pierson!" lustily and frequently; and was heard putting a number of meaningless questions, laughing and rallying Pierson till the two passed out of hearing unmolested. The lady then kissed a Cross passionately, and shivered Wilfrid's manhood by asking him whether he knew what love was. She went on:

"Never, never love a married woman! It's a past practice. Never! Thrust a spike in the palm of your hands drink scalding oil, rather than do that."

"The Prince Radocky is now safe," Wilfrid said.

"Yes, he is safe; and he is there, and I am here: and I cannot follow him; and when will he come to me?"

The tones were lamentable. She struck her forehead, after she had mutely thrust her hand to right and left to show the space separating her from her lover.

Her voice changed when she accepted Wilfrid's adieux, to whose fate in the deadly street she appeared quite indifferent, though she gave him one or two prudent directions, and expressed a hope that she might be of service to him.

He was set upon as soon as he emerged from the gateway; the cavalry cloak was torn from his back, and but for the chance circumstance of his swearing in English, he would have come to harm. A chill went through his blood on hearing one of his assailants speak the name of Barto Rizzo. The English oath stopped an arm that flashed a dagger half its length. Wilfrid obeyed a command to declare his name, his country, and his rank. "It's not the prince! it's not the Hungarian!" went many whispers; and he was drawn away by a man who requested him to deliver his reasons for entering the palace, and who appeared satisfied by Wilfrid's ready mixture of invention and fact. But the cloak! Wilfrid stated boldly that the cloak was taken by him from the Duchess of Graatli's at Como; that he had seen a tall Hussar officer slip it off his shoulders; that he had wanted a cloak, and had appropriated it. He had entered the gate of the palace because of a woman's hand that plucked at the skirts of this very cloak.

"I saw you enter," said the man; "do that no more. We will not have the blood of Italy contaminated—do you hear? While that half-Austrian Medole is tip-toeing 'twixt Milan and Turin, we watch over his honour, to set an example to our women and your officers. You have outwitted us to-night. Off with you!"

Wilfrid was twirled and pushed through the crowd till he got free of them. He understood very well that they were magnanimous rascals who could let an accomplice go, though they would have driven steel into the principal.

Nothing came of this adventure for some time. Wilfrid's reflections (apart from the horrible hard truth of Vittoria's marriage, against which he dashed his heart perpetually, almost asking for anguish) had leisure to examine the singularity of his feeling a commencement of pride in the clasping of his musket;—he who on the first day of his degradation had planned schemes to stick the bayonet-point between his breast-bones: he thought as well of the queer woman's way in Countess Medole's adjuration to him that he should never love a married woman;—in her speaking, as it seemed, on his behalf, when it was but an outcry of her own acute wound. Did he love a married woman? He wanted to see one married woman for the last time; to throw a frightful look on her; to be sublime in scorn of her; perhaps to love her all the better for the cruel pain, in the expectation of being consoled. While doing duty as a military machine, these were the pictures in his mind; and so well did his routine drudgery enable him to bear them, that when he heard from General Schoneck that the term of his degradation was to continue in Italy, and from his sister that General Pierson refused to speak of him or hear of him until he had regained his gold shoulder-strap, he revolted her with an ejaculation of gladness, and swore brutally that he desired to have no advancement; nothing but sleep and drill; and, he added conscientiously, Havannah cigars. "He has grown to be like a common soldier," Adela said to herself with an amazed contemplation of the family tie. Still, she worked on his behalf, having, as every woman has, too strong an instinct as to what is natural to us to believe completely in any eccentric assertion. She carried the tale of his grief and trials and his romantic devotion to the Imperial flag, daily to Countess Lena; persisting, though she could not win a responsive look from Lena's face.

One day on the review-ground, Wilfrid beheld Prince Radocky bending from his saddle in conversation with Weisspriess. The prince galloped up to General Pierson, and stretched his hand to where Wilfrid was posted as marker to a wheeling column, kept the hand stretched out, and spoke furiously, and followed the General till he was ordered to head his regiment. Wilfrid began to hug his musket less desperately. Little presents—feminine he knew by the perfumes floating round them,—gloves and cigars, fine handkerchiefs, and silks for wear, came to his barracks. He pretended to accuse his sister of sending them. She in honest delight accused Lena. Lena then accused herself of not having done so.

It was winter: Vittoria had been seen in Milan. Both Lena and Wilfrid spontaneously guessed her to be the guilty one. He made a funeral pyre of the gifts and gave his sister the ashes, supposing that she had guessed with the same spirited intuition. It suited Adela to relate this lover's performance to Lena. "He did well!" Lena said, and kissed Adela for the first time. Adela was the bearer of friendly messages to the poor private in the ranks. From her and from little Jenna, Wilfrid heard that he was unforgotten by Countess Lena, and new hopes mingled with gratitude caused him to regard his situation seriously. He confessed to his sister that the filthy fellows, his comrades, were all but too much for him, and asked her to kiss him, that he might feel he was not one of them. But he would not send a message in reply to Lena. "That is also well!" Lena said. Her brother Karl was a favourite with General Pierson. She proposed that Adela and herself should go to Count Karl, and urge him to use his influence with the General. This, however, Adela was disinclined to do; she could not apparently say why. When Lena went to him, she was astonished to hear that he knew every stage of her advance up to the point of pardoning her erratic lover; and even knew as much as that Wilfrid's dejected countenance on the night when Vittoria's marriage was published in the saloon of the duchess on Lake Como, had given her fresh offence. He told her that many powerful advocates were doing their best for the down-fallen officer, who, if he were shot, or killed, would still be gazetted an officer. "A nice comfort!" said Lena, and there was a rallying exchange of banter between them, out of which she drew the curious discovery that Karl had one of his strong admirations for the English lady. "Surely!" she said to herself; "I thought they were all so cold." And cold enough the English lady seemed when Lena led to the theme. "Do I admire your brother, Countess Lena? Oh! yes;—in his uniform exceedingly."

Milan was now full. Wilfrid had heard from Adela that Count Ammiani and his bride were in the city and were strictly watched. Why did not conspirators like these two take advantage of the amnesty? Why were they not in Rome? Their Chief was in Rome; their friends were in Rome. Why were they here? A report, coming from Countess d'Isorella, said that they had quarrelled with their friends, and were living for love alone. As she visited the Lenkensteins—high Austrians—some believed her; and as Count Ammiani and his bride had visited the Duchess of Graatli, it was thought possible. Adela had refused to see Vittoria; she did not even know the house where Count Ammiani dwelt; so Wilfrid was reduced to find it for himself. Every hour when off duty the miserable sentimentalist wandered in that direction, nursing the pangs of a delicious tragedy of emotions; he was like a drunkard going to his draught. As soon as he had reached the head of the Corso, he wheeled and marched away from it with a lofty head, internally grinning at his abject folly, and marvelling at the stiff figure of an Austrian common soldier which flashed by the windows as he passed. He who can unite prudence and madness, sagacity and stupidity, is the true buffoon; nor, vindictive as were his sensations, was Wilfrid unaware of the contrast of Vittoria's soul to his own, that was now made up of antics. He could not endure the tones of cathedral music; but he had at times to kneel and listen to it, and be overcome.

On a night in the month of February, a servant out of livery addressed him at the barrack-gates, requesting him to go at once to a certain hotel, where his sister was staying. He went, and found there, not his sister, but Countess Medole. She smiled at his confusion. Both she and the prince, she said, had spared no effort to get him reinstated in his rank; but his uncle continually opposed the endeavours of all his friends to serve him. This interview was dictated by the prince's wish, so that he might know them to be a not ungrateful couple. Wilfrid's embarrassment in standing before a lady in private soldier's uniform, enabled him with very peculiar dignity to declare that his present degradation, from the General's point of view, was a just punishment, and he did not crave to have it abated. She remarked that it must end soon. He made a dim allusion to the littleness of humanity. She laughed. "It's the language of an unfortunate lover," she said, and straightway, in some undistinguished sentence, brought the name of Countess Alessandra Ammiani tingling to his ears. She feared that she could not be of service to him there; "at least, not just yet," the lady astonished him by remarking. "I might help you to see her. If you take my advice you will wait patiently. You know us well enough to understand what patience will do. She is supposed to have married for love. Whether she did or not, you must allow a young married woman two years' grace."

The effect of speech like this, and more in a similar strain of frank corruptness, was to cleanse Wilfrid's mind, and nerve his heart, and he denied that he had any desire to meet the Countess Ammiani, unless he could perform a service that would be agreeable to her.

The lady shrugged. "Well, that is one way. She has enemies, of course."

Wilfrid begged for their names.

"Who are they not?" she replied. "Chiefly women, it is true."

He begged most earnestly for their names; he would have pleaded eloquently, but dreaded that the intonation of one in his low garb might be taken for a whine; yet he ventured to say that if the countess did imagine herself indebted to him in a small degree, the mention of two or three of the names of Countess Alessandra Ammiani's enemies would satisfy him.

"Countess Lena von Lenkenstein, Countess Violetta d'Isorella, signorina Irma di Karski."

She spoke the names out like a sum that she was paying down in gold pieces, and immediately rang the bell for her servant and carriage, as if she had now acquitted her debt. Wilfrid bowed himself forth. A resolution of the best kind, quite unconnected with his interests or his love, urged him on straight to the house of the Lenkensteins, where he sent up his name to Countess Lena. After a delay of many minutes, Count Lenkenstein accompanied by General Pierson came down, both evidently affecting not to see him. The General barely acknowledged his salute.

"Hey! Kinsky!" the count turned in the doorway to address him by the title of his regiment; "here; show me the house inhabited by the Countess d'Isorella during the revolt."

Wilfrid followed them to the end of the street, pointing his finger to the house, and saluted.

"An Englishman did me the favour—from pure eccentricity, of course—to save my life on that exact spot, General," said the count. "Your countrymen usually take the other side; therefore I mention it."

As Wilfrid was directing his steps to barracks (the little stir to his pride superinduced by these remarks having demoralized him), Count Lenkenstein shouted: "Are you off duty?" Wilfrid had nearly replied that he was, but just mastered himself in time. "No, indeed!" said the count, "when you have sent up your name to a lady." This time General Pierson put two fingers formally to his cap, and smiled grimly at the private's rigid figure of attention. If Wilfrid's form of pride had consented to let him take delight in the fact, he would have seen at once that prosperity was ready to shine on him. He nursed the vexations much too tenderly to give prosperity a welcome; and even when along with Lena, and convinced of her attachment, and glad of it, he persisted in driving at the subject which had brought him to her house; so that the veil of opening commonplaces, pleasant to a couple in their position, was plucked aside. His business was to ask her why she was the enemy of Countess Alessandra Ammiani, and to entreat her that she should not seek to harm that lady. He put it in a set speech. Lena felt that it ought to have come last, not in advance of their reconciliation. "I will answer you," she said. "I am not the Countess Alessandra Ammiani's enemy."

He asked her: "Could you be her friend?"

"Does a woman who has a husband want a friend?"

"I could reply, countess, in the case of a man who has a bride."

By dint of a sweet suggestion here and there, love-making crossed the topic. It appeared that General Pierson had finally been attacked, on the question of his resistance to every endeavour to restore Wilfrid to his rank, by Count Lenkenstein, and had barely spoken the words—that if Wilfrid came to Countess Lena of his own free-will, unprompted, to beg her forgiveness, he would help to reinstate him, when Wilfrid's name was brought up by the chasseur. All had laughed, "Even I," Lena confessed. And then the couple had a pleasant petitish wrangle;—he was requested to avow that he had came solely, or principally, to beg forgiveness of her, who had such heaps to forgive. No; on his honour, he had come for the purpose previously stated, and on the spur of his hearing that she was Countess Alessandra Ammiani's deadly enemy. "Could you believe that I was?" said Lena; "why should I be?" and he coloured like a lad, which sign of an ingenuousness supposed to belong to her set, made Lena bold to take the upper hand. She frankly accused herself of jealousy, though she did not say of whom. She almost admitted that when the time for reflection came, she should rejoice at his having sought her to plead for his friend rather than for her forgiveness. In the end, but with a drooping pause of her bright swift look at Wilfrid, she promised to assist him in defeating any machinations against Vittoria's happiness, and to keep him informed of Countess d'Isorella's movements. Wilfrid noticed the withdrawing fire of the look. "By heaven! she doubts me still," he ejaculated inwardly.

These half-comic little people have their place in the history of higher natures and darker destinies. Wilfrid met Pericles, from whom he heard that Vittoria, with her husband's consent, had pledged herself to sing publicly. "It is for ze Lombard widows," Pericles apologized on her behalf; "but, do you see, I only want a beginning. She thaerst for ze stage; and it is, after marriage, a good sign. Oh! you shall hear, my friend; marriage have done her no hurt—ze contrary! You shall hear Hymen—Cupids—not a cold machine; it is an organ alaif! She has privily sung to her Pericles, and ser, and if I wake not very late on Judgement. Day, I shall zen hear—but why should I talk poetry to you, to make you laugh? I have a divin' passion for zat woman. Do I not give her to a husband, and say, Be happy! onnly sing! Be kissed! be hugged! only give Pericles your voice. By Saint Alexandre! it is to say to ze heavens, Move on your way, so long as you drop rain on us r—you smile—you look kind."

Pericles accompanied him into a caffe, the picture of an enamoured happy man. He waived aside contemptuously all mention of Vittoria's having enemies. She had them when, as a virgin, she had no sense. As a woman, she had none, for she now had sense. Had she not brought her husband to be sensible, so that they moved together in Milanese society, instead of stupidly fighting at Rome? so that what he could not take to himself—the marvellous voice—he let bless the multitude! "She is the Beethoven of singers," Pericles concluded. Wilfrid thought so on the night when she sang to succour the Lombard widows. It was at a concert, richly thronged; ostentatiously thronged with Austrian uniforms. He fancied that he could not bear to look on her. He left the house thinking that to hear her and see her and feel that she was one upon the earth, made life less of a burden.

This evening was rendered remarkable by a man's calling out, "You are a traitress!" while Vittoria stood before the seats. She became pale, and her eyelids closed. No thinness was subsequently heard in her voice. The man was caught as he strove to burst through the crowd at the entrance-door, and proved to be a petty bookseller of Milan, by name Sarpo, known as an orderly citizen. When taken he was inflamed with liquor. Next day the man was handed from the civil to the military authorities, he having confessed to the existence of a plot in the city. Pericles came fuming to Wilfrid's quarters. Wilfrid gathered from him that Sarpo's general confession had been retracted: it was too foolish to snare the credulity of Austrian officials. Sarpo stated that he had fabricated the story of a plot, in order to escape the persecutions of a terrible man, and find safety in prison lodgings vender Government. The short confinement for a civic offence was not his idea of safety; he desired to be sheltered by Austrian soldiers and a fortress, and said that his torments were insupportable while Barto Rizzo was at large. This infamous Republican had latterly been living in his house, eating his bread, and threatening death to him unless he obeyed every command. Sarpo had undertaken his last mission for the purpose of supplying his lack of resolution to release himself from his horrible servitude by any other means; not from personal animosity toward the Countess Alessandra Ammiani, known as la Vittoria. When seized, fear had urged him to escape. Such was his second story. The points seemed irreconcilable to those who were not in the habit of taking human nature into their calculations of a possible course of conduct; even Wilfrid, though he was aware that Barto Rizzo hated Vittoria inveterately, imagined Sarpo's first lie to have necessarily fathered a second. But the second story was true: and the something like lover's wrath with which the outrage to Vittoria fired Pericles, prompted him to act on it as truth. He told Wilfrid that he should summon Barto Rizzo to his presence. As the Government was unable to exhibit so much power, Wilfrid looked sarcastic; whereupon Pericles threw up his chin crying: "Oh! you shall know my resources. Now, my friend, one bit of paper, and a messenger, and zen home to my house, to Tokay and cigarettes, and wait to see." He remarked after pencilling a few lines, "Countess d'Isorella is her enemy? hein!"

"Why, you wouldn't listen to me when I told you," said Wilfrid.

"No," Pericles replied while writing and humming over his pencil; "my ear is a pelican-pouch, my friend; it—and Irma is her enemy also?—it takes and keeps, but does not swallow till it wants. I shall hear you, and I shall hear my Sandra Vittoria, and I shall not know you have spoken, when by-and-by I tinkle, tinkle, a bell of my brain, and your word walks in,—'quite well?'—'very well! '—sit down'—'if it is ze same to you, I prefer to stand'—'good; zen I examine you.' My motto:—'Time opens ze gates: my system: 'it is your doctor of regiment's system when your twelve, fifteen, forty recruits strip to him:— 'Ah! you, my man, have varicose vein: no soldier in our regiment, you!' So on. Perhaps I am not intelligible; but, hear zis. I speak not often of my money; but I say—it is in your ear—a man of millions, he is a king!" The Greek jumped up and folded a couple of notes. "I will not have her disturbed. Let her sing now and awhile to Pericles and his public: and to ze Londoners, wiz your permission, Count Ammiani, one saison. I ask no more, and I am satisfied, and I endow your oldest child, signor Conte—it is said! For its mama was a good girl, a brave girl; she troubled Pericles, because he is an intellect; but he forgives when he sees sincerity—rare zing! Sincerity and genius: it may be zey are as man and wife in a bosom. He forgives; it is not onnly voice he craves, but a soul, and Sandra, your countess, she has a soul—I am not a Turk. I say, it is a woman in whom a girl I did see a soul! A woman when she is married, she is part of ze man; but a soul, it is for ever alone, apart, confounded wiz nobody! For it I followed Sandra, your countess. It was a sublime devotion of a dog. Her voice tsrilled, her soul possessed me, Your countess is my Sandra still. I shall be pleased if child-bearing trouble her not more zan a very little; but, enfin! she is married, and you and I, my friend Wilfrid, we must accept ze decree, and say, no harm to her out of ze way of nature, by Saint Nicolas! or any what saint you choose for your invocation. Come along. And speed my letters by one of your militaires at once off. Are Pericles' millions gold of bad mint? If so, he is an incapable. He presumes it is not so. Come along; we will drink to her in essence of Tokay. You shall witness two scenes. Away!"

Wilfrid was barely to be roused from his fit of brooding into which Pericles had thrown him. He sent the letters, and begged to be left to sleep. The image of Vittoria seen through this man's mind was new, and brought a new round of torments. "The devil take you," he cried when Pericles plucked at his arm, "I've sent the letters; isn't that enough?" He was bitterly jealous of the Greek's philosophic review of the conditions of Vittoria's marriage; for when he had come away from the concert, not a thought of her being a wife had clouded his resignation to the fact. He went with Pericles, nevertheless, and was compelled to acknowledge the kindling powers of the essence of Tokay. "Where do you get this stuff?" he asked several times. Pericles chattered of England, and Hagar's 'Addio,' and 'Camilla.' What cabinet operas would he not give! What entertainments! Could an emperor offer such festivities to his subjects? Was a Field Review equal to Vittoria's voice? He stung Wilfrid's ears by insisting on the mellowed depth, the soft human warmth, which marriage had lent to the voice. At a late hour his valet announced Countess d'Isorella. "Did I not say so?" cried Pericles, and corrected himself: "No, I did not say so; it was a surprise to you, my friend. You shall see; you shall hear. Now you shall see what a friend Pericles can be when a person satisfy him." He pushed Wilfrid into his dressing-room, and immediately received the countess with an outburst of brutal invectives—pulling her up and down the ranked regiment of her misdeeds, as it were. She tried dignity, tried anger, she affected amazement, she petitioned for the heads of his accusations, and, as nothing stopped him, she turned to go. Pericles laughed when she had left the room. Irma di Karski was announced the next minute, and Countess d'Isorella re-appeared beside her. Irma had a similar greeting. "I am lost," she exclaimed. "Yes, you are lost," said Pericles; "a word from me, and the back of the public is humped at you—ha! contessa, you touched Mdlle. Irma's hand? She is to be on her guard, and never to think she is lost till down she goes? You are a more experienced woman! I tell you I will have no nonsense. I am Countess Alessandra Ammiani's friend. You two, you women, are her enemies. I will ruin you both. You would prevent her singing in public places— you, Countess d'Isorella, because you do not forgive her marriage to Count Ammiani; you, Irma, to spite her for her voice. You would hiss her out of hearing, you two miserable creatures. Not another soldo for you! Not one! and to-morrow, countess, I will see my lawyer. Irma, begone, and shriek to your wardrobe! Countess d'Isorella, I have the extreme honour."

Wilfrid marvelled to hear this titled and lovely woman speaking almost in tones of humility in reply to such outrageous insolence. She craved a private interview. Irma was temporarily expelled, and then Violetta stooped to ask what the Greek's reason for his behaviour could be. She admitted that it was in his power to ruin her, as far as money went. "Perhaps a little farther," said Pericles; "say two steps. If one is on a precipice, two steps count for something." But, what had she done? Pericles refused to declare it. This set her guessing with a charming naivete. Pericles called Irma back to assist her in the task, and quitted them that they might consult together and hit upon the right thing. His object was to send his valet for Luigi Saracco. He had seen that no truth could be extracted from these women, save forcibly. Unaware that he had gone out, Wilfrid listened long enough to hear Irma say, between sobs: "Oh! I shall throw myself upon his mercy. Oh, Countess d'Isorella, why did you lead me to think of vengeance! I am lost! He knows everything. Oh, what is it to me whether she lives with her husband! Let them go on plotting. I am not the Government. I am sure I don't much dislike her. Yes, I hate her, but why should I hurt myself? She will wear those jewels on her forehead; she will wear that necklace with the big amethysts, and pretend she's humble because she doesn't carry earrings, when her ears have never been pierced! I am lost! Yes, you may say, lookup! I am only a poor singer, and he can ruin me. Oh! Countess d'Isorella, oh! what a fearful punishment. If Countess Anna should betray Count Ammiani to-night, nothing, nothing, will save me. I will confess. Let us both be beforehand with her—or you, it does not matter for a noble lady."

"Hush!" said Violetta. "What dreadful fool is this I sit with? You may have done what you think of doing already."

She walked to the staircase door, and to that of the suite. An honourable sentiment, conjoined to the knowledge that he had heard sufficient, induced Wilfrid to pass on into the sleeping apartment a moment or so before Violetta took this precaution. The potent liquor of Pericles had deprived him of consecutive ideas; he sat nursing a thunder in his head, imagining it to be profound thought, till Pericles flung the door open. Violetta and Irma had departed. "Behold! I have it; ze address of your rogue Barto Rizzo," said Pericles, in the manner of one whose triumph is absolutely due to his own shrewdness. "Are two women a match for me? Now, my friend, you shall see. Barto Rizzo is too clever for zis government, which cannot catch him. I catch him, and I teach him he may touch politics—it is not for him to touch Art. What! to hound men to interrupt her while she sings in public places? What next! But I knew my Countess d'Isorella could help me, and so I sent for her to confront Irma, and dare to say she knew not Barto's dwelling—and why? I will tell you a secret. A long-flattered woman, my friend, she has had, you will think, enough of it; no! she is like avarice. If it is worship of swine, she cannot refuse it. Barto Rizzo worships her; so it is a deduction—she knows his abode—I act upon that, and I arrive at my end. I now send him to ze devil."

Barto Rizzo, after having evaded the polizia of the city during a three months' steady chase, was effectually captured on the doorstep of Vittoria's house in the Corso Francesco, by gendarmes whom Pericles had set on his track. A day later Vittoria was stabbed at about the same hour, on the same spot. A woman dealt the blow. Vittoria was returning from an afternoon drive with Laura Piaveni and the children. She saw a woman seated on the steps as beggarwomen sit, face in lap. Anxious to shield her from the lacquey, she sent the two little ones up to her with small bits of money. But, as the woman would not lift her head, she and Laura prepared to pass her, Laura coming last. The blow, like all such unexpected incidents, had the effect of lightning on those present; the woman might have escaped, but after she had struck she sat down impassive as a cat by the hearth, with a round-eyed stare.

The news that Vittoria had been assassinated traversed the city. Carlo was in Turin, Merthyr in Rome. Pericles was one of the first who reached the house; he was coming out when Wilfrid and the Duchess of Graatli drove up; and he accused the Countess d'Isorella flatly of having instigated the murder. He was frantic. They supposed that she must have succumbed to the wound. The duchess sent for Laura. There was a press of carriages and soft-humming people in the street; many women and men sobbing. Wilfrid had to wait an hour for the duchess, who brought comfort when she came. Her first words were reassuring. "Ah!" she said, "did I not do well to make you drive here with me instead of with Lena? Those eyes of yours would be unpardonable to her. Yes, indeed; though a corpse were lying in this house; but Countess Alessandra is safe. I have seen her. I have held her hand."

Wilfrid kissed the duchess's hand passionately.

What she had said of Lena was true: Lena could only be generous upon the after-thought; and when the duchess drove Wilfrid back to her, he had to submit to hear scorn: and indignation against all Italians, who were denounced as cut-throats, and worse and worse and worse, males and females alike. This way grounded on her sympathy for Vittoria. But Wilfrid now felt toward the Italians through his remembrance of that devoted soul's love of them, and with one direct look he bade his betrothed good-bye, and they parted.

It was in the early days of March that Merthyr, then among the Republicans of Rome, heard from Laura Piaveni. Two letters reached him, one telling of the attempted assassination, and a second explaining circumstances connected with it. The first summoned him to Milan; the other left it to his option to make the journey. He started, carrying kind messages from the Chief to Vittoria, and from Luciano Ramara the offer of a renewal of old friendship to Count Ammiani. His political object was to persuade the Lombard youth to turn their whole strength upon Rome. The desire of his heart was again to see her, who had been so nearly lost to all eyes for ever.

Laura's first letter stated brief facts. "She was stabbed this afternoon, at half-past two, on the steps of her house, by a woman called the wife of Barto Rizzo. She caught her hands up under her throat when she saw the dagger. Her right arm was penetrated just above the wrist, and half-an-inch in the left breast, close to the centre bone. She behaved firmly. The assassin only struck once. No visible danger; but you should come, if you have no serious work."

"Happily," ran the subsequent letter, of two days' later date, "the assassin was a woman, and one effort exhausts a woman; she struck only once, and became idiotic. Sandra has no fever. She had her wits ready—where were mine?—when she received the wound. While I had her in my arms, she gave orders that the woman should be driven out of the city in her carriage. The Greek, her mad musical adorer, accuses Countess d'Isorella. Carlo has seen this person—returns convinced of her innocence. That is not an accepted proof; but we have one. It seems that Rizzo (Sandra was secret about it and about one or two other things) sent to her commanding her to appoint an hour detestable style! I can see it now; I fear these conspiracies no longer:—she did appoint an hour; and was awaiting him when the gendarmes sprang on the man at her door.

"He had evaded them several weeks, so we are to fancy that his wife charged Countess Alessandra with the betrayal. This appears a reasonable and simple way of accounting for the deed. So I only partly give credit to it. But it may be true.

"The wound has not produced a shock to her system—very, very fortunately. On the whole, a better thing could not have happened. Should I be more explicit? Yes, to you; for you are not of those who see too much in what is barely said. The wound, then, my dear good friend, has healed another wound, of which I knew nothing. Bergamasc and Brescian friends of her husband's, have imagined that she interrupted or diverted his studies. He also discovered that she had an opinion of her own, and sometimes he consulted it; but alas! they are lovers, and he knew not when love listened, or she when love spoke; and there was grave business to be done meanwhile. Can you kindly allow that the case was open to a little confusion? I know that you will. He had to hear many violent reproaches from his fellow-students. These have ceased. I send this letter on the chance of the first being lost on the road; and it will supplement the first pleasantly to you in any event. She lies here in the room where I write, propped on high pillows, the right arm bound up, and says: 'Tell Merthyr I prayed to be in Rome with my husband, and him, and the Chief. Tell him I love my friend. Tell him I think he deserves to be in Rome. Tell him—' Enter Countess Ammiani to reprove her for endangering the hopes of the house by fatiguing herself. Sandra sends a blush at me, and I smile, and the countess kisses her. I send you a literal transcript of one short scene, so that you may feel at home with us.

"There is a place called Venice, and there is a place called Rome, and both places are pretty places and famous places; and there is a thing called the fashion; and these pretty places and famous places set the fashion: and there is a place called Milan, and a place called Bergamo, and a place called Brescia, and they all want to follow the fashion, for they are giddy-pated baggages. What is the fashion, mama? The fashion, my dear, is &c. &c. &c.:—Extract of lecture to my little daughter, Amalia, who says she forgets you; but Giacomo sends his manly love. Oh, good God! should I have blood in my lips when I kissed him, if I knew that he was old enough to go out with a sword in his hand a week hence? I seem every day to be growing more and more all mother. This month in front of us is full of thunder. Addio!"

When Merthyr stood in sight of Milan an army was issuing from the gates.

CHAPTER XLI

THE INTERVIEW

Merthyr saw Laura first. He thought that Vittoria must be lying on her couch: but Laura simply figured her arm in a sling, and signified, more than said, that Vittoria was well and taking the air. She then begged hungrily for news of Rome, and again of Rome, and sat with her hands clasped in her lap to listen. She mentioned Venice in a short breath of praise, as if her spirit could not repose there. Rome, its hospitals, its municipal arrangements, the names of the triumvirs, the prospects of the city, the edicts, the aspects of the streets, the popularity of the Government, the number of volunteers ranked under the magical Republic—of these things Merthyr talked, at her continual instigation, till, stopping abruptly, he asked her if she wished to divert him from any painful subject. "No, no!" she cried, "it's only that I want to feel an anchor. We are all adrift. Sandra is in perfect health. Our bodies, dear Merthyr, are enjoying the perfection of comfort. Nothing is done here except to keep us from boiling over."

"Why does not Count Ammiani come to Rome?" said Merthyr.

"Why are we not all in Rome? Yes, why! why! We should make a carnival of our own if we were."

"She would have escaped that horrible knife," Merthyr sighed.

"Yes, she would have escaped that horrible knife. But see the difference between Milan and Rome, my friend! It was a blessed knife here. It has given her husband back to her; it has destroyed the intrigues against her. It seems to have been sent—I was kneeling in the cathedral this morning, and had the very image crossing my eyes—from the saints of heaven to cut the black knot. Perhaps it may be the means of sending us to Rome."

Laura paused, and, looking at him, said, "It is so utterly impossible for us women to comprehend love without folly in a man; the trait by which we recognize it! Merthyr, you dear Englishman, you shall know everything. Do we not think a tisane a weak washy drink, when we are strong? But we learn, when we lie with our chins up, and our ten toes like stopped organ-pipes—as Sandra says—we learn then that it means fresh health and activity, and is better than rivers of your fiery wines. You love her, do you not?"

The question came with great simplicity.

"If I can give a proof of it, I am ready to answer," said Merthyr, in some surprise.

"Your whole life is the proof of it. The women of your country are intolerable to me, Merthyr: but I do see the worth of the men. Sandra has taught me. She can think of you, talk of you, kiss the vision of you, and still be a faithful woman in our bondage of flesh; and to us you know what a bondage it is: How can that be? I should have asked, if I had not seen it. Dearest, she loves her husband, and she loves you. She has two husbands, and she turns to the husband of her spirit when that, or any, dagger strikes her bosom. Carlo has an unripe mind. They have been married but a little more than four months; and he reveres her and loves her.".... Laura's voice dragged. "Multiply the months by thousands, we shall not make those two lives one. It is the curse of man's education in Italy? He can see that she has wits and courage. He will not consent to make use of them. You know her: she is not one to talk of these things. She, who has both heart and judgement—she is merely a little boat tied to a big ship. Such is their marriage. She cannot influence him. She is not allowed to advise him. And she is the one who should lead the way. And—if she did, we should now be within sight of the City."

Laura took his hand. She found it moist, though his face was calm and his chest heaved regularly. An impish form of the pity women feel for us at times moved her to say, "Your skin is as bronzed as it was last year. Sandra spoke of it. She compared it to a young vine-leaf. I wonder whether girls have really an admonition of what is good for them while they are going their ways like destined machines?"

"Almost all men are of flesh and blood," said Merthyr softly.

"I spoke of girls."

"I speak of men."

"Blunt—witted that I am! Of course you did. But do not imagine that she is not happy with her husband. They are united firmly."

"The better for her, and him, and me," said Merthyr.

Laura twisted an end of her scarf with fretful fingers. "Carlo Albert has crossed the Ticino?"

"Is about to do so," Merthyr rejoined.

"Will Rome hold on if he is defeated?"

"Rome has nothing to fear on that side."

"But you do not speak hopefully of Rome."

"I suppose I am thinking of other matters."

"You confess it!"

The random conversation wearied him. His foot tapped the floor.

"Why do you say that?" he asked.

"Verily, for no other reason than that I have a wicked curiosity, and that you come from Rome," said Laura, now perfectly frank, and believing that she had explained her enigmatical talk, if she had not furnished an excuse for it. Merthyr came from the City which was now encircled by an irradiating halo in her imagination, and a fit of spontaneous inexplicable feminine tenderness being upon her at the moment of their meeting, she found herself on a sudden prompted to touch and probe and brood voluptuously over an unfortunate lover's feelings, supposing that they existed. For the glory of Rome was on him, and she was at the same time angry with Carlo Ammiani. It was the form of passion her dedicated widowhood could still be subject to in its youth; the sole one. By this chance Merthyr learnt what nothing else would have told him.

Her tale of the attempted assassination was related with palpable indifference. She stated the facts. "The woman seemed to gasp while she had her hand up; she struck with no force; and she has since been inanimate, I hear. The doctor says that a spasm of the heart seized her when she was about to strike. It has been shaken—I am not sure that he does not say displaced, or unseated—by some one of her black tempers. She shot Rinaldo Guidascarpi dead. Perhaps it was that. I am informed that she worshipped the poor boy, and has been like a trapped she-wolf since she did it. In some way she associated our darling with Rinaldo's death, like the brute she is. The ostensible ground for her futile bit of devilishness was that she fancied Sandra to have betrayed Barto Rizzo, her husband, into the hands of the polizia. He wrote to the Countess Alessandra—such a letter!—a curiosity!—he must see her and cross-examine her to satisfy himself that she was a true patriot, &c. You know the style: we neither of us like it. Sandra was waiting to receive him when they pounced on him by the door. Next day the woman struck at her. Decidedly a handsome woman. She is the exact contrast to the Countess Violetta in face, in everything. Heart-disease will certainly never affect that pretty spy! But, mark," pursued Laura, warming, "when Carlo arrived, tears, penitence, heaps of self-accusations: he had been unkind to her even on Lake Orta, where they passed their golden month; he had neglected her at Turin; he had spoken angry words in Milan; in fact, he had misused his treasure, and begged pardon;—'If you please, my poor bleeding angel, I am sorry. But do not, I entreat, distract me with petitions of any sort, though I will perform anything earthly to satisfy you. Be a good little boat in the wake of the big ship. I will look over at you, and chirrup now and then to you, my dearest, when I am not engaged in piloting extraordinary.'—Very well; I do not mean to sneer at the unhappy boy, Merthyr; I love him; he was my husband's brother in arms; the sweetest lad ever seen. He is in the season of faults. He must command;

he must be a chief; he fancies he can intrigue poor thing! It will pass. And so will the hour to be forward to Rome. But I call your attention to this: when he heard of the dagger—I have it from Colonel Corte, who was with him at the time in Turin—he cried out Violetta d'Isorella's name. Why? After he had buried his head an hour on Sandra's pillow, he went straight to Countess d'Isorella, and was absent till night. The woman is hideous to me. No; don't conceive that I think her Sandra's rival. She is too jealous. She has him in some web. If she has not ruined him, she will. She was under my eyes the night she heard of his marriage: I saw how she will look at seventy! Here is Carlo at the head of a plot she has prepared for him; and he has Angelo Guidascarpi, and Ugo Corte, Marco Sana, Giulio Bandinelli, and about fifty others. They have all been kept away from Rome by that detestable ——-, you object to hear bad names cast on women, Merthyr. Hear Agostino! The poor old man comes daily to this house to persuade Carlo to lead his band to Rome. It is so clearly Rome—Rome, where all his comrades are; where the chief stand must be made by the side of Italy's Chief. Worst sign of all, it has been hinted semi-officially to Carlo that he may upon application be permitted to re-issue his journal. Does not that show that the Government wishes to blindfold him, and keep him here, and knows his plans?"

Laura started up as the door opened, and Vittoria appeared leaning upon Carlo's arm. Countess Ammiani, Countess d'Isorella, and Pericles were behind them. Laura's children followed.

When Merthyr rose, Vittoria was smiling in Carlo's face at something that had been spoken. She was pale, and her arm was in a sling, but there was no appearance of her being unnerved. Merthyr waited for her recognition of him. She turned her eyes from Carlo slowly. The soft dull smile in them died out as it were with a throb, and then her head drooped on one shoulder, and she sank to the floor.

CHAPTER XLII

THE SHADOW ON CONSPIRACY

Merthyr left the house at Laura's whispered suggestion. He was agitated beyond control, for Vittoria had fallen with her eyes fixed on him; and at times the picture of his beloved, her husband, and Countess Ammiani, and the children bending over her still body, swam before him like a dark altar-piece floating in incense, so lost was he to the reality of that scene. He did not hear Beppo, his old servant, at his heels. After a while he walked calmly, and Beppo came up beside him. Merthyr shook his hand.

"Ah, signor Mertyrio! ah, padrone!" said Beppo.

Merthyr directed his observation to a regiment of Austrians marching down the Corso Venezia to the Ticinese gate.

"Yes, they are ready enough for us," Beppo remarked. "Perhaps Carlo Alberto will beat them this time. If he does, viva to him! If they beat him, down goes another Venetian pyramid. The Countess Alessandra—" Beppo's speech failed.

"What of your mistress?" said Merthyr.

"When she dies, my dear master, there's no one for me but the Madonna to serve."

"Why should she die, silly fellow?"

"Because she never cries."

Merthyr was on the point of saying, "Why should she cry?" His heart was too full, and he shrank from inquisitive shadows of the thing known to him.

"Sit down at this caffe with me," he said. "It's fine weather for March. The troops will camp comfortably. Those Hungarians never require tents. Did you see much sacking of villages last year?"

"Padrone, the Imperial command is always to spare the villages."

"That's humane."

"Padrone, yes; if policy is humanity."

"It's humanity not carried quite as far as we should wish it."

Beppo shrugged and said: "It won't leave much upon the conscience if we kill them."

"Do you expect a rising?" said Merthyr.

"If the Ticino overflows, it will flood Milan," was the answer.

"And your occupation now is to watch the height of the water?"

"My occupation, padrone? I am not on the watch-tower." Beppo winked, adding: "I have my occupation." He threw off the effort or pretence to be discreet. "Master of my soul! this is my occupation. I drink coffee, but I do not smoke, because I have to kiss a pretty girl, who means to object to the smell of the smoke. Via! I know her! At five she draws me into the house."

"Are you relating your amours to me, rascal?" Merthyr interposed.

"Padrone, at five precisely she draws me into the house. She is a German girl. Pardon me if I make no war on women. Her name is Aennchen, which one is able to say if one grimaces;—why not? It makes her laugh; and German girls are amiable when one can make them laugh. 'Tis so that they begin to melt. Behold the difference of races! I must kiss her to melt her, and then have a quarrel. I could have it after the first, or the fiftieth with an Italian girl; but my task will be excessively difficult with a German girl, if I am compelled to allow myself to favour her with one happy solicitation for a kiss, to commence with. We shall see. It is, as my abstention from tobacco declares, an anticipated catastrophe."

"Long-worded, long-winded, obscure, affirmatizing by negatives, confessing by implication!—where's the beginning and end of you, and what's your meaning?" said Merthyr, who talked to him as one may talk to an Italian servant.

"The contessa, my mistress, has enemies. Padrone, I devote myself to her service."

"By making love to a lady's maid?"

"Padrone, a rat is not born to find his way up the grand staircase. She has enemies. One of them was the sublime Barto Rizzo—admirable—though I must hate him. He said to his wife: 'If a thing happens to me, stab to the heart the Countess Alessandra Ammiani.'"

"Inform me how you know that?" said Merthyr.

Beppo pointed to his head, and Merthyr smiled. To imagine, invent, and believe, were spontaneous with Beppo when has practical sagacity was not on the stretch. He glanced at the caffe clock.

"Padrone, at eleven to-night shall I see you here? At eleven I shall come like a charged cannon. I have business. I have seen my mistress's blood! I will tell you: this German girl lets me know that some one detests my mistress. Who? I am off to discover. But who is the damned creature? I must coo and kiss, while my toes are dancing on hot plates, to find her out. Who is she? If she were half Milan..."

His hands waved in outline the remainder of the speech, and he rose, but sat again. He had caught sight of the spy, Luigi Saracco, addressing the signor Antonio-Pericles in his carriage. Pericles drove on. The horses presently turned, and he saluted Merthyr.

"She has but one friend in Milan: it is myself," was his introductory remark. "My poor child! my dear Powys, she is the best—'I cannot sing to you to-day, dear Pericles'—she said that after she had opened her eyes; after the first mist, you know. She is the best child upon earth. I could wish she were a devil, my Powys. Such a voice should be in an iron body. But she has immense health. The doctor, who is also mine, feels her pulse. He assures me it goes as Time himself, and Time, my friend, you know, has the intention of going a great way. She is good: she is too good. She makes a baby of Pericles, to whom what is woman? Have I not the sex in my pocket? Her husband, he is a fool, ser." Pericles broke thundering into a sentence of English, fell in love with it, and resumed in the same tongue: "I—it is I zat am her guard, her safety. Her husband—oh! she must marry a young man, little donkey zat she is! We accept it as a destiny, my Powys. And he plays false to her. Good; I do not object. But, imagine in your own mind, my Powys—instead of passion, of rage, of tempest, she is frozen wiz a repose. Do you, hein? sink it will come out,"—Pericles eyed Merthyr with a subtle smile askew,—"I have sot so;—it will come out when she is one day in a terrible scene ... Mon Dieu! it was a terrible scene for me when I looked on ze clout zat washed ze blood of ze terrible assassination. So goes out a voice, possibly! Divine, you say? We are a machine. Now, you behold, she has faints. It may happen at my concert where she sings to-morrow night. You saw me in my carriage speaking to a man. He is my spy—my dog wiz a nose. I have set him upon a woman. If zat woman has a plot for to-morrow night to spoil my concert, she shall not know where she shall wake to-morrow morning after. Ha! here is military music—twenty sossand doors jam on horrid hinge; and right, left, right, left, to it, confound! like dolls all wiz one face. Look at your soldiers, Powys. Put zem on a stage, and you see all background people—a bawling chorus. It shows to you how superior it is—a stage to life! Hark to such music! I cannot stand it; I am driven away; I am violent; I rage."

Pericles howled the name of his place of residence, with an offer of lodgings in it, and was carried off writhing his body as he passed a fine military marching band.

The figure of old Agostino Balderini stood in front of Merthyr. They exchanged greetings. At the mention of Rome, Agostino frowned impatiently. He spoke of Vittoria in two or three short exclamations, and was about to speak of Carlo, but checked his tongue. "Judge for yourself. Come, and see, and approve, if you can. Will you come? There's a meeting; there's to be a resolution. Question—Shall we second the King of Sardinia, Piedmont, and Savoy? If so, let us set this pumpkin, called Milan, on its legs. I shall be an attentive listener like you, my friend. I speak no more."

Merthyr went with him to the house of a carpenter, where in one of the uppermost chambers communicating with the roof, Ugo Corte, Marco Sana, Giulio Bandinelli, and others, sat waiting for the arrival of Carlo Ammiani; when he came Carlo had to bear with the looks of mastiffs for being late. He shook Merthyr's hand hurriedly, and as soon as the door was fastened, began to speak. His first sentence brought a grunt of derision from Ugo Corte. It declared that there was no hope of a rising in Milan. Carlo swung round upon the Bergamasc. "Observe our leader," Agostino whispered to Merthyr; "it would be kindness to give him a duel." More than one tumult of outcries had to be stilled before Merthyr gathered any notion of the designs of the persons present. Bergamasc sneered at Brescian, and both united in contempt of the Milanese, who, having a burden on their minds, appealed at once to their individual willingness to use the sword in vindication of Milan against its traducers. By a great effort, Carlo got some self-mastery. He admitted, colouring horribly, that Brescia and Bergamo were ready, and Milan was not; therefore those noble cities (he read excerpts from letters showing their readiness) were to take the lead, and thither on the morrow-night he would go, let the tidings from the king's army be what they might.

Merthyr quitted the place rather impressed by his eloquence, but unfavourably by his feverish look. Countess d'Isorella had been referred to as one who served the cause ably and faithfully. In alluding to her, Carlo bit his lip; he did not proceed until surrounding murmurs of satisfaction encouraged him to continue a sort of formal eulogy of the lady, which proved to be a defence against foregone charges, for Corte retracted an accusation, and said that he had no fault to find with the countess. A proposal to join the enterprise was put to Merthyr, but his engagement with the Chief in Rome saved him from hearing much of the marvellous facilities of the plot. "I should have wished to see you to-night," Carlo said as they were parting. Merthyr named his hotel. Carlo nodded. "My wife is still slightly feeble," he said.

"I regret it," Merthyr rejoined.

"She is not ill."

"No, it cannot be want of courage," Merthyr spoke at random.

"Yes, that's true," said Carlo, as vacantly. "You will see her while I am travelling."

"I hope to find the Countess Alessandra well enough to receive me."

"Always; always," said Carlo, wishing apparently to say more. Merthyr waited an instant, but Carlo broke into a conventional smile of adieu.

"While he is travelling," Merthyr repeated to Agostino, who had stood by during the brief dialogue, and led the way to the Corso.

"He did not say how far!" was the old man's ejaculation.

"But, good heaven! if you think he's on an unfortunate errand, why don't you stop him, advise him?" Merthyr broke out.

"Advise him! stop him! my friend. I would advise him, if I had the patience of angels; stop him, if I had the power of Lucifer. Did you not see that he shunned speaking to me? I have been such a perpetual dish of vinegar under his nose for the last month, that the poor fellow sniffs when I draw near. He must go his way. He leads a torrent that must sweep him on. Corte, Sana, and the rest would be in Rome now, but for him. So should I. Your Agostino, however, is not of Bergamo, or of Brescia; he is not a madman; simply a poor rheumatic Piedmontese, who discerns the point where a united Italy may fix its standard. I would start for Rome to-morrow, if I could leave her—my soul's child!" Agostino raised his hand: "I do love the woman, Countess Alessandra Ammiani. I say, she is a peerless woman. Is she not?"

"There is none like her," said Merthyr.

"A peerless woman, recognized and sacrificed! I cannot leave her. If the Government here would lay hands on Carlo and do their worst at once, I would be off. They are too wary. I believe that they are luring him to his ruin. I can give no proofs, but I judge by the best evidence. What avails my telling him? I lose my temper the moment I begin to speak. A curst witch beguiles the handsome idiot—poor darling lad that he is! She has him—can I tell you how? She has got him—got him fast!—The nature of the chains are doubtless innocent, If those which a woman throws round us be ever distinguishable. He loves his wife—he is not a monster."

"He appears desperately feverish," said Merthyr.

"Did you not notice it? Yes, like a man pushed by his destiny out of the path. He is ashamed to hesitate; he cannot turn back. Ahead of him he sees a gulf. That army of Carlo Alberto may do something under its Pole. Prophecy is too easy. I say no more. We may have Lombardy open; and if so, my poor boy's vanity will be crowned: he will only have the king and his army against him then."

Discoursing in this wise, they reached the caffe where Beppo had appointed to meet his old master, and sat amid here and there a whitecoat, and many nods and whispers over such news as the privileged journals and the official gazette afforded.

Beppo's destination was to the Duchess of Graatli's palace. Nearing it, he perceived Luigi endeavouring to gain a passage beside the burly form of Jacob Baumwalder Feckelwitz, who presently seized him and hurled him into the road. As Beppo was sidling up the courtway, Luigi sprang back; Luigi made a rush; Jacob caught them both, but they wriggled out of his clutch, and Luigi, being the fearfuller, ran the farthest. While he was out of hearing, Beppo told Jacob to keep watch upon Luigi, as the bearer of an amorous letter from a signor of quality to Aennchen, the which he himself desired to obtain sight of; "for the wench has caused me three sleepless nights," he confessed frankly. Jacob affected not to understand. Luigi and Beppo now leaned against the wall on either side of him and baited him till he shook with rage.

"He is the lord of the duchess, his mistress—what a lucky fellow!" said Luigi. "When he's dog at the gates no one can approach her. When he isn't, you can fancy what!"—"He's only a mechanical contrivance; he's not a man," said Beppo. "He's the principal flea-catcher of the palace," said Luigi—"here he is all day, and at night the devil knows where he hunts."—Luigi hopped in a half-circle round the exacerbated Jacob, and finally provoked an assault that gave an opening to Beppo. They all ran in, Luigi last. Jacob chased Beppo up the stairs, lost him, and remembered what he had said of the letter borne by Luigi, for whom he determined to lie in waiting. "Better two in there than one," he thought. The two courted his

Aennchen openly; but Luigi, as the bearer of an amorous letter from the signor of quality, who could be no other than signor Antonio-Pericles, was the one to be intercepted. Like other jealous lovers, Jacob wanted to read Aennchen's answer, to be cured of his fatal passion for the maiden, and on this he set the entire force of his mind.

Running up by different staircases, Beppo and Luigi came upon Aennchen nearly at the same time. She turned a cold face on Beppo, and requested Luigi to follow her. Astonished to see him in such favour, Beppo was ready to provoke the quarrel before the kiss when she returned; but she said that she had obeyed her mistress's orders, and was obeying the duchess in refusing to speak of them, or of anything relating to them. She had promised him an interview in that little room leading into the duchess's boudoir. He pressed her to conduct him. "Ah; then it's not for me you come," she said. Beppo had calculated that the kiss would open his way to the room, and the quarrel disembarrass him of his pretty companion when there. "You have come to listen to conversation again," said Aennchen. "Ach! the fool a woman is to think that you Italians have any idea except self-interest when you, when you... talk nonsense to us. Go away, if you please. Good-evening." She dropped a curtsey with a surly coquetry, charming of its kind. Beppo protested that the room was dear to him because there first he had known for one blissful half-second the sweetness of her mouth.

"Who told you that persons who don't like your mistress are going to talk in there?" said Aennchen.

"You," said Beppo.

Aennchen drew up in triumph: "And now will you pretend that you didn't come up here to go in there to listen to what they say?"

Beppo clapped hands at her cleverness in trapping him. "Hush," said all her limbs and features, belying the previous formal "good-evening." He refused to be silent, thinking it a way of getting to the little antechamber. "Then, I tell you, downstairs you go," said Aennchen stiffly.

"Is it decided?" Beppo asked. "Then, good-evening. You detestable German girls can't love. One step—a smile: another step—a kiss. You tit-for-tat minx! Have you no notion of the sacredness of the sentiments which inspires me to petition that the place for our interview should be there where I tasted ecstatic joy for the space of a flash of lightning? I will go; but it is there that I will go, and I will await you there, signorina Aennchen. Yes, laugh at me! laugh at me!"

"No; really, I don't laugh at you, signor Beppo," said Aennchen, protesting in denial of what she was doing. "This way."

"No, it's that way," said Beppo.

"It's through here." She opened a door. "The duchess has a reception to-night, and you can't go round. Ach! you would not betray me?"

"Not if it were the duchess herself," said Beppo; "he would refuse to satisfy man's natural vanity, in such a case."

Eager to advance to the little antechamber, he allowed Aennchen to wait behind him. He heard the door shut and a lock turn, and he was in the dark, and alone, left to take counsel of his fingers' ends.

"She was born to it," Beppo remarked, to extenuate his outwitted cunning, when he found each door of the room fast against him.

On the following night Vittoria was to sing at a concert in the Duchess of Graatli's great saloon, and the duchess had humoured Pericles by consenting to his preposterous request that his spy should have an opportunity of hearing Countess d'Isorella and Irma di Karski in private conversation together, to discover whether there was any plot of any sort to vex the evening's entertainment; as the jealous spite of those two women, Pericles said, was equal to any devilry on earth. It happened that Countess d'Isorella did not come. Luigi, in despair,—was the hearer of a quick question and answer dialogue, in the obscure German tongue, between Anna von Lenkenstein and Irma di Karski; but a happy peep between the hanging curtains gave him sight of a letter passing from Anna's hands to Irma's. Anna quitted her. Irma, was looking at the superscription of the letter, an the act of passing in her steps, when Luigi tore the curtains apart, and sprang on her arm like a cat. Before her shrieks could bring succour, Luigi was bounding across the court with the letter in his possession. A dreadful hug awaited him; his pockets were ransacked, and he was pitched aching into the street. Jacob Baumwalder Feckelwitz went straightway under a gas-lamp, where he read the address of the letter to Countess d'Isorella. He doubted; he had a half-desire to tear the letter open. But a rumour of the attack upon Irma had spread among the domestics and Jacob prudently went up to his mistress. The duchess was sitting with Laura. She received the letter, eyed: it all over, and held it to a candle.

Laura's head was bent in dark meditation. The sudden increase of light aroused her, and she asked, "What is that?"

"A letter from Countess Anna to Countess d'Isorella," said the duchess.

"Burnt!" Laura screamed.

"It's only fair," the duchess remarked.

"From her to that woman! It may be priceless. Stop! Let me see what remains. Amalia! are you mad? Oh! you false friend. I would have sacrificed my right hand to see it."

"Try and love me still," said the duchess, letting her take one unburnt corner, and crumble the black tissuey fragments to smut in her hands.

There was no writing; the unburnt corner of the letter was a blank.

Laura fooled the wretched ashes between her palms. "Good-night," she said. "Your face will be of this colour to me, my dear, for long."

"I cannot behave disgracefully, even to keep your love, my beloved," said the duchess.

"You cannot betray a German, you mean," Laura retorted. "You could let a spy into the house."

"That was a childish matter—merely to satisfy a whim."

"I say you could let a spy into the house. Who is to know where the scruples of you women begin? I would have given my jewels, my head, my husband's sword, for a sight of that letter. I swear that it concerns us. Yes, us. You are a false friend. Fish-blooded creature! may it be a year before I look on you again. Hide among your miserable set!"

"Judge me when you are cooler, dearest," said the duchess, seeking to detain the impetuous sister of her affection by the sweeping skirts; but Laura spurned her touch, and went from her.

Irma drove to Countess d'Isorella's. Violetta was abed, and lay fair and placid as a Titian Venus, while Irma sputtered out her tale, with intermittent sobs. She rose upon her elbow, and planting it in her pillow, took half-a-dozen puffs of a cigarette, and then requested Irma to ring for her maid. "Do nothing till you see me again," she said; "and take my advice: always get to bed before midnight, or you'll have unmanageable wrinkles in a couple of years. If you had been in bed at a prudent hour to-night, this scandal would not have occurred."

"How can I be in bed? How could I help it?" moaned Irma, replying to the abstract rule, and the perplexing illustration of its force.

Violetta dismissed her. "After all, my wish is to save my poor Amaranto," she mused. "I am only doing now what I should have been doing in the daylight; and if I can't stop him, the Government must; and they will. Whatever the letter contained, I can anticipate it. He knows my profession and my necessities. I must have money. Why not from the rich German woman whom he jilted?"

She attributed Anna's apparent passion of revenge to a secret passion of unrequited love. What else was implied by her willingness to part with land and money for the key to his machinations?

Violetta would have understood a revenge directed against Angelo Guidascarpi, as the slayer of Anna's brother. But of him Anna had only inquired once, and carelessly, whether he was in Milan. Anna's mystical semi-patriotism—prompted by her hatred of Vittoria, hatred of Carlo as Angelo's cousin and protector, hatred of the Italy which held the three, who never took the name Tedesco on their tongues without loathing—was perfectly hidden from this shrewd head.

Some extra patrols were in the streets. As she stepped into the carriage, a man rushed up, speaking hoarsely and inarticulately, and jumped in beside her. She had discerned Barto Rizzo in time to give directions to her footman, before she was addressed by a body of gendarmes in pursuit, whom she mystified by entreating them to enter her house and search it through, if they supposed that any evil-doer had taken advantage of the open door. They informed her that a man had escaped from the civil prison. "Poor creature!" said the countess, with womanly pity; "but you must see that he is not in my house. How could three of you let one escape?" She drove off laughing at their vehement assertion that he would not have escaped from them. Barto Rizzo made her conduct him to Countess Ammiani's gates.

Violetta was frightened by his eyes when she tried to persuade him in her best coaxing manner to avoid Count Ammiani. In fact she apprehended that he would be very much in her way. She had no time for chagrin at her loss of power over him, though she was sensible of vexation. Barto folded his arms and sat with his head in his chest, silent, till they reached the' gates, when he said in French, "Madame, I am a nameless person in your train. Gabble!" he added, when the countess advised him not to enter; nor would he allow her to precede him by more than one step. Violetta sent up her name. The man had shaken her nerves. "At least, remember that your appearance should be decent," she said, catching sight of blood on his hands, and torn garments. "I expect, madame," he replied, "I shall not have time to wash before I am laid out. My time is short. I want tobacco. The washing can be done by-and-by, but not the smoking."

They were ushered up to the reception-room, where Countess Ammiani, Vittoria, and Carlo sat, awaiting the visitor whose unexpected name, cast in their midst at so troubled a season, had clothed her with some of the midnight's terrors.

CHAPTER XLIII

THE LAST MEETING IN MILAN

Barto Rizzo had silence about him without having to ask for it, when he followed Violetta into Countess Ammiani's saloon of reception. Carlo was leaning over his mother's chair, holding Vittoria's wrist across it, and so enclosing her, while both young faces were raised to the bowed forehead of the countess. They stood up. Violetta broke through the formal superlatives of an Italian greeting. "Speak to me alone," she murmured for Carlo's ear and glancing at Barto: "Here is a madman; a mild one, I trust." She contrived to show that she was not responsible for his intrusion. Countess Ammiani gathered Vittoria in her arms; Carlo stepped a pace before them. Terror was on the venerable lady's face, wrath on her son's. As he fronted Barto, he motioned a finger to the curtain hangings, and Violetta, quick at reading signs, found his bare sword there. "But you will not want it," she remarked, handing the hilt to him, and softly eyeing the impression of her warm touch on the steel as it passed.

"Carlo, thou son of Paolo! Countess Marcellina, wife of a true patriot! stand aside, both of you. It is between the Countess Alessandra and myself," so the man commenced, with his usual pomp of interjection. "Swords and big eyes,—are they things to stop me?" Barto laughed scornfully. He had spoken in the full roll of his voice, and the sword was hard back for the thrust.

Vittoria disengaged herself from the countess. "Speak to me," she said, dismayed by the look of what seemed an exaltation of madness in Barto's visage, but firm as far as the trembling of her limbs would let her be.

He dropped to her feet and kissed them.

"Emilia Alessandra Belloni! Vittoria! Countess Alessandra Ammiani! pity me. Hear this:—I hated you as the devil is hated. Yesterday I woke up in prison to hear that I must adore you. God of all the pits of punishment! was there ever one like this? I had to change heads."

It was the language of a distorted mind, and lamentable to hear when a sob shattered his voice.

"Am I mad?" he asked piteously, clasping his temples.

"You are as we are, if you weep," said Vittoria, to sooth him.

"Then I have been mad!" he cried, starting. "I knew you a wicked virgin—signora contessa, confess to me, marriage has changed you. Has it not changed you? In the name of the Father of the Saints, help me out of it:—my brain reels backwards. You were false, but marriage—It acts in this way with you women; yes, that we know—you were married, and you said, 'Now let us be faithful.' Did you not say that? I am forgiving, though none think it. You have only to confess. If you will not,—oh!" He smote his face, groaning.

Carlo spoke a stern word in an undertone; counselling him to be gone.

"If you will not—what was she to do?" Barto cut the question to interrogate his strayed wits. "Look at me, Countess Alessandra. I was in the prison. I heard that my Rosellina had a tight heart. She cried for her master, poor heathen, and I sprang out of the walls to her. There—there—she lay like a breathing board; a woman with a body like a coffin half alive; not an eye to show; nothing but a body and a whisper. She perished righteously, for she disobeyed. She acted without my orders: she dared to think! She will be damned, for she would have vengeance before she went. She glorified you over me—over Barto Rizzo. Oh! she shocked my soul. But she is dead, and I am her slave. Every word was of you. Take another head, Barto Rizzo your old one was mad: she said that to my soul. She died blessing you above me. I saw the last bit of life go up from her mouth blessing you. It's heard by this time in heaven, and it's written. Then I have had two years of madness. If she is right, I was wrong; I was a devil of hell. I know there's an eye given to dying creatures, and she looked with it, and she said, the soul of Rinaldo Guidascarpi, her angel, was glorifying you; and she thanked the sticking of her heart, when she tried to stab you, poor fool!"

Carlo interrupted: "Now go; you have said enough."

"No, let him speak," said Vittoria. She supposed that Barto was going to say that he had not given the order for her assassination. "You do not wish me dead, signore?"

"Nothing that is not standing in my way, signora contessa," said Barto; and his features blazed with a smile of happy self-justification. "I have killed a sentinel this night: Providence placed him there. I wish for no death, but I punish, and—ah! the cursed sight of the woman who calls me mad for two years. She thrusts a bar of iron in an engine at work, and says, Work on! work on! Were you not a traitress? Countess Alessandra, were you not once a traitress? Oh! confess it; save my head. Reflect, dear lady! it's cruel to make a man of a saintly sincerity look back—I count the months—seventeen months! to look back seventeen months, and see that his tongue was a clapper,—his will, his eyes, his ears, all about him, everything, stirred like a pot on the fire. I traced you. I saw your treachery. I said—I, I am her Day of Judgement. She shall look on me and perish, struck down by her own treachery. Were my senses false to me? I had lived in virtuous fidelity to my principles. None can accuse me. Why were my senses false, if my principles were true? I said you were a traitress. I saw it from the first. I had the divine contempt for women. My distrust of a woman was the eye of this brain, and I said—Follow her, dog her, find her out! I proved her false; but her devilish cunning deceived every other man in the world. Oh! let me bellow, for it's me she proves the mass of corruption! Tomorrow I die, and if I am mad now, what sort of a curse is that?

"Now to-morrow is an hour—a laugh! But if I've not been shot from a true bow—if I've been a sham for two years—if my name, and nature, bones, brains, were all false things hunting a shadow, Countess Alessandra, see the misery of Barto Rizzo! Look at those two years, and say that I had my head. Answer me, as you love your husband: are you heart and soul with him in the fresh fight for Lombardy?" He said this with a look penetrating and malignant, and then by a sudden flash pitifully entreating.

Carlo feared to provoke, revolted from the thought of slaying him. "Yes, yes," he interposed, "my wife is heart and soul in it. Go."

Barto looked from him to her with the eyes of a dog that awaits an order.

Victoria gathered her strength, and said: "I am not."

"It is her answer!" Barto roared, and from deep dejection his whole countenance radiated. "She says it— she might give the lie to a saint! I was never mad. I saw the spot, and put my finger on it, and not a madman can do that. My two years are my own. Mad now, for, see!

"I worship the creature. She is not heart and soul in it. She is not in it at all. She is a little woman, a lovely thing, a toy, a cantatrice. Joy to the big heart of Barto Rizzo! I am for Brescia!"

He flung his arm like a banner, and ran out.

Carlo laid his sword on a table. Vittoria's head was on his mother's bosom.

The hour was too full of imminent grief for either of the three to regard this scene as other than a gross intrusion ended.

"Why did you deny my words?" Carlo said coldly.

"I could not lie to make him wretched," she replied in a low murmur.

"Do you know what that 'I am for Brescia' means? He goes to stir the city before a soul is ready."

"I warned you that I should speak the truth of myself to-night, dearest."

"You should discern between speaking truth to a madman, and to a man."

Vittoria did not lift her eyes, and Carlo beckoned to Violetta, with whom he left the room.

"He is angry," Countess Ammiani murmured. "My child, you cannot deal with men in a fever unless you learn to dissemble; and there is exemption for doing it, both in plain sense, and in our religion. If I could arrest him, I would speak boldly. It is, alas! vain to dream of that; and it is therefore an unkindness to cause him irritation. Carlo has given way to you by allowing you to be here when his friends assemble. He knows your intention to speak. He has done more than would have been permitted by my husband to me, though I too was well-beloved."

Vittoria continued silent that her head might be cherished where it lay. She was roused from a stupor by hearing new voices. Laura's lips came pressing to her cheek. Colonel Corte, Agostino, Marco Sana, and Angelo Guidascarpi, saluted her. Angelo she kissed.

"That lady should be abed and asleep," Corte was heard to say.

The remark passed without notice. Angelo talked apart with Vittoria. He had seen the dying of the woman whose hand had been checked in the act of striking by the very passion of animal hatred which raised it. He spoke of her affectionately, attesting to the fact that Barto Rizzo had not prompted her guilt. Vittoria moaned at a short outline that he gave of the last minutes between those two, in which her name was dreadfully and fatally, incomprehensibly prominent.

All were waiting impatiently for Carlo's return.

When he appeared he informed his mother that the Countess d'Isorella would remain in the house that night, and his mother passed out to her abhorred guest, who, for the time at least, could not be doing further mischief.

It was a meeting for the final disposition of things before the outbreak. Carlo had begun to speak when Corte drew his attention to the fact that ladies were present, at which Carlo put out his hand as if introducing them, and went on speaking.

"Your wife is here," said Corte.

"My wife and signora Piaveni," Carlo rejoined. "I have consented to my wife's particular wish to be present."

"The signora Piaveni's opinions are known: your wife's are not."

"Countess Alessandra shares mine," said Laura, rather tremulously.

Countess Ammiani at the same time returned and took Vittoria's hand and pressed it with force. Carlo looked at them both.

"I have to ask your excuses, gentlemen. My wife, my mother, and signora Piaveni, have served the cause we worship sufficiently to claim a right—I am sorry to use such phrases; you understand my meaning. Permit them to remain. I have to tell you that Barto Rizzo has been here: he has started for Brescia. I should have had to kill him to stop him—a measure that I did not undertake."

"Being your duty!" remarked Corte.

Agostino corrected him with a sarcasm.

"I cannot allow the presence of ladies to exclude a comment on manifest indifference," said Corte. "Pass on to the details, if you have any."

"The details are these," Carlo resumed, too proud to show a shade of self-command; "my cousin Angelo leaves Milan before morning. You, Colonel Corte, will be in Bergamo at noon to-morrow. Marco and Angelo will await my coming in Brescia, where we shall find Giulio and the rest. I join them at five on the following afternoon, and my arrival signals the revolt. We have decided that the news from the king's army is good."

A perceptible shudder in Vittoria's frame at this concluding sentence caught Corte's eye.

"Are you dissatisfied with that arrangement?" he addressed her boldly.

"I am, Colonel Corte," she replied. So simple was the answering tone of her voice that Corte had not a word.

"It is my husband who is going," Vittoria spoke on steadily; "him I am prepared to sacrifice, as I am myself. If he thinks it right to throw himself into Brescia, nothing is left for me but to thank him for having done me the honour to consult me. His will is firm. I trust to God that he is wise. I look on him now as one of many brave men whose lives belong to Italy, and if they all are misdirected and perish, we have no more; we are lost. The king is on the Ticino; the Chief is in Rome. I desire to entreat you to take counsel before you act in anticipation of the king's fortune. I see that it is a crushed life in Lombardy. In Rome there is one who can lead and govern. He has suffered and is calm. He calls to you to strengthen his hands. My prayer to you is to take counsel. I know the hour is late; but it is not too late for wisdom. Forgive me if I am not speaking humbly. Brescia is but Brescia; Rome is Italy. I have understood little of my country until these last days, though I have both talked and sung of her glories. I know that a deep duty binds you to Bergamo and to Brescia—poor Milan we must not think of. You are not personally pledged to Rome: yet Rome may have the greatest claims on you. The heart of our country is beginning to beat there. Colonel Corte! signor Marco! my Agostino! my cousin Angelo! it is not a woman asking for the safety of her husband, but one of the blood of Italy who begs to offer you her voice, without seeking to disturb your judgement."

She ceased.

"Without seeking to disturb their judgement!" cried Laura. "Why not, when the judgement is in error?"

To Laura's fiery temperament Vittoria's speech had been feebleness. She was insensible to that which the men felt conveyed to them by the absence of emotion in the language of a woman so sorrowfully placed. "Wait," she said, "wait for the news from Carlo Alberto, if you determine to play at swords and guns in narrow streets." She spoke long and vehemently, using irony, coarse and fine, with the eloquence which was her gift. In conclusion she apostrophized Colonel Corte as one who had loved him might have done. He was indeed that figure of indomitable strength to which her spirit, exhausted by intensity of passion, clung more than to any other on earth, though she did not love him, scarcely liked him.

Corte asked her curiously—for she had surprised and vexed his softer side—why she distinguished him with such remarkable phrases only to declare her contempt for him.

"It's the flag whipping the flag-pole," murmured Agostino; and he now spoke briefly in support of the expedition to Rome; or at least in favour of delay until the King of Sardinia had gained a battle. While he was speaking, Merthyr entered the room, and behind him a messenger who brought word that Bergamo had risen.

The men drew hurriedly together, and Countess Ammiani, Vittoria and Laura stood ready to leave them.

"You will give me, five minutes?" Vittoria whispered to her husband, and he nodded.

"Merthyr," she said, passing him, "can I have your word that you will not go from me?"

Merthyr gave her his word after he had looked on her face.

"Send to me every two hours, that I may know you are near," she added; "do not fear waking me. Or, no, dear friend; why should I have any concealment from you? Be not a moment absent, if you would not have me fall to the ground a second time: follow me."

Even as he hesitated, for he had urgent stuff to communicate to Carlo, he could see a dreadful whiteness rising on her face, darkening the circles of her eyes.

"It's life or death, my dearest, and I am bound to live," she said. Her voice sprang up from tears.

Merthyr turned and tried in vain to get a hearing among the excited, voluble men. They shook his hand, patted his shoulder, and counselled him to leave them. He obtained Carlo's promise that he would not quit the house without granting him an interview; after which he passed out to Vittoria, where Countess Ammiani and Laura sat weeping by the door.

CHAPTER XLIV

THE WIFE AND THE HUSBAND

When they were alone Merthyr said: "I cannot give many minutes, not much time. I have to speak to your husband."

She answered: "Give me many minutes—much time. All other speaking is vain here."

"It concerns his safety."

"It will not save him."

"But I have evidence that he is betrayed. His plans are known; a trap is set for him. If he moves, he walks into a pit."

"You would talk reason, Merthyr," Vittoria sighed. "Talk it to me. I can listen; I thirst for it. I beat at the bars of a cage all day. When I saw you this afternoon, I looked on another life. It was too sudden, and I swooned. That was my only show of weakness. Since then you are the only strength I feel."

"Have they all become Barto Rizzos?" Merthyr exclaimed.

"Beloved, I will open my mind to you," said Vittoria. "I am cowardly, and I thought I had such courage! Tonight a poor mad creature has been here, who has oppressed me, I cannot say how long, with real fear—that I only understand now that I know the little ground I had for it. I am even pleased that one like Barto Rizzo should see me in a better light. I find the thought smiling in my heart when every other thing is utterly dark there. You have heard that Carlo goes to Brescia. When I was married, I lost sight of Italy, and everything but happiness. I suffer as I deserve for it now. I could have turned my husband from this black path; I preferred to dream and sing. I would not see—it was my pride that would not let me see his error. My cowardice would not let me wound him with a single suggestion. You say that he is betrayed. Then he is betrayed by the woman who has never been unintelligible to me. We were in Turin surrounded by intrigues, and there I thanked her so much for leaving me the days with my husband by

Lake Orta that I did not seek to open his eyes to her. We came to Milan, and here I have been thanking her for the happy days in Turin. Carlo is no longer to blame if he will not listen to me. I have helped to teach him that I am no better than any of these Italian women whom he despises. I spoke to him as his wife should do, at last. He feigned to think me jealous, and I too remember the words of the reproach, as if they had a meaning. Ah, my friend! I would say of nothing that it is impossible, except this task of recovering lost ground with one who is young. Experience of trouble has made me older than he. When he accused me of jealousy, I could mention Countess d'Isorella's name no more. I confess to that. Yet I knew my husband feigned. I knew that he could not conceive the idea of jealousy existing in me, as little as I could imagine unfaithfulness in him. But my lips would not take her name! Wretched cowardice cannot go farther. I spoke of Rome. As often as I spoke, that name was enough to shake me off: he had but to utter it, and I became dumb. He did it to obtain peace; for no other cause. So, by degrees, I have learnt the fatal truth. He has trusted her, for she is very skilful; distrusting her, for she is treacherous. He has, therefore, believed excessively in his ability to make use of her, and to counteract her baseness. I saw his error from the first; and I went on dreaming and singing; and now this night has come!"

Vittoria shadowed her eyes.

"I will go to him at once," said Merthyr.

"Yes; I am relieved. Go, dear friend," she sobbed; "you have given me tears, as I hoped. You will not turn him; had it been possible, could I have kept you from him so long? I know that you will not turn him from his purpose, for I know what a weight it is that presses him forward in that path. Do not imagine our love to be broken. He will convince you that it is not. He has the nature of an angel. He permitted me to speak before these men to-night—feeble thing that I am! It was a last effort. I might as well have tried to push a rock."

She rose at a noise of voices in the hall below.

"They are going, Merthyr. See him now. There may be help in heaven; if one could think it! If help were given to this country—if help were only visible! The want of it makes us all without faith."

"Hush! you may hear good news from Carlo Alberto in a few hours," said Merthyr.

"Ask Laura; she has witnessed how he can be shattered," Vittoria replied bitterly.

Merthyr pressed her fingers. He was met by Carlo on the stairs.

"Quick!" Carlo said; "I have scarce a minute to spare. I have my adieux to make, and the tears have set in already. First, a request: you will promise to remain beside my wife; she will want more than her own strength."

Such a request, coming from an Italian husband, was so great a proof of the noble character of his love and his knowledge of the woman he loved, that Merthyr took him in his arms and kissed him.

"Get it over quickly, dear good fellow," Carlo murmured; "you have something to tell me. Whatever it is, it's air; but I'll listen."

They passed into a vacant room. "You know you are betrayed," Merthyr began.

"Not exactly that," said Carlo, humming carelessly.

"Positively and absolutely. The Countess d'Isorella has sold your secrets."

"I commend her to the profit she has made by it."

"Do you play with your life?"

Carlo was about to answer in the tone he had assumed for the interview. He checked the laugh on his lips.

"She must have some regard for my life, such as it's worth, since, to tell you the truth, she is in the house now, and came here to give me fair warning."

"Then, you trust her."

"I? Not a single woman in the world!—that is, for a conspiracy."

It was an utterly fatuous piece of speech. Merthyr allowed it to slip, and studied him to see where he was vulnerable.

"She is in the house, you say. Will you cause her to come before me?"

"Curiously," said Carlo, "I kept her for some purpose of the sort. Will I? and have a scandal now? Oh! no. Let her sleep."

Whether he spoke from noble-mindedness or indifference, Merthyr could not guess.

"I have a message from your friend Luciano. He sends you his love, in case he should be shot the first, and says that when Lombardy is free he hopes you will not forget old comrades who are in Rome."

"Forget him! I would to God I could sit and talk of him for hours. Luciano! Luciano! He has no wife."

Carlo spoke on hoarsely. "Tell me what authority you have for charging Countess d'Isorella with... with whatever it may be."

"A conversation between Countess Anna of Lenkenstein and a Major Nagen, in the Duchess of Graatli's house, was overheard by our Beppo. They spoke German. The rascal had a German sweetheart with him. She imprisoned him for some trespass, and had come stealing in to rescue him, when those two entered the room. Countess Anna detailed to Nagen the course of your recent plotting. She named the hour this morning when you are to start for Brescia. She stated what force you have, what arms you expect; she named you all."

"Nagen—Nagen," Carlo repeated; "the man's unknown to me."

"It's sufficient that he is an Austrian officer."

"Quite. She hates me, and she has reason, for she's aware that I mean to fight her lover, and choose my time. The blood of my friends is on that man's head."

"I will finish what I have to say," pursued Merthyr. "When Beppo had related as much as he could make out from his sweetheart's translation, I went straight to the duchess. She is an Austrian, and a good and reasonable woman. She informed me that a letter addressed by Countess Anna to Countess d'Isorella fell into her hands this night. She burnt it unopened. I leave it to you to consider whether you have been betrayed and who has betrayed you. The secret was bought. Beppo himself caught the words, 'from a mercenary Italian.' The duchess tells me that Countess Anna is in the habit of alluding to Countess d'Isorella in those terms."

Carlo stretched his arms like a man who cannot hide the yawning fit.

"I promised my wife five minutes, though we have had the worst of the parting over. Perhaps you will wait for me; I may have a word to say."

He was absent for little more than the space named. When he returned, he was careful to hide his face. He locked the door, and leading Merthyr to an inner room, laid his watch on the table, and said: "Now, friend, you will see that I have nothing to shrink from, for I am going to do execution upon myself, and before him whom I would, above all other men, have think well of me. My wife supposes that I am pledged to this Brescian business because I am insanely patriotic. If I might join Luciano tomorrow I would shout like a boy. I would be content to serve as the lowest in the ranks, if I might be with you all under the Chief. Rome crowns him, and Brescia is my bloody ditch, and it is deserved! When I was a little younger—I am a boy still, no doubt—I had the honour to be distinguished by a handsome woman; and when I grew a little older, I discovered by chance that she had wit. The lady is the Countess Violetta d'Isorella. It is a grief to me to know that she is sordid: it hurts my vanity the more. Perhaps: you begin to perceive that vanity governs me. The signora Laura has not expressed her opinion on this subject with any reserve, but to Violetta belongs the merit of having seen it without waiting for the signs. First—it is a small matter, but you are English—let me assure you that my wife has had no rival. I have taunted her with jealousy when I knew that it was neither in her nature to feel it, nor in mine to give reason for it. No man who has a spark of his Maker in him could be unfaithful to such a woman. When Lombardy was crushed, we were in the dust. I fancy we none of us knew how miserably we had fallen—we, as men. The purest—I dare say, the bravest—marched to Rome. God bless my Luciano there! But I, sir, I, my friend, I, Merthyr, I said proudly that I would not abandon a beaten country: and I was admired for my devotion. The dear old poet, Agostino, praised me. It stopped his epigrams—during a certain time, at least. Colonel Corte admired me. Marco Sana, Giulio Bandinelli admired me. Vast numbers admired me. I need not add that I admired myself. I plunged into intrigues with princes, and priests, and republicans. A clever woman was at my elbow. In the midst of all this, my marriage: I had seven weeks of peace; and then I saw what I was. You feel that you are tired, when you want to go another way and you feel that you have been mad when you want to undo your work. But I could not break the chains I had wrought, for I was a chief of followers. The men had come from exile, or they had refused to join the Roman enterprise:—they, in fact, had bound themselves to me; and that means, I was irrevocably bound to them. I had an insult to wipe out: I refrained from doing it, sincerely, I may tell you, on the ground that this admired life of mine was precious. I will heap no more clumsy irony on it: I can pity it. Do you see now how I stand? I know that I cannot rely on the king's luck or on the skill of his generals, or on the power of his army, or on the spirit in Lombardy: neither on men nor on angels. But I cannot draw back. I have set going a machine that's merciless. From the day it began working, every moment has added to its force. Do not judge me by your English eyes: other lands, other habits; other habits, other thoughts.

And besides, if honour said nothing, simple humanity would preserve me from leaving my band to perish like a flock of sheep."

He uttered this with a profound conviction of his quality as leader, that escaped the lurid play of self-inspection which characterized what he had previously spoken, and served singularly in bearing witness to the truth of his charge against himself.

"Useless!" he said, waving his hand at anticipated remonstrances. "Look with the eyes of my country; not with your own, my friend. I am disgraced if I do not go out. My friends are disgraced if I do not head them in. Brescia—sacrificed!—murdered!—how can I say what? Can I live under disgrace or remorse? The king stakes on his army; I on the king. Whether he fights and wins, or fights and loses, I go out. I have promised my men—promised them success, I believe!—God forgive me! Did you ever see a fated man before? None had plotted against me. I have woven my own web, and that's the fatal thing. I have a wife, the sweetest woman of her time. Goodnight to her! our parting is over."

He glanced at his watch. "Perhaps she will be at the door below. Her heart beats like mine just now. You wish to say that you think me betrayed, and therefore I may draw back? Did you not hear that Bergamo has risen? The Brescians are up too by this time. Gallant Brescians! they never belie the proverb in their honour; and to die among them would be sweet if I had all my manhood about me. You would have me making a scene with Violetta."

"Set the woman face to face with me!" cried Merthyr, sighting a gleam of hope.

Carlo smiled. "Can she bear my burden though she be ten times guilty? Let her sleep. I have her here harmless for the night. The Brescians are up:—that's an hour that has struck, and there's no calling it to move a step in the rear. Brescia under the big Eastern hill which throws a cloak on it at sunrise! Brescia is always the eagle that looks over Lombardy! And Bergamo! you know the terraces of Bergamo. Aren't they like a morning sky? Dying there is not death; it's flying into the dawn. You Romans envy us. Come, confess it; you envy us. You have no Alps, no crimson hills, nothing but old walls to look on while you fight. Farewell, Merthyr Powys. I hear my servant's foot outside. My horse is awaiting me saddled, a mile from the city. Perhaps I shall see my wife again at the door below, or in heaven. Addio! Kiss Luciano for me. Tell him that I knew myself as well as he did, before the end came. Enrico, Emilio, and the others—tell them I love them. I doubt if there will ever be but a ghost of me to fight beside them in Rome. And there's no honour, Merthyr, in a ghost's fighting, because he's shotproof; so I won't say what the valiant disembodied 'I' may do by-and-by."

He held his hands out, with the light soft smile of one who asks forgiveness for flippant speech, and concluded firmly: "I have talked enough, and you are the man of sense I thought you; for to give me advice is childish when no power on earth could make me follow it. Addio! Kiss me."

They embraced. Merthyr said no more than that he would place messengers on the road to Brescia to carry news of the king's army. His voice was thick, and when Carlo laughed at him, his sensations strangely reversed their situations.

There were two cloaked figures at different points in the descent of the stairs. These rose severally at Carlo's approach, took him to their bosoms, and kissed him in silence. They were his mother and Laura. A third crouched by the door of the courtyard, which was his wife.

Merthyr kept aloof until the heavy door rolled a long dull sound. Vittoria's head was shawled over. She stood where her husband had left her, groping for him with one hand, that closed tremblingly hard on Merthyr when he touched it. Not a word was uttered in the house.

CHAPTER XLV

SHOWS MANY PATHS CONVERGING TO THE END

Until daylight Merthyr sat by himself, trying to realize the progressive steps of the destiny which seemed like a visible hand upon Count Ammiani, that he might know it to be nothing else than Carlo's work. He sat in darkness in the room where Carlo had spoken, thinking of him as living and dead. The brilliant life in Carlo protested against a possible fatal tendency in his acts so irrevocable as to plunge him to destruction when his head was clear, his blood cool, and a choice lay open to him. That brilliant young life, that fine face, the tones of Carlo's voice, swept about Merthyr, accusing him of stupid fatalism. Grief stopped his answer to the charge; but in his wise mind he knew Carlo to have surveyed things justly; and that the Fates are within us. Those which are the forces of the outer world are as shadows to the power we have created within us. He felt this because it was his gathered wisdom. Human compassion, and love for the unhappy youth, crushed it in his heart, and he marvelled how he could have been paralyzed when he had a chance of interceding. Can a man stay a torrent? But a noble and fair young life in peril will not allow our philosophy to liken it to things of nature. The downward course of a fall that takes many waters till it rushes irresistibly is not the course of any life. Yet it is true that our destiny is of our own weaving. Carlo's involvements cast him into extreme peril, almost certain death, unless he abjured his honour, dearer than a life made precious by love. Merthyr saw that it was not vanity, but honour; for Carlo stood pledged to lead a forlorn enterprise, the ripeness of his own scheming. In the imminent hour Carlo had recognized his position as Merthyr with the wisdom of years looked on it. That was what had paralyzed the older man, though he could not subsequently trace the cause. Thinking of the beauty of the youth, husband of the woman who was to his soul utterly an angel, Merthyr sat in the anguish of self-accusation, believing that some remonstrance, some inspired word, might have turned him, and half dreading to sound his own heart, as if an evil knowledge of his nature haunted it.

He rose up at last with a cry. The door opened, and Giacinta, Vittoria's maid, appeared, bearing a lamp. She had been sitting outside, waiting to hear him stir before she intruded. He touched her cheek kindly, and thought that one could do little better than die, if need were, in the service of such a people. She said that her mistress was kneeling. She wished to make coffee for him, and Merthyr let her do it, knowing the comfort there is to a woman in the ministering occupation of her hands. It was soon daylight. Beppo had not come back to the house.

"No one has left the house?" Merthyr asked.

"Not since—" she answered convulsively.

"The Countess d'Isorella is here?"

"Yes, signore."

"Asleep?" he put the question mournfully, in remembrance of Carlo's "Let her sleep!"

"Yes, signore; like the first night after confession."

"She resides, I think, in the Corso Venezia. When she awakens, let her know that I request to have the honour of conducting her."

"Yes, signore. Her carriage is still at the gates. The countess's horses are accustomed to stand."

Merthyr knew this for a hint against his leaving, as well as against the lady's character.

"Let your mistress be assured that I shall on no account be long absent at any time."

"Signore, I shall do so," said Giacinta.

She brought him word soon after, that Countess d'Isorella was stirring. Merthyr met Violetta on the stairs.

"Can it be true?" she accosted him first.

"Count Ammiani has left for Brescia," he replied.

"In spite of my warning?"

Merthyr gave space for her to pass into the room. She appeared undecided, saying that she had a dismal apprehension of her not having dismissed her coachman overnight.

"In spite of my warning," she murmured again, "he has really gone? Surely I cannot have slept more than three hours."

"It was Count Ammiani's wish that you should enjoy your full sleep undisturbed in his house," said Merthyr, "As regards your warning to him, he has left Milan perfectly convinced of the gravity of a warning that comes from you."

Violetta shrugged lightly. "Then all we have to do is to pray for the success of Carlo Alberto."

"Oh! pardon me, countess," Merthyr rejoined, "prayers may be useful, but you at least have something to do besides."

His eyes caught hers firmly as they were letting a wild look of interrogation fall on him, and he continued with perfect courtesy, "You will accompany me to see Countess Anna of Lenkenstein. You have great influence, madame. It is not Count Ammiani's request; for, as I informed you, it was his wish that you should enjoy your repose. The request is mine, because his life is dear to me. Nagen, I think, is the name of the Austrian officer who has started for Brescia."

She had in self-defence to express surprise while he spoke, which compelled her to meet his mastering sight and submit to a struggle of vision sufficient to show him that he had hit a sort of guilty consciousness. Otherwise she was not discomposed, and with marvellous sagacity she accepted the forbearance he assumed, not affecting innocence to challenge it, as silly criminals always do when they are exposed, but answering quite in the tone of innocence, and so throwing the burden by an appearance of mutual consent on some unnamed third person.

"Certainly; let us go to Countess Anna of Lenkenstein, if you think fit. I have to rely on your judgement. I quite abjure my own. If I have to plead for anything, I am going before a woman, remember."

"I do not forget it," said Merthyr.

"The expedition to Brescia may be unfortunate," she resumed hurriedly; "I wish it had not been undertaken. At any rate, it rescues Count Ammiani from an expedition to Rome, and his slavish devotion to that priest-hating man whom he calls, or called, his Chief. At Brescia he is not outraging the head of our religion. That is a gain."

"A gain for him in the next world?" said Merthyr. "I believe that Countess Anna of Lenkenstein is also a fervent Catholic; is she not?"

"I trust so."

"On behalf of her peace of mind, I trust so, too. In that case, she also must be a sound sleeper."

"We shall have to awaken her. What excuse—what am I to say to her?"

"I beg you to wait for the occasion, Countess d'Isorella. The words will come."

Violetta bit her lip. She had consented to this extraordinary step in an amazement. As she contemplated it now, it seemed worse than a partial confession and an appeal to his generosity. She broke out in pity for her horses, in dread of her coachman, declaring that it was impossible for her to give him the order to drive her anywhere but home.

"With your permission, countess, I will undertake to give him the order," said Merthyr.

"But have you no compassion, signor Powys? and you are an Englishman! I thought that Englishmen were excessively compassionate with horses."

"They have been known to kill them in the service of their friends, nevertheless."

"Well!"—Violetta had recourse to the expression of her shoulders—"and I am really to see Countess Anna?"

"In my presence."

"Oh! that cannot be. Pardon me; it is impossible. She will decline the scene. I say it with the utmost sincerity: I know that she will refuse."

"Then, countess," Merthyr's face grew hard, "if I am not to be in your company to prompt you, allow me to instruct you beforehand."

Violetta looked at him eagerly, as one looks for tidings, with an involuntary beseeching quiver of the strained eyelids.

"No irony!" she said, fearing horribly that he was about to throw off the mask of irony.

This desperate effort of her wits at the crisis succeeded.

Merthyr, not knowing what design he had, hopeless of any definite end in tormenting the woman, and never having it in his mind merely to punish, was diverted by the exclamation to speak ironically. "You can tell Countess Anna that it is only her temporal sovereign who is attacked, and that therefore—" he could not continue.

"Some affection?" he murmured, in intense grief.

His manly forbearance touched her whose moral wit was too blunt to apprehend the contempt in it.

"Much affection—much!" Violetta exclaimed. "I have a deep affection for Count Ammiani; an old friendship. Believe me! believe me! I came here last night to save him. Anything on earth that I can do, I will do—on my honour; and do not smile at that—I have never pledged it without fulfilling the oath. I will not sleep while I can aid in preserving him. He shall know that I am not the base person he has conceived me to be. You, signor Powys, are not a man to paint all women black that are a little less than celestial—are you? I am told it is a trick with your countrymen; and they have a poet who knew us! I entreat you to confide in me. I am at present quite unaware that Count Ammiani runs particular—I mean personal danger. He is in danger, of course; everyone can see it. But, on my honour—and never in my life have I spoken so earnestly, my friends would hardly recognize me—I declare to you on my faith as a Christian lady, I am ignorant of any plot against him. I can take a Cross and kiss it, like a peasant, and swear to you by the Madonna that I know nothing of it."

She corrected her ardour, half-exulting in finding herself carried so far and so swimmingly on a tide of truth, half wondering whether the flowering beauty of her face in excitement had struck his sensibility. He was cold and speculative.

"Ah!" she said, "if I were to ask my compatriots to put faith in a woman's pure friendship for a man, I should know the answer; but you, signor Powys, who have shown us that a man is capable of the purest friendship for a woman, should believe me."

He led her down to the gates, where her coachman sat muffled in a three-quarter sleep. The word was given to drive to her own house; rejoiced by which she called his attention deploringly to the condition of her horses, requesting him to say whether he could imagine them the best English, and confessing with regret, that she killed three sets a year—loved them well, notwithstanding. Merthyr saw enough of her to feel that she was one of the weak creatures who are strong through our greater weakness; and, either by intuition or quick wit, too lively and too subtle to be caught by simple suspicion. She even divined that reflection might tell him she had evaded him by an artifice—a piece of gross cajolery; and said, laughing: "Concerning friendship, I could offer it to a boy, like Carlo Ammiani; not to you, signor Powys. I know that I must check a youth, and I am on my guard. I should be eternally tormented to discover whether your armour was proof."

"I dare say that a lady who had those torments would soon be able to make them mine," said Merthyr.

"You could not pay a fairer compliment to some one else," she remarked. In truth, the candid personal avowal seemed to her to hold up Vittoria's sacred honour in a crystal, and the more she thought of it, the more she respected him, for his shrewd intelligence, if not for his sincerity; but on the whole she fancied him a loyal friend, not solely a clever maker of phrases; and she was pleased with herself for thinking such a matter possible, in spite of her education.

"I do most solemnly hope that you may not have to sustain Countess Alessandra under any affliction whatsoever," she said at parting.

Violetta had escaped an exposure—a rank and naked accusation of her character and deeds. She feared nothing but that, being quite indifferent to opinion; a woman who would not have thought it preternaturally sad to have to walk as a penitent in the streets, with the provision of a very thick veil to cover her. She had escaped, but the moment she felt herself free, she was surprised by a sharp twinge of remorse. She summoned her maid to undress her, and smelt her favourite perfume, and lay in her bed, to complete her period of rest, closing her eyes there with a child's faith in pillows. Flying lights and blood-blotches rushed within a span of her forehead. She met this symptom promptly with a medical receipt; yet she had no sleep; nor would coffee give her sleep. She shrank from opium as deleterious to the constitution, and her mind settled on music as the remedy.

Some time after her craving for it had commenced, an Austrian foot regiment, marching to the drum, passed under her windows. The fife is a merry instrument; fife and drum colour the images of battle gaily; but the dull ringing Austrian step-drum, beating unaccompanied, strikes the mind with the real nature of battles, as the salt smell of powder strikes it, and more in horror, more as a child's imagination realizes bloodshed, where the scene is a rolling heaven, black and red on all sides, with pitiable men moving up to the mouth of butchery, the insufferable flashes, the dark illumination of red, red of black, like a vision of the shadows Life and Death in a shadow-fight over the dear men still living. Sensitive minds may be excited by a small stimulant to see such pictures. This regimental drum is like a song of the flat-headed savage in man. It has no rise or fall, but leads to the bloody business with an unvarying note, and a savage's dance in the middle of the rhythm. Violetta listened to it until her heart quickened with alarm lest she should be going to have a fever. She thought of Carlo Ammiani, and of the name of Nagen; she had seen him at the Lenkensteins. Her instant supposition was that Anna had perhaps paid heavily for the secret of Carlo's movements an purpose to place Major Nagen on the Brescian high-road to capture him. Capture meant a long imprisonment, if not execution. Partly for the sake of getting peace of mind—for she was shocked by her temporary inability to command repose—but with some hope of convincing Carlo that she strove to be of use to him, she sent for the spy Luigi, and at a cost of two hundred and twenty Austrian florins, obtained his promise upon oath to follow Count Ammiani into Brescia, if necessary, and deliver to him a letter she had written, wherein Nagen's name was mentioned, and Carlo was advised to avoid personal risks; the letter hinted that he might have incurred a private enmity, and he had better keep among his friends. She knew the writing of this letter to be the foolishest thing she had ever done. Two hundred and twenty florins—the man originally stipulated to have three hundred—was a large sum to pay for postage. However, sacrifices must now and then be made for friendship, and for sleep. When she had paid half the money, her mind was relieved, and she had the slumber which preserves beauty. Luigi was to be paid the other half on his return. "He may never return," she thought, while graciously dismissing him. The deduction by mental arithmetic of the two hundred and twenty, or the one hundred and ten florins, from the large amount Countess Anna was bound to pay her in turn, annoyed her, though she knew it was a trifle. For this lady, Milan, Turin, and Paris sighed deeply.

When he had left Violetta at her house in the Corso, Merthyr walked briskly for exercise, knowing that he would have need of his health and strength. He wanted a sight of Alps to wash out the image of the woman from his mind, and passed the old Marshal's habitation fronting the Gardens, wishing that he stood in the field against the fine old warrior, for whom he had a liking. Near the walls he discovered Beppo sitting pensively with his head between his two fists. Beppo had not seen Count Ammiani, but he had seen Barto Rizzo, and pointing to the walls, said that Barto had dropped down there. He had met him hurrying in the Corso Francesco. Barto took him to the house of Sarpo, the bookseller, who possessed a small printing-press. Beppo described vividly, with his usual vivacity of illustration, the stupefaction of the man at the apparition of his tormentor, whom he thought fast in prison; and how Barto had compelled him to print a proclamation to the Piedmontese, Lombards, and Venetians, setting forth that a battle had been fought South of the Ticino, and that Carlo Alberto was advancing on Milan, signed with the name of the Piedmontese Pole in command of the king's army. A second, framed as an order of the day, spoke of victory and the planting of the green, white and red banner on the Adige, and forward to the Isonzo.

"I can hear nothing of Carlo Alberto's victory," Beppo said; "no one has heard of it. Barto told us how the battle was fought, and the name of the young lieutenant who discovered the enemy's flank march, and got the artillery down on him, and pounded him so that—signore, it's amazing! I'm ready to cry, and laugh, and howl!—fifteen thousand men capitulated in a heap!"

"Don't you know you've been listening to a madman?" said Merthyr, irritated, and thoroughly angered to see Beppo's opposition to that view.

"Signore, Barto described the whole battle. It began at five o'clock in the morning."

"When it was dark!"

"Yes; when it was dark. He said so. And we sent up rockets, and caught the enemy coming on, and the cavalry of Alessandria fell upon two batteries of field guns and carried them off, and Colonel Romboni was shot in his back, and cries he, 'Best give up the ghost if you're hit in the rear. Evviva l'Italia!'"

"A Piedmontese colonel, you fool! he would have shouted 'Viva Carlo Alberto!'" said Merthyr, now critically disgusted with the tale, and refusing to hear more. Two hours later, he despatched Beppo to Carlo in Brescia, warning him that for some insane purpose these two proclamations had been printed by Barto Rizzo, and that they were false.

It was early on the morning of a second day, before sunrise, when Vittoria sent for Merthyr to conduct her to the cathedral. "There has been a battle," she said. Her lips hardly joined to frame the syllables in speech. Merthyr refrained from asking where she had heard of the battle. As soon as the Duomo doors were open, he led her in and left her standing shrinking under the great vault with her neck fearfully drawn on her shoulders, as one sees birds under thunder. He thought that she was losing courage. Choosing to go out on the steps rather than look on her, he was struck by the sight of two horsemen, who proved to be Austrian officers, rattling at racing speed past the Duomo up the Corso. The sight of them made it seem possible that a battle had been fought. As soon as he was free, Merthyr went to the Duchess of Graatli, from whom he had the news of Novara. The officers he had seen were Prince Radocky and Lieutenant Wilfrid Pierson, the old Marshal's emissaries of victory. They had made a bet on the bloody field about reaching Milan first, and the duchess affected to be full of the humour of this bet in order to conceal her exultation. The Lenkensteins called on her; the Countess of Lenkenstein, Anna, and Lena; and they were less considerate, and drew their joy openly from the source of his misery—a dreadful house for Merthyr to remain in; but he hoped to see Wilfrid, having heard the duchess rally Lena concerning the deeds of the white umbrella, which, Lena said, was pierced with balls, and had been preserved for her. "The dear foolish fellow insisted on marching right into the midst of the enemy with his absurd white umbrella; and wherever there was danger the men were seen following it. Prince Radocky told me the whole army was laughing. How he escaped death was a miracle!" She spoke unaffectedly of her admiration for the owner, and as Wilfrid came in she gave him brilliant eyes. He shook Merthyr's hand without looking at him. The ladies would talk of nothing but the battle, so he went up to Merthyr, and under pretext of an eager desire for English news, drew him away.

"Her husband was not there? not at Novara, I mean?" he said.

"He's at Brescia," said Merthyr.

"Well, thank goodness he didn't stand in those ranks!"

Wilfrid murmured, puffing thoughtfully over the picture they presented to his memory.

Merthyr then tried to hint to him that he had a sort of dull suspicion of Carlo's being in personal danger, but of what kind he could not say. He mentioned Weisspriess by name; and Nagen; and Countess Anna. Wilfrid said, "I'll find out if there's anything, only don't be fancying it. The man's in a bad hole at Brescia. Weisspriess, I believe, is at Verona. He's an honourable fellow. The utmost he would do would be to demand a duel; and I'm sure he's heartily sick of that work. Besides, he and Countess Anna have quarrelled. Meet me;—by the way, you and I mustn't be seen meeting, I suppose. The duchess is neutral ground. Come here to-night. And don't talk of me, but say that a friend asks how she is, and hopes—the best things you can say for me. I must go up to their confounded chatter again. Tell her there's no fear, none whatever. You all hate us, naturally; but you know that Austrian officers are gentlemen. Don't speak my name to her just yet. Unless, of course, she should happen to allude to me, which is unlikely. I had a dismal idea that her husband was at Novara."

The tender-hearted duchess sent a message to Vittoria, bidding her not to forget that she had promised her at Meran to 'love her always.'

"And tell her," she said to Merthyr, "that I do not think I shall have my rooms open for the concert to-morrow night. I prefer to let Antonio-Pericles go mad. She will not surely consider that she is bound by her promise to him? He drags poor Irma from place to place to make sure the miserable child is not plotting to destroy his concert, as that man Sarpo did. Irma is half dead, and hasn't the courage to offend him. She declares she depends upon him for her English reputation. She has already caught a violent cold, and her sneezing is frightful. I have never seen so abject a creature. I have no compassion at the sight of her."

That night Merthyr heard from Wilfrid that a plot against Carlo Ammiani did exist. He repeated things he had heard pass between Countess d'Isorella and Irma in the chamber of Pericles before the late battle. Modestly confessing that he was 'for some reasons' in high favour with Countess Lena, he added that after a long struggle he had brought her to confess that her sister had sworn to have Countess Alessandra Ammiani begging at her feet.

By mutual consent they went to consult the duchess. She repelled the notion of Austrian women conspiring. "An Austrian noble lady—do you think it possible that she would act secretly to serve a private hatred? Surely I may ask you, for my sake, to think better of us?"

Merthyr showed her an opening to his ground by suggesting that Anna's antipathy to Victoria might spring more from a patriotic than a private source.

"Oh! I will certainly make inquiries, if only to save Anna's reputation with her enemies," the duchess answered rather proudly.

It would have been a Novara to Pericles if Vittoria had refused to sing. He held the pecuniarily-embarrassed duchess sufficiently in his power to command a concert at her house; his argument to those who pressed him to spare Vittoria in a season of grief running seriously, with visible contempt of their intellects, thus: "A great voice is an ocean. You cannot drain it with forty dozen opera-hats. It is something found—an addition to the wealth of this life. Shall we not enjoy what we find? You do not wear out a picture by looking at it; likewise you do not wear out a voice by listening to it. A bird has wings;—here is a voice. Why were they given? I should say, to go into the air. Ah; but not if grandmother is ill. What is a grandmother to the wings and the voice? If to sing would kill,—yes, then let the puny thing be silent! But Sandra Belloni has a soul that has not a husband—except her Art. Her body is husbanded; but her soul is above her body. You would treat it as below. Art is her soul's husband! Besides, I have her promise. She is a girl who will go up to a loaded gun's muzzle if she gives her word. And besides, her husband may be shot to-morrow. So, all she sings now is clear gain."

Vittoria sent word to him that she would sing.

In the meantime a change had come upon Countess Anna. Weisspriess, her hero, appeared at her brother's house, fresh from the field of Novara, whither he had hurried from Verona on a bare pretext, that was a breach of military discipline requiring friendly interposition in high quarters. Unable to obtain an audience with Count Lenkenstein, he remained in the hall, hoping for things which he affected to care nothing for; and so it chanced that he saw Lena, who was mindful that her sister had suffered much from passive jealousy when Wilfrid returned from the glorious field, and led him to Anna, that she also might rejoice in a hero. Weisspriess did not refrain from declaring on the way that he would rather charge against a battery. Some time after, Anna lay in Lena's arms, sobbing out one of the wildest confessions ever made by woman:—she adored Weisspriess; she hated Nagen; but was miserably bound to the man she hated. "Oh! now I know what love is." She repeated this with transparent enjoyment of the opposing sensations by whose shock the knowledge was revealed to her.

"How can you be bound to Major Nagan?" asked Lena.

"Oh! why? except that I have been possessed by devils."

Anna moaned. "Living among these Italians has distempered my blood." She exclaimed that she was lost.

"In what way can you be lost?" said Lena.

"I have squandered more than half that I possess. I am almost a beggar. I am no longer the wealthy Countess Anna. I am much poorer than anyone of us."

"But Major Weisspriess is a man of honour, and if he loves you—"

"Yes; he loves me! he loves me! or would he come to me after I have sent him against a dozen swords? But he is poor; he must, must marry a wealthy woman. I used to hate him because I thought he had his eye on money. I love him for it now. He deserves wealth; he is a matchless hero. He is more than the first swordsman of our army; he is a knightly man. Oh my soul Johann!" She very soon fell to raving. Lena was implored by her to give her hand to Weisspriess in reward for his heroism—"For you are rich," Anna said; "you will not have to go to him feeling that you have made him face death a dozen times for your sake, and that you thank him and reward him by being a whimpering beggar in his arms. Do, dearest! Will you? Will you, to please me, marry Johann? He is not unworthy of you." And more of this hysterical hypocrisy, which brought on fits of weeping. "I have lived among these savages till I have ceased to be human—forgotten everything but my religion," she said. "I wanted Weisspriess to show them that they dared not stand up against a man of us, and to tame the snarling curs. He did. He is brave. He did as much as a man could do, but I was unappeasable. They seem to have bitten me till I had a devouring hunger to humiliate them. Lena, will you believe that I have no hate for Carlo Ammiani or the woman he has married? None! and yet, what have I done!" Anna smote her forehead. "They are nothing but little dots on a field for me. I don't care whether they live or die. It's like a thing done in sleep."

"I want to know what you have done," said Lena caressingly.

"You at least will try to reward our truest hero, and make up to him for your sister's unkindness, will you not?" Anna replied with a cajolery wonderfully like a sincere expression of her wishes. "He will be a good husband.. He has proved it by having been so faithful a—a lover. So you may be sure of him. And when he is yours, do not let him fight again, Lena, for I have a sickening presentiment that his next duel is his last."

"Tell me," Lena entreated her, "pray tell me what horrible thing you have done to prevent your marrying him."

"With their pride and their laughter," Anna made answer; "the fools! were they to sting us perpetually and not suffer for it? That woman, the Countess Alessandra, as she's now called—have you forgotten that she helped our Paul's assassin to escape? was she not eternally plotting against Austria? And I say that I love Austria. I love my country; I plot for my country. She and her husband plot, and I plot to thwart them. I have ruined myself in doing it. Oh, my heart! why has it commenced beating again? Why did Weisspriess come here? He offended me. He refused to do my orders, and left me empty-handed, and if he suffers too," Anna relieved a hard look with a smile of melancholy, "I hope he will not; I cannot say more."

"And I'm to console him if he does?" said Lena.

"At least, I shall be out of the way," said Anna. "I have still money enough to make me welcome in a convent."

"I am to marry him?" Lena persisted, and half induced Anna to act a feeble part, composed of sobs and kisses and full confession of her plight. Anna broke from her in time to leave what she had stated of herself vague and self-justificatory, so that she kept her pride, and could forgive, as she was ready to do even so far as to ask forgiveness in turn, when with her awakened enamoured heart she heard Vittoria sing at the concert of Pericles. Countess Alessandra's divine gift, which she would not withhold, though in a misery of apprehension; her grave eyes, which none could accuse of coldness, though they showed no emotion; her simple noble manner that seemed to lift her up among the forces threatening her; these expressions of a superior soul moved Anna under the influence of the incomparable voice to pass over envious contrasts, and feel the voice and the nature were one in that bosom. Could it be the same as the accursed woman who had stood before her at Meran? She could hardly frame the question, but she had the thought sufficiently firmly to save her dignity; she was affected by very strong emotion when Vittoria's singing ended, and nothing but the revival of the recollection of her old contempt preserved her from an impetuous desire to take the singer by the hand and have all clear between them; for they were now of equal rank to tolerating eyes. "But she has no religious warmth!" Anna reflected with a glow of satisfaction. The concert was broken up by Laura Piaveni. She said out loud that the presence of Major Weisspriess was intolerable to the Countess Alessandra. It happened that Weisspriess entered the room while Laura sat studying the effect produced by her countrywoman's voice on the thick eyelids of Austrian Anna; and Laura, seeing their enemy ready to weep in acknowledgment of their power, scorned the power which could never win freedom, and broke up the sitting, citing the offence of the presence of Weisspriess for a pretext. The incident threw Anna back upon her old vindictiveness. It caused an unpleasant commotion in the duchess's saloon. Count Serabiglione was present, and ran round to Weisspriess, apologizing for his daughter's behaviour. "Do you think I can't deal with your women as well as your men, you ass?" said Weisspriess, enraged by the scandal of the scene. He was overheard by Count Karl Lenkenstein, who took him to task sharply for his rough speech; but Anna supported her lover, and they joined hands publicly. Anna went home prostrated with despair. "What conscience is in me that I should wish one of my Kaiser's officers killed?" she cried enigmatically to Lena. "But I must have freedom. Oh! to be free. I am chained to my enemy, and God blesses that woman. He makes her weep, but he blesses her, for her body is free, and mine,— the thought of mine sets flames creeping up my limbs as if I were tied to the stake. Losing a husband you love—what is that to taking a husband you hate?" Still Lena could get no plain confession from her, for Anna clung to self-justification, and felt it abandoning her, and her soul fluttering in a black gulf when she opened her month to disburden herself.

There came tidings of the bombardment of Brescia one of the historic deeds of infamy. Many officers of the Imperial army perceived the shame which it cast upon their colours, even in those intemperate hours, and Karl Lenkenstein assumed the liberty of private friendship to go complaining to the old Marshal, who was too true a soldier to condemn a soldier in action, however strong his disapproval of proceedings. The liberty assumed by Karl was excessive; he spoke out in the midst of General officers as if his views were shared by them and the Marshal; and his error was soon corrected; one after another reproached him, until the Marshal, pitying his condition, sent him into his writing-closet, where he lectured the youth on military discipline. It chanced that there followed between them a question upon what the General in command at Brescia would do with his prisoners; and hearing that they were subject to the rigours of a court-martial, and if adjudged guilty, would forthwith summarily be shot, Karl ventured to ask grace for Vittoria's husband. He succeeded finally in obtaining his kind old Chief's promise that Count Ammiani should be tried in Milan, and as the bearer of a paper to that effect, he called on his sisters to get them or Wilfrid to convey word to Vittoria of her husband's probable safety. He found Anna in a swoon, and Lena and the duchess bending over her. The duchess's chasseur Jacob Baumwalder Feckelwitz had been returning from Moran, when on the Brescian high-road he met the spy Luigi, and acting promptly under the idea that Luigi was always a pestilential conductor of detestable correspondence, he attacked him, overthrew him, and ransacked him, and bore the fruit of his sagacious exertions to his mistress in Milan; it was Violetta d'Isorella's letter to Carlo Ammiani. "I have read it," the duchess said; "contrary to any habits when letters are not addressed to me. I bring it open to your sister Anna. She catches sight of one or two names and falls down in the state in which you see her."

"Leave her to me," said Karl.

He succeeded in extracting from Anna hints of the fact that she had paid a large sum of her own money to Countess d'Isorella for secrets connected with the Bergamasc and Brescian rising. "We were under a mutual oath to be silent, but if one has broken it the other cannot; so I confess it to you, dearest good brother. I did this for my country at my personal sacrifice."

Karl believed that he had a sister magnificent in soul. She was glad to have deluded him, but she could not endure his praises, which painted to her imagination all that she might have been if she had not dashed her patriotism with the low cravings of vengeance, making herself like some abhorrent mediaeval grotesque, composed of eagle and reptile. She was most eager in entreating him to save Count Ammiani's life. Carlo, she said, was their enemy, but he had been their friend, and she declared with singular earnestness that she should never again sleep or hold up her head, if he were slain or captured.

"My Anna is justified by me in everything she has done," Karl said to the duchess.

"In that case," the duchess replied, "I have only to differ with her to feel your sword's point at my breast."

"I should certainly challenge the man who doubted her," said Karl.

The duchess laughed with a scornful melancholy.

On the steps of the door where his horse stood saddled, he met Wilfrid, and from this promised brother-in-law received matter for the challenge. Wilfrid excitedly accused Anna of the guilt of a conspiracy to cause the destruction of Count Ammiani. In the heat of his admiration for his sister, Karl struck him on the cheek with his glove, and called him a name by which he had passed during the days of his disgrace, signifying one who plays with two parties. Lena's maid heard them arrange to meet within an hour, and she having been a witness of the altercation, ran to her mistress in advance of Wilfrid, and so worked on Lena's terrors on behalf of her betrothed and her brother, that Lena, dropped at Anna's feet telling her all that she had gathered and guessed in verification of Wilfrid's charge, and imploring her to confess the truth. Anna, though she saw her concealment pierced, could not voluntarily forego her brother's expressed admiration of her, and clung to the tatters of secrecy. After a brief horrid hesitation, she chose to face Wilfrid. This interview began with lively recriminations, and was resulting in nothing—for Anna refused to be shaken by his statement that the Countess d'Isorella had betrayed her, and perceived that she was listening to suspicions only—when, to give his accusation force, Wilfrid said that Brescia had surrendered and that Count Ammiani had escaped.

"And I thank God for it!" Anna exclaimed, and with straight frowning eyes demanded the refutation of her sincerity.

"Count Ammiani and his men have five hours' grace ahead of Major Nagen and half a regiment," said Wilfrid.

At this she gasped; she had risen her breath to deny or defy, and hung on the top of it without a voice.

"Tell us—say, but do say—confess that you know Nagen to be a name of mischief," Lena prayed her.

"I will say anything to prevent my brother from running into danger," Anna rejoined.

"She is most foully accused by one whom we permitted to aspire to be of our own family," said Karl.

"Yet you, Karl, have always been the first to declare her revengeful," Lena turned to him.

"Help, Karl, help me," said Anna.

"Yes!" cried her sister; "there you stand, and ask for help, meanest of women! Do you think these men are not in earnest? Karl is to help you, and you will not speak a word to save him from a grave before night, or me from a lover all of blood."

"Am I to be the sacrifice?" said Anna.

"Whatever you call it, Wilfrid has spoken truth of you, and to none but members of our family; and he had a right to say it, and you are bound now to acknowledge it."

"I acknowledge that I love and serve my country, Lena."

"Not with a pure heart: you can't forgive. Insult or a wrong makes a madwoman of you. Confess, Anna! You know well that you can't kneel to a priest's ear, for you've stopped your conscience. You have pledged yourself to misery to satisfy a spite, and you have not the courage to ask for—" Lena broke her speech like one whose wits have been kindled. "Yes, Karl," she resumed; "Anna begged you to help her. You will. Take her aside and save her from being miserable forever. You do mean to fight my Wilfrid?"

"I am certainly determined to bring him to repentance leaving him the option of the way," said Karl.

Lena took her sullen sister by the arm.

"Anna, will you let these two men go—to slaughter? Look at them; they are both our brothers. One is dearer than a brother to me, and, oh God! I have known what it is to half-lose him. You to lose a lover and have to go bound by a wretched oath to be the wife of a detestable short-sighted husband! Oh, what an abominable folly!"

This epithet, 'short-sighted,' curiously forced in by Lena, was like a shock of the very image of Nagen's needle features thrust against Anna's eyes; the spasm of revulsion in her frame was too quick for her habitual self-control.

At that juncture Weisspriess opened the door, and Anna's eyes met his.

"You don't spare me," she murmured to Lena.

Her voice trembled, and Wilfrid bent his head near her, pressing her hand, and said, "Not only I, but Countess Alessandra Ammiani exonerates you from blame. As she loves her country, you love yours. My words to Karl were an exaggeration of what I know and think. Only tell me this;—if Nagen captures Count Ammiani, how is he likely to deal with him?"

"How can I inform you?" Anna replied coldly; but she reflected in a fire of terror. She had given Nagen the prompting of a hundred angry exclamations in the days of her fever of hatred; she had nevertheless forgotten their parting words; that is, she had forgotten her mood when he started for Brescia, and the nature of the last instructions she had given him. Revolting from the thought of execution being done upon Count Ammiani, as one quickly springing out of fever dreams, all her white face went into hard little lines, like the withered snow which wears away in frost. "Yes," she said; and again, "Yes," to something Weisspriess whispered in her ear, she knew not clearly what. Weisspriess told Wilfrid that he would wait below. As he quitted the room, the duchess entered, and went up to Anna. "My good soul," she said, "you have, I trust, listened to Major Weisspriess. Oh, Anna! you wanted revenge. Now take it, as becomes a high-born woman; and let your enemy come to your feet, and don't spurn her when she is there. Must I inform you that I have been to Countess d'Isorella myself with a man who can compel her to speak? But Anna von Lenkenstein is not base like that Italian. Let them think of you as they will, I believe you to have a great heart. I am sure you will not allow personal sentiment to sully your devotion to our country. Show them that our Austrian faces can be bright; and meet her whom you call your enemy; you cannot fly. You must see her, or you betray yourself. The poor creature's husband is in danger of capture or death."

While the duchess's stern under-breath ran on hurriedly, convincing Anna that she had, with no further warning, to fall back upon her uttermost strength—the name of Countess Alessandra Ammiani was called at the door. Instinctively the others left a path between Vittoria and Anna. It was one of the moments when the adoption of a decisive course says more in vindication of conduct than long speeches. Anna felt that she was on her trial. For the first time since she had looked on this woman she noticed the soft splendour of Vittoria's eyes, and the harmony of her whole figure; nor was the black dress of protesting Italian mourning any longer offensive in her sight, but on a sudden pitiful, for Anna thought: "It may at this very hour be for her husband, and she not knowing it." And with that she had a vision under her eyelids of Nagen like a shadowy devil in pursuit of men flying, and striking herself and Vittoria worse than dead in one blow levelled at Carlo Ammiani. A sense of supernatural horror chilled her blood when she considered again, facing her enemy, that their mutual happiness was by her own act involved in the fate of one life. She stepped farther than the half-way to greet her visitor, whose hands she took. Before a word was uttered between them, she turned to her brother, and with a clear voice said:

"Karl, the Countess Alessandra's husband, our old, friend Carlo Ammiani, may need succour in his flight. Try to cross it; or better, get among those who are pursuing him; and don't delay one minute. You understand me."

Count Karl bowed his head, bitterly humbled.

Anna's eyes seemed to interrogate Vittoria, "Can I do, more?" but her own heart answered her.

Inveterate when following up her passion for vengeance, she was fanatical in responding to the suggestions of remorse.

"Stay; I will despatch Major Weisspriess in my own name," she said. "He is a trusty messenger, and he knows those mountains. Whoever is the officer broken for aiding Count Ammiani's escape, he shall be rewarded by me to the best of my ability. Countess Alessandra, I have anticipated your petition; I hope you may not have to reproach me. Remember that my country was in pieces when you and I declared war. You will not suffer without my suffering tenfold. Perhaps some day you will do me the favour to sing to me, when there is no chance of interruption. At present it is cruel to detain you."

Vittoria said simply: "I thank you, Countess Anna."

She was led out by Count Karl to where Merthyr awaited her. All wondered at the briefness of a scene that had unexpectedly brought the crisis to many emotions and passions, as the broken waters of the sea beat together and make here or there the wave which is topmost. Anna's grand initiative hung in their memories like the throbbing of a pulse, so hotly their sensations swarmed about it, and so intensely it embraced and led what all were desiring. The duchess kissed Anna, saying:

"That is a noble heart to which you have become reconciled. Though you should never be friends, as I am with one of them, you will esteem her. Do not suppose her to be cold. She is the mother of an unborn little one, and for that little one's sake she follows out every duty; she checks every passion in her bosom. She will spare no sacrifice to save her husband, but she has brought her mind to look at the worst, for fear that a shock should destroy her motherly guard."

"Really, duchess," Anna replied, "these are things for married women to hear;" and she provoked some contempt of her conventional delicacy, at the same time that in her imagination the image of Vittoria struggling to preserve this burden of motherhood against a tragic mischance, completely humiliated and overwhelmed her, as if nature had also come to add to her mortifications.

"I am ready to confess everything I have done, and to be known for what I am," she said.

"Confess no more than is necessary, but do everything you can; that's wisest," returned the duchess.

"Ah; you mean that you have nothing to learn." Anna shuddered.

"I mean that you are likely to run into the other extreme of disfavouring yourself just now, my child. And," continued the duchess, "you have behaved so splendidly that I won't think ill of you."

Before the day darkened, Wilfrid obtained, through Prince Radocky's influence, an order addressed to Major Nagen for the surrender of prisoners into his hands. He and Count Karl started for the Val Camonica on the chance of intercepting the pursuit. These were not much wiser than their guesses and their apprehensions made them; but Weisspriess started on the like errand after an interview with Anna, and he had drawn sufficient intelligence out of sobs, and broken sentences, and torture of her spirit, to understand that if Count Ammiani fell alive or dead into Nagen's hands, Nagen by Anna's scrupulous oath, had a claim on her person and her fortune: and he knew Nagen to be a gambler. As he was now by promotion of service Nagen's superior officer, and a near relative of the Brescian commandant, who would be induced to justify his steps, his object was to reach and arbitrarily place himself over Nagen, as if upon a special mission, and to get the lead of the expedition. For that purpose he struck somewhat higher above the Swiss borders than Karl and Wilfrid, and gained a district in the mountains above the vale, perfectly familiar to him. Obeying directions forwarded to her by Wilfrid, Vittoria left Milan for the Val Camonica no later than the evening; Laura was with her in the carriage; Merthyr took horse after them as soon as he had succeeded in persuading Countess Ammiani to pardon her daughter's last act of wilfulness, and believe that, during the agitation of unnumbered doubts, she ran less peril in the wilds where her husband fled, than in her home.

"I will trust to her idolatrously, as you do," Countess Ammiani said; "and perhaps she has already proved to me that I may."

Merthyr saw Agostino while riding out of Milan, and was seen by him; but the old man walked onward, looking moodily on the stones, and merely waved his hand behind.

CHAPTER XLVI

There is hard winter overhead in the mountains when Italian Spring walks the mountain-sides with flowers, and hangs deep valley-walls with flowers half fruit; the sources of the rivers above are set about with fangs of ice, while the full flat stream runs to a rose of sunlight. High among the mists and snows were the fugitives of Brescia, and those who for love or pity struggled to save them wandered through the blooming vales, sometimes hearing that they had crossed the frontier into freedom, and as often that they were scattered low in death and captivity. Austria here, Switzerland yonder, and but one depth between to bound across and win calm breathing. But mountain might call to mountain, peak shine to peak; a girdle of steel drove the hunted men back to frosty heights and clouds, the shifting bosom of snows and lightnings. They saw nothing of hands stretched out to succour. They saw a sun that did not warm them, a home of exile inaccessible, crags like an earth gone to skeleton in hungry air; and below, the land of their birth, beautiful, and sown everywhere for them with torture and captivity, or death, the sweetest. Fifteen men numbered the escape from Brescia. They fought their way twice through passes of the mountains, and might easily, in their first dash Northward from the South-facing hills, have crossed to the Valtelline and Engadine, but that in their insanity of anguish they meditated another blow, and were readier to march into the plains with the tricolour than to follow any course of flight. When the sun was no longer in their blood they thought of reason and of rest; they voted the expedition to Switzerland, that so they should get round to Rome, and descended from the crags of the Tonale, under which they were drawn to an ambush, suffering three of their party killed, and each man bloody with wounds. The mountain befriended them, and gave them safety, as truth is given by a bitter friend. Among icy crags and mists, where the touch of life grows dull as the nail of a fore-finger, the features of the mountain were stamped on them, and with hunger they lost pride, and with solitude laughter; with endless fleeing they lost the aim of flight; some became desperate, a few craven. Companionship was broken before they parted in three bodies, commanded severally by Colonel Corte, Carlo Ammiani, and Barto Rizzo. Corte reached the plains, masked by the devotion of Carlo's band, who lured the soldiery to a point and drew a chase, while Corte passed the line and pushed on for Switzerland. Carlo told off his cousin Angelo Guidascarpi in the list of those following Corte; but when he fled up to the snows again, he beheld Angelo spectral as the vapour on a jut of rock awaiting him. Barto Rizzo had chosen his own way, none knew whither. Carlo, Angelo, Marco Sana, and a sharply-wounded Brescian lad, conceived the scheme of traversing the South Tyrol mountain-range toward Friuli, whence Venice, the still-breathing republic, might possibly be gained. They carried the boy in turn till his arms drooped long down, and when they knew the soul was out of him they buried him in snow, and thought him happy. It was then that Marco Sana took his death for an omen, and decided them to turn their heads once more for Switzerland; telling them that the boy, whom he last had carried, uttered "Rome" with the flying breath. Angelo said that Sana would get to Rome; and Carlo, smiling on Angelo, said they were to die twins though they had been born only cousins. The language they had fallen upon was mystical, scarce intelligible to other than themselves. On a clear morning, with the Swiss peaks in sight, they were condemned by want of food to quit their fastness for the valley.

Vittoria read the faces of the mornings as human creatures base tried to gather the sum of their destinies off changing surfaces, fair not meaning fair, nor black black, but either the mask upon the secret of God's terrible will; and to learn it and submit, was the spiritual burden of her motherhood, that the child leaping with her heart might live. Not to hope blindly, in the exceeding anxiousness of her passionate love, nor blindly to fear; not to bet her soul fly out among the twisting chances; not to sap her great maternal duty by affecting false stoical serenity:—to nurse her soul's strength, and suckle her womanly weakness with the tsars which are poison—when repressed; to be at peace with a disastrous world for the sake of the dependent life unborn; lay such pure efforts she clung to God. Soft dreams of sacred nuptial tenderness, tragic images, wild pity, were like phantoms encircling her, plucking at her as she went, lest they were beneath her feet, and she kept them from lodging between her breasts. The thought that her husband, though he should have perished, was not a life lost if their child lived, sustained her powerfully. It seemed to whisper at times almost as it were Carlo's ghost breathing in her ears: "On thee!" On her the further duty devolved; and she trod down hope, lest it should build her up and bring a shock to surprise her fortitude; she put back alarm.

The mountains and the valleys scarce had names for her understanding; they were but a scene where the will of her Maker was at work. Rarely has a soul been so subjected to its own force. She certainly had the image of God in her mind.

Yet when her ayes lingered on any mountain gorge, the fate of her husband sang within it a strange chant, ending in a key that rang sounding through all her being, and seemed to question heaven. This music framed itself; it was still when she looked at the shrouded mountain-tops. A shadow meting sunlight on the long green slopes aroused it, and it hummed above the tumbling hasty foam, and penetrated hanging depths of foliage, sad-hued rock-clefts, dark green ravines; it became convulsed where the mountain threw forward in a rushing upward line against the sky, there to be severed at the head by cloud. It was silent among the vines.

Most painfully did human voices affect her when she had this music; speech was a scourge to her sense of hearing, and touch distressed her: an edge of purple flame would then unfold the vision of things to her eyes. She had lost memory; and if by hazard unawares one idea was projected by some sudden tumult of her enslaved emotions beyond known and visible circumstances, her intelligence darkened with am oppressive dread like that of zealots of the guilt of impiety.

Thus destitute, her eye took innumerable pictures sharp as on a brass-plate: torrents, goat-tracks winding up red earth, rocks veiled with water, cottage and children, strings of villagers mounting to the church, one woman kneeling before a wayside cross, her basket at her back, and her child gazing idly by; perched hamlets, rolling pasture-fields, the vast mountain lines. She asked all that she saw, "Does he live?" but the life was out of everything, and these shows told of no life, neither of joy nor of grief. She could only distantly connect the appearance of the white-coated soldiery with the source of her trouble. They were no more than figures on a screen that hid the flashing of the sword which renders dumb. She had charity for one who was footsore and sat cherishing his ankle by a village spring, and she fed him, and not until he was far behind, thought that he might have seen the white face of her husband.

Accurate tidings could not be obtained, though the whole course of the vale was full of stories of escapes, conflicts, and captures. Merthyr learnt positively that some fugitives had passed the cordon. He came across Wilfrid and Count Karl, who both verified it in the most sanguine manner. They knew, however, that Major Nagen continued in the mountains. Riding by a bend of the road, Merthyr beheld a man playing among children, with one hand and his head down apparently for concealment at his approach. It proved to be Beppo. The man believed that Count Ammiani had fled to Switzerland. Barto Rizzo, he said, was in the mountains still, and Beppo invoked damnation on him, as the author of those lying proclamations which had ruined Brescia. He had got out of the city later than the others and was seeking to evade the outposts, that he might join his master—"that is, my captain, for I have only one master;" he corrected the slip of his tongue appealingly to Merthyr. His left hand was being continually plucked at by the children while he talked, and after Merthyr had dispersed them with a shower of small coin, he showed the hand, saying, glad of eye, that it had taken a sword-cut intended for Count Ammiani. Merthyr sent him back to mount the carriage, enjoining him severely not to speak.

When Carlo and his companions descended from the mountains, they entered a village where there was an inn recognized by Angelo as the abode of Jacopo Cruchi. He there revived Carlo's animosity toward Weisspriess by telling the tale of the passage to Meran, and his good reasons for determining to keep guard over the Countess Alessandra all the way. Subsequently Angelo went to Jacopo for food. This he procured, but he was compelled to leave the man behind, and unpaid. It was dark when he left the inn; he had some difficulty in evading a flock of whitecoats, and his retreat from the village was still on the Austrian side. Somewhat about midnight Merthyr reached the inn, heralding the carriage. As Jacopo caught sight of Vittoria's face, he fell with his shoulders straightened against the wall, and cried out loudly that he had betrayed no one, and mentioned Major Weisspriess by name as having held the point of his sword at him and extracted nothing better than a wave of the hand and a lie; in other words, that the fugitives had retired to the Tyrolese mountains, and that he had shammed ignorance of who they were. Merthyr read at a glance that Jacopo had the large swallow and calm digestion for bribes, and getting the fellow alone he laid money in view, out of which, by doubling the sum to make Jacopo correct his first statement, and then by threatening to withdraw it altogether, he gained knowledge of the fact that Angelo Guidascarpi had recently visited the inn, and had started from it South-eastward, and that Major Weisspriess was following on his track. He wrote a line of strong entreaty to Weisspriess, lest that officer should perchance relapse into anger at the taunts of prisoners abhorring him with the hatred of Carlo and Angelo. At the same time he gave Beppo a considerable supply of money, and then sent him off, armed as far as possible to speed Count Ammiani safe across the borders, if a fugitive; or if a prisoner, to ensure the best which could be hoped for him from an adversary become generous. That evening Vittoria lay with her head on Laura's lap, and the pearly little crescent of her ear in moonlight by the window. So fair and young and still she looked that Merthyr feared for her, and thought of sending her back to Countess Ammiani.

Her first question with the lifting of her eyelids was if he had ceased to trust to her courage.

"No," said Merthyr; "there are bounds to human strength; that is all."

She answered: "There would be to mine—if I had not more than human strength beside me. I bow my head, dearest; it is that. I feel that I cannot break down as long as I know what is passing. Does my husband live?"

"Yes, he lives," said Merthyr; and she gave him her hand, and went to her bed.

He learnt from Laura that when Beppo mounted the carriage in silence, a fit of ungovernable wild trembling had come on her, broken at intervals by a cry that something was concealed. Laura could give no advice; she looked on Merthyr and Vittoria as two that had an incomprehensible knowledge of the power of one another's natures, and the fiery creature remained passive in perplexity of minds as soft an attendant as a suffering woman could have:

Merthyr did not sleep, and in the morning Vittoria said to him, "You want to be active, my friend. Go, and we will wait for you here. I know that I am never deceived by you, and when I see you I know that the truth speaks and bids me be worthy of it Go up there," she pointed with shut eyes at the mountains; "leave me to pray for greater strength. I am among Italians at this inn; and shall spend money here; the poor people love it." She smiled a little, showing a glimpse of her old charitable humour.

Merthyr counselled Laura that in case of evil tidings during his absence she should reject her feminine ideas of expediency, and believe that she was speaking to a brave soul firmly rooted in the wisdom of heaven.

"Tell her?—she will die," said Laura, shuddering.

"Get tears from her," Merthyr rejoined; "but hide nothing from her for a single instant; keep her in daylight. For God's sake, keep her in daylight."

"It's too sharp a task for me." She repeated that she was incapable of it.

"Ah," said he, "look at your Italy, how she weeps! and she has cause. She would die in her grief, if she had no faith for what is to come. I dare say it is not, save in the hearts of one or two, a conscious faith, but it's real divine strength; and Alessandra Ammiani has it. Do as I bid you. I return in two days."

Without understanding him, Laura promised that she would do her utmost to obey, and he left her muttering to herself as if she were schooling her lips to speak reluctant words. He started for the mountains with gladdened limbs, taking a guide, who gave his name as Lorenzo, and talked of having been 'out' in the previous year. "I am a patriot, signore! and not only in opposition to my beast of a wife, I assure you: a downright patriot, I mean." Merthyr was tempted to discharge him at first, but controlled his English antipathy to babblers, and discovered him to be a serviceable fellow. Toward nightfall they heard shots up a rock-strewn combe of the lower slopes; desultory shots indicating rifle-firing at long range. Darkness made them seek shelter in a pine-hut; starting from which at dawn, Lorenzo ran beating about like a dog over the place where the shots had sounded on the foregoing day; he found a stone spotted with blood. Not far from the stone lay a military glove that bore brown-crimson finger-ends. They were striking off to a dairy-but for fresh milk, when out of a crevice of rock overhung by shrubs a man's voice called, and Merthyr climbing up from perch to perch, saw Marco Sana lying at half length, shot through hand and leg. From him Merthyr learnt that Carlo and Angelo had fled higher up; yesterday they had been attacked by coming who tried to lure there to surrender by coming forward at the head of his men and offering safety, and "other gabble," said Marco. He offered a fair shot at his heart, too, while he stood below a rock that Marco pointed at gloomily as a hope gone for ever; but Carlo would not allow advantage to be taken of even the treacherous simulation of chivalry, and only permitted firing after he had returned to his men. "I was hit here and here," said Marco, touching his wounds, as men can hardly avoid doing when speaking of the fresh wound. Merthyr got him on his feet, put money in his pocket, and led him off the big stones painfully. "They give no quarter," Marco assured him, and reasoned that it must be so, for they had not taken him prisoner, though they saw him fall, and ran by or in view of him in pursuit of Carlo. By this Merthyr was convinced that Weisspriess meant well. He left his guide in charge of Marco to help him into the Engadine. Greatly to his astonishment, Lorenzo tossed the back of his hand at the offer of money. "There shall be this difference between me and my wife," he remarked; "and besides, gracious signore, serving my countrymen for nothing, that's for love, and the Tedeschi can't punish me for it, so it's one way of cheating them, the wolves!" Merthyr shook his hand and said, "Instead of my servant, be my friend;" and Lorenzo made no feeble mouth, but answered, "Signore, it is much to my honour," and so they went different ways.

Left to himself Merthyr set step vigorously upward. Information from herdsmen told him that he was an hour off the foot of one of the passes. He begged them to tell any hunted men who might come within hail that a friend ran seeking them. Farther up, while thinking of the fine nature of that Lorenzo, and the many men like him who could not by the very existence of nobility in their bosoms suffer their country to go through another generation of servitude, his heart bounded immensely, for he heard a shout and his name, and he beheld two figures on a rock near the gorge where the mountain opened to its heights. But they were not Carlo and Angelo. They were Wilfrid and Count Karl, the latter of whom had discerned him through a telescope. They had good news to revive him, however: good at least in the main. Nagen had captured Carlo and Angelo, they believed; but they had left Weisspriess near on Nagen's detachment, and they furnished sound military reasons to show why, if Weisspriess favoured the escape, they should not be present. They supposed that they were not half-a-mile from the scene in the pass where Nagen was being forcibly deposed from his authority: Merthyr borrowed Count Karl's glass, and went as they directed him round a bluff of the descending hills, that faced the vale, much like a blown and beaten sea-cliff. Wilfrid and Karl were so certain of Count Ammiani's safety, that their only thought was to get under good cover before nightfall, and haply into good quarters, where the three proper requirements of the soldier—meat, wine, and tobacco—might be furnished to them. After an imperative caution that they should not present themselves before the Countess Alessandra, Merthyr sped quickly over the broken ground. How gaily the two young men cheered to him as he hurried on! He met a sort of pedlar turning the bluntfaced mountain-spur, and this man said, "Yes, sure enough, prisoners had been taken," and he was not aware of harm having been done to them; he fancied there was a quarrel between two captains. His plan being always to avoid the military, he had slunk round and away from them as fast as might be. An Austrian common soldier, a good-humoured German, distressed by a fall that had hurt his knee-cap, sat within the gorge, which was very wide at the mouth. Merthyr questioned him, and he, while mending one of his gathered cigar-ends, pointed to a meadow near the beaten track, some distance up the rocks. Whitecoats stood thick on it. Merthyr lifted his telescope and perceived an eager air about the men, though they stood ranged in careless order. He began to mount forthwith, but amazed by a sudden ringing of shot, he stopped, asking himself in horror whether it could be an execution. The shots and the noise increased, until the confusion of a positive mellay reigned above. The fall of the meadow swept to a bold crag right over the pathway, and with a projection that seen sideways made a vulture's head and beak of it. There rolled a corpse down the precipitous wave of green grass on to the crag, where it lodged, face to the sky; sword dangled from swordknot at one wrist, heels and arms were in the air, and the body caught midway hung poised and motionless. The firing deadened. Then Merthyr drawing nearer beneath the crag, saw one who had life in him slipping down toward the body, and knew the man for Beppo. Beppo knocked his hands together and groaned miserably, but flung himself astride the beak of the crag, and took the body in his arms, sprang down with it, and lay stunned at Merthyr's feet. Merthyr looked on the face of Carlo Ammiani.

EPILOGUE

No uncontested version of the tragedy of Count Ammiani's death passed current in Milan during many years. With time it became disconnected from passion, and took form in a plain narrative. He and Angelo were captured by Major Nagen, and were, as the soldiers of the force subsequently let it be known, roughly threatened with what he termed I 'Brescian short credit.' The appearance of Major Weisspriess and his claim to the command created a violent discussion between the two officers. For Nagen, by all military rules, could well contest it. But Weisspriess had any body of the men of the army under his charm, and seeing the ascendency he gained with them over an unpopular officer, he dared the stroke for the charitable object he had in view. Having established his command, in spite of Nagen's wrathful protests and menaces, he spoke to the prisoners, telling Carlo that for his wife's sake he should be spared, and Angelo that he must expect the fate of a murderer. His address to them was deliberate, and quite courteous: he expressed himself sorry that a gallant gentleman like Angelo Guidascarpi should merit a bloody grave, but so it was. At the same time he entreated Count Ammiani to rely on his determination to save him. Major Nagen did not stand far removed from them. Carlo turned to him and repeated the words of Weisspriess; nor could Angelo restrain his cousin's vehement renunciation of hope and life in doing this. He accused Weisspriess of a long evasion of a brave man's obligation to repair an injury, charged him with cowardice, and requested Major Nagen, as a man of honour, to drag his brother officer to the duel. Nagen then said that Major Weisspriess was his superior, adding that his gallant brother officer had only of late objected to vindicate his reputation with his sword. Stung finally beyond the control of an irritable temper, Weisspriess walked out of sight of the soldiery with Carlo, to whom, at a special formal request from Weisspriess, Nagen handed his sword. Again he begged Count Ammiani to abstain from fighting; yea, to strike him and disable him, and fly, rather—than provoke the skill of his right hand. Carlo demanded his cousin's freedom. It was denied to him, and Carlo claimed his privilege. The witnesses of the duel were Jenna and another young subaltern: both declared it fair according to the laws of honour, when their stupefaction on beholding the proud swordsman of the army stretched lifeless on the brown leaves of the past year left them with power to speak. Thus did Carlo slay his old enemy who would have served as his friend. A shout of rescue was heard before Carlo had yielded up his weapon. Four haggard and desperate men, headed by Barto Rizzo, burst from an ambush on the guard encircling Angelo. There, with one thought of saving his doomed cousin and comrade, Carlo rushed, and not one Italian survived the fight.

An unarmed spectator upon the meadow-borders, Beppo, had but obscure glimpses of scenes shifting like a sky in advance of hurricane winds.

Merthyr delivered the burden of death to Vittoria. Her soul had crossed the darkness of the river of death in that quiet agony preceding the revelation of her Maker's will, and she drew her dead husband to her bosom and kissed him on the eyes and the forehead, not as one who had quite gone away from her, but as one who lay upon another shore whither she would come. The manful friend, ever by her side, saved her by his absolute trust in her fortitude to bear the burden of the great sorrow undeceived, and to walk with it to its last resting-place on earth unobstructed. Clear knowledge of her, the issue of reverent love, enabled him to read her unequalled strength of nature, and to rely on her fidelity to her highest mortal duty in a conflict with extreme despair. She lived through it as her Italy had lived through the hours which brought her face to face with her dearest in death; and she also on the day, ten years later, when an Emperor and a King stood beneath the vault of the grand Duomo, and the organ and a peal of voices rendered thanks to heaven for liberty, could show the fruit of her devotion in the dark-eyed boy, Carlo Merthyr Ammiani, standing between Merthyr and her, with old blind Agostino's hands upon his head. And then once more, and but for once, her voice was heard in Milan.

George Meredith – A Concise Bibliography

Novels
The Shaving of Shagpat (1856)
Farina (1857)
The Ordeal of Richard Feverel (1859)
Evan Harrington (1861)
Emilia in England (1864), republished as Sandra Belloni in 1887
Rhoda Fleming (1865)
Vittoria (1867)
The Adventures of Harry Richmond (1871)
Beauchamp's Career (1875)
The House on the Beach (1877)
The Case of General Ople and Lady Camper (1877)
The Tale of Chloe (1879)
The Egoist (1879)
The Tragic Comedians (1880)
Diana of the Crossways (1885)
One of our Conquerors (1891)
Lord Ormont and his Aminta (1894)
The Amazing Marriage (1895)
Celt and Saxon (1910)

Poetry
Poems (1851)
Modern Love (1862)
The Lark Ascending (1881)
Poems and Lyrics of the Joy of Earth (1883)
The Woods of Westermain (1883)
A Faith on Trial (1885)
Ballads and Poems of Tragic Life (1887)
A Reading of Earth (1888)
The Empty Purse (1892)
Odes in Contribution to the Song of French History (1898)
A Reading of Life (1901)
Selected Poems of George Meredith (1903, author's supervision)
Last Poems (1909)

Essays
Essay on Comedy (1877)

www.ingramcontent.com/pod-product-compliance
Lightning Source LLC
Chambersburg PA
CBHW070535260626
47161CB00002B/392